The Collected
Ronald Standish,
Sleuth

The Collected Ronald Standish, Sleuth

Tiny Carteret

Ronald Standish

Ask for Ronald Standish

and

the Short Story
'The Horror at Staveley Grange'

Sapper
(Herman Cyril McNeile)

LEONAUR

The Collected
Ronald Standish, Sleuth
Tiny Carteret
Ronald Standish
Ask for Ronald Standish
and the Short Story 'The Horror at Staveley Grange'
by Sapper
(Herman Cyril McNeile)

FIRST EDITION

First published under the titles
The Saving Clause (extract)
Tiny Carteret
Ronald Standish
and
Ask for Ronald Standish

Leonaur is an imprint
of Oakpast Ltd

ISBN: 978-1-78282-405-3 (hardcover)
ISBN: 978-1-78282-406-0 (softcover)

http://www.leonaur.com

Contents

The Horror at Staveley Grange

1

A fact pointing in a certain direction is just a fact: two pointing in the same direction become a coincidence: three—and you begin to get into the regions of certainty. But you must be very sure of your facts.

Thus ran Ronald Standish's favourite *dictum*: and it was the astonishing skill with which he seemed to be able to sort out the facts that mattered from the mass of irrelevant detail, and having sorted them out, to interpret them correctly, that had earned him his reputation as a detective of quite unusual ability.

There is no doubt that had he been under the necessity of earning his own livelihood, he would have risen to a very high position at Scotland Yard; or, if he had chosen to set up on his own, that his career would have been assured. But not being under any such necessity, his gifts were known only to a small circle of friends and acquaintances. Moreover, he was apt to treat the matter as rather a joke—as an interesting recreation more than a serious business. He regarded it in much the same light as solving a chess problem or an acrostic.

In appearance he was about as unlike the conventional detective as it is possible to be. Of medium height, he was inclined to be thick-set. His face was ruddy, with a short, closely-clipped moustache—and in his eyes there shone a perpetual twinkle. In fact most people on first meeting him took him for an army officer. He was a first-class man to hounds, and an excellent shot; a cricketer who might easily have become first class had he devoted enough time to it, and a scratch golfer. And last, but not least, he was a man of very great personal strength without a nerve in his body.

This, then, was the man who sat opposite to me in a first-class carriage of a Great Western express on the way to Devonshire. On the spur of the moment that morning, I had rung him up at his club in London—on the spur of the moment he had thrown over a week's cricket, and arranged to come with me to Exeter. And now that we were actually in the train, I began to wonder if I had brought him on a wild-goose chase. I took the letter out of my pocket—the letter that had been the cause of our journey, and read it through once again, it ran:

> Dear Tony, I am perfectly distracted with worry and anxiety. I don't know whether you saw it in the papers, and it's such ages since we met, but I'm engaged to Billy Mansford. And we're in the most awful trouble. Haven't you got a friend or someone you once told me about who solves mysteries and things? Do, for pity's sake, get hold of him and bring him down here to stay I'm nearly off my head with it all—Your distracted Molly.

I laid the letter on my knee and stared out of the window. Somehow or other I couldn't picture pretty little Molly Tremayne, the gayest and most feckless girl in the world, as being off her head over anything. And having only recently returned from Brazil I had not heard of her engagement—nor did I know anything about the man she was engaged to. But as I say, I rang up Standish on the spur of the moment, and a little to my surprise he had at once accepted.

He leant over at that moment, and took the letter off my knee.

"The Old Hall," he remarked thoughtfully. Then he took a big-scale ordnance map from his pocket and began to study it.

"Three miles approximately from Staveley Grange."

"Staveley Grange," I said, staring at him. "What has Staveley Grange got to do with the matter?"

"I should imagine—everything," he answered. "You've been out of the country, Tom, and so you're a bit behindhand. But you may take it from me that it was not the fact that your Molly was distracted that made me give up an excellent I.Z. tour. It was the fact that she is engaged to Mr. William Mansford."

"Never heard of him," I said. "Who and what is he?"

"He is the younger and only surviving son of the late Mr. Robert Mansford," he answered thoughtfully. "Six months ago the father was alive—also Tom, the elder son. Five months ago the father died: two months ago Tom died. And the circumstances of their deaths were, to put it mildly, peculiar."

8

"Good heavens!" I cried, "this is all news to me."

"Probably," he answered. "The matter attracted very little attention. But you know my hobby, and it was the coincidence of the two things that attracted my attention. I only know, of course, what appeared in the papers—and that wasn't very much. Mansford senior and both his sons had apparently spent most of their lives in Australia. The two boys came over with the Anzacs, and a couple of years or so after the war they all decided to come back to England. And so he bought Staveley Grange. He had gone a poor man of distinctly humble origin: he returned as a wealthy Australian magnate. Nine months after he stepped into the house he was found dead in his bed in the morning by the butler. He was raised up on his pillows and he was staring fixedly at a top corner of the room by one of the windows. And in his hand he held the speaking tube which communicated with the butler's room. A postmortem revealed nothing, and the verdict was that he had died of heart failure. In view of the fact that most people do die of heart failure, the verdict was fairly safe."

Ronald Standish lit a cigarette.

"That was five months ago. Two months ago, one of the footmen coming in in the morning was horrified to find Tom sprawling across the rail at the foot of the bed—stone dead He had taken over his father's room, and had retired the previous night in the best of health and spirits. Again there was a postmortem—again nothing was revealed, And again the same verdict was given—heart failure. Of course, the coincidence was commented on in the press, but there the matter rested, at any rate as far as the newspapers were concerned. And therefore that is as much as I know. This letter looks as if further developments were taking place."

"What an extraordinary affair," I remarked, as he finished. "What sort of men physically were the father and Tom?"

"According to the papers," answered Standish, "they were two singularly fine specimens. Especially Tom."

Already we were slowing down for Exeter, and we began gathering our suitcases and coats preparatory to alighting. I leant out of the window as we ran into the station, having wired Molly our time of arrival, and there she was sure enough, with a big, clean-cut man standing beside her, who, I guessed, must be her fiance. So, in fact, it proved, and a moment or two later we all walked out of the station together towards the waiting motor car. And it was as I passed the ticket collector that I got the first premonition of trouble. Two men standing on

9

the platform, who looked like well-to-do farmers, whispered together a little significantly as Mansford passed them, and stared after him with scarcely veiled hostility in their eyes.

On the way to the Old Hall, I studied him under cover of some desultory conversation with Molly. He was a typical Australian of the best type: one of those open-air, clear-eyed men who came over in their thousands to Gallipoli and France. But it seemed to me that his conversation with Ronald was a little forced: underlying it was a vague uneasiness—a haunting fear of something or other. And I thought he was studying my friend with a kind of desperate hope tinged with disappointment, as if he had been building on Ronald's personality and now was unsatisfied.

That some such idea was in Molly's mind I learned as we got out of the car. For a moment or two we were alone, and she turned to me with a kind of desperate eagerness.

"Is he very clever, Tom—your friend? Somehow I didn't expect him to look quite like that!"

"You may take it from me, Molly," I said reassuringly, "that there are very few people in Europe who can see further into a brick wall than Ronald. But he knows nothing, of course, as to what the trouble is—any more than I do. And you mustn't expect him to work miracles."

"Of course not," she answered. "But oh! Tom—it's—it's damnable."

We went into the house and joined Standish and Mansford, who were in the hall.

"You'd like to go up to your rooms," began Molly, but Ronald cut her short with a grave smile.

"I think, Miss Tremayne," he said quietly, "that it will do you both good to get this little matter off your chests as soon as possible. Bottling things up is no good, and there's some time yet before dinner."

The girl gave him a quick smile of gratitude and led the way across the hall.

"Let's go into the billiard room," she said. "Daddy is pottering round the garden, and you can meet him later. Now, Billy," she continued, when we were comfortably settled, "tell Mr. Standish all about it."

"Right from the very beginning, please," said Ronald, stuffing an empty pipe in his mouth. "The reasons that caused your father to take Staveley Grange and everything."

Bill Mansford gave a slight start.

"You know something about us already then."

"Something," answered Ronald briefly. "I want to know all."

"Well," began the Australian. "I'll tell you all I know. But there are many gaps I can't fill in. When we came back from Australia two years ago, we naturally gravitated to Devonshire. My father came from these parts, and he wanted to come back after his thirty years' absence. Of course he found everything changed, but he insisted on remaining here and we set about looking for a house. My father was a wealthy man—very wealthy, and his mind was set on getting something good. A little pardonable vanity perhaps—but having left England practically penniless to return almost a millionaire—he was determined to get what he wanted regardless of cost. And it was after we had been here about six months that Staveley Grange came quite suddenly on to the market. It happened in rather a peculiar way. Some people of the name of Bretherton had it, and had been living there for about three years. They had bought it, and spent large sums of money on it: introduced a large number of modern improvements, and at the same time preserved all the old appearance. Then as I say, quite suddenly, they left the house and threw it on the market.

"Well, it was just what we wanted. We all went over it, and found it even more perfect than we had anticipated. The man who had been butler to the Brethertons was in charge, and when we went over, he and his wife were living there alone. We tried to pump them as to why the Brethertons had gone, but they appeared to know no more than we did. The butler—Templeton—was a charming old bird with side-whiskers; his wife, who had been doing cook, was a rather timorous-looking little woman—but a damned good cook.

"Anyway, the long and short of it was, we bought the place. The figure was stiff, but my father could afford it. And it was not until we bought it, that we heard in a roundabout way the reason of the Brethertons' departure. It appeared that old Mrs. Bretherton woke up one night in screaming hysterics, and alleged that a dreadful thing was in the room with her. What it was she wouldn't say, except to babble foolishly about a shining, skinny hand that had touched her. Her husband and various maids came rushing in, and of course the room was empty. There was nothing there at all. The fact of it was that the old lady had had lobster for dinner—and a nightmare afterwards."

"At least," added Mansford slowly, "that's what we thought at the time."

11

He paused to light a cigarette.

"Well—we gathered that nothing had been any good. Templeton proved a little more communicative once we were in, and from him we found out, that in spite of every argument and expostulation on the part of old Bretherton, the old lady flatly refused to live in the house for another minute. She packed up her boxes and went off the next day with her maid to some hotel in Exeter, and nothing would induce her to set foot inside the house again. Old Bretherton was livid."

Mansford smiled grimly.

"But—he went, and we took the house. The room that old Mrs. Bretherton had had was quite the best bedroom in the house, and my father decided to use it as his own. He came to that decision before we knew anything about this strange story, though even if we had, he'd still have used the room. My father was not the man to be influenced by an elderly woman's indigestion and subsequent nightmare. And when bit by bit we heard the yarn, he merely laughed, as did my brother and myself.

"And then one morning it happened. It was Templeton who broke the news to us with an ashen face, and his voice shaking so that we could hardly make out what he said. I was shaving at the time, I remember, and when I'd taken in what he was trying to say, I rushed along the passage to my father's room with the soap still lathered on my chin. The poor old man was sitting up in bed propped against the pillows. His left arm was flung half across his face as if to ward off something that was coming: his right hand was grasping the speaking-tube beside the bed. And in his wide-open, staring eyes was a look of dreadful terror."

He paused as if waiting for some comment or question, but Ronald still sat motionless, with his empty pipe in his mouth. And after a while Mansford continued:

"There was a postmortem, as perhaps you may have seen in the papers, and they found my father had died from heart failure. But my father's heart, Mr. Standish, was as sound as mine, and neither my brother nor I were satisfied. For weeks he and I sat up in that room, taking it in turns to go to sleep, to see if we could see anything—but nothing happened. And at last we began to think that the verdict was right, and that the poor old man had died of natural causes. I went back to my own room, and Tom—my brother—stayed on in my father's room. I tried to dissuade him, but he was an obstinate fellow, and he had an idea that if he slept there alone he might still perhaps get to the bottom of it. He had a revolver by his side, and Tom was a man who could hit the pip out of the ace of diamonds at ten yards. Well, for a week nothing happened. And then one night I stayed chatting with him for a few moments in his room before going to bed. That was the last time I saw him alive. One of the footmen came rushing in to me the next morning, with a face like a sheet—and before he spoke I knew what must have happened. It was perhaps a little foolish of me—but I dashed past him while he was still stammering at the door—and went to my brother's room."

"Why foolish?" said Standish quietly.

"Some people at the inquest put a false construction on it," answered Mansford steadily. "They wanted to know why I made that assumption before the footman told me."

"I see," said Standish. "Go on."

"I went into the room, and there I found him. In one hand he held the revolver, and he was lying over the rail at the foot of the bed. The blood had gone to his head, and he wasn't a pretty sight. He was dead, of course—and once again the postmortem revealed nothing. He also was stated to have died of heart failure. But he didn't, Mr. Standish."

Mansford's voice shook a little. "As there's a God above, I swear Tom never died of heart failure. Something happened in that room—something terrible occurred there which killed my father and brother as surely as a bullet through the brain. And I've got to find out what it was: I've *got* to, you understand—because,"—and here his voice faltered for a moment, and then grew steady again—"because there are quite a number of people who suspect me of having murdered them both."

"Naturally," said Standish, in his most matter-of-fact tone. "When a man comes into a lot of money through the sudden death of two people, there are certain to be lots of people who will draw a connection between the two events."

He stood up and faced Mansford.

"Are the police still engaged on it?"

"Not openly," answered the other. "But I know they're working at it still. And I can't and won't marry Molly with this cloud hanging over my head. I've got to disprove it."

"Yes, but, my dear, it's no good to me if you disprove it by being killed yourself," cried the girl. Then she turned to Ronald. "That's where we thought that perhaps you could help us, Mr. Standish. If only you can clear Billy's name, why—"

She clasped her hands together beseechingly, and Standish gave her a reassuring smile.

"I'll try, Miss Tremayne—I can't do more than that. And now I think we'll get to business at once. I want to examine that bedroom."

2

Ronald Standish remained sunk in thought during the drive to Staveley Grange. Molly had not come with us, and neither Mansford nor I felt much inclined to conversation. He, poor devil, kept searching Ronald's face with a sort of pathetic eagerness, almost as if he expected the mystery to be already solved.

And then, just as we were turning into the drive, Ronald spoke for the first time.

"Have you slept in that room since your brother's death, Mansford?"

"No," answered the other, a little shamefacedly. "To tell the truth, Molly extracted a promise from me that I wouldn't."

"Wise of her," said Standish tersely, and relapsed into silence again.

"But you don't think—" began Mansford.

"I think nothing," snapped Standish, and at that moment the car drew up at the door.

It was opened by an elderly man with side whiskers, whom I placed as the butler—Templeton. He was a typical, old-fashioned manservant of the country-house type, and he bowed respectfully when Mansford told him what we had come for.

"I am thankful to think there is any chance, sir, of clearing up this terrible mystery," he said earnestly. "But I fear, if I may say so, that the matter is beyond earthly hands." His voice dropped, to prevent the two footmen overhearing. "We have prayed, sir, my wife and I, but there are more things in heaven and earth than we can account for. You wish to go to the room, sir? It is unlocked."

He led the way up the stairs and opened the door.

"Everything, sir, is as it was on the morning when Mr. Tom—er—died. Only the bedclothes have been removed."

He bowed again and left the room, closing the door.

"Poor old Templeton," said Mansford. "He's convinced that we are dealing with a ghost. Well, here's the room, Standish—just as it was. As you see, there's nothing very peculiar about it."

14

Ronald made no reply. He was standing in the centre of the room taking in the first general impression of his surroundings. He was completely absorbed, and I made a warning sign to Mansford not to speak. The twinkle had left his eyes: his expression was one of keen concentration. And, after a time, knowing the futility of speech, I began to study the place on my own account.

It was a big, square room, with a large double bed of the old-fashioned type. Over the bed was a canopy, made fast to the two bedposts at the head, and supported at the foot by two wires attached to the two corners of the canopy and two staples let into the wall above the windows. The bed itself faced the windows, of which there were two, placed symmetrically in the wall opposite, with a writing table in between them. The room was on the first floor in the centre of the house, and there was thus only one outside wall—that facing the bed. A big open fireplace and a lavatory basin with water laid on occupied most of one wall; two long built-in cupboards filled up the other. Beside the bed, on the fireplace side, stood a small table, with a special clip attached to the edge for the speaking-tube. In addition there stood on this table a thing not often met with in a private house in England. It was a small, portable electric fan, such as one finds on board ship or in the tropics.

There were two or three easy chairs standing on the heavy pile carpet, and the room was lit by electric light. In fact the whole tone was solid comfort, not to say luxury; it looked the last place in the world with which one would have associated anything ghostly or mysterious.

Suddenly Ronald Standish spoke.

"Just show me, will you, Mansford, as nearly as you can, exactly the position in which you found your father."

With a slight look of repugnance, the Australian got on to the bed.

"There were bedclothes, of course, and pillows which are not here now, but allowing for them, the poor old man was hunched up somehow like this. His knees were drawn up: the speaking-tube was in his hand, and he was staring towards that window."

"I see," said Standish. "The window on the right as we look at it. And your brother now. When he was found he was lying over the rail at the foot of the bed. Was he on the right side or the left?"

"On the right," said Mansford, "almost touching the upright."

Once again Standish relapsed into silence and stared thoughtfully round the room. The setting sun was pouring in through the windows, and suddenly he gave a quick exclamation. We both glanced at him and he was staring up at the ceiling with a keen, intent look on his face. The next moment he had climbed on to the bed, and, standing up, he examined the two wire stays which supported the canopy. He touched each of them in turn, and began to whistle under his breath. It was a sure sign that he had stumbled on something, but I knew him far too well to make any comment at that stage of the proceedings.

"Very strange," he remarked at length, getting down and lighting a cigarette.

"What is?" asked Mansford eagerly.

"The vagaries of sunlight," answered Standish, with an enigmatic smile. He was pacing up and down the room smoking furiously, only to stop suddenly and stare again at the ceiling.

"It's the clue," he said slowly. "It's the clue to everything. It must be. Though what that everything is I know no more than you. Listen, Mansford, and pay careful attention. This trail is too old to follow: in sporting parlance the scent is too faint. We've got to get it renewed: we've got to get your ghost to walk again. Now I've only the wildest suspicions to go on, but I have a feeling that that ghost will be remarkably shy of walking if there are strangers about. I'm just gambling on one very strange fact—so strange as to make it impossible to be an accident. When you go downstairs I shall adopt the role of advising you to have this room shut up. You will laugh at me, and announce your intention of sleeping in this room tonight. You will insist on clearing this matter up. Tom and I will go, and we shall return later to the grounds, where I see there is some very good cover. You will come to bed here—you will get into bed and switch out the light. You will give it a quarter of an hour, and then you will drop out of the window and join us. And we shall see if anything happens."

"But if we're all outside, how can we?" cried Mansford.

Standish smiled grimly. "You may take it from me," he remarked, "that if my suspicions are correct the ghost will leave a trail. And it's the trail I'm interested in—not the ghost. Let's go and don't forget your part."

"But, my God! Standish—can't you tell me a little more?"

"I don't know any more to tell you," answered Standish gravely. "All I can say is—as you value your life don't fall asleep in this room. And don't breathe a word of this conversation to a soul."

Ten minutes later he and I were on our way back to the Old Hall.

True to his instructions Mansford had carried out his role admirably, as we came down the stairs and stood talking in the hall. He gave it to be understood that he was damned if he was going to let things drop: that if Standish had no ideas on the matter—well, he was obliged to him for the trouble he had taken—but from now on he was going to take the matter into his own hands. And he proposed to start that night. He had turned to one of the footmen standing by, and had given instructions for the bed to be made up, while Ronald had shrugged his shoulders and shaken his head.

"Understandable, Mansford," he remarked, "but unwise. My advice to you is to have that room shut up."

And the old butler, shutting the door of the car, had fully agreed.

"Obstinate, sir," he whispered, "like his father. Persuade him to have it shut up, sir—if you can. I'm afraid of that room—afraid of it."

"You think something will happen tonight, Ronald," I said as we turned into the Old Hall.

"I don't know, Tom," he said slowly. "I'm utterly in the dark—utterly. And if the sun hadn't been shining today while we were in that room, I shouldn't have even the faint glimmer of light I've got now. But when you've got one bit of a jigsaw, it saves trouble to let the designer supply you with a few more."

And more than that he refused to say. Throughout dinner he talked cricket with old Tremayne: after dinner he played him at billiards. And it was not until eleven o'clock that he made a slight sign to me, and we both said goodnight.

"No good anyone knowing, Tom," he said as we went upstairs. "It's an easy drop from my window to the ground. We'll walk to Staveley Grange."

The church clock in the little village close by was striking midnight as we crept through the undergrowth towards the house. It was a dark night—the moon was not due to rise for another three hours—and we finally came to a halt behind a big bush on the edge of the lawn from which we could see the house clearly. A light was still shining from the windows of the fatal room, and once or twice we saw Mansford's shadow as he undressed. Then the light went out, and the house was in darkness: the vigil had begun.

For twenty minutes or so we waited, and Standish began to fidget uneasily.

"Pray heavens! he hasn't forgotten and gone to sleep," he whispered to me, and even as he spoke he gave a little sigh of relief. A dark

17

figure was lowering itself out of the window, and a moment or two later we saw Mansford skirting the lawn. A faint hiss from Standish and he'd joined us under cover of the bush.

"Everything seemed perfectly normal," he whispered. "I got into bed as you said—and there's another thing I did too. I've tied a thread across the door, so that if the ghost goes in that way we'll know."

"Good," said Standish. "And now we can compose ourselves to wait. Unfortunately we mustn't smoke."

Slowly the hours dragged on, while we took it in turns to watch the windows through a pair of night glasses. And nothing happened—absolutely nothing. Once it seemed to me as if a very faint light—it was more like a lessening of the darkness than an actual light—came from the room, but I decided it must be my imagination. And not till nearly five o'clock did Standish decide to go into the room and explore. His face was expressionless: I couldn't tell whether he was disappointed or not. But Mansford made no effort to conceal his feelings: frankly he regarded the whole experiment as a waste of time.

And when the three of us had clambered in by the window he said as much.

"Absolutely as I left it," he said. "Nothing happened at all."

"Then, for heaven's sake, say so in a whisper," snapped Standish irritably, as he clambered on to the bed. Once again his objective was the right hand wire stay of the canopy, and as he touched it he gave a quick exclamation. But Mansford was paying no attention: he was staring with puzzled eyes at the electric fan by the bed.

"Now who the devil turned that on," he muttered. "I haven't seen it working since the morning Tom died." He walked round to the door. "Say, Standish—that's queer. The thread isn't broken—and that fan wasn't going when I left the room."

Ronald Standish looked more cheerful.

"Very queer," he said. "And now I think, if I was you, I'd get into that bed and go to sleep—first removing the thread from the door. You're quite safe now."

"Quite safe," murmured Mansford. "I don't understand."

"Nor do I—as yet," returned Standish. "But this I will tell you. Neither your father nor your brother died of heart failure, through seeing some dreadful sight. They were foully murdered, as, in all probability you would have been last night had you slept in this room."

"But who murdered them, and how and why?" said Mansford dazedly.

18

"That is just what I'm going to find out," answered Standish grim-ly.

******

As we came out of the breakfast-room at the Old Hall three hours later, Standish turned away from us. "I'm going into the garden to think," he said. "I have a sort of feeling that I'm not being very clever. For the life of me at the moment I cannot see the connection between the canopy wire that failed to shine in the sunlight, and the electric fan that was turned on so mysteriously. I am going to sit under that tree over there. Possibly the link may come."

He strolled away, and Molly joined me. She was looking worried and *distraite*, as she slipped her hand through my arm.

"Has he found out anything, Tom?" she asked eagerly. "He seemed so silent and preoccupied at breakfast."

"He's found out something, Molly," I answered guardedly, "but I'm afraid he hasn't found out much. In fact, as far as my brain goes it seems to me to be nothing at all. But he's an extraordinary fellow," I added, reassuringly.

She gave a little shudder and turned away.

"It's too late, Tom," she said miserably.

"Oh! if only I'd sent for you earlier. But it never dawned on me that it would come to this. I never dreamed that Bill would be suspected. He's just telephoned through to me: that horrible man McIver—the inspector from Scotland Yard—is up there now. I feel that it's only a question of time before they arrest him. And though he'll get off—he must get off if there's such a thing as justice—the suspicion will stick to him all his life. There will be brutes who will say that failure to prove that Bill did it, is a very different matter to proving that he didn't. But I'm going to marry him all the same, Tom—whatever he says. Of course, I suppose you know that he didn't get on too well with his father."

"I didn't," I answered. "I know nothing about him except just what I've seen."

"And the other damnable thing is that he was in some stupid money difficulty. He'd backed a bill or something for a pal and was let down, which made his father furious. Of course there was nothing in it, but the police got hold of it—and twisted it to suit themselves."

"Well, Molly, you may take it from me," I said reassuringly, "that Bob Standish is certain he had nothing to do with it."

"That's not much good, Tom," she answered with a twisted smile.

"So am I certain, but I can't prove it."

With a little shrug of her shoulders she turned and went indoors, leaving me to my own thoughts. I could see Standish in the distance, with his head enveloped in a cloud of smoke, and after a moment's indecision I started to stroll down the drive towards the lodge. It struck me that I would do some thinking on my own account, and see if by any chance I could hit on some solution which would fit the facts. And the more I thought the more impossible did it appear: the facts at one's disposal were so terribly meagre.

What horror had old Mansford seen coming at him out of the darkness, which he had tried to ward off even as he died? And was it the same thing that had come to his elder son, who had sprung forward revolver in hand, and died as he sprang? And again, who had turned on the electric fan? How did that fit in with the deaths of the other two? No one had come in by the door on the preceding night: no one had got in by the window. And then suddenly I paused, struck by a sudden idea. Staveley Grange was an old house—early sixteenth century; just the type of house to have secret passages and concealed entrances. . . . There must be one into the fatal room: it was obvious.

Through that door there had crept some dreadful thing—some man, perhaps, and if so the murderer himself—disguised and dressed up to look awe-inspiring. Phosphorus doubtless had been used—and phosphorus skilfully applied to a man's face and clothes will make him sufficiently terrifying at night to strike tenor into the stoutest heart. Especially someone just awakened from sleep. That faint luminosity which we thought we had seen the preceding night was accounted for, and I almost laughed at dear old Ronald's stupidity in not having looked for a secret entrance. I was one up on him this time.

Mrs. Bretherton's story came back to me—her so-called nightmare—in which she affirmed she had been touched by a shining skinny hand. Shining—here lay the clue—the missing link. The arm of the murderer only was daubed with phosphorus; the rest of his body was in darkness. And the terrified victim waking suddenly would be confronted with a ghastly shining arm stretched out to clutch his throat.

A maniac probably—the murderer: a maniac who knew the secret entrance to Staveley Grange: a homicidal maniac—who had been frightened in his foul work by Mrs. Bretherton's shrieks, and had fled before she had shared the same fate as the Mansfords. Then and there I determined to put my theory in front of Ronald. I felt that I'd stolen a march on him this time at any rate.

I found him still puffing furiously at his pipe, and he listened in silence while I outlined my solution with a little pardonable elation.

"Dear old Tom," he said as I finished. "I congratulate you. The only slight drawback to your idea is that there is no secret door into the room."

"How do you know that?" I cried. "You hardly looked."

"On the contrary, I looked very closely. I may say that for a short while I inclined to some such theory as the one you've just put forward. But as soon as I saw that the room had been papered I dismissed it at once. As far as the built-in cupboard was concerned, it was erected by a local carpenter quite recently, and any secret entrance would have been either blocked over or known to him. Besides McIver has been in charge of this case—Inspector McIver from Scotland Yard. Now he and I have worked together before, and I have the very highest opinion of his ability. His powers of observation are extraordinary, and if his powers of deduction were as high he would be in the very first flight. Unfortunately he lacks imagination. But what I was leading up to was this. If McIver failed to find a secret entrance, it would be so much waste of time looking for one oneself. And if he had found one, he wouldn't have been able to keep it dark. We should have heard about it sharp enough."

"Well, have you got any better idea," I said a little peevishly. "If there isn't any secret door, how the deuce was that fan turned on?"

"There is such a thing as a two-way switch," murmured Ronald mildly. "That fan was not turned on from inside the room: it was turned on from somewhere else. And the person who turned it on was the murderer of old Mansford and his son."

I stared at him in amazement.

"Then all you've got to do," I cried excitedly, "is to find out where the other terminal of the two-way switch is? If it's in someone's room you've got him."

"Precisely, old man. But if it's in a passage, we haven't. And here, surely, is McIver himself. I wonder how he knew I was here?"

I turned to see a short thick-set man approaching us over the lawn.

"He was up at Staveley Grange this morning," I said. "Mansford telephoned through to Molly."

"That accounts for it then," remarked Standish waving his hand at the detective. "Good-morning, Mac."

"Morning, Mr. Standish," cried the other. "I've just heard that

21

you're on the track, so I came over to see you."

"Splendid," said Standish. "This is Mr. Belton—a great friend of mine—who is responsible for my giving up a good week's cricket and coming down here. He's a friend of Miss Tremayne's."

McIver looked at me shrewdly.

"And therefore of Mr. Mansford's, I see."

"On the contrary," I remarked. "I never met Mr. Mansford before yesterday.

"I was up at Staveley Grange this morning," said McIver, "and Mr. Mansford told me you'd all spent the night on the lawn."

I saw Standish give a quick frown, which he instantly suppressed.

"I trust he told you that in private, McIver."

"He did. But why?"

"Because I want it to be thought that he slept in that room," answered Standish. "We're moving in deep waters, and a single slip at the present moment may cause a very unfortunate state of affairs."

"In what way?" grunted McIver.

"It might frighten the murderer," replied Standish. "And if he is frightened, I have my doubts if we shall ever bring the crime home to him. And if we don't bring the crime home to him, there will always be people who will say that Mansford had a lot to gain by the deaths of his father and brother."

"So you think it was murder?" said McIver slowly, looking at Standish from under his bushy eyebrows.

Ronald grinned. "Yes, I quite agree with you on that point."

"I haven't said what I think!" said the detective.

"True, McIver—perfectly true. You have been the soul of discretion. But I can hardly think that Scotland Yard would allow themselves to be deprived of your valuable services for two months while you enjoyed a rest cure in the country. Neither a ghost nor two natural deaths would keep you in Devonshire."

McIver laughed shortly.

"Quite right, Mr. Standish. I'm convinced it's murder: it must be. But frankly speaking, I've never been so absolutely floored in all my life. Did you find out anything last night?"

Standish lit a cigarette.

"Two very interesting points—two extremely interesting points, I may say, which I present to you free *gratis* and for nothing. One of the objects of oil is to reduce friction, and one of the objects of an electric fan is to produce a draught. And both these profound facts have a very direct bearing on. . ." He paused and stared across the lawn. "Hullo! here is our friend Mansford in his car. Come to pay an early call, I suppose."

The Australian was standing by the door talking to his *fiancée*, and after a glance in their direction, McIver turned back to Ronald.

"Well, Mr. Standish, go on. Both those facts have a direct bearing on—what?"

But Ronald Standish made no reply. He was staring fixedly at Mansford, who was slowly coming towards us talking to Molly Tremayne. And as he came closer, it struck me that there was something peculiar about his face. There was a dark stain all round his mouth, and every now and then he pressed the back of his hand against it as if it hurt.

"Well, Standish," he said with a laugh, as he came up, "here's a fresh development for your ingenuity. Of course," he added, "it can't really have anything to do with it, but it's damned painful. Look at my mouth."

"I've been looking at it," answered Ronald. "How did it happen?"

"I don't know. All I can tell you is that about an hour ago it began to sting like blazes and turn dark red."

And now that he had come closer, I could see that there was a regular ring all round his mouth, stretching up almost to his nostrils and down to the cleft in his chin. It was dark and angry-looking, and was evidently paining him considerably.

"I feel as if I'd been stung by a family of hornets," he remarked. "You didn't leave any infernal chemical in the telephone, did you, Inspector McIver?"

"I did not," answered the detective stiffly, to pause in amazement as Standish uttered a shout of triumph.

"I've got it!" he cried. "The third point—the third elusive point. Did you go to sleep this morning as I suggested, Mansford?"

"No, I didn't," said the Australian, looking thoroughly mystified. "I sat up on the bed puzzling over that darned fan for about an hour, and then I decided to shave. Well, the water in the tap wasn't hot, so—"

"You blew down the speaking-tube to tell someone to bring you some," interrupted Standish quietly.

"I did," answered Mansford. "But how the devil did you know?"

"Because one of the objects of a speaking-tube, my dear fellow, is to speak through. Extraordinary how that simple point escaped me. It only shows, McIver, what I have invariably said: the most obvious points are the ones which most easily elude us. Keep your most private papers loose on your writing-table, and your most valuable possessions in an unlocked drawer, and you'll never trouble the burglary branch of your insurance company."

"Most interesting," said McIver with ponderous sarcasm. "Are we to understand, Mr. Standish, that you have solved the problem?"

"Why, certainly," answered Ronald, and Mansford gave a sharp cry of amazement. "Oil reduces friction, an electric fan produces a draught, and a speaking-tube is a tube to speak through secondarily; primarily, it is just—a tube. For your further thought, McIver, I would suggest to you that Mrs. Bretherton's digestion was much better than is popularly supposed, and that a brief perusal of some chemical work, bearing in mind Mr. Mansford's remarks that he felt as if he'd been stung by a family of hornets, would clear the air."

"Suppose you cease jesting, Standish," said Mansford a little brusquely. "What exactly do you mean by all this?"

"I mean that we are up against a particularly clever and ingenious murderer," answered Standish gravely. "Who he is—I don't know; why he's done it—I don't know; but one thing I do know—he is a very dangerous criminal. And we want to catch him in the act. Therefore, I shall go away today; McIver will go away today; and you, Mansford, will sleep in that room again tonight. And this time, instead of you joining us on the lawn—we shall all join you in the room. Do you follow me?"

"I follow you," said Mansford excitedly. "And we'll catch him in the act."

"Perhaps," said Standish quietly. "And perhaps we may have to wait a week or so. But we'll catch him, provided no one says a word of this conversation."

"But look here, Mr. Standish," said McIver peevishly. "I'm not going away today. I don't understand all this rigmarole of yours, and ..."

"My very good Mac," laughed Standish. "you trot away and buy a ticket to London. Then get out at the first stop and return here after dark. And I'll give you another point to chew the cud over. Mrs. Bretherton was an elderly and timorous lady, and elderly and timorous ladies, I am told, put their heads under the bed-clothes if they are frightened. Mr. Mansford's father and brother were strong virile men, who do not hide their heads under such circumstances. They died, and Mrs. Bretherton lived. Think it over—and bring a gun tonight."

For the rest of the day we saw no sign of Ronald Standish. He had driven off in the Tremayne's car to the station, and had taken

McIver with him. And there we understood from the chauffeur they had both taken tickets to London and left the place. Following Ronald's instructions, Mansford had gone back to Staveley Grange, and announced the fact of their departure, at the same time stating his unalterable intention to continue occupying the fatal room until he had solved the mystery. Then he returned to the Old Hall, where Molly, he and I spent the day, racking our brains in futile endeavours to get to the bottom of it.

"What beats me," said Mansford, after we had discussed every conceivable and inconceivable possibility, "is that Standish can't know any more than we do. We've both seen exactly what he's seen; we both know the facts just as well as he does. We're neither of us fools, and yet he can see the solution—and we can't."

"It's just there that he is so wonderful," I answered thoughtfully. "He uses his imagination to connect what are apparently completely disconnected facts. And you may take it from me, Mansford, that he's very rarely wrong."

The Australian pulled at his pipe in silence.

"I think we'll find everything out tonight," he said at length. "Somehow or other I've got great faith in that pal of yours. But what is rousing my curiosity almost more than how my father and poor old Tom were murdered is who did it? Everything points to it being someone in the house—but in heaven's name, who? I'd stake my life on the two footmen—one of them came over with us from Australia. Then there's that poor old boob Templeton, who wouldn't hurt a fly—and his wife, and the other women servants, who, incidentally, are all new since Tom died. It beats me—beats me utterly."

For hours we continued the unending discussion, while the afternoon dragged slowly on. At six o'clock Mansford rose to go: his orders were to dine at home. He smiled reassuringly at Molly, who clung to him nervously; then with a cheerful wave of his hand he vanished down the drive. My orders were equally concise: to dine at the Old Hall—wait there until it was dark, and then make my way to the place where Standish and I had hidden the previous night.

It was not till ten that I deemed it safe to go; then slipping a small revolver into my pocket, I left the house by a side door and started on my three-mile walk.

As before, there was no moon, and in the shadow of the undergrowth I almost trod on Ronald before I saw him.

"That you, Tom?" came his whisper, and I lay down at his side. I could dimly see McIver a few feet away, and then once again began the vigil. It must have been about half-past eleven that the lights were switched on in the room, and Mansford started to go to bed. Once he came to the window and leaned out, seeming to stare in our direction; then he went back to the room, and we could see his shadow as he moved about. And I wondered if he was feeling nervous.

At last the light went out, and almost at once Standish rose.

"There's no time to lose," he muttered. "Follow me—and not a sound."

Swiftly we crossed the lawn and clambered up the old buttressed wall to the room above. I heard Ronald's whispered greeting to Mansford, who was standing by the window in his pyjamas, and then McIver joined us, blowing slightly. Climbing walls was not a common form of exercise as far as he was concerned.

"Don't forget," whispered Standish again, "not a sound, not a whisper. Sit down and wait."

He crossed to the table by the bed—the table on which stood the motionless electric fan. Then he switched on a small electric torch, and we watched him eagerly as he took up the speaking-tube. From his pocket he extracted what appeared to be a hollow tube some three inches long, with a piece of material attached to one end. This material he tied carefully round the end of the speaking-tube, thereby forming a connection between the speaking-tube and the short hollow one he had removed from his pocket. And finally he placed a cork very lightly in position at the other end of the metal cylinder. Then he switched off his torch and sat down on the bed. Evidently his preparations were complete; there was nothing to do now but wait.

The ticking of the clock on the mantelpiece sounded incredibly loud in the utter silence of the house. One o'clock struck—then half-past—when suddenly there came a faint pop from near the bed which made me jump violently. I heard Ronald drawing his breath sharply and craned forward to see what was happening. There came a gentle rasping noise, as Standish lit his petrol cigarette lighter. It gave little more light than a flickering glimmer, but it was just enough for me to see what he was doing. He was holding the flame to the end of the hollow tube, in which there was no longer a cork. The little pop had been caused by the cork blowing out. And then to my amazement a blue flame sprang from the end of the tube, and burnt steadily. It burnt with a slight hiss, like a Bunsen burner in a laboratory—and it gave about the same amount of light. One could just see Ronald's face

26

looking white and ghostly; then he pulled the bed curtain round the table, and the room was in darkness once again.

McIver was sitting next to me and I could hear his hurried breathing over the faint hiss of the hidden flame. And so we sat for perhaps ten minutes, when a board creaked in the room above us.

"It's coming now," came in a quick whisper from Ronald. "Whatever I do—don't speak, don't make a sound."

I make no bones about it, but my heart was going in great sickening thumps. I've been in many tight corners in the course of my life, but this silent room had got my nerves stretched to the limit. And I don't believe McIver was any better. I know I bore the marks of his fingers on my arm for a week after.

"My God! look," I heard him breathe, and at that moment I saw it. Up above the window on the right a faint luminous light had appeared, in the centre of which was a hand. It wasn't an ordinary hand—it was a skinny, claw-like talon, which glowed and shone in the darkness. And even as we watched it, it began to float downwards towards the bed. Steadily and quietly it seemed to drift through the room—but always towards the bed. At length it stopped, hanging directly over the foot of the bed and about three feet above it.

The sweat was pouring off my face in streams, and I could see young Mansford's face in the faint glow of that ghastly hand, rigid and motionless with horror. Now for the first time he knew how his father and brother had died—or he would know soon. What was this dismembered talon going to do next? Would it float forward to grip him by the throat—or would it disappear as mysteriously as it had come?

I tried to picture the dreadful terror of waking up suddenly and seeing this thing in front of one in the darkened room; and then I saw that Ronald was about to do something. He was kneeling on the bed examining the apparition in the most matter of fact way, and suddenly he put a finger to his lips and looked at us warningly. Then quite deliberately he hit at it with his fist, gave a hoarse cry, and rolled off the bed with a heavy thud.

He was on his feet in an instant, again signing to us imperatively to be silent, and we watched the thing swinging backwards and forwards as if it was on a string. And now it was receding—back towards the window and upwards just as it had come, while the oscillations grew less and less, until, at last it had vanished completely, and the room once more was in darkness save for the faint blue flame which still burnt steadily at the end of the tube.

"My God!" muttered McIver next to me, as he mopped his brow with a handkerchief, only to be again imperatively silenced by a gesture from Standish. The board creaked in the room above us, and I fancied that I heard a door close very gently: then all was still once more.

Suddenly with disconcerting abruptness the blue flame went out, almost as if it had been a gas jet turned off. And simultaneously a faint whirring noise and a slight draught on my face showed that the electric fan had been switched on. Then we heard Ronald's voice giving orders in a low tone. He had switched on his torch, and his eyes were shining with excitement.

"With luck we'll get the last act soon," he muttered. "Mansford, lie on the floor, as if you'd fallen off the bed. Sprawl: sham dead, and don't move. We three will be behind the curtain in the window. Have you got handcuffs, Mac," he whispered as we went to our hiding place. "Get 'em on as soon as possible, because I'm inclined to think that our bird will be dangerous."

McIver grunted, and once again we started to wait for the unknown. The electric fan still whirred, and looking through the window I saw the first faint streaks of dawn. And then suddenly Standish gripped my arm; the handle of the door was being turned. Slowly it opened, and someone came in shutting it cautiously behind him. He came round the bed, and paused as he got to the foot. He was crouching—bent almost double—and for a long while he stood there motionless. And then he began to laugh, and the laugh was horrible to hear. It was low and exulting—but it had a note in it which told its own story. The man who crouched at the foot of the bed was a maniac.

"On him," snapped Ronald, and we sprang forward simultaneously. The man snarled and fought like a tiger—but madman though he was he was no match for the four of us. Mansford had sprung to his feet the instant the fight started, and in a few seconds we heard the click of McIver's handcuffs. It was Standish who went to the door and switched on the light, so that we could see who it was. And the face of the handcuffed man, distorted and maniacal in its fury, was the face of the butler Templeton.

"Pass the handcuffs round the foot of the bed, McIver," ordered Standish. "and we'll leave him here. We've got to explore upstairs now."

McIver slipped off one wristlet, passed it round the upright of the bed and snapped it to again. Then the four of us dashed upstairs.

"We want the room to which the speaking-tube communicates," cried Standish, and Mansford led the way. He flung open a door, and then with a cry of horror stopped dead in the doorway.

Confronting us was a wild-eyed woman, clad only in her night-dress. She was standing beside a huge glass retort, which bubbled and hissed on a stand in the centre of the room. And even as we stood there she snatched up the retort with a harsh cry, and held it above her head.

"Back," roared Standish. "back for your lives."

But it was not to be. Somehow or other the retort dropped from her hands and smashed to pieces on her own head. And a scream of such mortal agony rang out as I have never heard and hope never to hear again. Nothing could be done for her; she died in five minutes, and of the manner of the poor demented thing's death it were better not to write. For a large amount of the contents of the retort was hot sulphuric acid.

★★★★★★

"Well, Mansford," said Standish a few hours later, "your ghost is laid, your mystery is solved, and I think I'll be able to play in the last match of that tour after all."

We were seated in the Old Hall dining-room after an early break-fast and Mansford turned to him eagerly.

"I'm still in the dark," he said. "Can't you explain?"

Standish smiled. "Don't see it yet? Well—it's very simple. As you know, the first thing that struck my eye was that right-hand canopy wire. It didn't shine in the sun like the other one, and when I got up to examine it, I found it was coated with dried oil. Not one little bit of it—but the whole wire. Now that was very strange—very strange indeed. Why should that wire have been coated with oil—and not the other? I may say at once that I had dismissed any idea of psychic phenomena being responsible for your father's and brother's death. That such things exist we know—but they don't *kill* two strong men.

"However, I was still in the dark; in fact, there was only one ray of light. The coating of that wire with oil was so strange, that of itself it established with practical certainty the fact that a human agency was at work. And before I left the room that first afternoon I was certain that that wire was used to introduce something into the room from outside. The proof came the next morning. Overnight the wire had been dry; the following morning there was wet oil on it. The door was intact; no one had gone in by the window, and, further, the fan was going. Fact number two. Still, I couldn't get the connection. I admit that the fact that the fan was going suggested some form of gas—introduced by the murderer, and then removed by him automatically. And then you came along with your mouth blistered. You spoke of feeling as if you'd been stung by a hornet, and I'd got my third fact.

"To get it presupposed a certain knowledge of chemistry. Formic acid—which is what a wasp's sting consists of—can be used amongst other things for the manufacture of carbon monoxide. And with that the whole diabolical plot was clear. The speaking-tube was the missing link, through which carbon monoxide was poured into the room, bringing with it traces of the original ingredients which condensed on the mouthpiece. Now, as you may know, carbon monoxide is lighter than air, and is a deadly poison to breathe. Moreover, it leaves no trace—certainly no obvious trace. So before we went into the room last night, I had decided in my own mind how the murders had taken place. First from right under the sleeper's nose a stream of carbon monoxide was discharged, which I rendered harmless by igniting it. The canopy helped to keep it more or less confined, but since it was lighter than air, something was necessary to make the sleeper awake and sit up.

"That is precisely what your father and brother did when they saw the phosphorescent hand—and they died at once. Mrs. Bretherton hid her face and lived. Then the fan was turned on—the carbon monoxide was gradually expelled from the room, and in the morning no trace remained. If it failed one night it could be tried again the next until it succeeded. Sooner or later that infernal hand travelling on a little pulley wheel on the wire and controlled from above by a long string, would wake the sleeper—and then the end—or the story of a ghost."

He paused and pressed out his cigarette.

"From the very first also I had suspected Templeton. When you know as much of crime as I do—you're never surprised at anything. I admit he seemed the last man in the world who would do such a thing—but there are more cases of Jekyll and Hyde than we even dream of. And he and his wife were the only connecting links in the household staff between you and the Brethertons. That Mrs. Templeton also was mad had not occurred to me, and how much she was his assistant or his dupe we shall never know.

"She has paid a dreadful price, poor soul, for her share of it; the mixture that broke over her was hot concentrated sulphuric acid mixed with formic acid. Incidentally from inquiries made yesterday, I discovered that Staveley Grange belonged to a man named Templeton some forty years ago. This man had an illegitimate son, whom he did not provide for—and it may be that Templeton the butler is that son—gone mad. Obsessed with the idea that Staveley Grange should be his perhaps—who knows? No man can read a madman's mind."

He lit another cigarette and rose.

"So I can't tell you why. How you know and who: why must remain a mystery for ever. And now I think I can just catch my train."

"Yes, but wait a moment," cried Mansford. "There are scores of other points I'm not clear on."

"Think 'em out for yourself, my dear fellow," laughed Ronald. "I want to make a few runs tomorrow."

Tiny Carteret

Tiny Carteret stretched out a hand like a leg of mutton and picked up the marmalade. On the sideboard what remained of the kidneys and bacon still sizzled cheerfully on the hot plate: by his side a cup of dimensions suitable for a baby's bath gave forth the fragrant smell of coffee. In short, Tiny Carteret, half-way through his breakfast.

The window was wide open, and from the distance came the ceaseless roar of the traffic in Piccadilly. In the street just below, a gentleman of powerful but unmelodious voice was proclaiming the merits of his strawberries: whilst from the half-way mark came the ghastly sound of a cornet solo. In short, a service flat in Curzon Street.

The marmalade stage with Tiny was always the letter-opening stage, and as usual, he ran through the pile in front of him before beginning to read any of them. A couple of obvious bills: three more in feminine hands which proclaimed invitations of sorts with the utmost certainty—and then one over which he paused. The writing was a man's: moreover, it was one which he knew well although it was many months since he had seen it. Neat: decisive: strong—it gave the character of the writer with absolute accuracy.

"Ronald, by Jove!" muttered Tiny to himself. "And a Swiss postmark. Now what the dickens is the old lad doing there?"

He slit open the envelope, propped the letter against the coffee-pot, and began to read, it ran:

My Dear Tiny—

I know that at this time of year Ranelagh and Lords form your happy hunting-grounds, as a general rule by day, whilst at night you are in the habit of treading on unfortunate women's feet in divers ballrooms. Nevertheless, should you care to strike out on a new line, I think I can promise you quite a bit of fun out here. At least when I say here, this will be our starting-point. Where the trail may lead to, *Allah* alone knows. Seriously, Tiny, I have need of you. There is not going to be any poodle faking about it: in fact, the proposition is going to be an extremely tough one. So don't let's start under false pretences. There is going to be the devil of a lot of danger in it, and I want someone with a steady nerve, who can use a revolver if necessary, who has a bit of weight behind his fists and knows how to use 'em.

If the sound of this appeals to you send me a wire at once, and I will await your arrival here.

Yours ever, Ronald Standish.

P.S.—A good train leaves the Gare de Lyons at 9.10 p.m. Gives you plenty of time for dinner in Paris."

Tiny pulled out his case and thoughtfully lit a cigarette. A faint twinkle in his eyes showed that he appreciated the full significance of the postscript: Ronald Standish knew what his answer would be as well as he did himself. Even as the trout rises to the may-fly, so do the Tiny Carterets of this world rise to bait such as was contained in the body of the letter. And just because he knew he was going to swallow it whole, he played with it mentally for quite a time. He even went through the farcical performance of consulting his engagement book. For the next month he had not got a free evening—a thing he had been fully aware of long before he opened the book. In addition, such trifles as Ascot and Wimbledon loomed large during the daylight hours. In fact, he reflected, as he uncoiled his large bulk from the chair, the number of lies he would have to tell in the near future would probably fuse the telephone.

And at this period it might be well to give some slight description of him. The nickname Tiny was of course an obvious one to give a man who had been capped fifteen times for England playing in the scrum. But though he was extraordinarily bigly made, he was at the same time marvellously agile, as men who played him at squash found to their cost. He could run a much lighter man off his feet, without turning a hair himself. The last half of the war had found him in the Coldstream: then, bored with peace-time soldiering he had sent in his papers and taken to sport of every description, which, fortunately for him, the possession of five thousand a year enabled him to do with some ease.

That he was extremely popular with both men and women was not to be wondered at: he was so completely free from side of any sort. In fact, many a net had been spread in the sight of the wary old bird by girls who would have had no objection to becoming Mrs. Tiny. But so far beyond flirting outrageously with all and sundry he had refused to be caught, and now at the age of thirty he was still as far from settling down as ever.

Once again he glanced at Standish's letter. It had been sent from the Grand Hotel at Territet, a spot which he recalled as being on the Lake of Geneva. And once again he asked himself the same question— what on earth was Ronald Standish doing there of all places? Territet was associated in his mind with tourists and pretty little white steamers on the lake. Also years ago he had played in a tennis tournament there. But Ronald was a different matter altogether.

It had been said of Standish that only the Almighty and he himself knew what his job was, and that it was doubtful which of the two it would be the more difficult to find out from. If asked point blank he would stare at the speaker with a pair of innocent blue eyes and remark vaguely—"Damned if I know, old boy." For months on end he would remain in London leading the ordinary life of a man of means, then suddenly he would disappear at a moment's notice, only to reappear just as unexpectedly. And any inquiries as to where he had been would probably elucidate the illuminating answer that he had just been pottering round. But it was to be noticed that after these periodical disappearances his morning walk for a few days generally led towards that part of Whitehall where Secretaries of State live and move and have their being. It might also be noticed—if there was anyone there to see—that when Ronald Standish sent in his name he was not kept waiting.

Even with Tiny Carteret he had never been communicative, though they were members of the same clubs and the closest of friends. The farthest he had ever gone was to murmur vaguely something about intelligence. And it was significant that at the time of the Arcos raid the first question he had asked *before* opening the paper which contained the news, was the number of men who had been rounded up. Significant also that on two occasions after he had returned from these strange trips of his he had been absent from London for a day, once at Windsor and the other time at Sandringham.

At the moment he had been away for about a month. He had disappeared in his usual unexpected manner, leaving a Free Forester team one man short as a result. Which in itself was sufficient to show that the matter was important, for cricket was a mania with him. And yet Territet of all places! Tiny Carteret scratched his head and rang the bell.

"I'm leaving London, Murdoch," he said, when his valet appeared. "I'm going to Switzerland."

"Switzerland, sir?" The man looked at him as if he had taken leave of his senses. "At this time of year?"

"Even so, Murdoch," answered Tiny with a grin. "But I shan't want you."

"Very good, sir. And when will you be leaving?"

At that moment the telephone bell rang.

"See who it is, Murdoch. And then find out if I'm in."

The valet picked up the receiver, and Tiny heard a man's voice coming over the wire.

"Yes, sir. This is Mr. Carteret's flat. I will see if he is in."

He covered the mouthpiece with his hand and turned to his master.

"A Colonel Gillson, sir, wishes to speak to you."

"Gillson," muttered Tiny. "Who the devil is Gillson?"

He took the receiver from Murdoch.

"Hullo! Carteret speaking."

"Good morning." The voice was deep and pleasant. "I am Gillson. Speaking from the Home Office. Would you be good enough to come round and see me this morning any time before noon? The matter is somewhat urgent."

Tiny's face expressed his bewilderment.

"Sure you've got the right bloke?" he said. "The Home Office is a bit out of my line."

The man at the other end laughed.

"Quite sure," he answered. "You needn't be alarmed. Ask for Room 73."

"All right," said Tiny. "I'll be round about half-past eleven."

"Now what the dickens does Colonel Gillson of the Home Office want with me, Murdoch?" he remarked thoughtfully, as he hung up the receiver. "And where is the Home Office, anyway?"

"A taxi-driver might know that, sir," said Murdoch helpfully. "But to go back, sir, for the moment: when will you be leaving?"

Tiny lit a cigarette, and blew out a great cloud of smoke.

"Tomorrow," he said at length. "That will leave me today to tell the necessary lies in, and get my reservations."

"How long shall I pack for, sir?" inquired his man.

Tiny gave a short laugh.

"Ask me another," he said. "I'm darned if I know, Murdoch. Give me enough to last a fortnight anyway. And one other thing." He turned at the door. "Get that Colt revolver of mine oiled and cleaned, and pack it in the centre of my kit."

He went down the stairs chuckling gently at the look of scandalized horror on his valet's face. Revolvers! Switzerland in the middle of the London season! Such things were simply not done, as Murdoch explained a little later to his wife.

"Hindecent, I calls it: positively hindecent. Why we were dining out every night."

But Tiny Carteret, supremely unconscious of the regal pronoun, was strolling happily along Clarges Street. The morning was perfect: London looked her best, but no twinge of regret assailed him at leaving. There were many more mornings in the future when London would look her best, but a hunt with Ronald Standish was not a thing a man could hope for twice. And as he turned into Piccadilly he found himself trying to puzzle out what the game was going to be.

The Lake of Geneva! Could it be something to do with the League of Nations? And Bolshevism? He rather hoped not. Unwashed international Jews, plentifully covered with hair and masquerading as Russians, failed to arouse his enthusiasm.

"Hullo! Tiny. If you want to kiss me, do you mind doing it somewhere else."

He came out of his reverie to find himself towering above a delightful vision in blue.

"Vera, my angel," he said, "I eat dirt. For the moment my brain was immersed in the realms of higher philosophy."

"You mean you were wondering if it was too early for a drink at your club," she answered. "Anyway don't forget next weekend."

"Ah! next weekend. Now that's a bad affair—next weekend. For tomorrow, most ravishing of your sex, I leave for Switzerland."

"You do what?" she cried, staring at him.

"Leave for Switzerland," he grinned. "I am going to pick beautiful mountain flowers—roses, and tulips and edelweisses and all that sort of thing."

"Tiny! You must be mad! What about our party?"

"I know, my pet. My heart is as water when I think of it. But it is the doctor's orders. He says I require building up."

"There's a girl in it," she said accusingly.

"Thumbs crossed—there isn't. You are the only woman in my life. Good God! my dear—it is a quarter past eleven. I must hop it. Think of me, Vera, in the days to come—alone with chamois—yodelling from height to height in my endeavours to please the intelligent little fellows. Would you like me to yodel now?"

"For Heaven's sake don't. And I think you are a perfect beast."

Tiny took out his handkerchief and began to sob loudly.

"Jilted!" he boomed in a loud voice, to the intense delight of a crowd of people waiting close by for a motor-bus. "Jilted by a woman for whom I have given up my honour, my fortune, even my morning beer."

"You unspeakable ass," she cried, striving vainly not to laugh. "Go away at once. And I hope you get mountain sickness, and die in an avalanche."

He resumed his interrupted walk feeling rather guilty. He knew that the girl he had just left had engineered the week-end party simply and solely on his account, and he had gone and let her down. Now it would be to her even as gall and wormwood, and she really was a darling.

"In fact, young fellow," he ruminated, "you must go easier with the little pretties in future. It's a shame to raise false hopes in their sweet young hearts. And one of these days you'll get it in the neck yourself."

He hailed a passing taxi and told the man to drive to the Home Office. Vera Lethington was forgotten: the immediate and interesting problem was, What did Colonel Gillson want with him? Presumably it must be something to do with Ronald Standish, since he could think of no other possible reason for the summons.

He asked for Room 73, and on giving his name was at once shown up. Seated at the desk was a hatchet-faced man with an enormous nose, who rose as he entered. He was very tall, and his eyes, keen and steady, seemed to take in every detail of his visitor at a glance.

"Mornin', Carteret," he said, and the words were short and clipped. "Take a pew. I suppose you know why I rang you up."

"Well, since I haven't been copped in a nightclub raid, Colonel, I can hazard a pretty shrewd guess," answered Tiny with a grin.

The other man smiled faintly.

"That's a matter for Scotland Yard. Incidentally you were having a pretty good time at the Fifty-Nine last Tuesday."

Tiny gazed at him in amazement.

"How the devil do you know? You weren't there, were you?"

"I was not," laughed Gillson. "Nature has endowed me with a nasal organ which renders me somewhat conspicuous. So I do not frequent clubs of that sort."

"Then how did you know?" persisted Tiny.

"Had you been stopping in London," said the other quietly, "now that I know you are a friend of Standish, I should have given you a word of warning about that club."

"You assume I am not stopping on then," said Tiny.

"Naturally," answered Gillson. "A man with fifteen caps would hardly be likely to."

"Oh! that's rot, Colonel. But you still haven't told me how you knew I was there."

"I've got a list, my dear boy, of every single soul who was in that club that night. Your waiter gave it to me."

"Well, I wish the damned fellow had concentrated more on his waiting and less on making a list. He slopped soup all over my trousers."

"Seeing it was the first time he had waited I don't suppose he was too bad," said the other quietly. "A bad spot that, Carteret: a festering sore. I don't mean because they sell liquor out of hours: that by comparison is nothing. But it is the centre. . ." He paused and lit a cigarette. "Well, I wouldn't be surprised if in the course of the next few weeks you didn't find yourself back there again—shall we say professionally."

"This is all deuced intriguing, Colonel," said Tiny. "Can't you be a bit more explicit?"

"All in good time, my dear fellow. Let us first get down to the immediate future. I assume you are leaving tomorrow."

"Quite right," answered Tiny. "Provided I can get reservations."

Colonel Gillson opened a drawer in his desk.

"I've got them all here," he said calmly. "And your ticket as well."

"The devil you have," spluttered Tiny, half inclined to be annoyed. "And supposing I hadn't been going tomorrow."

The older man looked at him steadily for a moment or two.

"Then I should have made a very bad mistake in my judgment of human nature," he said quietly. "A mistake which would have disappointed me greatly."

"Thank you, sir," answered Tiny, all his irritation gone. "That's a very decent thing to say."

"Now then," said the other, "we'll get down to brass tacks. You will go by the 10.45 train from Victoria: your seat is booked in Pullman S.2. Take the Golden Arrow to Paris: then go to Philippe's Restaurant in the Rue Danou. You know it?"

"Can't say I do, Colonel."

"You will find it one of the most delightful restaurants in Paris. The *homard à la maison* is one of the wonders of the world. It is a small place, but travelling as you are by the Golden Arrow you will almost certainly be the first arrival, so that you will have no trouble over getting a table."

"If there is, I'll mention your name."

"Under no circumstances will you do anything of the sort, Carteret," said the other quietly. "Under no circumstances are you to mention to a soul that you have seen me today. Do you remember that French notice in the war—'*Mefiez vous. Taisez vous. Les oreilles de l'ennemi vous écoutent.*'"

He smiled a little at the look of astonishment on Tiny's face.

"My dear fellow," he continued, "don't think I'm being melodramatic. But in our trade the first rule, the second rule, and the last rule are all the same. Never say a word more than is necessary. And to mention my name there would not only be unnecessary, but might be suicidal. You don't suppose, do you, that I am giving you these detailed instructions merely to ensure that you have a good dinner?"

"Well—no," laughed Tiny. "I don't. But you must remember, Colonel, that this sort of work is a new one on me. Anyway what is going to happen when I've got down to the *homard à la maison*?"

"A message will be given to you either verbally or in writing: which I do not know, and exactly when I do not know. If in writing commit it to memory, and destroy the paper."

"Who will give me this message?" asked Tiny.

"A man," said the other. "Don't ask me to tell you what he will look like, for I haven't the faintest idea. Have you got it clear so far?"

"Perfectly," said Tiny.

"When you've had your dinner you will go to the Gare de Lyons in time to catch the 9.10 train for Switzerland. I have reserved you a berth in a sleeper, and it is more than probable, Carteret, that when you come to inspect that reservation and all that goes with it you will consign me to the nethermost depths of the pit."

"What do you mean, Colonel?" said the bewildered Tiny.

"You will find out in due course," answered the other with a grin. "But there is one thing, young fellow, and don't you forget it." The grin had departed. "Under no circumstances whatever are you to alter your bunk—not even if the rest of the coach is empty."

"Right you are, sir. I can't profess to understand what it is all about at the moment, but I know an order when I hear one. I sleep"—he glanced at the paper in his hand—"in Number 8 bunk. Hullo! the ticket is only as far as Lausanne."

"That is where you get out," said Gillson. "A room has been already taken for you at the Ouchy Palace Hotel. Go there, and then Standish will take over the ordering of your young life."

He rose, to show that the interview was over.

"But, dash it all, Colonel," pleaded Tiny, "can't you give me some idea as to what the game is?"

Gillson shook his head.

"You will find out all that it is good for you to know, at the time when it is good for you to know it. Believe me, my dear fellow, this reticence doesn't imply any lack of confidence on my part. But there are certain occasions when real genuine ignorance is worth untold gold. Standish is playing the hand at the moment, and you are a very important card. It must be left to him to decide when he is going to play you, and how he is going to play you. But if it is any comfort I can tell you one thing. I'd give a year's screw if some divine act of Providence would blast away a lump of my cursed nose. For with that landmark gone I could have faked my face sufficiently to go in your place."

"That sounds all right, anyway," laughed Tiny. "Any message for Ronald?"

And as he asked the question the telephone rang on the desk.

"Wait a moment," said the colonel. "Hullo!"

Tiny watched him idly as he stood there with the receiver to his ear. The lean hatchet face seemed frozen into a mask, so expressionless was it: only the eyes were glowingly alive. At last the voice from the other end ceased, and Gillson spoke.

"Can you come up at once, Dexter? You can. Good."

He replaced the instrument, and then stood motionless for more than a minute staring out of the window.

"Any message for Ronald," he said at length. "Yes, Carteret; there will be. You can tell him that Jebson has been murdered in the same way as the others. Wait a little. Dexter is coming, and we'll hear all about it. Incidentally, you know Dexter. You'd better dun him for another pair of trousers."

"You mean he was the waiter at the Fifty-Nine?"

But the other appeared not to have heard. With his hands in his pockets he was pacing up and down the office, his head thrust forward, his chin sunk on his chest, whilst Tiny leaned against the desk smoking. He did not speak again: he was busy with his own thoughts. So there was murder in the business, was there?... And more than one at that. And almost as if it was an echo of what was passing through his mind Colonel Gillson suddenly ceased his restless pacing and spoke.

"Don't be under any delusions, young Carteret. We're up against the big stuff this time with a vengeance."

He swung round as a knock sounded on the door.

"Come," he called, and a man entered whom Tiny recognised at once as the waiter.

"Morning, Dexter," said Gillson. "Bad affair this. You know Mr. Carteret, I think. He tells me you spoilt his trousers for him."

The newcomer grinned at Tiny.

"Sorry about it, Mr. Carteret. If only you'd stuck to kippers it would have been all right." He grew serious again and turned to Gillson. "You're right, sir: it is a bad affair. Am I to. . ." He glanced hesitatingly at Tiny.

"Carry on, Dexter. Mr. Carteret is now one of us."

"Well, sir, Jebson as you know was our permanency at the Fifty-Nine. He's been there now for over three months, and up to yesterday he was convinced that not a soul suspected he was not a genuine waiter. I saw him myself at lunchtime and he told me so. He's been waiting on two of the private rooms upstairs, and for over a fortnight nothing of any importance has taken place. Just the usual young fool, with the usual woman. But last night he told me he was expecting something of interest. That little swine Giuseppi who owns the place had been running in and out of one of his two rooms the whole morning, cursing and swearing and saying that this was wrong and that was wrong—a thing he never did for his ordinary *clientèle*. And then Jebson, happening to pass Giuseppi's office, heard him on the telephone ordering masses of orchids. Mauve orchids," he added meaningly.

Once again he paused and glanced at Tiny, as if doubtful whether to proceed.

"Mr. Carteret understands, Dexter, that any name he may hear mentioned in this office is as inviolate as if it was in confession," said Gillson quietly.

"Very good, sir," continued Dexter. "He at once appreciated the possible significance: the flowers had been mauve orchids the time before."

"Mauve orchids," said Tiny slowly. "Mauve orchids! Good Lord! it's impossible."

"What is impossible?" asked Gillson quietly.

"Nothing, sir, nothing. It was only a wild idea that flashed through my mind. Just a strange coincidence."

"The longer you are in this job, my boy, the more will you realise that nothing is impossible," said Gillson. "Well, Dexter: was it she?"

"That's the devil of it, sir—we don't know. Jebson did—but Jebson is dead. We don't know if it was Lady Mary."

Gillson's eyes were fixed on Tiny—a faintly quizzical look in them.

"Nothing is impossible, Carteret," he repeated quietly. "So that was the idea that had flashed through your mind."

"No: no, Colonel—nothing of the sort. Heavens! Nothing would induce Mary Ridgeway to go to a private room at the Fifty-Nine."

"And yet she was there six weeks ago alone with a man," said Gillson.

"Damn it, Colonel," said Tiny angrily, "this is going beyond a joke. Mary is a great personal friend of mine."

"Do you really imagine, Carteret," said the older man coldly, "that I should take the trouble to make a statement of that sort about any woman, whether she was a friend of yours or whether she wasn't, unless I knew it to be true? Well, Dexter?"

"That's all, sir. That's the sickening part of it. Jebson, poor devil, has been done in."

Tiny took a step forward.

"Look here, sir," he said to Gillson, "I apologise for my last remark. But you *cannot* mean to tell me that even if Lady Mary was there you hold her in any way responsible for this man Jebson's death?"

"Most certainly not," answered Gillson at once. "Such an idea never crossed my brain for a second. The person who is responsible for Jebson's death, is the man with whom Lady Mary—if it was she—was having supper. And he is the man we want, or perhaps I should say— one of the many men we want."

Tiny sank into a chair, his brain whirling. The whole thing was too preposterous. And yet—was it? Statements made in this quiet office seemed to carry with them a definite conviction which shook him. And Gillson had quietly said in the most matter-of-fact voice that six weeks ago she *had* been to the Fifty-Nine alone with a man. If so— what about last night?

He had been dancing with her at a house in Berkeley Square, and it had struck him more than once during the evening that she had seemed unusually *distraite*—so much so, in fact, that he had pulled her leg about it. And then at half-past eleven she had pleaded a headache and left. Nothing much to go on so far, it was true: but it was the matter of the mauve orchids that worried him, and that—he cursed himself now for not having kept a better guard on his tongue—had made him say what he did. Mary adored mauve orchids: all her friends knew it: half the world knew it on the evidence of Aunt Tabitha in *Society Snippets*.

And yet the whole thing seemed too preposterous. She was undoubtedly an unconventional girl, but there were certain things at which she would draw a very fast line. And it seemed to Tiny that dining in a private room at a place like the Fifty-Nine alone with a man was most emphatically one of them. Unless she had to: unless she had no alternative. He lit a cigarette thoughtfully, and then conscious that Gillson was eyeing him shrewdly he pulled himself together. His sudden remark could easily be attributed to the matter of mauve orchids: for the moment at any rate he saw no necessity to mention what he knew of her movements the previous night. Dexter was speaking, and Tiny forced himself to listen.

"Just the same way, sir—the same in every detail. He was an unmarried man and he lodged in a back road off Hammersmith Broadway. The woman who keeps the house heard him come in about two o'clock—she is sure about that because she happened to be awake at the time and the clock in her room struck the hour. Then she dozed off only to be woken up about an hour later by a choking sort of cry. Half shout—half moan is how she described it to me. Then there came the sound of a heavy fall in the room above her—the room which belonged to Jebson. Thinking he might be ill she put on her dressing-gown and ran upstairs. Then apparently she threw a faint at what she saw.

"I really don't blame her, sir," went on Dexter. "I saw the poor devil this morning and he was a pretty ghastly sight. He was in his pyjamas, half in and half out of bed. One hand was thrown up as if to ward something off, and his face was contorted hideously. Just like the others. Teeth bared: and only the whites of his eyes showing."

"Was the light on or off when the woman went in?" asked Gillson.

"On, sir. He was evidently just getting into bed."

"And the window?"

"Wide open."

"Would it be possible, without great difficulty, for someone outside to get in through the window?

"Quite impossible, sir, unless a ladder was used. But the room looks out at the back of the building. And about three yards away there is a sort of outhouse place. Nothing would be easier than for an agile man to scramble up on the roof of the outhouse, from where he could see straight into Jebson's room."

"Quite." Gillson nodded thoughtfully. "And where was it this time?"

"In the chest."

"Where was what?" cried Tiny.

"This is the fourth affair of this sort that has taken place," said Gillson. "In each case the appearance of the victims has been the same—distorted features, teeth set in a rigid snarl, only the whites of the eyes showing. And in each case somewhere or other on the body there has been a small scratch. But on no occasion has the thing with which the scratch was made been found. You found nothing, did you, Dexter, this time?"

"Not a thing, sir, though I went over the room with a fine toothcomb."

"But have you no explanation, Colonel?" asked Tiny.

"I certainly have an explanation as far as it goes. Unfortunately that isn't very far. That these four men were murdered I have no doubt, and they were murdered in precisely the same way. They were killed by the introduction into their system of some form of unknown poison, probably of the snake venom variety. It was injected through the scratch, and the ghastly expression on their faces was due to the agony of the muscular contortion as they died. But how was it injected? How was the scratch made?"

"Blowpipe and poisoned dart," suggested Tiny.

"You can blow a dart out of a pipe, Carteret," said the other, "but I have yet to hear of a person who can suck it back again. If it had been done that way we should have found the darts."

44

"That's true," agreed Tiny. "I suppose it couldn't have been done by actually introducing a snake into the room."

"Impossible, Mr. Carteret," said Dexter. "At least—almost impossible. I wouldn't say that anything was quite impossible in this case. But there are a number of difficulties over such a solution. How was it got into the room: how was it got away again? Besides, so far as I know there is no known brand of snake whose bite causes practically instantaneous death. Well, you aren't going to tell me that if Jebson found that he had been bitten by a snake he was going to do nothing about it until he died twenty minutes or so later."

"Surely," said Tiny, "the same objection applies to whatever it was that did it. You can't have a hole made in your chest without knowing it."

"Precisely," remarked Gillson. "To my mind that is the essence of the entire thing. And it is such an amazing feature of all the cases that there can be only one solution. Consider the facts. Four trained officers—each of them scratched by something: each of them taking some period of time—how long we do not know—to die, and yet not one of them doing anything during that period, either to call for help or even to write a message on a piece of paper. It is incredible: it is preposterous unless we assume one of two things. Either the poison is to all intents and purposes instantaneous, or they attached no importance to the initial puncture."

Dexter nodded his head thoughtfully.

"I get your meaning, sir. Though it doesn't seem to make things any easier," he added ruefully. "By what possible method could the scratch be made to seem accidental, and yet not be accidental?"

"When you have solved that, Dexter, you have solved the problem. But of one thing I am certain. None of those poor devils connected the pain they were suffering—pain which must have increased to agony at the end—with the thing that pricked them. If they had—with their training, their sense of duty—they would have left some record of it."

"Mightn't it be possible," put in Tiny, "that they did leave some message? And then, once they were dead, the murderer, who could then afford to take his time, destroyed it. From what you say, Dexter, the old lady fainted. Isn't it feasible that the murderer, who was concealed in the room the whole time, took the chance and calmly hopped it?"

"Doesn't get over my initial difficulty, Carteret," said Gillson. "What about that period of time between the puncture and death? Do you mean to tell me that Jebson was going to allow some strange man in his bedroom to stab him in the chest, and not raise Cain?"

"It's the devil," said Dexter. "Because whether it seemed an accident or whether it didn't, they had to make certain of doing it last night. I'm sure of that, though of course we've got no proof."

Tiny lit a cigarette.

"What should make you so sure of that?" he asked quietly.

"I believe he found out something whilst he was waiting," said the other. "And then perhaps he gave himself away—who knows? At any rate they did him in before he could make his report."

"Well, really, my dear fellow," remarked Tiny, "if you'll forgive my saying so, it seems a piece of the wildest guesswork. Why you should assume that there is any connection between this poor devil's death in Hammersmith, and a party in a private room at the Fifty-Nine is beyond my diminutive brain. And you, Colonel, went so far as to say that the man giving the party actually did it."

"Not so, Carteret: I said he was responsible for it. Which is rather different."

"A matter of words, sir. But I cannot forget either—going back a bit in the discussion—that the name of a great personal friend of mine was mentioned as possibly having been in that room. Well, put it how you will—though I quite realise that what is said inside these four walls is sacred—it's a pretty serious matter. Following it to its logical conclusion, Colonel, it boils down to this. That whoever the lady was who was present, she took part in some conversation with the others who were present which resulted in the murder of the man who was waiting on them. Am I right?"

Colonel Gillson took a couple of turns up and down the room: then he swung round and faced Tiny.

"I see that I shall have to alter my decision, Carteret." He glanced at his watch. "Come and have lunch with me at the Rag, and I'll put you wise."

CHAPTER 2

"Now you'll understand, Carteret, that what I'm going to tell you is for your ears and your ears alone."

The two men were seated in a corner of the smoking-room with coffee and brandy on the table in front of them.

"Fire ahead, Colonel. I don't mind confessing that I'm deuced curious. And you have my promise that I shan't say a word to a soul."

"I'll make it as short as possible," began Gillson. "And you had better realise right away from the start that a great deal of what I am going to say is in the nature of conjecture or even guesswork. Certain bald facts stick out, and on those pegs we have had to build up our theory. How much of that theory is right, and how much wrong, only time will show. And reading between the lines of a letter Standish wrote me, I think the time is pretty close at hand.

"However, let's get on with it. About five years ago there was a series of extraordinary and apparently disconnected crimes. They were not confined to England: in fact some of the most remarkable of them took place abroad. To take only a few at random. The murder of Rodrigo, the Spanish millionaire banker, in his house in Madrid; the death of Steiner, the German coal magnate, in Essen; Vanderstum the Dutchman, who was shot late one night when going back from a dinner-party in Amsterdam; Leyland, one of our own millionaires who was brutally done to death in an hotel in Liverpool—there are four that spring to my mind. And as I say, at first there seemed no connection between them. But if you go a little deeper into it you will find one factor that is common to all. In each of the four cases I have mentioned the death of the victim was of inestimable value to certain other people. I won't bore you with the why and the wherefore, but the bald fact remains that no tears were shed by various vested interests when they died. Don't misunderstand me: I don't mean the same vested interest in each case—I mean four different ones."

"I get you perfectly, Colonel," said Tiny.

"About that time, too, strange rumours began to go round in the underworld. At first the police paid no attention to them: then it was found that the same stories were being circulated in Paris and Berlin and all over the continent. It was the rumour of a thing which has long been the subject of sensational fiction—namely the super-criminal. The Napoleon of crime had at last arrived—the man who sat at the centre of things and pulled the strings while others did the work.

"For a long time I refused to believe it, but at length the evidence became so overwhelming that I had no alternative but to agree. Somewhere or other there was a controlling influence at work, though whether it was one man or several we didn't know. Nor do we know today. But after having sifted all the information we could lay our hands on, and rejected every scrap which seemed in the smallest degree doubtful, we came to the definite conclusion that a new factor in crime had arisen and a damned dangerous factor too. In short, we were confronted with a central body of unscrupulous and clever men who were prepared—at a price—to do your crimes for you."

"Good Lord! Colonel—it sounds incredible."

"Nevertheless it is the truth," said the other gravely. "It is a lamentable fact, but when you come into the realms of high finance a good many standards seem to change. And though I do not say for a moment that the people who stood to be ruined by Leyland, for instance, would ever have gone to the length of murdering him themselves, they were by no means averse to somebody else doing it for them. Of course, to a certain extent all this is conjecture. Not one of the many men who, I believe, were collectively responsible for Leyland's death has ever said a word. Naturally not. Though it is possibly suggestive that one of them—a man well known and well respected—has since committed suicide for no apparent reason."

"But what I don't understand," interrupted Tiny, "is how the dickens they set about it. How did they get in touch with this central body?"

"I don't suppose they did for a moment: the central body got in touch with them. My dear Carteret, if our theory is correct we are dealing with people whose brains are quite the equivalent of our own. We are dealing with an organisation which has ramifications and spies all over the place through whom it collects its information. And I believe what happened was this. Someone—some underling—cautiously approached one of the men who were up against Leyland. Probably no mention of the word murder was made. Probably all that was said was that for some large sum of money it could be guaranteed that Leyland would change his policy. Which shows, mark you, if my supposition is correct, that they are no ordinary type of criminal. Hardheaded business men don't part with their cash on vague promises, unless the man who makes them is pretty convincing. Anyway—still sticking to our theory—the fact remains that they did stump up, and Leyland was murdered."

"Have you any proof that they stumped up?" asked Tiny.

"No actual proof. But it is a significant fact that the bank account of the man who committed suicide shows that he drew out a sum of five thousand pounds about a week before Leyland was murdered—a proceeding so foreign to his usual habits that the cashier remarked on it."

"But surely something should be done about it."

"My dear fellow," said the other, with a short laugh, "one of the first things you find out in this game is the difference between knowing and proving. You won't believe it, but the police know of four men at large in London today—two of them members of first-class clubs—who have all committed murder. But they can't prove it, so nothing can be done. However, that is a digression: let's return to our friends. We dug and we delved: we tried channels known to us and channels unknown to us. We pieced together information received from every imaginable quarter and after a time things did begin to look a little clearer. But always did we come up against one impenetrable wall—the wall that we still haven't succeeded in climbing. Where is the big man? Who is the big man? At this minute we could lay our hands on half a dozen underlings, but where is the boss?"

"Interrupting you for a moment, Colonel," said Tiny, "did they use this poison on any of the cases you have mentioned?"

"No. That little joy is of comparative recent date. And you will be amazed when I tell you what we are now convinced was the first occasion it was used—at any rate in this country. Do you remember the sudden death of Prometheus just before the Cambridgeshire two years ago when the horse was at evens?"

"Do I not?" said Tiny grimly. "I stood to win a monkey over the double with Galloping Lad."

"Precisely. And there were a good many other people besides you who had backed Galloping Lad for the Cesarewitch. In fact if Prometheus had won, the bookies would have had the skinning of their lives."

"But, Colonel, you surely don't imply that there was foul play, do you? The horse was just found dead in his box one morning."

"Exactly. Doubled up in the most dreadful contortions—teeth bared, head a mass of bruises where the poor brute had hurled itself against the walls in his agony, and the stable-boy with a fractured skull in the corner of the box, due to the horse having kicked him in its frenzy."

"Of course," said Tiny, "the case is coming back to me. When the boy was fit to be examined he swore on his Bible oath that he hadn't heard a sound till the horse started bucking and rearing in the box. Then he had rushed in and been kicked. That was it, wasn't it?"

"That was it. And I've mentioned the case only because, though we didn't know it at the time, I am convinced now that that was the first time this poison was used. It was a new one on us then: no one thought of looking for any puncture, and anyway it would have been very hard to find in a horse's coat. The vet was completely nonplussed, but the horse was dead, and that was all there was to it. The boy was put through a searching cross-examination later, but he stuck to the same story. He said that he had been asleep as usual in front of the door of the box: that he was a very light sleeper, and that no one could possibly have got to the horse without waking him. And so after a while, though a lot of people maintained that the horse had been tampered with, the accepted verdict was that it had died of some inexplicable disease of the heart which had attacked it suddenly."

"Hold hard a minute, Colonel. Does this poison leave no trace?"

"No chemical trace. But it affects the muscles of the heart, tautening them up and in non-medical language bringing on acute cramp. Hence the agony which the victims suffer just before death."

"It sounds awfully jolly," murmured Tiny. "Do you mind if I have another spot of brandy? But the point I can't get at is this. If the boy was speaking the truth: if the door of the loose box was shut—how was the poison administered?"

"Don't ask me, Carteret: frankly I don't know. The window was open: the top half of the door consisted of bars as usual. If a poisoned dart was used on that occasion we should never have found it in the straw even if anyone had thought of looking for it. But—let's get on. It is really immaterial whether the poor brute was killed that way or not: there are other far more important things at stake. And perhaps the most important is the fact that from about that time we began to notice a subtle difference in the activities of the gang—a difference which brought Standish and me in more directly than before. Until then the matter had been essentially a police affair: now they began to interest themselves in political affairs. True only if big money was likely to be available: but it was a new departure, and one which made things even more serious."

He paused and lit a cigarette: then abruptly he turned to Tiny.

"Have you ever heard of Felton Blake?"

"Never—to the best of my knowledge," answered Tiny.

"Felton Blake is one of the most perfect examples of the criminal mind that exists today. From his appearance you would put him down as a successful lawyer or doctor. He is a clean-shaven, dark, distinctly good-looking man of about forty-five. He has a large house in Hampstead, where he entertains lavishly and well. He states, should the question arise, that he is a merchant broker, and he does, in fact, run an office somewhere down in the city. An absolute blind, of course: in reality the man is the most dangerous blackmailer in Europe. He is completely devoid of pity: the most usurious money-lender is a tender-hearted woman compared to him. Once his claws are into a human being, the poor wretch can say goodbye to hope. He is a member of this gang, and a very prominent one. And"—once again he paused—"he is the man with whom Lady Mary Ridgeway was having supper at the Fifty-Nine six weeks ago."

"Good God!" muttered Tiny. "Are you sure, sir?"

"Jebson—the man who was murdered last night—though not then waiting on the private room, made it his business to be hanging round when Blake left. He had seen him go in: had seen that he had a lady with him, but had not been able to see her face. He succeeded as she left: it was Lady Mary."

"But, Great Scott! Colonel—what the devil can it mean? Is he trying to blackmail her? If so, what for? I mean—she's a cheery soul: does damned fool things at times. But—blackmail Mary. I can't believe it."

"Is it any harder to believe than the mere fact that she was there?"

"Do you think she has written some letters or something like that? And he's got hold of them? Because if so I'll go and break every bone in the swine's body."

The older man smiled faintly.

"A very natural instinct, Carteret—but one which I fear you will have to repress. I gather you know Lady Mary pretty well, don't you?"

"I do," said Tiny and then hesitated. "Look here, Colonel," he burst out, "you've been pretty frank with me: I'll return the compliment. I didn't say anything in your office, but after all there is no good having half confidences. Of course—there may be nothing in it. I was dancing with her last night, and she was frightfully glum all through the evening. Not a bit her usual self—in fact I pulled her leg about it. And then at half-past eleven she suddenly coughed up something about a headache and pushed off. Moreover, she bit me good and proper when I suggested running her home."

"I am glad you told me, Carteret," said Gillson quietly. "As you say there may be nothing in it; at the same time it shows us that she might have been there."

"But, damn it—why should she be there?" exploded Tiny.

"That is what I would give a good deal to know," answered Gillson. "We can assume one thing at any rate: she did not go there because she wanted to—she went because she had to. Therefore Blake has some hold over her: or..."

"Or what?" demanded Tiny.

"She went there on behalf of somebody else."

"That's much more likely," remarked Tiny. "She's the most kind-hearted creature in the world: do anything for a pal."

The other glanced cautiously round the room: then he bent forward, and his voice was hardly above a whisper.

"You saw a good deal of Princess Olga when she was over here three years ago, didn't you?"

For a moment or two Tiny stared at him blankly.

"I did," he said at length. "But firstly, how do you know; and secondly, what has that got to do with it?"

"My dear fellow," said Gillson shortly, "don't be dense. Do you imagine that when a princess who is shortly to become Queen of Bessonia comes over here on a visit we don't know who she goes about with? And as to what it has to do with it—possibly a lot. I think I'm right in saying that she and Lady Mary became very great friends."

"You are," agreed Tiny. "Very great friends indeed."

"Six weeks ago Lady Mary returned from a visit to Bessonia where she had stayed with the king and queen. A few days later she has supper with a notorious blackmailer in a private room at the Fifty-Nine—admittedly a thing which only the greatest provocation would cause her to do. Now do you see what I'm getting at?"

"I gather that your implication is that she is acting on behalf of the queen. But I don't see that it takes us much further."

"It doesn't—and that is where you come in. Had Jebson not been murdered, it might have been a different matter. As it is, you've got to do what you can. But first of all get the points clear in your mind. As I told you the activities of the gang have of recent months tended to become political. Add to that the fact that at the present moment Bessonia is the open powder-keg of Europe. The overthrow of the king and queen would undoubtedly cause a grave crisis: but there are people who would pay a lot of money to bring it about. There is the major side of the case: now for the minor. Has Felton Blake got some hold over the king and queen—or over the queen alone—which if used in the proper quarter might bring about that overthrow? And is Lady Mary acting as an emissary of the queen to buy off Blake, or to persuade him to hold his hand? That's what I want to find out: that's what I believe Jebson *did* find out last night. And was murdered for his pains."

He paused and lit a cigarette, while Tiny sat motionless, staring at him.

"Understand, Carteret, that only two other men in the world—on our side at any rate—know what I've been telling you. One is Ronald Standish. Dexter knows nothing save the obvious fact that Lady Mary had supper with Felton Blake. His is purely the police side of the show: this is our end of it."

"But surely, Colonel," said Tiny at length, "in a case of such gravity as this something could be done with this man Blake. Couldn't he be run in—on a faked charge if necessary?"

The other shook his head.

"You can't run a man in on a faked charge in this country, Carteret. At least not in peace-time. And as to a genuine charge against the swine—he's far too clever. Blake only deals in those cases where the consequences to the victim if he did come forward and lay information would be such that he simply daren't do it. There are probably forty people today, any one of whom could get that blackguard sent to prison for fifteen years. But not one of them will do it. Some day, of course, a social benefactor will come along who will murder Blake. And then he will be tried for his life and probably hanged. But until that moment arrives we have got to fight Blake with legitimate weapons."

"Exactly what do you want me to do?" asked Tiny.

"I would suggest that you call round and see Lady Mary this afternoon—ostensibly to say goodbye to her. Or to inquire if her headache is better. Then I leave it entirely to you. Find out what you can. Even the certainty that she was at the Fifty-Nine last night would be something."

"Can't say I like it much, Colonel."

"You are free to back out now, Carteret. You are not under my orders. But I think you are viewing the thing from the wrong aspect. Don't get into your head the idea that I am asking you to spy on her. We are entirely on her side—and the more we know the more we can help her. If only people who are up against the Blakes of this world would realise that—Lord! what a difference it would make."

"Yes: I quite see that. All right—I'll have a dip at it. But don't expect too much, sir. Mary is not an easy person to pump. By the way—you don't happen to know the number of the private room, do you?"

The other rose.

"Wait here. I'll telephone and find out."

He threaded his way through the now half-empty room, leaving Tiny with his brain whirling. It was the extraordinary inside knowledge about other people's movements that Gillson had which amazed him. And yet he had seemed to take it quite as a matter of course. Then his mind switched over to the immediate problem. Deep down he felt instinctively that Mary had been to the Fifty-Nine the night before. She had been so utterly unlike her usual self that there must have been something pretty drastic to account for it. And suddenly he became quite definitely aware of the fact that the thought of Mary having supper with Felton Blake affected him considerably more than if it had been Vera Lethington for example. The idea that there could be anything between them was simply laughable; and yet. . . . Why the Fifty-Nine? Why a private room? Surely if there was anything in this idea of Gillson's—if Mary was acting as a go-between for the Queen of Bessonia—she could have sent for Blake to come to her house.

His mind went back to the time three years ago when as Princess Olga he had seen a lot of her. Several little *partis carrés* with Mary and a cheery fellow about his own age. What the deuce was his name? He could remember him perfectly distinctly—a tall fair bloke with hair that crinkled naturally. Joe something or other. Funny now that he came to think of it, but he'd never seen him since. Seemed to have disappeared completely. Probably out in Kenya, or one of the colonies. What the devil was his name? Joe. . . .

"Room number 7."

Tiny came out of his reverie to find Gillson standing beside him.

"Right, Colonel!" He got up. "It's a quarter past three now: I'll probably drift in to see her about half an hour before cocktail time. Best chance of finding her alone. And I'll let you know if I find out anything. Incidentally do the arrangements for tomorrow still hold?"

"They do," said the other. "And I know no more than you do what will happen afterwards. There is only one bit of advice I can give you—keep your eyes skinned. For unless I'm much mistaken the time is coming when you'll want 'em in the back of your head."

Tiny grinned cheerfully.

"Sounds good to me, sir. The only thing I'm not frantically set on is this poison stuff. Your description of the symptoms sounded most entertaining."

But there was no answering smile on the other's face.

"Take care, my boy," he said gravely. "There's no jest about this matter. And I'd like you to add to the fifteen next winter. Don't forget: *sleep* with one eye open. And ring me up tonight at eight o'clock and tell me what you've found out. . . . Sloane 1234 is the number."

Tiny strolled along Pall Mall still puzzling over the elusive name. At times it was on the tip of his tongue: then it was gone again. He would ask Mary when he saw her: she'd remember. Joe. . . Joe. . . . Though, after all, what the devil did it matter? There were vastly more important things to think about, not the least being the method of tackling Mary. From a fairly profound knowledge of her he realised that he would have to walk warily. If she got the impression that he was coming as a sort of emissary of the police the probability was that she would go straight off the deep end. And small blame to her: he would feel the same himself. And yet he saw quite clearly that what Gillson had said was right. Whatever was the reason of her meeting Felton Blake, it was better for her that it should be known. The point was—would she tell him?

He glanced at his watch: two hours still to put through. It was too early for tea: besides he felt as if he had only just finished lunch. And as he stood cogitating on what to do at the corner opposite the Athenaeum a magnificent Rolls-Royce swung past him and turned up towards Piccadilly Circus. Unconsciously he glanced at the people in it: then his eyes narrowed. For one of them was a clean-shaven, dark, distinctly good-looking man who might have been a successful lawyer: the other was Mary herself.

She had not seen him, but that fleeting glimpse had been enough for him to see the expression on her face. And it had been like a frozen mask: the man at her side might have been non-existent.

He felt instinctively that her companion was Felton Blake, though he had never seen the man before in his life. And he began to feel annoyed. Was Mary insane? In many ways it was more indiscreet of her to drive alone with the man than to have supper with him. Where one person might find out the latter, to drive alone with him in the middle of the season was proclaiming the thing to a hundred. Her features were far too well known: moreover, as far as he could see she was making no attempt whatever to conceal them.

He turned and strolled back the way he had come, and almost immediately ran into Gillson on his way to the Home Office.

"Has that man Felton Blake got a yellow Rolls limousine with an aluminium bonnet?" he demanded shortly.

"I should think it's more than likely," answered the other. "He's rich enough to keep a dozen. Why?"

"Because if he has he's just passed me at the corner there with Lady Mary alone in the car with him. Damn it! Colonel—the girl has gone mad. I must say she was looking at the swab as if he was something out of cheese. But fancy her doing such a thing! In May, in London, in the middle of the afternoon!"

"Don't forget one thing, Carteret, in your quite natural peevishness. Very few people except his actual victims know what Blake really is. You may not have met him, but he is a man who is received in very good society. So that it is not quite the howling indiscretion it seems to you. Where are you going?"

"White's—until it's time for me to go and see her."

"I'll find out about that question of the car and ring you up. So long."

But when twenty minutes later one of the pages told him he was wanted on the telephone he felt it was almost unnecessary to go. He *knew* the man was Felton Blake: and Gillson's voice from the other end telling him that the description fitted Blake's car only confirmed a certainty.

He went moodily back into the smoking-room and flung himself into a chair. The club was empty, a fact for which he was profoundly thankful. He felt in no mood for conversation: he wanted to try and get things straight in his head. And after a time one fact began to stand out very clearly. If Jebson had been murdered by this mysterious poison because he had overheard something the night before, it was obvious that he himself would be in danger of a similar attention, if it became known that Mary had confided in him. Not that that mattered in the slightest. Tiny was as much without fear as a man may be, and so long as he could help Mary nothing else counted. But he also was no fool, and the prospect of dying in the manner Gillson had described failed to appeal to him in the slightest degree. At the same time if four skilled police officers had all been caught, the odds were pretty strongly against his escaping.

He wished now that he had asked Gillson more details about the other three. Surely by comparing the four cases some factor common to all must emerge, from which it would be possible to deduce something. And yet the only deduction that seemed to have been made so far was that the puncture in each case must have seemed accidental to the victim. He quite saw the reasoning behind the conclusion: at the same time there seemed to be some grave difficulties in accepting such a conclusion. If it had genuinely seemed accidental, then surely in each case it must have been pure chance whether it came on or not. If, for instance, some form of poisoned spike had been fixed somewhere in the room, it would be an absolute fluke if the victim pricked himself on it. And if it was fixed in something he was bound to use— his tooth-brush say—it certainly would not seem accidental. Besides, only the most eccentric people use toothbrushes on their stomachs. And that was where Jebson had got it.

At last he gave it up and sent for some tea. He would probably solve the mystery personally, he reflected grimly, and until then there was not much good worrying. The utmost he could hope for was that if he was cast for the part of number five he would have the time to pass on some warning for the benefit of number six.

At a quarter past five he left the club and hailed a taxi. And while he waited for the machine, mindful of Gillson's instructions, he stared fixedly at the passers-by, most of whom seemed to resent it strongly. But with the exception of a bishop, who Tiny regarded with certainty as the murderer in disguise, they seemed comparatively harmless.

He gave the driver the address, and sat down with care. Beyond the fact, however, that the machine was obviously on the verge of complete disintegration, he could see no cause for alarm. No spikes stuck out anywhere, and though the cushion felt as if it was stuffed with tin-tacks he arrived at his destination without any perforation of the skin. And then came the first check. Her ladyship was in, but the butler was not sure if she wished to see anyone at the moment. She had come in with a headache, and had left word that she did not wish to be disturbed.

"That's a nuisance, Simmonds," said Tiny. "Because I'm leaving England tomorrow."

"Leaving England, sir! I dare say that would make a difference. I'll ask her ladyship."

"What's that, Tiny?" A door at the end of the hall opened and the girl herself put her head out. "Leaving England! Come in and tell me about it. But no one else, Simmonds."

"Very good, my lady."

Tiny followed her into her own particular *sanctum*, and she closed the door.

"It's sweet of you to see me, Mary dear," he said, taking both her hands. "How's the head?"

"As an excuse it serves, Tiny. I felt I couldn't bear that chattering cocktail crowd this evening. Sit down and tell me about this sudden change of plan. What are you leaving England for? You said nothing about it last night."

"I only decided this morning," he answered, sinking into a chair and pulling out his cigarette-case. "And then you very nearly altered my plans."

"I did? What *do* you mean?"

"Whilst communing with nature opposite the Athenaeum this afternoon I narrowly escaped death from a large yellow Rolls. And in that Rolls, Mary dear, I perceived you complete with gentleman friend."

He spoke lightly, but the sudden tightening of her lips did not escape him.

"I never saw you, Tiny." Her voice expressed only the most perfunctory interest. "But since you did escape death, why this strange move? And where are you going?"

"A sudden whim, my dear. I'm joining a very great pal of mine in Switzerland, and we're going on a walking tour. We might even pop over the border and go into Bessonia."

"Bessonia! Walking tour! My dear Tiny, what has come over you?" She was staring at him in genuine amazement, as if she could hardly believe her ears.

"Sounds a bit grim, doesn't it?" he laughed. "However, that's the programme. I wonder," he added carelessly, "if the queen would remember me."

"Of course she does, Tiny," she said slowly. "She talked a lot about you when I was there, Give me a cigarette, like a dear."

He handed her the box and struck a match. But he noticed that it was quite an appreciable time before she seemed to be aware of either.

"Tiny," she said, when he had sat down again, "are you serious? Are you really going on a walking tour?"

"Like the headache, my dear—as an excuse it serves. By the way," he went on, "it's funny how little things worry one. I've been trying the whole afternoon to think of the name of that bloke who used to play about with us such a lot when she was over here. I can't get farther than Joe."

"Joe Denver," she said. "I suppose you don't know where he is, Tiny?"

Was it his imagination, or did he detect a certain eager tenseness in the question?

"Not a notion, my dear. I've never seen him since those days. I've a sort of idea he was in Kenya or something like that."

"I wonder if there is any way of getting in touch with him," she went on.

"I suppose an advertisement in the papers would do it in time. But is there any special reason for doing so?"

"Oh! no. I just wondered." She passed her hand over her forehead.

"Mary, dear, you're looking tired," he said quietly. "And worried. Is there anything I can do to help? You know you've only got to say the word."

"You're a dear, Tiny," and her voice was weary. "But there is nothing, old lad, that you or anybody else can do, I fear me."

"Then there is something the matter," he said insistently. "Can't you tell me, dear?"

"That's the devil of it: I can't. And even if I did it wouldn't do any good."

For a moment he hesitated: then he took the plunge.

"Mary, is it anything to do with that bloke you were driving with this afternoon?"

She pressed out her cigarette.

"Tiny, drop it, please. I can't tell you. Let's change the subject. What have you been doing today?"

"I lunched with a lad at the Rag," he said. It seemed to him that the moment had come to go at it bald-headed. "One of these mysterious sort of birds who move about behind the scenes, and appear to know everything. He was very full of a murder that took place last night. Some man down Hammersmith way—a waiter."

"It hardly seems of surpassing interest," she remarked.

"He was a waiter at the Fifty-Nine Club, and apparently. . . Mary dear—"

Every vestige of colour had left her face, and as he sprang towards her she swayed in her chair. Then she pulled herself together and pushed him away.

"It's all right, Tiny. Stupid of me. I suddenly felt faint. I'm not very fit these days. Tell me about this murder."

"There is very little to tell. The man was killed by some new and hitherto unknown poison. The only point of interest is that apparently he wasn't a waiter at all, but some secret service agent."

And once again every vestige of colour left her cheeks.

"Why on earth should they want a secret service agent at the Fifty-Nine?" she asked at length.

Tiny shrugged his shoulders as if the matter had already begun to bore him, though his heart was aching for her. What was the best thing to do? Should he put all his cards on the table? Should he tell her exactly what he suspected and implore her to confide in him what the trouble was? Finally he decided to temporize.

"Ask me another, my dear. I believe some pretty rum things go on in the private rooms there."

"It was a waiter for one of the private rooms, was it?"

"Number 7," he said, and stared straight at her. But by this time she had controlled her expression, and the shot missed.

"Poor fellow," she said. "Do you think that dark deeds of treason were being discussed in the room, and that he overheard them?"

"Nobody seems to know what went on in the room, or even who was there, because he never sent in a report. In fact, the only thing that seems to have come out up to date is that the table was decorated with mauve orchids."

"My dear Tiny," she said lightly, "what on earth are you looking at me like that for? Why shouldn't the table be decorated with mauve orchids?"

"Mary dear," he answered steadily, "I'm going to chance it. I must. Was it you who was having supper in that room last night?"

"You must be mad, Tiny," she cried angrily.

"I wish I was, Mary. Listen, my dear, for it's got to be told. This bloke I was lunching with today simply appalled me with his inside knowledge. For instance, he knows that you had supper at the Fifty-Nine Club in a private room about six weeks ago with a notorious blackmailer called Felton Blake."

"Go on, please," she remarked icily. "I was always given to understand that women's names were not bandied about in men's clubs."

"My dear," he pleaded, "for God's sake, get it right. There was no question of your name being bandied about. We were having a private talk after lunch."

"The upshot of which appears to be that you, a man whom I have always regarded as a friend, come round here to spy on me. I suppose whatever you find out will be added to this gentleman's inside knowledge."

"Mary," he cried passionately, "you can't think I'd be such a swine as that. Don't you see, my dear, that if you are in trouble—if this swab has a hold over you in any way—it's vital that someone should help you."

"What I see is the most unwarrantable interference in my private affairs. I foolishly imagined that if I did choose to have supper six weeks ago at the Fifty-Nine it was my concern and nobody else's."

"Even if the man you had supper with is a notorious blackmailer?" asked Tiny.

"Even if he is a murderer, forger and thief rolled into one. What business is it of anyone else's?" she cried passionately. "And anyway, what are you driving at now? Even if I did have supper last night at the Fifty-Nine, am I supposed to be responsible for this so-called waiter's death?"

Tiny got up a little wearily.

"Then you won't tell me, Mary dear? You won't let me help you."

For a moment her eyes softened: then she shook her head.

"I wish I could, Tiny: how I wish I could. Forgive me, old man— I've been talking out of my turn a bit. I didn't mean all that about spying on me: I do know you were trying to help. But it's useless, my dear—useless."

"Mary, my dear," he stammered, "would it be useless if I were in— well, in a position to look after you?"

"Bless his heart: he's proposing." She gave a tender little laugh. "Bend down, Tiny." For a moment or two she stared at him: then she kissed him on the lips. "Now run away, my dear, and forget all about it."

And Tiny, being a man of understanding, went away. Just once by the door he turned round and looked at her, and it seemed to him that she looked weary unto death. Then a little blindly he went out into the sunlit street.

CHAPTER 3

That it had been Lady Mary Ridgeway with Felton Blake the previous night he was convinced. True, she had not actually admitted it, but her whole demeanour simply shouted the fact. And as he walked moodily back to his club he tried vainly to puzzle the thing out.

Tiny Carteret knew probably as much about Lady Mary Ridgeway as any other man, and a good deal more than most. He knew all her friends: they were both in the same set. And if anybody was likely to have heard of any undesirable entanglement in the past it was he. As he argued it to himself if she was in Felton Blake's power it must be due to his possession of something incriminating belonging to her. And that as far as he could see could only be letters. . . . Love letters. Further, they must be letters written either to some hopeless outsider, or to a married man. Otherwise, though possibly injudicious, there would be nothing incriminating about them.

The question of the outsider he dismissed at once: the mere thought of such a thing in connection with Mary was laughable. And the married man solution seemed almost as blank a wall. He made, of course, no pretence whatever to such an extremely intimate inside knowledge of her life, and there might have been some man . . . might even be one now. And a letter might have got mislaid, or been stolen by a valet and sold to Blake. But somehow or other—rightly or wrongly—Tiny felt that if it had been so rumours of it would have got about, at any rate in her own immediate set. And there had never been such a rumour—not the suspicion or hint of one: that he knew.

He tried another line—could it be money trouble? If possible— even more absurd. Mary was very well off, and her father the duke was an extremely wealthy man, who adored her. Besides, Gillson had said nothing about Blake being a moneylender.

At which point in his reflections he realised that he didn't seem to be making much progress. Incriminating letters and money trouble removed there didn't seem to be a great deal left. And quite naturally his thoughts turned along the other line; the line at which Gillson had hinted that morning. Was she acting as a go-between for the queen?

If it was so he was in deeper waters than ever. Impossible though it was to arrive at any conclusion if it was Mary herself involved, it was doubly impossible if it was the queen. And yet the more he thought of it the more likely did it seem to him. In the first place the mere fact that Gillson had suggested it as a likely solution weighed with him. Never in his life had Tiny Carteret been so impressed by a man's personality as he had been that morning. It wasn't only the fact that the fellow had seemed to know such an astounding amount about one's personal movements, he reflected: it was the indefinable atmosphere of power about him . . . inscrutable to a certain extent, and yet quite prepared to throw all his cards on the table if it suited him. And a damned hard man to bluff.

But apart from Gillson having considered it a possibility, Tiny himself was inclining towards the idea. The difficulty of imagining Mary herself to be the victim, necessitated finding another. And it was a significant fact that the first time she had had supper with Felton Blake was immediately on her return from Bessonia. Odd remarks, to which he had attached no importance at the time, came back to him—remarks made casually during the last few weeks by pals of both sexes.

"Mary seems a bit off her oats." "Mary doesn't seem a bit herself these days." And one in particular. "My dear, I believe you've fallen in love with a Bessonian."

Trifles: laughed off as soon as made, but now taking on a new significance in Tiny's brain. What had happened to Mary during her visit there? He would have given all he possessed to know. In the answer to that question lay the solution.

He ordered a gin and bitters and picked up an evening paper. One of the headlines caught his eye—

Critical Situation in Bessonia. Increasing Tension.

His eye travelled down the column.

The situation in Bessonia is appreciably graver than it was twenty-four hours ago. As yet there are no visible signs of discontent and things are proceeding normally. But this state of affairs exists only on the surface. To anyone acquainted with the Bessonian temperament it is obvious that a clash must come soon between the Royalist party and the International group, and what the issue will be no one can say. At the moment the army remains loyal.

He put down the paper, and lit a cigarette. Like the majority of his fellow-countrymen, the internal affairs of remote foreign states bored him to extinction. He dimly remembered that he had heard a man at dinner a few nights ago saying something about the condition of Bessonia, but he had paid no attention. And it began to strike him now that if his surmise over Lady Mary was right, it was high time he ceased to pay no attention. He glanced round the room and saw the very man he wanted—Squire Straker, foreign editor of the *Planet*.

"Straker, old hearty," he called out, "in return for a few minutes of your valuable time I will donate you with a pink gin. Is it a bargain?"

"Hullo! Tiny." The other lounged over—a big loosely made man with a European reputation. "Don't often see you in here at this hour."

"Straker, I crave for knowledge. Knowledge about Bessonia. Get on with it."

The other looked at him curiously.

"Rather a new departure for you, isn't it? What do you want to know about it? If the shooting is good, or what?"

"I want to know briefly, old lad, what the political situation is there. I have just read in this rag—oh! it's one of yours, is it—that a clash is imminent between the Royalist party and the Industrial group. Why?"

Squire Straker sat down and began to fill an ancient pipe.

"If you are really interested, Tiny, I can give you the situation in a nutshell. It is not at all complicated: it is a situation which has occurred innumerable times in those small Latin states in the past, and which will occur innumerable times in the future. Political intrigue is as the breath of life to them, though I am bound to say that in this case the matter is rather more serious than usual. You probably don't remember that when the old king died five years ago, there was a very large party in Bessonia who were in favour of the place becoming a republic. The party was led by a gentleman named Berendosi, who is an extremely able man—possibly the ablest they've got. And had that party had its way Berendosi would undoubtedly have been the first president. Well—it didn't have its way, and the present bloke Peter became king. But Berendosi is not the type of man to let trifles of that sort deter him, and though he was defeated in the first round he was by no manner of means knocked out. He went on working and plotting behind the scenes, until he got a severe jolt in the second round too.

"That was when the king got married. The queen, as you probably know, is a most divinely pretty creature, and she absolutely knocked the entire population endways. They raved about her, and Peter's stock soared sky high. Never had he been so popular: never had his position seemed more secure. And Berendosi looked on, smiling behind his hand. Only too well did he know his own countrymen: only too well did he know the rapidity with which the pendulum swings with people of their temperament. He could afford to bide his time. A word here, a hint there: a rumour spread and then contradicted—but by that time the damage was done. And so it went on, like drops of water wearing away a stone, until a new and completely unexpected development took place about three months ago. Am I boring you?"

"Very far from it," said Tiny.

"Up to that time the hints and innuendoes started by Berendosi and his group had been entirely political. You know the sort of thing I mean—that So-and-So was accepting bribes: that the king was grossly extravagant: that the people were being overtaxed in order that corrupt ministers might line their pockets. And then, as I say, came the change. It was done very gradually, and at first our correspondent out there—who by the way is an extremely able man—disregarded it. But after a time he could do so no longer: the rumours became so persistent. And though they varied in small details the main gist was the same: the queen was being unfaithful to her husband."

Tiny Carteret sat up with a jerk: then sank back in his chair again.

"Go on," he said quietly.

"Now you can see at once," continued Straker, "the vast importance of the move. The Industrial party—which is another name in that country for the Republican party—and Berendosi do not care the snap of a finger if she is unfaithful or if she isn't. But the other party—the Royalist party—would literally be split from top to bottom if it were proved that she was. In fact Berendosi would have obtained everything he wants. The cement binding the Royalist party together, is the beauty and the home life and all the rest of it of the king and queen. Once that cement was removed: once the rumour was proved true the party would simply disintegrate."

"And do you think it is true?" asked Tiny slowly.

The other shrugged his shoulders.

"The king is not a particularly prepossessing specimen," he answered. "And queens are no different to ordinary women except that considerably more publicity surrounds their lives. No, Tiny: I can't tell you—I don't know. All I can tell you is that if the rumour becomes currently believed, it doesn't matter whether it's the truth or whether it isn't: the result will be the same. It may take longer—but in the end Berendosi will win. Of course, were it possible to prove such a thing—spectacularly, which as far as I can see it isn't, why then..."

Again he shrugged his shoulders.

"What then?" said Tiny.

"Well, it wouldn't be a question of in the end. The thing would be over in an hour, and one would never be surprised with people of the Bessonian temperament if the punishment awarded the erring lady was short and drastic. No, Tiny—that would be a very serious matter. We do not want Berendosi in power there for many reasons into which I haven't got time to go now. And as long as the matter remains in the region of rumour I don't think we shall have Berendosi in power. But if by some unfortunate chance that girl has been indiscreet, and Berendosi holds proof of it—proof which would carry conviction to the masses—it's all up. He is just biding his time now, and preparing the ground. Then when he's ready, he'll strike."

He finished his drink and rose.

"So long, old boy: this is the hour when my chief labour commences."

He shambled out of the room like a great bear, leaving Tiny staring thoughtfully out of the window. And such is the constitution of the human mind that it was not problems of high politics in the Near East that occupied the latter's thoughts, but something very much more personal. Why had not Gillson told him all this at lunch? That Squire Straker should be in possession of information unknown to Gillson was absurd. Gillson must have known all about these rumours, but not a word had he said. And Tiny began to feel irritated. He had all the independent man's dislike of being kept in the dark. Surely if he was a fit and proper person to play at all, the least he could expect was to be given full information. Why should he be used as a cat's paw? And then as suddenly as his irritation had arisen, it evaporated. Gillson's words in his office that morning recurred to him.

"There are certain occasions when real genuine ignorance is worth untold gold."

Presumably this had been one of them. Not only was he to be kept in the dark as to what was going to happen to himself on the other side, but also as to what was happening to other people. Yet, surely it would have been better had he known the rumours before he went round to see Mary. He could have asked her point blank: he could have. . .

And what would have been the result? He lit a cigarette thoughtfully, and a faint smile twitched round his lips. What would have been the result? Nothing: a flat denial. He knew Mary well enough for that, and so apparently did that darned fellow Gillson. Had he gone round there evidently bursting with official information, Mary would have shut up like an oyster. And so Gillson had deliberately sent him round to see her full of genuine ignorance, in the hope that she would turn to him for help. The problem that occupied Straker occupied Gillson too. Was there any definite proof of the rumour in existence? That is what he had been sent to find out, and that is what he had not succeeded in finding out.

At least, not for certain. That Squire Straker's information was of vital importance he realised. It provided a central peg on which the whole thing hung together connectedly. There *was* proof in existence, and Felton Blake held it. And Mary *was* acting on behalf of the queen to get it back. The other difficulties—the private room in the Fifty-

Nine, the motor drive which the two had taken together—seemed capable of explanation once that central fact was conceded. They were trifles compared with the main thing.

He glanced at his watch: five minutes to eight. What was he going to say to Gillson over the telephone? He had no proof: only a strong intuition. He might be wrong—wildly wrong. He might be jumping to the most absurd conclusion. And yet, once granted Mary herself was not the victim, which was even more absurd, what other possible conclusion was there?

He was still undecided as he called up Sloane 1234: still undecided when he heard Gillson's deep voice from the other end.

"Nothing for certain, Colonel," he said.

"We can't always deal in certainties, Carteret, in our trade. Did you find out anything at all?"

He answered with another question.

"Do you know Squire Straker by any chance?"

"Of course I do." Gillson seemed surprised. "Why do you ask?"

"I've just been having a long talk with him over the state of affairs in a certain country."

Was it Tiny's imagination, or did a very faint chuckle come from the other end of the wire?

"Have you indeed? I hope you were interested."

"I think you might have been a little more explicit, Colonel, at lunch today."

"Possibly, Carteret. But don't forget it is still only in the rumour stage. The point, however, now is this. What opinion, if any, have you arrived at?"

Tiny weighed his words carefully.

"I believe that your conjecture is right. I believe that the lady is acting for someone whose name I won't mention. But it's only belief: I haven't a vestige of proof."

"I see. Well, my dear fellow, we're moving in deep waters; and unless I'm much mistaken you shortly will be moving in deeper ones. Goodnight and good luck to you."

Tiny replaced the receiver, and went back to the smoking-room. A bunch of members hailed him as he came in, but he was in no mood for club back-chat. He wanted to get things straightened out in his mind; so making some excuses he went into the coffee-room and ordered dinner. And during his solitary meal he attempted the straightening process, though it would be idle to pretend he got very far with it.

The whole affair was such a complete upheaval, and such an extremely rapid one. In the course of twelve hours he had been transported from the even tenor of his ways and landed in the centre of an atmosphere of murder and blackmail. And one of his companions was Mary. That was the most staggering part of the whole business: Mary mixed up with such a bunch! It seemed incredible: almost as incredible as it would have seemed to him this morning if someone had told him he was going to propose to her.

There was no doubt about it; he had done so. And now he tried to think how he would be feeling if she hadn't turned him down. To depart from the habits of a lifetime and propose to a girl was clear proof of what an upheaval had taken place. And yet he wasn't at all certain that he had wanted to be turned down. Mary was unquestionably a darling, and that kiss she had given him. . . .

"Give me my bill," he said savagely: the thought of Mary alone in a private room with any man, let alone Felton Blake, had suddenly become unspeakable.

"I'll write her," he reflected, as he strolled back to his rooms. "Write her tonight, and tell her I meant it. That it wasn't a spasm induced by a desire to help her."

And because he was very busy with his thoughts, he failed to notice a man who was lingering aimlessly not far from his front door, and who vanished rapidly as he entered. Nor could he possibly have known that shortly afterwards the man expended the sum of twopence on a telephone call to Hampstead.

He sat down at his desk, and pulled a sheet of paper towards him. From the next room came the sound of Murdoch finishing his packing, and for awhile he remained motionless, gnawing the end of his penholder. Then he began to write.

Mary Dear—

Ever since I saw you this afternoon I've been feeling distracted. I know you're in trouble; I know I could help you if only you would let me. You pulled my leg about proposing to you, but believe me, Mary, I meant it. I know I'm every sort and condition of an ass, while you're just—Mary. No need to say more. I think I've always loved you, dear: but it was seeing you up against it today that made me cough it up.

However, let all that be for the time. Can't I do anything to help? Please let me. You can tell me as much or as little as you like: I'll go into it blind if it's for you. This letter should arrive first post tomorrow, and if you telephone me on its receipt I'll cancel all my arrangements with regard to Switzerland. Or a letter to the Ouchy Palace Hotel at Lausanne will bring me back at once. One can get through in a day, and if necessary I can always fly.

Mary dear, I beg of you to think very deeply. Are you being wise trying to tackle this business—whatever it is—alone? Can't I help you? I know I'm repeating myself, but, my dear, I do feel so terribly strongly about it. We've played a lot together in the past, Mary: we've always been damned good pals. And if you can't turn to a pal when you're up against it, it's a pretty hopeless state of affairs.

Yours ever, my dear one, Tiny.

He re-read it: then slipped it into an envelope and stamped it.

"Murdoch," he called out, "take this out and post it at once."

"Very good, sir: and the packing is practically finished."

The man withdrew, and Tiny flung himself into a chair and lit a cigarette. Would the letter have any effect, or would she still go on playing the hand alone? And even as he asked himself the question there came the faint purring of an engine through the open window. He rose idly, and crossing the room, looked out. Drawn up by the kerb was a yellow Rolls limousine with an aluminium bonnet.

"Well, I'm damned," he muttered. "Things move."

The door opened behind him and he swung round. Standing in the entrance was Felton Blake.

For a moment or two they eyed one another in silence: then Tiny spoke.

"May I ask who you are, and what you are doing here?"

"I think you already know who I am, Mr. Carteret," answered the other. "But to prevent any possibility of error I will introduce myself. My name is Blake."

"How did you get in?" said Tiny curtly.

"I walked through a door which your man had considerately left open."

"Then would you be good enough to walk out again, and pretty damned quick at that."

Felton Blake put his hat and gloves on a chair.

"You disappoint me, Mr. Carteret," he said suavely. "I thought you were sufficiently a man of the world not to adopt such a foolish attitude. It can lead us nowhere, and I have come round here expressly to have a talk with you."

"I have not the slightest wish to talk to you in any place or at any time," said Tiny icily.

"I can't say from the standard of your conversation," answered Blake, "that I have much desire to talk to you either. But sometimes these boring entertainments become regrettable necessities."

Tiny mastered his anger, which was rapidly rising: it occurred to him that up to date he had not shone in the interview.

"It would be interesting to know what possible necessity there can be for a conversation between you and me," he remarked.

"That sounds a little better," said Blake. "And since this isn't a stage melodrama—shall we sit down?"

"As you like. There is a chair. I prefer to stand."

"Now, Mr. Carteret—I must ask you for an explanation. You called on Lady Mary Ridgeway this afternoon, did you not?"

Once again Tiny began to see red.

"Give you an explanation," he cried. "Why the devil should I?"

"Assuredly there is no reason at all," said the other suavely, "if you had confined yourself to calling. But it becomes a different matter when, during your call, you slander me. I understand that you alluded to me as a notorious blackmailer."

Tiny stood very still: that Mary would pass on his remarks to Blake was a development he had not anticipated.

"I am waiting, Mr. Carteret, for an explanation—and an apology."

And suddenly it dawned on Tiny that the position was undeniably awkward. The man confronting him, as Gillson had said, might have been a successful lawyer: certainly he looked the acme of respectability.

"You have proof, of course, of your astounding statement," continued Blake.

Which was exactly what Tiny had not got.

"You seem very silent, Mr. Carteret. Come, sir, I insist on an explanation."

"No explanation is necessary for speaking the truth," said Tiny, lighting a cigarette.

"So you adhere to it," remarked the other softly. "And your proof?"

70

"Is there any good in prolonging this discussion, Mr. Blake," answered Tiny. "It bores me excessively. Of proof in the accepted sense of the word I have none. Nevertheless I repeat my assertion: you are a notorious blackmailer. And there is the door."

"Not quite so fast, my young friend," snarled the other. "Have you ever heard of the law of libel?"

"Cut it out, you poor fish," laughed Tiny. "As a bluff that is unworthy of a child of ten. You go into a law court to defend your lily-white character! I think not, Mr. Blake—somehow. Besides, where is your own proof? Even you would hardly ask Lady Mary to go into the witness-box, I presume."

For a moment Blake was silent: in a sudden fit of rage he had put up a bluff, and no one knew better than he that the bluff had been called successfully. Some other line would have to be adopted with this very direct young man.

"Mr. Carteret," he said, "you are perfectly right. Nothing, of course, would induce me to ask Lady Mary to do such a thing. At the same time I think you will agree that it is a little disconcerting, when I am doing my best to help her over some extremely ticklish negotiations, for me to be libelled in such a way."

"Leaving out the question of libel for the moment, Mr. Blake, may I ask the nature of these negotiations?"

"I regret that I am not at liberty to pass that on," answered Blake.

"Leaving that out too then for the moment, I would be greatly obliged if you would tell me why it is necessary to take her to such an impossible place as a private room at the Fifty-Nine Club?"

Felton Blake eyed him narrowly.

"Your information is good, Mr. Carteret."

"Damn my information," cried Tiny angrily. "What I want to know is how you dare compromise a girl in her position by doing such a thing."

Blake raised his eyebrows.

"Dare! Rather a strong word. You don't suppose, do you, that I dragged her there against her will? Nor can you really suppose that with her knowledge of the world she didn't know what she was doing."

"I refuse to believe that she went there willingly," said Tiny doggedly.

"Did she tell you so?" asked Blake quietly. "No: I see she didn't. Mr. Carteret—I am going to put my cards on the table."

71

"How many of them?" said Tiny with a short laugh.

"All that I can," answered the other. "As I said before, your information is good. Moreover, I can hazard a pretty shrewd guess as to its source. That, however, is neither here nor there. To be brief then, I am not acting, as you seem to suppose, against Lady Mary: I am acting on her behalf. I too have sources of information at my disposal, and it so happens that I am in a position where I may be able to render her a considerable service. But in order to do so it is essential that she and I should be left—if I may put it that way—in peace. Come, Mr. Carteret—I'm going to ask you a straight question. Your information came from Colonel Gillson, didn't it?"

"I refuse to say who it came from," said Tiny.

"And he sent you round to Lady Mary to find out what you could?"

"You seem to have everything cut and dried," remarked Tiny.

"Now I solemnly warn you and him as well that any outside interference at the moment may prove fatal. I speak in all earnestness. I am, believe me, on your side, and I therefore beg of you to remember what I say. If you don't, the consequences will be on your head—and on Lady Mary's."

Tiny stared at him thoughtfully: on the face of it the man was sincere. And yet. . .

"Touching the little matter of the waiter who was murdered," he remarked.

"I can assure you, Mr. Carteret, that I have never been more surprised in my life than when Lady Mary told me about it." He gave a short laugh. "I hope in addition to being a blackmailer, I am not suspected of that. Because, unfortunately for your kindly suggestion, I have a perfect alibi."

"When did Lady Mary tell you I had been to see her?"

"She rang me up as soon as you left: you had alarmed her so much. Hence my visit to you tonight. Mr. Carteret—I beg of you be guided by me in this matter. The issues are altogether too serious."

He rose, and glancing through the open door into Tiny's bedroom he saw the half-packed suitcases.

"You're going out of Town?" he asked.

"Didn't Lady Mary tell you that also?" said Tiny sarcastically.

"No," returned the other. "Her mind was too much occupied with other things."

"Yes, Mr. Blake: I'm going out of Town. I'm going for a walking tour—in Bessonia."

Just for an instant Felton Blake stood as if carved out of stone. Then he spoke.

"Bessonia," he said. "A most interesting country. I trust you will have a good time. Goodnight, Mr. Carteret; I have enjoyed our chat greatly."

He went down the stairs and crossed the pavement to his car. He had given his chauffeur the night off, and now he felt rather relieved that he had done so. For Felton Blake was one of those men who could concentrate better when quite alone. Why on earth had Lady Mary said nothing to him about this trip to Bessonia? And was there any special significance in it? For Gillson's knowledge of all sorts and conditions of things he had the most profound respect, and his reason for sending Carteret round to see her was clear in view of the friendship between them. But surely if he suspected anything he would not send an untried man like that to Bessonia. Anyway, what could he do? What could anyone do? The thing was fool-proof as far as he could see: moreover it was within the law.

Felton Blake smiled gently to himself. The soft purr of the engine soothed him with its hundred *per cent* efficiency—he liked efficiency because it engendered success. And success was his god. The means by which it was attained mattered nothing: the fact that at the moment he was engaged in driving one of the most infamous bargains a man can drive troubled him not at all. The only thing that concerned him was whether he had bluffed Tiny Carteret sufficiently.

There was no doubt that his interview with Lady Mary had caused him a distinct shock. Even he had not suspected that the information on the other side was as good as it evidently was. And one point struck him as being so important that it would have to be cleared up. Was it he personally who was being watched—or was it the Fifty-Nine Club? And since so far as he knew there was no reason why he should be honoured with such an attention, it rather pointed to the latter as being correct. Which was annoying: distinctly annoying. Almost as annoying as this extraordinary murder of the waiter. For one of the few truthful remarks he had made in his interview with Carteret had been when they talked about it.

He had been absolutely amazed when Lady Mary had told him about it. At first, in fact, he had refused to believe it—had assured her that she must be mistaken. And then when she had still persisted he could only come to the conclusion that it was an extraordinary coincidence. Unless. . . .

He frowned slightly: the train of thought suggested by that word did not please him. For if it was not a coincidence, it could only mean one thing—the presence in England of the last man he wanted to see at the moment. And even then it was hard to understand. Why should he have murdered an inoffensive waiter?

He ran the car into his garage: then he let himself into his house. And the first thing he saw was a black Homburg hat lying on the hall table. For a moment he stood very still: that hat was the answer to the question. His "unless" had been justified.

He opened the door of his study and went in. Seated in an easy chair, smoking a cigarette, was a peculiar-looking individual. At first sight he appeared to be a man of about forty, but on closer inspection he might have been considerably more. He had a high domed forehead rendered the more noticeable because of his absolute lack of hair, and from beneath it there stared two unwinking blue eyes. And to complete the picture, on his shoulder there sat a small monkey which chattered angrily on Blake's entrance.

"Good evening, Zavier," said Blake. "This is an unexpected pleasure."

"Be quiet, Susan," said the other in a curiously gentle voice. "Don't you know our friend Felton by now?" He turned to Blake. "So you are surprised at seeing me?"

"I thought you were still at headquarters," remarked Blake. "What brings you over here?"

"A desire to see you, my dear fellow, amongst other things. All goes well?"

"Very well. Though I am bound to confess, Zavier, that the intelligence of our English police has been sadly underrated. They know too much."

"And today they would have known considerably more save for my presence. You're a damned fool, Blake—and I have but little use for damned fools. All I can say is—that I trust you stop short at foolishness. Otherwise...."

"What do you mean?" Blake's lips were strangely dry.

"Is it conceivable," said the other, and his voice was softer than ever, "that you did not realise that your waiter of last night was a police spy?"

"Good God!" muttered Blake. "So it was you, then?

"Who removed him? Oh! yes—it was I who did that."

"But, why?" stammered Blake. "What was the object?"

"It was nothing to do, I assure you, with your conversation with the young lady. There were one or two indiscretions, but nothing sufficient to warrant such a drastic step as that."

"What do you mean?" said Blake slowly. "What do you know of my conversation with Lady Mary?"

"My dear fellow, I listened with interest to every word." Zavier smiled faintly. "Charming! Charming! But I fear your suit does not progress as rapidly as you wish."

At last Blake found his voice.

"You listened," he shouted angrily. "You cursed spy. Where did you listen from?"

"You are exciting Susan again," remarked the other gently. "I must really beg of you to control yourself."

He pacified the excited little animal, while Blake with a great effort pulled himself together.

"There are secrets of mine, my dear Blake, that even you do not know. And one of them concerns the private room so prettily decorated with mauve orchids last night. A delightful girl, Blake—delightful. But what a fool you are! Even should she be insane enough to marry you, do you really think you would be happy? The daughter of a duke!"

"That's my affair," said Blake sullenly. "What I want to know is how much you heard."

"It's just because your waiter happened to find out how I heard that he died. So I fear your curiosity will not be gratified. You were saying, however, that the English police know too much. What precisely did you mean?"

"For one thing, they know that I have twice given supper to Lady Mary at the Fifty-Nine."

"Well—what of it?" remarked the other. "It is not a criminal offence. Though what obscure idea was at the bottom of your mind in so doing is beyond me."

"I want to put her under a still greater obligation to me," explained Blake.

"My denseness must be pardoned," said Zavier, "but I confess I do not quite follow."

"Well—if there was a police raid, it would be a bit awkward for her."

"I see. You mean the next time you sup there, there *will* be a police raid. A remarkably local police raid staged by Felton Blake, and from the unfortunate consequences of which she will be saved by Felton Blake." He began to laugh softly. "My God! what a fool you are! However, if it amuses you that's all that matters. To return to the point: what else do they know?"

"That man Gillson is wise to the fact that there is something in the wind between Lady Mary and me."

"Somewhat naturally. My dear fellow, I don't want to be rude but the Lady Marys of English society do not have supper with people like you because they want to, but because they have to."

Felton Blake's face turned a deep red.

"Go to hell, Zavier," he snarled. "I'm sick of your damned sneers. And here's one for you. I believe he suspects the truth."

"So," said Zavier, pulling the monkey's ears, and staring at Blake. "And what makes you think that?"

"He sent a man called Carteret, who is a great friend of Lady Mary's, round to pump her this afternoon. Scared her out of her life—especially over the murder of the waiter. I've just been round to see him, and the last thing he said to me was that he was going for a walking tour in Bessonia, and was starting tomorrow."

"What sort of a man is he?"

"A great big fellow. A Rugby international."

"Size matters but little," said Zavier gently, "should it be necessary to remove him. I alluded more to his intelligence."

"Not very high, I should think." He was staring half fascinated at the other man. "You'll fail, you know, one day, Zavier. Last night was the fifth."

"One almost loses count," returned Zavier. "And as to failure, Blake, the only being who never fails is the one who never tries. But to come back to this man Carteret. If your description of him is accurate, I don't think it matters if he takes a walking tour in Bessonia or not."

"I didn't say it did," said Blake. "But it points to the fact that Gillson suspects."

"What if he does? What we propose to do is strictly constitutional." He rubbed his hands together. "Quite legal, in fact."

"Have you any further information with regard to dates?"

"I was talking to Berendosi three days ago. He thinks in two or possibly three months. By then he calculates that there will be no one in Bessonia who won't have heard the rumour. And that will be the time to spring the proof on them—or what they will regard as the proof. It will also give him time to mature his own plans." His shoulders began to shake silently. "What about yours, my friend," he murmured. "It strikes me you will have to press forward with your love-making."

"What do you mean?" demanded Blake irritably.

"Just this. What little chance you have of being united in holy matrimony to Lady Mary will assuredly vanish altogether when she finds you've sold her a pup. To put it another way. It is within the bounds of possibility that she might sacrifice herself to save her friend; but it is completely off the map to think that she would marry you once the revolution has taken place. That strikes home, doesn't it, Blake? And so while we are on the subject, my friend, I will tell you what I really came round here to say. From one or two remarks I heard last night, it seemed to me that you are in that condition of maudlin imbecility with regard to the girl that one usually associates with a boy of eighteen. And when that is combined with the passion of a man of your age the situation becomes grave. Anything might happen. You might even, to attain your desire, really do what you have told her you are going to do. In which case, believe me, Blake, the honeymoon would not be of long duration." His voice had dropped almost to a whisper. "As I said—one almost loses count."

The unwinking blue eyes were fixed on Felton Blake, who moistened his lips with his tongue.

"You needn't be afraid," he muttered. "I won't let you down."

"Somehow or other I don't think you will," agreed Zavier, with a short laugh.

He opened his case and extracted a thin Russian cigarette. It was the only brand he ever smoked, and his daily allowance of ten was as invariable as all his habits.

"By the way, Blake," he continued, "did you know that Standish is in Switzerland?"

"How did you find out?" asked the other quickly.

"Various Continental papers have as you know the custom of publishing the names of guests staying at the better hotels. He is staying at the Grand Hotel at Territet."

"Has it any significance, do you think?" demanded Blake.

"My experience of Standish is that anything he does has a certain significance. So I made a point of staying a weekend at the hotel, where I had made one or two inquiries. He seems to be just aimlessly putting through time there, and to put through time aimlessly is not a characteristic of Standish. So I at once arrived at the conclusion that he was doing nothing of the sort."

"Good God! do you think he's found out anything?"

"You mean as to where our cosy home is? To be quite frank with you, Blake, the possibility had crossed my mind. But now, after what you tell me about Gillson, I am almost inclined to think that he may be there merely on the Bessonian question."

Felton Blake heaved a sigh of relief.

"Then we needn't worry. On that point neither he nor anybody else can do anything to interfere with us. But if he had found head-quarters. . . ."

"He still has to get inside," remarked Zavier, pressing out his ciga-rette. "And that as you know, my dear Blake, presents certain difficul-ties. In fact to do it in safety without knowing how, is as nearly impos-sible as a thing can be." He rose to his feet. "Well, Susan—a little walk will be good for both of us."

"When do you return, Zavier?"

"Tomorrow. So possibly I shall travel with your friend Carteret. Yes—I go back tomorrow. There are two or three big deals maturing, which I want to get through before the business with Berendosi. And on the Roumanian question I may require you. I think you have a little private information concerning two members of their cabinet which should prove useful. Well, goodnight, and may the course of your young love run smooth."

And his faint mocking laugh was still echoing in Blake's ears, long after the front door had banged behind him.

CHAPTER 4

Age cannot wither nor custom stale the incredible tedium of the journey from Calais to Paris. It is possible that for those who are about to gaze on that most delectable of cities for the first time the thrill of anticipation may suffice to tide them over those three interminable hours. But for the rest—*on s'ennui.*

Tiny was one of the rest. Normally he always flew to France, but on this occasion he was not his own master. The day had started badly, with a brief telephone message from Mary.

"My dear," she had said, "I adore your letter, and I'm not at all sure I don't adore you. But you can't do anything, really you can't. Now run along like a good boy or you'll miss your train."

At that she had rung off, and when he tried to get through to her again only her maid had answered. Then a grim visaged woman using her dressing-case as a battering-ram winded him badly at Victoria, and then glared at him furiously when he invoked Allah in his agony. In fact, everything seemed to have gone wrong.

Half-way to Dover had found him already regretting that he had ever left London. It seemed to him that if he went on badgering Mary long enough, she would be bound to tell him what the trouble was, and that therefore his place was near her and not flying about Switzerland. That momentary look on Blake's face the previous night, when he had drawn a bow at a venture and mentioned Bessonia, had confirmed his opinion. That *was* the root of the whole trouble, and he wished he had taxed her with it directly. Then she might have spoken.

The train was slowing down for Amiens, when he threw aside his paper and glanced round the Pullman. It was filled with the usual cosmopolitan crowd, and he was just picking up a magazine when the attendant handed him a note, scribbled in pencil and written evidently while the train was in motion, it ran:

Dear Mr. Carteret, have you quite forgotten me? I am sitting directly behind you, two chairs away. Nada Mazarin.

His brows wrinkled: who the devil was Nada Mazarin? Then he turned round and looked at the writer who smiled, as she caught his eye, and indicated the seat opposite her own which happened to be free. Her face was small and *piquante*, and Tiny remembered having caught a glimpse of her on the boat, and wondering vaguely if he didn't know her. And the worst of it was, he couldn't place her even now.

He rose at once and took the vacant seat.

"It is incredibly *gauche* of me to admit it," he said, "but though I remember you perfectly, I cannot for the life of me think when and where I had the pleasure of meeting you."

"You didn't see much of me, Mr. Carteret," she answered, with only the faintest of foreign accents. "You and Mr. Denver made the four with Lady Mary and—you know who."

Tiny leaned back in his chair: now he had got the whole thing.

"Of course," he cried. "How infernally stupid of me not to remember."

Countess Nada Mazarin—that was who it was. She had been lady-in-waiting, or female of the bedchamber—Tiny was a bit vague on the correct nomenclature in such matters—to Princess Olga when she had been over in England three years ago. He recalled her perfectly: he'd seen her several times at Claridges with the princess. And as she justly remarked she had been a bit left out of things: the others had formed a square party.

"Lady Mary told me you were crossing today, so I wondered if by chance we should go by the same service."

"And when did you see Lady Mary?" he asked, holding out his cigarette-case to her.

"No, thank you," she said. "But please smoke yourself. I've seen a lot of her during the few days I've been in London."

Tiny looked at her thoughtfully: proof seemed to be mounting on proof.

"Should I be right in assuming that it was in order to see her that you went to London?" he remarked.

Her face betrayed no surprise at his question.

"I wonder how much you know, Mr. Carteret," she said quietly.

"If what I knew depended on what Mary had told me," he remarked a little bitterly, "it would be mighty little. To be truthful, Countess, I *know* nothing. But I've guessed a good deal. Come: won't you be frank with me. You know I'm to be trusted."

"It's not a question of that, my dear man," she answered wearily. "Tell me—what have you guessed? From what Mary said to me last night you seem to know a good deal about her doings."

"I know," said Tiny grimly, "that she has been doing the most amazingly injudicious things with a man who is a blackguard of the first water."

"He's not as bad as that surely," she protested, her eyes dilating.

"My dear Countess, personally I know nothing about the swine except what I've been told. But, believe me, there are no flies on my informant. You don't suppose, do you, that I even knew Mary had been to the Fifty-Nine with the blighter. I was told it, and it was the man who told me that, and a lot of other things too, who put me wise as to Felton Blake's character."

"But, Mr. Carteret, he's doing all he can for Mary."

Tiny gave a short laugh.

"Countess, your look belies you. You don't trust the blighter any more than I do. If he's doing all he can for Mary, he's also doing it for himself at the same time. And that's what I can't get the hang of—

having guessed, shall we put it, as much as I have." He leaned across the table towards her. "Let's quit this beating about the bush. Mary is acting for someone whose name we won't mention, isn't she?"

She gave an almost imperceptible nod.

"I thought so." Tiny sat back in his chair; it was a relief to have absolute confirmation at last. "I was sure of it. But why the dickens Mary couldn't tell me herself is what beats me."

"Mr. Blake is doing all he can for her," said the countess after a pause.

"That's one point in the gentleman's favour anyway. Though from what I've heard of him, I should never have expected him to be so altruistic."

For perhaps half a minute she stared out of the window in silence: then she suddenly turned to him.

"Why should you assume that he is being altruistic?" she said slowly.

"You mean he's going to make her pay? Well, it's quite in keeping with the blighter's character. And if Mary is in want of money, there are stacks of her pals who will rally round the old flag."

"You're dense, my friend," said his companion. "Money isn't the only method of paying."

For a moment or two Tiny stared at her blankly: then, as her meaning got home he half rose from his chair.

"But, good God!" he stuttered, "you're mad. It's impossible. It's. . . . . it's . . . an outrage on decency. You mean that Mary might—might marry that—that excrescence! You're joking."

"I don't say she will, Mr. Carteret," she said gently. "But, if I'm any judge of human nature, that is what he is working for."

"Ah! that's a different matter." Tiny sat back relieved. "Jove! but you gave me a shock, Countess. And why should you think that's his game?"

"I've seen them together," she answered. "I've seen him looking at her when he thought he was unobserved, and a score of little things like that."

"The insolent blackguard," fumed Tiny. "Of course she knows nothing about it?"

"If you mean by that, that he hasn't said anything to her—quite right. But Mary is very much a woman, my friend."

"You mean, she's guessed what he's up to?"

"Is there any woman in the world who doesn't guess a thing like that? Though, mind you, she's said nothing to me about it."

"But you aren't hinting, are you, that there's a possibility of Mary agreeing?" he cried, aghast.

And once again she stared out of the window before she replied.

"Supposing that was the only price he would accept," she said at length.

"Surely there is no man living who could be such a swine," he muttered. "And surely," he went on slowly, "there is no one living who could ask such a sacrifice of another person."

"I know what you mean," she answered quietly. "And if things were quite as obvious as they seem to us, there would be a great deal of justification in your remark. The someone whose name we won't mention has no inkling of that side of the case. Nor had I till I came over this time."

"Then you must tell that someone, Countess," said Tiny gravely. "At once: the instant you get back."

"Tell her what, my friend? Believe me, it isn't quite so easy as it appears to you. As I told you, Mary has said nothing to me. All I have to go on is my own intuition. And supposing Mary laughed the whole idea to scorn. She's loyal to the core, you know, and she loves that someone dearly."

"You mean she might deliberately sacrifice herself," said Tiny, and his voice was low. "Good God! There must be some other way out. Can't you tell me, Countess, what the trouble is? Damn it! I might think of some alternative: I'm not an absolute fool."

She shook her head wearily.

"Believe me, Mr. Carteret, there is absolutely nothing you or any-one else can do. Except this man Blake. He is literally our only hope. You see it's not a question of brawn and muscle, or even of brain. It's a question of being in touch with certain people, of having certain inside information. And only he possesses it. *Mon Dieu!*" she put her hand to her forehead. "I think I shall go distracted at times. One feels so utterly helpless—like a fly in a spider's web. And the spider is sitting there, just biding its time."

"Ah! Countess, what a delightful surprise. I had no idea that you were on the train."

A thick-set man with an aquiline nose had paused beside their table.

"Nor I, that you were, *Signor.*"

The new-comer turned a pair of shrewd eyes on Tiny, and deliberately studied him before replying.

"You have had a good time in London, I trust?" he said suavely.

"Thank you," she answered. "London at this time of the year is always delightful."

He lingered for a few moments shooting little quick glances at Tiny between each platitude: then he moved on into his own coach.

"How very funny, *mon ami*," said the countess, "that I should have been speaking about the spider just then. For that man is the spider himself."

"Indeed," cried Tiny. "Who is he?"

"A man called Berendosi," she answered. "The most implacable enemy of our someone that exists. But I don't suppose you have ever heard of him."

"On the contrary, Countess: I have. You know," he added with a smile, "I am not quite so ignorant of affairs in other countries as the average Englishman is always reputed to be."

"I would give a good deal to know what he's been doing in England," she said thoughtfully. "I suppose," she gave a little laugh, "you wouldn't like to perform a thoroughly meritorious action and drop the brute out of the window!"

"He looks the irrepressible type who would bounce back," he answered with a smile. "Hullo! we're nearly there. Now, look here, Countess, will you promise me one thing? If you should find that I can be of the smallest assistance—and you never know, I might be— will you drop me a line to the Ouchy Palace Hotel, Lausanne. I'll make arrangements to get it with a minimum of delay whether I'm in Lausanne or not."

"I promise," she said. "And don't take what I said about Mary too seriously. I may be completely wrong."

But that was just what it was impossible for him to do. As he drove to Philippes it rang in his brain: as he sat in the empty restaurant the thought kept dancing through his mind till it almost seemed to be written on the cloth in front of him. Mary married to Blake! Mary married to Blake!

It was inconceivable: hideous: monstrous. And yet as he forced himself to think it over dispassionately he had to admit that even stranger *misalliances* had taken place. The man at any rate looked a gentleman, and he had plenty of money. And then he recalled the expression on her face when she had passed him in the Rolls.

He ordered another Martini and lit a cigarette. That settled it.

There could be no willingness on the part of a girl who looked like that. Quite obviously she disliked the man intensely. And that being the case she was not going to marry him even if it necessitated killing Blake with his own hands.

He shook himself angrily: what the devil was the use of thinking along those lines? You can't go running round London murdering people whose proposed nuptials you disapprove of. And if Mary had made up her mind, he knew the futility of trying to dissuade her. Besides, she would probably do it at a registrar's office and no one would know anything about it till it was all over.

The room was beginning to fill up, but Tiny hardly noticed it, so engrossed was he in his own thoughts. He ordered dinner automatically, and ate it scarcely conscious of what the dishes were. Which was manifestly unfair to superlative cooking. And it was not until the coffee and brandy were in front of him that he suddenly remembered that someone was to meet him there. This ghastly question of Mary had driven everything else out of his head.

He glanced round the restaurant: every table was full. And certainly no one that he could see looked in the very slightest degree like the possible bearer of a message. He was the only solitary diner present: all the other tables had parties. He looked at his watch: half-past eight. In a few minutes he would have to start for the station.

"Monsieur Carteret?"

A waiter was standing by his table, and Tiny nodded.

"A note for *M'sieur.*"

He took the envelope from the tray, and for a moment or two he hesitated. Should he open it at once, or wait till he got in the taxi? And then he realised that if by any chance he was being spied on it would seem far more natural to do the former.

Inside was a sheet of paper on which was scrawled a single sentence.

Tell R.S. that D. is being shadowed.

He looked round the neighbouring tables: no one seemed to be paying any attention to him. Then he beckoned the waiter.

"Who gave you this note?" he demanded.

"A gentleman who came to the door, *M'sieur.* He just looked in and when he saw you he gave me the note."

"Right, thank you. Give me my bill, please."

He tore the message into tiny pieces and dropped them in his coffee cup. The R.S. obviously referred to Ronald Standish, but who D. was he had no idea. Presumably Ronald would, however, and having poured some more coffee over the scraps of paper to obliterate them still further, he rose and left.

It was in the taxi that he suddenly remembered Gillson's remark about the sleeper, and he began to wonder why the temporary possession of Number 8 bunk was going to fill him with gloom and despondency. Presumably it must have something to do with the occupant of Number 7, and he groaned mentally. The night was hot, and the thought of being cooped up with some odoriferous male was not pleasant. Still his orders were quite definite, though as it happened they proved to be unnecessary. For when he got to the station he found that the train was crowded and every other berth in the coach was full. But of the possessor of Number 7 there was no sign.

He tipped the porter, and then got out and stood on the platform. The usual bunches of people seeing off others stood chattering in little groups under the glare of the arc lights, and Tiny watched them idly. There were two or three obvious English people, but for the most part they consisted of French or Italians. Two monks in brown cowls paced gravely up and down, and he wondered what their particular order was. And then just as he was beginning to hope that for once Gillson's arrangements had miscarried, and that he was going to have the compartment to himself, a strange trio advanced along the platform.

The centre one of the three was being, if not supported, at any rate helped by the other two, and a terrible premonition of impending doom assailed Tiny. And the next moment it ceased to be a premonition—it became a certainty: the trio had stopped at the entrance to the sleeper. Then one man pushed and another pulled, and the centre one shot inside. The occupant of Number 7 had arrived.

Breathing a short invocation to Heaven to give him strength to bear his cross, Tiny entered the carriage and walked along the corridor to his compartment. And what he saw shook him to the marrow. The gentleman reclining on Number 7 would have shaken anyone to the marrow.

He was a fat puffy-looking individual of about forty, with a greasy unhealthy complexion. At the moment he was breathing hard, and his eyes were roving wildly from side to side like those of a frightened rabbit. He was making periodical remarks in a language unknown to Tiny, and one of his companions was answering him in the same tongue. The third man looked and evidently was an Englishman.

It was he who first saw Tiny, and he grinned slightly.

"Had to make him a bit screwed, or we'd never have got him here," he said, joining Tiny in the corridor. "Still, he'll sleep all the better."

"Thank Heaven for that, anyway," Tiny grunted.

"He's scared out of his life," muttered the man. "And I don't wonder. Not sorry to be shot of this show myself."

"I suppose you realise that I haven't the slightest idea what you are talking about," said Tiny.

The man stared at him in amazement.

"Good God!" he cried. "Ain't you. . . Hullo! Train's off. Hop it, Jim."

They scrambled on to the platform, leaving Tiny gazing moodily at his bedfellow. And the more he gazed the less he liked it. So far as he could see the gentleman had no redeeming feature. At the same time, in view of what Gillson had said, he was evidently one of the pawns in the game, though where he fitted in it was impossible to say.

The arrival of the attendant settled one point: he, too, was going to Lausanne. Moreover, he was going in his own fashion. Not for him the comparative comfort of pyjamas and sheets, but something far more primitive. He did, it is true, remove his shoes, having first, with great difficulty, shut the window. Then, swaying slightly, he turned a rather glazed eye on Tiny and pointed to the top bunk.

Assuming that he was asking a question Tiny shook his head and pointed to the lower. But that apparently was not what he wanted. Still continuing to point at the bunk with one hand, he beckoned to Tiny with the other.

"Come," he ejaculated solemnly. "Come."

"Oh! you want me to turn in, do you," said Tiny. "Well, laddie, we're going to have the window open whether you like it or not."

He entered the compartment, and the instant he was inside the man shut and bolted the door. Then he bolted the door into the washing-place, made a strange grunting noise which Tiny took to mean goodnight, collapsed on the lower berth and began to breathe stertorously.

But not for long: the sound of Tiny opening the window galvanized him into frenzied activity. He sprang off the bed pouring out a flood of unintelligible words, and shut it again. Then gesticulating wildly he turned to Tiny, and said "No" with great distinctness six times. After which effort he fell down.

"Yes, but look here," said Tiny, when he'd helped him to his feet, "there's not an atom of air in the carriage. *Pas de l'air. Fenêtre. Ouvrir. Insanitaire. Oui. Non.*"

"No. No. No," answered the man. "Danger."

"Rot," cried Tiny angrily. "You can't have the window shut on a hot night like this."

But the man had collapsed on his bunk again, still repeating No at intervals, and Tiny stared at him nonplussed. He knew that by the regulations for all railways abroad, the man was within his rights in insisting on having the window shut. He also knew that despite all those regulations he was going to have it open. Already the carriage was becoming stuffy and airless, and to go all through the night in such an atmosphere was a physical impossibility.

And then he had an idea. The man was half tight: once he was asleep nothing would be likely to wake him. So he hoisted himself carefully into the top bunk, and began to undress. From below came the gentle music of the sleeper, but he decided to give it a little longer. So he lit a cigarette, and opened a magazine. But after ten minutes he felt he could stand it no more. He carefully inspected his companion in the mirror, and having listened to his snores for a while he decided the time was ripe. With great caution he descended to the floor: in a moment the window was open. And—the sleeper still slept.

Tiny returned to his berth, and shortly began to yawn himself. And being one of those fortunate individuals who can sleep soundly in a train, he soon switched out the lights, leaving only the dim blue one in the centre of the roof just above him burning.

Now, as has been said, Tiny Carteret was a man whose nerves were just about as strong as a man's nerves may be. He had, like many of us, suffered moments of intense fright during the war, and again like most of us those moments had passed into the limbo of forgotten things. But it is to be doubted if the thing that happened in that sleeper some two hours afterwards will ever fade from his mind.

At first he thought he was having a nightmare: in fact, such a peculiar thing is the human brain that during the few seconds in which it happened he very distinctly said to himself—"It's that lobster." For suddenly a hand clutched his arm, and as he opened his eyes he saw not six inches away the face of the man below. Only the whites of his eyes were showing: his lips were drawn back from his teeth in a hideous snarl. And in the eerie blue light it seemed to him that he was looking at a skull.

Suddenly the man uttered a dreadful cry, which sounded to Tiny like "*Bazana*." Then the face disappeared.

For what seemed an eternity Tiny lay there, with the sweat pouring off him as if he was in a Turkish bath. Then with a great effort he forced himself to switch on the lights. He leaned over the edge of his bunk: the man was sprawling face downwards on the floor. And instinctively Tiny knew he was dead.

He got down and turned him over. There was no doubt about it: that strange word "*Bazana*" was the last he would ever utter. His face was contorted with agony: his arms and legs were rigid. And for a space Tiny stood looking at him dully, hardly able to realise what had happened.

The whole thing was so astoundingly sudden, and Tiny's brain was not at its best at the moment of waking. But at last he pulled himself together and rang the bell for the attendant, who came after a slight delay and tried the door.

"Come in," called Tiny. "*Entrez.*"

"*C'est fermé, M'sieur.*"

Of course: the door had been locked. Tiny remembered now: the dead man had locked it himself. He opened it and the conductor came in.

"*Mon Dieu!*" he cried, as he noticed the body. Then he drew back with a cry of horror as he saw that terrible distorted face.

"*Qu'est-ce-que y est arrivé?*"

And Tiny could only shrug his shoulders helplessly. What was there to say? Every symptom seemed to tally with Gillson's description of the mysterious murders, but how was it possible in this case? How could a man be murdered in a train travelling at sixty miles an hour when he was locked into a sleeper? The thing was incredible; preposterous.

The *chef du train* had arrived by this time, and after one look at the body had departed rapidly to see if there was a doctor on the train. As luck would have it there was, and two minutes later he returned with a young Englishman.

"Good God!" he cried, "the poor devil must have been in absolute torture before he died. What happened, sir?" He turned to Tiny.

"I can tell you nothing," answered Tiny. "I was in the top bunk and I was suddenly awakened by feeling his hand on my arm. His face was convulsed with agony, and then he crashed to the floor. I realised at once, of course, that he was dead. So I rang for the attendant."

"You know him? Was he a friend of yours?"

"I've never seen him before in my life," said Tiny.

Once more the doctor stooped over the dead man, and suddenly he gave a little exclamation.

"Hullo! I wonder what that mark is on his hand? It's been made fairly recently."

Tiny bent down to look: sure enough on the back of the man's right hand was a small puncture that looked as if it had been made by a thorn. Further evidence: and yet—how could it be so? Vaguely he heard the others talking: realised that the doctor in a mixture of English and French was telling the *chef du train* that nothing could be done: that the man was dead and that his body had better be removed from the train at the next stop.

"Dijon," said the worried official, and then with the attendant he lifted the body back on to the bunk and covered the ghastly face with a blanket.

"What was the cause of it, do you think, doctor?" asked Tiny.

"Without a postmortem it is impossible to say," replied the other. "But from what you tell me, taking into account the rapidity of the thing and the contortion of the features, I should say that almost certainly it is a case of advanced disease of the heart. Look here," he went on, "I've got a carriage to myself, and I have also got a spot of Scotch. You'd better come along with me, at any rate as far as Dijon."

"I think I will," said Tiny. "It's shaken me a bit, I confess. I'll put some clothes on."

"Right you are," cried the doctor. "I'll wait in the corridor."

"Is it true that a poor fellow is dead?"

A deep voice from the doorway made them both swing round: standing there was one of the monks Tiny had noticed on the platform in Paris. His hands were clasped in front of him: the brown cowl still covered his head.

"I regret to say that it is," said the doctor. "But, reverend Father, he is not a pretty sight to look at."

"My son," answered the other, "one must learn to disregard the outer shell, and pay attention only to the inner spirit."

He drew back the blanket, and for a while his lips moved silently. Then having made the sign of the cross, as abruptly as he had come, he vanished.

"I suppose it's grossly materialistic of me," said the doctor, "but I'm blowed if I see what good that has done. However—doubtless I'm wrong."

"Look here," said Tiny, getting into his coat, "do you think the French authorities are likely to detain me at Dijon?"

He took his watch down from the hook: ten minutes to twelve— not three hours since they had left. Dijon, so far as he remembered, was about four and a half hours from Paris, and to be shot out there in the middle of the night was not a pleasant thought.

"I really don't see why they should," said the doctor. "You can do no earthly good. Of course they may keep you there on some formality. At the same time I should say the cause of death is obvious. Heart, as I told you. Come along, if you're ready. A drink will do us both good."

Tiny shut the door, and the attendant locked it at once. Then he followed the doctor along the train, his brain buzzing with the problem. What had happened? What could have happened? Had it not been for the mark on the dead man's hand, he would have been inclined to think that the doctor was right, and that death had been due to natural causes. But now the coincidence was too extraordinary. And yet how in Heaven's name had the poor devil been got at?

A possibility struck him. Had he got up and gone along the corridor for some reason? That would presuppose that the murderer was lurking outside on the bare chance that such a thing would happen. Unlikely—but at any rate it did present a solution.

Another idea. Was it conceivable that this man had been one of the users of the poison himself, and had been carrying with him whatever it was that they employed to commit their murders. Then, accidentally while he was asleep, he had run it into his own hand, and being half drunk had not awakened when he did so? If so, the implement would still be in the dead man's berth, or in one of his pockets.

For awhile he debated whether he should say anything about it to the doctor. And then it occurred to him that to suggest the possibility of foul play could do no good, and might involve him in extremely awkward complications. For on the face of it to the ordinary outsider the only person who could have murdered the man was himself.

No: it was impossible to say anything. All he could do was to hope that the French authorities would come to the same conclusion as the doctor, and attribute the man's death to natural causes. If they didn't, and detained him for a postmortem, he would have to grin and bear it. As he reflected a little cynically, it would only be in keeping with the whole state of affairs at the moment.

But luck proved to be in at Dijon. Fortunately for Tiny one of the station officials spoke fluent English, and helped by the doctor's professional opinion, they merely asked his name and destination and then allowed him to proceed. But one thing of interest did come to light. The dead man was a Russian named Demeroff. And as Tiny got back into the train he wondered if he was the man referred to as D. in the letter he had received at Philippes. If so, the shadowing was pretty efficient...

There was no sign of Ronald Standish on the platform at Lausanne, so he chartered a car and drove to the Ouchy Palace Hotel. And there, as Gillson had said, he found that a room had been reserved for him.

"There is a letter for you, sir," said the clerk. "Delivered by hand."

It was from Ronald and was as terse as the one he had received in Paris.

Do not let Demeroff out of your sight. Mid-day—the bar.

Tiny smiled grimly: it struck him that the writer would require more than one cocktail when he heard the news.

"There was another gentleman coming, sir, I believe," said the clerk inquiringly. "A Russian."

"I fear that he has been unavoidably detained," answered Tiny quietly.

The morning passed slowly: try as he would he couldn't get the thought of that ghastly distorted face out of his mind. And try as he would he couldn't get any nearer to solving the problem of how it had been done. Ronald's note knocked the bottom out of his theory that the thing was accidentally self-administered, because it seemed to show that the dead man had been on their side.

At twelve o'clock precisely Ronald Standish came into the bar. His face was expressionless, but Tiny knew by the way he walked that his nerves were a little on edge.

"What's this, Tiny, I hear at the office? Demeroff not come?"

"And I'm afraid he never will, Ronald. He died in the train last night: his body is at Dijon."

For a moment or two Standish said nothing: then he spoke—very deliberately.

"If," he remarked, "I ever did lose my temper, I would now swear without repeating myself for five minutes. How did they get him? Tell me exactly what happened."

He listened in silence while Tiny ran through everything from the receipt of the note in Paris to the examination at Dijon.

"You assume they got him, Ronald," he said in conclusion. "So do I, because of the mark in his hand. But if you can tell me how the devil they did it I'll be much obliged."

"What time did you say it was when you looked at your watch?" asked the other.

"Ten to twelve," said Tiny. "But what's that got to do with it?"

"Everything," answered Standish quietly. "Oh! Tiny, Tiny, if only we as a race, didn't like fresh air so much! Still, it can't be helped."

"What can't be helped?" said Tiny peevishly. "You're not going to tell me that he was murdered through the open window of a train travelling at sixty miles an hour."

"No, old lad, I'm not. He was murdered through the open window of a train standing stationary by a platform. All the fast expresses on that line stop at Laroche halfway between Paris and Dijon to change engines. It was then they got him. You were asleep and so was he. And that's when the poison was inserted. He was a bit drunk so the prick never woke him. And it wasn't until after the train had started that the poison began to work."

"Good God!" muttered Tiny. "Then I'm responsible for the poor devil's death. He said it was dangerous to open the window, but I never dreamt he meant that."

"How should you?" answered Standish. "You needn't worry, Tiny: he was a nasty piece of work, and it was only a question of time before they got him. But, if only I could have seen him for five minutes! You see, to put the matter in a nutshell, he was blowing the gaff. I don't know how much Gillson has told you; anyway I'll fill in the gaps later, but the man who was murdered last night was a member of the gang we are after. And our people had got at him in Paris. His journey here was simply and solely to split on his former pals. From the note you got at Philippes our people realised the danger. But naturally no one thought of the damned window."

"How did they get at him, Ronald? How was it done?"

"If I could tell you that, Tiny, I should have solved one problem that is worrying us all. Obviously the man who did it got out of his carriage at Laroche, saw his opportunity and seized it. If the window had been shut, of course he couldn't have done it."

He lit a cigarette thoughtfully.

"*Bazana*. I wonder if there's any significance. Was he trying to tell you something?"

"Quite possibly," said Tiny. "And don't forget that's only what it sounded like to me. The poor blighter's teeth were clenched, and with the noise of the train it may not have been that at all."

"Let's have another spot, Tiny. Because we've got to decide what we're going to do. I hear incidentally that you agree with Gillson and me that Lady Mary is acting as go-between."

"How do you know that?" said Tiny with some surprise.

"I got a cable in code from Gillson yesterday."

"Well, if we wanted any further confirmation I got it in the Golden Arrow yesterday," said Tiny. "Do you by any chance know a Countess Mazarin?"

"I know who you mean, though I don't know the lady personally."

"Well, she admitted it to me. By God! Ronald," he went on savagely, "something has got to be done to get Mary out of the clutches of that excrescence Felton Blake. The countess actually told me that she thought he was in love with her."

Standish raised his eyebrows.

"He aims high," he remarked. "Still, I wouldn't be surprised if you aren't right."

"Berendosi was on the train too," said Tiny.

"I heard he'd been in England. Lord! Tiny, I'm at a dead end." He got up and started pacing up and down, his hands deep in his trouser pockets. "If only Lady Mary or the Mazarin woman would tell us what the mystery was! Though, to be perfectly frank, I don't know that it would do us much good. They've got some form of proof—faked or otherwise, it matters not—which they are going to spring at the last moment."

"And Mary thinks Blake can get it back for her?"

"Presumably. Otherwise why should she be mixed up in it at all. That's where the devil of it comes in. Of course he is double-crossing her."

"Why should you think that?" said Tiny slowly.

"My dear fellow, it's obvious. If this proof lies out here in the hands of Berendosi's crowd, you don't suppose they are going to give it up to help Blake's love affair. But as a matter of fact, I don't think for a moment it is out here. It's locked up in Felton Blake's safe. Otherwise why should he have come into it at all? He was no good to them: they didn't want him if they held it themselves. No: he started the hare himself. He holds the trump card, though he is probably pretending to

Lady Mary that he is moving heaven and earth to help her."

"I'd like to wring the blighter's neck," grunted Tiny.

"So would a good many other people," said Standish with a short laugh. "But it's hardly worthwhile being hanged for exterminating vermin. No: it's the other one that I want, Tiny: the big man. And I hoped to get on his trail through Demeroff. You see, one of the most extraordinary things about this gang is the elusiveness of its members. It sounds fantastic, but I can assure you that sometimes I have been tempted to think that they hold the secret of becoming invisible. Not once, but a dozen times have people we wanted vanished from practically under our noses. It is incredible."

"Disguise of some sort, I suppose."

"You can take it from me that it's got to be a pretty useful disguise to deceive our fellows. And yet—they've done it. Why only a week ago in Paris, we hunted two of them to ground in a smallish hotel in the Rue Tivoli. Men were posted at every entrance, but they got away—slipped clean through our fingers. It's positively uncanny."

"And have you no idea of the whereabouts of their headquarters?"

"I believe it to be somewhere in this country. In fact, I'm almost sure it is."

"Well, old lad, you're the commanding officer for this expedition," said Tiny. "What does A do, beyond lighting an Abdullah?"

And at that moment a page boy entered the bar with a telegram.

"Monsieur Carteret?"

"That's me," said Tiny, taking the envelope.

He glanced through the message: then with a laugh he handed it to Standish.

"That would seem to give us a pointer, Ronald."

For the wire which had been handed in in Paris ran as follows:

"Can you go Hotel Royal Dalzburg at once. Mazarin."

"As you say, Tiny," said Standish, "it seems to give us a pointer. Well—the capital of Bessonia is a delightful spot. And since Demeroff's removal prevents us getting direct at their headquarters, perhaps we'll do it through the side track of Berendosi's little scheme. But I wonder what the lady can have discovered in Paris to cause her to send that."

CHAPTER 5

Dalzburg, as Ronald Standish had said, was a delightful place, and when they arrived there the next day it was looking its loveliest. The picturesque old town, dominated by the Palace standing on the wooded heights behind it, was bathed in the early-morning sunshine, as they rattled over the cobbled bridge which spans the river. But at the moment their thoughts were centred on the mundane questions of baths and food, and it was not until eleven o'clock that they sauntered forth from the hotel for a stroll round.

It was Tiny's first visit to the place, though Standish knew it well. And since they had found nothing further at the hotel to explain the countess's telegram in any way, there seemed to be nothing to do except kick their heels and wait. Presumably in time its reason would become clear.

"I seem to remember," said Standish after a while, "that they make a not indifferent brand of beer. What about it, Tiny?"

"Lead me to it, old boy. These damned continental sleepers give me a mouth like a lime kiln."

They found a vacant table at a shady *café* on the main *boulevard* and sat down. The place was full of people bent on the same errand, and as luck would have it, their immediate neighbours were not tourists but natives of the place.

"You'll often get more reliable information from the apparently idle chatter in a place like this," said Standish, "than from a score of agents. But you must be able to speak the lingo."

"How many can you speak, Ronald?" asked Tiny curiously.

"About fifteen, old boy," laughed the other. "They seem to come naturally to me."

He half closed his eyes, and leaning back in his chair he relapsed into silence. To the casual observer he seemed almost asleep: in reality every sense was alert. Times out of number had he played this same game, and even if it was only once in twenty that anything tangible rewarded his efforts, it was at any rate good practice in the language.

The first essential was to shut out as far as possible the people who were obviously useless to him, and long practice had enabled him to do this in the most amazing way. He could deliberately, as it were, shut down parts of his brain, till only one particular conversation came through, while the rest seemed merely an aimless buzz. And now, having cut out a nursemaid with children on his right, and a loving couple on his left, he concentrated on two men sitting at the table just behind him as being the only possible source of interest.

At first he drew blank: they were discussing some recent reconstruction scheme in the business belonging to one of them. The other he gathered was interested financially: the matter of a mortgage cropped up. Influential men evidently: men of substance. And he was just preparing to relax and get on with his beer, when a name caught his attention. One of them mentioned Berendosi.

But luck was out: both at once lowered their voices, and strain his ears as much as he could he was unable to catch more than an odd word here and there. Suddenly, however, one of them made a remark which he heard perfectly and which riveted his attention.

"There. That man the other side of the street. The tall Englishman. I tell you it's obvious."

He opened his eyes and looked across the road. There was no mistaking whom they were alluding to: there was only one man who could possibly be an Englishman. And even as he was idly speculating as to what was obvious, he heard a sudden exclamation from beside him. He glanced round: Tiny Carteret had half risen from his seat and was staring at the Englishman himself.

Now Standish was a man who thought quickly, and though he was completely in the dark himself as to why two prominent Bessonians and Tiny should both be interested in the same man, his brain reacted instinctively.

"Sit down, Tiny," he said curtly. "Don't pay any attention to that man across the road. I'll explain later."

A little bewildered, Tiny obeyed, and once again Standish leaned back in his chair. Had the two men behind him noticed Tiny's movement? If so, goodbye to any chance of hearing any more. Apparently they had not, and stray snatches of their conversation came to him.

"Undoubted. . . Gregoroff saw him. . . Hotel Royal. . . . Must be the same man. . . . There won't be much trouble. . . Berendosi must see him. . ."

And then their voices became mere whispers, and not another word could he hear, during the remaining ten minutes they sat at their table.

"I will now have another beer," said Standish, as he watched their retreating backs.

"What was the great idea, Ronald?"

"Well, old boy, it was obvious that you knew or thought you knew the Englishman on the other side of the street. It was equally obvious that the two men who have just left were interested in him too, as they were talking about him. And I thought I might hear a good deal more if your mutual interest wasn't paraded too obviously."

"What did you hear?"

"Only snatches of conversation. He is stopping at the Royal, and he is obviously the same man. Same as what I can't tell you. They also are anxious for Berendosi to see him. Not much, I admit, but one often finds that little clues like that help one later. Now—your turn. Who did you think he was?"

"Three years ago when Princess Olga, as she then was, was over in London, there were four of us who used to get about a good bit together. She, Mary, myself, and a fellow called Joe Denver. And unless I'm very much mistaken that was Joe Denver himself. A bit more tanned, but I'm almost certain it was him—same walk and everything. And if it was him, it is the most extraordinary coincidence, because Mary and I were only talking about him the other afternoon, and wondering where he was. And here he is apparently stopping at the same hotel."

Ronald Standish lit a cigarette, and stared thoughtfully across the sunny street.

"That's interesting, Tiny—very interesting. I wonder if at last something tangible is in sight."

"What do you mean?" asked the other.

"I wonder if the thing isn't a coincidence at all—except that you and Lady Mary should have been talking about him. But is it his presence here that was the cause of the wire you got yesterday?"

"By Jove!" cried Tiny, "that's possible."

"It's more than possible, old boy—it's probable. But we must not go too fast. Let's take the points. Something must have inspired that wire. And when we find a man staying at the hotel we are told to come to, who was a friend of the queen's in days gone by and is now an object of great interest to Berendosi and his lot, surely there must be some connection. It's stretching coincidence too far altogether to imagine there isn't. I wonder, Tiny: I wonder. Are we on the verge of something that isn't merely guesswork?"

"Mark you, I won't swear that it was Joe Denver," said Tiny.

Standish glanced at his watch.

"Well, it's about time for *tiffin*. Let's go back to the pub and see."

They found him in the corner of the lounge, and all doubts were set at rest immediately. For the instant he saw Tiny he jumped to his feet.

"Carteret—by all that's wonderful. What brings you here?"

"I might almost ask the same," said Tiny. "By the way, Denver, let me introduce you. This is Standish. Well, old boy, how goes it? It's a long time since we met."

"Over three years. I've been in the back of beyond since then. This is my first leave."

"Are you spending it all here?" asked Standish casually.

"I don't know," said Denver a little curtly. "It depends."

He turned to Tiny, and asked after Lady Mary, while Standish studied him covertly with shrewd blue eyes. An expert in sizing up a man, he preferred to listen rather than to talk. And it soon became obvious to his trained observation that this good-looking youngster's nerves were on edge. There was an air of unrest about him, and once or twice he glanced round the lounge almost nervously.

That there was something the matter with him was clear: that he was not inclined to be communicative was also clear—his curt answer to Standish's question proved that. But being a past master in the art of getting things out of uncommunicative people, he was content to bide his time. That this youngster was involved in the matter in some way he was convinced: as he had said to Tiny, the coincidence if it were not so would be too amazing. Besides, his whole demeanour simply shouted the fact that something was up.

Suddenly Denver started to his feet angrily. He was glaring across the lounge, and Standish followed the direction of his glance. Two men were sitting at a small table, who looked away immediately they saw they were observed.

"I'll give that damned fellow a thick ear soon," said Denver furiously.

"Steady, old lad," said Tiny, pulling him back into his chair. "What's all the worry?"

"You see that pasty-faced swab over there with a dial like a suet pudding? Well, that fellow he's with is the fourth man he's brought in here for the express purpose of looking at me." He grinned a little sheepishly as if ashamed of his temper. "I don't resemble any blinking prince, do I, travelling *incognito*?"

"Are you sure you're not imagining it?" said Standish quietly.

"Absolutely certain. It started the very morning I arrived. That's three days ago. I was sitting in here, when pasty face arrived on the scene, and sat down at the next table. At first he took no notice of me: he certainly hadn't looked at me as he sat down. And then just as I was lighting a cigarette I found him staring at me. He turned away at once, but for the next ten minutes he did nothing but study my face when he thought I wasn't looking. After that I got a bit fed up, so I wandered to the bar. And the first thing he did—I could see it reflected in the mirror—was to go over to the reception clerk and ask who I was. I'm certain it was that because the fellow opened the visitors' book. I didn't think much more about it at the time, but since then he's led in four different blokes, with the express purpose of letting them see me. Damn it! I may not be a prize beauty, but I'm not a bally freak, am I?"

"You've never been here before, have you, Denver?" said Standish thoughtfully.

"Never in my life," said the other. "Anyway, what's that got to do with it?"

"I was only wondering. At any rate it seems perfectly clear that your pasty-faced friend is interested in you for some reason or other. Perhaps you bear a strong resemblance to some local celebrity. By Jove!"—he paused as if struck with a sudden idea—"I wonder if that can be the reason. You don't know von Emmerling, by any chance?"

"Never heard of him in my life. Why?"

"I wondered if he had written and asked you to come here."

"Nobody wrote and asked me to come here. I only decided at the very last moment and got off the boat at Brindisi. Who is von Emmerling, anyway?"

But Standish seemed to have lost interest in the matter.

"It doesn't matter," he said. "Evidently as you don't know him, that can't be the reason."

"But," persisted the other, "if there was any reason why this bloke should ask me here, that may account for the other thing."

"Von Emmerling," said Standish, "is one of the big German film magnates. And I believe he is going to stage one of his productions here. Moreover I know he is on the look-out for a tall fair Englishman, and it occurred to me as a possibility that he might have approached you on the matter."

Tiny glanced at Standish out of the corner of his eye, but his face was expressionless.

"Afraid it doesn't fit," said Denver. "Still it's possible you may be right. These blokes may be sizing me up from that point of view, though I fear they'll be disappointed. And incidentally that reminds me." He leaned forward in his chair. "By Jove! Standish, I wonder if you have hit it. Yesterday morning, when I was on the other side of the river strolling along the bank, a most persistent merchant with a camera came badgering me. Wanted to take my photo: no need to pay if I wasn't satisfied with the result. You know—all the usual palaver. I told him to go to hell, but for all that he took a couple. And it was only when I threatened to fling his cursed machine in the river and him after it that he vamoosed."

Once again Tiny glanced at Standish: in his eyes there was the faintest perceptible gleam of satisfaction. But his voice when he answered was as expressionless as ever.

"It certainly looks as if I might be right," he said. "Anyway, I wouldn't let the matter worry you. Well, I don't know about you fellows but I'm going to have a bite of lunch. See you afterwards, Denver."

"The plot thickens a little, Tiny," he went on as they sat down to lunch.

"Who on earth is von Emmerling?" demanded the other.

"He wasn't too bad, was he?" laughed Standish. "Realising our young friend was a bit nervy and touchy when asked a direct question I invented the gentleman on the spur of the moment. And I must say he justified his birth, even if he has complicated things. Because if Denver is speaking the truth it was a sheer fluke that he came here."

"I don't quite follow," said Tiny.

"My dear fellow, it's obvious. Had someone—I don't care who, asked him here, it would presuppose that that someone knew him. But if he came absolutely by chance, it's damned difficult to understand. Why should anyone be concerned with the arrival of an unknown Englishman who has never been here before? Unless..."

"Unless what?" demanded the other.

"And why bother about his photograph?" went on Standish, disregarding the question. "It's puzzling. Unless. . ."

Once again he paused, and this time Tiny did not interrupt.

"Tell me, Tiny"—he lowered his voice and leaned over the table—"when you and he and Lady Mary used to go about, was there anything between him and the fourth member of the party?"

"I see what you're driving at," said Tiny slowly. "Not as far as I know, Ronald. We played round a bit, and he may have been a bit keen on her. But that's all. Only, of course, I'm the world's most almighty mutt at spotting anything of that sort."

"Then I can't understand it," said Standish. "It beats me. I suppose Gillson put you wise to the state of affairs out here."

"Squire Straker did."

"Same thing. Well, what had occurred to me was that young Denver might have been indiscreet with a certain lady—written a letter or something of that sort—and these blokes have found out about it. I admit that there are a lot of difficulties—not the least of them being, how they know him. I mean if there is some letter that has fallen into the wrong hands—if, in other words, that is where Mr. Felton Blake comes in—you can't recognise a man through his handwriting. So why this excitement over him?"

"Assuming for the moment, Ronald, that you're right, and that there was more in it than I thought, mightn't it be possible that the indiscretion has been committed since he came here? That a certain lady has met him on the quiet and been spotted."

"Possible," agreed the other, "but it won't account for everything. He has only been here three days, and this song and dance started two months ago. No, Tiny: there's the deuce of a lot more in this than meets the eye. And as far as I can see our only hope is to persuade someone to talk. At present we're working in the dark. Lead Denver on after lunch, if you can. Mention of the lady in question will come quite naturally from you. And this is no time for half measures. I've got a feeling in my bones that things will shortly come to a head. By Jove! don't look round, but do you know who has just come in? Berendosi himself."

"Do you know him?" said Tiny.

"Only by sight."

"I was introduced to him in the train to Paris. It may prove useful."

"He's coming this way. If he doesn't recognise you, you recognise him. As you say, he may be useful."

As luck would have it he went to the next table. Preceded by the *maître d'hôtel*, and surrounded by other lesser minions, the great man was piloted to his seat, and having ordered his meal he glanced round the room. And the first person his eyes fell on was Tiny.

For a moment he stared at him with a puzzled look: then he came across.

"Surely we met in the Golden Arrow?" he said courteously.

"Quite right, *Signor*," said Tiny, "though I hardly expected you to remember me."

"You were with our charming Countess Nada," remarked the other. "I had no idea you were proposing to honour us with a visit."

"I'm just wandering at random," said Tiny carelessly. "By the way, may I introduce Mr. Standish—Signor Berendosi."

"Your first visit, Mr. Standish?" said Berendosi politely.

"No: I have been here several times. I love Dalzburg."

"It is indeed a beautiful spot," agreed Berendosi. "A little unhealthy sometimes, but one cannot have everything."

"How true," said Standish. "And one can always take suitable pre-cautions against—er—ill health."

For a moment the eyes of the two met and measured: then with a murmured banality Berendosi resumed his seat. And even as he did so Joe Denver passed the table.

"Have you finished, you fellows?" he remarked. "If so, come and have some coffee with me outside. Who was the bird who was talking to you?" he went on as they left the room. "The method of his entry seemed to indicate he was a big noise."

"That was Signor Berendosi," said Standish quietly. "Probably the most influential man in this country. And the most dangerous."

"Oh! What's he up against?"

"The existing system, Denver," said Standish. "The Royal House, the king and—the queen."

Denver paused with a cigarette halfway to his mouth, and stared at him.

"What's that you say?" he said. "Up against the king and the queen. Why?"

"Because he wants to turn this country into a republic of which he will be the President."

"But has he any chance of succeeding?" demanded Denver.

Standish shrugged his shoulders.

"You never can tell, my dear fellow, in spots like this. These people are not as we are, you know. And a small thing, such as say some bit of gossip or scandal against the queen, might prove very dangerous."

"What the hell are you talking about?" said Denver angrily. "Scan-dal against the queen! Such a thing is impossible. Ask Carteret. He knows her."

"My dear fellow," said Standish soothingly, "you are surely man enough of the world to know that it isn't the truth that counts, but what people believe is the truth. I should be the last person to believe anything against such a very charming lady: nevertheless, the bald fact remains that Berendosi and the very influential group who are back-ing him have started insidious rumours about the queen."

"I'll break the damned swine's neck for him," said the youngster through clenched teeth.

"Don't be such an ass, boy," said Standish sternly but not unkindly. "You're in a country now, where if they wish, you go into prison first and the charge comes on in a year or two. You've got to keep your head and your temper, or you'll be for it. Now I'm going to ask you an absolutely straight question. Why are you so very upset over what I've told you?"

"Wouldn't any decent fellow be?" answered the other.

"That's not good enough," said Standish. "I don't wish to probe into your private affairs, but there are times when it is necessary. And this is one of them. There are international questions at stake which render it essential. Now what are the facts? You, returning from the back of beyond, as you said yourself, after three years, decide suddenly to come here. Why?"

"I suppose I can please myself, can't I?" said the youngster angrily.

"For God's sake, Denver," said Standish gravely, "don't take it that way. Try and understand that I am not being gratuitously offensive and impertinent: try and understand that there are far bigger questions at stake than your feelings or mine."

"But how on earth can my movements have anything to do with them?" demanded Denver.

"I'm damned if I know, and that's what I'm trying to find out. I don't mind confessing to you now that there is no such person as von Emmerling. I invented him to find out one thing from you, and I succeeded. Your coming here was a sudden decision: no one had asked you. Very well then—what am I as an outside observer confronted with? The very significant fact, that the group of men who are at the bottom of the conspiracy against the queen, are also keenly interested in an unknown Englishman arriving in Dalzburg for the first time. And I ask myself: Why?"

"What possible connection can there be between the two things?" said Denver.

"None—but for one other fact. The Englishman in question at one time knew the queen very well. Steady now: don't lose your temper. As I told you before—it's not the truth that counts, and these people are capable of faking anything. Can you think of any letter which has passed between you and the lady concerned, and which by some wild stretch of imagination might be construed into something compromising?"

For a moment Denver hesitated: then he shook his head.

"I've never written to the lady in my life," he said.

"Well, do you think it possible," persisted Standish, "that the lady in question might have written to you and the letter has gone astray?"

"That, of course, is possible," answered Denver in a low voice. "Good God! Standish, you don't think, do you, that I may have caused her any harm?"

"Not wittingly, my dear fellow, but we've got to try and find a solution to certain facts. And I tell you frankly that I cannot help thinking that the Berendosi crowd are in the possession of some definite piece of evidence which they propose to use against the queen. And further, I cannot help thinking that you by coming here have played straight into their hands, because I believe that evidence concerns you."

"But how could they possibly know me? I've never been here before."

"That is not an insuperable difficulty," said Standish. "Berendosi's machinations have been going on for years. What more likely then, than that, when the future consort of the king was in London he had her watched? And it was there that you were seen by someone who recognised you again here."

For a moment or two he stared at the youngster, with eyes that were full of understanding, for Joe Denver's expression was plain to read.

"We are all out for one thing, young Denver," he went on gravely: "to protect the honour of a lady. And I've been very frank with you. Will you be equally frank with me?"

"What do you want to know?" said the other.

"Just this. Assuming for the moment that I am right: assuming for the moment that a letter from the lady to you had gone astray, can you give me any idea as to the terms it would have been couched in. I mean," he went on with a smile, "would it have started 'Dear Mr. Denver'?"

For a while Joe Denver stared in front of him: then he got up suddenly.

"I loved her," he said quietly, "as I didn't believe it was possible for a man to love a woman. And I think—I know, she felt the same about me. And I came here in the hopes that perhaps I might catch a glimpse of her, now and then, as she drove through the streets. I shall be in my room if you want me: this has got to be talked over. And understand one thing, Standish. I am prepared to do anything—anything to help."

"Well, I'm damned," said Tiny as Denver disappeared. "He kept mighty dark about it."

"You didn't expect him to put it in the papers, did you?" Standish gave a short laugh. "You may be a darned fine player of Rugby football, old lad, but as an observer of human nature you are not in the international class. Hell, Tiny, and once again Hell. This is a devilish serious matter."

"We're not certain yet, Ronald."

"If by that you mean we've no absolute proof, you're right. But short of that, I'm as certain of it as I ever could be of anything. You take my word for it, Tiny—a letter was written and it's fallen into the wrong hands. Lord! It's as plain as a pike-staff. That accounts for the photographer taking snapshots of him. When the time is ripe they will publish the letter in one of their rotten rags—probably in the original handwriting, and on the page opposite the snapshots of the man to whom the letter was sent. Strengthens their case enormously: just the sort of thing the public eats. They'll pretend, of course, to take some action against the editor, but the mischief will have been done. I wish to Heaven the youngster had never come here, though it's too late to worry about that now."

Tiny lit a cigarette thoughtfully.

"So you think Felton Blake in some way got hold of a compromising letter written to young Denver," he said after a while. "Bit difficult to account for, Ronald. If Denver had received one, and had then mislaid it, it wouldn't be so hard. But it's almost incredible to believe that the lady would have left it lying about, and the only other alternative is that it was tampered with in the post."

"Blotting-paper," said Standish. "An unscrupulous floor waiter or chambermaid reads the letter in a looking-glass. Then realising who the writer is he at once sees the financial value of the thing, and in the fullness of time it finds its way into Felton Blake's hands."

He drained his coffee and began to fill a pipe.

"Don't think that I'm not fully alive to the difficulties, Tiny," he went on. "There are many. If my blotting-paper theory is right, why didn't Denver get the letter? An answer to that is that possibly the lady on second thoughts tore the letter up and never sent it. Then there's another point: how does the lady in question know anything about it? Has Berendosi told her? Has he already held it over her head? If so, it seems a very unnecessary thing to do. The one thing I should have thought he would not do is to give his victim any warning until he is ready to strike. And yet even with all the difficulties—it must be the solution; it must be."

"Look here, Ronald, would it do any good if I went and saw the queen. I don't know how it's done, as I've never been in the habit of calling on queens. But if we can find out the correct procedure I'm sure she'd see me, and I might be able to find out something."

"A darned good idea, Tiny: darned good. Here's Berendosi: ask him. He'll know the ropes. And you can make the request without arousing any suspicion."

"Are you making a long stay, Mr. Carteret?"

Berendosi paused by their table, and glancing up Tiny saw that his eyes were fixed on the chair just vacated by Joe Denver.

"It depends, *Signor*," he answered. "By the way, I wonder if you could help me over something?"

"I shall be delighted," said the other. "In what way can I assist you?"

"Won't you sit down and join us in some coffee?"

"You are very kind."

He seated himself, and leaned forward attentively.

"Two or three years ago in London," said Tiny, "I had the honour of seeing a good deal of Her Majesty the queen before she was married. And if it is not presumption on my part I would so like to renew my acquaintance. I was wondering if perhaps you could tell me whether such a thing is possible; and if so, how I should set about it."

For a moment or two Berendosi sat as if carved in stone, his eyes fixed on Tiny's face.

"Certainly such a thing is possible," he said quietly. "And equally certainly I can help you. I feel sure Her Majesty would be delighted to see you again. As a matter of fact I am going to the palace this afternoon, and if you would care to come with me I am sure I can arrange an audience. It will of course only be an informal one."

"That is more than good of you," said Tiny.

"And would Mr. Standish care to come as well?"

"I fear I cannot," said Standish. "I have very urgent letters to write."

"And your other friend—the good-looking boy?"

With a wave of his hand he indicated the empty coffee cup.

"He unfortunately has fulfilled your warning to me, *Signor*, concerning bad health," said Standish gravely. "He's got a very sharp attack of fever: I'm going up to him now."

"I would," said Berendosi suavely. "It would be a pity if in spite of his fever he suddenly appeared."

Ronald Standish's eyes twinkled: though he disliked the man his quickness appealed to him.

"He is far too well brought up a patient for that," he answered. "Well, Tiny, I shall see you later. *Adieu, Signor.*"

Berendosi watched him in silence as he went up the stairs: then he turned to Tiny.

"So that is the celebrated Ronald Standish, is it?" he remarked. "I am glad to have met him."

"Celebrated!" Tiny raised his eyebrows. "I should hardly have thought he was that."

"His reputation is European. Not perhaps amongst the *hoi polloi*, but in those circles that count." An enigmatic smile twitched round his lips. "Well, I trust your young friend's fever will have abated: these sudden attacks are most disconcerting, aren't they?"

"A sort of malaria he got in Africa," said Tiny carelessly.

"Then, of course, it would be unwise for him to meet Her Majesty," agreed Berendosi. "One should always be careful in cases of malaria to avoid anything which might send the patient's temperature up."

"I hardly see why meeting the queen should do that, *Signor,*" said Tiny, staring him straight in the face.

"No? Well, well, perhaps you're right. Anyway the situation does not arise—this afternoon."

He rose from his chair.

"Well, Mr. Carteret, if you are ready, we might start. My car is waiting outside the hotel."

He relapsed into silence as soon as they moved off and Tiny was not sorry: he wanted to think. It was the personal side of the thing that hit him considerably more than it did Ronald Standish. To him the fact that these two had been in love with one another merely complicated the practical difficulties of the situation: they were just two strangers. But to Tiny they were two old friends.

He found himself wondering if Mary had known at the time. Of course she had: trust a woman for spotting anything of that sort. And now that he too looked back he began to remember little things which should have told him the condition of affairs: small pointers he had ignored at the time but which now seemed ridiculously obvious.

"I loved her, as I didn't believe it was possible for a man to love a woman."

Joe Denver's words rang in his brain, and suddenly he looked at the man sitting beside him. And a great desire took possession of him to hit that man's face and continue hitting it hard and often and then again some. For the full swinishness of the thing had struck him for the first time. Not only was he going to exploit a big love for his own ends, but he was going to do it in such a way that the woman would be held up to shame and obloquy. And his great desire grew even greater.

"Have you ever played rugger, *Signor?*" he asked as the car swung through the palace gates.

"Rugger, Mr. Carteret? I am afraid I don't quite understand."

"Football, *Signor,*" said Tiny dreamily. "And sometimes a man goes down on the ball when there are eight large forwards who want that ball."

"It sounds most unpleasant," said Berendosi politely.

"It is: most unpleasant." A gentle smile spread over Tiny's face. "You should play rugger, *Signor.* I am sure you would enjoy it."

"Presumably you play forward yourself, Mr. Carteret."

"I do," said Tiny.

"Then when I am next in England I must come and watch you. I should like to see what happens to the man who goes down on the ball before I start playing myself."

"They have an open grave ready dug for him," murmured Tiny.

"I think then that I will be one of the eight forwards," said Berendosi.

"You aren't a big enough man, *Signor,*" remarked Tiny quietly, and at that moment the car stopped.

If Berendosi appreciated the insult he showed no sign beyond a faint smile. He gave a curt order to his chauffeur and then led the way past a sentry who saluted. And the first thing that struck Tiny was that even among members of the household itself, his companion was evidently, as Joe Denver put it, the big noise. Footmen and underlings of all descriptions sprang up and bowed obsequiously as he passed, and Berendosi took not the slightest notice of any of them.

"Now if you wait in there, Mr. Carteret"—he indicated a small ante-room—"I will see what I can do."

Left to himself, Tiny studied his surroundings. The room looked out over the town and river towards the snow-capped mountains away to the north. Just in front lay the garden, and beyond it came the woods which covered the lower part of the hill. Much like an ordinary

English country house, he reflected, set in beautiful surroundings. And he was just wondering if he dared to smoke, when a girl appeared in the doorway.

"Her Majesty will be delighted to see you, Mr. Carteret," she said with a smile. "Come along this way."

He followed her down a corridor, until they reached a room at the end.

"Signor Berendosi is with her," said the girl as she opened the door.

They were standing by the window as he entered, and the queen greeted him with a charming smile.

"This is a real pleasure, Mr. Carteret," she said as he bent and kissed her hand. "I could hardly believe my ears when Signor Berendosi told me you were here."

"It is more than good of Your Majesty to remember me," said Tiny.

"One doesn't forget old friends like that," she answered. "Mary was out here with me a few weeks ago."

"A pity that your visit and hers did not coincide, Mr. Carteret," said Berendosi suavely. "It would have been quite a reunion for Her Majesty."

"Where are you staying, Mr. Carteret?" asked the queen.

"At the Royal Hotel, ma'am," said Tiny.

"With a very well-known compatriot of his, Your Majesty," remarked Berendosi. "Ronald Standish. And another friend who has gone down with fever. I didn't catch his name, Mr. Carteret."

Tiny had realised it would come sooner or later: had realised indeed that the main reason why Berendosi had taken the trouble he had was to see what effect Joe Denver's name would have on the queen. And there was no way out of it. Manifestly he couldn't pretend not to know.

"Someone else you knew in London, Your Majesty," he said quietly. "A great friend of Mary's—Joe Denver."

Just for a moment her eyes dilated—her body grew rigid: just for a moment she gave herself away to the lynx-eyed man who was watching her. Then she recovered herself.

"Of course. I remember him perfectly," she answered. "I do hope he's not bad."

"No, no," said Tiny. "Just a sudden return of malaria."

"Should he not be better tonight, Mr. Carteret," remarked Berendosi with a faintly mocking smile, "I can give you the name of my own doctor. And now if Your Majesty will graciously excuse me I have some important papers to attend to. My car, Mr. Carteret, will be waiting for you."

He backed from the room, and the door had barely closed behind him before her whole demeanour changed.

"Drop the queen business, Tiny," she cried. "Let's go back three years. Tell me about—about Joe Denver. Is he really ill?"

"He's not ill at all," said Tiny with a smile. "But I think it was better, don't you, that he shouldn't meet you before the extremely astute eyes of the gentleman who has just left us."

"You guessed, did you," she said softly. "Or did Mary tell you?"

And then somewhat to his relief she went on without waiting for an answer.

"I must see him again, Tiny: I simply must."

"But, Olga," he cried, "such a thing would be madness just now."

"Why?" she demanded. "Nobody else knows. It's no different to my seeing you."

For a moment he stared at her in amazement: what on earth was she talking about?

"But with Berendosi on the look out," he stammered, "it would be dangerous to a degree."

"That pig of a man is always on the look out," she cried. "And I can easily fool him. I must, Tiny: I must see him."

"Perhaps it could be arranged," he said at length, more to gain time than anything else. Was it possible that she was in ignorance of the whole plot? Certainly from the way she was talking it looked like it.

"It must be: it must be. I've never seen him, Tiny, since those days in London."

"But you've written to him," he said.

She shook her head.

"Never," she said, and he looked at her blankly.

"Not even in those days in London?" he persisted.

And once again she shook her head.

"I've never written to him in my life," she repeated.

"Are you sure you didn't and then tear the letter up?"

He saw her give a little frown of annoyance, and he realised that it must seem to her he was being *gauche*. But it was imperative to find out the truth: if the answer to the last question was again in the negative Ronald's theory fell to pieces. And it was—emphatically.

"I've never put pen to paper to him, Tiny," she said. "Why do you ask? You're mysterious, you know," she went on a little petulantly. "Like Mary when she was out here. And Nada—do you remember her? She has just been over to England."

"I travelled back to Paris with her," he said.

And then she switched back to Joe Denver. How was he? What did he look like? How long was he going to stay? And Tiny answered almost mechanically, so dumbfounded was he at the new turn of events.

At length she dismissed him, having first extracted a half promise that somehow or other he was to bring Joe Denver to see her. He had not the heart to refuse point blank; she was so desperately in earnest and so wistfully pretty.

"I will do what I can," he said gently, and just for a moment her mouth trembled.

"Half an hour is not much in a lifetime, Tiny," she whispered.

He left her standing by the window—a slim girlish figure in white—and went in search of the car. He found it waiting for him, with Berendosi inside perusing some papers.

"It was good of you to wait, *Signor*," he remarked as he got in.

"Not at all, Mr. Carteret. And I hope your audience with Her Majesty was a pleasant one."

"Very, thank you."

"With two such old acquaintances it was bound to be," murmured the other. "By the way, the mention of your young friend's name seemed to upset the queen a little."

"I didn't notice it," said Tiny curtly.

"Indeed!" A faint smile flickered round the other's lips. "Perhaps it was my imagination." He turned suddenly and faced Tiny. "Mr. Carteret: it might be as well if we all understood one another. I am not under the delusion that you have come to Dalzburg to gaze upon our charming scenery. And therefore I would be glad if you would convey a message from me to the excellent Standish. So long as you confine yourselves to our scenery we shall be delighted and honoured to have you with us. But should other activities begin to take place—well, then, Mr. Carteret, I am convinced we should discover some irregularity in both your passports. Do I make myself clear?"

"I don't know about Standish, but my passport is in perfect order," said Tiny.

"Mr. Carteret! Really! Your lack of intelligence pains me. Ah! here we are. Well—you won't forget my little message. *Adieu!*"

The car rolled off, and Tiny entered the hotel, where he found Standish waiting for him in the lounge.

"Come into the bar, Ronald," he said. "I need a drink."

"Did you see her?" asked the other as they crossed the lounge.

"I did. And alone. She swears that she never wrote a line to him—not even one that she subsequently tore up. So unless she's forgotten, your blotting-paper theory goes down the drain. Moreover, she seems to be in complete ignorance that there is anything in the air at all."

Standish stared at him nonplussed. "That makes things a bit harder, doesn't it? And did you enlighten her?"

"I thought it better not to," said Tiny. "There's another thing also," he went on, "our friend Berendosi was kind enough to tell me that should the spirit move him he will fake up some irregularity on our passports, presumably with the idea of making us leave the country."

"That possibility—like the poor—has always been with us," said Standish with a short laugh. "And, 'pon my soul, Tiny, I don't know that we're doing much good here. I've got half a mind to go back to England and try from the Felton Blake end. I don't remember ever having felt so completely up against a blank wall. And of course we must get young Denver out of the country. I've told him that already. Hullo! there is a lady who seems to know you just entered."

Tiny swung round: Countess Nada was coming towards them.

"Mr. Carteret," she said a little breathlessly, "where is Mr. Denver?"

"I left him up in his room about half an hour ago," said Standish.

"Go and see if he's still there," she cried. "And then don't let him out of your sight."

The barman was looking at them curiously, though he could not have heard the actual words.

"Countess," said Tiny, "may I introduce Mr. Standish—Countess Mazarin."

"Go, please—go," she said urgently. "It is vital."

"Give the countess a cocktail, Tiny," said Standish, and left the bar.

"It was because of Denver you sent me that wire?" said Tiny when he had ordered the drinks.

"Yes, of course," she cried. "I'll tell you everything in a moment. Oh! he couldn't tell, but nothing more cruel could have happened than that he should come here."

She put her hand suddenly on his arm.

"It's too late," she whispered. "They've got him."

Ronald Standish was crossing the lounge, and his face was grave.

"His room is empty," he said as he sat down, "and the floor waiter tells me he dashed out wildly about twenty minutes ago after receiving a note. Here is the envelope: I found it in the paper basket."

He held it out to the countess, who studied the writing for a moment.

"I thought as much," she said wearily. "Sonia Gregoroff. One of the ladies-in-waiting and in Berendosi's pay. Oh! how cruel. You see, I got back from Paris a few moments after you left the queen, Mr. Carteret. And she told me he was here. And she told me that she could not understand. . . ." She passed her hand over her forehead. "I'm going distracted. I flew down here. . . ."

"Don't let us lose our heads, Countess," said Standish quietly. "You are certain about the writing on the envelope?"

"Absolutely," she cried. "I'd know it anywhere."

"That settles it then. There are many questions I'd like to ask you, but they must wait. The first vital necessity is for you to get back to the queen. Stay with her: remain glued to her side. Above all things see that those two don't meet alone. And if you find out anything telephone me here, or send a message. But—*keep them apart*."

With a little nod she rose at once.

"I understand perfectly," she said. "I'll go now."

"A stout-hearted girl, that," remarked Standish as she left the hotel. "By Jove! Tiny, we're up against some pretty useful odds. Still it's not the first time."

He started to fill his pipe, staring idly at the cosmopolitan crowd that thronged the lounge outside.

"What's our next move, Ronald?" said Tiny after awhile.

"It's a bit difficult to decide, old boy. Beyond the fact that he has been decoyed out of the hotel by a note written by Gregoroff's daughter, we don't know anything. He may be up at the palace now: he may be anywhere. Until we can get some further information there is nothing to be done as far as I can see."

"Do you think they've kidnapped him?"

"I wouldn't put it a bit beyond them. And if so, the proverbial needle in the bundle of hay would be easier to find. Unless somebody blows the gaff. You see, Tiny, we're at a hopeless disadvantage. In England one could go to the police: here it would be absolutely useless. We can't even go to the embassy. On the first hint of our doing anything like that Berendosi's threat would be put into execution, and our passports would be found irregular. So we've got to play a lone hand, in which the first vital trick is to get Denver out of the country."

He gave a short laugh.

"Nice easy hurdle for the kick off, isn't it? Still I've got faith in the countess. She's loyal to the core, and she's got her head screwed on the right way. If anyone can find things out, she will."

A prophecy which was duly fulfilled twenty minutes later when a page boy brought Tiny a note. It was short and to the point.

Mr. Denver was seen with Sonia Gregoroff driving in closed car towards Gregoroff's castle. Queen knows nothing as yet. Fear some devilry. Get him out of the country.

"On the face of it a somewhat tall order," said Standish with a grin. "However, we may as well have a dip at it."

"Sure thing," agreed Tiny. "How do you propose we should set about dipping?"

"Well, as I see it, it's like this," said Standish. "Whatever the communication was that the lady wrote him, he evidently smelt no rat. He left the hotel without any suspicions. Moreover, he took no kit with him. One of two things therefore is going to happen. Either they will keep him unsuspicious by means of some plausible story, in which case he will probably be allowed the run of the grounds: or having got him there they will drop the pretence and he will find himself a virtual prisoner. In the first event there should be no difficulty in communicating with him."

"And in the second?" murmured Tiny.

Ronald Standish knocked out his pipe.

"It will be considerably harder," he remarked shortly.

Chapter 6

"My dear Gregoroff, you seem absurdly jumpy. What on earth is the matter with you?"

Berendosi, his cigar drawing evenly between his teeth, surveyed his companion with amused contempt.

"It's this fellow Standish coming here," said the other uneasily. "It looks as if he must know something."

"He can know the lot for all I care," remarked Berendosi with a short laugh. "What does it matter? You know," he went on after a pause, "I'm really rather sorry for Standish. It's pathetic to see a man of his ability endeavouring to make bricks with such a ridiculously small quantity of straw."

"He might give us a lot of trouble," said Gregoroff.

"How can he?" demanded Berendosi. "Even granted that he knows everything, which I think is doubtful, what can he do? As I told his large friend only an hour ago, I should have no hesitation, if I deemed it necessary, of cutting short their visit here. In fact, I think I shall anyway do so tomorrow. If your charming daughter is successful, as I am sure she will be, they will be better out of the country. That Mazarin woman is no fool: it will only be a question of time before she suspects we've got young Denver here. And then I don't want Standish to take any diplomatic action. It might complicate things."

He strolled to the window and stared over the country that lay, spread out like a map, before him.

"A fine view you've got from here, Gregoroff," he said thoughtfully.

His face was as impassive as usual, but into his eyes there had come a sudden gleam. For Paul Berendosi was allowing himself a rare luxury: he was day dreaming. After long years he saw his life's ambition within his grasp: so far as he could see nothing could upset his calculations. If it had been a good thing before, the providential arrival of the young man himself now made it a certainty. The thing was foolproof, and he had said no more than the truth when he had remarked to Gregoroff that he didn't care if Standish knew everything.

Therein lay the beauty of the scheme: the hand could be played with all the cards on the table. The ground was prepared: his spies and underlings had done their work well. Now all that remained was the one culminating thing which would split the country from top to bottom. Bloodshed perhaps: what of it? No man can step suddenly into supreme power without some payment.

With an effort he came out of his reverie: Gregoroff was speaking.

"What of Zavier? Is he coming?"

"As soon as I heard your news I wired him at once. He should be here at any moment."

"What do you make of that man, Berendosi?"

"It is hard to say, my friend. Undoubtedly a gentleman whom I would sooner have for me than against me." He glanced through the window. "And here, unless I am much mistaken, is your daughter."

A big red car had turned off the main road, and was coming up the winding drive to the castle.

"I wonder if she has been successful."

He leaned still further out, as the car stopped by the front door.

"Yes—she has. Our young friend is with her. Now under no circumstances, Gregoroff, must he see me; at any rate until our little play is staged. I am under no delusions as to what Standish will have told him about my poor self. And I am not at all certain that it would not be better for you to keep out of the way also. However, we will wait until we see your daughter, and find out what she has to say."

He swung round as the door opened, and a dark, striking-looking girl came in.

"Bravo! my dear Sonia," he cried. "You have done admirably. How did you manage it?"

She gave a short laugh.

"I sent him a note saying that someone very dear to him was in grave danger, and would he come at once. And he came."

"Yes, but what of the Englishman—Standish. Does he know where he's gone?"

"No, I asked him that in the car. You see the note was given to him when he was alone: I saw to that. Standish was in the bar, waiting for the big man."

"And the note itself?"

"Was in Denver's pocket. It is now torn up."

"Admirable, my dear, admirable," said Berendosi. "But how did you explain to him about the grave danger?"

"I admitted that it was a fib," she laughed, "put in to make sure that he came. And then I pitched him the yarn we arranged. That it was unsafe for him to see her at the palace, but that I was arranging a meeting for them here. He swallowed it whole."

"And you don't think anyone knows he is here?"

"I'm sure no one does. I took every precaution, and made him sit right back in the car."

"Excellent. Not that it matters very much, but it saves trouble. Did you find out anything of interest from the young man?"

"A lot," she said, lighting a cigarette. "He was simply frantic to know what all the mystery was. Evidently this man Standish has told him that something is in the wind, and that you are at the bottom of it. He talked about a letter written by her to him."

"So he doesn't know the truth," said Berendosi softly. "And apparently Standish doesn't know it either. That is most interesting.

116

Undoubtedly, my dear Gregoroff, Standish and his friend leave this country tomorrow."

"And this man Denver?" asked the girl.

"Remains here—until the end. Though I don't think it is necessary, I have already taken the precaution of closing every frontier to him. But that is only in case he should escape from here, which is an unlikely eventuality. By the way, what is he doing now?"

"Dreaming of the meeting to come," she said with a sneer.

"Well, I think, my dear, that it wouldn't be a bad thing if you went and dreamt with him. I should hate him to dream anywhere near a telephone if he was alone."

"I'll go," she said at once. "And I suppose neither of you will appear till after it's over."

"That's right," answered Berendosi. "Till then we leave him entirely to you."

"A girl in a thousand, my dear fellow," he said, as the door closed behind her. "You are to be congratulated on such a daughter."

"How long are we going to keep him here, Berendosi?" said the other.

"As I said before—until the end," said Berendosi curtly. "Though if it is of any comfort to you, I think that moment is considerably nearer than we at one time anticipated. A lot will depend on what Zavier says."

"Indeed!"

They both swung round: the man was standing in the door, the monkey perched on his shoulder.

"And what is this new development you wired me about?" he asked.

"Come in, Monsieur Zavier," cried Berendosi. "I am delighted to see you. The new development is nothing more nor less than the arrival in the country of the young man himself."

"So." Zavier took a chair, and lit one of his little cigarettes. "That is interesting. And when did he come?"

"A few days ago, whilst I was in England. Gregoroff recognised him."

"And where is he now?"

"In this house. A small trap was laid for him into which he obligingly walked. Yes—he is in this house, and in this house he will remain."

"You propose to keep him as a prisoner, do you? I should have thought that better results might have been obtained by leaving him at large."

"But for one fact you are quite right," agreed Berendosi. "But we have some other English visitors who complicate things somewhat. You may perhaps have heard of Ronald Standish?"

Zavier's eyes half closed.

"So he has arrived too, has he? But surely they didn't come together."

"No. But I cannot help thinking that there is a very close connection between the two things. By some means or other Standish found out that Denver was here. So he at once came himself. And though I have since found out that he doesn't know the truth, he is very near it. That being the case it is obvious that his first idea would be to get Denver out of the country. And though of course that can be prevented it might give rise to unpleasantness with the British Embassy. So taking everything into consideration I thought it best to bring him here."

He held up his hand for silence as footsteps passed the door, and Denver's cheerful laugh rang out.

"He seems in excellent spirits," remarked Zavier in some surprise; and Berendosi smiled.

"He has at present no idea of what the future holds in store for him," he remarked. "In fact he thinks he is going to meet a certain lady here after dinner tonight."

Zavier stared at him for a moment or two in silence.

"And why not?" he said thoughtfully. "Such a meeting might be made use of."

"It was the first idea I had," remarked Berendosi, "but I dismissed it for two reasons. First it gives away his presence here, and secondly I doubt greatly if the lady would come. Gregoroff is not *persona grata* with her. But I have staged what I think you will agree is a most entertaining little performance, and one which will benefit us even more than her Majesty's presence. I don't know if you have met our host's charming daughter?"

"I have not yet had that pleasure," answered the other.

"The same build, the same colouring as our gracious queen. In fact when dressed in the same way it would be difficult if one could not see their faces to tell which was which."

Zavier nodded appreciatively.

"An understudy. Excellent. And the window wide open."

"Better than that, my friend: far better than that. But—wait and see. It may, of course, not come off. If so, there is no harm done. He will anyway cease to be in good spirits when he discovers he has been trapped. To return to more important matters. This young man's unexpected arrival has rather altered things. And although nothing could have suited our plans better, it has introduced certain difficulties. He can, of course, be kept here, and will be kept here till he is no longer required, but with a man in Standish's position instituting inquiries and pushing them hard, there is bound to be a considerable hue and cry. It will naturally be done through the embassy. And so I would like to curtail the time before we strike as much as possible. Everything is in train: I was only waiting because for many reasons September is the most suitable time of year. But Denver's presence overrides everything. Therefore I propose to do the thing immediately—that is, say, in a fortnight. Does that suit you?"

"Anything, my dear *Signor*, suits me," said Zavier languidly, "so long as the money is forthcoming. But I doubt," he continued with a little chuckle, "if it will suit Felton Blake."

Berendosi frowned.

"Is he likely to give trouble?"

"People with whom I deal never give trouble," remarked Zavier. "But, as I think I told you before, one of his conditions was that he should be allowed to further his ridiculous love affair. To return, however, to Standish for the moment. You say he does not know the truth."

"At present—no. How long that state of affairs will continue I can't say—nor does it really matter very much. As a matter of fact I was surprised when I found out he didn't. Countess Mazarin—a lady who has no affection for me—was travelling with his friend Carteret to Paris the day before yesterday, and I fully expected she had told him. But—apparently not. And so, my dear Monsieur Zavier, if you would be good enough to deliver the goods within the next few days I think we shall soon be able to congratulate ourselves on a successfully planned and still more successfully executed *coup*."

"I shall await the result with interest, *Signor*," murmured Zavier, glancing at his watch. "And since there would appear to be nothing further to discuss, I think I will return to my hotel. Unless, that is, you could give me a little dinner here?"

"Delighted," said Gregoroff. "We three will feed alone, leaving the stage set for the other two."

He gave an odious chuckle, and Zavier glanced at him thoughtfully. An unpleasant specimen, he reflected: a hanger-on, a cringer. For Berendosi he had the respect that one strong, unscrupulous man feels for another of the same kidney: for Gregoroff he felt nothing but contempt. But his face was expressionless as he spoke.

"I shall be interested to see the play," he said suavely.

"You have fixed everything?" asked Berendosi.

"Everything," answered Gregoroff. "The curtain rises at ten. And in case the leading man becomes annoyed with his part, I have six strong supers in readiness to soothe him down."

"There is the castle you want."

Andrew Mackintosh, correspondent for the *Planet*, halted his ancient Fiat and indicated the place with a large hand.

"I will drive no nearer, for this damned machine makes a noise like a tank. And may God help you on your nefarious undertaking. I will await you here."

"Good for you, Andy," said Standish, getting out of the car. "But we may be the devil of a time."

"Mon—the night is warm, and I have a flask. But dinna forget that I have a wife and bairns, and if trouble arises, as I'm thinking it will, we are perfect strangers. I will turn the car round, and I will wait till dawn. But if you're no here before then, I shall be away back to Dalzburg."

"Stout fellow," said Standish. "Come on, Tiny: it's dark enough to start."

From the back of the car he took out a coil of rope which he slung over his shoulder.

"Got your torch, Tiny? And little Willie? Right—come on."

He had from the first decided against taking fire-arms, and little Willie was the substitute. And no mean substitute either. It consisted of a piece of stout rubber with a lump of lead at the end, which when connected with the base of a man's skull, produced oblivion for as long or short a period as desired. It also produced oblivion in silence, an essential factor if they were to succeed that night.

It was Mackintosh who had suggested the rope, and lent them a coil of his own.

"It may be no use," he had remarked, "but it's no trouble to carry, and maybe it will come in handy. Supposing they mean to keep him there, they will put him in a top room. And perhaps you can find a way of getting it up to him. But it's going to be a difficult and a dangerous business."

A fact of which they were both aware. Not that the danger deterred them: as Standish had pointed out, it was not danger in the accepted sense of the word. But it was essential that they should not be caught because of the consequences. They were putting themselves outside the pale of even Bessonian law: they were doing a thing which rendered them liable to sample the inside of a prison for months. And once there, there they would remain until everything was over.

So strongly did Standish feel it that he again impressed it on Tiny as they moved cautiously forward.

"It's got to be stealth, Tiny," he muttered. "Stealth and cunning all the time. We must only use force as absolutely our last resource."

The ground rose fairly abruptly from the road, which helped them considerably as far as cover was concerned, and a steep bank about six feet high on the edge of the drive allowed them to get to within thirty yards of the castle. Fortunately for them there was no moon, and they could lie against the bank with their heads above it without fear of being seen. A light was filtering out from two rooms, one almost directly in front of them on the ground floor, the other some way to the left on the first. Heavy curtains covered both windows, so that it was impossible to see who was inside, though once a man put his head out of the upper one and stared round.

Suddenly a woman's laugh rang out from the room opposite, and they heard Denver's voice in answer.

"Evidently they haven't aroused his suspicions yet," whispered Standish in Tiny's ear. "Hullo! the other light has gone out."

Once more silence fell, broken only by the low murmur of conversation from across the drive. Five minutes passed—ten, when Tiny gripped Standish's arm.

"Look," he whispered. "Away to the left. Someone smoking."

Sure enough from some distance away there came the even glow of a cigarette. The smoker was standing motionless: they could see the little lines of light as he lifted it to and from his mouth.

"In front of us, Tiny," breathed Standish in his ear. "Between the man smoking and the room where Denver is. There are half a dozen of them."

They peered into the darkness, and at last he picked them up. They were standing bunched together not far from the window, and it seemed to him they were waiting? But, what for?

Boom! From a clock tower above rang out the first note of the hour, and instantly things began to happen. The smoker flung away his cigarette: two shadowy figures detached themselves from the group opposite and moved swiftly towards the window. There they paused, and began adjusting something that looked like a tripod. And when at length the last note of the clock had quivered into silence, all was as before save that the smoker no longer smoked, and the thing that looked like a tripod was in position.

"Standing by for the clock," muttered Standish, "to cover the noise. What's going to happen now?"

They had not long to wait for the answer. Suddenly the curtains parted, and a woman's arm showed for a moment through them. They saw two men spring forward to the tripod: then the curtains swung back revealing the whole room. And for a moment they could hardly believe their eyes. Seated beside the table, a look of stupefied amazement on his face, was Joe Denver. On her knees at his feet, her arms thrown round him, her face buried against his chest was a woman. It might have been a *tableau vivant* representing "The anguish of a woman in love." And even as they watched in astonishment there came the blinding flash of magnesium, and the mystery was solved. A flashlight photograph had been taken.

"Ronald," whispered Tiny, "it's the queen."

"Rot," said Standish. "It's someone whose back view looks like the queen. We've got to get that camera. Hullo! things move."

The door of the room opened and Gregoroff stood there, his eyes blazing. And slowly the woman rose from her knees and faced him, trembling.

"So, *Madame*," he thundered, "I have caught you, have I?"

"Holy Smoke," muttered Ronald, "that wheeze came out of the ark with Noah. But we've got to miss it for a bit, Tiny. The camera man is away to the left. After him."

Like shadows they faded into the darkness. From behind them came the sound of Gregoroff's angry voice, and Joe Denver's stammered answers, but they paid no attention. The camera was their objective, and they caught its owner, a little rat of a man, just as he was turning in at the front door. He gave one squeal like a frightened rabbit; then Tiny's vast hand closed over his mouth.

"Take the camera, Ronald," he said in a low voice. "I've collared the excrescence."

"Right, old boy. I've got it. And here's the plate."

There came the crack of breaking glass—the sound of the pieces being thrown into the bushes. Then—

"What now, Ronald? What are we to do with this thing?"

"We've got to dot him one, Tiny. Otherwise he'll give us away. Hold his head forward."

And with the skill born of practice Ronald Standish laid him out.

"Into the bushes with him. And his camera too. Now we've got to get young Denver out of it."

They reached the cover of the bank again, and crept back to their original point of vantage. Two of the men who had been outside the window were now inside the room, but they could see the other four in readiness close at hand. The girl was no longer there: only Gregoroff, still simulating righteous anger, faced the utterly bewildered youth.

"I assure you, sir, there is some extraordinary mistake," Denver was saying. "I have never met your wife before in my life."

"You expect me to believe that," sneered Gregoroff. "You expect me to believe that my wife asked a perfect stranger to dine with her! Explain why you came, if what you say is true."

"I came to..." Denver paused: then he threw back his head. "Damn you," he shouted, "go to Hell. It doesn't matter why I came. What are you going to do with me?"

"We will decide that later," said Gregoroff icily. "In the meantime you shall be shown your quarters for the night. Take him away."

"Let's rush 'em, Ronald," muttered Tiny, but Standish shook his head.

"Odds too great, old boy. Eight of them, and the betting is they've got guns. We must wait and hope for the best. But, by God! they're a bunch of swine."

The two men rushed Denver out of the room, and Gregoroff leant back in his chair shaking with laughter.

"My dear," he chuckled as the door opened and his daughter came in, "I congratulate you. He doesn't know whether he is on his head or his heels, in fact he has visions of fighting a duel with me. Where are the others?"

"Just coming," she said, lighting a cigarette. "I think it went off very well."

"Capitally: capitally. Ah! my dear Berendosi, the stage has lost a shining light."

He pointed to his daughter, and Berendosi bowed.

"In order that we may enjoy it more fully," he murmured. "So it was successful. You hear that, Zavier?"

And Tiny suddenly found Standish's hand on his arm.

"That man who has just come in, Tiny." His voice was shaking with excitement. "With the monkey on his shoulder. Can it be possible? Damn it! it must be." He relapsed into silence. "Let's listen."

"Admirable," said Zavier. "And where is the young man now?"

"Where he is likely to remain for a time," laughed Berendosi. "Locked in upstairs. Those men needn't wait, Gregoroff. Well," he continued as the group outside the window dispersed, "I think we have every reason to congratulate ourselves. Everything has gone off without a hitch. I would keep up the fiction as long as you can, Gregoroff, though I fear he is bound to suspect sooner or later."

"You intend to produce him at the crucial moment, I presume," said Zavier.

"Exactly. I fear he may have an unpleasant time at the hands of my outraged fellow-countrymen, but it will be in an excellent cause. Well, Zavier—I think we might return to Dalzburg. Goodnight, dear lady, and a thousand thanks for your assistance."

He bowed over her hand, and the three men left the room. And shortly after the girl followed them.

"It's now or never, Tiny," said Standish. "They've put him up in that tower; you can see the light. Are you on?"

"You bet I'm on," grunted the other. "Let's move."

Keeping in the shadow beyond the light thrown from the window, they darted across the drive and into the now empty room. The door was open and Standish peered out. From one end of the passage came voices, and without hesitation he led the way in the opposite direction till he came to a flight of stairs. And a moment or two later they were both on the first landing.

"Passages too damned well lit," he muttered. "We've got to make the fourth floor at least."

They darted up the next flight: then the third, and there Standish paused. From above them came the sound of voices and the chink of money.

"They will be guarding his door," he whispered to Tiny. "Wade in—but do it silently. My God! look out."

Flattened into a little recess, hardly daring to breathe, they watched Gregoroff himself go past them so close that they could almost have touched him. He went up the next flight, and they heard his voice.

"All right, is he?"

"Fought like a madman," came the answer, "but he's quieter now.

He started trying to break the door down, but I guess he hurt himself more than the door."

"You'll be relieved in a couple of hours. Leave him alone unless he starts shouting. Then gag him."

Once again Gregoroff passed close to the recess where Standish and Tiny were crouching, and they waited until his footsteps died away downstairs.

"Now, Tiny," whispered Standish, "we've got to hurry. That camera merchant may come to at any moment. But for Heaven's sake—no noise."

Cautiously—step by step—they crept up the last flight. And this time luck was with them: the passage, save for one light under which two men were playing cards, was in darkness. They were engrossed in their game, and the thing was over in a flash. Two dull thudding blows, and the card players rolled gently off their chairs on to the floor.

"I've got the key," said Standish, "and that must be the door where the light is. By Gad! old boy, I believe we're going to pull it off."

He turned the lock, and they went in to find Joe Denver sitting disconsolately on his bed. He sprang to his feet with a cry of amazement when he saw who they were, but Standish silenced him at once.

"Move, young fellow, and move quickly. Good Lord! what's that?"

Through the open window came an uproar from below, and he looked out.

"Tiny, they've found the camera bloke. It will have to be the rope."

He darted to the door and locked it: already the sound of footsteps could be heard rushing up the stairs.

"Put that wardrobe against the door," he said curtly. "I'll fix this."

He lashed one end of the rope to a leg of the bed, and threw the rest of the coil out of the window.

"Now, Denver, down you go. Don't argue, damn you: move. Go into the main road and get into a car you'll find there. We're after you at once."

Crash after crash was coming from the other side of the door, and it was obvious it could not hold much longer.

"After him, Tiny. Quick, man, quick."

He gave him two seconds: then he too clambered out and started to swarm down. And even as he dropped out of sight, the door above him gave way.

"Drop freely," he shouted; all pretence of concealment was useless now. "They'll cut the rope."

But luck held. The heavy wardrobe delayed their pursuers sufficiently to let Denver and Tiny reach the ground, and when at last they did get to the rope and cut it Standish had only some ten feet to fall.

"Run like hell," he said curtly.

Panting and breathless they reached the car to find Mackintosh had started the engine.

"I thought I observed a slight commotion," he remarked as they fell in. "We'll have to hop it, boys: yon man Gregoroff has a powerful car."

"And, by Jove! Andy," said Standish, when they had covered a couple of miles, "he's let it loose. Give her every ounce you can."

"Hopeless, mon, hopeless. But bide a while: there's a turn a little way ahead."

Suddenly he swung the car right-handed up a narrow lane, and then switched off his lights.

"He has a Hispano," he explained; "I could never have got away from him. What happens if he spots us?"

"We fight," said Standish tersely. "Here they come."

Exhaust open, head-lights flaring, the car roared past them crammed with men, and not until the noise of the engine had died away in the distance did they breathe freely again.

"And now," remarked Mackintosh, "we go back on our tracks. We can make a detour which will bring us into Dalzburg by another road. Otherwise I'm thinking we may meet them coming back."

The castle was blazing with lights as they approached, and suddenly Mackintosh cursed under his breath. Three men were standing across the road holding out their arms.

"Drive at 'em, Andy," cried Standish. "Denver, get down: hide."

And Andy Mackintosh drove at them, all out. Came a thud on the mudguard, a brief vision of jumping, swearing men and the castle was left behind them.

"And me—a respectable married journalist," groaned Andy. "I'm hoping they did not get my number."

"You see the trouble you've caused, young fellah," said Standish to Denver with a laugh. "However, it looks as if the first hurdle was safely over."

"For Heaven's sake tell me what it's all about," cried the youngster. "My brain is in an absolute whirl."

"All in good time," said Standish. "Let's get back first."

"But they'll be watching the hotel," said Denver.

"That's why we're not going there. Or at any rate you're not. You are going to bed down, any way for a time, with the excellent Andy."

"And after that comes the second hurdle," said that worthy gloomily. "Dinna forget that."

"You damned old croaker," laughed Standish, "we'll think of something."

But though he spoke cheerfully, he was far from feeling it. No one realised better than he did that the second hurdle was going to be considerably harder than the first. For it consisted of getting Joe Denver out of the country. Luck, astounding luck, had been with them so far: how long would it last? Obviously every frontier post would be watched, and Denver would simply be arrested on some trumped-up charge and returned to Berendosi. It was true that he might lie hidden for a time with Andy Mackintosh, but that was only postponing the evil. And two things made him unwilling to leave him there longer than absolutely necessary. First, it seemed probable that Berendosi would get him and Tiny out of the country as soon as possible, which would mean leaving Denver on his own. And second, though Andy had not hesitated for a moment to come in with them, he was, as he had said, a respectable married journalist, not too well off at that. And the last thing Standish wanted to do was to get him into trouble.

The devil of it was that the problem seemed almost insoluble. And yet there must be some way of smuggling the youngster out. One trouble was that he did not speak a word of the language. Still, surely there must be some method. But he was still racking his brains for an answer when the car drew up at Mackintosh's house.

It was past one, and the street was deserted. There was no sign of anyone watching the house, so that even if the men they had driven at had got the number of the car, as yet it had not been traced.

"I'll put the car away," said Andy. "You go in."

His wife opened the door to them: a homely, sweet-faced Scotch woman.

"But you've got him," she cried. "Good. Come in, and have a drink."

"You've guessed right there, Mrs. Andy," laughed Standish. "And here's the young blighter who is responsible for all the trouble."

She smiled at Joe Denver, and then led the way upstairs.

"I thought it would be safer above," she explained, "in case they started to watch the house."

"You're a marvel," cried Standish. "We would never have pulled it off without you and Andy. Now, young fellow," he went on, "let's hear how they got you to walk into their parlour so easily."

"They sent me a note to say that . . . that . . ." He hesitated for a moment and glanced at Mrs. Mackintosh.

"You can speak out freely," said Standish. "Mrs. Andy knows."

"To say that the queen was in danger, and would I go at once. There would be a car waiting in the square, and I was to tell no one."

"And into that singularly obvious trap," laughed Standish, "you walked with both your great flat feet. Ah! well, perhaps I'd have done the same."

"But what was the meaning of all that damned foolery?" cried Denver. "That flashlight photograph, and the rest of it."

"Young fellah," said Standish gravely, "we're in pretty deep waters—you especially. The whole of this evening's performance was staged with the express purpose of getting a photograph of you with a woman in your arms, who in colouring and size might easily have been the queen."

"The infernal swine," said Denver savagely. "What are we to do about it?"

"Don't worry about the photograph. Tiny and I attended to that. The point to be decided is what are we to do about you."

"Aye," said Andy, helping himself to whisky. "That's the point."

"We've got to get you out of the country somehow, Denver, and do it damned quick. For if they get you a second time, they'll keep you."

"But if you've smashed the photo what does it matter?" cried Denver. "They won't get another."

"Perhaps not," agreed Standish. "But there's something else behind it all, though at present we don't know what. It's not a letter; Tiny found that out. What is it? Countess Mazarin could tell us. . ."

"Which reminds me," interrupted Mrs. Andy. "I rang her up as you told me, and promised to ring her up again if all went well."

"Bit late, isn't it, my dear," said her husband doubtfully.

"She told me to ring her whatever time you came back," she said.

"Well, be careful what you say, Mrs. Andy," warned Standish. "Telephones at this hour of the night are dangerous."

"I feel as if I was in a sort of daze," cried Denver as she left the room. "The whole thing seems like some mad nightmare."

"It's going to be madder soon," said Andy gravely. "It's getting mighty near, if I'm any judge."

"What is?" asked Denver.

"Hell let loose. Civil war. Well, my dear, did you get through?"

"I did. And she's coming here."

"The devil she is," said Andy uneasily. He went to the window and peered out. "I don't see anyone at present, but pray the Lord she's not followed."

"Hardly likely, Andy, at this hour," said Standish. "They've got no cause to suspect her."

"Mon, this place is a hot-bed of spies and intrigue," answered the other. "And the palace is the worst spot of the lot. However, we can but hope for the best."

"And at any rate, Andy, we'll know at last. That's worth running a bit of risk for. Though it's not going to help us over this blighter's immediate future."

"But what's the difficulty?" cried Denver. "I'll go tomorrow, if you want me to."

Standish laughed shortly.

"My dear boy," he said, "every frontier has been closed to you days ago. There are no strings you can pull at all, Andy, I suppose?"

"I've been racking my brains, Ronald, and I'm just phased. It's a fair snorter. He can stop here, of course, but after a time the servants are bound to talk."

"No, no, Andy," said Standish, "if we can't get him away we must find somewhere else. If necessary he must go like the Biblical gentleman, into the mountains with the ravens."

Andy shook his head.

"They'll go through the country with a tooth-comb," he said.

"I seem a damned popular bird," remarked Denver ruefully. "What exactly are they going to do with me when they do get me?"

"Produce you as an exhibit at the psychological moment," said Standish. "Though now that that photograph is destroyed it seems to me you lose a good deal of your value. Unless. . . . "

And at that moment the front-door bell rang.

"It's the countess," said Andy, peering through the window. "I'll go and let her in."

"Thank Heaven you've got him," she cried a little breathlessly as she entered the room. "I've made all the arrangements for a fast car to get him away."

"Hopeless, Countess," cried Standish. "The frontier will be closed.

We should simply play into their hands."

"But we must get him away," she said. "We *must*. What happened tonight?"

He told her briefly, and when he'd finished she opened her bag.

"The only comfort," concluded Standish, "is that the photo was destroyed."

"Comfort," she cried. "Precious little comfort, Mr. Standish. The one they took tonight may have been destroyed, but this one hasn't."

She threw a faded print on the table, and they crowded round.

"Good God!" said Standish. "So that's the trouble. How did you get hold of this?"

"But I don't understand," muttered Denver, scarlet to the roots of his hair. "It's the day I said goodbye to her. What damned ineffable swine took this?"

"Steady, Denver," cried Standish. "Don't tear it up. It's more serious even than I thought, but at any rate we know what we're up against, at last."

"But who took the damned thing?" said Denver between his teeth.

"Immaterial, young fellow," remarked Standish shortly. "Good Lord! you might both have posed specially for it."

Which was no more than the truth. For the photograph showed a little glade in a wood. Two people were standing in it, their arms round one another. Their profiles were towards the camera, and the woman was looking up into the man's face with an expression which caused the warm-hearted Mrs. Andy to wipe her eyes surreptitiously, and whisper, "You poor bairns." For the woman in the photograph was the queen: the man was the youngster who now stood with his back to them, staring out of the window.

"At any rate," repeated Standish, "we know what we're up against. Now, Countess, we'd very much like to hear your side of the story, because there is a good deal that is still mighty obscure. And incidentally, Denver, come away from that window. Your face is a darned sight too well known in this country."

Chapter 7

"There's not much to tell," she began. "I got it about two months ago by sheer luck. I had been out motoring one day, driving my own car, and I ran out of petrol. I was miles from a garage, but as luck would have it I was only about ten minutes' walk from the Castle of

Birenden, which is Berendosi's country house. It was a case of needs must, or else nothing would have induced me to ask the brute for anything. But if I was to get home at all I'd have to borrow some petrol from him. It was a pitch dark night, and stiflingly hot, and the house was in darkness save for one room on the ground floor, from which a light shone out through partially drawn curtains. I knew the place fairly well, because Berendosi entertains lavishly, and the room which was lit up was either the dining-room or his study. And acting on the spur of the moment, instead of ringing the bell, I crossed the lawn towards it. I intended to ask him for the petrol, and for a man to carry it to the car.

"When I got close to I heard voices, and I don't quite know why, I hesitated for a moment or two. Somehow I had expected to find him alone and now it looked as if he had a dinner-party. And then I heard one remark of Berendosi's that made me go cold all over.

"'What about that for proof, Gregoroff? Our gracious majesty herself.'

"Now I give you my word that up to that moment I'd had no intention of spying or listening. I had crossed the lawn quite openly with no pretence at concealment, and in another second I should have appeared in the open window. I'd really forgotten all about everything except that I'd run out of petrol. And to hear a remark like that suddenly when one wasn't in the least expecting it, brought me up with a start.

"My first inclination was to go back and ring the front-door bell, but I soon decided not to. Eavesdropping it might be but I was going to find out all I could. Evidently I had not been seen crossing the lawn, and if anyone came to the window and I was discovered, I should have to put as good a face on the matter as I could. So I crept a little closer until I could just see into the room. There were three of them inside: Berendosi, Gregoroff and a third whom I had never seen before. He was the most strange-looking individual—completely bald with a high, domed forehead. But the most peculiar thing about him was that on his shoulder there sat a little monkey, which he fondled continuously. Did you say anything, Mr. Standish?"

"Go on, Countess. It will keep."

"This man was smoking a cigarette and watching the other two, who were poring over something that was lying on the desk in the centre of the room.

"'Marvellous,' said Gregoroff at length. 'My dear Paul, I congratulate you. And you also, *Monsieur.*'

"Then he picked the thing up, and I saw what it was—an unmounted photograph. I didn't know what to do. At first I didn't understand what it was all about. I couldn't see what the photograph was, though I guessed from Berendosi's remark that it was a snapshot of the queen. But as they went on talking I realised that it must be more than that.

"'Do you know who the young man is, Monsieur Zavier?' asked Berendosi of the bald-headed man.

"'I have forgotten,' he answered. 'I was told, but for the moment it has slipped my memory. I can, however, easily find that out, and let you know.'

"They talked on for a while, and then Gregoroff lit a cigarette.

"'A quarter of a million is a lot of money, *Monsieur,*' he said to this man Zavier.

"'A lot is a relative term,' answered the other. 'My dear sir,' he added contemptuously, 'you don't suppose I deal in children's saving accounts, do you? That is my figure, and you can take it or leave it. I told Signor Berendosi weeks ago that I would deliver the goods as I had promised. There is a proof of it: though to be on the safe side,' he added with a smile, 'it is only an unfixed proof, which will fade. But at the appointed time you shall have the genuine article. And it is for you to arrange that time: it is not my affair.'

"You can imagine, Mr. Standish, that by this time I was nearly crazy. I still had no idea what was in the picture, beyond the fact that there was a man and Olga. But it was pretty clear that if a quarter of a million was the price, there must be something more in it than that. And I stood there racking my brains as to how I could get hold of it and see. They had left it lying on the desk: in two seconds I could have darted in and picked it up. And I very nearly did. After all they couldn't hurt me, and at any rate I should know the worst.

"And then, just as I was nerving myself to do so, the whole sky was lit up by lightning and almost simultaneously came the crash of thunder overhead. It was one of our usual mountain storms, but it was a particularly fierce one. There was no rain, but the wind got up like a tornado. The curtains flapped wildly: the monkey jibbered, but all that I had eyes for was that photograph. For it had blown off the desk, and was lying just inside the window not a yard away from me. And then I had a stroke of luck. There came another terrific gust of wind and the lamp blew over. So I made one grab at the photo and fled. The lightning was almost continuous, so I kept in as close to the house as I could. Two of them had dashed into the garden and were peering round in every direction, leaving the other one, I suppose, to attend to the lamp. But I dodged along as quickly as I could and they neither of them saw me. And at last I got in among the trees bordering the drive, and felt safe."

"Well done, Countess," said Standish. "It was a ticklish situation. And they have never suspected you?"

"I'm sure they don't. They imagine it blew away in the gale. At any rate a car came along as I was standing there, and I borrowed some petrol and drove home in a sort of daze. What was to be done about it? And the more I thought the more hopeless did it appear. I'd got one print it was true, but there must be others in existence. And so beyond making myself half sick with worry I'd really accomplished nothing.

"There was no one I could turn to for help. I didn't say a word, of course, to Olga—that would have been too cruel. She could have done nothing, and if the blow had got to fall it might just as well be unexpected. And it was no good trying to console myself with the idea that the picture was harmless since it had been taken before Olga's wedding. Berendosi is far too clever a man to let a trifle like that bother him. I was distracted until, out of the blue came Mary Ridgeway. She was someone I could confide in, at any rate.

"Judge, then, of my amazement when I found she knew all about it and was dumbfounded to find that I did. It appeared that a man in London—you know, Mr. Carteret, Felton Blake—had written to her begging for an interview. She had met him at some party or another, and since he said it was of vital importance that he should see her she allowed him to call. He apparently went straight to the point and produced a copy of the photo.

"She was as much bowled over as I was when she saw it, and demanded how he came to have such a thing. He told her it had come into his possession by roundabout means."

"More than likely," said Standish dryly.

"So she asked him what he was going to do with it.

"'Why burn it, of course,' he answered, and did so then and there.

"'But then why, Mr. Blake, bother to come and show it to me?' she cried.

"'Because, Lady Mary,' he explained, 'I wanted to show you the intense gravity of the situation. To make a print there must be a film. And I have the best of reasons for believing that that film is in existence.'"

"The very best," said Standish with a short laugh.

"You mean..." she said, staring at him.

"Shall I tell you the rest? Our Mr. Felton Blake, appalled by the vileness of the scoundrel who had taken such a photograph, ranged himself on the side of virtue. He somehow or other would get hold of that film: he somehow or other would see that it was destroyed, and any other prints that might be in existence."

"As a matter of fact, he has found one more print," she said.

"It would be equally easy for him to find a dozen," said Standish grimly. "My dear Countess, I am not a wealthy man, but I would cheerfully wager a thousand pounds to a sixpence that I could lead you to that film now. It is where it has always been—in Felton Blake's safe."

"But if that is so," she cried pathetically, "it's our last hope gone. Or do you think he's only trying to make it seem harder, so as to..."

Her eyes met Tiny's and he laughed savagely.

"So as to ingratiate himself with Mary?" he said.

"More than likely," said Standish. "But don't delude yourself into thinking that when the ingratiating period can no longer be prolonged he is going to hand over the film. Unless, of course. . . Do you really think, Tiny, that the swine is in love with Lady Mary?"

Tiny waved his hand at the countess.

"There is my informant," he said shortly.

"Yes, Mr. Standish, I do," she answered.

"Then it is possible that Felton Blake might drive the bargain. It's quite in keeping with the man's character. If she will marry him, then she gets the film as a wedding present."

"The ineffable swine," muttered Tiny.

"Agreed, old lad," said Standish. "But we've got to take the facts as they are. And I'm bound to say they look just about as grim as they can."

"But, good God!" exploded Joe Denver, "we can put the police on to him."

"What for?" asked Standish quietly. "What are you going to charge him with? Having that photograph in his possession doesn't constitute a crime. That's the devil of it, young fellah. As I see the matter at present, they are absolutely within the law."

He relapsed into silence, tapping his teeth with the stem of his pipe.

"Let's try and get things in order," he remarked at length. "Somehow or other Blake has got hold of an incriminating photograph. As the countess quite rightly observed, the fact that it was taken before a certain marriage is of no account. Berendosi, as she says, is far too clever a man to let that worry him. So little in fact does it do so that he is prepared to pay a quarter of a million for it to this man Zavier. . . . . And Zavier is a very interesting gentleman."

"I gathered you had seen him before tonight," said Tiny.

"He did me the honour of being somewhat curious over my movements when I was staying in Territet. I don't think he realised I had spotted his interest, but it is a game which two can play. Then he vanished, and I dismissed him from my mind. But now we hear from the countess that he was the actual man who offered the photo to Berendosi months ago. Very interesting."

"Why particularly?" demanded Tiny.

"Do you suppose that Felton Blake would have given away the handling of a show involving a quarter of a million unless he had to? That he would have passed it over to one of the smaller fry—one of his own equals? Not he. He would have negotiated himself, and pocketed the whole of the boodle. Don't you see what that means, Tiny? It means, unless I am vastly mistaken, that at last we have found our bird. Zavier is the big man. However, that will all keep for the moment. Let us concentrate on the immediate issue. Andy, you are more in touch with things here than we are. What is your candid opinion of the situation?"

The journalist puffed thoughtfully at his pipe.

"With that film in his possession," he said at length, "Berendosi has the game in his hands. It's fool proof. Things are on the edge of a precipice now: with that photograph comes the landslide."

"But why?" cried Denver. "All he can do is to show it to his friends."

"Laddie," answered Andy gravely, "he can show it to the whole country. What is to prevent him having thousands of copies made, till your face is as familiar as Charlie Chaplin's? He can distribute them broadcast through the land. And had Ronald not smashed the plate tonight there would have been a pair. The plot is as clear as the nose on your face. And your arrival here has given it the finishing touch. Not only will they distribute the photograph, but they will produce the original."

"I agree with you, Andy," said Standish. "It's incredibly simple, and

135

incredibly sure. *And it must not be.* But how the devil we're going to prevent it, I, at the moment, do not see. By the way, Countess, how did you know Mr. Denver was here?"

"I told my very greatest friend, Mr. Standish, about the photograph and showed it to her. And she by chance saw Mr. Denver here in the hotel. She thought she recognised him, and when she saw the name in the book she knew at once. So she wired me in Paris and I wired Mr. Carteret. I hoped he would be able to persuade him to go at once, if I couldn't. And now it's too late. . ."

"Don't be too sure of that. There must be some way."

"Look here," said Denver quietly, "don't go ahead too fast. If that entrancing exhibition of beastliness Berendosi is going to flood the country with copies of that photograph, I'm going to be here."

"Very understandable, old lad," said Standish, "but it won't do. Any man would feel the same. But it's one of those cases where not only could you do no good, but you'd do an enormous amount of harm. It would at once appear as proof that the affair was still going on. No; I sympathize with you. But if we can manage it you have got to be removed from here. And it's easier said than done."

"Well, if you've all quite finished talking," said Mrs. Andy quietly, "I'll tell you how to do it."

"Good for you, Maggie," said her husband, reaching for the whisky. "Come into the office, boys, for you can bet it is all settled."

And when twenty minutes later Standish and Tiny strolled back to their hotel, it seemed to them that there was at least a sixty *per cent* chance of her scheme succeeding. Denver had remained with the Mackintoshs: the countess had gone home, and the most searching examination had failed to reveal any sign of men watching the house. In fact, up to date everything seemed to have gone splendidly, and yet Standish seemed gloomy and depressed.

"It's worse—far worse than I thought, Tiny. It's foolproof, as Andy said—once they get that photo, even if young Denver isn't in the country. A letter would have been bad enough, but that photo—why, good Lord! it's a cinch. And we don't want a change of regime here."

"I wonder how they got it," said Tiny.

"That we shall probably never know. She was well known by sight, of course, and someone must have followed them that day. But all that is only of academic interest. The only thing that matters is that they *have* got it, or rather Felton Blake has."

"I suppose that is certain, Ronald. You don't think that possibly that man Zavier has taken it over by now. Or even Berendosi himself."

"I've thought of that, and it is undoubtedly a possibility. But I'll tell you my reasons for thinking Blake still has it. He got it in the first place, otherwise he would never have come into the game at all. Now from every point of view it is to his advantage to hang on to it as long as he can. The more time he gets with Lady Mary, the better for him. And once that film is out of his possession, the show here might be sprung under his feet at any moment."

"It seems sound," said Tiny. "Gad! I'd like to wring the swine's neck. Ronald, we've damned well got to do these blighters down."

"And so say all of us, laddie," answered the other with a short laugh. "Honestly, Tiny, I don't see how we're going to do it. But there's one thing that is intriguing me at the moment. What line is our friend Berendosi going to adopt when he sees us? Because he must know that it was we who did the trick."

They turned into the hotel, and Standish gave a short chuckle.

"Obvious police spy the first," he muttered, "lurking in corner of lounge. And behold! he moves at speed. Come into my room, Tiny, for a nightcap. I'm thinking we may have a visitor, and I wouldn't like you to miss the fun."

And sure enough a few minutes later there came a knock on the door.

"My dear *Signor*," cried Standish, as he opened it, "this is indeed an unexpected surprise. And—er—pleasure. Will you join us in a little whisky?"

Berendosi, still fully dressed save that he had substituted a dressing-gown for his coat, came into the room and shut the door.

"Mr. Standish," he said shortly, "do we put the cards on the table, or not?"

"Surely in lives as blameless as ours, there should never be anything to conceal," remarked the other. "What about a *deoch-an-dorriss*?"

Berendosi waved away the proffered drink.

"It isn't poisoned," said Tiny mildly. "We still maintain our English habits even in this country."

"Will you kindly be silent?" snapped Berendosi. "When I wish you to speak I will tell you."

"Indeed," said Tiny ominously. "And when I wish you to speak to me like that, I will tell you. But if you do it again, you rat-faced swab, I'll take you by the scruff of the neck and hang you out of the window."

"Steady, Tiny," said Standish with a grin, as Berendosi recoiled against the wall. "But you really must remember, *Signor*, that my friend is very large, and choose your words accordingly. Now what can we do for you?"

With an effort the other recovered his composure.

"I would prefer to discuss the matter alone with you, Mr. Standish. Your very large friend is, I should imagine, more suited to the football field than to a matter of this sort."

"The interview is not of my seeking," said Standish curtly. "And I know of nothing that I wish to discuss with you alone."

"So be it," remarked Berendosi, with a shrug of his shoulders. "I gather then, from the tone of your remarks, that you do not propose to put your cards down. It seems a waste of time, but have it your own way. A few hours ago, Mr. Standish, you and your friend here forcibly entered the house of a colleague of mine, and removed a young man whom I require. Where is he?"

"Am I to understand that this young man whom we are reputed to have removed was being detained against his will?" asked Standish.

"Come, come, Mr. Standish," said Berendosi irritably, "what is the use of this pretence? We are alone together: we all know the facts of the case. As a clever man, don't you think it would be as well to have a perfectly straight discussion, and then we can all go to bed?"

"I am waiting," remarked Standish quietly.

"You are a man whose knowledge of the political situation in Europe is profound. I am well aware that England does not desire any change of government here: nevertheless, that change is coming. You know that as well as I do: hence your presence here. You also know that by one of those strange turns of Fate, this young man Denver is a very important person in that change. Therefore you remove him. Good! I admire you for it. But, Mr. Standish, I require him back. Where is he?"

Standish laughed gently.

"Your ideas of argument are rather crude, *Signor*. Even supposing for a moment that this extraordinary assertion of yours is right, and that we removed Denver, we must have done it because we wished to hide him. Why then should we completely negate what we've done by telling you where we have hidden him? I don't quite see what we get out of it."

"Then I will explain," said the other. "And I am relieved to see that we both know where we stand. The point you raise is a perfectly fair one: the answer, however, is simple. As you will doubtless have guessed, every frontier post has already been closed to Mr. Denver. He can leave the country neither by car, by rail, nor by air. As a further precaution, his passport is being temporarily taken care of for him. In fact, Mr. Standish, you will not believe the activity that took place on his utterly unexpected arrival. I mention these points merely to show that we are in earnest. Very well then: I will come to the point. For how long do you think it would be possible for this young man, whose description has been widely circulated and who cannot speak a word of the language, to remain hidden?"

"I was never much good at riddles," murmured Standish.

"Sooner or later he is bound to be found. And," continued the other slowly, "it is for you to decide whether it shall be sooner or later."

"I may be dense," said Standish, "but I still fail to see the *quid pro quo.*"

"Mr. Standish—as a lover of law and order, I know you will be grieved to hear that a dastardly crime has been committed tonight. At a house belonging to a high state official two miscreants nearly killed an inoffensive photographer, forced their way in, stunned two of the old family retainers and then decamped—for all I know with large quantities of valuables. Justice cries aloud for the names of these criminals, in order that they may be punished. Do you see now where the *quid pro quo* comes in? Should you decide on it's being sooner, I don't think the names of the criminals are ever likely to be disclosed. Should you decide on it being later—well, one of the criminals was a thick-set man of medium height, the other was a very large friend of his. Do I make myself clear?"

"Perfectly," answered Standish. "There is, however, one point that strikes me, *Signor.* When these two villains are haled before the law to answer for their sins, they will naturally give a reason for their scandalous behaviour. They will say what the photographer was doing, and people will wonder why. They will say who was there and all sorts of embarrassing and awkward things, which will doubtless get into the papers."

"My dear Mr. Standish, can you possibly believe for an instant that a man in my responsible position, knowing as I do the unsettled state of the country, would allow such a thing as that to get into the papers? You quite pain me. Think of the terrible example to the youth of the land. No, I fear that the two miscreants would have no chance of stating their case until later—considerably later. And I may further say that amongst other reforms which are urgently needed here the state of our prisons leaves much to be desired."

"So that's it, is it?" said Standish, lighting a cigarette.

"That is it, Mr. Standish. I do not think I can make it any clearer. As I said before, sooner or later Mr. Denver will be found. For reasons into which we need not enter I would prefer it to be sooner. I therefore offer you the two alternatives. If you make it sooner there is a most comfortable train *de luxe* which leaves for Paris tomorrow night: if the other, well, as I said, our gaols are not all they might be."

"And what do you propose to do with Denver when you get him?"

"I can assure you that he will be treated with the utmost consideration," answered the other. "Be reasonable," he continued as Standish said nothing. "As a clever man you know that I hold the top trumps: I've got a winning hand. And clever men cut their losses under those circumstances. Hand over the young man to me and clear out. And when things are more settled, believe me we shall be only too delighted to welcome you back to our country."

"Sooner and later are relative terms, *Signor*," remarked Standish abruptly. "By when is this decision to be made?"

For an instant a gleam of triumph showed in Berendosi's eyes, but his voice was quite casual as he answered.

"Shall we say lunchtime tomorrow, or rather today? I have a most boring function to attend in a few hours at the aerodrome—the inauguration of the new service between here and Le Bourget. So lunch will suit me admirably."

"All right," said Standish, opening the door. "I will tell you then."

"But let there be no misunderstanding, Mr. Standish," remarked the other. "I must have proof."

"You shall have proof," said Standish coldly, ignoring Berendosi's outstretched hand.

"Strange men—you English." The Bessonian's hand fell to his side. "I thought you were always reputed to take a beating like a sportsman."

"Only if that beating comes from a sportsman. Signor Berendosi, it would be idle to pretend that I don't know your game. But it would be equally idle to pretend that I do not consider you a cad of the first order. A man who deliberately sets out to obtain his ends by blackening the reputation of a perfectly innocent woman in the eyes of the

140

whole world, is not a man whose hand I would ever shake."

He turned to Tiny as the door closed, and gave a short laugh.

"I feel a little better for that, Tiny. Lucky he suggested lunch: we shall know by then."

"But if it doesn't come off—are you going to tell the swine?"

"That he's at Andy's? Yes. It's not fair to them. What Berendosi said is right—they're bound to find him in a place like this. The servants would give it away. And don't be under any delusions as to what he said about our going to jug. That was no bluff. And though we may be precious little use out of prison, we'd be even less inside. So one way or the other we'll tell him at lunch. And I'll go round to the Embassy in the morning and get Bunny Rogers to feed, for I'm thinking that if we do pull it off Berendosi will be as sore as if he'd sat in a hornets' nest. So a little diplomatic flavouring at the meal may be helpful. Well, goodnight, old lad. We'd better get a few hours' sleep."

But though he undressed and got into bed sleep would not come. Round and round in his brain the problem twisted and turned, and when the broad light of day was streaming through the window it was still unsolved. How was the negative of that photo to be procured? And mixed up with it was another even more important factor. How was he to get a line on Zavier and hold it?

He felt that his reasoning was correct with regard to that gentleman. Even if he was not the biggest man of all, he was considerably nearer that position than Felton Blake. And though he had made no effort to trace him from Territet—his suspicions then had not been aroused—he was under no delusions as to what would in all probability have happened if he had. Time and again had he and others got on the trail of men who they knew belonged to the gang, in the hope of tracking them to their headquarters: time and again had those men vanished as completely as if the earth had swallowed them up. True they had only been underlings, but if underlings could shake skilled men off their heels, how much more easily could a man in Zavier's position.

He recalled a case where a man who was known to be a forger in the employ of the gang was purposely allowed his freedom in the hopes that he would lead them to their quarry. That man had got on the boat train at Victoria: he had not got off at Dover. At least Inspector Mead had been prepared to swear he hadn't. And yet the run had been non-stop. That it was a disguise of some sort was obvious, since no man can disappear into thin air. But what was this disguise that—

not in one isolated case but in several—could completely hoodwink some of the shrewdest men living?

At last he gave up any attempt at sleep and, lighting a cigarette, he pulled up a chair to the open window. For the moment he had to dismiss the bigger problem from his mind and concentrate on the smaller—how to obtain the negative from Felton Blake. And after a while he began to laugh gently to himself: there was only one possible method. Clearly Blake would not hand it over voluntarily: therefore, there was no good asking for it. Equally clearly there was no good attempting to obtain it by force: Blake was a powerful man who would certainly be armed, and who also had an alarm on his desk which sounded in the rooms of two large men-servants. He remembered that fact from a previous interview he had had with him when tempers had become a little frayed. And since those two methods were both ruled out, there remained only one other—the negative must be stolen.

He began to pace thoughtfully up and down the room: was it feasible? It was a risk—a very grave risk: on that point he was under no delusions. If he was caught he would be treated exactly the same as any ordinary burglar: therefore he must not be caught. But burglary was a skilled profession and up to date he had not served an apprenticeship at it. And yet it was worth taking a big chance—the issues at stake were so big. Moreover, it was quite possible that once he got inside Blake's safe other things would come to light—things that might lead him to the headquarters of the gang.

He argued it out in his mind, weighing up the chances. Given favourable conditions he could deal with the safe, but it was not going to be an easy matter to get those conditions. Gentlemen of Felton Blake's mode of living took considerable precautions over their houses. Still, there was no device yet invented by human brain, that could not be circumvented by the same agency, and the more he thought of it the more did it seem to him the only way. In fact, when he went downstairs after his coffee and rolls his mind was made up: he was going to try and steal the negative.

Berendosi was in the lounge, and greeted him affably. He apparently bore no ill feeling over Standish's final remark of a few hours previously: garbed in a frock-coat and top-hat he oozed complacency.

"A tedious performance," he remarked, "but *pro bono publico.*"

"A most apt quotation," said Standish politely. "You are making a speech?"

"A few words only. Well—at lunch then, we will resume our talk."

"Precisely," answered the other with a faint smile. "At lunch."

Thinking over the bigger problems had almost driven the immediate point at issue from his mind. And now as he watched Berendosi enter his car he began to feel doubtful. Would the thing come off? Its principal hope of success lay in the calm audacity of the scheme, but now that the actual moment had arrived he didn't feel quite so confident as he had done the previous night. Right under Berendosi's nose as Andy had gleefully exclaimed, but was the nose big enough to hide it? And at that moment Tiny hove in sight.

"Go off, old man, to the aerodrome," he said, "and see what happens. I'm going to the embassy."

He found George Potter pretending to work, and was at once taken in to the ambassador.

"Hullo! Standish," cried the latter. "Delighted to see you. What brings you here, though it isn't hard to guess?"

He listened in silence while Standish told him the whole story, and his face grew graver and graver.

"Mackintosh is right," he said at the conclusion. "It means the end. And probably a lot of bloodshed. What on earth induced the boy to come here?"

"That is the least part of it, sir," remarked Standish. "It is this damned photograph."

"Well, don't get yourself into trouble, my dear fellow. And take George along with you to lunch. Gad! I'd give something to see friend Berendosi's face if you pull it off. And if the blighter gets gay with you and your pal, George can put it on to me. In fact, he'd better stop with you till you go."

It was midday when they got back to the hotel, and a quarter of an hour later Tiny came in grinning all over his face, with Andy Mackintosh.

"Thumbs up, Ronald," he cried. "Went without a hitch."

"A verra impressive spectacle," said Andy gravely. "In fact I lapsed into journalese. Like a giant dragon-fly with gossamer wings outstretched the flying bird lay motionless, gleaming silver in the sunshine. Soon it would spring to life, and soaring into the blue empyrean, bear its living cargo over the snow-capped peaks towards the smiling fields of France, gliding smoothly under the master hand of the keen-eyed bird-man in control. And then the great Berendosi himself drew nigh.

In a few well-chosen words he painted a dazzling picture of the future, with Dalzburg not the least important link in the world flying route. And what of the men who made such things possible: the intrepid pilot: the clear-brained, efficient mechanic...."

"For the love of *Allah*, Andy, shut your mouth on a drink," laughed Standish. "For here, if I mistake not, is the bird himself. George, my boy, we're going to have some fun. Have you ever seen a finer example of '*l'État, c'est moi*'?"

And undoubtedly at the moment Paul Berendosi was feeling that life was good. The ceremony had gone off swimmingly: the cheers of the onlookers still rang in his ears. And to crown everything, a plain-clothes officer had told him as he alighted at the hotel that the young Englishman he wanted had returned to his room. Evidently Standish had seen wisdom: now all that remained was to get him and his boring friend out of the country as soon as possible. He glanced into the bar, and for a moment a slight feeling of uneasiness assailed him. The party in there seemed very hilarious considering they had been beaten all along the line. Someone from the embassy, he reflected, and the correspondent of one of the English papers. And at that moment Standish hailed him.

"I trust everything went well, *Signor?*"

"Admirably, thank you."

He moved on, his uneasiness increasing. Why on earth were the four of them looking so pleased? Standish must know that Denver had returned to the hotel. And just then the police officer came up to him.

"May I have a word with you, your Excellency?" he said in a low voice. "There is some mistake. The young man upstairs is in possession of his passport, and it is in perfect order. And he is not even an Englishman: he is French."

"What's that?" snarled the other. "Are you certain?"

"But of course, Excellency. I have just been speaking to him."

"Who is he, you fool? Go and find out."

So Standish was trying the funny stuff, was he? And a sudden burst of laughter from the bar seemed to bear out the fact. He moved a few steps to one side so that he could see in: the four men were examining something intently.

"Come and have a look, *Signor*," called out Standish. "It's an excellent one of you, and I know your interest in photography."

Without a word he joined them: an advance press proof of the

144

morning's proceedings lay on the table. There was the aeroplane, the passengers, himself, the crowd, but what the devil was the jest?

"Quite good," he said indifferently.

"Particularly of the mechanic," murmured Standish blandly. "And I hear you said some very nice things about clear-brained, efficient mechanics."

Berendosi stood very still: a sudden ghastly suspicion had assailed him.

"It was verra lucky that such an able substitute could be found at the last moment," said Andy gravely. "It would have been terrible, *Signor*, if your impassioned eloquence had been wasted."

"May I ask exactly what you are talking about?" said Berendosi quietly.

"Didn't you hear?" boomed Tiny cheerfully. "That's too bad. Just as everything was ready, what should occur but that the mechanic felt the urge for a drink upon him. So back he trotted to the hangar with his tongue hanging out. And there who should he find but another man ready, aye ready! to take his place."

"And the lucky thing was that he had already gone through the necessary formalities," said Standish. "Because this noble fellow who was prepared to sacrifice himself that another man should not thirst, had in some extraordinary manner lost his passport. But since most people look more or less alike in goggles and a crash-helmet, the point escaped the notice of the aerodrome authorities."

For perhaps ten seconds Berendosi stared at Standish with a look of smouldering fury in his eyes. What had happened was clear. The man upstairs was the real mechanic, for whom they had substituted Denver at the last moment. And now Denver was gone beyond recall. How they had fixed it mattered not: the one salient fact remained that he had been completely outwitted. Moreover, in the presence of the others it was impossible to show the furious rage that was seething in him.

"How very interesting," he said at length.

"I was sure you would find it so," remarked Standish affably. "Will you join us in a little lunch?"

"I thank you—no," answered the other. "You leave tonight?"

"I do."

"Then I will say goodbye."

"*Au revoir* is more suitable, Signor Berendosi. I shall return."

And once again the eyes of the two men met.

CHAPTER 8

That, up to date, luck had been with them all along the line Ronald Standish was the first to admit. The comparative similarity of build between Denver and the mechanic: the fact that Denver held a pilot's ticket and so was fully capable of taking over the job: above all, the sportsmanship of Laval the French pilot in agreeing to the change, was a combination of circumstances they could hardly hope to strike again. But it was a good omen: the first hurdle, even if it was the least formidable, had been cleared. Joe Denver was out of the country. Now they were faced with the second. And it was after dinner was over that Standish broached the subject to Tiny.

"Are you prepared to take a pretty useful risk, old lad?" he said quietly.

The restaurant car was empty save for the staff having a meal behind the partition at the end.

"We've run one or two already," laughed the other, "so a few more won't hurt."

"After you went to bed last night I got thinking," went on Standish. "Thinking about this damned negative. Tiny—there is only one way to get it, and that is to steal it."

Tiny raised his eyebrows.

"Not too bally easy, old man, is it? I should imagine a man of Blake's type takes fairly good precautions against burglary."

"Undoubtedly he does. Hence the risk. But there is no other way. He won't give it to us: we can't take it by force, so we've got to get it by stealth if we get it at all."

"Seems sound enough reasoning," agreed Tiny. "How do you propose to set about it?"

"I know his house, and I know the room in which he keeps his safe. It is a ground-floor room looking out on to the garden, and as far as I can recollect there are some trees fairly close to the window. The first thing we've got to do is to get him out of the way. And there, Tiny, Lady Mary comes in. She must contrive to keep him clear of the house for at least two hours round about midnight. Then we'll have a dip at it. I can manage the safe if I've got the time. And if by any chance we are heard—he keeps a couple of tame bruisers about the place, disguised as footmen—we'll wade into 'em, or cut and run."

"Sounds easy: too easy. Still, it's worth chancing."

"The chief risk is if some zealous Hampstead policeman catches us in the act. If we are just seen by some of his staff, however good a description of us is circulated, I don't think we shall be implicated. There are times," he added with a wink, "when Scotland Yard can be very dense."

"And when do you suggest we should do it?"

"On the first possible occasion," said Standish. "Time is becoming one of the most vital factors in this matter. And I propose we should try tomorrow night. Always provided, that is, that we can get hold of Lady Mary."

"Shouldn't be much difficulty about that. I know she will be in Town, and she'll cancel any engagement to help us. Incidentally, what do we do about young Joe?"

Standish shrugged his shoulders.

"There's nothing much to be done. I'm damned sorry for the boy, but other people have been in love before and got over it. We'll go round to Laval's flat when we get to Paris, pick him up and take him over to England. I can probably help to square matters over his passport."

He lit a cigarette and leaned back in his seat.

"Gad! Tiny, it would be great if we could pull it off. Just great, with..."

He paused suddenly, eyes narrowed, staring over Tiny's head. Then he went on—

"all the odds against us."

"What's stung you, Ronald?"

"One of the biggest of those odds, who for the moment had slipped my mind. Our friend Zavier is on the train, though I certainly never noticed him get on at Dalzburg. And he's watching us, Tiny!"

"How do you know?"

"He was standing in the corridor of the next coach, and for a moment our eyes met."

He called for the bill, and a few minutes later they returned to their carriage. Sleeping berths had been impossible, and they had a first-class compartment to themselves.

"Be careful, old man," he said abruptly, as Tiny prepared to throw his coat, which he had left to mark his place, into the rack. "Don't touch anything. Apparently nothing has been moved, but..."

His eyes were searching every corner of the carriage, and after awhile he drew on a pair of gloves.

"We may be several kinds of ass, Tiny, but I don't trust railway trains when members of this fraternity are about. We've been in the restaurant car for a good two hours, and this carriage has been empty."

He ran his fingers gently over the upholstery, while the train rocked and swayed through the darkness. And not until he had explored every corner did he at length sit down.

"False alarm this time," he said. "But it alters things a little for to-night. We mustn't both sleep at the same time: that's obvious. We'll shut the door into the corridor, and we'll open the window. But for the love of Pete if it's your watch don't forget to shut it whenever we stop at a station."

But nothing happened throughout the night. Once, when they had stopped at some comparatively small and ill-lit place, it had seemed to Tiny that something had hit the window, but the blow was so soft that he couldn't have sworn to it. And peering out he could see nothing, so he dismissed it as imagination. Once also during another period when he was on duty a peculiar-shaped shadow showed for a moment in the corridor—a shadow so indefinite that it might have been thrown by a sack. But it disappeared as abruptly as it had come, and when he glanced out the corridor was empty. And so without event they arrived in Paris.

"You deal with the kit, Tiny," said Standish, as the train ran into the Gare de Lyon. "I'm sprinting like a hare for the barrier to see if I can spot our friend."

But when Tiny joined him there, he shook his head a little ruefully.

"I didn't," he said. "And I saw every soul who came off that train."

"If your idea over the headquarters being in Switzerland is right," remarked Tiny, "he may have got off there."

"Possibly," agreed Standish. "And yet I have a sort of hunch that his goal is the same as ours—Felton Blake."

He gave Laval's address to the taxi-driver.

"I may be wrong, but I don't think they would trust a thing so important as that negative to the post. Moreover, a man of Blake's type trusts no one. He will want to see the colour of his money before he parts. Still, it's guesswork. The only thing we know is that Zavier has disappeared for the time as far as we are concerned."

They found Laval having his breakfast and introduced themselves.

"It was to me a great pleasure," he remarked when Standish began to thank him for what he had done. "When the so charming Madame Mackintosh tell me her scheme and I realise zat the honour of a lady is at stake—*que voulez vous?* It was so easy. And I arrange the affair of the passport here. I say my mechanic he is ill, and zat this gentleman—a qualified pilot—he take his place at ze last moment so as not to disappoint ze passengers."

"Splendid, Monsieur Laval," cried Standish. "A thousand thanks. And where is he now?"

"He sleep late, I think, in zat room."

He crossed the passage, and knocked on the door of a room opposite. And then, receiving no answer, he flung it open.

"He is not here. *Probablement* he is gone out. Ah! but here is a note. Let us see what he say.

Dear Monsieur Laval,—
My warmest thanks for all that you have done. I looked into your room but you were sleeping so I did not awaken you. Tell Standish when you see him that I have gone to London. I'll square the passport business somehow. And tell him I'll get what we want. Again many thanks.

He laid the letter down on the table, and Standish re-read it, frowning thoughtfully.

"A nuisance—that," he said. "You don't know his address in London, Tiny, I suppose? Or his club?"

"Not a notion. Why?"

"My dear old lad, Joe Denver is an excellent youngster. But the last thing I want is to have him blundering round Felton Blake. And that's what he evidently means to do. It's going to completely queer our pitch. He'll do no good: and he'll put Blake on his guard."

"I should think it is more than likely he will go and see Mary," said Tiny. "What about getting her on the 'phone?"

"That's a good idea. May we put through a London call, Monsieur Laval?"

"But assuredly. It is in the hall."

"Tell her, Tiny, that if ever she sees Denver she must tell him from us to do absolutely nothing until he sees us. Tell him to come to the club at six to-night."

"And what about Felton Blake tonight?" said Tiny, hanging up the receiver.

"Tell her what we want to do. But be guarded."

The call went through quickly, and in less than three minutes Tiny heard Simmonds' voice from the other end.

"Speaking from Paris, Simmonds. Mr. Carteret. I want Lady Mary urgently."

"Her ladyship is out of London, sir. Not returning until lunchtime."

"Give him the message about Denver," said Standish, as Tiny repeated it. "Not Felton Blake."

"Simmonds," went on Tiny, "you remember Mr. Denver. Tall, fair gentleman with curly hair. You do. Good. If he comes to call on Lady Mary today tell him that he is to do nothing until he sees Mr. Standish. Got that? And tell him to be at my club at six."

He listened while the butler repeated the message, and then rang off.

"So far, so good," said Standish. "We couldn't have passed a message through him about Felton Blake. We must wire."

He sat down and pulled a telegraph form towards him.

"How's this?" he said a few moments later.

We want F.B. out of his house tonight from eleven till one. Please arrange. Urgent and vital. Tiny.

"That ought to do it," said Tiny. "And she'll pull it off if it is humanly possible."

"My man can take it for you at once," said Laval. "The bureau is just around the corner. And first he shall get you some hot water for a shave."

"Excellent," cried Standish. "And then we must catch the ten o'clock boat train."

"*Pour les pauvres, Messieurs.*"

Two nuns were standing in the passage, and the speaker, as if to account for their unexpected appearance, added almost apologetically—"*La porte était ouverte.*"

The three men each handed over a note, and then, while one of the nuns carefully entered the amounts in a little book, Laval led the way to the bathroom. And for a moment the nuns were alone. So that there was no one to see the sudden quick movement with which the top telegraph form of the pad was detached, carefully folded, and put away in a bag. And when Laval returned they were standing meekly waiting for his signature in their book before leaving as silently as they had arrived. Nor was there anyone to see that instead of continuing their house to house visitation the two nuns walked swiftly away to where a large car was waiting, and paused by it just long enough to say "*Dix heures*"—and to place the piece of paper in a hand extended through the window—the hand of a man on whose shoulders sat a small monkey.

The car rolled off, and Boris Zavier studied the telegraph form. He saw at once the imprint of the pencil, which had been made when the wire had been written, but realising the impossibility of deciphering it in a moving car he re-folded it and placed it in his pocket book. Then he lay back and began to think. For the events of the last few days had shaken his nerve badly.

The first had been the Demeroff affair. That the Russian had been coming to Lausanne with the express purpose of meeting Standish he now knew, and though he had acted in time it had been a very close shave. But the disquieting part of the thing was that it proved that what he had said to Felton Blake was wrong. It was not only the Bessonian affair that had brought Standish to Switzerland: it was something much bigger. That the existence of his organisation was known to the authorities was obvious: activities on such a scale as he had carried them out could only be inspired by one controlling brain. And it struck him with a sort of cynical humour that it would be amusing if this—one of the least of his schemes—should prove to be the one that revealed to whom the brain belonged.

It was the abduction of this boy Denver that worried him. Not that he really cared in the slightest whether Berendosi succeeded or failed: save for the money involved the whole thing bored him. But what did matter was the fact that Standish and his friend must have seen him at Gregoroff's place.

He cursed himself now for ever having attended such an absurd farce, but at the time he did not know Standish was in Dalzburg. Had he had an inkling of the fact nothing would have induced him to go. For he was under no delusions with regard to the Englishman: he was not a man to be trifled with. Once let him suspect and he would pass his suspicions on. And it seemed to him more than likely that he suspected already.

It had been a pure accident, that momentary glimpse in the restaurant-wagon, but the result of that accident had alarmed him more than he cared to admit even to himself. Was it merely coincidence that one or the other of them had been awake all through the night? Was it merely coincidence that the door into the corridor had been closed, and the windows shut whenever he had alighted from the train? And finally, was it merely coincidence that Standish should have been standing by the barrier watching the passengers intently as they left the station? The fact that he had passed within two feet of him in safety was beside the point: all that mattered was whether these precautions had been due to that accidental glimpse in the train. And being a man who never believed in underrating the odds on the other side, he came quite definitely to the conclusion that it would be better to assume it was not a coincidence, and make his plans accordingly. Standish and his friend Carteret suspected him: therefore, they must be dealt with, and at once.

The car pulled up at the door of a luxurious flat, and Zavier alighted. They were going by the ten o'clock train: he would go by the one at midday. And that would leave him comfortable time to see if the wire contained information of any importance. It proved unexpectedly easy to decipher: the writer had evidently pressed hard with his pencil. And when the complete message lay before him on his desk, for awhile he stared thoughtfully out of the window. Then a faint smile curled round his lips, and he rubbed his hands gently together.

"Excellent," he murmured: "Excellent."

And with the smile still on his face he went into his dressing-room.

At half-past five Tiny rang the bell of Lady Mary's house, and the door was opened by Simmonds.

"Her ladyship is not at home, sir," he said. "She left a note for you."

"Did she get my wire?" asked Tiny.

"She got a wire, sir, when she returned at lunch-time."

"Has Mr. Denver been here?"

"No, sir: no sign of him. Will you come in, sir, and read the note: you might like to write an answer."

Tiny went into the *boudoir* and as he glanced round the familiar room he gave a short laugh. Only four days since he had last been there: only four days since he had felt her lips on his for the first time—but what a lot of water had flowed under the bridge since then.

"A whisky and soda, sir?" suggested the butler.

"Thank you, Simmonds," he said, sitting down and opening the note, it ran:

My Dear,—I have done what you asked in your wire. But what on earth is the idea? I gather from your telephone message to Simmonds that Joe Denver must be safely out of Dalzburg.

Nada Mazarin wrote me from Paris to say he was there, and that she had travelled with you. It's distracting that I can't see you today, but I've got an engagement I simply cannot break. I'm dying to hear all your news: come round and see me first thing tomorrow.—Mary.

P.S.—There has been no sign of Joe here.

He crossed to her desk as the butler came in with the drink.

"If I may say so, sir," he said with the familiarity of an old servant, "her ladyship seems to have been very worried lately. Not at all her usual self."

"You are quite right, Simmonds. She has been. By the way, has a gentleman called Blake been here at all?"

"Once or twice, sir," he said. "Might I ask, sir, if he is—er—a friend of yours?"

"A friend of mine!" cried Tiny. "Emphatically he is not."

"I am not surprised, sir," said Simmonds quietly. "Will you ring if you require another drink, sir?"

So even the servants had noticed it, reflected Tiny savagely as the door closed. And any lingering doubts he might have had about the night's work ahead vanished. That negative had *got* to be obtained.

He pulled a sheet of paper towards him, he wrote:

Mary Dear,—
Well done. I'll come round and see you tomorrow and maybe— though I don't promise—it will see the end of all our troubles. I've got lots to tell you. —Tiny.

He sealed the envelope and finished his drink. Then he rang the bell.

"Give this to Lady Mary, Simmonds, will you? And if by any chance Mr. Denver does arrive, my telephone message to you still holds. Send him round to my club without fail."

Ronald Standish was waiting for him in the smoking-room.

"Fortunately it is the more important of the two things that has come off," was his comment when he heard Tiny's news. "And we can only hope that young Denver postpones his visit till tomorrow. I put through a call to the Folkestone passport people, and he'd arrived all right by the one o'clock boat. And after they had satisfied themselves he was British they let him go on. He was very insistent apparently on getting to London as soon as possible—strangely insistent was the phrase they used. However, we can only hope for the best."

153

"Did you find out anything at the Yard?" asked Tiny.

"Not a thing. I described Zavier in detail, and clearly he is a new one on them. Which proves just nothing at all. Then I went along and saw Gillson, and gave him a *résumé* of our doings. In fact I whispered to him of our expedition tonight. At first he tried to dissuade me: said the risk was too great. But after awhile he agreed that it was the only possible solution. Not that he can do much if we're caught," he added with a short laugh. "We're definitely putting ourselves outside the pale of the law. And, 'pon my soul, Tiny, I don't know if it is fair to you. You are only a volunteer, so to speak: it's not your palaver."

"Go to blazes, you ass," cried Tiny. "Unless you want a rough house here and now."

"Right ho!" grinned the other. "I'm not denying you won't be damned useful, but it's only fair to warn you that there is going to be the devil of a risk."

"How are you going to open the safe if we do get in?" said Tiny.

"One of my little secrets that you don't know," answered Standish. "You shall after dinner."

"And since it will probably be our last," laughed Tiny, "we'd better make it a good one."

It was nine o'clock when they left the club, and there was still no sign of Joe Denver. During the meal they had both been unusually silent: as the time drew nearer the bald fact that, if they were caught, it would without a shadow of doubt mean a term of imprisonment, began to obtrude itself with increasing clearness. But neither of them had the slightest intention of drawing back.

They drove to Standish's flat. There was at least an hour to put through before they dared start, but there were several preparations to be made. First he went to the safe in the corner of the room, and from it he extracted a rolled-up green wallet of the type used for motoring tools. Then he drew the blinds, before opening it out on the table.

"This room is overlooked," he said with a grin. "And I'd hate any-one to think that this represented my normal method of livelihood."

Inside was a complete set of safe-opening tools. Braces, bits—all the paraphernalia of the professional cracksman lay gleaming in the electric light.

"Good Lord! old man," cried Tiny. "Where did you get that lot?"

"I got them in the States from a professional user of them," laughed the other, "as a small token of gratitude for something I did for him. According to him they weren't quite up to his form, and he was getting some others. Moreover, he showed me how to use 'em."

He rolled up the wallet again and put it in his pocket.

"Now—two masks." He rummaged in a drawer. "Here are two that will do."

"Are we taking any weapons?" asked Tiny.

"I think not, old lad. Certainly not guns. Burglary is one thing: shooting is another. No: we'll stick to the perfectly efficient fist, if we're caught in the act, and then run like stags. For the trouble is that we daren't go in my car. We'd have to leave it some distance from the house, and a car untended for two hours or so would have the police on it at once. We'll just take a taxi to somewhere near the house and then walk."

It was half-past ten when they decided they could start, and a quarter of an hour later they dismissed their machine at Swiss Cottage. If Blake was meeting Lady Mary at eleven, he would have left his house already and the coast would be clear.

They walked along Eton Avenue, comparatively dimly lit after the glare of Finchley Road behind them. And after about a quarter of a mile Standish turned left-handed up an even quieter road. They were in the centre of one of the wealthy residential quarters of Hampstead, and the houses on each side of them proclaimed the fact. Solid, comfortable and above all eminently respectable, they seemed to personify their solid, comfortable and eminently respectable owners.

"There is the spot we want," said Standish. "Number 12."

They paused opposite it on the other side of the road. It was in darkness save for a light from one of the top windows. To the right of it as they looked lay the garage, and over the top of it they could see some trees.

"Up and at it, Tiny," chuckled Standish. "Take your last look at London as a free man. My God! what's that?"

For suddenly there had come a ghastly strident shriek of agony, and it had seemed to proceed from the house they were watching. A window was flung up behind them, and a man peered out. With a quick pressure on his arm Standish indicated to Tiny that they should walk on. But the scream was not repeated, and after strolling a few yards, they retraced their steps.

"Was that from Blake's house?" said Tiny.

"Sounded like it. We must wait now for a bit: it's probably alarmed the neighbourhood. Hullo! what's this?"

Once again he gripped Tiny's arm and the pair stood motionless under a tree. A man had come out of the gate of Number 12, and keeping in the shadow of the trees was walking rapidly towards Eton Avenue. It was quite impossible to recognise him: a hat pulled well down over his forehead obscured his features even if they had been visible at the distance. But not till the sound of his steps had died away did they move.

"Our friend would seem to have other visitors tonight," said Standish thoughtfully. "Things grow interesting."

"Well, the alarm doesn't seem to have spread," remarked Tiny. "And the place is deserted. What about it?"

They crossed the road some fifty yards from Blake's house, and strolled gently towards it. The man who had looked out had shut the window again: the moment was propitious. And with one quick glance round Standish turned in at the gate, and moved swiftly towards the garage.

There was a space of nearly a yard between the garage and the wall that divided Number 12 from the next house, and in a second they were both standing in it. It afforded perfect cover, and gave them a direct approach to the garden without the slightest chance of being seen. A certain amount of old rubbish had collected in it, and Standish picked his way carefully: it was not the time to play football with old oil cans. But nothing untoward occurred, and they reached the shadow of the trees without mishap.

To their right lay the garden: in front of them and a little to the left was the back of the house. It, too, was in complete darkness, and after a while they began to creep cautiously towards it.

"It's the room with the big French windows," whispered Standish. "The second one we come to."

They were close to it when he paused suddenly, and Tiny, glancing at him, could just see that he was frowning.

"Why are the windows open, Tiny?" he breathed, "when there is no light in the room? There is something damned funny about this show."

They could see the curtains moving gently in the slight breeze. No sound came from inside: the place seemed ominously quiet. And then they both shrank against the wall: a telephone bell was ringing in the room.

"Back to the trees," said Standish urgently. "Someone will probably answer it."

But no one did, and after a few more abortive attempts the operator gave it up. Silence settled once again save for the faint rustle of the leaves above their heads. They allowed five minutes: then for the second time they crept towards the window. There was no good delaying: every moment of time was valuable.

"I'll get on to the safe at once, Tiny," whispered Standish. "You lock the door, and then stand by the window. Great Scott! look there."

He had parted the curtains, and was crouching down staring at the floor. The wood was of a light colour inside the window, and stretching out from the edge of the carpet a dark stain was visible. And even as they looked at it, it altered its shape.

With a sudden exclamation he switched on a small electric torch: then his eyes dilated.

"My God!" he muttered. "It's blood. For Heaven's sake be careful where you tread."

Holding his torch in front of him he stepped into the room. And there they stood, motionless: the failure to answer the telephone was explained.

Lying on his back, with legs and arms sprawling, was Felton Blake, and driven up to the hilt in his heart was a dagger. The blood had welled out, soaking into the carpet and finally reaching the woodwork, though now it had ceased to flow.

"That scream we heard," muttered Tiny. "It must have been his."

But Standish shook his head.

"No man killed like that would scream. It was instantaneous."

He bent and felt one of the dead man's hands. "He's been dead some time. Hold those curtains together: I'm going to get some light on the scene."

He crept noiselessly away and in a moment there came the click of a switch. And once again they stood motionless, too stunned to speak. For the door of the big safe was open, and the contents were flung in wild confusion all over the carpet. But it was not empty. Lying half inside it, his head wedged in a corner, with teeth bared and only the whites of his eyes showing, was Joe Denver. No need to ask the cause of his death: both of them recognised it only too well. Somewhere on him they would find the death scratch: he had been murdered even as Demeroff and the others had been murdered. And it was his dying scream they had heard from the other side of the road.

"So that's what he meant when he said he'd get the negative somehow," said Standish gravely. "Poor young devil! And I don't know that I blame him."

"You think he killed Blake?" said Tiny.

Standish pointed to the key which was in the safe door.

"I think that he killed Blake, and then took the key from him. Blake has been dead for more than an hour: Denver for less than a quarter."

"And the man we saw leaving killed Joe?"

"Possibly, though we have no proof. Possibly there is some infernal device in the safe itself." He was drawing on his gloves as he spoke. "But now we've got to get a move on. We don't want to be discovered here if we can avoid it. The first point is—did he find the negative?"

Gently they pulled the twisted body on to the carpet, and then swiftly and methodically Standish went through his pockets.

"No sign of it," he muttered.

"If he'd found it he would have destroyed it," said Tiny, but though they searched every corner of the room, the paper basket and the fireplace, they could find no traces of it anywhere.

"Useless, Tiny. He'd surely have destroyed it here by the safe, if he destroyed it at all."

He was peering at the carpet with his torch held close.

"Nothing: nothing at all. And even a film leaves some residue if it is burnt."

At length he straightened up.

"He didn't get it, Tiny, and that means it isn't here."

"Then what do we do now?"

"We collect these papers," said Standish quietly. "Every one of them probably means some poor devil's happiness. Our burglary shall have some result, anyway."

He crammed them into his pockets till they bulged, while Tiny stood by him. Some result perhaps—but it was only a side issue. As far as they were concerned it had all been wasted; the negative was still in existence. And a damned good man had been killed. Of Felton Blake he gave no thought: men such as he deserved to die. But in his imagination he could see the youngster going feverishly through the safe: he could feel the despair that must have gripped him as he drew blank. And then—the end—the ghastly agonizing end.

"Tiny."

He glanced up at the sharp whisper: Standish was by the window looking at the floor.

"What is it?"

"You didn't tread in the blood here, did you?"

"No." He crossed the room and joined the other.

"Look there," said Standish.

In the crimson patch, clear and distinct was a footmark.

"Someone has been watching us," he continued gravely. "The waters grow deeper."

CHAPTER 9

"So it's hopeless, Tiny: they've beaten us."

"I must say, Mary dear, that at the moment it looks rather like it."

It was eleven o'clock the following morning, and the two of them were in her *boudoir*. He had told her the whole story of what had happened since they last met, and she in her turn had filled in one or two blanks.

"You see, Tiny," she said, "I knew the man was a sweep, and I can't pretend that in one way the news of his death isn't a profound relief. At the same time I did think he was genuinely trying to get it."

"But how dared such an excrescence fall in love with you?" he demanded.

"My dear man," she said with a short laugh, "I don't know about love. But he was received in a lot of places, and I think he thought that marrying a duke's daughter would enable him to be received in more."

"Would you really have married him," he said curiously, "if he had produced the negative?"

"Heaven knows," she answered. "Anyway, the point does not arise. It's the thought of Joe that upsets me so much. They must have been both lying there when I telephoned."

"It was you, was it? We were just outside the window, and it startled us some."

"My dear, I was getting wild with anxiety. I'd arranged for him to meet me here at ten-thirty. And when eleven came with no sign of him I rang up. Tiny—what *are* we to do?"

She rose restlessly and stood by the fireplace.

"Dunno, Mary dear," he said. "I'm absolutely beat."

"Can't Mr. Standish suggest something?"

"I haven't seen him today," said Tiny. "He was going round to see Gillson, and I told him I was coming here."

"I wish she had seen him once. Olga and Joe," she added with a faint smile as she saw the puzzled look on his face. "I'm jumping a bit this morning: nerves all on edge."

"It was impossible, my dear," he answered gravely. "Every other person you meet there is a spy."

"And to think he did it for nothing: that is the wicked part of it. Oh! Tiny, we can't let it be in vain: we *can't*."

"The Lord knows, dear, that those are my sentiments too. And Ronald's as well. But it's the devil and all of a proposition."

"And it will be the end of all things if that photo is published?"

It was a question, but he could see she was clutching at a straw of hope.

"My dear," he said, "as you know, my acquaintance with Bessonian politics is microscopic. All I can tell you is that both Ronald and that fellow Andy Mackintosh, who I was telling you about, view the case as hopeless if Berendosi gets hold of that negative. And now that we've drawn blank in Blake's safe it might be anywhere."

Simmonds opened the door, and entered with a card on a salver.

"Tiny," cried the girl, "it's your pal—Mr. Standish. Show him in at once, Simmonds. Do you think he's thought of something new?"

"We'll soon hear if he has."

He turned as Ronald Standish came in, and it seemed to him as if there was a certain suppressed excitement in the other's face.

"Something fresh," he cried. "Oh! by the way, you two haven't met, have you? My fellow-criminal, Mary . . ."

"Mr. Standish," she said eagerly, "you look as if there was a new development."

"I won't go so far as to say that, Lady Mary," answered Standish, "but we have just obtained a piece of information which *might* lead us somewhere. May I smoke?"

"Please do."

He lit a cigarette, while the others waited breathlessly.

"Tiny, of course, will have told you everything that happened last night. How young Denver went to interview Blake in order to get the negative, and when Blake refused to part he killed him. He took the keys, opened the safe, and later was murdered himself. So much is clear. From now it becomes a question of surmise, with only one fact standing out as certain. And that fact is that the man we saw leaving Blake's house shortly after we heard Denver's scream was either the murderer or knew that he had been murdered."

"Now that action on his part is understandable: he would naturally clear off for fear the scream should attract people to the place. But what is not so understandable is why they should have murdered

160

Denver at all."

"Perhaps Joe had found it," said Tiny, "and he murdered him to get it back."

"The first thought that occurred to me, but there is one insuperable difficulty. We know that poison and its method of working. Take Demeroff: take other cases. It requires at least a quarter of an hour to act. During that quarter of an hour if Denver had found the negative, he might and probably would have destroyed it. Would the murderer, then, dare to have risked it? The film was far more important to him than killing Denver. In fact, the last thing he wanted to do was to kill Denver: he is much more value to the other side alive than dead."

"Anyway he *did* kill him, Ronald—so there is no more to be said."

"But did he *mean* to, Tiny?"

"You mean it was an accident."

"Yes and no. He meant to kill someone—but not Denver. He killed the wrong man."

"But, good Heavens! old man, it's impossible. And anyway, who did he mean to kill?"

"Me," said Standish quietly. "And possibly you."

"But do you mean to say he didn't know he was killing Denver?"

"That is what I mean to say. I admit it sounds wild—almost fantastic. Nevertheless, can you give me any reason whatsoever why the other side should commit such a suicidal act from their point of view as to kill a man who was vitally important to them?"

"I can't. But neither can I give you any reason why they should have imagined we were going to be there at all."

"Let's go on with our surmise, and put ourselves in the other bloke's place—in Zavier's place. Zavier knows that we are fully aware of the existence of that negative: he knows we connect Blake with it: he knows we are in London. Surely his first assumption would be that we would seek an interview with Blake and do our best to get it. He may not have thought we would go as far as burglary, but he must assume on our trying to obtain it. He therefore lays his plans accordingly. He instructs a subordinate—or possibly that was Zavier himself last night—and proceeds, in some mysterious way, which I frankly admit I cannot explain, to lie up for us. First he removes the negative to avoid any possibility of danger to it: then probably in conjunction with Blake he sets the scene. He obviously cannot be present—that would give the whole thing away. And if the plan comes off Blake is safe, because my death would appear as all the other deaths have appeared to be, due to heart trouble.

"Then comes the one thing he had not anticipated. Instead of us appearing, Joe Denver turns up. . . He, as I say, was not there: he was probably hanging about somewhere to see what happened. Nothing at all might have occurred, in which case he would try again next night. Suddenly he hears the scream, and goes in. To his horror he finds Blake murdered and the wrong man dead in the safe. He waits only to remove whatever there was in that room to cause death to Denver, and bolts."

"But, Mr. Standish," cried the girl, "I don't quite see how all this helps. Even if you are right, this man Zavier has the negative. And that's all that matters."

"Sorry to be so long: I'm coming to that now. As you say, that is all that counts, but I wanted to start from the beginning. As I said, he then bolts: we know that—we saw him. Which brings us to the second very peculiar incident, as peculiar in its own way as the killing of Denver. What brought him back again? As Tiny has probably told you, Lady Mary, we saw his footprints in the blood by the window. Why did he return?"

"How do we know it was the same man?" said Tiny.

"Well, it can't have been a policeman or any ordinary outsider: in either of those cases the alarm would have been raised at once. Therefore if it wasn't the same man it was at any rate someone who knew what had happened and so must have been one of the gang. And since the film was safe as far as they were concerned, what object was served by his coming back? This morning I got a possible answer.

"You remember, Tiny, that I took away all the papers from Blake's safe. This morning I went through them with Gillson. Ye gods! the half of that man's vileness has not been thought of. There were letters in his possession belonging to people whose names are household words, and who he has been bleeding to death. Needless to say we burned the lot, with the exception of one most interesting one."

He took from his pocket a legal-looking document.

"This is the lease of 11 Gregory Street. The landlord is, or rather was, Felton Blake: the tenants are three in number. A bookmaker has an office on the first floor: there is a branch of some wholesale hardware store on the second. But the basement is let to an organisation with a somewhat strange name—the Universal Benevolent Society.

"At first sight admittedly there is nothing very peculiar about it, but when we studied it a little closer an interesting point emerged. The first two 'lets' are drawn up in the orthodox legal fashion with rent and all the usual conditions stated, but for the Universal Benevolent Society the document is simply worthless. From a business point of view it has no value whatever. In fact it is not a lease.

"Knowing Felton Blake's characteristics, this seemed strange. He was not the type of man to let the Universal or any other benevolent society have an office without paying for it. And when Gillson's secretary, who was in the room at the time, happened to remember where Gregory Street was, the matter began to take shape. To cut it short, this house abuts on to the back of the Fifty-Nine Club, and the basement therefore is on the level of the dance floor.

"Now you know, Tiny, that for some time past the police have had that club under close supervision. And there have been two or three strange incidents there. The other night, for instance, a man who was well known as a trafficker in drugs came to the club and was spotted by one of our men there, who tipped the wink to his companion upstairs. There was no question of arresting the man—he was only one of the smaller fry: but as a matter of interest they kept an eye on him. Our fellow downstairs was acting as a waiter, and so was not in the room the whole time. And it so happened that he did not actually see this man leave his table. But at some period during the evening he did so, and he did not return. Moreover, he did not go out by the front entrance."

"Your point is, then," said Tiny, "that there is some form of communication between the club and this house in Gregory Street?"

"Exactly. And my further point is that it was to obtain this document, which he had forgotten in the excitement of the moment, that our friend of last night returned. He knew the police would spot it as soon as they came to go through it carefully: and he knew that in a few hours the police must discover the murders and take possession of all the papers. And so he came back to get it, only to find us in occupation."

"But where is all this leading us to, Mr. Standish?" cried the girl, a little impatiently.

"It does seem a bit beside the mark, I agree, Lady Mary," said Standish with a smile, "but I've very nearly finished. You see it has put the gentleman in an awkward quandary. Assuming—and one must make assumptions in a case like this—assuming he has the negative in his possession, his first instinct, realising we are on the trail, would be to take it direct to Berendosi and pocket the money. But he now knows that we are in possession of this information about 11 Gregory Street. He knows that the Universal Benevolent Society has served its turn and must close down. Dare he therefore leave the country until he has closed it down? Which is not likely to be a matter that can be done in two or three hours.

"And so, if you want some fun, go to the Fifty-Nine tonight. Anyway, Tiny, you must go even if Lady Mary doesn't, and you must get a table from which you can command a view of the staircase. At one o'clock the club will be raided, though I promise you that your names shall not appear. At a little before one there will be a certain activity round the office of the Universal Benevolent Society, which I hope may bolt the badger. And even though a raid is on in the club he can only bolt that way. If, as I hope and believe, our badger is Zavier himself, you will recognise him. Then tip the wink to the Inspector in charge of the raid: we'll do the rest."

"But is he likely to have the negative on him, Mr. Standish?" said the girl.

"More than likely. What safer place could there be from his point of view? There is nothing criminal about it. But if by chance we pull it off, I fear that an accident will happen to it."

"By Jove! it sounds possible, old man," cried Tiny. "I'll be there."

"So will I," said the girl excitedly.

"Easy does it," warned Standish. "Don't for Heaven's sake let's build on it. It may come off: there's a bare chance of it's coming off—but that's all."

"Anyway there is a chance," she said. "Which is more than we thought a little while ago."

"What is your part in the show, Ronald?" asked Tiny.

"I shall be with the Number 11 party. It is essential that you should mark one exit while I take the other, because we are the only people who know him."

"Always provided it is Zavier."

"Always provided it is Zavier," agreed Standish, getting up to go. "And somehow, Tiny, I believe we shall find that it is. This whole business is too big for a subordinate. Well—I must be off. And if I don't see you again, be at the Fifty-Nine from midnight onwards. And—*don't* build on it."

But it was well-nigh impossible not to. All through luncheon they fluctuated between hope and despair, and the afternoon seemed to drag on leaden wheels. There was an account of the previous night's tragedy in all the midday papers, but somehow naturally it told them nothing they did not know already. The police, as usual, were in possession of a valuable clue, and further developments were expected at any moment.

At four o'clock Standish rang up.

"Developments, Tiny," he said, "and hopeful ones. There is considerable activity round Number 11. Two car loads of suit-cases and packages of various sorts have been removed, and have been followed to their new destination, where we can lay our hands on them at any time."

"Can't you raid the place now?" asked Tiny.

"Got no warrant. And no magistrate would issue one on our present knowledge. Cheer up, old lad: I'm feeling more confident."

At last midnight came. Their table was almost next to the foot of the stairs leading to the street, which they had insisted on having much to the amazement of the head waiter, who pointed out that it was the worst in the room. The cabaret show was just starting, and having ordered kippers and a bottle they tried to watch it, without, however, much success. Apart from the fact that they had both seen it before, they were far too keyed up to pay any attention.

"What happens in a raid, Tiny?" asked the girl.

"My dear, it's a perfectly harmless proceeding. Some large men will appear on the stairs, and other large men will walk gracefully round the room taking our names and addresses. Hullo! do you see that waiter over there—the one attending to the woman with magenta hair? He is police—one Dexter by name."

And at that moment the man turned and caught Tiny's eye. It was the flicker of an eyelid that he gave, rather than a wink, before he resumed his job, but it was vaguely comforting. It seemed to establish a sort of liaison with the imperturbable Gillson and the powers that be generally.

"Is it my imagination, Mary," said Tiny after awhile, "or is there an air of tension about the place? Giuseppi has been in twice talking to the head waiter, and it strikes me the staff seems uneasy."

He glanced at his watch.

"Quarter of an hour to go. Gad! I wish I knew what was happening next door."

The show was over: dancing had started again. And now there was no mistaking it: something was in the air. Giuseppi had come in again and was gesticulating in a corner with his second in command, while the waiters in their vicinity listened eagerly. Then abruptly the band stopped.

The head waiter issued rapid orders to his underlings: Giuseppi stepped into the middle of the floor.

"Ladies and gentlemens," he called out, "ze police. ."

"Quite so," came a deep genial voice from the stairs, "the police."

A dead silence settled on the room.

"I must ask you, ladies and gentlemen, please to keep your seats. You will not be put to any inconvenience. I shall require your names and addresses, and I may say that I shall view any Mr. Smith of Birmingham with grave suspicion. In the last raid I undertook there were six."

There was a general laugh as he came down the stairs, leaving two men in uniform standing at the top. And the first table he stopped at was Tiny's.

"I need hardly ask your name, sir," he said with a twinkle in his eye. "I've watched you too often at Twickenham. If you see your man, wait till I am talking to him, and then come up to me and ask if you can go."

The whole sentence was spoken without the faintest change of inflection, while the inspector was apparently writing in his book.

"I get you," said Tiny, in the same tone of voice, and the Inspector passed on.

A general buzz of conversation had broken out: the inspector's jovial manner had put everyone in a good temper except Giuseppi whose agitation was obvious. In fact, it seemed to Tiny that it was out of all proportion to what might have been expected from the anticipation of a hundred-pound fine. He watched him closely, and soon he noticed that he was shooting continual little bird-like glances at a far corner of the room. There was a small alcove there containing a table where he had sometimes sat himself, and beyond it was a door with frosted glass marked "Private." He had always assumed it was Giuseppi's office, but now he began to wonder. He made a quick calculation: Gregory Street lay beyond that side of the room. And at that moment he noticed a man with a small pointed beard sitting at a table by himself not far from the alcove.

To Zavier he bore not the slightest resemblance as far as he could see. This man's hair was plentiful while Zavier was bald: moreover Zavier was clean shaven. But those were trifles: wigs were easy to obtain.

What did count was, that whether this man was Zavier or not, he had not been at that table ten minutes previously. Of that fact Tiny was certain. He had happened to notice on glancing round the room earlier that the table next to the one this man now occupied contained a well-known actress in the party, and it had momentarily attracted his attention in that direction. And he was convinced he would have noticed this bearded man if he had been there.

It was the wildest guesswork: he realised that. The man might have been away for a moment, or dancing. But no: he couldn't have been dancing. The cabaret show had been on most of the time. And suddenly he made up his mind.

"Mary—I'm going to chance it," he said. "It may be the most ungodly bloomer, but I can't help that."

"Do you think you've spotted him, Tiny?" she cried eagerly.

"It's that bloke over there with a beaver, sitting next the table where Paula Rayne is. I swear he has only just sat down there."

"Go on, Tiny: it's worth it every time."

He waited until the inspector was about to reach him: then he rose and crossed the room.

"I say, Inspector," he remarked, "is there any jolly old reason why one shouldn't push off?"

He glanced at the man, who was staring at him with unwinking blue eyes.

"Are you quite certain you want to go, sir?" said the inspector quietly.

"I'm never quite certain about anything, dear old lad," laughed Tiny, and at that moment it happened. He had one glimpse of a face distorted with fury glaring into his: then both he and the inspector were on their backs on the floor with the table on top of them and the cloth round their heads.

They scrambled up swearing: the man had disappeared. And after a pause of stupefied silence, everyone near them began talking at once.

"Up there."

"That's where he went."

"Towards the private room."

One of the constables had come running down the stairs, but it was Tiny who headed the pursuit, closely followed by the inspector. They darted along the passage to find a frightened waiter cowering up against the wall.

"Where did he go?" shouted Tiny.

"In there, sir," stammered the man.

And even as he threw himself against the door he noticed it was Number 7.

"Locked," cried Tiny. "All together, boys."

Which proved an admirable prophecy. For at the precise moment they charged the door, it was opened from the inside. And once again the inspector and Tiny found themselves on the floor, with the addition this time of a large constable. They picked themselves up: confronting them was a vacuous-looking youth with an eye-glass, while at the table there sat an extremely frightened girl.

"I say," he bleated, "has the whole place gone bug house? First of all there comes a man with a beard, who locks the door and vanishes through the wall. . ."

"What part of the wall?" snapped the inspector.

"Just there: by the fire-place. . ."

In a couple of strides the inspector reached the spot and hit it with his fist.

"Hollow," he cried. "Once again, sir: all together."

They felt it crack under their weight, and with the third charge it gave way, revealing a narrow brick passage.

"Careful, sir," said the Inspector warningly, as Tiny started along it. "He's probably a dangerous customer."

He turned to the constable. "Get everyone out of the room, except the two who were in there first. Now, sir."

Cautiously they moved forward. The room behind gave them some light to begin with, but after awhile the passage bent left-handed, and almost at once they felt cooler air on their faces. With a grunt the inspector hurried forward: in front of them was a chink of light.

"The damned fellow has done us, sir," he said. "There was a third bolt-hole."

They had emerged into a deserted mews. An old lean-to shed concealed the entrance to the passage: a solitary gas lamp supplied the illumination. Not a soul was in sight, though there was a certain amount of traffic in the street at the end. The spot where they stood formed a *cul-de-sac*, and once again the inspector swore under his breath.

"Staffordale Street," he said. "And we've lost him right enough. Haven't got anyone posted there at all. How did you spot him, sir?" he added curiously.

"I took a chance," said Tiny. "I knew he had not been long at that table: in fact he suddenly arrived."

"Well, he was our bird evidently. Come on, sir: we'd best be getting back. Useless going along the mews: he's got clean away."

They retraced their steps along the passage. The vacuous youth was still declaiming loudly against life in general, and even Tiny, sore though he was at being baulked, couldn't help smiling. To bring a girl out to supper in a private room and then have dozens of people playing leapfrog through it is a trifle disconcerting, to say the least of it.

"Got away, Mary," he said gloomily as he joined her. "There was a secret door in Number 7—the room where you fed with Blake. And he did a bolt through it. Of course that beard was false, and the wig too."

"You'd better wait, sir," said the inspector, coming up to their table. "I'll soon have finished with the rest of these people, and then we'll clear the place. Mr. Standish is here: I've told him about it."

And at that moment they saw him threading his way through the tables towards them.

"Pretty sickening," he said. "Especially after you'd spotted him, Tiny. Evidently Zavier right enough: the inspector mentioned those light-blue eyes of his."

"What are you going to do now, Mr. Standish?" asked the girl.

"Keep a watch at every port for a man with eyes like that," he answered. "Nothing else to be done."

"How went things with you, Ronald," said Tiny. "Did you find out anything?"

"Enough to jug the whole lot," said the other grimly. "We've got one of them under lock and key now. The Universal Benevolent Society still retained on its premises enough drugs to dope an army. The rest they had got rid of this afternoon, as I told you, by taxi. In addition we found the remains of what was obviously a forger's plant in a cellar off the basement. Damn it!" he continued, thumping his fist on the table, "if we'd been one minute earlier we'd have caught him. Or if the police hadn't had to appear to act legally we'd have done it. You see you can't force an entrance to a place without either a warrant or some very good excuse. So as we couldn't get the first, we had to fall back on the second. A little straw was lit and thrown down outside the basement, and that gave us the pretext of fire. It also gave the alarm inside.

"We forced a window, and rushed below. A pale-faced youth was sitting at a table, who rose and demanded what we wanted. We told him we thought the house was on fire, and at that moment I noticed the butt of one of those tiny cigarettes Zavier always smokes. Moreover, it was still smouldering, while the youth had a Gold Flake in his mouth.

"'Where is the man who was here with you?' I cried.

"He denied it, and I pointed to the butt end in front of him. He turned a bit green about the gills when he saw it, but he still continued to stick to his story. In fact he began to bluster, and demanded by what right we dared to intrude.

"'Look at this, sir,' sang out the sergeant to me, and our friend turned greener still.

"'This' was a mass of charred paper in the grate, in which quite a number of fragments were unburned. And anyone could tell at a glance that it was the paper used for counterfeiting banknotes.

"'How came this paper in your possession?' I said, but he merely shook his head. He was only a paid clerk, and knew nothing about it.

"All this time I was wandering round the room trying to find the second exit. That Zavier had been there just before we came, I knew. He couldn't have got out by the stairs, therefore there must be another door. And after a few moments I found it. There was a bookshelf in one corner, and on closer inspection it proved to be a blind. It swung back, revealing a cellar beyond leading out of a passage. The music from here was plainly audible, and while the police searched the cellar I tried to find the communicating door. But it was concealed too well."

"I'll bet it is behind that door marked 'Private,'" said Tiny.

"Probably. Anyway we'll get it from this side, once they've emptied the place. They've had months, you see, to make a good job of things."

"What chance is there of catching Zavier, now?" asked the girl.

"Not so good as half an hour ago, I'm afraid," he admitted. "No good blinding ourselves to the facts. From one point of view this raid has been a brilliant success: but from the point of view that concerns us most it's been a failure. He's slipped through our fingers once again. And the only ray of comfort that I see is that he is bound to try and leave the country sooner or later with the negative on him. He would never dare risk sending it by post to Berendosi. He'll want to see the colour of his money before he hands it over."

The inspector approached the table.

"I've interviewed Giuseppi, sir," he said, "and he either can't or won't say a thing. He is terrified out of his life. Swears he knows nothing about the house next door."

"That's a lie," said Tiny. "You bring him down here, Inspector, and ask him what's behind that glass door over there."

"I'm going to explore that now," said the other.

He signalled to one of his men to fetch the Italian.

"Now, Giuseppi," he remarked curtly, as the proprietor appeared, "we're going to have a little further exploration. Where does that door lead to?"

"To my private room," wailed the other. "I give you my word, sare, ze word of an Italian, zat zere is noddings zere."

"I'd sooner have the key, thank you," laughed the inspector. "Come on, Giuseppi," he added sternly. "Get a move on. If you don't open that door at once I'll break it down."

Protesting volubly the little man produced a bunch of keys and led the way across the room, with the others behind him. And after much fumbling he at length got the door open. It was a small plainly furnished room. Against one wall stood an ordinary roll-top desk: for the rest a couple of easy chairs completed the contents, except for some overcoats which hung on pegs from the wall. And Tiny, happening to glance at Giuseppi, saw that it was at these he was staring.

"What the devil is this?" said Standish suddenly.

He was bending over the paper basket, from which he proceeded to pull out a number of pieces of torn brown cloth. Some of them had been ruthlessly slashed with scissors: others had been ripped by hand. And in a corner of the room was another heap of similar fragments.

They all stared at the Italian, who shrugged his shoulders deprecatingly.

"*Signors*," he said, "it is an old dressing-gown of mine. There are times, you understand, when I take off ze coat and ze waistcoat..."

"Why have you ripped it to pieces?" said Standish curtly.

"It is old, sare. Besides zis afternoon suddenly he annoy me. I like not his colour. I snatch him off: I tear him up."

"You're a pretty bad liar, my lad," said Standish. "Though I frankly admit I can't quite spot where it comes into the general scheme. However, that may come later. Where is the communicating door, Giuseppi?"

"Zere is no such sing, sare," he protested. "Zat is all brick wall behind."

"Get out of the light," snapped the inspector, and pushing the Italian on one side he proceeded to make a minute inspection. And at last he gave a cry of triumph.

"Here we are, Mr. Standish. You can see the crack in the woodwork. Now, see here, Giuseppi—we've wasted enough time already. Get that open, and do it at once. Very well, if you won't—I'll send for a pickaxe."

"Wait a moment, Inspector," said Standish. "Here is a small keyhole."

It was barely visible in the pattern of the wood: anyone not looking for it would never have found it.

"And here's the key that fits it," remarked the inspector quietly, as he examined Giuseppi's bunch. "Do you still pretend you know nothing about it?"

He inserted it in the lock, and gave a heave with his shoulder. Without a sound a part of the wall swung outwards, revealing a passage on the other side.

"Who's there?" came a stern voice, and into the light there stepped a police sergeant in uniform, who saluted as soon as he saw the inspector.

"Number 11 Gregory Street," said Standish. "And what is that I see on the floor?"

He bent and picked up a long brown cord with a tassel at each end.

"This would seem to belong to your dressing-gown, Giuseppi," he said quietly. "One wonders why it should be this side of the door."

Chapter 10

"Well, sir," said the inspector half an hour later, "I don't know that there is anything more to be done here. It's been a magnificent round up."

"Except for the one big fish," answered Standish a little bitterly.

"We'll get him, sir. With those blue eyes of his it's only a question of time."

"And that's the one thing we can't afford at the moment," said the other. "However, as you say it's been very successful as far as it goes. Go through all those books and papers, will you, and let me know anything you may find."

"I will, sir. Goodnight. Goodnight, your ladyship."

The four of them were standing on the pavement outside the entrance to the club. Giuseppi, still protesting volubly, and the youth from Number 11, had both been removed to the police station: the street was empty save for one belated taxi, which Standish inspected carefully before entering.

"I'm taking no risks this trip," he remarked, after giving Lady Mary's address to the driver. "Zavier must be mad as a civet cat with you and me, Tiny. We've completely smashed his organisation here in England, to say nothing of collaring thousands of pounds' worth of dope."

"I wonder if that little sweep Giuseppi is really as ignorant of things as he pretended to be," said Tiny.

"Of course he wasn't ignorant of the fact that those two places have been run in conjunction for months. But I'm not at all sure he wasn't speaking the truth when he said he knew nothing about Zavier. I tried him suddenly with the name, as you heard, and though I watched him closely I believe his ignorance there was genuine. It's a damned interesting business, and if it wasn't for the other affair I should be loving life."

"It's that that is worrying me so frightfully," said the girl. "We don't seem to be any better off there."

The taxi had stopped outside her house.

"Cheer up, Lady Mary," he cried. "We haven't lost yet by a long chalk."

But his face was grave and preoccupied as they drove back to Tiny's rooms.

"What do you think his next move will be, Ronald?"

"He will either try and leave the country at once, or he'll have a dip at you and me. My own candid opinion is the latter. You and I are the only two people who have seen him, and who know him for what he is. All the other people who have had dealings with him— Berendosi and the rest of them—have no idea whatever that he is a cold-blooded murderer. We do, and as long as we are alive he's not safe. We've broken up his show here, so the probability is that once he is out of the country it will be some time before he returns. And that is why I think he will try and do us in before he goes. He's desperate, and he'll run a big risk to get us out of the way. So for the love of Allah, old man, keep your eyes skinned."

"I'll do that all right. It's this cursed negative I'm thinking of."

"I agree. But the two things march together. If he gets us goodbye to any chance of ever seeing it."

The taxi pulled up, and Tiny got out. He cast a searching look up and down the street: as far as he could see there wasn't a soul in sight.

"Good night, old lad," said Standish. "Inspect your room with a microscope: sleep with your window shut: and meet me at Gillson's office at eleven tomorrow. We may hear something fresh about to-night's raid."

But though Tiny undressed he could not sleep. It was already dawn: his thoughts kept whirling chaotically. Round and round in a vicious circle they went, always finishing up with the negative. Had it all been in vain? Was this swine Zavier going to do them after all?

He went over the events of the night once more, Surely some-where amongst the mass of papers they had obtained, they would find something which would put them on his trail. And then those bits of torn brown cloth. He had noticed that Ronald Standish had seemed strangely interested over them. Again and again his eyes had returned to the basket with a thoughtful look in them, as if he felt some clue lay there. And yet what could it be? That Giuseppi had lied over the dressing-gown was obvious, but beyond that it did not seem to advance them much.

In a way it was Mary he felt most sorry for. She had done so much—striven so hard, and though she had said very little, he knew how bitterly she had felt the disappointment. What a darling she was! He rose and began to pace up and down the room. Once or twice the previous day words had been trembling on the tip of his tongue—words he had bitten back. Instinctively he had felt that until this matter was settled one way or the other she would resent anything at all personal. Afterwards it would be different, and somehow he felt distinctly hopeful. There had been a moment in the taxi coming home, and another at supper before the raid, when he thought he had read the unmistakable message in her eyes. But for the time being all that must be in abeyance: to get on with the job was the order of the day.

At last he heard Murdoch moving about, and ringing the bell he ordered some breakfast. He wanted exercise: for the past week he seemed to have been permanently sitting in trains. And a brisk four miles finishing up with a bathe at the R.A.C. made life seem distinctly better.

It was still some time before he was to meet Standish at the Home Office, and going into the smoking-room he glanced over the morning papers. "The Hampstead Mystery," as it was called, occupied a prominent place in them all, and he picked up the *Daily Leader*.

"There is no doubt," ran the paragraph, "that Mr. Felton Blake was first stabbed by the young man who was found dead by the safe.

The fingerprints on the handle of the dagger proves this conclusively. So that over his death there is no mystery. The strange part of the affair is the death of the murderer, who is at present unidentified. What happened in that room while the owner of the house lay dead on the floor? The safe was empty. What happened to the papers in the safe? Above all, who was the third man whose footprint was found in the blood by the window, a footprint which could not have been made by either of the dead men?"

He laid down the paper, and lit a cigarette. Precisely: what had happened to him? It was a question they all wanted answered. And then his thoughts turned to Standish's theory. Could it be correct, could it be that Joe Denver's death was an error, and unintentional? If so, what was this diabolical contrivance they were up against that murdered blindly?

It seemed almost incredible, and yet he was forced to admit that there was some force in Standish's argument. Once granted the negative had first been removed, why kill Denver? What possible object could it serve? No one but a madman murders needlessly.

At length he rose: he would go round and see Ronald. Then they could go together to meet Gillson. The more he thought over things the more hopelessly befogged did he feel: sitting still was an impossibility. He walked quickly, hardly noticing the greetings of two or three men he knew who passed him. And it was not until he turned into the street where Standish lived that he paused, his eyes narrowed, a sudden dreadful presentiment clutching at him. For outside his friend's house a crowd had gathered, and two policemen were standing in the door.

He elbowed his way through the people, heedless of angry remarks, and approached one of the constables.

"What has happened?" he said. "I was just coming round to see the gentleman who lives here."

"Well, sir," answered the man gravely, "I'm afraid you won't be able to. He's dead: burned to death."

"What!" shouted Tiny. "Good God! man, it's impossible. Why, I only left him three or four hours ago."

"Sorry, sir, but it's the truth. Fire engine's been gone some time."

"Can I go in?" said Tiny dazedly.

"No admittance, sir, unless the inspector gives permission," said the constable firmly.

"Where is the inspector? Ah! there he is."

It was the same officer who had raided the Fifty-Nine, and the instant he saw Tiny he beckoned him in.

"This is a bad business, sir," he said gravely.

"But it's unbelievable," cried Tiny. "Mr. Standish—burned to death."

The inspector looked at him queerly.

"There's a bit more in this than meets the eye, sir. It's the rummiest fire I've ever seen."

"Damn the fire. Is he dead?"

"Yes, sir: he's dead, I'm sorry to say. Do you want to see him? It's not a pretty sight."

He followed the officer dazedly: the thing was so utterly unexpected that he felt stunned. It was inconceivable, a fantastic nightmare: he'd wake up soon, and find he'd been dreaming.

"There, sir." The inspector opened the door of the room from which Ronald and he had started for their expedition to Felton Blake, and it was a moment or two before he could force himself to enter. The smell of smouldering wood was heavy in the air: the charred and blackened desk, dripping with water from the fire engine, was still smoking. But it was not on that that his eyes were riveted: it was on the twisted figure lying by the hearth-rug. The knees were drawn up almost to the chin, and by one blistered hand there lay the remnant of the cloth which had covered the little table standing by the arm-chair—the table on which his reading-lamp had always stood. It had been a fad of Ronald's—an oil lamp to read by, and now it lay smashed to pieces on the floor beside the body.

Here too everything was sopping wet: the rug, the chair, the body itself had all come under the hose. And at last with an effort he took a few steps forward and looked at the face. It was burned beyond recognition: a gruesome, terrible sight.

"My God! Inspector," he muttered, "it's awful. When did it happen?"

"Early this morning, sir," said the other.

"We went back with Lady Mary, and then he dropped me, and came on here."

"That would be about it, sir. It was dawn when the man on duty on this beat, saw smoke coming out of the window. He rang up the fire station at once, and they had no difficulty in putting it out. Apparently the oil was concentrated in a pool by his head, and was already nearly burned out. Then in the ordinary course of events the Yard was notified. Now I was still working on the papers we got tonight, but as soon as I heard where the fire was I made a point of coming round myself. As you see, the features are unrecognisable. But that's the suit he was wearing: and that's the tie and tiepin he had on last night."

"Moreover," said Tiny, stooping down and looking at one of the hands, "that is his signet ring."

"It's Mr. Standish, sir, right enough," went on the other gravely. "But it's a mighty queer thing. I'd very much like to know what happened. The doctor suggests that he tried to beat out the flames with his hands: but it won't do, sir—it don't hold together."

"Why do you say that, Inspector?" said Tiny slowly.

"Try and reconstruct it, sir, and you'll see for yourself. Mr. Standish wasn't an invalid, or a cripple. He wasn't a man who suffered from heart trouble or fainting fits. There is that cloth by his hand, so it's clear that it was pulling it off the table that upset the lamp. But why should he pull the cloth off the table?"

"He might have fainted," suggested Tiny, "and clutched at the table to save himself."

"Even then, sir, a faint is a faint. That"—he pointed to the blackened face—"didn't take place in a minute, nor yet in two. Do you mean to tell me, that the agony which must have been caused by a burn like that wouldn't have brought him to. And then he wouldn't have gone on lying there. He'd have dashed about the room: he'd have shouted, put his coat over his head—done something, at any rate."

"What do you suggest, then?" said Tiny.

"He was dead before he fell, sir. It's another of the same cases. We know all about them at the Yard, and if Mr. Standish was right, and it's that man that gave us the slip who is at the bottom of them, it's he who was responsible for this. We know that poison acts suddenly at the last moment, and I believe that as he died he, as you said, clutched at the table, pulled off the cloth as he fell, and upset the lamp. But he was dead before he was burned."

"I believe you are right, Inspector," said Tiny slowly.

A cold, over-mastering rage was getting hold of him, the more dangerous because he was a man who was slow to anger. First Denver: then Ronald—his greatest friend.

"By the living God above," he went on quietly, "I'll get even with the fiend who did this thing. If it's Zavier, then Zavier shall pay to the uttermost farthing. If it's someone else, I'll get him if it takes me years."

The inspector shook his head gravely.

"Be careful, sir. For unless I'm much mistaken, you are the next on the list."

"So much the better," said Tiny, his jaw set like a steel trap. "And even if I swing for it, Inspector, I'll kill the man who did this, so that his screams will be heard at the other end of London."

He turned on his heel abruptly, and left the room. Through the crowd outside he passed as if they were non-existent, and hailed a taxi. He would see Mary first, then he would put his affairs in order. And after that. . .

"I must see her ladyship, Simmonds. I can't help it if she is still in bed. Ask her to put on a wrap and come down to the *boudoir*."

Something in his face precluded further argument, and the butler went off to find Lady Mary's maid. And a few minutes later she came downstairs.

"What is it, Tiny?" she cried anxiously. "What's happened?"

"They've got Ronald," he said grimly. "Murdered him last night after he got back to his rooms."

Slowly the colour ebbed from her face, as she stared at him speech-lessly.

"I've just been round there, and seen the dear old chap's body," he went on in the same ominous voice.

She listened in silence while he told her what had happened: then she went up to him and put her hands on his shoulders.

"I'm dreadfully sorry," she said gravely. "Sorry for him, and sorry for you too, old Tiny, for I know what pals you were. But it's not going to alter our plans, is it?"

"How do you mean, Mary?" he said.

"I mean that we—you and I—go on just the same," she cried. "We won't give up hope till the end."

"You bet your life we won't," he answered savagely. "There are several items now on Mister Zavier's account which have got to be settled. But there's just one thing, Mary dear, I'd like to say."

He hesitated a moment, and she didn't hurry him: only looked steadily into his eyes.

"I'm under no delusions," he went on quietly, "as to my capabili-ties. I'm a pretty average damned fool, and if this swine can catch a man like Ronald napping, the chances are that he will catch me as well."

Her hands tightened on his shoulders, but she still said nothing.

"I hadn't meant to say anything at present," he continued, "but this has altered things. You see, dear, as Ronald said last night after we left you, he and I were bound to be the object of Zavier's attentions, and now that he has been got it's my turn next. And in case he succeeds again I'd like you to know that what I said the other day wasn't a jest. I meant it with every fibre of my being. I love you."

"Same here, Tiny," she answered quietly. "In fact I've done so for a considerable time," she added with a little laugh.

"Mary, my dear."

His arms went round her, and for a moment or two she let him hold her with his lips on hers. Then very gently she pushed him away.

"For we'd never look each other straight in the face again," she said, "if we didn't do our damndest to beat this brute. So this is dangerous, old man—too dangerous altogether. It makes one want to ease up."

"My dear," he said, "believe me there was no thought of that in my mind."

"There was in mine, Tiny. Do you suppose, dear man, that I don't realise the danger you are running. And the mere thought of it makes me sick. So I want you to realise that I'm in it with you. Two heads are better than one, and it's more than likely I can help."

He looked at her doubtfully.

"I don't like it, my dear," he said slowly. "It's an infernal risk."

"Dry up," she laughed. "I don't know that I'll be able to do anything, but I'm going to have a shot at it. Now first of all let's try and see exactly where we stand."

"Not much difficulty about that, dear," he said shortly. "Zavier is after me, and I'm after Zavier. And if I was making a book I know which of the two would start favourite. I'm no match for the swine in cunning. Moreover, the devil of it is that as far as I can see it's a question of sitting down and waiting for him to strike. One can't go wandering through the streets of London looking for a man with light-blue eyes."

"If he strikes, Tiny," she said thoughtfully, "he's going to strike soon. He's not going to stop in this country a day longer than he can help. So we've just got to sit in one another's pockets for the next few days. Perhaps he'll make a slip: that's all we can hope for. You go round now to the Home Office and see this pal of yours there. Find out if anything fresh has materialized, and then come back here for lunch."

"Right you are, my dear." He caught her in his arms once again. "You adorable person," he muttered, and was gone.

He glanced up and down the street as he left, though he realised the futility of the precaution. If skilled men had failed to spot the enemy, he was hardly likely to succeed. Then he chartered a taxi and drove to the Home Office. He found Gillson as quiet and impassive as ever, studying the documents obtained in last night's raid.

"By God! Colonel," he burst out, "this is a foul business. I still simply can't believe it."

"Pretty grim, Carteret," said the other gravely. "I heard you'd been round."

"Do you agree with the Inspector that he was murdered?" asked Tiny.

"Looks remarkably like it," answered Gillson. "Well—that is the end of it."

"End of it be damned," cried Tiny. "You don't imagine I'm going to let this drop now, do you? Zavier may get that negative through to Berendosi—that I'm afraid he's bound to do now. But he's killed my best pal, and either he or I are going to follow Ronald."

"Good for you, Carteret." A gleam of approval showed in Gillson's eyes. "But I'm afraid you will find the dice loaded pretty heavily against you."

"No one realises that more than I do," said the other doggedly. "But it just can't be helped. Have you found out anything from those?"

He pointed to the papers on the table.

"A lot," answered Gillson. "Enough to put half a dozen of them in prison for a long stretch, But of the one vital thing we wanted—not a word. There is nothing that gives us a clue to Zavier, or his main headquarters."

A clerk entered with a type-written sheet of paper.

"Will that do, sir?" he said handing it to Gillson, who read it.

"That is all right," he answered. And then, on a sudden impulse he passed it to Tiny, it ran:

A shocking tragedy occurred in the early hours of this morning, which but for the prompt action of the Fire Brigade might have ended in a disastrous fire. Smoke was seen issuing from one of the rooms of 10 Hooper Street by a constable on duty. He gave the alarm at once, and the outbreak was soon extinguished. Unfortunately the owner of the rooms, Mr. Ronald Standish, perished in the flames. His body was discovered afterwards so badly burned as to be practically unrecognisable. Identification was only possible through the deceased man's clothes and his signet ring. The accident appears to have been caused by an oil reading-lamp upsetting.

Without a word Tiny handed it back, and not until the clerk left the room did he speak.

"For the Press, I suppose," he said. "Why no word about the murder?"

"What's the good?" answered the other. "There is enough hue and cry already without adding to it."

He rose and stood by the window, hands deep in his trouser pockets, and Tiny contemplated his back with rising anger.

"Damn it! Colonel," he exploded at length, "you seem to take the old chap's murder pretty calmly."

"How else is one to take it, Carteret?" said Gillson. "There is no good running round in small circles biting the blotting paper. They've got Ronald, and there is no more to be said."

"Isn't there, by Jove," cried the other. "Do you imagine I'm going to let the matter drop?"

"Well—what do you propose to do?"

"Find this man Zavier if it takes me the rest of my life."

"How are you going to set about it? Look here, my dear fellow," went on Gillson kindly, "I know what you are feeling: I know you are mad with rage. But don't let that distort your vision. As I've told you, the dice are loaded far too heavily against you. And for any chance of success we have got to get them a bit more evenly balanced."

"How do you suggest we should do it?" demanded Tiny.

"Ever done any big-game shooting, Carteret?"

Tiny stared at him in amazement.

"No—never."

"First you get a nice tree, and in that tree you build yourself a place where you can sit. Then you get a goat and you put it on the ground not far from the tree. Then you wait for the tiger to come and feed. And then you shoot the tiger—perhaps."

He swung round and faced Tiny, with the glint of a smile in his eyes.

"See the point?"

"Can't say I do."

"You are the goat. Only I'd prefer that you come out of the performance alive."

"Deuced considerate of you, Colonel," said Tiny with a grin.

"The flying fellers did it in the war," went on the other. "Sent slow machines over the Boche lines fairly low to attract the wily Hun. Then when Fritz was engaged in what looked like a soft job our fast fighters, who had been up much higher, came down on top of him. Bait, young Carteret—that is what you have got to be. Provided, of course, you feel like going on with it."

"You can take that for granted," answered Tiny quietly.

"Good for you. Though I tell you quite candidly that I don't think the decision lies in your hands. Whether you want to or not, you'll have to go through with it: the other bloke is going to see to that. He wants your head on a charger, and he won't feel safe until he's got it."

"Quite a number of people seem to share your opinion," remarked Tiny resignedly. "But there's one point, since we are on the subject, that might be a bit clearer. The goat we know, and the tiger, but who is the bird who is going to sit in the tree?"

"I'll see to that, Carteret," said the other. "You'll have to trust me there implicitly. All I propose to tell you is that he's the best man available, and if it is humanly possible he won't let you down."

"Well, if that's all you can tell me, I suppose I'll have to be content with it. What do you want me to do?"

"Nothing," answered the other. "Just live your ordinary life as if this affair had never been. Of what to warn you against, I know no more than you. We're still as much in the dark as ever as to how he commits these murders. So take every precaution you can, and we can only hope for the best. If he thinks you've dropped the thing, he may get careless."

He rose and held out his hand.

"Good luck, Carteret. It's not a pleasant job: in fact it's damned unpleasant. But I'd like to feel we'd got a bit of our own back over Ronald."

"By Gad! you're right, sir," cried Tiny. "So the motto is, *Business as usual.*"

"That's it," said the other, and Tiny turning at the door saw that Gillson was already immersed again in the documents in front of him.

He walked slowly along the passage and out into the street. That Gillson was right, he realised. Since the chances of his finding Zavier in London were infinitesimal, the only thing to do was to wait until Zavier found him. And that was a simple matter, especially if he lived his normal life. His rooms were known: his club was known: there was no secrecy about his movements. In fact it all seemed delightfully simple—a feeling doubtless shared by the goat.

He paused in the Park, and looked behind him. Was one of that hurrying crowd the man with the gun who was sitting in the tree? And was another of them the tiger? And then he realised suddenly that he was doing a foolish thing. When it is business as usual, one does not stop and peer into the faces of passers-by. If he was going to play the part he would play it properly. He would blot out the events of the last few days from his mind as Gillson had said. Was it not beer time, and there was at least an hour before he was due to lunch with Mary.

He strolled along Pall Mall, and turned into his club. Already the news about Ronald seemed to have got round, and he was immediately besieged by members clamouring for details. Mindful of the official statement he had been shown he made no mention of the word murder, and as soon as he could he shook them off and buried himself behind a paper. Here at any rate he could relax: Zavier couldn't get him in his own club.

And that brought him back to the question of Mary. When they had decided to join forces, he had not seen Gillson. The whole thing had been vague and indefinite. Now a very different complexion had been put on the matter. In the *rôle* of goat which he now had to fill, the one place of all others where she must not be was anywhere near him. The danger was far too great.

He hesitated for awhile as to whether he would ring her up and say he was not coming to lunch, but thinking it over he decided to go after all. There was a lot to explain to her, and it could not be done over the telephone. But lunch was going to be positively their last appearance together until things were settled one way or the other. She would make a fuss about it, he knew, but her objections would have to be got over. It would cramp his style and spoil his nerve far too much if he felt there was any risk for her. The game had got to be played as a lone hand, with the man in the tree a shadowy figure in the background.

At a quarter to one he left the club, wondering what was the best way to persuade her. If he stressed the danger side of it it was quite sufficient to make a girl like her all the more determined to face it with him. And if he did not there was no valid reason why she should back out. And he was still undecided when he pressed the bell. He would have to stress the point that it would make it more difficult for him.

Mechanically he handed his hat and stick to Simmonds, and walked towards the *boudoir*, suddenly to become aware that the butler was delivering himself of startled noises.

"What's the matter?" he said turning round. "Her ladyship is expecting me to lunch, isn't she?"

"But, sir," stammered the man, "Her ladyship went with you to Paris by the midday boat train."

Tiny stood very still. The statement was so staggeringly unexpected, that for a moment or two his brain refused to act. All that he was conscious of was the monotonous ticking of the hall clock.

"What in Heaven's name are you talking about?" he got out at length. "To Paris—with me?"

"Well, sir, I'll tell you what happened. And Janet here can bear me out."

Tiny looked round to see that the maid had appeared, and was looking at him in amazement.

"About half an hour after you left this morning, sir," went on the butler, "a lady called. She wanted to see her ladyship and she told me to say that she was a friend of a Countess Mazarin. Also that it was urgent, and that she had just come from you. She held a letter in her hand, sir, which however, she did not give to me. I at once told Janet, and as her ladyship was dressed she came down immediately. She took the letter, and read it through standing here in the hall. And then, sir, though it didn't strike me at the time, not thinking that anything could be wrong, a most extraordinary expression came on her face. She had half turned her back on the other lady, and only I could see it. It was—how shall I say, sir—sort of half puzzled and amazed. And then it changed. Her frown went away, and she got that look, sir, that I remember when she was a kiddy, and was told not to do a thing she wanted to do. She'd made up her mind.

"'There's only just time to catch the train,' she said, turning to the other lady. 'Will you walk into my parlour?' she went on, and it was such a funny thing for her to say, that I stared at her—'Will you walk into my parlour while I throw a few things into a bag?'

"She went upstairs, sir, and for some reason Janet wasn't there. Anyway she was down again in a minute carrying her little dressing-case. Then she went into the *boudoir*, and the two of them came out together.

"'I hadn't expected to go to Paris at quite such short notice,' she said as she passed me, 'I do hope Mr. Carteret will catch the train.'

"And that's all I know, sir. But you will understand how surprised

I was to see you."

"What on earth can it all mean?" said Tiny dazedly. "I never had the slightest intention of going to Paris."

Mechanically he had opened the door of the *boudoir*, and now he stood staring round the room. A letter was lying on the writing-table, and as his eyes fell on it they slowly dilated in amazement. Then, heedless of the two servants, he darted across the room and picked it up, it ran:

A scrawl, dear, to say that the most extraordinary development has taken place. The bearer of this note is a pal of Nada Mazarin, who is in Paris now. She wants us both to go over there by the eleven o'clock boat train. Hotel Majestic. Will catch it if I possibly can. Tiny.

He stood by the table as if carved out of stone while the two servants watched him anxiously.

"Is this the note that woman brought?" he asked at length.

"From the glimpse I got of the envelope, sir," said Simmonds, "it looks the same writing."

"I suppose we are not all mad," remarked Tiny.

He read through the note once again: then with a hopeless gesture he threw it back on the desk. *For the writing was the writing of Ronald Standish.*

"For the love of *Allah*, Simmonds, give me a drink. I've got to try and think this thing out."

He threw himself into a chair. What on earth did the thing mean? Why should Ronald write a letter to her and sign it "Tiny" after he was dead? For a time a wild hope surged up in him. Did it mean that Ronald was alive: that the scorched and blackened body had belonged to someone else? But he soon dismissed the possibility, principally because he failed to see, even with the wildest stretch of imagination, what possible object could have been served by sending such a note if it was Ronald who had done it. He would have known that Mary would spot it at once as a forgery.

A forgery: the thing was a forgery. That was obvious. Someone had written her a note purporting to come from him, and had committed the trifling error of employing the wrong writing. How it had happened was beside the point: even the fact that it was Ronald's writing was not the main issue—as far as he knew Mary had never seen it. But she had sampled his own often enough. Therefore, she had realised it was a forgery. Why, then, had she gone to Paris?

And gradually light dawned on him. Deliberately, and with her eyes open she had walked into the trap. Her remark to the woman which had stuck in Simmonds' mind came back to him.

"Will you walk into my parlour?"

He supplied the end without difficulty. With complete disregard of danger she had elected to play the *rôle* of the fly, in an endeavour to locate the spider. He could see it all: the puzzled frown as she first read the letter: the sudden set of that small jaw as she came to a decision. And then the calm carrying through of the thing so that the woman should not suspect that she suspected.

"You priceless kid," he muttered ecstatically.

She had left the letter there on the desk on purpose that he should see it. She knew that the instant he did, he would realise the error, and act accordingly. And she had been careful not even to telephone him, for fear of rousing the woman's suspicions. All the information he required was given by the note.

Exactly: and the fact started another train of thought. What was their object in getting Mary to Paris. Obviously as bait for him. It was Gillson's plan over again, only this time he was to be the tiger and Mary the goat. And suddenly he began to laugh: they did not lack audacity.

He grew grave again. Astoundingly plucky though she was, this was no show for a girl to be in alone. It was time he got a move on. The Hotel Majestic was his destination, and at once. Gillson's instructions must go by the board: this development altered everything. Mary was first, second and last. The two o'clock service would not get him there until ten, which was too late. A special aeroplane was the only thing.

"Get me a car, Simmonds," he cried. "At once. Then ring up the Home Office."

He would speak to Gillson, explaining what had happened. But when he got through Gillson was not to be found, nor had he arrived at his club. And so he scribbled a note, and gave it to Simmonds to send round. Then, the car having arrived, he started for Croydon, nearly knocking down a man from the Telephone Exchange as he ran down the steps.

"Bloke seems in a bit of an 'urry," said the man. "Is this 'ere the habode of Lady Mary Ridgeway?"

"It is," said Simmonds. "And what might you be wanting?"

186

"She's put in a complaint about the hextension of 'er telephone. Lead me to it, Gussie."

"In there," remarked Simmonds coldly. "And kindly reserve your funny business for them that appreciate it."

"Try sitting on a drawing pin, Adolphus," laughed the other. "You look dead from the neck down. This room, is it?"

He went to the instrument, and for a few moments Simmonds watched him from the door. Then he stalked majestically to his own quarters.

And with his departure the interest of the telephone operator in his job faded rapidly. His eyes darted round the room, to rivet themselves on the note Tiny had thrown down on the desk. And if Tiny had been amazed, this man seemed literally dumbfounded as he read the letter.

A door opened somewhere, and he returned to the instrument.

"Seems all right now, Clarence," he said as Simmonds reappeared. "Only I won't guarantee it if you breathe down it. So long, matey."

Two hours later the second private aeroplane of the day rose from Croydon. Moreover, its occupant bore a striking resemblance to a certain very temporary member of the London telephone staff.

CHAPTER 11

It was seven o'clock that night that Tiny realised how completely he had blundered. Since five he had been sitting in the entrance-hall of the Majestic, watching the door. A consignment of Americans from London had arrived by the Golden Arrow: a few more people had come by the ordinary boat train, but of Mary there had been no sign. And at last he saw what a fool he had been. The other side had never had any intention of her going to the Majestic at all.

He marvelled that such an obvious point could have escaped him. How could they let Mary meet him in a crowded hotel lounge? Believing as they did that the letter they had forged to her was in his writing, they would assume that she was quite unsuspicious. But at the first word she spoke to Tiny she would realise the whole trap. That, naturally, was the way they must look at it.

So it boiled down to the fact that he had come at maximum speed to the one spot in the whole of Europe where there was not the slightest chance of finding her. And the point now arose as to what would be the next move on their part. That Zavier would know by this time that he had come to the Majestic was practically a certainty.

Any one of the men—or women—sitting round him might be a spy. So what was going to happen now?

He could do nothing himself except sit and wait. It was the *rôle* of the goat to perfection, and had it not been for the maddening anxiety over Mary he could have obtained a certain amount of cynical amusement out of it. But what were they doing with her? Common sense told him that it was unlikely she would come to any physical harm: from Zavier's point of view such a thing would be foolish, because it was unnecessary. And as long as she continued to act her part of suspecting nothing she would, at any rate, be safe. Nevertheless, the mere thought of her playing a lone hand drove him nearly crazy with worry. She might be literally anywhere: she might not even be in Paris. If he could even know that it would be something.

And it was at that stage in his reflections that happening to look up he saw one of Cook's couriers standing by the concierge's desk. The man caught his eye at the same moment, and after a momentary hesitation saluted. And it suddenly dawned on Tiny that not only was he from the Gare du Nord, but that he was the identical man who had on one occasion looked after Mary and a pal of hers who was ill, when they were going to Nice. Tiny had gone as far as Paris with them himself, and he recognised the man perfectly. He was evidently fixing up some luggage question, and acting on a sudden impulse Tiny crossed and spoke to him. Only a hundred-to-one chance? but still a chance. Had he seen Mary?

"Lady Mary Ridgeway, sir? Why, funnily enough—I did. I was standing outside, where you get a taxi, and I saw her plain."

"Was anyone with her?"

"Another lady, sir. They got into a car and drove off."

"What sort of a car?"

"A big private one, sir. One of the large Renaults."

"You didn't hear where they went?"

"No, sir: I didn't. They just got in and the car went straight away."

The man hesitated a moment, and looked at Tiny curiously.

"Seemed to me, sir, as if her ladyship was expecting someone. She kept looking round over her shoulder, and peering into the crowd."

Tiny thanked him and resumed his seat. Of course, she'd been looking for him. He should have met the train, not sat doing nothing in the hotel. And yet as things panned out he couldn't have done much good. Following a Renault is somewhat beyond the powers of a Paris taxi. For all that he cursed himself for not having been there:

he would have stopped the whole thing then and there.

In an overwhelming wave all his fears had come back to him. There was something ominous about that big car driving straight away, without a word to the driver. Just one more link in the skilfully constructed chain that seemed to be tightening round them. And there was a ruthless efficiency about it all that made him feel helpless. If only he could do something, and not merely have to sit and wait.

At length he went in to dinner. Either there would be a further development soon, or they were going to try and get him in the hotel: anyway food was indicated. He had had nothing to eat since breakfast, and hunger is a bad preparation for a crisis. And he felt instinctively that one was approaching: Zavier would not delay an instant longer than necessary. He glanced round the room wondering if any of his fellow-diners were even shadowing him. Most of them were in evening clothes, and it was at the others that he principally directed his attention. But after a while the futility of the proceeding struck him, and he concentrated on his meal. They could recognise him, and he couldn't recognise them; at that it had to be left.

Suddenly he became aware that a new-comer had sat down at the next table. He was a thin, sandy haired little man, and his clothes—although scrupulously neat—showed signs of wear. The elbow he lifted as he studied the menu shone suspiciously in the light, and Tiny shrewdly suspected that the seat of his trousers would reveal the same story. In short, not the type of customer one would expect at the Majestic, and for that reason Tiny studied him covertly.

After a while he realised the man was shooting quick little bird-like glances at him, and instantly all his suspicions were aroused. Was the next move about to start? He continued his dinner calmly, only moving his chair just sufficiently to enable him to watch the man more easily. A feeling of relief had come over him: anything was better than inaction. And he felt certain the new-comer was one of the players.

It was ten minutes, however, before the game started, and then the opening gambit was so unexpected that he almost decided he had been mistaken.

"I suppose, sir, you can't tell me what has happened in the Yorkshire and Middlesex match?"

Tiny stared at him blankly: so the man was English.

"I'm afraid I can't," he said at length. "You are interested in cricket?" he added perfunctorily.

"Very. I play for my bank here."

A bank clerk, was he? And bank clerks do not generally dine at the Majestic.

"Am I right, sir, in supposing that you are Mr. Carteret, the Rugby player?"

Getting down to it, reflected Tiny, but what the deuce was coming next?

"My name is Carteret," he answered briefly.

"I thought so," said the other. "It was lucky I'd seen your photograph so often in the papers, otherwise I might not have been able to help the lady."

"What's that; you're saying?" said Tiny tensely.

"There's danger, sir, danger. Finish your dinner quickly and come to the bar. I daren't talk here."

"I've finished," said Tiny. "I'll wait for you there."

He settled his bill, and left the room. Then he went to the bar where the other joined him almost immediately.

"Now, sir," he said, after a cautious glance round. "I'll tell you all I know. I'd been on my bicycle to see some friends outside Paris, and I came back through the Porte de la Gare. That would be about half-past six. Drawn up by the side of the road was one of the big Renaults, and inside it were two ladies. Something had evidently gone wrong, because the bonnet was up and the chauffeur and another man were bending over the engine. Just as I got alongside, one of the ladies got out and went and stood by the two men. She seemed to be talking to them earnestly.

"Well, I don't know why, but I happened to look at the other one who was still inside the car, and it fairly gave me a shock. She was staring at me fixedly, and suddenly she deliberately opened the window and dropped her vanity bag on the road. Deliberately, sir: no question of an accident. Of course, that attracted my attention still more. I was pushing my machine at the time, and I stopped at once and handed back the bag.

"She took it, and at the same instant, I felt a twisted note pushed into my hand.

"'*Merci*,' she said.

"'Not at all,' I answered.

"'Thank God! you're English,' she muttered. 'Give that to Mr. Carteret—Majestic Hotel. There's danger. It's urgent.'

"'The football player?' I asked.

"'That's the one,' she answered, and then she gave a smile. 'Thank you so much for picking it up.'

"For a moment I couldn't understand: then I saw the other lady was watching us. So I took off my hat, and mounted my bike."

"Have you got the note?" interrupted Tiny.

"Here it is, sir."

He handed the slip of paper to Tiny, who unrolled it eagerly. Inside, in a hurried scrawl which, however, was obviously Mary's, was the one word "Brig."

"What the devil does it mean?" he muttered.

"Well, Mr. Carteret," said the other a little apologetically, "I have to admit that I took a liberty. The whole thing was so strange that when I got out of sight I dismounted and opened the note. 'Brig,' I said to myself, 'that's a funny message.' And after a time I turned my machine and rode back again, to find that the car had gone. Now I happen to know one of the men at that gate very well—I use it a lot—and acting on an impulse I decided to have a talk with him. Quite casually I turned the conversation round to the big car.

"It appeared that the chauffeur had been cursing like blazes at the breakdown, because he had such a long drive in front of him. My pal had said that there was a second driver, and the chauffeur had remarked that they wanted three on such a trip.

"'Four hundred and fifty kilometres to the frontier,' he had grumbled, 'and another two hundred on.'

"Well, that was all I could get out of him, so I got on my bike again and went back to my rooms. Now it so happens that I'm a bit of a map fiend, and what with this curious message and the chauffeur's remarks, I got down some of my maps and had a look. And I can't help thinking I've solved it: in fact I'm sure I have."

"What do you make of it?" said Tiny eagerly.

"First of all, Mr. Carteret, take the gate they were leaving by—the Porte de la Gare. That's the gate you leave by for Dijon, and after that Switzerland."

He paused impressively, while Tiny possessed his soul in patience.

"Secondly," went on the little man, "the Swiss frontier is just about four hundred and fifty kilometres from Paris."

"By Jove!" said Tiny, as Ronald's words in Lausanne came back to him. "I believe you're right."

"Well, if I'm right so far, sir, I have solved it. Brigue, which is the Swiss end of the Simplon tunnel, is another two hundred or so kilometres farther on. They spell it both ways—Brigue and Brig."

He glanced at his watch.

"Just half-past eight, Mr. Carteret. There's a train at 9.10. If you hurry you can catch it."

For a moment Tiny hesitated. Was it genuine, or was it all part of some elaborate trap? And then with a shrug of his shoulders he made up his mind. Anything was better than staying on in the Majestic.

"I'm much obliged to you," he said, holding out his hand. "I'll go at once."

He hurried over to the *concierge's* desk to confirm the time of the train, and countermanded his room. A Frenchman with a small pointed, black beard was having an excited argument over something, but he politely stood on one side as Tiny approached.

"9.10, *Monsieur*. That is correct. Shall I get you a taxi?" He gave an order to a *chausseur*. "Will you be wanting a sleeper?"

He paused as the Frenchman made some remark.

"Because, if so, sir," he went on, "this gentleman suggests that you might perhaps care to share one with him."

"Thank you," said Tiny grimly. "I shall not be wanting a sleeper."

No more sleepers for him, he reflected, unless he knew his fellow-traveller. And a Frenchman with a beard struck him quite definitely as being a suspicious character under existing circumstances. Not that he could be, of course: he had been talking to the concierge before Tiny came up. But the principle held. No unknown men: certainly no unknown beavers.

"The taxi is here, sir," said the *concierge*, and the last words Tiny heard as he left the hotel were—"*Un autre, pour Monsieur.*"

The train was not full, and he had no difficulty in getting a first-class corner seat. On purpose he chose a compartment that was not empty: though he had no intention of sleeping he was not neglecting any precaution. And by no stretch of imagination could anyone already seated in one particular carriage selected at random, be involved in the matter: the coincidence would be too extraordinary.

He selected a corner next to the corridor, and it was just as the train started that he got a bit of a shock. Standing in the door of the next compartment was Black Beard. True—if looked at from one point of view there was nothing very surprising in the fact. From what the *concierge* had said the man was going to travel by this train, and probably he had been unable to get a sleeper. That was all there was to it, and yet. . .

Zavier, when the Fifty-Nine Club had been raided, had worn a beard. Was it possible that this man was Zavier himself? As far as he remembered his eyes were not blue, but he had taken very little notice of him at the Majestic. Anyway, that was a point which could easily be settled. He went into the corridor, and looked into the next compartment. The man had put on a pair of tinted glasses, and was reading a newspaper.

Tiny returned to his seat and shut the door. Was it Zavier? could it be? If so, was he going to strike on the train? His jaw set grimly. Ass he might be, but at any rate on this occasion he was forewarned. And he proposed to give the gentleman a run for his money. If only he was not in such an agonising condition of uncertainty over Mary....

Came Laroche, and his mind went back to the last time he had done this same journey. It was there, according to Ronald, they had got the Russian, and instinctively he kept his eyes glued on the small expanse of open window opposite him. Would some strange mysterious thing come through and strike him? Then he happened to glance into the corridor: the bearded man was standing outside his compartment watching him intently. For an instant he had a wild idea of tackling him then and there: but he dismissed it. So long as he kept his door shut nothing could get at him from that side at any rate, and his job was to get to Brigue.

At last the train started again and Tiny relaxed. Strong as his nerves were the strain was beginning to tell on him, and he found himself longing for the daylight. And then, to keep his mind occupied he tried to work out a plan of campaign for what he should do when he arrived at Brigue. He remembered the place hazily—a small typical Swiss town at the east end of the Rhone valley. It seemed the last place in the world where one would expect to meet with adventure, and yet the little clerk's solution appeared correct. Moreover, Ronald had said that the headquarters were somewhere in Switzerland.

But what to do when he got there was the problem. Presumably there would be no difficulty in tracing such a conspicuous car as a big Renault if it had already reached the place: and if the train got there first he could keep a look-out for it. After that events would have to shape themselves.

Dawn came at length and he stretched himself wearily. The bearded man had not appeared again: the halts at Dijon and the subsequent station had passed without incident. At Lausanne his fellow-travellers alighted, and from then on he had the carriage to himself. An attendant announced breakfast, and Tiny, after a moment's hesitation, rose and stepped into the corridor. After all, nothing much could happen in broad daylight. And the next instant he laughed softly to himself. The next compartment was empty: the bearded man was no longer there.

"Might have had an easier night, if I'd known that," he reflected. "The wretched fellow was probably a harmless commercial traveller."

At eleven o'clock they reached Brigue, and for a while he stood undecided on the platform. He had vaguely thought of the possibility of some message awaiting him, but there was no one who looked in the least like a messenger. He would have to make for the town and ask there. The local *gendarme*, however, proved the first difficulty. Doubtless the worthy man did his best, but at the end of five minutes all he could do was gravely to indicate the church. Then, with a hoarse grunt of satisfaction at having at last interpreted Tiny's question, he relapsed into his habitual stupor.

It was an hotel proprietor who stepped into the breach.

"Can I be of any assistance, sir?" he asked in perfect English.

Tiny heaved a sigh of relief.

"I'm trying to find out," he explained, "if a big Renault car has passed through here this morning? It would have come from Paris, with two ladies on board and two chauffeurs."

The other shook his head.

"Not that I'm aware of, sir. But I will make inquiries, and if you would care to come into the hotel, I can put you in an excellent position."

He led the way to a small beer garden fronting the main street.

"Now, sir," he said, "anyone coming from Paris must pass you here. The road forks down there to the left—one branch over the Simplon, the other over the Furka. So whichever pass they are going to take, they must come by here."

"Splendid fellow," cried Tiny. "Send out a magnum of ale."

And even as he spoke his eyes narrowed. A man had crossed the street some thirty yards away, and he could have sworn it was the bearded Frenchman of the Majestic. He half rose, then sank back again in his chair: the man had disappeared. It was useless to try and follow him, if not dangerous, but it gave Tiny a jolt. Why had he changed his carriage in the train, and what was he doing in Brigue?

The beer came and, with great rapidity, was gone. And after awhile Tiny began to feel drowsy. Periodically a car passed along the hot, airless street, but of the big Renault there was no sign. And with increasing frequency his head fell forward as he dozed. Which perhaps was just as well for his peace of mind. For had he been his usual alert self he might have noticed a strange phenomenon in the window of a house some thirty yards away. For curtains do not move suddenly when there is no wind unless someone is there touching them. And had that elementary fact penetrated Tiny's brain, he might have seen a small object which lay on the sill—circular and black: an object which bore a strange resemblance to the muzzle of a gun when pointed at the observer. And had he got as far as that he might have looked even more closely. In which case he might have caught a glimpse through the opening of the curtains of a black-bearded face peering motionless and patiently over the sights of a rifle. And the analogy of the tiger and the goat might have struck him unpleasantly. But none of these things happened: he dozed.

A hand on his shoulder awoke him with a start: the hotel proprietor was standing at his side.

"*Monsieur*," he said gravely, "I fear I have some bad news for you. Is your name Carteret?"

"It is," said Tiny, getting up. "What's the matter?"

And then he noticed that behind the speaker a monk was standing.

"There has been an accident, sir—a bad accident."

With a gesture he indicated the monk.

"My son," said the latter in a deep voice, "you must prepare for a shock. Early this morning there were brought to the monastery two men and two women. One of the men was dead, and one of the women: the others were badly injured. It appeared that their car had overturned at a dangerous corner, and fallen some thirty feet into a ravine. Two hours ago the injured lady recovered consciousness. She could barely speak, but she kept saying—'Monsieur Carteret—Brigue. Monsieur Carteret—Brigue.' So the Brother in charge sent me to see if I could find you."

"Get a car quick," said Tiny curtly.

"My son," answered the monk, "we have a car at the monastery. It is outside now."

"What about a doctor?"

"A doctor is with her now."

"Is there no hope?"

The monk crossed himself.

195

"It is in the hands of *le bon Dieu*. Come: the car is on the other side of the hotel."

Almost stunned by the unexpectedness of it, Tiny followed the monk. Mary dying: the thing was impossible.

"But how did it happen?" he cried distractedly.

Laboriously the monk wound up an ancient Fiat, and climbed in.

"On the road to Gletsch, my son, are many dangerous turnings. Moreover, in places it is very narrow. Last night in the mountains there was rain, and one stretch in particular became greasy. It was there that it happened. The car must have skidded: that is all we can think."

"Can't you get some more speed out of this cursed machine?" muttered Tiny.

"My son," said the other gently, "we are only a poor order. What little we have is given to *les pauvres*—not used in buying a new car."

"Sorry," grunted Tiny. "Only, you see I happen to be engaged to the lady. Do we pass the place where the accident occurred?"

"No. It is a mile beyond our doors. The villagers carried the bodies to us."

They drove in silence, till they came to a place like the side of a cliff, up which the road zigzagged. And it was when they were half way up that, looking down, Tiny saw below them another car with a solitary man in it. The driver's face was hidden by his hat, but a glance told him that the car was a Lancia, and therefore capable of some three times the speed of his present conveyance.

"There's a man behind us in a fast car," he said. "Do you mind if I ask him for a lift when he overtakes us?"

"Certainly," answered the monk. "I understand what you must be feeling. We will stop him when he passes us."

But though Tiny, glancing back from time to time, could see the other car it never appeared to get any nearer. The driver seemed to be deliberately regulating his speed by the Fiat, and after a while he resigned himself to his present conveyance. And then, at last, when he felt he could bear it no longer, his companion spoke.

"Nearly there," he said. "That building on the left is the monastery."

Tiny took a deep breath: in a few moments now he would know the worst. Was she still alive? Was there any hope? With a creaking of brakes the car pulled up, and he dashed to the door.

"Patience, my son," said the deep voice behind him. "We have rules in our fraternity which must be obeyed."

Chafing with impatience Tiny waited while the monk knocked three times on the door. And so completely impervious was he to everything save the thought of Mary, that he did not even notice that the Lancia had pulled up some twenty yards away, while the driver peered under the bonnet as if to discover some defect.

At length a small panel slid back and he saw a pair of eyes looking at him. Then his companion said something in a language he did not know, and the door was opened.

"Is the lady dead?" he cried in an agony of apprehension.

Once again there was a remark in an unknown tongue, and then the monk who had driven him turned to him with a smile.

"No, my son: she is not. And the doctor is most hopeful. Follow me."

He led the way along a stone corridor, with Tiny at his heels, until he came to a large vaulted room—a room which was divided into two parts by a steel grille.

"Wait here," he said. "I will find the doctor, and bring him to you."

His footsteps echoed on the stone flags till they died away in the distance. And Tiny, fuming at the delay strode up and down the room. Suddenly he paused. From the direction of the front door had come a short stifled groan. He listened intently: it was not repeated. And then, for the first time, he became aware of the deathly silence of the place. Not a sound of a voice: not a sound of any sort. The building was like a tomb. He walked over to the steel grille and examined it: it was let into the stone-work on each side, and reached right up to the ceiling. In each half of the room were a table and chair, and he concluded that it must be the place where the monks interviewed callers.

He turned round: would the doctor never come? A grille similar to the one he had been examining was slowly closing across the entrance to the room. For a moment he stood rigid—too amazed to move: then, with a shout, he dashed at it. And even as he reached it, it clanged home.

He tugged at it desperately: it was as immovable as the one in the centre of the room. And suddenly he realised the truth: the whole thing was a trap into which he had not only walked, but had galloped at full speed. Instinctively his hand went to his pocket, and he cursed savagely. His revolver was in his bag at the hotel.

"That simplifies matters, doesn't it, Mr. Carteret," came a suave voice, and he swung round.

Standing on the other side of the central grille was another monk—a monk with pale-blue, unwinking eyes. He was face to face with Zavier himself.

"Had you had your revolver I might have had to forgo the pleasure of a little chat with you," continued Zavier genially. "Dodging bullets in a room like this with nasty stone walls is not a pastime I care about."

"Damn you," said Tiny between his teeth. "How is Lady Mary?"

"As far as I know, in the very best of health," answered the other. "But whether she is still in Paris, or has returned to London I can't tell you."

"So the whole thing has been a lie from beginning to end."

A futile rage had seized him, which even the knowledge that Mary was safe did little to calm.

"Naturally," laughed Zavier. "But really, Mr. Carteret, you were a little too easy. I mean one does like a certain amount of run for one's money."

"What the devil are you going to do with me? Murder me, I suppose, like the others, you damned swine."

"I fear that that is your ultimate end undoubtedly," agreed Zavier. "You see, my dear Mr. Carteret, I have the gravest objection to people being at large who know me: or rather, I might put it, who associate me with my activities."

"Get it over, for God's sake," shouted Tiny. "You can play me like a sitting hen if you want to."

"True: very true. But at the moment I don't want to. As I said before, I should like a little chat. It is so rare, Mr. Carteret, that one has the chance of discussing things with one's adversaries in safety. And I have a little pardonable vanity, you know. Now the first time I met you was in the sleeper just after that foolish fellow Demeroff had paid the just penalty for his offence."

"So you were the monk, were you?" said Tiny, interested in spite of himself.

"I was the monk. And my object in visiting your compartment, my dear fellow, was not, believe me, to breathe a prayer over the dear departed, but to make quite sure that the right one of you had departed. By the way, that reminds me. From information I have received I am given to understand that considerable doubt exists in the minds of the authorities as to how these regrettable accidents take place. Am I right?"

198

"Go to hell," grunted Tiny.

"Well, if you won't answer, you won't. Still, my information is generally reliable. To turn to another subject. What do you think of this idea of mine for disguise purposes? You have no idea how free from suspicion a monk or a nun remains. If one twiddles a few beads, and mutters hoarsely under one's breath, the police of two continents hold up the traffic for you. Besides, on occasions, when the attentions of those who one wishes to avoid become too pressing, and ports are being watched and things like that, I have found but little difficulty in prevailing upon the master of some small tramp to smuggle me on board. I plead extreme poverty and thereby touch his heart. However, I fear I shall have to adopt something new in the future."

He sighed, and lit one of his little cigarettes.

"Yes, I shall have to think of something fresh. I could not destroy that cassock at the Fifty-Nine Club, and it can't be long before your admirable police appreciate its significance. In fact, I wouldn't be surprised if your friend Mr. Standish hadn't spotted the truth before his regrettable end. Burned to death. Poor fellow!"

"You nauseating hypocrite," snarled Tiny. "You know perfectly well he was not burned to death. You murdered him, as you murdered young Denver."

"Come, come, Mr. Carteret, believe me you are wrong there. True, the young man died, but I can assure you that it was the last thing I intended. You see, I happened to know that you and Standish proposed to pay Blake a visit, and it was for you that the scene was laid. And then your young friend Denver went and butted in in front of you."

"How did you know Standish and I were going there?"

"My dear sir, you underestimate my resources. For what other reason would you wire Lady Mary to get Blake out of his house from eleven to one. Useful, that wire—very useful. It gave me a specimen of your writing, which came in very handy for my little note to Lady Mary."

"Well, you're damned well wrong there, Zavier. Standish wrote that wire, and signed it with my name."

"Dear me! You don't say so." He seemed genuinely upset. "You can't believe how I dislike anything that savours of a blunder. So that letter to Lady Mary was in Standish's writing. You surprise me. Why then did she go to Paris?"

"To try and run you to earth," said Tiny savagely. "She knew it was a trap. . ."

"And she deliberately walked into it," said the other with an amused smile. "Plucky, but foolish. And I fear rather useless. Well, what message shall I give Signor Berendosi from you? Strange, isn't it, what a lot of trouble has been caused by such a small thing as that."

With a mocking laugh he held up the negative, and Tiny looked at it moodily. Heavens! what a consummate fool he had been. Looking back now he marvelled how he could ever have believed the so-called clerk's story in Paris for a second. And yet, at the time, it had seemed to ring true. And then the next one about the accident.

"Cheer up, Mr. Carteret," cried Zavier. "Admittedly you haven't been very bright, but though I say it myself I am a little bit above your form. And you have had a charming trip to a very delightful part of the country. I shall be leaving you shortly, and I don't quite know when anyone will find your . . . er . . . body. You see this place has served its purpose. From information I have received Mr. Standish was not the only person who had located my little home as being in Switzerland. And even as near as that, my dear fellow, is too near for my liking. So you will soon have the place entirely to yourself."

"So you definitely mean to kill me," said Tiny quietly.

"For what other reason do you suppose I have gone to the trouble and worry of bringing you out here," answered Zavier. "Had I had the time I should have done it in London. But I didn't: things were getting a little too hot. So it became necessary to devise some other method, though I frankly admit I never dreamed it would come off quite so successfully as it has. Well, *au revoir*, Mr. Carteret. You made me run very fast at the Fifty-Nine Club, but I bear you no ill-will."

With a wave of the hand he passed through a door which up till then Tiny had not noticed. He left it ajar, and Tiny stared at the aperture fascinated. It commanded the whole of his half of the room, and it was through there, he felt certain, that death would come. But how: in what form?

Suddenly an overmastering rage gripped him: he would not be butchered like a rat in a trap. He went to the grille that blocked the door, and hauled on it with all his great strength. Useless: the thing was a fixture, and he cursed savagely. Then he pulled himself together: there was no good losing his head. Surely something could be done, but his only hope lay in keeping cool. His eyes fell on the table. It was a big one with a stout top. Supposing he was to use it as a shield. True—it wouldn't keep out a bullet, but if Zavier had intended to shoot him surely he would have done so already. He turned it on its end, and placed it so that it shielded him from the aperture. Then getting the chair he sat down and lit a cigarette. Now at any rate he only had one opening to watch—the door in his half of the room.

The minutes dragged on: the silence seemed to grow more intense. And after a time a very natural psychological reaction set in. He fought against it, but it became stronger and stronger till he knew that shortly he would be unable to resist it. What was happening on the other side of the table in that part of the room he could not see? The thought became a craving: he must know.

He stood up, and moved cautiously back from his shield, thereby bringing more of the room into view. But there was still a large area that was hidden: to see that he would have to put his head round the table. After all, if it had to come, it had to—and the sooner the better. He could not go on for the rest of time in his present position. And he had just made up his mind to chance it, when he heard a peculiar scratching noise. It came from the other half of the room, and for a moment or two he listened intently.

Suddenly there came a grating sound, such as the leg of a chair might make when moved slightly on a stone floor. And with a pricking in his scalp Tiny realised that the crisis was at hand. Somebody or something was in the room.

Cautiously he approached his table: to know what it was had now become an imperative necessity. He would thrust his head out quickly, and have a snap look. Then back again under cover to form his plan. He did so, only to remain staring at what he saw.

"Well, I'm damned," he remarked: then he began to laugh. Seated on the back of the chair with its head cocked on one side was a small monkey, solemnly waving a toy Swiss flag, and dressed in a tiny coat.

"You funny little beast," he said. "Where in blazes have you sprung from?"

Like most men of his type he adored animals, and the ridiculous aspect of the situation struck him. There had he been sheltering behind heavy barricades, and the foe turned out to be a diminutive grey monkey!

"Come on, you little blighter," he cried, holding out his hand, and suddenly it put the end of the flagpole in a pocket of the coat so that its hands were free, ran down the chair and came sidling across the floor towards him. It got through the grille with ease, chattering hard. And he was on the point of stroking it when there came a frenzied shout from behind him.

201

"Don't touch it. For God's sake—don't touch the monkey. Kick it away."

And the voice was the voice of Ronald Standish.

Startled—the monkey paused, and as if in a dream Tiny aimed a blow at it with his shoe. With a shrill squeak of anger it scuttled away, back through the grille, and still half dazed with the sudden development, Tiny saw that Zavier, his face suffused with rage, had returned. And then things happened quickly: so quickly that looking back on it later Tiny was hard put to it to remember their exact order. The monkey darted to Zavier, who had removed his monk's disguise, and swarmed up one of his legs. Then it seemed to wave the flag. And the next instant Zavier was staring at one of his hands, with terror in his eyes. On it was a long red scratch.

"Come home to roost at last, Zavier, has it?" came Ronald's quiet voice. "The reward is just."

Tiny forced himself to turn round. Standing in the doorway behind the grille, in the garb of a monk, was the man he had believed dead and buried.

And then from the other half of the room came a shout of maddened rage.

"Behind the table, Tiny," roared Standish, and with a splintering crash a bullet imbedded itself in the wood. Almost simultaneously came a crack from the door, and a howl of pain from Zavier, followed by the noise of his revolver falling on the stone floor.

"If you bend to pick it up, Zavier, I'll plug your other hand," said Ronald quietly.

"For God's sake do," cried the other hoarsely, "before the poison has time to work."

And Standish laughed grimly.

"As I said before—the reward is just," he said. "Ah! would you?"

The two cracks rang out almost as one and then Ronald Standish lowered his gun.

"You can come out, Tiny," he said quietly. "The swine has cheated us after all."

And Tiny, stepping out from behind the table, understood. The monkey was chattering angrily on the chair, and beside it lay stretched the body of her master, a smoking revolver still clutched in his hand. Zavier had blown out his brains.

CHAPTER 12

"Touch and go, old lad," said Standish gravely. "I can't think what maggot atrophied my brain."

"For the love of Pete, explain, Ronald," cried Tiny. "At the moment my own is in the same condition."

They were back in the hotel at Brigue, and on the table between them was the toy Swiss flag. At first sight it looked harmless enough and the sort of thing to be expected on a birthday cake or a Christmas tree. But a closer examination dispelled the illusion. The little pole was about the length of an ordinary pencil, and half the thickness. It was hollow and made of the finest steel, and a small chain with a little band on the end—a band that was fitted to the monkey's arm—ensured that it could never be left behind.

A special grip like a tiny trigger guard had been made for the monkey's paw an inch from the end, and this grip was connected by a microscopic bar passing up the centre of the tube to a little plunger, on exactly the same principle as a bicycle pump. A slot rather more than two inches long allowed the grip to slide forward that amount towards the sharp end, thereby ejecting any fluid on the other side of the plunger. And at the sharp end there stuck out for the sixteenth of an inch a needle point.

"Damned neat," said Standish, a note of genuine admiration in his voice. "Look how beautifully the thing is made. It is nothing more nor less than a perfectly disguised hypodermic syringe. Who would ever suspect a monkey waving a flag? You'd merely think it was an accidental scratch."

"He must have spent months training the little brute."

"Probably. Though those small ones pick up tricks very quickly."

"I wonder what the poison is," said Tiny.

"They'll find that out at home fast enough," answered the other. "Probably some native concoction, such as they use on their poisoned darts."

He replaced it on the table and picked up a metal bar some three feet long. One end was curved to make it look like a walking-stick, but there the resemblance ceased.

"Exhibit Number two for Gillson's museum. Pull on that end, Tiny."

The thing was telescopic, each new length fitting inside the previous one. Its full length when extended was five yards, and it formed a bar quite sufficiently rigid to bear the weight of a little monkey.

"To introduce the beast into a room he could not reach otherwise," said Standish. "Ingenious: very. But I ought to have spotted it, Tiny."

"I'm blowed if I see how," cried the other.

"Go back a bit, old boy. I admit we had nothing to go on over Jebson: nor did we have anything that helped us over Demeroff. It was when we came to Felton Blake—or rather Joe Denver—that we weren't as clever as we ought to have been. You see, I was right when I said that that was an accident, and that he had meant to get us. Well, having got as far as that I should have pursued it to the logical end. And I didn't. I actually said to you, if you remember, that he had set the scene in Blake's room, and I oughtn't to have been so dense. He merely left the monkey in the room pending our arrival."

"Awkward for Blake," said Tiny.

"Why? He had a perfect alibi with Lady Mary if things had worked out according to plan. It was leaving young Denver out of the calculations that upset the whole arrangement."

"I still don't see why you should have suspected the monkey."

"Perhaps it is easy to be wise after the event," agreed Ronald. "But that, combined with the affair at my flat..."

"Who was it who was killed?" interrupted Tiny.

"Poor Stanhope—my man," said Standish gravely. "I found him dead when I got back that night. And I did some pretty quick thinking, Tiny. It seemed fairly probable that in murdering Denver they had got the wrong man: but when it came to Stanhope it was an absolute certainty. So what did it mean? The window was open: the light was on. Therefore if Zavier had been able to see into the room he would have spotted at once that it wasn't me. The logical conclusion therefore was that he couldn't see into the room, otherwise he wouldn't have murdered poor inoffensive Stanhope. Which carried me a further step forward: it wasn't necessary for Zavier to see his victim. Therefore there was some agent at work—not exactly a blind agent, but one that couldn't discriminate. And it is then, I think, that I was not very clever. I should have spotted it. What happened, of course, is easy to reconstruct now. Zavier from the road outside saw the light, and Stanhope's shadow. He assumed it was me and took a chance. He had brought the monkey in case: he must have gone straight from the Fifty-Nine to get it. He introduced the little brute by means of this stick, and that was that. . ."

"I wish I'd known, old boy. Jove! it gave me a turn the next day."

"Sorry, Tiny: but it had to be done. You had to be in ignorance. Otherwise you wouldn't have acted normally. You see, I had no idea what Zavier's next move was going to be."

"Did Gillson know?"

"Yes: he knew. It was a beastly job changing clothes with that poor devil, and then burning him enough to make him unrecognisable, but it had to be done. The stakes were too big to hesitate."

"What did you do then?"

"Shadowed you, old boy, disguised as a London telephone operative. And it was then that I read the note which got Lady Mary over to Paris. At first, I confess, I was completely dumbfounded: how had they come to make such a mistake? We now know: moreover, now we can see that it was that one mistake which has enabled us to pull the thing off. That—and your girl's priceless nerve. Had that message been in your handwriting she would assuredly have rung you up to confirm it. And then—no Paris: no dead Zavier: no film. But by acting as she did, she has let us win.

"As soon as I read it I made a few changes in my rig, and rushed down to Croydon. I found you had chartered a special plane, so I took another and followed you. But I did what you didn't do—I met the boat train at the Gare du Nord. Moreover, I had previously wired, and I had two of the best men in Paris with me. I saw Lady Mary get into a big car, and tipped them the wink. They followed her, and I came straight to the Majestic."

"I never saw you."

"You weren't intended to, Tiny," laughed the other. "I realised, of course, that the thing must be coming to a head. She was in Paris: you were at the Majestic: there would not be a moment's unnecessary delay. What I thought was going to happen was the receipt by you of a note from her—probably bogus—giving some specious reason why you should go to a certain spot. And I thought it more than likely that spot would be in Paris or just outside.

"Candidly, I felt no anxiety over her. She was under the immediate eye of the police, and even without that there was not the faintest object in doing her any harm. From Zavier's point of view she had served her purpose by getting you over, and he was far too clever a man to commit an unnecessary crime. You were his bird, and to come back to Gillson's metaphor I expected the arrival of the tiger at any moment. He arrived, or rather his emissary did, in the person of a very dear old friend of mine—one Perky Edwards.

"Perky is probably the finest pen-and-ink draughtsman alive today, but unfortunately for himself the medium he prefers is not acceptable to the powers that be. The police have a rooted objection to dud fivers, and as a matter of fact I didn't know Perky was out of prison till I saw him soaking you good and hearty in the bar."

"I thought the little swab was a bank clerk," laughed Tiny. "He told me he was."

"He looks rather like it, doesn't he? Well, clearly, the last round had begun. I didn't dare go into the bar myself—the place was so empty—but I'd made all the necessary arrangements. A man was outside the door to note any address you gave to a taxi driver: I was there in case you consulted the concierge. Which you did, and I must confess surprised me considerably. I had not expected Brigue to be your destination."

"But, good Lord!" cried Tiny, "you weren't that damned Frenchman with a beard, were you?"

"Guilty, old boy," laughed the other. "And your distaste for sharing a sleeper with me came as no surprise. However, if you were going to Brigue, obviously I'd have to go too. Whether they were going to try and do you in in the train, remained to be seen. Anyway I got into the next compartment."

"I know you did," said Tiny with a grin. "And to start with I thought you were Zavier himself."

"Now you've got to remember that I had no idea what particular yarn Perky had put across you," went on Standish. "But what I did know was that you were sitting in a position of considerable danger. So I went to ground in that hotel opposite and during the two hours you were here I had this veranda covered the whole time. Then the monk arrived, and with him came the first flood of light.

"I don't wonder you didn't spot it: you had no suspicion then of any trap. Whereas I knew the entire thing was a plant. I saw, at once, the significance of that heap of torn-up cloth we found at the Fifty-Nine, and the cord on the other side of the door. And so, later on, Zavier's remarks to you came as no surprise. Ingenious, you know, Tiny: he was perfectly right. It is the easiest of all disguises to assume and the least suspicious.

"You have probably guessed by now that it was I in the car following you, and so you have got most of the rest. As soon as you had gone into the so-called monastery I knocked in the same way, and though he was a bit suspicious at first he let me in. And then it was a question of move, and move quickly. I went for him, but before I outed him he gave tongue once."

"I heard him," said Tiny. "Just before the grille over the door shut."

"I put on his rig, and all through your interview with Zavier I was just outside in the passage. Perhaps it was an unfair risk to expose you to, but I was so desperately keen to find out his secret. Then he left, and you very wisely went to ground behind the table. Now from where I was I could watch the door by which he had left, and I saw that darned little monkey come in. And still my brain didn't click. Which is why I said, Tiny, it was touch and go. Gad! I'd never have forgiven myself if he had got you."

"What did make it click at the end?" said Tiny curiously.

"For some unaccountable reason there flashed through my mind the last word that man Demeroff had said in the sleeper. You remember you told me he called out what sounded like '*Bazana.*' And it suddenly dawned on me. What he had really shouted was '*Obezïana,*' which is the Russian for monkey. Whether in his half-drunken stupor he had seen the little brute come through the window at Laroche, or whether he knew Zavier's secret before, we shall never know. In view of his determination to have the window shut I should think the latter."

He got up and stretched himself, and a look of surprise dawned on his face.

"Bless my soul, if it isn't Lady Mary herself."

Tiny sprang to his feet.

"Where? It is, by Jove! Mary, dear," he called out, "what under the sun brings you here?"

She was in the street below, and turned at the sound of his voice.

"Tiny," she cried, "is it really you? My dear, I've been sick with anxiety. And Mr. Standish there too!"

"Oh! I'm not dead," he grinned. "Come right up and take a pew. We've been having a topping time."

She came up the steps towards them.

"You see, I went off with that woman to a house on the outskirts of Paris, where I had dinner. And after dinner she left me to go to the telephone. I waited and waited and she never returned, so after awhile I had a look round. My dear—the house was empty: there wasn't a soul in it. So I left, and met two men outside, who spoke to me. They were in the police, and I asked them what I should do. Their advice was to go back to Paris, and one of them got me a taxi. I drove straight to the Majestic, and found you'd come here. What was the idea?"

"To keep you out of the way, Lady Mary, sufficiently long to decoy Tiny here," said Standish. "Our friend the late Mr. Zavier was no slouch."

"Late?" She stared at him incredulously, and he nodded.

"He died unpleasantly a couple of hours ago, and left you this."

With a grave smile he produced the film from his pocket.

"I can't believe it," she said very low. "So we've won after all."

"Thanks entirely to you," he answered. "If you hadn't deliberately walked into the trap with your eyes open we shouldn't have this. What shall I do with it?"

"Burn it," she cried. "Burn the beastly thing at once."

In silence they watched it flare up and sizzle away: then Standish began to laugh.

"I've got an idea," he said. "It just breaks my heart to disappoint Berendosi. Supposing you two posed in a similar attitude, and we sent him the film of that."

"Men have died for less infamous suggestions," grinned Tiny. "However, we have no objection to you joining us at lunch provided you pay for it."

The Creaking Door

CHAPTER 1.

Ronald Standish lay back in his chair with a worried look on his usually cheerful face. In his hand he held a letter, which he read over for the second time before tossing it across to me.

"The devil and all, Bob," he said, shaking his head. "From what I saw in the papers a clearer case never existed."

I glanced at the note, it ran:

Dear Mr. Standish,—I do hope you will forgive a complete stranger writing to you, but I am in desperate trouble. You will probably remember a very great friend of mine—Isabel Blount, whom you helped some months ago. Well, it was she who advised me to come to you. Would it be possible for you to see me tomorrow after noon at three o'clock? I shall come, anyway, on the chance of finding you disengaged.

Yours sincerely,

Katherine Moody.

"Which means today, in a quarter of an hour," he said, as I laid down the note.

"And I fear it's pretty hopeless."

"You know who she is, then?" I remarked.

He nodded gravely and crossed to a corner of the room where a pile of newspapers was lying on a chair. And as I watched him I wondered, not for the first time what had made him take up the profession he had. A born player of games, wealthy, and distinctly good-looking, he seemed the last person in the world to become a detective. And yet that was what he was when one boiled down to hard facts. True, he picked and chose his cases, and sometimes for months on end he never handled one at all. But sooner or later some crime would interest him, and then he would drop everything until he had either solved it or was beaten. With the official police he was on excellent terms, which was not to be wondered at in view of the fact that on many occasions he had put them on the right track. At times some new man was tempted to smile contemptuously at the presumption of an amateur pitting himself against the official force, but the smile generally faded before long. For there was no denying that he had a most uncanny flair for picking out the points that mattered from a mass of irrelevant detail.

"It's bad to prejudge a case," he remarked, coming back with two papers, "but this looks pretty damaging on the face of it."

He pointed to a paragraph, and I ran my eye down it.

Shocking Tragedy in Leicestershire
Brutal Murder of Young Artist

A crime of unparalleled ferocity was committed yesterday in the grounds of Mexbury Hall, the home of Mr. John Playfair, who has lived there for some years with his ward, Miss Katherine Moody, and her companion. Standing amongst the trees, some way from the Hall and out of sight of it, there is a summer-house which commands a magnificent view over the surrounding country. And it was in this summer-house that the tragedy occurred.

It appears that for some weeks past Mr. Playfair has allowed a young artist named Bernard Power to use it as a studio. Yesterday, on returning in the afternoon from a motor trip, Mr. Playfair, while taking a stroll in the grounds, happened to pass by the summer-house, where he was horrified to see a red stream dripping sluggishly down the wooden steps that led to the door. He rushed in, to find the unfortunate young man lying dead on the floor with his head literally crushed in like a broken eggshell.

Touching nothing, he rushed back to the house, where he telephoned for the police and a doctor, who arrived post-haste.

The doctor stated, after examining the body, that Mr. Power had been dead about five hours, which placed the time of the crime at ten o'clock that morning. Then, with the help of Inspector Savage, who has charge of the case, the body was moved, and instantly the weapon with which the deed was done was discovered. A huge stone weighing over fourteen pounds was lying on the floor, and adhering to it were blood and several hairs that obviously had belonged to the dead man.

Mr. Playfair explained that the stone had originally come from an old heap which had been left over when the foundations of the summer-house had been laid. This particular one, he went on to say, had been used as a weight on the floor to prevent the door from banging when the artist wanted it open: he had suggested it to him some weeks previously.

It is clear that a particularly brutal murder has been committed, as any possibility of accident or suicide can be ruled out. The murderer must have approached from behind while the unfortunate young man was at work on his picture, and bashed in his head with one blow.

The police are in possession of several clues, and sensational developments are expected.

I looked at the date. It was yesterday's paper. Then I looked at the other paragraph he was indicating.

"These are the sensational developments," said Ronald, "which are doubtless responsible for Miss Moody's letter."

The police have lost no time in following up the clues they obtained in the shocking tragedy that occurred the day before yesterday at Mexbury Hall. It will be recalled that the body of a young artist named Bernard Power was found in the summer house with the head battered in a fashion which proved conclusively that a singularly brutal murder had been committed.

Yesterday Inspector Savage arrested a neighbouring landowner, Mr. Hubert Daynton, on the charge of being the murderer. It is understood that a stick belonging to the accused was found in the summer and the butt end of a cigarette of a brand he habitually smokes was discovered lying on the floor.

The accused protests his complete ignorance of the affair, a further developments are awaited hourly. Needless to say, Mr. Playfair, in whose grounds the tragedy occurred, is much upset, as the dead man was a *protegé* of his.

I put down the paper and glanced at my companion.

"It certainly seems pretty bad for Mr. Hubert Daynton," I said. "He seems to have gone out of his way to leave the evidence lying about."

"Exactly," Standish remarked. "Which may be a point in his favour.

However, there goes the bell. We'll hear what Miss Moody has to say."

The door opened, and his man ushered in a delightfully pretty girl of about twenty-one or two, who looked from one to the other of us with a worried expression on her face.

"Sit down, Miss Moody," said Ronald. "And let me introduce a great pal of mine, Bob Miller. You can say anything you like in front of him."

"I suppose you know what I've come about, Mr. Standish," cried the girl.

"I know what has appeared in the papers," said Ronald, "which summarises into the fact that Hubert Daynton has been arrested for the murder of an artist called Bernard Power in the summer-house of your guardian's place."

"But he never did it, Mr. Standish," she cried, clasping her hands together.

"So, I gather, he states. At the same time, the police seem to think otherwise. Now will you be good enough to fill in all the gaps, as far as you can, which have been left by the papers? And one thing I beg of you—don't keep anything back. It is absolutely imperative that I should have all the facts, even if they appear to you to be damaging."

"I will conceal nothing," she said. "You know from the papers that I live at Mexbury Hall with my guardian, and Hubert Daynton has the neighbouring house, Gadsby. Tower. He was often over with us, and we did the same thing at his place—"

"Was?" put in Ronald. "Do you imply anything by using the past tense?"

"During recent months matters have become a little strained," she said, a slightly heightened colour coming into her cheeks. "To be brief, he wanted to marry me, and my guardian didn't like the idea."

"Why not?" said Ronald bluntly. "Was there any particular reason, or just general disapproval?"

"I don't know," she answered, "Uncle John—he's not really any relation, of course—is very old-fashioned in some ways, and has the most absurd ideas about what girls ought to be told. But one thing is certain: the moment Hubert made it clear that he wanted to marry me, Uncle John's manner towards him changed completely."

"One further point, Miss Moody," said Ronald, with a faint smile. "What were your feelings on the subject?"

"Well," she answered frankly, "I didn't say I would and I didn't say

I wouldn't. He's rather a dear, and I like him immensely, but I can't say I'm in love with him. In addition, I'm terribly fond of Uncle John who has been a sort of mother and father to me, and the fact that he disapproved did influence me. There was an idea at the back of my mind, I think, that in time I might get him to change his mind about Hubert, which would have made a difference."

"I understand perfectly," said Ronald. "And that was the condition of affairs between you and Hubert Daynton at the time of his arrest?"

"I'm afraid it wasn't," she answered slowly. "Two months ago Bernard Power came to stay at the village inn. He was an artist, as you know, and in some way or other he got to know Uncle John. Now, my guardian is a photographic maniac—it is the one absorbing hobby of his life—and as Bernard went in for landscape work they seemed to find something in common. He was continually asking Bernard to dinner; and fitted him up, as you read in the papers, in the summer-house as a studio."

She paused for a moment, and glanced from Ronald to me.

"The poor man is dead now," she went on, "and if it wasn't for Hubert's sake, I'd say nothing. But there's no getting away from the fact that Bernard Power was a nasty bit of work. You both of you look thoroughly amazed, and you'll know what I mean when I say he was always pawing one, touching one's arm or something like that—a thing I loathe. But matters came to a head three days ago. I happened to be passing the summer-house when he called out to me to come and have a look at his picture.

"Without thinking, I went in. To do him justice, he was a very clever painter. And before I knew where I was, he'd seized me in his arms and was trying to kiss me. I was perfectly furious. I'd never given him the slightest encouragement. However, after I'd smacked his face as hard as I could, he let me go. And then I told him a few home truths and left."

Again she paused, and bit her lip.

"I left, Mr. Standish, and, as evil fortune would have it, I ran into Hubert paying one of his very infrequent visits, He had come over to see me about a spaniel I wanted. If only it had been an hour later it wouldn't have mattered; I should have recovered. As it was he saw, of course, that I was angry, and realising I'd come from the direction of the summer-house, he jumped at once to the correct conclusion.

"'Has that damned painter been up to his monkey tricks again?'

he cried.

"And very foolishly I told him what had happened. He was furious, and there's no denying that Hubert has a very nasty temper when roused. I regretted having said anything the moment the words were out of my mouth, but then it was too late. And it was only with the greatest difficulty that I prevented him going on then and there to put it across Bernard Power. I told him that I was quite capable of looking after myself, and that the matter was over and done with.

"In the middle of our conversation Uncle John joined us. He saw at once that something was up and asked what had happened. Hubert told him and he didn't mince his words, which got Uncle John's back up. And finally the two of them very nearly had a row.

"Uncle John's point of view was that he was the proper person for me to go to, and that it was no business of Hubert's. Hubert on the contrary said it was any decent man's business if some swab of a painter kissed a girl against her will. And then he made the damning statement that he personally proposed to interview Mr. Bernard Power the following morning."

"Did anyone else hear that remark besides you and your guardian?" asked Ronald.

"No one," she said. "Of that I'm positive."

"Why did he specify the following morning? Why didn't he go right away?"

"He had people coming to lunch, and it was getting late."

"And the following morning was the morning of the murder," said Ronald thoughtfully. "Now let's hear exactly what Daynton says took place."

"He says that he started from Gadsby Tower at half-past nine and walked over to the summer-house. He found Bernard Power had not yet arrived, so he lit a cigarette and waited for him—a cigarette which he admits he threw on the floor and put out with his shoe.

"Then Bernard Power came in, and apparently Hubert went for him like a pickpocket. He called him a leprous mess, and a few more things of that sort, and they had a fearful quarrel, in the course of which Hubert put his stick up against the wall, because he was afraid he might hit the other with it, and he was a much smaller man than Hubert. Then he left, and went back to his own house, which he reached at twenty past ten."

Ronald Standish nodded thoughtfully.

"Forgetting all about his stick," he remarked. "A very important point, that."

"He was so excited, Mr. Standish," said the girl. "I know the police think as you do, but surely it's understandable"

"My dear Miss Moody," he said with a smile, "you quite mistake my meaning. Now that I've heard your full story I think it tells enormously in his favour. It is certain that he must have discovered he had left his stick in the summer-house on his way back to Gadsby Tower. There is nothing that a man notices quicker. If, then, he had murdered Power he would at all costs have had to go back to get it. To leave such a damning piece of evidence lying about was tantamount to putting a noose round his neck. But what was more natural than that he, rather than renew the quarrel, should decide to leave it there, and get it some other time?"

"Then you don't think he did it?" she cried eagerly.

"What I may think," said Ronald guardedly, "is one thing. What we've got to prove is another. If he didn't do it—who did? The crime, according to the doctor's evidence, must have been committed very shortly after Daynton left the summer-house. It is, therefore, I think, a justifiable assumption that the murderer was near by during the interview, heard the quarrel, and seized the opportunity of throwing suspicion on somebody else. So that at any rate one line of exploration must be to find out if this man Power had an enemy who was so bitter against him that he wouldn't stick at murder. And from what you tell me of his manners with you, it would not be surprising if he has gone even further with some other girl. In which case there may be a man who was not as forbearing as Daynton."

"Then you'll help Hubert?" she cried.

"Certainly, Miss Moody," he said. "Now that I've heard the details my opinion is quite different. Bob and I will come down with you this afternoon. But before we start there are just one or two points I'd like cleared up. First—what were your movements on the day of the murder?"

"I stayed in the house till lunch; and in the afternoon I played tennis at a house five miles away."

"You had no communication with Daynton of any sort—over the telephone, for instance?"

"None."

"And Mr. Playfair—what did he do?"

"He went out on one of his photography expeditions. He started in the car about half-past eight in the morning, and was not back till

215

after lunch."

"One last point. You have already said that no one could have overheard the conversation between the three of you on the drive. But did you by any chance mention it to anybody afterwards?"

"No," she said. "I said nothing about it. And I'm sure Uncle John didn't either, as he was in the whole afternoon fiddling about with his latest camera."

"Then it must either have been an unfortunate coincidence for Bernard Power or—" He broke off and stared out of the window thoughtfully.

"Come along," he said, rousing himself at length. "Let's go down and look at this summer-house. I hope your nerves are good, Miss Moody. Bob generally drives, and never at less than sixty miles an hour."

Chapter 2.

The grounds of Mexbury Hall were extensive, and the summerhouse was a good quarter of a mile from the Hall itself. Trees surrounded it on three sides, affording admirable cover for anyone who wished to hide. The fourth was open, and gave a magnificent view over the country to the south. It was simply built of wood, with a sunblind that could be let down over the big window.

A policeman was on guard as we approached, and he looked doubtful when Ronald explained his business.

"Inspector's orders, sir, were that no one was to be allowed in. Still, I suppose you're different."

"Come in yourself, officer, and you'll see that I'm not going to touch anything. I take it nothing has been moved except the body?"

"Nothing, sir."

"Were you here yourself when the body was found?"

"I came with the inspector, sir."

Ronald knelt down by the wooden steps leading to the door, and carefully examined the ominous red stain. Then, with a shake of his head, he got up.

"Too late," he said, "Nothing to be got out of that now."

He pushed open the door and stepped inside. Then, according to his invariable custom, he stood absolutely motionless, with only his eyes moving from side to side as he absorbed every detail. On the easel stood the half-finished picture spattered with the dead man's blood. The overturned chair still lay where it had fallen as the artist had crashed to the floor.

"Not much doubt about what happened, sir," remarked the constable. "Never seen a clearer case in all my service. Fair battered to pieces, he was, poor gentleman."

"What's the meaning of this, Roberts?" said a gruff voice from outside. "I ordered you to admit no one."

Ronald Standish swung round. A choleric looking man in uniform was standing in the doorway.

"Inspector Savage, I take it?" Standish said genially. "I have been commissioned by Miss Moody to make a few inquiries on behalf of Mr. Daynton."

He held out his card, and the inspector grunted.

"I've heard of you, Mr. Standish," he remarked. "And if I was you I'd wash my hands of it. You'll get no credit out of this case."

"Perhaps not," agreed Ronald. "Still, when a lady asks one to do something for her it is hard to refuse."

"Kinder in the long run," said the other. "There's no good in raising false hopes in her mind. You've seen in the newspapers what we've discovered. What you may not know is that Daynton admits to having had a furious quarrel with the murdered man at the very time the deed was done."

"It was that fact, amongst others, my dear inspector, that caused me to take up the case. Surely no one out of a lunatic asylum would go out of his way to damn himself so completely if he had done the murder. His stick, I admit, he couldn't get over, since he was imbecile enough to leave it here; the cigarette stump is awkward. But why he should then add a quarrel which no one had heard is really more than one can swallow."

He was swinging the door backwards and forwards as he spoke, and I saw by the glint in his eye that he was hot on something.

"Very clever, Mr. Standish," laughed the Inspector, "but not quite clever enough. Both Miss Moody and Mr. Playfair knew of his intention. So how could he deny it? I say, sir, must you go on making that squeaking noise with the door?"

"Both ways, you notice," said Ronald. "It creaks when it opens and it creaks when it shuts. Moreover, it shuts of its own accord. Very interesting."

We stared at him in amazement, but he took no notice, and at last the inspector turned to go, with a significant glance at me.

"By the way, Inspector," said Ronald suddenly, "had the dead man got a brush in his hand?"

"No; but one was lying on the floor beside him."

"Was there any paint on it?"

For a moment the inspector looked nonplussed.

"I really couldn't tell you at the moment," he said, and Ronald shook his head.

"My dear fellow," he remarked, "you surprise me. Get hold of it and examine it. And if there's paint on it, sit down and think things over, bearing in mind the fact that the door creaks."

"And if there isn't paint on it?" said the other with ponderous sarcasm.

"There will be," answered Ronald quietly.

"Anything else you can suggest?"

"Yes; but I don't think you're likely to do it."

"What's that?"

"Release that unfortunate chap, Daynton."

"Release Daynton?" gasped the other.

"Why not? For I can assure you that he had no more to do with the murder of Bernard Power than you or I had."

"Then who did do it?"

"I promise you shall know at the first possible moment," said Ronald.

"Well, until I do," grinned the other, "Mr. Daynton remains under lock and key."

Ronald was silent as we strolled back to the house, and I knew him too well to interrupt his reverie.

"By the way, Bob," he said suddenly, as we neared the door, "say nothing—even to Miss Moody—about our thinking Daynton innocent. It might get round to the servants."

She met us on the drive, and with her was a man of about forty-five, who we correctly surmised was her guardian, Mr. Playfair.

"Well," she cried, after introducing us, "what luck?"

Ronald shook his head. "Early days yet, Miss Moody," he said gravely. "I've seen the inspector, and I'm bound to confess it doesn't look too good."

"I blame myself very much," said her guardian, "but never in my wildest imagination did I dream of such a tragedy occurring."

"In what way do you blame yourself, Mr. Playfair?" asked Ronald.

"In going out so early that morning. I ought to have waited here and been present at the interview. Hubert is such a hot headed chap."

"But, Uncle John, he didn't do it!" cried the girl.

"My dear," said the other sadly, "I wish I could think so. And let us hope that Mr. Standish succeeds in proving it. Candidly," he went on as she left us, "I wish she hadn't been to you. You understand how I mean it. The case is so painfully clear that I fear even you can do no good. And the sooner she realises it the better."

"Perhaps so," agreed Ronald. "As you say, it's a pity you went out as early as you did."

"Well, I wanted to get to Comber Ness by noon, and it's very nearly a four hours' run. I don't know whether my ward has told you," he went on, with a faint smile, "but I'm a most enthusiastic photographer. And I have just acquired a new toy. Are you by any chance interested?"

"Very," said Ronald. "I do a bit that way myself."

"Then come and have a drink, and I will show it to you." He led the way into the house and we followed him. "It is a stereoscopic camera," he explained, as he took it off a table in the hall. "And doubtless you know the principle on which it works. The two lenses are the same distance apart as one's eyes, and two negatives are taken at each exposure. Then by making positives and holding them in one of those machines that you probably remember from your early youth, the whole thing stands out as in real life."

"And you went over to Comber Ness to get a photograph," said Ronald.

"Exactly," said the other, and then gave a rueful laugh. "And didn't get it—at least, not what I wanted. I've only just got the machine. In fact, it was my first load of plates. Now, if you examine it, you will see a little number at one end of the plate-carrier. Every time you change a plate after taking a photo the number goes up one, so that you always know how many plates are left. The numbers range from one to twelve, and the night before Wilkinson, my butler, who is almost as keen as I am on it, happened to mention to me that number twelve was showing, which meant that there was only one more plate left. And I forgot all about it till I arrived at Comber Ness."

"But one exposure was surely enough?" said Ronald.

"Quite—if I hadn't wanted to take two different views. It is, as you know, one of the most celebrated beauty spots of England, and I had promised an American friend of mine two photographs taken from totally separate points. And I had only one plate. So there was nothing for it but to use the camera as an ordinary one by covering one lens with a cap and taking one view on half the plate, and then covering the other lens and taking the second view on the other half. But, of course, it spoiled things from a stereoscopic point altogether. However, I'm glad to say they both came out well. I left them to be developed that day, and they were sent up this afternoon with the other eleven."

He was examining some of the results as he was speaking, and at moment his ward came into the hall.

"Good Heavens! Uncle John," she cried, "this is hardly the time photographs."

"Sorry, dear," he said contritely. "The matter came up in the course of conversation with Mr. Standish. You see, this was the camera I was using that day at Comber Ness."

She seemed sorry at having spoken so sharply, and laid her hand on his shoulder.

"It's all right, old 'un," she said "So that's the new toy, is it? Can we see the pretty pictures?"

"I've got to make the positives first," he answered. "These are the negatives."

"Well, it's all beyond me. And I thought they were going to be much bigger. Each of them seems just the same size as that other camera takes—the little one."

"Quite right. This camera takes two identical pictures on every plate, each of which is the same size as the little one."

"And when were these very goo views of the grounds here taken?" said Ronald.

"Let the see. I think I took those the day before I went to Comber Ness."

"A very fine machine," cried Ronald. "They are so clear cut. And these two separate ones of Comber Ness. Beautiful! Beautiful! I should very much like prints of those myself, if you would be good enough."

"Certainly," said our host. "Delighted. And now I expect you'd like to see your rooms."

He led the way upstairs and, having told us the time of dinner, left us. And shortly after Ronald came sauntering into my room and sat on the bed.

"What do you make of it, Bob?" he said.

"Nothing at all," I answered. "And though you may be perfectly

220

clear in your own mind, old lad, that this man Daynton didn't do it, I don't see that you've got much forrader as to who did."

He made no reply, and was staring out of the window as the butler knocked to find out if there was anything we wanted.

"I hear you're very keen on photography, Wilkinson," said Ronald pleasantly.

"In a small way I dabble in it, sir."

"Mr. Playfair was telling me it was a great hobby of yours. What do you think of that new camera of his?"

"I've only seen it once, sir. He asked me to tell him the number showing at the end. Twelve it was, I remember. That was the night before the tragedy, sir. I do hope that you may be able to do something for poor Mr. Daynton. Such a nice gentleman, sir."

"I hope so, too, Wilkinson. By the way, Mr. Playfair does most of his developing himself, doesn't he?"

"Invariably, sir," said the butler, looking faintly surprised.

"But he had this last lot developed for him?" persisted Ronald.

"Yes, sir. He apparently lunched at Barminster on the day of the murder, and left them with a chemist there."

"Thank you, Wilkinson. No—nothing to drink."

The butler left the room, and I stared at him.

"You seem very interested in our host's photography," I said.

"Bob;" he remarked, "if you had just bought a new stereoscopic camera and had motored over a hundred miles for a view, would you suddenly be so overcome by a promise given to an American friend that you wouldn't use your new acquisition as such?"

"What in the name of fortune are you driving at?" I cried. "Anyway, whatever I might or might not do, we have seen what our host did. There's the proof in the negative. Why, good Lord, man, you can't suspect him."

"I didn't say I did. I merely asked a question. You see, Bob, one thing is perfectly clear. A man who was at Comber Ness in the morning and arrived at Barminster for lunch could not possibly have left here as late as ten o'clock."

"Very well, then?"

"A perfect alibi. But it would have been an equally good alibi if he had carried out the same timetable and taken a stereoscopic picture there instead of two separate views. So again I ask—why those two different views?"

"It must be the American," I cried.

"Must it? Or is it because he couldn't take a stereoscopic picture?"

"Then he couldn't have taken the other two?"

"Sound logic," he grinned. "Well, time to change, I suppose."

"Look here, Ronald," I almost shouted, "what do you mean?"

The grin departed, and he looked at me gravely. "It means," he said, "that we are dealing with a particularly dangerous and unprincipled man, whose only slip up to date is that he did not expend a penny-worth of oil on the hinges of the summer-house door."

And with that he left the room.

All through the evening his words kept recurring to me, and the more I thought of them the more amazing did they become. It seemed to me he must be wrong, and yet Ronald Standish was not in the habit of making a definite statement without good reason. And when, next morning, he suddenly announced his intention of returning to London, I was even more dumbfounded.

The girl was terribly disappointed, and it struck me that his attempts at consolation were very half-hearted. He seemed to have lost interest in the case, though he gave her a few perfunctory words of hope.

"I'll be back this evening, Miss Moody," he said, "and perhaps by then I may have something to report."

But I heard him expressing a different opinion to our host when she was out of hearing. For some reason he did not want me to go with him, and so I spent most of the day with her trying to cheer her up. It was a little difficult, since I manifestly could not allude to the amazing hints he had dropped the preceding evening. In fact, the more I thought of them the more fantastic did they seem. If Ronald had a fault it was that he sometimes seemed to go out of his way to find a complicated solution to a thing when a simple one fitted the facts. And for the life of me I could not see wherein lay the difficulty over our host's explanation of the two different photos on the one plate.

He returned about six, looking weary and dispirited, and my heart sank.

"Waste of time, I fear," he said, as we all met him in the hall. "I'm afraid it's a case of going back to London for good."

"And throwing up the case?" cried the girl.

"I fear I was to blame, Miss Moody, in speaking too hopefully in my rooms," he said. "So if you could give orders for our things to be packed, we'll be getting along. By the way, Mr. Playfair, don't forget those two photographs you promised me."

"I did them for you today," said our host. "I'll see if they are dry."

He left the hall, and for a moment we were alone.

"Got him, Bob," he said, and his eyes were blazing with excitement, "by an amazing piece of luck."

But he was his apathetic self when Playfair returned with the prints.

"Astoundingly good," he remarked, as he examined them. "How did you manage to do it, Mr. Playfair?"

"Do what?" cried the other, staring at him.

"Avoid taking the steamroller which has been standing idle in the centre of this particular view for the last ten days."

For a moment there was dead silence, and I saw that every atom of colour had left our host's face.

"I did not go to London today," went on Ronald. "I went to Comber Ness, where I took this photograph. Not fixed yet—but look at it."

He flung it on the table; it was the same as the other. But in the centre was a steamroller with a tarpaulin over it.

"You devil!" screamed Playfair, and made a dash for the passage leading to the back of the house.

"Hold him, Bob!" roared Ronald, and I collared him. He struggled like a maniac, but I kept him till Ronald came running back with the plate in his hand.

"He was going to destroy that," he cried. "Well, Mr. Playfair, have you any explanation as to why that steamroller is missing from your photo?" And then with a sudden shout—"Stop him, Bob!"

But it was too late. I felt his body relax in my arms, almost immediately after his hand came away from his mouth. Then he slithered to the floor—dead.

CHAPTER 3.

"I'm blowed if I see how you did it, Mr. Standish."

It was three hours later, and Inspector Savage was gazing at Ronald in undisguised admiration.

"By starting with a theory diametrically opposed to yours," said Ronald. "You were convinced Hubert Daynton had done it; I was convinced he hadn't. Then who had? My first idea was that the murderer was some man Power had wronged—probably over some woman. He had been hiding near by, and had taken advantage of the quarrel he heard to do the deed and throw the suspicion on someone else. Then I suddenly realised the enormous significance of the fact that the door creaked, and shut of its own accord.

"Now, Power was sitting at his easel some four yards from the door. Suppose the door was shut when the murderer entered; it would creak as he opened it. Suppose it was being kept open by the stone with which the deed was done; it would creak as it shut, after the stone was picked up. In either event it would creak.

"Now, what does anybody do who hears a door creak behind him—especially if there has just been a quarrel and the creak may mean that the other person has returned? He looks over his shoulder to see who it is. And if he sees some enemy of his, someone he has wronged, he does not continue his job with his back to the newcomer. But Power went on with his painting. Therefore the person he saw he did not regard as an enemy, but looked on as a friend. So much of a friend, in fact, that he did not object to this new arrival walking about behind his back—always an uncomfortable sensation unless your mind is completely at rest. And at once a very different complexion was put on the matter.

"Then came my interview with Mr. John Playfair, and the question of the two separate pictures of different views of Comber Ness on the one plate—the point that puzzled you so much, Bob. You remember that when I said it might be because he couldn't take a stereoscopic picture, you countered by saying that in that case he equally could not have taken the two separate views. Which was right, up to a point. He couldn't have taken either, but that doesn't prevent a negative appearing on a plate.

"The man was a skilled photographer, and he was faced with the necessity of proving to the world that he had been to Comber Ness. If he could do so he was safe. But since he had no intention of going anywhere near Comber Ness, what was he to do? He knew that if you take a negative and make a positive from it, you can produce a second negative in a dark room on exactly the same principle as you produce a print. But he had no stereoscopic picture of Comber Ness; he'd only just bought the machine. What he had got were two separate views taken with his smaller camera!

"So he makes two positives—you remember Miss Moody told us he was fiddling about in the dark room all the afternoon before the murder—and then he takes out his last stereoscopic plate. You see the importance of its being the last one; that accounted for his having to put them both on one plate. And that was why he took three unnecessary photos of his own grounds. On to that last plate he clips the two positives, side by side, exposes it in his dark room, and returns the plate to the camera. There is his alibi. He need never go near Comber Ness, and, in fact, he never did.

"He had Wilkinson's evidence that twelve was the number showing—you noticed there, Bob, the slight discrepancy between Playfair's statement and the butler's. He had the chemist's evidence that the plates were handed over to him to be developed; he had the hotel evidence that he lunched at Barminster.

"Exactly what he did we shall never know. He drove away at eight-thirty, and presumably concealed his car in some lane. Then he returned and hid near the summer-house. He was taking no risk up to date; if he was found there was no reason why he shouldn't be in his own grounds. And everything came off. He murdered Power, and drove quietly over to Barminster, where he lunched."

"But why, this cold-blooded murder of a man he apparently liked?" I asked.

"The usual reason," he answered. "Once or twice after dinner last night I caught the look in his eyes as they rested on the girl. He was in love with her himself, which can account for many things. Why he took up Power at all I can't tell you—possibly at the beginning he had some idea of choking off Daynton by making him jealous. Then he may have feared that instead of doing that the artist's attentions to the girl might have the opposite result and bring Daynton and the girl closer together. Or perhaps he may have become jealous of Power himself. Anyway, he saw his opportunity of getting rid of both of them. And but for the astounding piece of luck of my finding that steamroller where it was, he'd have gone darned near doing it. Being a clever man, he realised at once that his whole alibi had become worse than useless—it had become a rope round his neck. For what possible reason could there be, save the true one, for his saying he'd been to Comber Ness when he hadn't? That was why I was so off-hand today. At the first hint of suspicion he would have destroyed the plate and never given me the prints, trusting to the chemist's evidence that it had been a view of Comber Ness."

"Well, I'm sure I'm much obliged to you, Mr. Standish," said the inspector. "Mr. Daynton has already been released."

"And doubtless will provide the necessary consolation for Miss

Moody," said Ronald, with a smile. "For I don't think we need waste one second's pity on that singularly cold-blooded murderer."

And it wasn't until we were driving into London that he turned to me thoughtfully.

"I think the lie was justified, Bob, don't you?"

"What lie?" I said.

"That steamroller only arrived at Comber Ness early this morning."

The Missing Chauffeur

It was on a morning in late September that, happening to drop into Ronald Standish's rooms, I found a man with him whose face seemed familiar to me. He was sprawling in one of the easy chairs, smoking a cigarette, and he glanced up as I apologised for interrupting.

"You're doing nothing of the sort, old boy," said Ronald. "In fact, you've arrived at a very propitious moment. Do you know the Duke of Dorset, known to most of the dear old schoolfellows as Catface? This"—he waved a hand at me—"is Bob Miller."

The duke grinned cheerfully.

"I was up in town on business," he said, "and I suddenly remembered that Ronald sometimes did the sleuth act. So I called round to see him."

"Not much sleuthing about this," laughed Ronald. "Bob—we are rising in business. We've now become a registry office for servants."

"If somebody would explain," I murmured mildly, "it might be a little easier."

"Catface has lost his chauffeur," Ronald remarked. "Hence his visit. But tell Bob the story. I'd like to hear it again."

"It sounds a bit absurd, I must admit," said the Duke, "and there is probably some quite ordinary explanation. At the same time it's no use pretending that I'm not worried. My chauffeur has suddenly and mysteriously disappeared. He's been in our service for years; he was with my father. And he's vanished into thin air."

"It's this way, Bob," said Ronald. "The man's name is Williams, and he lives with his wife in a cottage on the estate. By the way, are there any children?"

"Two," said the duke. "A boy and a girl—about ten and eight years old."

"Well, it appears that the night before last Williams left his cottage just after seven o'clock, telling his wife that he was going down to the 'Bat and Ball' to have a pint—the 'Bat and Ball' being the chief pub in Medchester, which, as you know, is the village close to Catface's hovel. Apparently it was not an unusual thing for him to do, and Mrs. Williams thought nothing about it. But, as time went on and nine o'clock came with no sign of him, she began to get uneasy. So finally she rang up the 'Bat and Ball,' to find to her amazement that he had never been there. She still wasn't really alarmed. There was another pub to which he some times went. But that wasn't on the telephone, so all she could do was to wait. And wait she did until eleven o'clock, when she became genuinely frightened. So she put on a hat and went down into the village, a matter of ten minutes' walk. At that hour both the pubs were shut, but she beat up the two owners, only to find that her husband had not been to either of them that night.

"By this time, of course, she was in a thorough panic. She could only assume that her husband had been taken ill or had had a fit on the way. So she got the local constable out of bed, and armed with a lantern the two of them searched the road the whole way back to her cottage, without, however, finding any trace of him. And that is as far as we go at the moment. Her husband did not return during the night. He had not returned when Catface left for London yesterday after lunch. And such is the story of the missing chauffeur."

"Possibly he's back by now," I said.

"I told his wife to wire me at the club if he returned," said the duke. "You see, the extraordinary thing to my mind is that Williams, of all men, should act in such a way. It's as if one's butler suddenly stood on his head in the dining-room."

"Probably suffering from loss of memory," I remarked.

"But in that case surely he'd have been found yesterday!" he cried.

"Not of necessity, by any means," said Ronald. "It doesn't follow that he's remained in the neighbourhood. He had money. What was there to stop him wandering about all night, and then taking a train for somewhere?"

"The only station within miles is Croyde Junction," said the duke. "And he's as well known there as I am. Naturally I rang them up to ask, and no sign of him had been seen. I'm worried, old boy, not only because I'm genuinely attached to the fellow, but also because it's an infernal nuisance having to get a temporary chauffeur for the grand duke's visit."

He saw my look of bewilderment and explained.

"The Grand Duke Sergius is coming to stay with me next week. In the old pre-Bolshevik days he was one of the loud noises in Russia, and he was a great personal friend of my father's. And he has announced his intention of putting in two or three days with me during his stay in England."

"But do you think there is any connection between your chauffeur's disappearance and the grand duke's visit?" I asked.

He shrugged his shoulders.

"Probably I've got the wind up needlessly," he said, "but the possibility has occurred to me. He is a leader and mainspring of the Whites, and I know that his life has been threatened on several occasions."

"Still, it is difficult to see how abducting your chauffeur is going to help them to carry out their threat. They can't possibly know whom you are going to engage in his place. They can't, so to speak, force a man on you."

"I know all that," he agreed. "I've said it to myself over and over again. And still I can't get rid of the thought that there may be some connection."

"Have you taken any steps to get another man?" asked Ronald.

"I told my agent to write about it," he said. "Honestly, old boy, I wish you'd come down for a few days." He leaned forward in his chair. "It's possible—perhaps probable—that I'm talking through the back of my neck. But I am uneasy. If it wasn't for the grand duke the thing would be quite different; I shouldn't have worried you. But I'd never forgive myself if anything happened while he was staying with me. Why doesn't Miller come, too? I can give you both some shooting. And I'd feel easier if you'd cast your eye over things."

Ronald smiled. "I've got no objection to trying to hit a few in the beak, old boy," he said. "And I don't suppose Bob has either. But I frankly think you are worrying yourself most unnecessarily about this man's disappearance. I'm convinced myself you'll find that there is some quite simple explanation."

And at that we left it, after agreeing to motor down that afternoon.

The duke had arrived before us, and a glance at his face showed that further developments had taken place.

"I've got Mrs. Williams here, Ronald," he said. "I want you to hear what she has to say. I'm terribly afraid there has been foul play."

We followed him into a small writing-room, where a middle-aged woman, her eyes red with weeping, was waiting.

"Now, Mrs. Williams," he went on, "I want you to tell these gentlemen exactly what you've told me. They've come down from London especially to see if they can do anything to help you."

"I will, your Grace," she answered; "though I fear my poor Henry is beyond human aid. He'd never have gone away like that, without so much as a word to me, of his own free will."

"Supposing you just tell us everything, Mrs. Williams," said Ronald gently. "I have already heard from his Grace the bare facts of your husband's disappearance. Now I want to hear further details."

"Show Mr. Standish what you found today," said the duke. She fumbled in her bag, and finally produced a sheet of paper, which she handed to Ronald. On it was written the following sentence in block capitals:

MEET ME CROSSROADS 7.30

"And where did you find this?" asked Ronald, holding it up to the light.

"In my husband's livery, sir," she answered. "There was a hole in the top pocket, and as I was folding it up and putting it away this morning I felt this rustle in the lining."

"Which crossroads does it refer to?"

"There are crossroads halfway between the cottage and Medchester," said the duke.

"I see," said Ronald. "So for the moment, at any rate, we'll assume that that is the spot alluded to. Now, Mrs. Williams, you say you found this in your husband's livery. Did he wear it on the day he disappeared?"

"Yes, sir. He came in about six o'clock and changed."

"Was he in his usual spirits, or did he seem at all worried?"

"Not exactly worried, sir, but rather quiet like."

"In other words, different from what he generally was?"

"Well, yes, sir—he was a little. And yet not enough to make me remark on it at the time. Though what with one thing and another and getting the children to bed, I didn't have much chance of speaking."

"And he's said nothing to you in the last few days which could throw any light on this note?"

"Nothing, sir." And then she hesitated. "Well, there was one little thing, sir."

"Out with it," said Ronald. "It's the little things we want."

"Well, sir, about four days ago, or perhaps five, he did say to me that there was a lot of wicked scoundrels in the world. And he said it as if there was something at the back of his mind."

"Did you ask him what he meant?" cried the duke.

"I didn't, your Grace," she said. "He was just going out, and after that it slipped my memory."

"So there's really nothing more you can tell us, Mrs. Williams?" said Ronald.

"No, sir. I can't think of anything."

"And your children noticed nothing?"

"No, sir. I haven't told them yet. I've just let them think their daddy has gone away for two or three days." She clasped her hands together. "Oh, sir—do you think there's any hope?"

"Good Heavens! yes, Mrs. Williams," cried Ronald cheerfully. "You go back to your cottage and keep your spirits up. I shall probably be along that way shortly myself. By the way, there is one more question I want to ask you. Has your husband got any friends or acquaintances who are not English?"

"Not that I know of, sir," she answered. "If he has, he's never mentioned it to me."

"Thank you, Mrs. Williams. Now, don't forget what I said: keep cheerful."

"What do you make of it, Ronald?" said the duke, as the door closed behind her.

"Nothing at all at the moment," Ronald answered, "except the one significant fact in that note."

He put it on the table.

"Look at that seven. Have you ever seen an Englishman make a seven with a horizontal line across it? Whereas a lot of Europeans do. I don't say it's conclusive, but it's more than likely that the writer has lived a lot abroad. Question number two. Is it a man or a woman? No answer possible from what we've got at present. From what you tell me, Williams is not the sort of man who would play the fool with a girl."

"Most emphatically not," said the duke.

"But, on the other hand, he might be taken in by a sob-stuff story and think he could help, someone. So, as I said, we do not know if it's a man or a woman. All we can say is that the loss of memory theory is out of court, and that he left the house to keep a definite assignation."

"Which looks bad to me," said the duke. "For nothing will make me believe that he would not have communicated with me if he'd been able to."

"It has that appearance, Catface," agreed Ronald. "However, we may as well go and have a look at the place, though I don't suppose we'll find anything after such a lapse of time."

"I'll come with you," said the duke. "There is ample time before dinner."

We strolled across the park, and after we had gone about half a mile he pointed to two cottages ahead of us.

"One of those is Williams's," he remarked; "the other belongs to the head keeper."

"I think we'll start at the cross-roads first," said Ronald. "Has anybody except the local constable been over the ground?"

"I couldn't tell you," answered the duke. "I told my agent to do all he could, and to get in touch with the police at Dorchester. Incidentally—talk of the devil—Well, Johnson, any fresh developments?"

A middle-aged man in riding breeches was coming towards us, and his expression was grave.

"I'm sorry to say there are, your Grace," he said. "About thirty yards up the road leading to Cantrell's farm the undergrowth at one side is all beaten down. There is blood on the grass, and every appearance of a desperate struggle having taken place."

The duke turned to Ronald.

"That settles it," he remarked. "That's the spot we're making for."

He introduced us to the agent, and we all four walked on together.

"I was just coming to report to you," continued Johnson. "He must have been set on by someone in the darkness, and in the struggle gone swaying up that side road. That's Inspector Morrison from Dorchester in front of us now. It was he who discovered it."

The inspector saluted as we came up and led us to the spot. "Pretty clear what happened, your Grace," he said. "Though why anyone should want to assault Mr. Williams is beyond me. Case of mistaken identity, I suppose."

"Not that, Inspector," remarked Ronald, handing him the note. "This has just been found in his coat. He was deliberately decoyed here."

As he spoke he was peering at the ground carefully.

"Is this track much used?" he asked.

"Very little," answered Johnson, "and mainly by Cantrell."

"Has Cantrell got a car?"

"Yes—but it's been out of action for the last week. A big end went."

"Well, a car has been standing here comparatively recently. You can see the impression on the grass if you look closely."

He straightened up and his face was grave.

"Things look much worse than I thought, Catface," he said in a low voice. "It's hardly conceivable that the mark of that car at this particular spot should have no connection with the struggle. So it boils down to the fact that the whole affair was definitely planned. But why the deuce anybody should want to kidnap your chauffeur is a bit of a poser."

He turned to the inspector.

"You haven't by any chance heard of any foreigners being in the neighbourhood?" he asked.

The inspector shook his head, but Johnson swung round at once.

"Funny you should ask that, Mr. Standish. There's been a woman—quite young—staying at the 'Bat and Ball' recently. And two or three days ago she was joined by two men who arrived by car. They all left that night. By Jove! it was the very day of this affair, now that I come to think of it."

"But why do you imagine that they were foreigners?" asked Ronald.

"Cheadle—the landlord—told me they were," said Johnson. "Apparently they all spoke English perfectly, but amongst themselves they used some other language."

"Well, Inspector," said Ronald, "there's something for you to go on. That note was almost certainly written by a foreigner, and now we hear that three foreigners were staying at the 'Bat and Ball' on the day of Williams's disappearance and left in a car that night. Moreover, a car stood here recently."

"Not much proof anywhere, sir," said the inspector doubtfully.

"None at all," agreed Ronald. "But if there is no connection, it is an extraordinary chain of coincidence. If I were you, I'd try to get a description of those people from Cheadle, and put some quiet inquiries on foot. It's just within the bounds of possibility that someone might have noticed the number of their car."

He turned to the duke.

"And that, it seems to me, is all that we can do. Sorry not to be more helpful, old boy, but the business of tracking car and people is beyond me. It's a police job pure and simple."

"Supposing you're right, Ronald, do you think they've killed him?"

"I can't tell you. I don't know, There's a lot of blood about. The struggle was pretty desperate. All that one can do is to hope that he's only been laid out."

"Lord! but I wish I could get to the bottom of this," cried the duke in a worried voice. We were walking back over the park towards the house. "I'm infernally sorry for Williams—poor devil!" he went on—"but what's the object of the thing?"

"Well," said Ronald slowly, "it seems to me that there are two possible alternatives which suggest themselves at once. The first one is that they made some suggestion to him which he resented so much that they had this fight. The second one is rather more sinister. They decoyed him there in order to abduct him, so that someone else might be substituted in his place—someone who might prove more amenable to this suggestion."

The duke stopped and stared at him.

"What sort of suggestion?" he demanded.

"I did not think so at first," said Ronald, "but with these fresh developments, old boy, I am bound to admit that I'm beginning to agree with your original suspicion that it's got something to do with your visitor of next week. Otherwise the whole thing is absolutely incomprehensible."

"What the devil am I to do?" cried the other. "Shall I make some excuse and put him off?"

"You can hardly do that on what we've got up to date. We may be entirely wrong. All you can do is to vet the new man when he comes very thoroughly, and—"

He broke off suddenly.

"Hallo! a new development. What does Mrs. Williams want?" She was running across the grass towards us, waving her arms, and evidently in a state of considerable excitement.

"Your Grace," she gasped as she came up, "this has just come." In her hand she held a letter which she brandished in the air. "Steady, Mrs. Williams," he said soothingly. "Let's have a look at it."

"It's from Henry, sir." She turned to Ronald. "But look at the writing."

And Ronald was looking at the writing with a face grown suddenly grave. For its colour was reddish brown, and it looked as if the wrong end of a penholder had been used, so thick were the letters. The envelope was addressed to "Mrs. Williams, Lilac Cottage, Medchester," and was stained with mud and dirt.

"Read what's inside, sir," she cried.

The contents consisted of a double sheet of paper on which two words were written, also in reddish brown:—

Harvey petrol.

"Harvey!" cried the duke, who was looking over Ronald shoulder. "Why, that's the local garage."

"Is that so?" said Ronald thoughtfully. "You are sure this is your husband's writing, Mrs. Williams?"

"Positive, sir. Besides, I know the paper. You see that little W in the corner, and Henry always carried some in his pocket-book. And envelopes. What does it mean, sir?"

"Postmark—Belton. Where's Belton?"

"Next village to Medchester on the London road," said the duke

"Then, your Grace, he must be there," she cried. "But why has he used that funny-coloured ink? And why is the envelope so dirty?"

"I'm afraid you mustn't build on the hope that your husband is at Belton, Mrs. Williams," said Ronald gravely. "In fact, I'm sorry to have to tell, you some bad news."

"He's not dead, sir?" she said piteously.

"No, no. I don't think for a moment he's dead. But I'm afraid he's been badly hurt."

"Can I go to him, sir?" she cried.

"We don't know where he is, Mrs. Williams."

"But, look here, Ronald," said the duke, who had been studying the envelope, "the date of the postmark is today."

"Which shows that it was posted today, but not that it was written today. This letter was thrown out of the car in which he was travelling, and fell in the mud. Evidently today somebody found it and put it in the post."

"How on earth can you tell that?" demanded the duke incredulously.

But Ronald did not answer. Instead, he turned to the woman. "Will you leave this with me, Mrs. Williams? I'll take great care of it. And the instant we know anything about your husband we'll let you know."

"Very good, sir. I'm sure, sir, you will."

She curtsied, and went stumbling back to her cottage.

"Now, Ronald," cried the duke, when she was out of hearing, "how do you know this letter wasn't written today?"

"Because I recognised at once the ink that had been used. It's blood, Catface. And from the colour it's considerably more than one day old."

"Good God!" gasped the duke. "Are you sure?"

"Quite sure. Somehow or other Williams managed to write this, using his own blood as an ink. He knew that if his wife got it she would bring it to you. It must be a warning of sorts, but what it means is somewhat obscure."

"We always do get our petrol from Harvey." said the duke. "His is the only garage within miles."

Ronald put the letter carefully in his pocket.

"It's one of the most extraordinary cases I've ever struck," he said. "And at the moment I don't see one ray of light."

That state of affairs continued for the next week. The new chauffeur, a man by the name of Groves, arrived with the most impeccable references, two of them from people known personally to all of us. Harvey, whose garage we visited casually, proved to be a typical West Countryman with a jovial face and a cheery manner: a man who, if appearances ever count for anything, was as honest and straight as could be found in Dorsetshire. Cheadle, with whom we had a pint or two, gave us as closely as he could a description of the three foreigners, but, as Ronald had anticipated, it proved quite useless. It would have fitted a hundred people equally well. And the mystery of Williams's whereabouts remained as profound as ever.

It was not until two days before the grand duke's arrival that any further development took place. Ronald and I were strolling through the village on our way back to lunch, when Johnson, the duke's agent, came out of the "Bat and Ball" and hurried towards us.

"That woman is back," he said. "Returned this morning."

"Is she, by Jove?" cried Ronald. "We'll come in and have a drink. I'd like to have a look at her without her knowing it."

"Good morning, gentlemen," cried Cheadle, as we entered the bar. "That lady—"

"Three pints, Mr. Cheadle, please," interrupted Ronald quickly, at the same time giving him a warning frown. "And have something yourself."

The room was full of the usual crowd that gathers in a village inn at midday, and after a cursory glance round Ronald dismissed them. At the same time, he did not relax his caution.

"Not a word, please, Mr. Cheadle," he said, in a low voice. "I want to see that lady without raising her suspicions. Is she having lunch here?"

"Yes, sir."

"Then my friends and I will lunch here, too. Give me a table where I can get a good look at her."

And for half an hour, in the intervals of trying to masticate the so-called cold beef, we were able to study the woman at our leisure. And it must be admitted that the insult to our digestion was not worth it. Just a distinctly pretty young foreigner having lunch by herself in an English inn—that and nothing more. And yet the clue to so much lay under that tight-fitting little hat.

"Bob, I'm flummoxed," said Ronald, as we left the inn. "Absolutely flummoxed. Why has she come back? What is the connecting link? There must be one. No woman like that is going to stay at the 'Bat and Ball' for fun. But we've got no proof: nothing but two or there apparently unconnected facts. What is the link? Are we being damned stupid, or is it really something that we couldn't know yet?"

And that night I heard him pacing up and down, his room for hours, until at length I fell asleep.

CHAPTER 2.

Even now, after the lapse of years, I sometimes wake up sweating at the nearness of the thing. But for one tiny slip on their part, and Ronald's extraordinary quickness in realising its significance, one of the most atrocious crimes of modern times would have succeeded. Many garbled accounts have appeared in the Press. Now for the first time I will set down the real truth of that amazing plot.

It occurred on the second day of the grand duke's visit. A ceremonial call on a former British Ambassador who lived some fifty miles away had been arranged, and at eleven o'clock the car drew up at the door. Groves was driving, and seated beside him was the man who passed as the grand duke's secretary, but who was in reality a highly-placed secret service man. Behind sat the grand duke and his host. The car rolled away, some of the house party watching it depart. Nothing could have been more normal. And then two minutes after it had gone a chance remark of Johnson's threw the spark into the powder magazine.

"Never seen the duke so angry in my life," he said, "as he was with that new chauffeur a few minutes ago."

"What was the trouble?" asked someone perfunctorily.

"He'd let the car run practically dry of petrol."

"What's that?"

Ronald's voice came like a pistol shot, and then things moved.

"Bob—get the bus. Move, man, move!"

I raced towards the garage, and was back inside a minute with the Bentley, to find Ronald waiting. He boarded her whilst she was still moving, leaving a crowd of surprised guests staring after us. He flung himself down in the seat beside me, and with a little thrill I felt something hard in his pocket pressed against my thigh. Whilst I had got the car, he had got his revolver.

"The tank of Catface's car was full last night, Bob," he said quietly. "I had a look at it on purpose. Stamp on the gas, boy."

And three minutes later we were in the village. In front of us was the Rolls outside Harvey's garage, filling up from the petrol pump.

"Pull up just behind her," said Ronald.

His eyes were darting in every direction, but at the moment the scene looked harmless enough. The village street was almost deserted save for a powerful-looking racing car outside the "Bat and Ball," and Harvey and his assistant, who were manipulating the pump. The secret service man had descended and was standing by the window on the side of the grand duke. The chauffeur, having watched the filling for a few moments, had returned to the driving seat. At length the operation was over; the pipe was held up to let the last drops out; the gauze filter of the car was put back in the tank; the cap was screwed on. And a moment later they were away.

"Seems all in order, old boy," I said.

He did not answer; only stared after the back of the retreating car. And suddenly his eyes narrowed, and without a word he raced down the street after it. Stopped, picked something up in the road, and came back towards me like a madman.

"Get her going!" he roared. "And chase the Rolls."

He fell in beside me, and I saw that he held in his hand a gauze filter. Even then I didn't get it. Evidently the assistant had forgotten to put it back in the tank, and any time would do to return it. And at that moment the roar of the racing car behind us drowned our own machine.

"They're after us," said Ronald, through set teeth. "And they've got our legs. Saw the curtains moving in the inn and I knew we were being watched. The woman and two men."

"What shall I do?" I cried. "Let her all out?"

"Yes, until I tell you otherwise."

The road was twisty for the first mile, and we swung round corners with the other car on our tail. In the glass on the screen I could see their faces at times, and suddenly I saw one of them stand up and draw a revolver from his pocket.

"Look out," I howled. "They're trying gun work."

"Are they, by gosh?" said Ronald, kneeling up on the seat and facing backwards. "Two can play at that game. Swerve about a bit, Bob, till he's fired."

Came a crack and the pilot lamp shattered.

"Now keep her steady."

For about a hundred yards the road was straight, and I could see them all in the mirror. And then it happened. Ronald fired, and the car behind us seemed to swerve like a mad thing across the road. I had a vision in the glass of wheels upside down; heard a frightful crash; then silence save for the roar of our own engine.

"I burst their front tyre for them," said Ronald quietly, sitting down again. "And now then, Bob, every ounce of juice."

His face was cold and set, but I could feel the nervous tension of him. And still half dazed I drove on—drove as I have never driven before or since—drove till we saw a minute or two later the Rolls in front of us.

"Keep your horn going," he cried, standing up and waving his arms violently.

At last we saw Catface look round, then turn and give an order to Groves. The car slowed down and stopped.

"Pull up beside 'em, but stand by to move on," said Ronald.

We reached them, and Ronald yelled his orders.

"Fall into this car for your lives!" he shouted. "Hurry! For God's sake, hurry!"

They tumbled in a heap into the back of the Bentley.

"Drive on, Bob. Stamp on it again."

And I suppose I'd gone fifty yards when it happened. There came a deafening explosion, and the Rolls seemed literally to split in two. The whole of the back part flew in pieces, and what was left became in half a second a raging inferno of flames. For a while we watched it in awe-struck silence, and then the grand duke lit a cigarette and turned to his host.

"Cutting it a trifle fine, I think. Do all your cars do that, my dear fellow?"

"How did you find out, Ronald?" said the other shakily.

But Ronald was staring at Groves, who had turned as white as a sheet.

"Who got at you?" he said sternly. "And how much were you paid for emptying the tank?"

"Nothing, sir," he cried. "Before God, I swear it. It was a lady, your Grace, who had never seen His Royal Highness, and she begged me to stop the car in the village so that she could have a closer look at him. She wanted to take a photograph, and she suggested emptying the tank."

"You damned scoundrel!" roared the duke. "How came that infernal bomb or whatever it was into the car?"

"That he is not responsible for, old boy," said Ronald quietly. "Harvey's assistant is the man who did it. But whether he knew it was a bomb or not I can't say. Turn the car round, Bob. There are one or two little things to be cleared up."

And the first of them was soon done. The car that had pursued us had turned clean over and crashed down a steep bank, killing all three occupants.

"They started some shooting practice at us, as you can see," said Ronald, pointing to the shattered lamp. "So I retaliated, and was lucky enough to burst one of their front tyres."

"Assuredly, Mr. Standish," remarked the grand duke, "you seem to be a man after my own heart. Though I am still not quite clear why, if you saw the bomb being put in, you did not warn us at the time."

"Because, sir, I did not realise then that it was a bomb. I thought the assistant was putting back the gauze filter, and it was not until it fell off the back of the car as you drove off that I realised that what he had put in was something else. Sheer luck. No skill of mine. Had you gone another thirty yards before it slipped off, and rounded the corner out of sight, the death roll would have been in our camp, I fear. But—it did slip off, and I saw it. It was a certainty then as to what had happened, confirmed by their immediate pursuit of us."

And that is the true story of one of the most sensational cases of the past few years. Harvey's assistant proved to be almost a half-wit who had been bribed by one of the men to put the time bomb in the tank, having been told by him that it was a patent device for increasing mileage. And Williams, who had been kept a close prisoner in a house on the outskirts of London, returned to the duke's service. It transpired that the woman had made the same suggestion to him as she did to Groves, and on his refusing indignantly, the two men had sprung on him out of the darkness. She had previously pitched him some yarn about being persecuted, and he had met her on one or two occasions. In fact, the only remaining thing left to chronicle was the arrival, a few days later, at Ronald's rooms of a beautiful little clock. And on the back of it was engraved: "Guaranteed not to explode. Sergius."

The Haunted Rectory

The fact that Ronald Standish was amply provided with this world's goods was a great advantage to him in more ways than one. In the first place, it allowed him to pick and choose his cases, since the question of a fee did not enter into matters. He worked for the sheer interest of the thing, and the utmost I have ever known him ask were his out-of-pocket expenses. Often, indeed, he dispensed with these if his client was not well off. There was one example I remember in which they were considerable, but since he was working for a woman whose husband had been killed in the war, leaving her extremely poor, he refused to accept a penny.

But he derived benefit from his pecuniary position in another and not quite such an obvious manner. Acting completely on his own as he did, taking cases only when he felt like it (I have known periods of six months when he hasn't handled one at all), he was not habitually rubbing shoulders with the criminal classes in the way his professional confreres had to do. And, consequently, he was not known by sight to any large number of the people he was up against. Which, in view of the fact that no one looked less like a detective than he, was on certain occasions an immense help.

At the same time, there was but little reciprocity about the matter. It was the exact opposite to the old proverb Tom Fool. There were very few of the big men that Standish did not know by sight, and his was the type of memory that never forgot a face. He made a point of attending, as a casual spectator, any trial that promised to be of the slightest interest. But unless it justified its promise, he rarely stayed longer than was necessary to memorise the features of the prisoner. And so stored away in his brain was an immense gallery of portraits that he could inspect at will—an asset of incalculable value on occasions. And one such occasion was the strange case of the Haunted Rectory, a case which also illustrated his astounding quickness at spotting little things which other people missed. I was one of the other people!

It was early in April when he and I arrived at the small Cornish town of St. Porodoc. We were on a golfing holiday, and having sampled Saunton and Westward Ho! we wandered farther west till we reached a course which, according to its own members, at any rate, was better than either of them. And assuredly it was a beautiful piece of golfing country. Moreover, not being so widely known as its more illustrious neighbours, there was no crowd. In fact, Ronald found a certain amount of difficulty in getting a level game. His handicap was scratch, whereas I regret to state that mine has never descended into the realms of single figures. And since the Easter crowd had not yet arrived the field was a little limited. However, he played the best ball of the secretary and myself on two or three occasions, and it was at the nineteenth hole after one such match that the incidents I am about to relate started.

The secretary, Maxwell—a retired naval officer—was a man after our own hearts. And I remember that he was in the middle of a story when the door of the club-house swung open, and he stopped abruptly.

"Hallo, Vicar!" he sang out cheerily. "How's the ghost?" The newcomer was a charming-looking old man, with the fresh complexion that only years of living in the country can preserve. His grey hair was still plentiful; his eyes clear and bright, but at the secretary's question his expression clouded over.

"Worse and worse," he said ruefully. "Maguire says he's going."

"By Jove! That's bad," cried the other, with a whistle of surprise. "By the way, let me introduce our vicar—Mr. Greycourt. This is Mr. Standish and Mr. Miller."

The clergyman bowed and sat down.

"Yes—I think I will have something," he remarked. "I'm so worried I don't know what to do. The whole thing seems to me so absurd."

"It's certainly a pity if Maguire goes," said Maxwell. "And, by the same token, Standish, it's unfortunate it's Lent, otherwise you could have had a round or two with him. He'd have given you a good game."

"What's the trouble about Lent?" remarked Ronald.

"Maguire is my curate," explained the vicar, "and the dear fellow won't play golf in Lent. He says he'll see me through Easter, Maxwell, and then he won't stay any more."

"Which means he won't get a game on these links at all," said the secretary. "Surely something can be done to make him alter his mind, Vicar?"

"Excuse my butting in," said Ronald, with a smile, "but at the moment it's all rather confusing."

"And very boring, too, it must be, to a stranger," said the vicar apologetically.

"Not at all," cried Ronald. "Let's hear all about it, and possibly I might be able to suggest something."

"I'm sure I should be eternally grateful if you could," said the other. "Well, then, Maguire came to me some weeks ago—a delightful young fellow in every way—tall, upstanding, a typical British sportsman, and exactly the sort of man that we want today in the Church. So much did I feel that, in fact, that after he had been with me for two or three days I had a very serious conversation with him.

"'My boy,' I said, 'don't think for a moment that what I am going to say to you is inspired by anything but a sense of duty. The only reason that I applied for a curate is that with advancing years I find this straggling parish too much for my old legs. But I never dreamed that a man of your ability and charm of manner would arrive. You are wasted here, Maguire. You should be in some big centre, where your talent will not be hidden under a bushel.'

"He smiled and thanked me for the compliment. And then he explained his reasons for coming. It appeared that he had had a serious illness, and he thought a few months of Cornish air would pull him together.

"'Moreover, sir,' he went on with a smile, 'I must confess to another thing. The fame of the St. Porodoc links has reached as far as London. And once Lent is over, I hope to have many a round over the course.'"

"Is he a very star-turn golfer?" put in Ronald.

"Apparently he was in the running for his blue," said Maxwell, "so he must be fairly hot stuff. But he arrived after the beginning of Lent, so I've never seen him play. In fact, I've only seen him once, and then it was in the distance."

"I think he goes on the principle of keeping as far as possible from temptation," said the vicar with a smile. "I know nothing about the game myself, and so I fear I can't tell you how good he is, but he is certainly extraordinarily keen. However, that is only a side issue. To return to the main point: you must know, Mr. Standish, that I am unmarried, and the vicarage, though very comfortable, is too big for one man. And so when Maguire arrived I suggested to him that he should take up his quarters with me."

He paused to sip his drink, and it struck me that I had seldom met a more perfectly delightful old man.

"He fell in with the idea at once," the vicar continued, "and I placed at his disposal a sitting-room of his own. Our meals we take together, but I considered it essential that he should have his own den to go to when he wanted it. And for a week everything went swimmingly. Almost every evening we talked together for an hour or two before retiring, and then during the day he was out getting In touch with my parishioners.

"I think it was on the eighth day after he came that I noticed he was looking a little worried at breakfast, and asked him if anything was wrong.

"'Nothing, sir—nothing,' he answered, but I wasn't satisfied.

"'My dear boy,' I said, 'there's no good saying that. Something has upset you. Come now: out with it.'

"For a moment or two he hesitated; then he looked across the table at me.

"'It seems a ridiculous thing to say, sir,' he said, 'but is this house haunted?'

"I stared at him, speechless. It. was the last thing I expected him to say.

"'God bless my soul!' I cried at length, 'not that I've ever heard of. Why?'

"'Last night,' he said quietly, 'I awoke quite suddenly. The moon was shining through a chink in the curtains, and in its light, standing at the foot of the bed, I saw a man. At first I thought it was you, and I asked you what you wanted. And then, as I became more fully awake, I realised it wasn't you, but someone I had never seen. At once the thought of burglars entered my mind, and I sprang out of bed. And as I did so, the man vanished. I lit my candle to make sure. The room was empty. Then I looked at my watch. It was just two o'clock.'

"He resumed his breakfast, and for a moment or two I felt nonplussed. That the thing was merely a dream I felt convinced, but Maguire had spoken so quietly, and with such a complete absence of any excitement, that I hesitated to say so. And then took the words out of my mouth.

"'Probably a nightmare, sir,' he remarked 'and yet it was very real. Perhaps that second whack of cream with Martha's pastie last night. I mustn't fall again.'

"And so it passed off, and I thought no more about it until three days later, when it was my turn to be awakened—this time by footsteps outside my door. I slipped on a dressing-gown, and went into the passage. From the hall below me came the flickering light of a candle, and peering over the banisters I saw Maguire.

"'What is it?' I called out, and he looked up and saw me.

"'No nightmare now, sir,' he said a little shakily. 'I've had my visitor again, and this time he didn't vanish. He went through the door, and I followed him down here. And then he just disappeared into the wall.'

"'Come, come, Maguire,' I cried testily, 'this is absurd.'

"'So would I have said a week ago,' he answered gravely. 'Now I know it is not. Mr. Greycourt—this house is haunted.'

"'Then why have I never seen anything?' I demanded.

"He had no answer to that. He couldn't tell me. But I was unable to shake his conviction. I suggested he should change his bedroom, and he did so—at first with good results. For three or four nights nothing happened. Then the ghostly visitor appeared to him again. I sat up with him, but whenever I did so we saw nothing. And last night it came to him once more. I was awakened by a noise downstairs that sounded like a window shutting. Then I heard his footsteps outside my door. His face was white and his agitation was obvious.

"'It's getting on my nerves, sir!' he cried. 'I don't think I can go on much longer. It vanished into the wall again.'

"'I thought I heard a window bang,' I said, but he shook his head, so it was apparently something else that woke me. And, to cut a long story short, this morning at breakfast he told me that be felt he couldn't stay. He would remain to help me over the Easter celebrations, but after that he must go. Naturally I was greatly upset, but what can I do? The poor fellow is going to pieces. It is unfair to ask him to remain. But I shall never be able to replace him with anyone I like so well. And even if I did get a satisfactory successor, how do I know that the same thing won't happen to him?"

Ronald had listened with the closest attention to the vicar's story, and before making any comment he carefully filled his pipe.

"What servants have you, Mr. Greycourt?" he asked.

"Old Martha, who has been with me for years, is the cook. And I have a younger girl who does the rest of the work."

"Have either of them ever seen this ghost?"

"No. And no mention has been made of it to them. You know what servants are, and Maguire quite agreed with me that it would be folly to alarm them. But do you really believe in such manifestations, Mr. Standish?"

"Evidently your curate does," said Ronald dryly. "And as far as I myself am concerned I keep an open mind. Personally I have never seen one. At the same time, so many people of integrity have, at various times, vouched for their existence that it would be a bold man who denied their possibility. At the same time—"

He relapsed into thoughtful silence, and I looked at him curiously. The story was one of the last that I should have thought would have interested his practical brain.

"Then I suppose," said the vicar, rising, "that there is nothing to be done."

"As far as the departure of your curate is concerned, nothing that I can see," answered Ronald, "But if it would be of any assistance to you, I should be only too delighted to come up to your house and have a look round."

"Will you both come to lunch tomorrow and discuss it with Maguire?" he cried, and Ronald nodded.

"Thank you very much," he answered. "We'll be there."

"What do you really make of it?" said Maxwell as the door closed behind the old clergyman.

"Nothing at the moment," said Ronald. "But there is one possible point of interest. I don't profess to be well up in ghostly I lore, but from what I have read on the subject I have always believed that a ghost haunted a locality and not a person. Now in this case it is Maguire who is haunted. No one else has seen it now or ever before. It arrived, so to speak, with the curate. I wonder if it will depart with him?"

And once again he relapsed into silence, which remained unbroken till we all three rose to go and dress for dinner.

Chapter 2.

The vicarage, which we found next day without difficulty, was a rambling old house about half a mile from the top of the cliffs. A well-kept garden lay in front, and as we opened the gate a tall young man straightened up from a flower bed where he was working and came towards us with a smile.

"The vicar told me you were coming," he said; "he'll be in shortly. Excuse my not shaking hands, but gardening is not conducive to cleanliness. By the way, I'm Maguire."

"So I guessed," said Ronald genially. "This is a nasty experience of yours."

The curate's face clouded over. "Believe me, Mr. Standish," he remarked, "I wouldn't have worried that dear old man for the world. But I can't go on. I think my nerves are as strong as most people's, but this thing is wearing them to a frazzle. I daren't go to sleep now. I just lie awake wondering whether it's coming."

"Are you by any chance what the Scotch call fey?" said Ronald.

"I've never seen anything of the sort before," he cried. "But after this experience, I think I must be. You see, I'm the only person who has seen it. And the only conclusion I can come to is that I am what is technically known, I believe, as *en rapport* with this particular earth-bound spirit. So that when I arrived here it was able to manifest itself for the first time."

He made a sudden dart at a large snail, and picking it up threw it over the wall.

"Doubtless they fulfil some purpose," he remarked, "but they are a pest in a garden."

"How is your nocturnal visitor dressed?" asked Ronald, as we went into the house.

"As far as I can tell you, in brown," answered the other. "But I've really only seen his outline. He always eludes me, and then he vanishes just about there."

We were standing in the hall, and he pointed to a spot on one of the walls.

"Don't let's talk about it, if you don't mind. I try to forget it during the day. Come up to my room, and we'll wash our hands."

We followed him up the stairs into a large, airy bedroom, where he left us to get some hot water from the bathroom. And some what curiously I glanced round. There was the bed at the foot of which the ghostly visitor appeared; there near the window the bag of temptation—his golf clubs. A cheerful, sunny room—the last one would have associated with the supernatural. Then I happened to glance at Ronald's face. And to my amazement I saw on it the look I knew only too well, which was replaced by his usual imperturbable expression as

Maguire entered with the can. He had seen something, but what?

A few minutes later we descended to find the vicar waiting for us in the hall.

"Welcome!" he cried. "I hope Maguire has done the honours, and that you are ready for a real Cornish lunch?"

"I certainly am, Mr. Greycourt," said Ronald. "The links here give one an appetite. I understand you play, Mr. Maguire?"

"I'm frightfully keen on it," answered the curate. "But I don't play in Lent." He gave a deprecating smile. "However, I confess that I'm longing to loosen my arms again."

He gave a couple of practice swings as if to illustrate his remark. Then we all went into the dining-room and sat down.

"We must try to fix a round after Easter, if I'm still here," said Ronald, and Maguire nodded.

"By all means," he answered. "Though I fear the same proviso applies to me."

A slightly embarrassed silence settled on the table, which the vicar broke by inquiring how we liked the place. And thereafter throughout the meal the dangerous topic was safely avoided. No allusion was made to it, in fact, until after lunch, when Maguire had left the room to go to the telephone.

"I suppose you haven't succeeded in making him change his mind?" said our host.

Ronald shook his head.

"No, Mr. Greycourt. And I think I can safely say that it is better that he should not. The experience is evidently very real to him but I am hopeful that when he leaves here he will go somewhere where the manifestation will—er—cease. Somewhere, perhaps, where the food is not so rich."

His voice was expressionless, and the vicar nodded thoughtfully. "You think it's digestion?" he said.

"Perhaps so. In which case a change of diet may work the trick."

"I think it will do him a lot of good," remarked Ronald gravely. "Very plain diet: wholesome, of course, and at fixed hours. But don't mention it to him, Mr. Greycourt; he might think we were unfeeling."

"Of course not; of course not!" cried the worthy clergyman. "I shouldn't dream of doing so."

"And while I think of it, Vicar, there is one other thing I would like to suggest to you. If, during the few remaining days he is here, you should again hear him moving about at night—take no notice. Remain in your own room. It is a case, if I may say so, where the intervention of a third party does more harm than good."

"Perhaps you're right, Mr. Standish. I will do as you say. He must work out his own salvation. . . .Ah! my dear boy—parish matters?"

He smiled at Maguire, who had just returned.

"It's my cousin, sir. He is passing through Wadebridge again. Apparently the last consignment of cream was so much appreciated that he's going to call for some more."

"Splendid! Splendid! I hope he'll stay for tea. Are you playing golf, Mr. Standish?"

"Not this afternoon," answered Ronald. "Bob and I were thinking of having a walk along the cliffs."

"Good. You'll find them beautiful—very beautiful. And if you are near here, come in for tea also."

"What the dickens were you driving at?" I asked Ronald as we left the house. "Your remarks on Maguire's diet seemed to me to be pretty pointed."

"Getting quite bright, aren't you, Bob?" he said with a grin. And then the grin faded, and with compressed brows he swung along over the springy turf.

"I hope that dear old chap follows my advice," he said at length.

"That was another thing I couldn't understand," I remarked.

"Unless I'm much mistaken, you will within the next few days," he answered. "The vicar has come to no harm as yet, but it's only because he's been lucky."

"You mean he's in danger?" I said.

"Very grave danger," he said quietly.

His eyes were roving round the landscape as he spoke.

"But what from?" I demanded.

"That ghost. It would have been a bad thing for the vicar if he had happened to come out one night in time to see it, or rather not to see it. Let's walk over to the edge of the cliff there."

"You are an irritating devil," I said. "Can't you be more explicit? Give me some clue to what you are driving at!"

Once again he grinned faintly.

"Do you remember the snail our friend threw over the wall? A most instructive action, old boy, when coupled with that bag of golf clubs."

We had reached the top of the cliff, and stood peering down. A clearly-marked path led to the beach, and he nodded his head as if satisfied.

"It fits together, Bob," he remarked. "An old, old game, with one or two distinctly novel features in it. And, but for the snail, I might never have spotted it."

I refrained from profanity, and inquired mildly what he proposed to do next.

"Admire the beauties of nature, old boy, until the time arrives for us to get a look at Maguire's cousin. I feel he might help."

And not another word could I get out of him on the subject during our two hours' walk, a walk which I noticed was so planned that it brought us back to the vicarage about four o'clock. A car was standing outside the gate, and as we approached two men came down the path carrying a wooden packing-case. One was Maguire; the other, presumably, the cousin. And the instant he saw them, Ronald went dead lame.

"Twisted my ankle, I don't think," he muttered, sitting down on the bank. "Go on, Bob, and see if that second man has anything wrong with his nose."

I strolled on, and got level with the car just as it was starting. Maguire was talking earnestly to his companion, who was in the driver's seat, and as I came up to them they both looked at me. And with a queer little thrill I noticed that the cousin's nose had an odd kink in it, as if it had been broken and not set straight.

Almost immediately the car drove off, and Maguire crossed the road with a smile.

"Where is Mr. Standish?" he asked.

"He gave his ankle a bit of a turn," I said, "and I was just coming to ask for a little cold water."

"Of course," he cried. "We must get him indoors. Here he comes now."

Ronald was hobbling along the road, and called out cheerily:

"Quite all right. Don't worry. Thought for a moment I'd twisted it properly, but it's nothing at all."

"Sure you won't bathe it?" asked Maguire solicitously.

"Quite, thank you. I'll get straight on. It's no distance to the hotel."

"It's a pity my cousin has just gone. He could have given you a lift."

"Better to walk," said Ronald. "So you got the cream off, did you?"

"Yes, he's taken it with him. Well, Mr. Standish, we must try to fix that game some time."

"Sure thing," cried Ronald. "If I'm still here all you've got to do is to ring up the hotel."

With a cheerful wave of his hand, he limped on and the instant we were out of earshot he turned to me eagerly.

"Well! Had he?"

"Yes," I answered. "It looked as if it had been broken."

"Good," he cried. "I thought I recognised him, even at that distance. Bob, the plot thickens, or perhaps it would be more correct to say that it clears up."

"Who was he?" I demanded.

"The last time he was given free board and lodging at His Majesty's expense it was under the name of John Simpson. His real name, I think, is Robert Stenway, and he's just about as nasty a customer as you could wish to meet."

"Then what the dickens is he doing in this galley,"—I asked— "carting Cornish cream about for a curate?"

Ronald began to shake with laughter

"Bob," he remarked, "I take off my hat to you. Maguire is no more a curate than that Cornish cream is cream. And that being the case we will send a wire to my friend Inspector McIver, which, unless I am much mistaken, will bring him down here post-haste."

CHAPTER 3.

"If 'Snarkie' Stenway is in it, it's dope for a certainty," said McIver.

We were in our sitting-room the following afternoon, and Ronald nodded.

"I thought so myself," he remarked. "But this fellow Maguire is a new one on me, Mac."

"I can't spot him either from your description. Maybe I'll know him when I get a closer look at him. Or perhaps he's a genuine beginner."

"Then he shows astounding aptitude for it. Incidentally there he is, walking towards the post-office."

The inspector sprang to the window and peered out. Then he shook his head.

"No, I don't know him. Still, perhaps this is the beginning of an acquaintance that is destined to ripen."

"And no harm will be done by visiting the post office after he's gone," said Ronald. "People have been known to send wires from post offices, the imprints of which are left on the next form."

He strolled out of the room, and the inspector grinned at me. "No flies on him, Mr. Miller. How did he stumble on this?"

"Ask me another," I said. "I've been with him the whole time; I've seen everything he's seen; and all I can get out of him is that it was through seeing this man Maguire throw a snail over the wall."

McIver roared with laughter, and a few minutes later Ronald returned with a telegraph form in his hand.

"Virtue rewarded," he remarked. "It's to John Cuthbertson, Charing Cross Post Office. 'Shall have more cream tomorrow.'"

He threw the form on the table.

"A bit quicker than I thought. It means he'll be getting the cream tonight. Wherefore, Bob, if you want to see the ghost, a bit of shut-eye won't do anyone any harm. It may be an all-night job."

"I'll just arrange for a couple of men from Wadebridge in case of accidents," said McIver, "and then I'm of your way of thinking."

It was a pitch-dark night when we started at ten o'clock. The two local men had already been sent on with instructions to lie up by the road a few hundred yards short of the vicarage. And there we found them half an hour later.

"No one has passed, sir," said the sergeant, "and the light downstairs has just gone out."

"Good," said McIver. "Then we'll get closer and wait."

We approached cautiously, and finally went to ground in some bushes about thirty yards from the house. Light was coming from two of the bedrooms, and once Maguire came to his window and looked out. Then the lights were extinguished and our vigil began.

The wind had dropped. The only sound was the distant beating of the surf on the shore. And after a while I began to feel drowsy. It was a weary business waiting, with no possibility of a cigarette. And then, just as my head was nodding, I felt Ronald stiffen beside me. From the direction of the cliffs had come the call of a sea-bird. It was thrice repeated, and immediately the light in Maguire's room went on.

We waited tensely, our eyes straining into the darkness. And suddenly I heard Ronald's whisper in my ear: "There he is."

A figure was just discernible creeping along the side of the house. Then a light began to flicker in one of the downstairs windows. A candle was being carried down the stairs. And then the set, white face of Maguire himself came towards the window.

"Now," muttered McIver, and we all rose.

The window was opened, a bulky parcel was handed through, and at that moment we were on them. The man outside was so surprised that he showed no struggle at all. Not so Maguire. He fought with a cold ferocity that was almost inhuman. And it was not until Ronald knocked him out with a beauty on the point of the jaw that McIver got the handcuffs on him.

We stood breathing a bit heavily, when a plaintive voice from the stairs reminded us of the vicar.

"What is it?" he cried, standing there in his dressing-gown. 'What has happened?"

"We've laid your ghost for you, Mr. Greycourt," said Ronald reassuringly. "I'm afraid we made a bit of a noise over it."

"But I don't understand," said the other, dazedly. "Why is Maguire handcuffed?"

"Because he richly deserves to be," answered Ronald. "So you've come to, have you?" He glanced at the prisoner, who was glaring at him with eyes full of vindictive hatred. "Now, young man," he went on, sternly, "there's one question that you'd better answer, and answer darned quickly. Where is Maguire? For on your reply depends whether you're in the running for a six-foot drop."

"He's not croaked; we've got him hidden," snarled the other. "But"—he burst into a flood of hideous blasphemy—"I'll be even with you over this one day, Mr. Meddlesome."

"If you don't stop that language I'll gag you," snapped McIver. "Take 'em both into that room and keep 'em there," he ordered the sergeant.

"Now, sir," he continued, as the vicar joined us, "somewhat naturally, you're a bit surprised. But if you will come and have a look at the contents of this parcel you'll understand. You see these packets? Do you know what is inside them?"

He opened one, and the old man stared at the contents uncomprehendingly.

"Snow," went on the inspector. "Cocaine. Your so-called curate has been using your house for smuggling dope."

"I can't believe it!" cried the vicar. "How did you find it out?"

"Better ask Mr. Standish," laughed McIver. "He's the wizard in this case. And while he's telling you I'll just examine the room upstairs."

"It must have come as a shock to you, Mr. Greycourt," said Ronald quietly. "But once you realise that this man whom you have known as Maguire is not Maguire at all, and certainly not a clergyman, it will help. You see, I've got rather a suspicious nature, and a severely practical nature, and though I don't deny the possibility of ghosts, I'm sceptical about them. And I became more sceptical still when I found out that no one else had ever seen or heard of this apparition. So out of idle curiosity I asked myself what object would be served if there wasn't a ghost at all—if, in fact, the whole story was a lie. And one answer stuck out a yard. It would enable the man who invented the yarn to move about at night without incurring your suspicion. Which was suggestive, but was only a mere surmise on my part—a bare pos-sibility—when I came to have lunch with you. Then there occurred one of those strange little things on which the best-laid schemes go wrong. The man posing as Maguire seemed a delightful fellow: his personality seemed all that one would expect in a really sound sport-ing curate. And when in a moment of zeal he flung a snail over the wall, as one gardener to another I took to him more. Then we went up to his bedroom to wash. McIver," he sang out, "bring those golf clubs down, will you?"

"Right you are," answered the inspector. "And I've got a nice pot of cream as well."

He came down the stairs carrying the bag of clubs and a china jar.

"What do you want the clubs for?" he demanded.

"I happened to look at those clubs while he was getting some hot water," went on Ronald. "Try one, Bob; take that mashie."

Completely mystified, I took the club out of the bag, and then in an instant light dawned on me.

"Good Lord," I cried "it's a left-handed club!"

"Exactly. And he'd thrown the snail with his right hand; he poured out the water with his right hand; he swung his arms in the hall right-handed. In fact, here was a right-handed man, reputed to be a first-class golfer, with left-handed clubs. Which, as Euclid said, was absurd. So at once the case had to be examined from a fresh angle—the angle that this so-called Maguire was an impostor. And everything began to fit in. His refusal to play golf in Lent: obviously the easiest way of avoiding the exposure of his complete ignorance of the game. His de-cision to leave you after Easter, when Lent ends, and his excuse would no longer hold water. And then another, more ugly, thought arose— he could not have bought those clubs himself. No dealer would have sold a right-handed beginner left-handed clubs. Therefore they must belong to the real Maguire; and what had happened to him? And on that point, according to what this man says, I'm glad to hear he has not been murdered. But I didn't know that then, and so I warned you, Vicar, to let him ghost-walk by himself. Quite clearly he was a dangerous customer, a fact further proved by the way he fought tonight.

"The rest was easy. What possible purpose could bring a man of that sort down here—save smuggling? This house lends itself admirably to getting contraband from a boat lying off the coast. Moreover, you had been awakened on one occasion by a noise that you thought was like a window shutting. And when I heard that 'a cousin' was taking Cornish cream to London from here instead of buying it for himself, the thing became obvious. When, still further, I found that this so-called cousin was a notorious dope smuggler and criminal, the case was complete, and I wired for my old friend, Inspector McIver, with the result you've seen tonight."

"Clever trick, this, Mr. Standish," said the inspector. "Looks like a genuine pot of cream, doesn't it?"

He held out the jar: all that could be seen was a layer of the delicious stuff with its skin of faint golden yellow. And then with a spoon he scraped it away, revealing an inch underneath packet after packet of cocaine.

"In fact, a very ingenious plot, the memory of which may solace him through a few years of seclusion," he went on with a grin. "With your help, Vicar, we'll get Snarkie tomorrow, and that will conclude the entertainment."

And with the vicar's help we did. The worthy old gentleman lied as to the manner born with regard to where Maguire was when Stenway arrived, and personally helped him carry the cream we had made up to the car. And there McIver arrested him, while Ronald congratulated Mr. Greycourt on his ready tongue.

"Not at all, Mr. Standish," he answered, with a merry twinkle in his eye. "I said that Maguire was visiting one of my parishioners, whether willingly or not I saw no reason to state. And it may interest you to know that the police station is within the confines of my parish."

So ended a clever crime which, save for Ronald's quick eye, would never have been detected. Stenway got seven years: the other man, who turned out to be the son of a wealthy man in the Midlands, and who had been a wrong 'un from his birth, got five. It was the first offence that had brought him into actual contact with the police, but I shall be surprised if it is his last.

And as for the genuine Maguire, who, to do the scoundrels justice, had been quite well treated, he and I beat Ronald and Maxwell in a four-ball foursome only last week. After which we all dined with the vicar, concluding with a pot of cream. Only the cream was not limited to the top inch.

A Matter of Tar

One of the most useful assets in Ronald Standish's mental equipment was his extraordinary knowledge of out-of-the-way little tips that are not known to the man in the street. He seemed to have a positive storehouse of them locked away in his brain; in fact, he was a sort of living edition of one of those peculiar compendiums called "Do you know?" or some such title. An astounding memory had a great deal to do with it. Any new fact that struck him as being of interest was locked away and duly docketed in his mind ready for immediate production when required. And one of the best examples of this gift of his was shown in the case of the Fallconer diamonds. And though, as an instance of his powers of detection, it is perhaps not so illuminating as many others, it illustrates his quickness on the uptake and powers of observation to a very marked degree.

It was on an afternoon in early June that I wandered round to his rooms to find him in the middle of a telephone conversation.

"I shall expect you round at once," he said as I entered, and then he hung up the receiver.

"A lady visitor, Bob, is on her way," he remarked, "and from what I gathered over the telephone she is in a state of considerable agitation. Let us, therefore, endeavour to make the darned place a little more presentable to the feminine optic before she comes."

He threw a couple of niblicks into, the corner, and removed his cricket bag from a chair where it was in the process of being packed.

"A nuisance," he said. "I was going to have played tomorrow. But when Jumbo Dean has wished her on to us, I can't let him down."

"Do you want me to stay?" I asked. "It may be private."

"Wait and see, anyway," he said. "Her name is Miss Fallconer, which conveys rather less than nothing to me."

He reached for a copy of "Who's Who" and opened it. "Only one

Fallconer mentioned," he remarked, "and he has one daughter, so it may be him. A widower living at Oxbridge Place in the county of Sussex. He's a J.P., and has written two or three books on travel, so that one is not surprised that his club is the Travellers'. Age fifty-six. After which," he continued with a grin, "we shall probably find he's not our bird at all."

I strolled over to the window. A girl was just getting out of a taxi in the street below.

"Here she is," I said, "and there's a man with her. Both of 'em young."

A few moments later she came in, followed by her companion. They were a striking-looking couple, and I instinctively glanced at her left hand to see if they were engaged. They were not; there was no ring on her finger.

"How d'you do, Miss Fallconer?" said Ronald, going forward with hand outstretched. "May I introduce my friend, Bob Miller?"

She gave me a little nod, and then turned back to Ronald. "Good Heavens! Mr. Standish," she cried, "you're not a bit like what I imagined."

"Sorry about my face," laughed Ronald. "'Tis a poor thing, but mine own."

"I don't mean that at all," she answered, laughing also, "but it's all this."

She waved a hand round the room generally.

"Did you expect to find me immersed in a test tube?" said Ronald cheerfully. "Or peering at you out of the cupboard with a false nose on?"

He looked inquiringly at the man, who so far had not spoken.

"This is my cousin, Mr. Sanderson," she said, and Ronald pulled forward two chairs.

"Let's get down to it," he remarked. "You're evidently very worried, so there's no good wasting time."

She took a seat facing the window, and I studied her covertly. She was an extremely pretty girl, but, as Ronald had said, she looked anxious and troubled. One foot was tapping nervously on the floor, and once or twice as she talked she bit her lip as if to control her voice.

"It was Major Dean who advised me to come to you," she said. "You know him, don't you?"

"I know Jumbo very well," Ronald assured her. "And anything I can do for a pal of his will be a pleasure."

"Mr. Standish, Jack couldn't have done it—I know," she cried.

"I don't want to interrupt you, Miss Fallconer," said Ronald quietly, "but you must remember that I know absolutely nothing of the matter on which you have come to consult me. So may I ask you to begin at the beginning, and taking your own time, tell us everything that has happened? Everything, please, omitting nothing, however trivial it may seem to you."

He handed her his cigarette-case, but she shook her head.

"My father," she began, "is Mr. John Fallconer, and we live at Oxbridge Place."

Ronald glanced at me.

"It is the one in 'Who's Who' then. Go on."

"My mother died a few years after I was born, and since then, except for the time when I was at school, and one or two other gaps when he has been abroad, he and I have lived there by ourselves. He was a very wealthy man. Even today, though, of course, he's been hit like everybody else, father is still pretty well off."

"Is the place entailed?" put in Ronald. "I mean, on his death does the property go to you, or to the male next of kin?"

"To me," she said slowly, "unless he chose to make a will leaving it to someone else, which I don't think is likely."

"All right. That's quite clear," said Ronald. "Now we can get down to the real business."

"I say, Beryl, my dear," put in her cousin, "hadn't you better tell Mr. Standish something about old Jack before we come to last night? He must get it clear, you know, about everybody concerned."

"I suppose I had," she said. "Half a mile from us, Mr. Standish, there is a small chicken farm which is being run by a man called Jack Dalton. And"—she hesitated for a moment—"well—he's been the cause of the only quarrels father and I have ever had."

"Leave this bit to me, old thing," said Sanderson quietly. "Jack Dalton is a topper, Mr. Standish, but honesty compels me to admit that he's a damned bad chicken farmer. At least, the bally birds don't seem to pay, and as he's got practically no money at all of his own he's pretty impecunious. That, however, has not prevented what you have probably guessed already: the two of 'em are in love. But her respected male parent has old-fashioned ideas on the subject, and fails to see why his daughter should ante up the boodle for Jack's eggs. That's about it, isn't it, Beryl?"

She nodded.

"Yes, but there's another point," she said. "Jack feels just the same himself. He says he won't marry me unless he can make his farm pay."

"I see," said Ronald. "We have now got that relationship taped. Let's get on with it."

"The night before last—that is to say, Tuesday," she continued— "we had a small dinner-party. Harold was there and Jack…"

"So Jack is invited to the house, is he?" put in Ronald.

"Oh! yes," she cried. "Father likes him very much. He often shoots with us. It's only when I come in that the trouble arises. Where was I? Harold and Jack were there; the vicar and his wife, and Sir John and Lady Grantfield who brought Harold in their car."

Ronald looked inquiringly at Sanderson.

"I live about seven miles away, Mr. Standish," he explained. "And my car being temporarily out of action Sir John, very kindly, gave me a lift."

"Carry on, Miss Fallconer," said Ronald.

"After dinner," went on the girl, "father sprang a surprise on us. We were all sitting in the room that used to be the billiard-room, but which we have now converted into a sort of general living-room, when he suddenly produced from his pocket a large case. And inside it was the so-called Fallconer tiara. It used to belong to my mother, and it's always been a bit of a joke in the family. It's of great value, but perfectly hideous. The diamonds are magnificent stones, but the setting has to be seen to be believed. And it appeared that he had removed it from the local bank that very afternoon with the idea of bringing it up to London today to get it altered for my twenty-first birthday. I, of course, had seen it before, but the others hadn't, and it was passed round for everyone to have a look at. And then he proceeded to lock it up in a drawer in his big writing-desk, which stands in one corner of the room.

"'But surely, Fallconer,' said Sir John, 'you're not going to leave it there. Why, a child could open that drawer with a hair pin.'

"Father laughed.

"'Possibly,' he agreed, 'if there was any reason for him to try. But since we eight and the bank manager are the only people who know it's there, I'm not worrying.'

"And then we started to play bridge."

"No servant came in while it was being handed round?" asked Ronald.

"No; of that I'm certain," she said.

"Is this room on the ground floor?"

"Yes, but all the curtains were drawn."

"I see," said Ronald. "So it comes to this—that on Tuesday night your father put away this tiara in a locked drawer in his desk, and so far as either of you know no one but the eight people you have mentioned knew of its presence there."

"Precisely," said Sanderson.

"Now we come to yesterday," continued the girl. "Father and I were alone after dinner, and we both went to bed before eleven. He had intended to catch the early train to London this morning, and I'd been playing tennis and was tired. In addition to that—we'd—we'd had a row."

"What about?" asked Ronald.

For a moment or two she hesitated and glanced at her cousin. "Cough it up, old thing," he said. "There's no good hiding anything."

"It was about Jack again," she said. "And it was rather a bad one. Apparently he'd asked father to lend him some money in the afternoon. I know that he wanted more capital to extend his farm with, and I suppose he caught father at the wrong moment."

"I can't imagine why the silly ass didn't come to me," put in Sanderson.

"Well, Miss Fallconer," said Ronald, "let's hear what happened after you and your father went to bed."

"Just as I was falling asleep," she answered, "I heard what sounded like a heavy bump. I listened again, but it was not repeated. And then as I lay in bed something unusual struck me. For a while I couldn't make out what it was, and then at last I got it. A light was shining on the tree opposite my window, which had not been there before. So I got up and looked out. And to my amazement I found that the light came from the billiard-room.

"I looked at my clock. It was just after midnight. I wondered who on earth could be in there at such a time. And then I suddenly thought of the diamonds. So I put on a dressing-gown and went down."

"Good for you," cried Ronald approvingly.

"I opened the door," she continued, "and for a few seconds I thought the room was empty. And then happening to look towards the fire-place I saw father lying on the floor. I rushed over to him, fearing for one ghastly moment that he was dead. But I soon saw he wasn't, but was unconscious.

"I was too worried about him to think about the diamonds, as I thought he'd had some sort of a fit. So I roused the house, and we telephoned for the doctor, who came within twenty minutes, He made an examination, and then he gave me the biggest shock of all.

"'This is no fit,' he said. 'Your father has been knocked out with a weapon of some sort.'

"I stared at him stupidly. 'Knocked out!' I cried. 'Who by?'

"'That I can't tell you,' he answered, 'But he is in no danger, though he will probably be unconscious for several hours. The only thing to do is to get him to bed and make him as comfortable as possible.'

"And it was then that the diamonds came back to my mind. I rushed over to the desk, and found the drawer had been forced and it was empty. Evidently father had caught the burglar in the act of stealing the tiara, when the man had stunned him and escaped. A window was open. The whole thing seemed clear. So we got him upstairs and rang up the police station. There was no good in the doctor remaining, as there was nothing to be done till father came round. And so, finding myself alone except for the servants, I got on the telephone to Jack, to ask him if he'd come round and help me with the police."

Once again she hesitated, and glanced at her cousin. But he was apparently engrossed in the toe of his shoe.

"He was out," she went on after a while; "at least, I could get no answer. So I thought of Harold, forgetting his car was out of action. But he managed to raise one in the village and arrived at about the same time as the police."

"Which was at what hour?" asked Ronald.

"Ten minutes past one," said Sanderson, and Ronald made a note. "And at what time did Miss Fallconer telephone to you?" he asked.

"As near as makes no odds, twelve-thirty," answered Sanderson. "But it took me some little time to get dressed and rouse the owner of the village car."

"Quite," said Ronald, then, Miss Fallconer?"

"The police asked all sorts of questions, and, of course, I could tell them nothing," said the girl. "They rushed round the garden looking for footmarks; they examined the window-sill for finger prints. And then at four o'clock father recovered consciousness."

Ronald leaned forward, his eyes fixed on the girl's face.

"Oh! I know he didn't do it," she cried passionately. "It's all some ghastly mistake."

"Steady, Miss Fallconer," said Ronald quietly. "Let's hear all about it."

"Father accused Jack of having done it," she answered, controlling herself with an effort.

"His exact words, please."

"He said—'That damned young swine Dalton did it. He was masked but I recognised his coat.' Then he became all muzzy again."

"Recognised his coat," repeated Ronald thoughtfully. "Is there any particular significance in that remark?"

The girl had risen and gone to the window, and her cousin answered.

"Unfortunately there is, Mr. Standish," he said gravely. "When my uncle became coherent again he gave us fuller details. Apparently he had heard a noise in the billiard-room and had gone down to find out what it was. And there he saw a man bending over the desk in an overcoat which was unmistakable. We've all of us pulled Jack's leg about that garment of his, but he said it was an old friend. It had a sort of purplish tint about it which was like nothing else I've ever seen. In addition to that it was filthy dirty."

"In fact," said Ronald, "as you have just said, an unmistakable garment."

"Quite," said Sanderson.

"How very peculiar!" remarked Ronald dryly. "I somehow think that if I was going to break into a house I should not choose something to wear which would inevitably give me away if I was discovered."

"Just what I say," cried the girl eagerly.

"What is Dalton's explanation of the matter?"

"He says that the coat must have been stolen from his house by whoever did it."

"He absolutely denies that it was him?"

"Absolutely."

"Where was he when you rang him up, Miss Fallconer?"

"He says that he couldn't sleep and went out for a walk."

For a while Ronald was silent as he filled his pipe, and suddenly the girl went to him appealingly.

"Mr. Standish," she cried. "I know he didn't do it. Jack would never have hit father."

"My dear Miss Fallconer," he answered gravely, "whoever it was who stole the diamonds never had any intention of hitting your father when he started out. That was an entirely secondary thing done on the spur of the moment when Mr. Fallconer discovered him. Have they arrested Dalton?"

"Not when we left," she said. "But father has told the police everything. And I know they think he did it."

"Well, what do you want me to do, Miss Fallconer?" he asked.

"Come down with us, Mr. Standish, and see if you can't find out something to help him. Major Dean, who is staying near us, told me this morning that if anyone in England could save him you could."

"Jumbo exaggerates," said Ronald with a faint smile. "But I'll come and see what I can do."

"Thank you a thousand times," she cried. "Will you come in my car or go in your own?"

"In my own, thank you, Miss Fallconer. I'll be at Oxbridge Place as soon as possible."

"I've got to get that stuff from the chemist for father, Harold," she said at the door. "Will you be in St. James's Square in ten minutes?"

"All right, my dear," answered her cousin, picking up his hat as she went out. And then he paused, listening to make sure she had gone.

"Mr. Standish," he said gravely, "I fear you're going on a fruitless errand. I hadn't the heart to try and dissuade her from coming to you, and perhaps—who knows?—you may spot something which we've missed. But since you are, so to speak, acting for Jack, it's only fair that I should tell you what I have not mentioned to anybody. I'd been over in the bus yesterday, and dropped in on Jack just after his interview with my uncle. And he was in a furious rage. As a matter of fact, he's got the devil of a temper at times. And he announced not once, but two or three times, his intention of making the darned old swab, as he put it, sit up."

"Threats of that sort may mean a lot or nothing at all," remarked Ronald.

"I agree. But I fear you've hit the nail on the head. I don't think for one second he meant to strike my uncle, but I do think he intended to steal the diamonds. You see, the devil of it is that there are only four men except Mr. Fallconer himself who knew where the tiara was. And of those four the vicar and Sir John are obviously out of court, while I was in my house seven miles away. It's a hopeless case, I'm afraid. However, let's trust you won't think so."

With a nod he went out, and Ronald turned to me. "What do you make of it, Bob?"

"Frankly, old boy, very much what Sanderson does. Pretty black."

"It was very hot last night," he said enigmatically.

"What the dickens—" I began, but he was already in his bedroom throwing things into a bag.

"Pack a bag, Bob," he said. "I'll come and pick you up."

The whole way down he hardly spoke, and I wondered at his pre-occupation. To my mind the thing was obvious. Had someone been lurking outside the window on the night of the dinner-party and seen the tiara being handed round, surely he would have broken in on the Tuesday, and not waited till Wednesday—I said as much to Ronald.

"Some such idea had occurred to me," he said, with a faint smile. "Which, coupled with the fact that the night was hot, raises an interesting point."

"What point?" I demanded.

The smile grew more pronounced.

"Think it out," he said. "And surely there is Sanderson standing by the road?"

We pulled up as he waved to us.

"I got off at my house and waited for you," he said. "Will you come and have a drink before you go?"

"I've heard worse ideas," remarked Ronald.

"And perhaps you'd give me a lift afterwards," continued Sanderson as he led the way. "My bus is still out of commission. Confound it," he said, peering into the sideboard. "There isn't a siphon. Mrs. Burton," he shouted, going to the door, "siphon, please. A dear old woman," he continued as he came back, "but as deaf as a post."

A moment later she entered beaming, and carrying in her hand a small bottle done up in white paper.

"Here it is, sir," she said.

"What on earth is that?" he asked.

"The oil of eucalyptus you wanted this morning. The chemist did say that you'd bought some yourself, but I thought I'd get a bottle and make sure."

"Very kind of you, Mrs. Burton," said Sanderson, "but in the meantime what I want is a siphon."

She bustled away, and he turned to us apologetically.

"Sorry," he remarked. "She seems to get deafer every day. Perhaps you'd like a whisky and eucalyptus. As a matter of fact I thought I had a bit of a cold coming on this morning, and there's nothing like it, in my opinion."

The housekeeper returned with a siphon, and Sanderson poured out the drinks.

"Here's fortune," he cried. "And may you be able to help poor old Jack. We go past his cottage on the way to my uncle's house."

We finished our glasses and re-entered the car, with Sanderson sitting behind.

"You'll have to go slow over one bit," he said. "They're just tarring, and they're doing it damned badly, I think, with a particularly vicious sort of yellow grit on top of it."

We came to the place quite shortly, and though Ronald almost crawled the rattle of the tiny fragments on the back of the car was very audible.

"You're right," he said. "Damned badly. I'll have to—go even slower."

I glanced at him quickly. The pause in his last sentence had been very perceptible. And it was obvious to me that that was not what he had intended to say. But his expression was inscrutable and his next question quite casual.

"How long have they been at it?" he asked.

"They only started yesterday morning," answered Sanderson. "Now in about a mile we come to Jack's place. Are you going to stop there?"

"We might look in and see what he has to say," said Ronald, "though I fear it's not much use. I've been thinking the thing over on the way down, and it looks pretty hopeless to me."

And once again I glanced at him in surprise, though I said nothing.

"There's the cottage," said Sanderson. "And, by Jove! There's a constable there. I know him, too; he's a local fast bowler. Good evening, Paxton," he called out as we walked up the path to the house. "Any further developments?"

"Afraid there are, sir," answered the policeman. "They've arrested Mr. Dalton."

"The dickens they have!" said Sanderson, with a significant look at Ronald. "When did they do it?"

"Half an hour ago, sir. You see, we found the coat what the squire was talking about—that there overcoat of Mr. Dalton's. And in the pocket was the case what the diamonds had been in."

"And the diamonds?"

"Ain't found them, sir. Not a trace."

"Where was the coat found, officer?" asked Ronald.

"'Idden away, sir, be'ind one of the 'en 'ouses," answered the man. And then he hesitated. "I suppose as 'ow I didn't really ought to, but would you gentlemen like to have a look at it? It's in the 'all."

"I certainly would," said Ronald. "After all I've heard about this garment I'm most curious to see it. Great Scott!" he cried as he saw it, "no wonder you used to pull his leg over it."

He had taken it down, and was examining it carefully, and suddenly I saw that unmistakable gleam in his eyes which I knew only too well. He was hot on something, but no one except me would have noticed it.

"Interesting," he remarked. "Indeed, a coat of many colours. However, it opens up a field for research."

"What?" cried Sanderson incredulously. "That coat does? How?"

"It has recently been worn by a discharged soldier who has a pronounced limp and fair hair," said Ronald quietly. "I am beginning to see daylight. Bob," he continued, turning to me, "will you and Sanderson go on to Mr. Fallconer's house and wait for me? There are one or two inquiries I've got to make, but I hope to get there myself in time for dinner."

He got into the car and drove off, leaving us staring after him.

"Is he pulling our legs?" demanded Sanderson. "What's all that bilge about a discharged soldier? He couldn't possibly deduce that by looking at an old overcoat."

"It's astounding what he can get at," I answered, though I was wondering a bit myself. It seemed well-nigh impossible to have made such a deduction, and yet his voice had been perfectly serious. "Let's do what he says, anyway," I continued, "and wait for him at your uncle's house."

He took me by a short cut over the fields, and all the way he did nothing but hark back to Ronald's remark.

"What on earth are we to tell Beryl?" he said just before we reached our destination. "If his remark means anything at all it means that this discharged soldier is the criminal. But it would be a shame to raise her hopes and then find he was fooling."

"Let's just say that he's making few inquiries and hopes to join up for dinner," I said.

We found Beryl with her father, and she introduced me to him. "Delighted if you'll both stop and dine," he said when I told him about Ronald, "but I'm afraid he's wasting his time. The thing is as clear as a pikestaff, though I'd never have believed it of young Dalton.

No, no, my dear," he continued as his daughter began to protest, "we don't want to go over it all again. If he had given me back the tiara, and promised to leave the district and never see you again, I might have been lenient. But now justice must take its course."

"The police have searched for the diamonds?" I asked.

"Of course," he answered testily. "But what's the good? He wasn't going to leave 'em in the middle of the dining-room table. He had the whole night in which to hide the tiara. It may be buried anywhere in the countryside, near some landmark that he can recognise later."

And so it went on for an extremely uncomfortable hour. Mr. Fallconer, whose head was obviously still hurting him, grew more and more irritable, whilst his daughter, with a sort of pathetic faith in Ronald, continually stared out of the window down the drive. And at last came the welcome sight of the car. Not, frankly, that I hoped for anything, but the situation would now be settled one way or the other at any rate.

We all met him in the hall.

"Found the discharged soldier?" said Sanderson, with mild sarcasm.

"No," answered Ronald genially. "That, I fear, was a little flight of fancy indulged in on the spur of the moment. But what I have found is far more important."

And from his pocket he produced the tiara.

"The diamonds!" shouted Mr. Fallconer. "Where were they?"

But Ronald did not answer. His eyes, stern and relentless, were fixed on Sanderson, who, with an ashen face, plucked ceaselessly at his collar. And soon we were all looking at him.

"Need you ask?" said Ronald gravely. "I found them in your nephew's desk."

"It's a lie!" muttered Sanderson thickly. "It's a plot."

"The plot was yours, Sanderson," said Ronald, and his voice cut like a knife. "And a pretty rotten one, too. Why you poor fool, it was next door to obvious from the word go."

But the other waited to hear no more and, like a whipped cur, bolted from the house.

"Stop him!" roared his uncle. "Stop the damned young black guard!"

"Steady, Mr. Fallconer," said Ronald quietly. "You can always get him if you want to. But I would suggest your thinking things over calmly first. After all, he is your nephew, and the scandal will be considerable. But one thing, of course, should be done at once. You must ring up the police and tell 'em to let Jack Dalton go immediately. Explain things as you like, but he is as innocent as I am."

"I knew it!" cried the girl. "Though how you found out beats me."

"A very simple case, Miss Fallconer," he said, "and yet a case which showed an extraordinary mixture of skill and stupidity on the part of your cousin. The first point of interest was the fact that last night was very hot—the sort of night on which no one would dream of wearing an overcoat for warmth. I add those last words advisedly—for warmth.

"We now come to that blessed old coat—a most conspicuous garment; a garment about which. Dalton was used to being chaffed; a garment which would be instantly recognised by your father or by you. Well, now, it is conceivable that if he wanted the coat for warmth he might have chanced wearing it; but he didn't. Therefore what possible purpose could there be in his putting it on? If he proposed to steal your diamonds, it is the very last thing he would have worn. And so the obvious alternative solution was that it wasn't Dalton who was wearing the coat at all, but someone who wanted to impersonate him. So much was clear before we left London.

"Came the next question—who could this be? First, it was some man who knew the tiara was in your desk. That boiled us down to the four who dined with you, or someone looking through the curtains on the night of the party. Second, it was some man who knew Dalton intimately—so intimately that he knew all this jest about the coat. And that was one of the reasons which made it improbable that it was a casual burglar who had seen from outside. The other reason, as you pointed out, Bob, was that a casual man would have gone for it on the night of the party and not waited. So I considered your four guests; in fact, Mr. Sanderson considered them for me. And somewhat naturally I dismissed the vicar and Sir John Grantfield.

"Now we came to the first difficulty, for by this time I was frankly wondering about your nephew. On the face of it he had a perfect alibi. Mr. Fallconer had been attacked just after midnight. Miss Fallconer rang him up at twelve-thirty. His car was out of commission. He couldn't have walked seven miles in less than half an hour. He couldn't even have bicycled it unless he was a racing champion. He wouldn't have dared to ask for a stray lift, or even hire another car. And so if his car was really out of commission he was exonerated.

"Well, we called in on him on our way down. And then we went to Dalton's cottage, where we saw the coat. And on that celebrated garment there were some interesting marks. Behind the right shoulder were three or four splashes of new tar, and adhering to the tar were tiny fragments of yellow grit. Now, between Dalton's place and Sanderson's there is a stretch of new tar covered with yellow grit which they only commenced work on yesterday. So it appeared possible that the driver of an open car might have worn that coat when going over that stretch the marks were just where one would expect to find them. And the significance of the oil of eucalyptus struck me at once—a bottle of which Mrs. Burton had given him while we were there.

"Back I went and examined his car. True, it was out of commission, but a glance at the trouble showed that half an hour's work was all that was necessary to put it right. Then I looked at the back: no trace of tar. Then I searched in the rubbish heap and found this."

He took a blackened old rag out of his pocket and the reek of eucalyptus filled the room.

"The proof I wanted," he continued, and we stared at him in amazement. "The whole thing was clear. Your nephew had taken Dalton's coat, probably when he saw him yesterday afternoon. He repaired his car and drove to somewhere near here, going over the newly-laid tar and getting some on the coat. Then, having knocked you out and got the diamonds, he left the coat in Dalton's farm and drove back. Mrs. Burton, being deaf, never heard the car at all. Came a stroke of luck for him when you rang up, Miss Fallconer. To his mind it established his innocence. He then came over here in a hired car; went back this morning and again took his engine partially down. But a further point had to be dealt with: the back of his car was covered with tar splashes—noticeable splashes because of the yellow grit. He realised that if they were seen he was for it, since the work only started yesterday. And here he was clever. He happened to know a small fact which very few people do know.

"Unfortunately for him, I knew it too, and very nearly gave it away in the car, Bob. There is nothing so good for removing tar from paint-work as plain oil of eucalyptus. Moreover, no suspicion would be aroused by his asking for some, whereas if he bought one of the patent mixtures sold for the purpose—even if he could have got it in the village—questions might have been asked. And so when I found this rag in the rubbish beside the garage the whole chain of events was complete, and I decided to commit a small burglary myself, which very fortunately was successful. I had noticed a big desk in the room he had taken us to, and I decided to chance it. Picking locks is a little hobby of mine, and that one presented no difficulties."

"I think it's simply amazing, Mr. Standish," said the girl.

"Honestly—no, Miss Fallconer. Sheer luck was far too big a factor for me to take much credit. For there is no getting away from the fact that it was the fresh tar on the road and the eucalyptus being brought in by Mrs. Burton that solved the matter."

"Well, we're extremely grateful to you," said Mr. Fallconer. "Young Jack will be here at any moment now and will be anxious to thank you himself. But there is one point that occurs to me. What would have happened if I hadn't interrupted him? He's a man with a lot of money; he didn't want the diamonds for the cash they'd bring."

Ronald smiled faintly.

"Solving things that have happened is hard enough without trying one's hand at things that haven't. But I think I can hazard a guess. The tiara was destined for Dalton's house: taking the first opportunity, Sanderson would have planted it there, as the phrase goes."

"But in Heaven's name—why?" cried Mr. Fallconer. "What motive had he?"

Ronald's smile grew more pronounced, and he stared at the girl.

"A singularly charming one, if I may say so," he answered.

The House with the Kennels

"A young lady to see you, sir. Here is her card."

With a frown of annoyance Ronald Standish put down the golf bag he had just picked up and took the bit of pasteboard from his man.

"That's a nuisance, Bob," he said to me, and then he raised his eyebrows. "Miss Nancy Millington. I wonder if she is any relation of Tom Millington whom I've played cricket with. Show her in, Sayers."

The butler left the room and a moment later he ushered in a pretty girl of about twenty-five, who looked from one to the other "I wonder no longer," said Ronald, with a laugh. "And what can I do for Tom Millington's sister?"

"How did you know?" she cried, surprised.

"My dear Miss Millington—you're as alike as two peas. How is the old lad?"

"He's very well, Mr. Standish, and it was he who told me to come to you. He thinks I'm a half-wit for bothering you at all, and I'm not at all sure I don't think the same myself now that I'm here."

"Take a pew, bless you," said Ronald, "and let's hear all about it. Incidentally, this is Bob Miller."

"It all seems so trivial and stupid," she began, "when one starts, to put it into words, that probably you'll laugh at me the same as Tom did. But I can't help it. I feel I've got to get it off my chest. He and I, as perhaps you know, Mr. Standish, live together. We've got a house down at West Bilsington, which is a little village not far from Pulborough, in Sussex. Tom does a bit of farming in the intervals of playing cricket, and we've been there about four years.

"Most of the houses round us are small cottages belonging to labourers; in fact, the only big one in the neighbourhood is the rectory, which is a great barn of a place. And it is about the rectory that I've come to see you. A year ago the old vicar died. He was a man with considerable private means, and an awfully good sort. He and his wife used to do a lot of entertaining in a mild way—tennis and that sort of thing; and so, when he pegged out, we were all of us very concerned as to who was going to take his place.

"Well, I don't know how these things are arranged, but the next incumbent, or whatever they call it, hadn't got a bean to bless himself with. He's an extraordinarily nice man, and his wife is charming, but they found they couldn't possibly afford to live in the rectory. You want at least four servants, and they simply couldn't run to it. So they put it in the house-agent's hands, with no result until two months ago, when a Mrs. Hamilton took it, and the vicar and his wife moved into a cottage.

"Somewhat naturally, as you can guess, we were all very anxious to see the lady. The tennis court is the only decent one for miles, and we hoped the old *régime* would start again. Which is where we were disappointed. A week after Mrs. Hamilton arrived we discovered she was mad on dogs, and proposed to start kennels. She hung up notices all over the place to say that dogs would be taken in and boarded, and proceeded to cover the lawn with wired-in runs for them. And in addition to that, she actually brought half a dozen dogs of all varieties of breeds with her. I'm afraid all this is very boring," she added apologetically, "but I must begin at the beginning."

"Tell it your own way, Miss Millington," said Ronald.

"As you can imagine," she continued, "in a small village like ours everybody knows pretty well everything about everybody else. The butcher or someone passes things on to the cook and she does the rest. And it soon became known that Mrs. Hamilton's *ménage* was rather a funny one. For one thing, she had nothing but men servants; for another, two of them, at least, were foreigners. Of course, there was nothing in that—"

"Just one moment, Miss Millington," interrupted Ronald. "What age is this Mrs. Hamilton?"

"Forty—forty-five," said the girl.

"And is she English?"

"I wouldn't swear to it," she answered. "She speaks English perfectly, but once or twice it has seemed to me that she's got the trace of an accent."

"Is there a Mr. Hamilton?"

"If there is, he hasn't been down there, to my knowledge."

"I see," said Ronald. "Please go on."

"Another thing that soon became obvious was that she was a very unsociable sort of woman. I gave her a fortnight to settle in and then I went to call. She was quite polite and returned it a week later, but one could tell at once that it was only because she had to, and that she didn't intend to let it go any further. Not that I wanted it to, but she is our next-door neighbour, and in a little place like that one naturally wants to be friendly. She is always quite pleasant if she is on the lawn and I happen to be passing, but, she definitely gives you the impression that it's a case of bare politeness, and that she wishes to goodness you'd go away. The trouble is that I'm absolutely devoted to dogs, and I never can resist having a look at them when I go past the gate. Which is what caused the first thing that has brought me here today.

"Three weeks ago I was going into the village, and looking on to the lawn I saw her with a new arrival—a perfectly topping Irish terrier.

"'What a beauty!' I cried. 'What's his name?'

"'Cheaper,' she said. 'Because I got him cheaper than I expected.'

"The jest, I admit, was feeble, but it was such an extraordinary thing for her to make a joke at all that I went in and joined her.

"He is a good dog,' she went on. 'Quite the best Airedale I've seen for a long while.'

"I stared at her in amazement.

"'But, Mrs. Hamilton,' I cried, 'he's not an Airedale; he's an Irish terrier.'"

The girl paused for a moment, as if searching for the right words.

"I don't want to exaggerate, Mr. Standish," she went on, after a while, "but the effect was literally amazing. Admittedly, it was an incredible error for a dog-lover to make, but one would have expected her to laugh it off, or to pretend that she'd been fooling. After all, there is a certain similarity between the two breeds. It's not like mistaking a pug for a mastiff.

"She turned white with fury, and for a moment I actually thought she was going to hit me. A look came into her eyes that was positively venomous, and I stepped back a pace. And then she recovered herself.

"'Of course,' she said, with a forced laugh. 'How stupid of me!'

"I stayed on a few more minutes; then I left. And the more I thought over it the more I wondered. How could anyone who is keen on dogs make such a mistake? And why the fury when it was pointed out?

Because I hadn't imagined it, Mr. Standish! I can assure you of that.

"I talked it over with Tom, and he pooh-poohed the whole thing. He seemed to think that the lady had a bad temper naturally and was furious with herself at being caught out. Which was all right as far as it went, but it didn't answer my difficulty. How could a genuine dog-lover be caught out over such a thing?"

Ronald nodded, and I could see he was interested.

"And having got as far as that," continued the girl, "I went a bit farther. Was she a genuine dog-lover, and if she wasn't, what on earth was the object of all this elaborate pretence of kennels? Again Tom laughed at me. His contention, and I admit it is difficult to answer, was that no one but a congenital idiot would rent the rectory at a place like West Bilsington and install dogs all over the lawn unless they were fond of animals. If she wanted to bury herself there, why couldn't she do it without the dogs?"

"I can think of two very good reasons," said Ronald quietly, "but it's early days yet. This happened, you say, three weeks ago. I take it something further has occurred since?"

"Yesterday," she answered promptly. "And it was that that decided me to come and see you. It may be all rot. Tom shrieked with laughter when I told him, and probably you will too. I was passing the gate of the rectory about eleven o'clock in the morning, and I stopped as I nearly always do to have a look at the dogs. Suddenly, I don't know why, I happened to glance up at the house. And there, pressed against one of the top windows, was a face. The sun was shining on the room, and so I could see the features clearly and the expression of fear and terror on them. Then in a flash the face had gone, almost as if it had been dragged away by someone behind."

"Man or woman?" asked Ronald.

"An elderly man," she said. "I stayed there as long as I could, wondering if he would reappear, but he didn't."

Ronald lit a cigarette thoughtfully.

"Let's get this straight, Miss Millington," he said. "The lawn is between the road and the house, so the house must be a considerable distance from where you were standing. Now, can you really be sure that the expression on this man's face was one of fear and terror?"

"Just what Tom said," she answered. "In my own mind, Mr. Standish, I am perfectly sure. As I told you, the sun was shining on him, and in that momentary glimpse he stood out as clear as a photograph. Tom says that it is one of the servants who is sick, and, of course, he may be right. But if ever a man was appealing for help, that man was; I'm sure of it. So much so, in fact, that I very nearly told our local policeman when I got into the village. And then I thought I'd better ask Tom's advice first."

"I don't think the policeman would have been much use," agreed Ronald. "Your evidence is a little too thin, isn't it, for official action?"

"But you do believe me, don't you, Mr. Standish?"

"I certainly believe all you've told me," answered Ronald. "But what interpretation to put on it is a different matter. Terror and great pain might look much the same at a distance, and Tom's theory about the sick servant is quite possibly correct. Again, Mrs. Hamilton's anger over her mistake about the Airedale is also capable of an innocent solution."

"Which means you think there's nothing in it!" she cried, with keen disappointment in her voice.

"Not at all," Ronald assured her, "I am merely trying to show you that we mustn't be too hasty in jumping to conclusions; which is just what you, bless your heart, have done. You are convinced that Mrs. Hamilton is a fraud, to put it mildly, and that she and her gang of servants are holding some man prisoner, and probably torturing him."

He laughed, and after a moment she laughed too.

"Put like that, it does seem a bit absurd," she confessed. "And as Tom says, it would be ridiculous if she is a fraud to bother about the dogs."

"Now that," said Ronald, "is where I entirely disagree with Tom, for two reasons, as I said before. Either the whole thing is completely innocent and you've made a crashing bloomer, or something very like my melodramatic picture is the truth. As you rightly remarked, in a tiny place like that everybody is intensely curious, and if this Mrs. Hamilton is playing some deep game, it is essential for her to have an occupation which will account for her being there."

"But why dogs, if she knows nothing about 'em?" I put in.

"Reason number two," he answered. "If there are dirty doings going on in the house, what better guardians could she possibly find than a bunch of dogs that bark the place down if a stranger approaches the door? Especially at night."

"You're quite right, Mr. Standish," said the girl. "They make the most awful row. So you do think there's something in it?" she added.

"'Pon my Sam, Miss Millington, I don't know. I should say it's about a fifty-fifty chance. But I'll tell you what I'll do, if you like. Can you put Bob and me up for two or three nights?"

"Of course," she cried. "Only too delighted."

"Good! Then he and I will arrive with golf clubs complete, ostensibly to play round those very excellent links near Pulborough. And in the intervals of so doing we will cast a discerning eye on the denizens of the rectory."

"How splendid!" she said. "I'm so glad, Mr. Standish! Because I'm certain there is something wrong."

"Do you really think there is anything in it?" I asked when she had gone.

He shrugged his shoulders.

"On the one hand we have woman's intuition, which is never a thing to be sneezed at; on the other some first-rate golf. So, old lad, we score either way."

There would have been no mistaking the rectory even without the dogs on the lawn. The only large house in the village, it stood some forty yards back from the road and about the same distance from the church, from which it was separated by an old wall with a wicket gate in it. Trees ran along the rectory side of the wall; on the other lay part of the churchyard. So much was obvious as we drove slowly past, and then, just as we got to the gate, Ronald somewhat unexpectedly stopped the car.

"No time like the present, Bob," he said. "We'll do a bit of acting."

There was no one in the garden, but he pointed to the notice board for the benefit of anybody who might be watching from the house and led the way up to the front door. Immediately all the dogs started barking furiously, and I saw a curtain shake in one of the end rooms. We were being inspected.

"I see from the notice on the road," he said to the man who opened the door, "that you are prepared to receive dogs and board them. Can I see the owner of the place?"

"I will find out if she is in," answered the man, speaking with a pronounced foreign accent. He was a saturnine-looking fellow, dark-skinned and swarthy, and I put him down as an Italian.

He was away some time before he returned to say that Mrs. Hamilton would receive us, and to my surprise he seemed considerably agitated. However, we followed him through the hall to a room at the back of the house where we found the lady sitting at a desk, writing. She rose as we entered.

"I was just motoring past, madam," said Ronald with a bow, "and I happened to catch sight of your notice. I have a terrier in London, for whom I want to find a happy home for the next six months while I am abroad. Would you be prepared to take him?"

"Certainly," she answered. "My terms are half a guinea a week." They continued talking details for a time whilst I glanced round the room. It was just what one would have expected to find in such a house—sunny and comfortable, and the conviction began to grow on me that Miss Millington had made a mistake. Outside was another stretch of lawn with more dogs on it, and beyond that lay the kitchen garden.

"Then that is settled," I heard Ronald say. "I'll send the little chap down in a week or ten days."

She pressed the bell, which was answered by the same man who had let us in, and whom we again followed through the hall. We had penetrated the fortress, but it did not seem to me that we had gained much by it.

"Didn't it strike you," I said, as we got into the car, "that that blighter who let us in had been ticked off when he went to find out if she was at home?"

"Well done, Bob," said Ronald with a laugh. "You're getting on fine. But did it strike you as to why he'd been ticked off?"

"How on earth can I be expected to know that?" I cried.

"Didn't you notice any difference in his appearance when he returned to say that Mrs. Hamilton would see me?"

"I can't say that I did."

"Not so good, old boy. When he opened the door to us he was not wearing gloves. When he came back he was."

"One of her rules, I suppose, and he'd forgotten."

"Did you see his nails?"

"No, I didn't. What was the matter with them?"

He did not answer for a time, and when he did it was about, something completely different.

"Is it possible," he said, "that anybody could seriously think that a terrier eats a pound of dog biscuits twice a day? For that is what I told the lady my mythical hound consumed, and she swallowed it hook, bait, and sinker. I must say she was at pains to inform me that all practical details were left to the kennelman, but even so, Bob—a terrier, and two pounds of biscuits a day is a bit hot."

"Then you do think the show is crooked?"

"I said fifty-fifty to Miss Millington. Now..."

He fell into a brown study, which continued till we reached the Millingtons' house.

"The devil of it," he said as he stopped the engine, "is that we've got no excuse for going back there again, and it will be the deuce of a job to reconnoitre that house with dogs fore and aft, so to speak. I'd no idea she had more at the back."

Tom Millington came out to greet us grinning all over his face, and Ronald introduced me to him.

"Delighted to see you," he cried, "but I never thought Nancy would catch an old bird like you, Ronald, with her mare's nest."

Ronald smiled but said nothing, and we followed Millington into the house, where we were joined by his sister.

"Here are your wretched dupes, Nancy," he said. "The least you can do for them is to produce some whisky and soda."

"What time does the post go out?" asked Ronald.

"Six o'clock," said Millington. "You've plenty of time to catch it."

"Good. Well, Miss Millington, I've interviewed your girl friend."

"You've seen Mrs. Hamilton!" she cried. "How did you manage that?"

"I am sending her a non-existent terrier in a few days which eats two pounds of biscuits a day. At least I told her so and she didn't dispute the fact."

For a moment she looked bewildered Then she turned triumphantly on her brother.

"There you are, Tom. I knew she was a fraud."

"Just because she knows nothing about dogs doesn't prove she's a wrong 'un," he said obstinately.

"It doesn't prove it," agreed Ronald. "But from one or two little things I saw, I think the betting on it is quite sufficient for me to write to Scotland Yard and make a few inquiries on the matter. Only I must beg of you to say nothing about it to anyone. If we're wrong it's the most libellous thing to do. If we're right we don't want the smallest chance of giving the alarm. Which is why I do not propose to post the letter in the village box. The local postman would probably die of heart failure."

"Let's go and have a round," said Millington, now definitely impressed, "and you can post it on the way there. But what on earth can they be up to in a place like this?"

"That remains to be seen, old boy," answered Ronald. "Mrs. Hamilton and the man who opened the door are both new ones on me, so I've got no ideas as to their line of country. But if one of my surmises is correct, I think I could hazard a pretty shrewd guess."

And more than that he refused to say, though we were all itching with curiosity. We played golf that evening, and two rounds the next day, and never once did he allude to the matter. And then on the following morning came the reply from the Yard.

"Blank," said Ronald after he had read it. "Nothing is known about them. And I'm afraid I rather expected it. However, the point that now arises is what we're going to do about it—if anything."

"We must do something," cried the girl. "If they are criminals we can't let them stay on at the rectory."

"If you can tell me of any method by which we can turn 'em out," laughed Ronald, "we'll get down to it. We haven't got a vestige of proof, and if we managed to get into the house in search of it, it's we who become the criminals. No, Miss Millington, I fear it's no go at present. So I think I will go back to London and make a few further inquiries, leaving Bob, if you can bear him, to hold the fort at this end."

"We'd love Mr. Miller to stay on," she said, but I could tell she was disappointed.

"Keep your eyes skinned, Bob," said Ronald. "See without being seen, and don't let 'em suspect you."

Which was all very fine and large, as I said to the girl after he had gone. How on earth was I to see without being seen? I could not stand at the front gate, nor could I walk backwards and forwards past it for hours on end. A hiding place in the grounds was out of the question because of the dogs, so that altogether it seemed a somewhat tall order. And then at lunch she had a brain-wave.

"Do you, by any chance, sketch, Mr. Miller?"

"Not so that you'd notice it," I said. "Why?"

"Because if you could, sufficiently well not to make it ridiculous, I thought you might sit in the churchyard and draw the church. Then you'd have at any rate two sides of the house under observation."

Now, as a matter of fact, as a schoolboy I had done a certain amount of sketching in a mild way, and the advantages of her suggestion were obvious. The trouble was that it had been very mild, and my fear was that my effort would be so crude that anyone seeing it would know I was an impostor. Still, it seemed the only possibility, and after lunch we drove into Horsham for the necessary paraphernalia. Then, having obtained permission from the vicar, I proceeded to the churchyard.

One difficulty immediately presented itself. To even the most in-experienced eye there was only one feasible spot in which to set up my easel, from the point of view of drawing the church, and that spot was utterly unsuitable from the point of view of watching the rectory. However, undeterred by trifles of that sort, I selected a place which gave me the best observation post for the house and commenced work under the rheumy gaze of an incredibly old man who was pot-tering round tending the graves.

It was a beautifully warm afternoon and I soon began to feel infer-nally sleepy. What little cunning my hand had ever possessed seemed to have completely gone, and my preliminary effort looked like a cross between a Martello tower and a drunken lighthouse. The old man was immensely edified.

"Have 'e done much in that line, sir?" he mumbled, after he had inspected it long and carefully.

"Not for some time," I answered, with what dignity I could, hop-ing fervently that my audience would not increase.

He cupped his hand round his ear.

"What do 'e say?" he remarked. "I be terrible 'ard of 'earing."

"I said not for some time," I told him in a loud voice, and even as I spoke I realised that a man was watching me intently from one of the top windows of the rectory. He was not the one who had let Ronald and me in when we had called on Mrs. Hamilton, but he also looked like a foreigner. For an appreciable time he stood there staring at me. Then as suddenly as he had appeared he vanished, and a few moments later I saw him come out of the front door and walk towards the wicket gate. Evidently he was going to speak to me, which was the last thing I wanted. One glance at the effusion I had produced would give the whole show away. There was only one thing to be done, and I did it. I tore off the sheet, crumpled it into a ball and threw it away.

"A fine day for sketching," he remarked, as he came up. "And an excellent subject."

"Which, I fear, I did but scant justice to with my first attempt," I answered, lighting a cigarette. "In fact, I have thrown it away."

"What a pity," he said. "I would have liked to have seen it." He was looking round, and my heart sank. What on earth was I going to do if he picked it up and opened it? And suddenly, to my amazement, I realised it was no longer there. It had fallen between two graves, and now there was no sign of it. And then it dawned on me what had happened: the ancient had picked it up.

"Yonder octogenarian has removed the outrage," I said lightly.

"I really must see it," he remarked with a smile. "I assure you I am no mean critic. Hi—you!"

The old man took not the slightest notice, but continued pottering about with his hoe.

"He's as deaf as a post," I said. "But I am not at all anxious for it to be seen; it is altogether too bad."

"Artistic modesty," he cried, and to my alarm and annoyance he went up to the old chap. Which was devilish awkward. We could not have a bellowing match in the churchyard.

"Have you got the sketch the gentleman threw away?" he shouted.

"Aye, sir, it's a beautiful day," wheezed the other. "Just what we want at cherry-picking time."

"The sketch that you picked up, you old ass."

"The grass, sir. Maybe that could do with a drop of rain. Which, reminds me," he chuckled, "that I could do with a drop of summat myself. 'Tis powerful thirsty weather."

He hobbled away down the path, and I burst out laughing at the other's discomfiture. He looked completely nonplussed. And then the more sinister aspect struck me. Why was he so keen to inspect this sketch of mine that he had even displayed considerable bad taste over the matter? If ever a man had been told plainly that I did not want it looked at, he had. And yet he had persisted.' If he was so anxious to find out whether I was a genuine artist, it followed that he had reasons for fearing I might not be. Which was yet another proof that things were going on in the house which he wished to conceal. But he had quite recovered himself when he rejoined me.

"He certainly is a little hard of hearing," he remarked genially.

"Are you also interested in dogs?" I inquired.

"I fear not," he answered. "It is my aunt's hobby. Aren't you going to sketch any more?"

I had risen and started to pack up.

"Not today," I said. "I'm just beginning to think that our elderly friend's idea of a drop of Summat has much to commend it."'

I did not tell him that as nothing would induce me to draw a line under his eye there did not seem much object in prolonging the interview. Mrs. Hamilton was walking about amongst the dogs; it seemed unlikely that I should find out anything more. And so I left him standing there and started home. Did he suspect me? That was the point. Most certainly I suspected him, but was the converse true? His attempt to test me had been foiled by the old man's deafness. What was the final result in his mind?

"Aunt!" scoffed Nancy Millington, when I told them about it. "I don't believe it."

"I admit I've seldom seen two people who are less alike," I agreed. "Still, I don't see that that has much bearing on it either way!"

"It's another proof that they're crooked," she cried. "Why should he pretend to be her nephew when he isn't?"

"Hold hard, old soul," said her brother with a grin. "It is just possible, you know, that she is his aunt."

"Any message from Ronald?" I asked.

"Not a word," said the girl, and shortly after we all went to dress for dinner, a meal at which we endeavoured without conspicuous success to keep the conversation off the rectory.

It was the sudden furious barking of all the dogs at about eleven o'clock that gave Tom Millington the idea.

"What about doing a little observation by night from the churchyard, Miller? There's no moon, and it's nice and warm. We might find out something."

"I'm quite on," I said. "Let's go and change into some other clothes. And we'd better wear rubber shoes."

His sister wanted to come too, but with brotherly frankness he informed her that she would merely be a damned nuisance. And so half an hour later we two men found ourselves crouching amongst the graves as near to the wicket gate as we could get. The top rooms of the rectory on the side facing us were in darkness, though light was streaming out from two windows in front.

Not a breath of wind stirred; the night was absolutely still. The village, a few hundred yards down the road, was long since asleep. And I was just beginning to feel a strong craving for a cigarette, when with disconcerting suddenness a light went on in one of the downstairs rooms in front of us. A man, clearly visible through some thin curtains, had just come in, and I edged nearer Millington.

"That's my bird of this afternoon," I whispered.

He crossed to the French windows and flung them open, whilst we shrank back, though it was out of the question for him to see us as we were well in the shadow. For some time he stood there silhouetted against the light, and the smell of his cigar came to us distinctly.

"Nothing much the matter with that weed," breathed Millington in my ear. "Why can't the bally man go and smoke it somewhere else? It's making me envious."

Suddenly he swung round. Another man—the servant who had admitted Ronald and me—had entered the room carrying something in his hand. It looked like a piece of white paper, and he put it on the table. Then both men pored over it in silence for some minutes. At length my acquaintance of the afternoon produced a magnifying glass from his pocket, and continued his examination through that. And he was just straightening up when there came a startling interruption. A man's scream, instantly suppressed, rang through the night. And it came from the house.

With a snarl of rage my acquaintance dropped the magnifying glass and sprang to the door, followed by his companion. And in a flash Tom Millington was on his feet.

"Come on, Miller," he muttered. "I'm not standing for this. That scream was one of mortal terror."

We rushed through the wicket gate, and into the room. The door was open, and heedless of what noise we made we raced up the stairs. The passage was lit, and as we passed one of the rooms a pitiful moaning sound came from it. And Tom Millington without hesitation walked straight in.

For a moment there was dead silence, and we took in the whole scene. Lying in bed was a dazed man. Standing over him were Mrs. Hamilton and the two who had been in the room down stairs. And in the woman's hand was a hypodermic syringe. For just a second the sick man's eyes sought ours in an agony of supplication. Then they closed wearily and he sank back on the pillows.

"What is the meaning of this monstrous intrusion?"

Mrs. Hamilton had at length found her voice.

"What is the meaning of that poor devil?" I cried sternly, pointing at the bed.

"By Gosh it's the—artist," said her so-called nephew softly, getting between us and the door and ringing the bell.

"How dare you break into my house?" cried the woman, white with anger.

"Cut it out," said Millington curtly. "When one hears some poor wretch screaming in terror one doesn't stop to ring the front door bell. Well—what explanation have you?"

Out of the corner of my eye I saw that two more men had entered the room, and an ugly-looking couple of customers they were. Then I turned back to the woman, and just caught a meaning glance that passed between her and her nephew.

"You are evidently under some delusion, Mr. Millington," she remarked in a very different voice from her former one. "I still consider it an outrageous thing for you and your friend to come into my house unannounced at this time of night. But hearing what you did it is perhaps understandable. This poor man is suffering from an agonising and practically incurable complaint, and the only thing we can do to help him is to give him continual injections of morphia."

"What doctor is attending him?" said Millington stubbornly.

"Really, Mr. Millington! I confess I'm amazed at your question. What possible business can it be of yours? But if you wish to know, it is a specialist from Brighton. And now I must really request you to go. Otherwise I shall have to ask my nephew to ring for the police."

"Nephew?" came a genial voice from the door, and we all swung round. To my astonishment Ronald was standing there with three other men, one of whom—the speaker—I recognised as Inspector McIver of Scotland Yard.

"Well, well," he continued, "one lives and learns. I didn't know you went in for aunts. So you're up to your old games again, are you, Joe?"

"I don't know what the devil you're talking about, McIver," answered the other sullenly. "You fellows will never give a man any credit for trying to run straight. I'm helping my aunt with her dogs."

"Are you, now? And do you feed 'em on these?"

From his pocket McIver produced a piece of paper, which I recognised as being similar to the one the two men had been examining downstairs.

"I've struck some damn fool things in my life, Joe," he continued, "but actually to leave one lying about in a sitting-room with the window open wins in a canter."

I looked at the paper more closely. It was a five-pound note. And the next moment we were all of us mixed up in it. With a howl of fury the man called Joe had hurled himself on the footman.

"You thrice damned fool!" he screamed. "You've wrecked everything."

"Not quite," said McIver, when they were finally separated. "But each of you thinking the other had it saved me a lot of bother. Put the bracelets on all of 'em."

A sergeant entered the room.

"I've found the outfit, sir," he announced, but McIver took no notice. He had gone to the bed, and was staring at the unconscious man. And suddenly he gave a long whistle.

"Blest if it isn't Mr. Symington, the millionaire! He's supposed to have left for Paris three or four days ago. My sainted aunt, Joe, you'll be for it this time good and hearty. Forging bank-notes and abduction with violence will keep you occupied at the taxpayers' expense till it's time to redeem the three and a half *per cent* War Loan."

And at that instant the sick man opened his eyes.

"Save me," he muttered. "Forging my signature. Stop the cheques."

"All right, sir," said McIver soothingly. "Don't you worry your head about that. We've caught the whole bunch."

"Came down about my dog," whispered the other. "They must have sent faked letters to hotel."

His eyes shut, he seemed to sleep.

"What have you done to him?" said McIver sternly.

The woman shrugged her shoulders, she knew the game was up.

"Nothing serious," she said. "He's only bung full of morphia. I was speaking the truth when I told those guys that."

And then she stared at Ronald.

"What put you wise?" she asked.

"Apart from the small matter of Irish terriers and Airedales," he said, "the fox terrier has yet to be born that eats two pounds of biscuits a day."

"But you were wise to that before you left London," I remarked. "What made you wiser?"

It was an hour later, and we were having a final nightcap. Mr. Symington had been removed to a nursing home, the prisoners to a less comfortable destination.

"When I saw Joe Darlington," he answered. "At least, that was the name under which he last enjoyed His Majesty's hospitality. What his real name is I doubt if even he himself knows. He has several aliases, speaks four or five languages fluently, and is a natural criminal. And to think that he would sit in the country on a dog farm was to think the unthinkable. So I knew the show was crooked, a thing I had only guessed before.

"You remember I asked you if you'd noticed that other man's nails when he opened the door. Well, I had, and I'd seen they were stained and discoloured with acid. Such stains may come quite innocently; they may also come very much otherwise. They are almost invariably to be found on a forger's hands, and when I saw them I told you that if anything shady was going on I could give a pretty shrewd guess as to what it was. Seeing Darlington this afternoon made it to my mind a certainty. I don't think he has ever been actually in that line himself, but he would be an invaluable help in getting the notes distributed, which is more than half the battle. So I got on the 'phone to McIver, who arrived about two hours ago with his merry men. And the rest you know It was luck, of course, each of 'em thinking the other had the dud flyer, but we had them in any case."

"But what I still don't understand," I said, "is about this man Joe Darlington. You hadn't seen him before you went to London, so how could you 'phone McIver?"

Ronald grinned gently.

"My dear old boy," he said, "I never went to London. I had the very greatest faith in your ability to bolt any badger there might be. I was tolerably certain you had only to be in the vicinity of the house for half an hour for the suspicions of every inmate to be aroused. And I banked on it."

His voice changed suddenly.

"Oi be terrible 'ard of 'earing," he wheezed, producing my crumpled-up sketch from his pocket. "My sainted aunt, Bob, it might be anything from a joint of beef to a ship in distress at sea!"

The Third Message

"Sussex at the Oval; Oxford at Lord's. Which shall it be, Bob?"

Ronald Standish pushed back his chair from the breakfast table and started to fill his pipe.

"Neither—unless I'm much mistaken, old boy," I said from the window. "A warrior showing traces of excitement has just crossed the street and is making for the door. It looks like a job of work!"

The bell rang furiously, and a moment or two later Ronald's butler ushered in a visitor. He was a man of about thirty-five, dark and clean-shaven, and he was in a state of considerable agitation.

"Mr. Standish?" he inquired, looking from one to the other of us.

"That's me," said Ronald. "What can I do for you?"

"I must first of all apologise for coming at such an unearthly hour," he remarked, "but a very shocking tragedy has taken place. And re-membering that a friend of mine, Major Brewster—"

"Jim Brewster in the 10th Lancers?" put in Ronald.

"That's the man."

"I know him well. Please go on."

"Remembering, then, that he once told me that you were prepared sometimes to take on detective cases, I ventured to come straight away to you. Stavert is my name—Herbert Stavert."

"Take a chair, Mr. Stavert; and take your time," said Ronald. "But before you begin, I'll just have the debris cleared away."

He rang the bell, and while Sayers—his man—was removing the breakfast things, no more was said.

"Now," said Ronald, as the door closed, "let's hear all about it."

"To make things clear, Mr. Standish," began the other, "I must go back five months. Does the name Sir James Brackenbury convey any-thing to you?"

Ronald knit his brows.

"Brackenbury! Vaguely—yes. I know I've heard the name, but at the moment I can't connect it with anything. Wait—didn't he fall over a cliff and break his neck?"

"So I thought until last night," said the other, grimly. "Now I don't think that 'fall' is the right word. However, you shall hear the whole story and judge for yourself. Sir James Brackenbury was my uncle; he was also, in a sense, my employer. I used to live with him at Stalbridge Hall, doing for him what little secretarial work he required. But it was really only a nominal job; I was more a companion than a secretary. To be quite frank, he never got on with either of his sons, and when his wife died, about two years ago, he suggested that I should make the place my home.

"I deliberated for some time as to whether I should accept his offer. Again, to be quite frank, my uncle was a somewhat queer-tempered individual, and I was doubtful as to how we should get on. But jobs are hard to come by these days, and, to cut it short, I went—an action which was not approved of by either of my cousins. They made the most offensive insinuations, the more offensive because they were so obviously groundless. The property was entailed; the title must pass automatically, so what I was expected to get out of it I don't know. But I want to make it clear that the family atmosphere was not good.

"Well, for about fifteen months the arrangement continued. I ran the business of the estate; opened my uncle's correspondence, arranged his shooting parties, and so on. And, somewhat naturally, my uncle got into the habit of expressing himself pretty freely in front of me. Which brings me to the next family difference. It has, so far as I can see, no hearing on the matter, but I think it better to tell you everything. You must know, then, that the principal cause of my uncle's anger with his elder son Harry was that he refused to get married. The old man was frightened lest the title should ultimately come to Dick, the younger boy, whom he disliked far more than he did Harry."

"It certainly sounds a very happy family," commented Ronald dryly. "Did the two brothers dislike one another also?"

"They got on fairly well together so far as I know. Harry was in the Guards; Dick was in some motor business down in Brighton. And it was the old man's custom always to allude to him as 'that damned chauffeur'. Harry came twice while I was there for the shooting. Dick never entered the house. And that was the state of affairs at the beginning of last March, when, on opening my uncle's letters one morning, I found an extraordinary communication. It was typewritten, evidently on a cheap machine, by someone who was not an expert. The spacing was uneven, and some of the letters were irregular.

"'Place the papers on the seat by the summer-house.'

"That was the message. Just that and nothing more. I looked at the envelope; the postmark was a London one."

"One moment," interrupted Ronald. "Have you got that paper on you?"

"I have not," said Stavert. "You will understand why shortly. After breakfast I showed it to my uncle, commenting on its strangeness. And, to my amazement, the old man turned as white as a sheet.

"'Good Lord! Uncle James!' I cried. 'What's the matter?'

"He slowly recovered his colour, though I could see he was terribly shaken.

"'The devils,' he muttered at length, 'the foul devils! I'll be damned if I do. Let them do their worst.'

"'But who are you talking about?' I cried, bewildered.

"'Never you mind,' he said, and with that he tore the note into tiny pieces and flung them in the paper basket.

"'But are there any special papers?' I persisted, for I certainly had never heard of them.

"'You mind your own business,' he answered, and stumped out of the room.

"The next few days my uncle was unusually silent. Two or three times I tried to get him back on to the subject, but on each occasion he shut up like an oyster. And after a while the thing began to fade from my mind, when suddenly the tragedy occurred. About two miles from the house is an old disused quarry. My uncle was found at the bottom of it with his neck broken. It was easy to see what had happened. For some reason or other, he had been standing too near the edge; the ground had given way, and he had fallen. Death was instantaneous. The thing had happened at dusk, the body being found by a passing labourer about eight o'clock at night.

"Harry, of course, at once motored down, but Dick was out of England on business. I immediately told Harry the whole story of the letter. For the decision we had to make was whether or not I should allude to it at the inquest. And, rightly or wrongly, we decided not to. I felt that it was principally for my cousin to say, and he was very averse to mentioning anything.

"'It can't bring the poor old chap back to life,' was the line he took, 'and we'll have these confounded newspaper men round us like a swarm of bees. It is impossible to say that there is any connection between the two things. There are no marks indicating violence on the body. It's far better to have a verdict of accidental death returned.' And in due course it was, with the obvious rider about the danger of the quarry and the need for a more adequate fence."

"One moment, Mr. Stavert," said Ronald. "Was your uncle in the habit of taking long walks, and that one in particular?"

"Yes; it was a favourite direction of his."

"A fact which would be known or could be easily found out by the writer of that message?"

"Presumably so."

"Another point. Is the spot from which he fell visible for a long distance around?"

"No, it is not. There is a little dip there, and the usual path runs round the top of the dip. But it can, of course, be seen from below."

"I understand perfectly. It comes to this—that a man could hide in that dip and not be seen by anyone walking along the top of the quarry until he was close to him."

"That is so, Mr. Standish. From your questions I gather you think the verdict may have been wrong."

"I don't say that. But I most certainly think that you and your cousin acted wrongly in suppressing a very material piece of evidence."

"So do I—now," cried the other bitterly. "And this time it certainly won't be suppressed."

"This time?" said Ronald, staring at him. "You've received another of these messages, have you?"

"That's why I'm here, Mr. Standish. However, to go back. After the funeral, Harry and I went through everything in an endeavour to find anything which might possibly account for the letter. We found nothing—absolutely nothing. I, of course, knew where most of his papers were, but even in a drawer he kept permanently locked there were only a few faded letters and the draft of his will."

"What sort of letters?" demanded Ronald.

"Love letters—old ones—from a lady who did not become his wife," said Stavert. "I think you can dismiss the idea at once of their being the object of the communication, for the lady involved has been dead some years. And so we were forced to the conclusion that he had either destroyed these papers, whatever they were, or else that there was some secret hiding-place which we had not discovered."

"Again I must interrupt," said Ronald. "In Sir James's past life had there been any periods when he might have got mixed up with such a thing as a secret society, let us say, or with any organisation of a political or criminal character?"

"I'm glad you asked that question, because it was one of the first things we discussed. And beyond our knowledge that he had been pretty wild as a young man, and had been a lot in America, we could come to no conclusion. I think the correct way of putting it would be that, though we had no proof that he had become involved in anything of the sort, neither of us would have been surprised to hear that he had."

"I get you," remarked Ronald. "Please continue."

"Well, his death, of course, terminated my job and my life at Stalbridge Hall. Harry made a half-hearted suggestion that I should continue there, but it was clear that he didn't really mean it. And so I returned to London, where I have been since then until a week ago, when I got a letter from him asking me to go down and see him at once. He met me at the station with a peculiar look on his face, and the instant we got into the car he pulled this out of his pocket."

As he spoke Stavert handed an open envelope to Ronald, who took out the contents.

"'Place the papers on the seat by the summer-house.'"

"A facsimile, Mr. Standish, of the message his father had received, even to the extent, I should think, of being written on the same machine."

Ronald held it up to the light; then he examined it carefully through a magnifying glass. After which he laid it on the table. "Well—what happened then?"

"We discussed what was the best thing to do. Clearly we could not comply with the request, since there were no papers as far as we knew. Equally clearly we could not go to the police, since on the face of it the message did not seem one to cause alarm. It was only the fact that it was the second one that gave it its significance, and to admit that it was the second one was to admit that we had suppressed the first. So we finally decided that we would lie up in wait by the summer-house and see what happened. Whoever it was who had written the note would have to come and see if the papers were there, and we then proposed to nab him."

Ronald leaned forward expectantly: clearly he was interested.

"For six nights we waited. Nothing happened; no one came near

293

us. Once I thought I heard a movement in the undergrowth a little way off, but it may have been a fox. At any rate, our vigil was useless. And then came last night."

He paused and lit a cigarette, and I noticed that his hand was trembling a little.

"It was raining pretty hard after dinner, and Harry said that he'd be damned if he was going to get wet to the skin lying about in a damp wood. And so for the first time for a week we both went to bed. This morning, at seven o'clock, I was awakened by the footman, who was white and shaking.

"'For God's sake come at once, sir,' he said. 'Sir Harry is dead!'

"I sprang out of bed and dashed along to his room. He was sprawling on the floor, and there was a hole in the back of his head I could have put my fist in. When we turned him over it was obvious what had happened. The poor devil had been shot through the eye. So I immediately telephoned for the police and a doctor, and then, getting into a car, I came straight up to you."

Ronald raised his eyebrows.

"I suppose you waited to see the police, didn't you?"

"No. I left a message as to where I was going, and told the butler to say I'd be back by noon. I felt there was nothing I could do at the moment, and I desperately wanted your advice. Would it be possible for you to come back with me now in the car?"

"I will certainly do so," said Ronald. "But I think you must be prepared for a bit of a tail twisting from the police for bolting off like that. To put it mildly, it was a most irregular thing to do."

"I can't help that, Mr. Standish," said the other. "If I'd waited there, there would have been interminable delays and red tape. You know what the local police are, and I want the best opinion on the spot at once before half the clues are obliterated."

"What clues are there up to date?"

"I don't know. But there must be some. I refuse to believe that a man can be murdered without any traces being left. And I want you to find those traces."

Ronald rose.

"All right, we'll come with you. By the way—did no one hear the shot?"

"I heard nothing, and none of the servants mentioned it. So, presumably, no one did."

"Strange;" said Ronald thoughtfully.

"It's a big rambling house, and the servants' quarters are right at the other end."

"Still, it takes a good deal of nerve to discharge a gun in the middle of the night when a house is quiet. However—we'll see."

CHAPTER 2.

We reached Stalbridge Hall about midday, to find, as Ronald had anticipated, a very ruffled inspector. And his temper was not improved when he learned the reason of Stavert's absence. But after a while, having delivered himself of a suitable reprimand, he recovered sufficiently to tell us what he had found out.

"The murderer," he remarked, "entered the house by way of the library window. If you care to verify the fact, Mr. Standish, by means of some subtle deduction, we can go there and see."

"Thank you, Inspector," said Ronald cheerily, with a wink at me. "I feel it will be a waste of time after what you've found out yourself, but still it can do no harm."

The officer led the way to big room in one wing of the house. "If you look through the window," he continued, "you will see the marks of his footprints in the flower-bed outside. The ground is still damp and they are clearly visible. He then stood on the sill, and with a stout knife forced the hasp of the window: the damage to the woodwork is plain. In fact, he made no endeavour to conceal his mode of entry. There are traces of mud on the carpet, those nearest the window being particularly clear."

He had opened the window as he spoke, and Ronald began to examine everything in his usual methodical way while the inspector, with a barely concealed smile, watched him. And I must say that even I was a little surprised at the amount of time he took: the thing did indeed look obvious. The footprints outside, the mud on the window-sill and carpet, the splintered woodwork, all told their own tale.

"Have you deduced anything fresh?" demanded the Inspector a little sarcastically, as Ronald closed the window again.

"My dear Inspector, I'm sure you've seen everything there is to be seen," answered Ronald mildly. "As you say, he certainly seemed determined that we should know how he got in. By the way, was this window shut or open this morning?"

"Shut, but not bolted," said the other.

"I see," said Ronald. "Well—what then?"

"He proceeded to poison the dog—" continued the officer.

"What's that?" cried Stavert. "Rollo poisoned?"

"It was found lying dead in the hall just behind the banisters, and the doctor had no hesitation in saying it had been poisoned. You can see the body now."

We followed him into the hall, and there, lying half concealed behind the staircase, was a big Airedale. And a glance at the stiff, rigid legs was sufficient to confirm the doctor's diagnosis.

"Was he a good watch-dog?" asked Ronald.

"Excellent," said Stavert.

"If he hadn't been, there would have been no necessity to poison him," remarked the inspector, with a pitying glance at Ronald.

"Quite so, Inspector," he answered humbly. "Very stupid of me not to have thought of that."

The officer gave him a suspicious look, but Ronald's face was expressionless. And after a moment he led the way upstairs.

"We are now going to the room where the late baronet was murdered," he continued. "Once again the murderer has left traces of mud, which are plainly visible on the light carpet."

He flung open the door, and we walked in. The body, covered by a sheet, was lying on the bed, and Ronald lifted a corner and looked at the head. It was a ghastly wound, the only merciful thing being that death must have been absolutely instantaneous.

"I see that there's no trace of scorching on the face," he remarked. "Have you found the bullet?"

"Yes," said the inspector "It was embedded in the wall behind the bed. And here, I must confess, I am a little nonplussed, for to the best of my belief I have never seen such a bullet before."

He held it out to Ronald, whose face lit up the instant he saw it.

"I don't wonder, Inspector," he cried. "And this accounts for what was puzzling me. This bullet was fired from a weapon which is far more common in America than it is here—a compressed-air rifle. At close range it is as deadly as an ordinary gun, and, bar a hiss when fired, it makes no noise. That's why you heard nothing, Mr. Stavert, and also why there is no sign of scorching."

The inspector nodded portentously.

"I suspected something of the sort," he remarked.

"But have you any clue as to the murderer?" cried Stavely.

"At the moment—no," answered the inspector. "And that is where you may be of help, and that is the reason your absence this morning was very unfortunate. Time has been lost, and in a case like this every moment is of value. Now, Mr. Stavert, what we want to find in a case of this sort is the motive. It is clear that your cousin was murdered by someone who possessed a good working knowledge of the house. Do you know of anyone who had a grudge against him?"

"I knew very little of my cousin's life," said Stavert, "and still less of his friends and acquaintances. I know that he was very popular in his regiment."

"Mr. Stavert," interrupted Ronald, "I think you should tell the inspector at once what you told me. And while you do so I will have a further look round. Come along, Bob. Now," he continued as we went down the stairs, "let's go back to the library. I want to have a final look at it unhampered by that mutton-headed policeman."

Once again he studied the window-sill with the utmost care. Then he stood on it and examined the marks on the woodwork with his magnifying-glass. Then he looked at the flower-bed outside as if measuring its width in his mind's eye.

"Just shut the window, Bob," he said, and I did so, leaving him balanced precariously on the sill outside. He paused for a moment; then he jumped, landing a good yard short of the grass on the other side of the bed.

"What's the great idea?" I demanded, opening the window once more.

"Get up yourself and jump," he said. "Jump as far as you can. Leave the window open."

I did so, and found that I could clear the flower-bed with ease, owing to being able to crouch on the sill, while Ronald had had to stand upright.

"And now," he continued, "we will remove my footmarks, lest the worthy inspector should have a rush of blood to the head."

He smoothed them over with his stick, and was lighting a cigarette as the officer, followed by Stavert, appeared at the window.

"This is a most important development, Mr. Standish," he remarked.

"I thought you'd find it so," said Ronald.

"It presents us, of course, at once with the motive: revenge because the papers were not forthcoming."

"Exactly," cried Ronald. "But revenge on whose part?"

"The man who typed the message. Who else?"

"So that all you have to do is to lay your hands on him. It seems to me that you may find it a little difficult, in view of the fact that nobody knows what these papers consisted of."

"Nevertheless, it gives us one very important point to go on. This vendetta was not so much a personal one against the dead man, but it was more in the nature of a family feud. It is on Sir James's life, therefore, that we must concentrate rather than on his son's."

"Very true," murmured Ronald. "It is a pleasure and a privilege to work with you, Inspector. By the way, Mr. Stavert, was your uncle ever in Australia?"

"Yes, for a considerable time when he was a young man," answered Stavert in some surprise. "Why do you ask?"

"Well—it's a long shot. But I think you'll find that your cousin's murderer was a left-handed Australian, at least six feet tall—"

"With red hair and a slight stammer," snorted the inspector. "Really, Mr. Standish, this is hardly the moment for far-fetched jokes."

"I don't think Mr. Standish is joking, Inspector," said Stavert quietly, turning to Ronald. "What makes you think so?"

But Ronald was looking thoroughly annoyed. "I am not in the habit of making far-fetched jokes on occasions such as this," he remarked shortly. "As I say—that is my opinion; you can take it or leave it."

He turned on his heel, giving me an imperceptible signal to follow him.

"That will give 'em something to think about," he chuckled. "Hallo! Who is this, I wonder?"

A youngish man was coming rapidly along the path towards us, carrying a small suit-case in his hand.

"Is this true about poor old Harry?" he called out as soon as he saw us.

"Are you his brother?" asked Ronald, and he nodded.

"Yes. I got a wire this morning to say he was dead."

"He was murdered last night," said Ronald gravely.

"But in Heaven's name who wanted to murder the old chap?" cried the new baronet.

"That's what we want to find out," answered Ronald.

He glanced round. We were out of sight of the house.

"I would like a few words with you before you go on," he continued. "I am going to make a somewhat peculiar request to you, and before I do so it is necessary for me to tell you who I am and why I'm here."

Briefly he explained the situation, and as soon as he mentioned his name the other nodded.

"I've heard of you, Mr. Standish. No need of any further introduction."

"Good. Well, now you know that when your father died he had just received a letter telling him to put certain papers on the seat by the summer-house."

"Yes. I was told so afterwards."

"Your brother received a similar notification a week ago."

The other whistled.

"The devil he did! So there's a connecting link between the two cases. One, too, that makes it look as if my old governor was murdered."

He was staring at Ronald thoughtfully.

"Just so. And now it's going to be your turn."

He put down his suit-case and lit a cigarette.

"Look here, Mr. Standish, this seems to me to be getting beyond a joke. What are these papers, anyway? Hasn't anybody got an idea?"

"No one," said Ronald gravely. "But I think if you will do exactly what I say we shall be able to solve part of the mystery, at any rate. Are you by chance going to be married?"

We both stared at him in blank amazement. The question was so completely unexpected.

"I am not," the young man answered. "But what the deuce has that got to do with it?"

"I told you, didn't I, that I was going to make a peculiar request?" continued Ronald. "And I'm coming to it now. I must beg of you to trust me, and to believe that, strange though it may seem to you, it gives the surest and safest way of solving this murder. You are in grave danger, Sir Richard. Not, of course, at this moment; but it is there, hanging over you. And I want to it remove it as soon as possible. Will you, therefore, remember that you are going to be married in a fortnight? That, owing to your brother's death, the ceremony will be a quiet one, but that you don't propose to postpone it? And that after it is over you will be leaving for a lengthy honeymoon on the Continent? Further, and this is the most vital thing of all, you are not to tell a single soul that your story is not the truth."

The young baronet's eyes had been growing rounder and rounder as Ronald proceeded.

"Well I'm damned!" he muttered at length. "Do you really mean it?"

"Never more serious in my life," said Ronald quietly.

"But who am I supposed to be marrying?"

"There must surely be some girl, unknown to your cousin or the members of the household, who would fill the bill. Someone you've met at Brighton."

"All right," said the young man. "I suppose I can invent somebody, if you think it is absolutely essential."

"Absolutely," answered Ronald. "And it's still more essential that no one should have the faintest suspicion that it is an invention. You are going to be married in a fortnight. So get that idea into your head. And there is one thing further. Should you receive a similar communication about the papers, let me know immediately in London. But do not tell anyone else that you have let me know. On that, Sir Richard, your life may depend. The line you must take up is that you think the whole thing is rot, and if the writer of the message plays any tricks with you, you are quite capable of dealing with him. Do you get me?"

The other nodded.

"Perfectly; I'll do it."

"Good," said Ronald. "And not a word to a soul. Ah! here comes the inspector with your cousin. We'll stroll on."

"For the love of Pete, Ronald," I said, when we were out of earshot, "what is the great idea?"

"All holders of an old title should be married," he answered, with a grin. "Perhaps it will inspire him to do so in reality."

Then he grew serious again.

"But there are certainly points about this case, Bob, which render it almost unique in my experience. And it's very lucky that we met that youngster when we did. Let's pray that he can play his part."

CHAPTER 3.

During the next few days I found myself growing more and more bewildered over the whole thing. Try as I would, I could think of no explanation for this supposed marriage, and Ronald was not communicative. But as time went on, and more than a week elapsed since the murder, I noticed that he became a little uneasy. He would never go far from the telephone, and whenever a post arrived he went eagerly through his letters.

The verdict at the inquest had been the only one possible in the circumstances—"Murder by some person or persons unknown." The inspector had been congratulated on his reconstruction of the crime, especially his discovery of the type of weapon that had been used, and was now, according to the papers, hot on a clue.

It was on the tenth day that the telephone rang while we were at breakfast, and Ronald went to it. And I saw at once from his face that it was the message he had been waiting for.

"It's come, has it?" he said. "Excellent. Now listen to me, Sir Richard, and obey my instructions literally. You will be quite safe till tonight. I want you to be thoroughly bombastic about it the whole of today, and refuse point-blank to tell the police. Is your cousin with you? Coming back this afternoon? Tell him, of course, that you've received it, but do not let him keep watch with you tonight. Tell him that at dinner. You propose to be alone in your bedroom. No—don't tell anyone that you've rung me up. Now, there's a big set-in cupboard in your room; you've got to smuggle us into that somehow without anybody knowing. You can do that, can you, if we get down about nine, All right—the side door by the shrubbery. I remember it. And don't forget that it's vitally important that you should announce at dinner in front of the servants your determination to sleep alone."

"So it's worked, Bob," said Ronald, as he hung up the receiver. "The third message has been sent, though I was getting a bit worried. That supposed marriage was drawing rather too close."

"But what would that have had to do with it?" I demanded, scenting a chance of finding some ray of light in my mental fog.

"Well, it would have upset things rather if he'd had to admit he wasn't even engaged," said Ronald, with a grin. "Seems such a funny thing to lie about, doesn't it? Almost qualifies him for a mental home."

"Confound you, you know I don't mean that!" I cried.

But he only grinned the more. "Think it over, Bob. Use the old grey matter."

And I was still pondering at ten o'clock that night as I stood beside Ronald in the cupboard of Sir Richard's bedroom. He had got us in safely unseen by anyone, and there was nothing for it now but to wait. A footman came in to turn the bed down for the night, and at eleven o'clock the baronet came upstairs.

He stopped for a moment or two talking to his cousin outside, and we heard the latter begging him to be allowed to share the vigil. But Sir Richard was adamant, and after saying goodnight cheerfully, he came in and shut the door. And a few seconds later Stavert's door closed also.

"All right?" asked the youngster, coming over to the cupboard.

"Quite," said Ronald, in a low voice. "Get undressed, and go to bed. I want you to turn about in it so as to give it the normal appearance of having been slept in."

Ronald crossed the room, and noiselessly locked the door. Then, opening a bag he had brought down with him, he took out a life-size wax head and shoulders. He looked critically at the colour of the hair; then at the baronet's.

"Not too bad from memory," he muttered. "Now we'll set the scene."

We watched him as he carefully arranged a bolster and a pair of hunting boots under the bedclothes, moving them this way and that till the result was exactly like a body. Then he put the head sideways on the pillow and pulled up the sheet around it till only the hair and a bit of the forehead were visible. And finally he unlocked the door again and turned out the light.

"It might be better," he said "but it will serve. Into the cupboard with you, Sir Richard: all we can do now is to wait."

The house grew silent, though every crack of the boards sounded like a pistol-shot in the stillness. But is was not until the clock in the hall had just chimed two that I felt Ronald's hand tighten on my arm. A door had opened somewhere. I listened intently, though I could scarcely hear anything save the pounding of my own heart. And then quite distinctly came the sound of footsteps along the passage. They paused outside the room, and I heard Sir Richard draw in his breath sharply.

There came a low knock; then the door handle was tried. Some one was coming in: and tense with excitement I peered over Ronald's shoulder through the chink we had left open. I could hear nothing now: the footsteps made no sound on the carpet. And for what seemed an eternity we waited.

Suddenly a beam of light shone on the bed; and then everything happened quickly. There came a sharp whistling hiss, and the splintering noise of the wax mould breaking. And then the room was flooded with light. Ronald was standing by the switch with a revolver in his hand. Herbert Stavert, his teeth snarling like a trapped animal's, leant against the bed.

"I don't think we need trouble you any further," said Ronald calmly. "Ah! would you?"

302

A shot rang out, and Stavert, with an oath, dropped the gun he had raised and clutched his shattered wrist.

"So it was you, you swine," shouted Sir Richard. "By God! I wonder if they'll let me be present at the gallows?"

"There's no crime in shooting a dummy," muttered Stavert at length.

"From the word go, Stavert, I realised you were a fool," said Ronald deliberately. "But I should think that even you can't be such a complete imbecile as not to realise how utterly you've damned yourself by this performance. One question, and one question only, I would like to ask you from a point of academic interest. Did you murder your uncle? You refuse to answer? Perhaps you're right. You can only hang once; and your unfortunate cousin supplies the necessary evidence for that. Ring, Sir Richard, will you? We must get the police."

Chapter 4.

"I don't think," said Ronald, an hour later, when Stavert had been taken away, "that I have ever struck a crime which was in some respects so carefully thought out, and in others so incredibly bungled. The conception was brilliant; the execution simply puerile. He left so many clues lying about that one simply fell over them.

"Let us take the conception first, as he intended to do it. And for that we must go back to your father's death. You heard the question I asked him, but we may never know the answer. Was the whole thing an invention on Stavert's part, or did your father really receive that message? Stavert says he tore it up. It that the truth?

"My own impression is that it is. There would not seem to have been much object in his murdering his uncle, and thereby depriving himself of an easy job and a pleasant home. And so I think the balance of probability is that his story with regard to your father is correct. He did receive a message, and if he was murdered it was not by Stavert.

"Now come on to your brother. Stavert, finding that life in London was a very different proposition from his life here, began to think things over. He was hard up, and your brother was wealthy. And gradually the scheme must have taken shape in his brain. If he could avert all suspicion from himself by supplying a very plausible motive for some unknown person to have committed the crime, he was one step nearer the title. And one cannot deny that in outline his schemes was good. These mysterious papers, which were inherently quite probable, and the clear trail of a forced entry to the house—what more was necessary? And when in addition you realise the invaluable point, as far as he was concerned, that it did not throw suspicion on anybody in particular who would be able to prove his innocence, but merely on someone who could never be found, it must have looked a certainty to him. Then, of course, after a suitable lapse of time you would have been the next victim, and he steps into the whole shooting-box. Finally, he would send himself a similar message, and then by some strange piece of luck discover the papers. Faked, naturally, but good enough to end for ever the family tragedy.

"So sure was he, in fact, after having killed your brother, that he was safe, that he took the extra bold step of coming up to me. And he certainly told his story so convincingly that when I motored down with him I had not the slightest suspicion of the truth. But when I arrived on the scene and looked round, a very different aspect of affairs came to light.

"The first glaring error was the earth-mark on the window-sill. There was only one. Ostensibly the man had stood there some time while he worked at the catch. Why on earth should he stand on one leg? Then came the question of the dog: what was he doing all this while? He was found in the hall: why hadn't he barked? He must already have been dead. Who had killed him? Obviously someone in the house. And at once a different complexion came over the matter. Was it a servant, or who? I couldn't say at that time. But it was clear that there was a confederate, who had opened the window, after having first monkeyed with the catch as a blind, allowing the murderer to walk straight in, putting one foot on the sill. Further, he had then closed the window after the crime was committed, a point which I proved by the simple experiment of trying to jump the flower-bed. With the window shut no one could clear it; with it open it was easy. And there were no outgoing footsteps in the earth.

"So far so good. But now a very pertinent point arose. Why this elaborate and obvious trail? Why didn't the confederate inside merely open the front door? There could be no reason for it save one—it was a false trail. The error lay in the fact that is was far too obviously false. It was condemned as soon as you looked into it. And it knocked out the possibility of two people being involved.

"We were getting warm then. The murderer couldn't get into the house without a confederate. If there had been a confederate he would have opened the front door. Therefore there was no confederate. So the murderer must have been inside the house. How did that fit in?

And I soon saw that it fitted perfectly.

"The murderer stood on the inside of the sill before his shoes were muddy, and cut the woodwork round the catch. Then he opened the window, cleared the flower-bed, came back and shut the window. Then, realising he was supposed to be a stranger, he poisoned the dog. Previous to that, in all probability, he had murdered your brother, who might otherwise have been aroused by the noise. Who was it?

"Who was most likely to have been able to go into your brother's room in the middle of the night without arousing his suspicions? Who was most likely to have in his possession an expensive and very rare gun? It was beginning to look obvious. So I made a ridiculous statement about a left-handed Australian to throw him off the scent; and then luckily met you, when I surprised you by my matrimonial suggestion. I saw at once that by that method we could bring things to a head. If my suspicions were right, he would have to strike, and strike quickly. Which he did, with the result we know."

"Hold hard a minute, Standish," cried Sir Richard. "Why should my supposed marriage make him strike quickly?"

Ronald grinned gently.

"My dear fellow," he said, "messages ordering papers to be placed in the summer-house can be delivered to grown men. But they lose much of their efficacy if delivered to the twins in a bassinet."

Mystery of the Slip Coach

"Well, I'll be danged. She's signalled through, and yet she's stopping, though she's late already. Be there summat up?"

The stationmaster of Marley Junction scratched his head, and stared at the oncoming express which was now slowing down rapidly.

"Isn't she supposed to stop?" Ronald Standish asked.

"No, sir; she ain't. There be a slip coach for here, but main part goes through."

Rows of heads were already protruding from carriage windows as the train came to a standstill, and the guard got out.

"What's the matter, Joe?" demanded the stationmaster.

"Murder's the matter," was the unexpected answer; and with a lift of his eyebrows Ronald turned to the other member of our little party.

"You seem to be having a busy time of it, Inspector," he said, and with an expression of relief the two railway officials turned round.

"Are you the police, sir?" cried the guard.

"I'm Inspector Grantham of Scotland Yard," answered the other, "What's that you say? Murder!"

"Yes, sir. And I'll be pleased if you can come this way, for we're a lot behind time. He's in the slip coach."

We followed him to the rear of the train, paying no attention to the excited conjectures of the passengers, several of whom had got out on the platform. And as we got to the back carriage an irascible-looking, elderly man, who might have been a retired colonel, an old clergyman and his wife, and a young man of perhaps thirty, with a worried expression on his face, descended.

The inspector paused for a moment.

"This coach is separate from the rest of the train, I take it?" he said. "There's no connecting corridor?"

306

"That's so, sir," said the guard, "as you can see. No one can pass farther than my van, which is just in front of it."

"Then get the coach uncoupled. And all passengers, please, who were in this coach must wait."

He entered, and we followed him along the corridor of the carriage. The stationmaster had gone off to give the necessary orders; the guard accompanied us.

"Everything is as it was found, sir," he said. "After the train was stopped I travelled in this coach myself."

"Why did the train stop? I thought this was fast to Downwater?"

"Communication cord was pulled, sir, by the reverend gentleman."

The inspector nodded.

"We'll go into that later," he said. "Where's the body?"

For answer, the guard opened the door of the centre compartment. On the seat by the opposite window was sprawling the body of a man. One hand hung limply downwards, and on the cushion and the carpet lay an ominous red pool. A glance was sufficient to show that he was dead, and that the cause of death was a wound in the head. The window was shut; his, suit-case littered up the rack; and in the opposite corner to the body a pair of wash-leather gloves was lying on the seat.

Suddenly Ronald gave a whistle.

"Good Lord!" he cried, "it's old Samuel Goldberg, the book maker."

"You know him?" said the inspector.

"I've betted with him from time to time," Ronald answered. "But all in due course, for you'll have to do something about this train, Grantham. Why not let it go on with a relief guard and run this coach into a siding."

The inspector nodded, and a few moments later the express was speeding on her way, whilst the slip coach, with us still on board, was shunted off the main line.

"Yes—I knew him, Grantham," said Ronald. "He was a bookmaker, and quite a decent fellow. Great Scott! What's that mess?"

He was studying the woodwork of the door with a puzzled expression.

"Why—it's the remains of a raw egg! Here are bits of the shell on the carpet. And there's the place it hit the door. What an extraordinary thing to find in a railway carriage. Did you notice it, guard, when you came in?"

"Can't say as 'ow I did, sir. I was so worried and bemused that I didn't think of little things like that. When I sees there was nothing to be done for the poor gentleman I just shut the door again and started the train off after telling the driver to stop her here."

"And you shut the window, too?"

"No, sir. The window was shut already. Both the window and the door was shut when I got here."

"I think we'd better start our investigation, Mr. Standish," said the inspector. "We can come back again later to the body. Pull down the blinds"—he turned to the stationmaster—"and lock the carriage up. No one is to enter it."

We found the other occupants of the coach pacing about the platform. The young man had joined up with the clergyman and his wife; the irascible military man was fuming visibly.

"I hope you'll hurry this business as much as possible," he cried irritably. "I'm judging hounds this afternoon, and I shall be late. I may say that I knew nothing about it till the train was stopped."

"Quite, sir, quite," said the inspector soothingly. "But in view of the fact that a man has been found dead in circumstances which preclude natural causes, you will appreciate that I must make inquiries. Now, sir," he turned to the clergyman, "I understand that it was you who pulled the communication cord and stopped the train. Presumably, therefore, it was you who first discovered the body. Will you tell me all you know? First—your name, please."

"I am the Reverend John Stocker," said the old man, "of the parish of Meston, not far from here. And really I fear I can tell you but little of this terrible affair. I was reading in my carriage—"

"Which compartment did you occupy, Mr. Stocker?"

"Let me see—which was it, my love?" he asked his wife.

"The third-class one—two away," she answered promptly.

"Please proceed," said the inspector, making a note.

"It so chanced," continued the clergyman, "that I happened to glance out of the window at a passing train. It was travelling in the same direction as ourselves, at about the same speed, on the next line. I watched it idly, as we very slowly overtook it, when suddenly, to my amazement, I saw some people in the train beckoning to me. They were shouting and pointing, and though, of course, I could not hear what they said, it seemed to me by their agitation that something must be wrong, and that, whatever that something was, it was in our train.

So I got up and walked along the corridor to find, to my horror, the body of that unfortunate man."

"What did you do then?" said the Inspector.

"I pulled the communication cord."

"Did you go into the carriage?"

"No, I did not. The door was shut, and the sight had unnerved me."

"And what happened then?"

"This gentleman"—he indicated the hound judge—"came out from his compartment at the other end of the carriage, and I called to him. He came at once, and I showed him what had happened. By that time, of course, the train was slowing up."

"Quite correct," barked the other. "I went—"

"One moment, sir, if you please," said the inspector. "Your name?"

"Blackton—Major Blackton. Late of the Gunners."

"Now, sir. When you saw the dead man what did you do?"

"Opened the door, and went in to make certain, though, when you've seen as many men shot through the head as I have, it was obvious to me at first sight that he was beyond aid."

"Did you shut the window?"

"No, sir, I did not. The window was already shut. I noticed it particularly, because I remember thinking to myself what an odd thing it was that a man should be travelling with both door and window shut on a hot day like this."

The inspector nodded thoughtfully.

"Any more you'd like to say, sir?"

"Naturally, my first thought," continued Major Blackton, "was that it was a case of suicide."

"Why naturally?"

"Damn, man. I hadn't shot the feller, and it wasn't likely the *padre* had, and at that time I thought we were the only people in the coach. However, when I found no sign of any weapon on the floor or the seat I realised it couldn't be suicide. That wound caused instantaneous death, or I'm no judge of such matters, so that by no human possibility could he have got rid of the gun."

Once again the Inspector nodded.

"You said, sir," he remarked after a pause, "that at that time you thought you were the only people on the coach. When did you find you weren't?"

"Just before the train stopped, when that young man joined us

309

in the corridor. And it seems to me that he might be able to tell you something, because he'd been talking to the dead man."

"How do you know that?"

"Because he said so. 'Good God!' he said, 'what's happened? I was only talking to him ten minutes ago.' Then he had another look and said: 'What on earth has he done that for?' And by that time the train had stopped and the guard took charge."

He glanced at his watch.

"That's positively all I can tell you, Inspector, so with your permission I'll get away."

"Sorry, sir," said the inspector quietly, "but at the present juncture that is quite impossible. You don't seem to realise," he continued a little sternly, "that a man has, so far as we know, just been murdered under conditions that render it imperative that the other occupants of the coach should place themselves unreservedly at the disposal of the police. Other points may arise over which I shall want to see you later. And now, before interrogate the other gentleman, there is one further question. Did either of you two gentlemen hear the sound of a shot?"

"I certainly didn't," said Major Blackton, "but then I was at the far end of the coach."

"I didn't, either." The clergyman glanced at his wife. "Did you, my love?"

She shook her head decidedly.

"I heard nothing," she said. "Nothing at all."

"Thank you, madam." He beckoned to the young man. "Now, sir, will you tell me what you know of this affair? First—your name?"

"Carter—Harry Carter."

"Did you know the dead man?"

"I did," said Carter quietly.

"What was his name?"

"Samuel Goldberg."

"Had you spoken to him since leaving London?"

"I had a long talk with him. That's what made it so amazing because he seemed his usual self when I left his compartment."

The inspector consulted his notebook.

"You said to Major Blackton: 'What on earth has he done that for?' or words to that effect. What did you mean by that remark?"

Carter stared at him.

"Just what I said. I couldn't make out why he should commit

suicide."

"Why should you assume it was suicide?"

Carter stared at him even harder. "What else could it have been? Unless it was an accident."

"It was neither suicide nor an accident, Mr. Carter. Goldberg was murdered."

"Murdered? But who by?"

"That is what we are endeavouring to find out. Now, Mr Carter, am I to understand that you didn't hear Major Blackton and the guard talking in the corridor after the train started again and saying it was murder?"

"I did not, and for a very good reason. I returned almost at once to my own compartment to try and think out how this very unexpected development was going to affect me."

The inspector stopped writing and glanced at Standish. Then he looked steadily at Carter.

"Mr. Carter," he said gravely, "it is my duty to say one thing to you. We are investigating a case of murder, and everything points to the fact that the murderer was one of the people who travelled from London in that slip coach. You need not tell me anything that might, in certain eventualities, incriminate you."

Carter stared at him in amazement.

"Good God!" he burst out at length, "you aren't suggesting that I had anything to do with it?"

"I am suggesting nothing," answered the inspector shortly. "I am merely pointing out your possible future position. And having done so I will now ask you in what way Goldberg's death could affect you? You need not answer if you don't wish to."

"But, of course, I wish to. I've got nothing to hide. I owed him money, and I was wondering whether his suicide—as I then thought it was—would wipe out this debt."

"Had your discussion with him previously concerned this debt?"

"It had," said Carter.

"Was it an acrimonious interview?" asked the Inspector mildly.

"Well, when you ask your bookie not to press for payment and he cuts up rough, it's not very pleasant."

"And it terminated some ten minutes before you found that Goldberg had, as you thought, committed suicide?"

"That's right."

"May I ask how much was the sum involved?"

"A thousand pounds."

Inspector Grantham tapped his teeth with his pencil. "One final question, Mr. Carter. Did you know that Goldberg was going to travel by this train?"

"I hadn't an idea of it until I found him in the same coach."

The inspector rose and closed his notebook with a snap. "That is all for the present," he said, and then, for the first time, Ronald spoke.

"I should like to ask you two or three other questions, Mr. Carter. When you had your interview with Goldberg, did you sit by the door?"

"I did—in the opposite corner to him. By Jove! now I come to think of it, I've left my gloves there!"

"Was the window open?"

Carter thought for a moment.

"It was: wide."

"And the door?"

"Shut."

"Now, Mr. Carter, I want you to think carefully. Did he throw a raw egg at you?"

Carter stared at Ronald with a look of utter amazement, which changed to an angry flush.

"Are you trying to be funny? Because, if so, it seems to me neither the time nor the place. A raw egg? Why the devil should he throw one at me?"

"Exactly," said Ronald. "Why the devil should he? Well Grantham, what do you propose to do now?"

The inspector, who had frowned slightly at Ronald's last question, again took charge.

"I'm afraid I must request you three gentlemen, and you, too, madam, to remain here for a little while yet. I know, sir, I know about your hound show, but this is even more important. Guard, come with me. And you too, Mr. Standish—if you care to."

We returned to the slip coach and the guard unlocked the door. Then, leaving him on the platform, we entered the carriage.

"What do you make of it, Mr. Standish?" said the Inspectors

"At the moment, Grantham, remarkably little," said Ronald "There are one or two very strange features about the case. Have you come to any conclusion yourself?"

"Only to the obvious one that Goldberg was murdered by some one who was in this coach. Further than that I would not care to go, though it would be idle to deny that of the four occupants the most likely is Carter. Of course, it is possible that there was someone else in the carriage who escaped when the train stopped but there are two grave difficulties to put up against that theory. First, it was the clergyman who pulled the communication cord. Surely, the murderer would have done it himself. And even if he didn't, but had seized on this unlooked-for chance of escaping, he would have been bound to be seen by people in the train. I mean, one knows that when a train stops unexpectedly everyone's head goes out of the window."

"And what about the egg?" remarked Ronald thoughtfully.

"Confound the egg!" cried Grantham irritably. "You've got it on the brain."

"I have," agreed Ronald, unperturbed. "But before we go any farther, let us examine the compartment thoroughly again."

I watched them from the corridor for ten minutes, and at the end of that time the inspector came out and joined me.

"Nothing of value; no trace of any weapon."

"And no trace of any more eggs," said Ronald. "Now, don't get angry, Inspector. I'm not fooling. But when an extremely bizarre fact intrudes itself on one it is advisable not to overlook it. Now, have you ever heard of a man carrying one raw egg about with him? Frequently have I known people to take half a dozen or even three in a paper bag, but not one. There isn't even a paper bag. Was he, then, carrying this solitary egg in his hand or in his pocket? However, let us go on a little further. Assuming for the moment that he had got this one egg, why did he throw it at the door? It seems a strange pastime."

"Your second point is easier to answer than your first," said the Inspector. "Goldberg was unarmed, and when he looked and saw the murderer standing in the carriage he threw the first thing that came to hand."

"This solitary egg." Ronald stared at him thoughtfully. "Was he holding it, studying its beauty? Or was it on the seat beside him? However, perhaps I am over-stressing the point. Where are you off to now?"

"To get on with the case, Mr. Standish," answered the inspector tersely. "I don't know how or why that egg got there, but I do know that that man was murdered. Almost certainly the murderer flung the weapon out of the window, but it is just possible he did not. So my first move will be to search the baggage of the four people I have detained."

"Splendid," said Ronald quietly. "Have I your permission to wait here a little longer? There are one or two more points I would like to look into, and I will, of course, pass on anything to you."

With a faint smile the inspector departed and Ronald turned to me.

"There's something very rum, Bob—very rum indeed about this affair. Apart from the egg, who shut the window? Did Goldberg, after Carter had left him? Did the murderer, either before or after he'd done it? Or is Carter lying? I don't think he is."

Ronald was talking half to himself.

"To place too much reliance on faces is dangerous, but I don't think he is. His evidence has the ring of truth. And I ask you—would he have left his gloves here if he'd done it?"

He went back into the compartment and stood staring round.

"The clergyman—what about him? And our military friend? As things are, the clergyman is the more likely, as the other had to pass the door to get to this compartment. Moreover, we only have the clergyman's word that he saw people beckoning to him from the other train. It's unlikely, of course, but it's conceivable that he, too, was in debt to Goldberg, and has staged a pretty piece of acting the innocent after killing him. Means his wife is in collusion with him, but stranger things have happened. But it's that damned egg that beats me."

"Well, old boy," I said, "I admit it's very peculiar as you say, but it seems to me we've got to accept it as a fact that Goldberg was in possession of one raw egg. I mean, it isn't likely the murderer came with an egg in one hand and a gun in the other."

Ronald spun round and stared at me.

"Great Scott! Bob," he cried, "I believe—"

He broke off abruptly, and dashed into the next compartment, where he opened and shut the window several times, while I looked on in blank amazement. What on earth there was in my semi-jocular remark that had caused this activity was beyond me, butt I knew better than to ask. And then he returned to the scene of the murder, and kneeling down on the floor by the door he examined the sticky mess of shell and yolk on the carpet.

"Hopeless," he muttered, "hopeless; but—ah!"

He was carefully picking out a piece of shell, which he placed on the seat. The search continued: two other pieces were selected, which, after a further scrutiny, he roughly joined together.

"Do you see, Bob?" he cried.

314

I did and I didn't. Stamped in violet ink on the fragments were some letters. On one piece was written "atch"; on the other, "ways." Presumably part of the name of the firm where the egg had been bought, and I said so. But what further light that fact threw on the matter was beyond me, and I said that, too.

He put the bits of shell into an empty match-box, as there came the sound of people getting into the carriage.

"Perhaps you're right, Bob; we'll see," he said, slipping the box into his pocket.

Inspector Grantham was coming along the corridor, and with him was a man carrying a small black bag. A doctor obviously, but the thing that struck me at once was the expression of subdued triumph on the inspector's face.

"Here you are, doctor," he said. "And as soon as you've made your preliminary examination I'll have the body moved to a waiting-room."

Then, as the doctor entered the compartment, he joined us in the corridor.

"I've found the revolver, Mr. Standish," he remarked complacent-ly.

"You have, have you?" said Ronald. "Where?"

"In one of Carter's suit-cases."

"Was it loaded?"

"No, but there was a half-open packet of ammunition. And that's better than your raw egg, I'm thinking."

"How does he account for its being there?" demanded Ronald, ignoring the gibe.

"He doesn't. He simply says he was taking it down to the country with him."

"Which," said Ronald, "is probably the truth."

"Of course it is," agreed the inspector. "I don't suppose for a moment that he brought it on the train to shoot Goldberg, but with Goldberg in the same carriage with him he yielded to the temptation. Come, come, Mr. Standish," he went on good humouredly, "you're very smart and all that, but really there is no good trying to pretend that there is any mystery here. Goldberg was shot by someone in this carriage. Carter admits having had a bad quarrel with him; Carter is in possession of a revolver and ammunition. Moreover, no sign of arms can be found on the other three people concerned. The thing is as plain a pikestaff."

And I saw that Ronald looked worried.

"Too plain, Grantham," he said. "Altogether too plain. But if you're right there's only one place Carter ought to be sent to, and that's a lunatic asylum. The man must be crazy. Why on earth didn't he throw the gun out of the window?"

The Inspector shrugged his shoulders.

"Like your raw egg, Mr. Standish, I can't tell you," he remarked. "Well, doctor?"

"Killed instantaneously, of course," said the other, joining us. "If you will have the body moved Inspector, I will carry on at once."

The inspector bustled off, followed by the doctor, and Ronald turned to me.

"Bad, Bob; damned bad," he said, and I have seldom seen him look so grave.

"You think Carter did it?" I asked.

"I am as certain as I can be of anything that he didn't," he answered quietly. "But on the face of it, Carter's position is about as serious as it could well be."

And so Carter evidently realised. We found him in the custody of a policeman, and the instant he saw us he sprang to his feet.

"Look here, sir," he cried to Ronald, "I don't know who you gentlemen are, but I assume you're something to do with the police. Well, all I can tell you is that I swear before Heaven I had no more to do with the death of Samuel Goldberg than you had! I often take a revolver with me when I go down to stay with my uncle. I'm a very keen shot, and potting at rabbits is marvellous practice."

"I believe you, Carter," said Ronald, holding out his hand. "But there's no good blinding yourself to the fact that a combination of circumstances has put you in a very awkward corner."

Carter's expression, which had cleared at Ronald's first words, clouded again.

"It's hideous," he cried passionately. "It's like a nightmare. I'm not a fool, and I see the gravity of the situation. Someone in the carriage must have shot him and I'm found with a gun. But if I'd done it should I have kept the revolver?"

"Exactly what I said to the inspector," said Ronald, with a grave smile. "But you may depend on one thing—"

He broke off.

"Hallo! Grantham doesn't look too happy."

The inspector was coming along the platform with a puzzled

frown.

"Well, Mr. Carter," he said, "I must apologise."

"What do you mean?" Carter almost shouted.

"The bullet doesn't fit your revolver."

For a moment or two there was dead silence. Then Ronald stepped up to Carter and clapped him on the shoulder.

"Congratulations," he said. "Well out of a nasty position."

"Thanks," said Carter quietly. "I don't want to go through another half-hour like that again. I don't blame you in the slightest degree, Inspector; it must have looked a cert to you. But you can imagine my feelings, knowing I hadn't done it."

"I apologise again," said the inspector. "But, damn it," he burst out, "who did? Well, it will be a question of searching the line till we find the revolver that that bullet does fit."

"You never will," remarked Ronald, lighting a cigarette.

"Why not?" demanded Grantham.

"Because it isn't there."

"I suppose you're going to tell me next that Goldberg wasn't shot at all," said the inspector sarcastically.

"No, not that. But once again I am going to suggest to you that you consider in all its aspects the extraordinary phenomenon of the raw egg."

"Any other points?" asked the inspector, impressed in spite of himself.

"Two," said Ronald. "First—the strange fact that the window was open when Carter's interview with Goldberg finished, and was shut when the body was found. Second—that Carter is certainly not the only person in the world who owes Goldberg money."

"Damn it!" exploded Grantham, "I believe you know who did it."

"No, I don't," said Ronald emphatically. "Moreover, it is quite possible I never shall. But we'll see. Once again congratulations, Carter, on a lucky escape. If that bullet had fitted your gun you would have been in the soup. Come on, Bob; here's our train coming. I've just got time to ask the guard of the express one question."

And the only remark he made to me the whole way up to London added considerably to my mental confusion.

"Well done, Bob," he said. "You solved that in masterly fashion."

"I solved it!" I spluttered.

"Of course you did, old boy. When you said the murderer had an egg in one hand and a revolver in the other."

★★★★★★

For the next few days I did not see him at all. The newspapers, naturally, were full of the case, and interviews were published with all four of the other occupants of the carriage. In fact, "The Mystery of the Slip Coach" appealed immensely to the man in the street, owing to the strange circumstances of the crime.

And it certainly was a baffling affair. As far as the public was concerned, it was obvious that one of the four people in the coach was guilty, and in most clubs betting on the final result was frequent. And it was inevitable that Carter should prove the favourite in spite of the fact that the shot did not fit his revolver. The vicar and his wife were a delightful old pair who had lived a blameless life for years at Meston; Major Blackton turned out to be an extremely wealthy man who had just returned to England after a prolonged absence abroad, and who had never heard of Goldberg in his life.

"You mark my words," said a man one day to me, "young Carter did it, and he's a mighty deep 'un. Shall I tell you how? He had a second revolver. D'you get me? The gun he shot Goldberg with he bunged out of the window, leaving the other one to be found."

The trouble was that in spite of an army of searchers no trace of another gun could be found. A large reward was offered by the police, without producing any result, and another theory was started. Carter must have had a confederate who picked up the revolver when it was thrown from the train. And that held the field for quite a time, till it was conclusively proved that Goldberg had only decided to go by that train on the very morning in question, and that it was, therefore, utterly impossible for Carter to have known about it in time to make any such arrangements.

Another source of information from which the police had hoped to derive some help proved of no assistance. The people in the other train, who had first seen the body, could say nothing which threw any more light on matters. They were two young men, one of whom was standing up at the window watching the express as it gradually overtook them. He had seen the body sprawling on the seat and realising that something was amiss, he had, with his companion, attracted the vicar's attention. But of one thing they were positive: the window of Goldberg's carriage was shut. And as time went on it began to look as if the mystery would prove insoluble, which would have been unpleasant for Carter. For there was no doubt that a large percentage of the public believed that in some way or other he had done it. And even though that belief was only due to the fact that it was most unlikely that any of the other three was guilty—that it was arrived at by a process of elimination, and was not the result of any positive evidence—it made things no better for him.

And then one morning I got a phone message from Ronald, asking me to go round to his rooms. He was not in when I got there, but somewhat to my surprise, I found Inspector Grantham.

"Morning, Mr. Miller," he said gloomily. "I hope Mr. Standish has found out something, for this case isn't doing me any good."

"I know he doesn't think it was Carter," I said.

"Then who could it have been?" he cried. "But I can't arrest him. We haven't a shred of evidence. If only we could find the gun it was done with."

The door opened and Ronald entered.

"Come in, Mr. Meredith," he said, nodding to us. "Here are the other two gentlemen who I know will be interested in our little venture."

A morose-looking individual entered as he was speaking, who contemplated us suspiciously.

"You remember, Bob," Ronald went on, "our ideas about a chicken farm. Well—I've found the very spot, and Mr. Meredith is quite willing to sell."

"Give me my figure, and you can have it tomorrow," said the newcomer. "Not that it isn't a good proposition: it is. But I haven't the money to run it. I'll have a drop of Scotch, thank you."

I glanced at the inspector as Ronald filled a glass, but his face was impassive. Only the faintest of winks showed that he realised something was up, but I knew he was as much in the dark as I was.

"Here's how," said Meredith, and drained his drink. "Well, gentlemen, do we talk business?"

"No time like the present," said Ronald cheerfully, ringing the bell. "Take away that empty glass, will you, Sayers," he told his man, "and bring in some more clean ones. Now, Mr. Meredith, I understand Hatchaways is for sale, and that the price you are asking is fifteen hundred pounds?"

"That is correct," agreed the other, his eyes sparkling greedily.

"And it is not mortgaged nor encumbered in any way?"

"No; the property is quite clear."

The door opened, and Sayers came in carrying some more glasses. And as he put them down I saw him nod to Ronald.

319

"Have you had to borrow any money on the place, Mr. Meredith?" continued Ronald.

"You'll pardon me, Mr. Standish, but I don't see that that has anything to do with you," said Meredith truculently.

"You didn't borrow, for instance, from Samuel Goldberg, who has recently been murdered?"

Meredith gave one uncontrollable start. Then he pulled himself together.

"Never heard of the man till I saw his death in the paper."

"Strange," said Ronald quietly. "He was a complete stranger to you, maybe?"

"Absolute."

"Then why, Meredith, did you throw that egg through his open window on the Downwater express as his carriage came level with yours?"

Meredith lurched to his feet and tried to bluster. But there was sick fear in his face and Grantham moved towards the door.

"It's a cursed lie," he said thickly.

"Oh, no, it isn't," answered Ronald sternly. "On the shell of the egg you threw are fingerprints: on the glass you've just drunk from are fingerprints. And those fingerprints are identical. There's your man, Grantham. He murdered Samuel Goldberg by shooting him through the head from the other train."

For a moment there was silence, and then with a roar of rage Meredith whipped a revolver out of his pocket. But he was too late. Grantham was on him like a flash.

"And that is the gun, Inspector," continued Ronald, calmly, "that I told you you would not find on the permanent way."

★★★★★★

"I wish to Heaven you'd elucidate, old boy," I said a few minutes later, "for it's the smartest thing I've ever known."

Ronald filled his pipe thoughtfully.

"You may remember, Bob," he said, "that after your illuminating remark I went into the next compartment and started monkeying about with the window. Now, there are two main types of fitting in trains. The more common has a long strap, and with that sort, when the strap has been pulled to the full extent, an outward push on the bottom of the window is necessary to keep it shut. The other type has no strap, but a slot in the top sash which, when pulled up to the full extent, automatically remains there. And that was the type used in the slip coach.

"You may also remember how I harped on the raw egg. I could not place it, Bob; every instinct in me rebelled against the thought that Goldberg carried one raw egg with him. Then you made the remark about the murderer carrying it. Once again it was incredible if the murderer was in the carriage. He wouldn't come in, plaster an egg on the door, and then shoot Goldberg. But, supposing the murderer hadn't been in the carriage—what then? For a considerable time another train had been running parallel with the express, and at about the same speed.

"Supposing a man in that other train had seen Goldberg sitting in his compartment, and to attract his attention had thrown an egg through the open window, what would be Goldberg's reaction? He would get up to shut the window, to prevent more eggs following. Supposing that then the egg-thrower shot him through the brain. Now you and I have seen men killed instantaneously in France, and if you cast your mind back you will remember that quite a number threw up their arms and fell backwards. What would have happened if Goldberg's fingers had been in the notch of the window? Just what did happen in this case: he shut the window with his last convulsive jerk, thereby making it appear impossible for him to have been shot from anywhere except inside the carriage, which was, of course, an incredible piece of luck for the murderer.

"So on that hypothesis I started. You heard me say to Grantham that I might never find the man who did it, and but for luck which now turned against him I never should have. My starting point, naturally, was the other train and its occupants. Now the last station at which it had stopped, before the murder had been committed, was Pedlington, and so there I repaired. I made inquiries with the utmost caution, because it was essential that nothing should get into the papers if we weren't going to alarm our bird, whoever he was. And after talking to the stationmaster I and getting in touch with the guard of the tram, facts began to accumulate, though it was a slow business.

"The first thing I found out was that the train was comparatively empty—so empty that the guard was able to remember more or less accurately how the passengers were seated. And the important thing was to ascertain how many compartments had only one occupant. There were only three to his certain knowledge: one with a woman, two each with a man. More than that he could not say, except that the woman was very old.

"Now came the wearisome search. I eliminated the woman, and concentrated on the men. I went to every station after Pedlington at which the train stopped, and got in touch with the ticket collector. It was still an absolute toss-up if I could spot my man. If it was someone carrying a few eggs in a paper bag it was hopeless. And then came an astounding stroke of luck. The collector at Marlingham—four stations beyond Pedlington—remembered a man who got out there with a basket of eggs and who asked the way to some farm.

"Bob, I was getting warm. Off to the farm I went, and found that a man called Meredith, who owned a chicken farm called Hatchaways, not far from Pedlington itself, had been there. And now I knew I'd got him. You remember the letters on the broken shell—'atch' and 'ways.' He was my bird, but he was still a long way from the net.

"So back to Pedlington, where I posed as a man with a certain amount of money who was interested in chicken farming. And I met Master Meredith, who thought he had found a sucker. Further inquiries revealed the fact that he was in bad financial straits, and was only too ready to sell. Further inquiries also revealed the very significant and unusual fact that he always carried a Colt revolver in his pocket wherever he went—a habit, he said, he got into while out West. So I staged the little performance this morning. Marshall, from the Yard, the fingerprint expert, was outside, and when Sayers nodded to me I knew that there was no mistake.

"Just one of those strange crimes that nearly came off. It wasn't premeditated, of course. By a mere freak of fate the two trains ran side by side for some time, and Meredith saw the chance of getting rid of the man to whom he owed money in such a way that no suspicion could fall on him. And when Goldberg shut the window as he died, Meredith must have thought himself absolutely safe. Which," he concluded, "he would have been if he'd thrown a banana and not an egg."

The Second Dog

One of the most dangerous mistakes you can make in any investigation is to start with a preconceived idea.

Thus one of Ronald Standish's favourite maxims, and seldom has its truth been better demonstrated than in the case of the murder of Daniel Benton, when, but for the lucky chance of Ronald's presence at Croxton Hall for the annual cricket match, an innocent man might well have gone to the gallows.

The thing happened on the night of our arrival. The house-party was a big one, comprising as it did most of our eleven, and several of the Free Foresters whom we were playing next day. Bill Maybury, our host, was in his usual good form, and we were just going in to dinner when the butler, looking very perturbed, came in and whispered something in his ear.

"Daniel Benton murdered!" cried Maybury. "Good God! Who did it?"

The butler hesitated for a moment.

"There's a rumour, sir," he said, "that Sergeant Johnston is arresting young Joe Drury."

Bill Maybury looked very grave.

"Young Drury." he repeated. "When did it happen, Parker?"

"I've just heard the news, sir. The postman brought it."

"The devil!" said Maybury. "Ronald, this looks like something in your line. I don't know any details, but from what Parker says our fast bowler tomorrow is on the verge of being arrested for murder. I don't believe he did it for a moment," he went on. "He's a hot-tempered boy, and there's no love between him and that blackguard Benton." He pulled himself up. "Still, if the man's dead, I suppose one oughtn't to call him a blackguard."

A silence had fallen on the room at the mention of the word 'murder', and Ronald broke it.

"Let's hear a bit more, Bill. Who was the dead man, and who is this young Drury?"

"Daniel Benton," said Maybury, "came to these parts about three years ago, and took a small house about a mile from here. And though the poor devil seems to be dead there is no use in pretending that he will be the slightest loss. In fact, not to mince words, I have seldom in my life met a bigger swine. In his early days he was a seafaring man, and what induced him to settle in the depths of the country I don't know. However, he took the house for five years. He seemed to have a certain amount of money, and his principal method of spending it was down his throat. And when he had drink on board that man was a devil incarnate. He was immensely powerful, with a great ragged black beard, and about twice a week he used to go round to the 'Grey-hound' and have a bout. The other men loathed him, but they were all afraid of him. He'd sit in the corner of the bar speaking to no one till he got well sprung: then the trouble would begin. He delighted in picking a quarrel. He was a foul-mouthed brute, and the fellows here, though no more squeamish than most, were utterly disgusted by him. He couldn't get out a sentence without an oath in it, and his stories were invariably connected with his own unsavoury past.

"But even that," he continued, "wouldn't have mattered so much if he could have kept his hands to himself. Twice, he's been before the bench for inflicting grievous bodily harm on two of the lads. The first time we fined him; the second we gave him three months. But each time it was the same thing: he started sneering at someone until the victim lost his temper and struck him. Then Benton would wade into him and half kill him."

"What a delightful member of the community," said Ronald.

"You're right, old boy," said Maybury, "and if young Drury has killed him it's no more than he deserves. At the same time, that's not going to help the boy much."

"Was there any special animosity between the two?"

"That's the devil of it," answered our host. "There was. Drury was one of the two he laid out. The boy was walking out with little Nellie Seymour, and one day they met Benton. And that night Benton came into the bar, and started making foul innuendoes about them, Drury, of course, flared up and went for him, but it was simply pitiful, I believe. He's quite a well-built, strong lad, but he was like a child in that brute's hands. That was the case we gave him three months for, because of the provocation.

"Benton half murdered him, which was damned galling to his pride. And that, coupled with what had previously been said about Nellie and him, drove him wild, and he started uttering foolish threats—'he'd do the swine in' and that sort of thing. It came to my ears, and when I met him one day I told him to quit it and not be an ass. To keep out of Benton's way as much as possible; to avoid the fellow. But, from what I understand, it has been proving very difficult. Benton, somewhat naturally, regarded Drury as the cause of his imprisonment, and has been seizing every opportunity of sneering at him and making his life a hell."

"When did Benton come out of prison?" asked Ronald.

"Two months ago," said Maybury. "And there's no doubt about it, it's made him worse."

"I wonder how he was killed," remarked Ronald.

"I'll ring for Parker and see if he knows. Parker," he said as the butler entered, "what was Benton killed with? Was he shot?"

"I don't know, sir," answered the man. "All the postman said was that the room was like a shambles. But I've just heard, sir," he went on, "that young Drury turned up at the 'Greyhound' in a terrible condition about an hour ago. Bleeding he was, and all muzzy like, but he wouldn't say anything. He just had a couple and then stumbled off home."

"By Gad! that looks bad," said Maybury gravely. And then he looked tentatively at Ronald, "I suppose, old man, you wouldn't like to..."

"Of course, I will," said Ronald. "Let's go and see if there's anything to be found out."

"Thanks, Ronald," said Maybury gratefully. "Sergeant Johnston is an excellent man, but I'd like that boy to have the very best possible chance. You fellows go and have dinner; we'll have something when we get back."

"Coming, Bob?" said Ronald.

"You bet," I cried, and a few minutes later we started off with Maybury in his car.

It was a beautiful starlit night. The air was cool after a heavy shower that had fallen about six o'clock, and it seemed hard to realise in the peaceful countryside that we were on our way to a scene of murder. But as we drove along the main road we overtook people in twos and threes hurrying along and evidently bound for the same destination as ourselves.

"There's Benton's house," said Maybury, suddenly pointing ahead; and in the glare of the headlights we could see a crowd already gathered in the road. They parted as we drew up by the gate, and a stolid policeman on duty saluted as he recognised Maybury.

"Bad business, sir," he said. "The sergeant's hinside now with the hinspector. Stand back there," he cried, as two or three of the more daring spirits tried to follow us in.

"Good evening, Sergeant Johnston," said Maybury, addressing a stout, florid-faced man who was standing in the hall. "This is a bad show."

"Very bad indeed, sir," answered the sergeant, touching his hat. "Inspector Merrifield is here, but it's just one of those obvious cases."

A tall, thin man in plain clothes came out of one of the rooms and looked at us keenly.

"This is Mr. Maybury, sir," said the sergeant. "One of our bench of magistrates."

"A terrible affair, Inspector," said Maybury. "And I've taken the liberty of bringing Mr. Standish, who is staying with me. He's very well known at Scotland Yard: and since I hear there is some talk of young Drury being implicated in this business, I hope you'll let him have a look round."

"I've heard of you, Mr. Standish," said the inspector none too graciously. "And if you think you're going to get anything out of this business you're sadly mistaken! The whole thing is obvious.'

"For all that, I'd like just to have a look, Inspector," said Ronald genially. "Though I'm sure you've spotted everything there is to see."

The inspector flung open the door of the room behind him, and we all went in.

"Everything is as it was," remarked the inspector, "except that I've drawn the curtains because of the crowd outside."

Ronald nodded shortly, and we all stood silently looking round. Lying on the floor against the wall opposite to us was a huge, black-bearded man. His open eyes seemed to glare at us horribly: his mouth had set itself into a snarl. One great hairy hand lay outstretched on the carpet: the other was clenched round the metal shaft of a spear, which stuck out from his chest. Just above him a similar weapon had been half wrenched from the wall and now dangled precariously from one support. The blood, which had ceased to flow, had collected in a pool by his side, and the whole effect was incredibly gruesome.

"The spear was driven clean through him," said the inspector. "The point is sticking out of his back."

"You presumably know what sort of a spear that is," remarked Ronald.

The other raised his eyebrows.

"Whatever sort it is," he answered, "it was sufficient to kill him, and that's all that matters to me."

"Perhaps you're right," said Ronald quietly. "Still, it is instructive. I think you said, Bill, that the dead man had been a sailor, so that accounts for him having harpoons about the room."

"That's what they get whales with, isn't it?" cried the inspector.

"It is," said Ronald. "And I see that the one with which he was killed was hanging by the side of its companion, which is still on the wall."

"Excellent," remarked the inspector with a faint smile. "The companion which Benton was trying to get down when he was murdered."

"Ever tried to throw a harpoon, Inspector?" asked Ronald mildly.

"I can't say I have. Why?"

"I only wondered," said Ronald still more mildly. "You have a shot at it one day and you'll be surprised at the result. However, what's all this about young Drury?"

"Have you seen all you want to see in here?" said the inspector with a touch of sarcasm.

"For the moment, yes," answered Ronald.

"Then we might go to another room, and I'll tell you what happened."

He led the way across the hall, and we followed.

"See that no one goes into that room," he ordered the constable at the door and the man saluted.

"Well, gentlemen," he said, "it's one of those cases which solves itself automatically. I'm sorry for young Drury, who, Sergeant Johnston tells me, is a good lad, and who seems to have had the utmost provocation. However, the law is the law, and justice must take its course. It seems, then, that Drury has a dog to which he is very attached. It's a mongrel of sorts—"

"I know the animal," cried Maybury. "It's an intelligent little beast."

"This afternoon," continued the inspector, "the dog appears to have been out on its own. (I may say, gentlemen, that what I am about to tell you is at present only hearsay from the constable, but I shall, of course, have it all substantiated.) While the dog was out it met Benton, and whether it barked at him or whether he was in a rage and recognised it as belonging to Drury, I don't know. What is clear, however, is that he picked up a big stone, threw it at the dog and broke one of its legs."

"The damned swine!" said Maybury.

"Not content with that," went on the inspector, "he caught the dog, and wrote a note, which he fastened to its collar—a note which Drury showed to several men in the 'Greyhound'. 'Next time I'll break its—head.'

"That was about six o'clock, for Drury had been away for the afternoon and only found out what had happened when he returned. He was in a white rage."

"Somewhat naturally," cried Maybury.

"And," continued the other, without heeding the interruption, "spent half an hour uttering wild threats against Benton. Also, though usually, I understand, an abstemious lad, he drank several whiskies, which still further inflamed him. Then he left the 'Greyhound' with the avowed intention of coming here and having it out. He did come here, arriving at about seven o'clock."

"You know that for certain?" said Ronald.

The inspector nodded. "This man Benton has an old woman called Betsy who cooks for him and does the work of the house. We'll send for her in a moment, if you like, and she will tell you herself. At any rate, he let him in, and he joined Benton in the room opposite, from which shortly after she heard the sound of furious quarrelling, followed by blows. She hung about in the hall, too frightened to go in, and after a while the noise ceased. So she returned to the kitchen to get supper ready.

"She was there for about a quarter of an hour, and then started to carry the meal into the dining-room. And as she was crossing the hall she heard a loud voice, which she swears was not Benton's. And the words that she heard are, I fear, about as damning to Drury as they could well be.

"'Three bells in the second dog, you swine.'

"Of course, she may not have got the sentence absolutely right. It might have been three bricks, or something of that sort, but on one point she remains absolutely unshaken: the phrase 'the second dog' was used.

"She waited—listening—and a moment or two later heard a sound as if something had been thrown against the wall. Then all was silent, and she continued with the supper, which was ready at a quarter to eight, when she went in to tell Benton, and found what you have seen. She rushed out screaming, and fortunately ran straight into Sergeant Johnston, who communicated at once with me. And that, gentlemen, is the whole damning story in a nutshell. Young Drury arrived just before eight at the 'Greyhound' in a state of terrible agitation, and very badly knocked about."

"By Gad! it looks bad," cried Maybury. "What do you think, Ronald?"

"That I'd like to speak to Betsy," he said.

"She can't tell you any more than I've already done," snapped the inspector.

"Perhaps not," remarked Ronald quietly. "But I'd still like to see her."

The inspector made a sign to the sergeant, who left the room. "So your theory, I take it, Inspector," said Ronald, "is some what as follows. Young Drury came here at seven o'clock, and proceeded to have a furious row with the dead man. Moreover, they came to blows, when presumably Drury was knocked about. Then—well, what happened then?"

"Drury left in a flaming rage," said the inspector, "a rage which grew more intense with every step he took until it mastered him, and he determined to kill Benton. He returned, and managed—how I can't say—to get one of the harpoons down from the wall. Benton, realising his intention, tried to get the other, but was struck down before he could succeed."

"And then young Drury helped himself to rum," murmured Ronald.

"So you saw that glass, did you?" grunted the other.

"Well, Inspector," cried Ronald with a smile, "I am not completely blind. And since it is improbable they were drinking together, the rum must have been consumed after Benton was killed, as a nerve bracer."

"What on earth does that signify?" said the other. "It doesn't alter facts."

"It depends on what are facts," said Ronald. "Ah! Betsy," he swung round as the door opened and an old woman came in, followed by the sergeant, "there are one or two questions I want to ask you: How long have you been in this house?"

"Three years, sir," she mumbled. "Ever since he came." She jerked a thumb at the room opposite.

"And during those three years did he ever have anyone to stay?"

"No, sir; no one."

"Many visitors by day?"

"No, sir: he didn't like strangers. He had special bolts fitted to all the windows just after he came here," said the old crone. "He used to lock up most particular each night: always did it himself."

"Thank you, Betsy. Oh! one more question. This voice that you heard shouting about the second dog—could you recognise whose it was?"

"No, sir; I couldn't. But it must have been young Joe Drury."

"Which shows how singularly dangerous a witness of that sort can be," said Ronald as she left the room. "It must have been young Joe Drury. Why?"

We all stared at him, the inspector with a barely concealed sneer.

"Are you suggesting that it wasn't young Drury?" he demanded.

"Certainly," said Ronald calmly. "You may take it from me that Drury had no more to do with Benton's death than I had."

"But, damn it!" exploded the other, "that remark Betsy overheard practically proves it was him."

"On the contrary," said Ronald, "it practically proves it wasn't."

"Then who the devil was it?"

"That is more than I can tell you at this stage of the proceedings," answered Ronald cheerfully. "But I don't think there will be much trouble about laying our hands on him when we want him. And I very much doubt, Inspector, if you will find that it turns out to be a hanging matter. Now, if you don't mind, I would like one more look at the room where he was killed."

We followed him across the passage, the inspector looking at the sergeant and winking significantly. But Ronald, even if he noticed, paid not the smallest attention. Quietly and systematically he was examining the wall near the door, and at last the inspector could stand it no longer.

"Looking for fingerprints?" he inquired

"Something of the sort," said Ronald. "Ah! here it is, as I thought."

We crowded round him to look. The paper had been torn away at the spot where he was pointing, and the plaster behind was showing. The hole was about an inch deep, and looked as if it had been made by the sharp corner of a cupboard or desk.

"I commend that hole to you, Inspector," he remarked. "Also the fact that some of the plaster has trickled out on to the floor, a state of affairs which I am sure Betsy would have rectified had she noticed it. Now, surely with that to go on, and the rum, and the fact that Benton was killed round about half-past seven, you ought to be able to lay your hands on your man. It's a pity that you've allowed the villagers to obliterate every footprint for miles around, otherwise we might have got some more evidence, but you've got enough to go on. And while I think of it—be careful with the gentleman when you get him—because I think you will find that he is quite as powerful as the man he killed."

The inspector, who had flushed angrily at Ronald's remarks, controlled himself with an effort.

"What a lovely story it would make, wouldn't it?" he remarked. "Has he brown or blue eyes?"

Ronald smiled cheerfully.

"That I'm afraid I can't tell you. But he's tanned and weather-beaten, about the same height as myself, walks with a slight roll, and possibly has a beard."

But the inspector had had enough, and with an angry snort he left the room.

"If you've got the time to play round with this fooling, Mr. Standish, I haven't. I wish you goodnight."

"What are you going to do?" asked Ronald.

"Interview young Drury," snapped the other. "And I wish you luck of your bearded, weather-beaten roller."

"A pig-headed individual," said Ronald as he departed. "A little lesson will do him no harm."

"But are you honestly serious, old boy?" cried Maybury as we walked to the car.

"My dear Bill," answered Ronald quietly, "I can assure you of one thing. However big a swine a man was I wouldn't jest in the room where he lay dead."

"Then how the devil you've done it beats me," said our host. "I saw all you saw."

Ronald smiled. "Mustn't ask me to explain the doings just yet, Bill," he said. "Besides, we haven't caught our bird. Do you mind if we drive to the 'Greyhound'? We may as well begin our inquiries there."

"Can you get it, Bob?" said Maybury as we started.

"Haven't an earthly," I confessed. "But then I never have."

The car pulled up at the "Greyhound" and Ronald got out.

"I shan't be long," he said and disappeared inside. A minute later he was out again with a pleased look on his face. "Luck right in," he remarked. "Drive slowly towards Tetterbury," he told the chauffeur, "and stop the moment I tell you to."

"We've landed him quicker than I expected," he said, getting in with us at the back. "And if you don't mind we'll take him up to your place and hear his story. But don't alarm him till we get him there."

The car, headlights blazing, drove slowly on. And I suppose we'd gone about a mile when suddenly I felt my pulses quicken. In front of us, in the middle of the road was a thick-set man walking with a pronounced roll.

"Our bird," said Ronald quietly. "Stop when you come abreast of him."

He had a bundle slung over his shoulder, and as the car approached he swung round. And I heard Maybury whistle under his breath; the man had a beard.

"Want a lift, mate?" sang out Ronald. "Hop in beside the driver."

"Thank you, gentlemen," he said. "I'm bound for Tetterbury."

"We'll send you on there later," said Ronald. "I expect you could do with a bit of grub first. To the Hall," he told the chauffeur.

"Well, it's never been Tom Dixon's way to refuse a good offer. Thank you, gents, I don't mind if I do."

"I told the landlord at the 'Greyhound' to tell that ass Merrifield to come up there too," said Ronald in a low voice. "Hope you don't mind, Bill."

"My dear man," answered Maybury, "I'm too puzzled to mind anything. The whole thing has me beat."

Which applied equally to me.

The house-party was assembled in the hall when we arrived, and Ronald jumped out quickly to warn them to say nothing. And so it was a silent group which stared curiously at the man who stood blinking a little in the light. He was clearly puzzled, and when Ronald shut the front door behind him he made a quick movement as if he expected a trap.

"Sit down, Dixon," said Ronald quietly. "What you did this evening has got to be explained, you know."

"What are you getting at, mister?" he growled. "I've done nothing this evening."

And at that moment Inspector Merrifield, looking completely mystified, came into the hall.

"What's this the landlord tells me?" he began, and then he saw Dixon standing sullenly in the centre of the group.

"Good Lord!" he muttered, staring at him foolishly. "Who's that?"

"The man I was telling you about, Inspector," said Ronald, with a faint twinkle in his eyes. "And he is just going to tell us why he killed Benton."

With an oath the man lurched forward.

"It's a...lie," he shouted. "I don't know who you mean."

"Don't be a fool, Dixon," said Ronald sternly. "Your only chance is to make a clean breast of it. And to show you how useless it is to lie I'll tell you exactly what took place. This evening you arrived at Benton's house. Through the open window you saw him sitting in his room drinking. Then you either climbed in through the window or, opening the front door, you walked through the hall to his room, where you confronted him with the remark, 'Three bells in the second dog, you swine!'

"He recognised you at once, and in some way managed to get at one of the harpoons on the wall behind him, which he flung at you. It missed and, hitting the wall, fell at your feet. You picked it up, and as he tried to get the second you hurled it. And. Dixon, you did not miss. Then you took a glass, poured yourself out some rum, drank it, and left the house."

The man who had been listening with ever increasing amazement and fear collapsed limply in a chair.

"Strike me pink, mister!" he muttered, "were you watching from the road? You're plumb right, but it was him or me."

"I know that," said Ronald quietly, "and that's why we want to hear what led up to this affair."

The inspector stepped forward.

"I must caution you," he said, "that anything you say will be used in evidence against you."

Dixon looked at him contemptuously.

"Copper, are you? That's all right, mister. If there's any justice in this country they'll do nothing to me for killing a black-hearted devil who should have been dead this last thirty years. From what I've heard down in the pub yonder he made himself pretty well hated round these parts, but you can take it from me, gentlemen, that he was a Sunday-school marm compared to what he was like in the old days.

"Bully Benton he was known as, and well did he deserve the nick-name. Even when he was sober he had the temper of a fiend, but when he was drunk the man was uncontrollable. He was as strong as two ordinary men, and the life he lived kept him fit in spite of his drinking bouts. He owned a whaler, and that's not work for the weakling.

"I first met Bully Benton in '97 in a low-down joint in Sydney. He'd just come back from a cruise and he had money to burn. And from the very first we hated one another. I reckon I'm no plaster saint myself, but there are limits, gentlemen. And he was over it. Some of the stories I could tell you about him you wouldn't believe. Once when he was drunk he soaked a cat in oil and set light to it, and there are a score of other things he did which made one wonder if the man was sane.

"We steered clear of one another as much as we could. Though I says it myself, I was one of the few men that Bully had a wholesome respect for. We never actually came to a scrap, but I was no chicken in those days and the result might have surprised him. He knew it too, and that was enough for him, though it made him hate me all the more. I suppose, mister, there's not a thing as a wet about? I reckon I'm not much of a hand at talking."

Bill Maybury pressed the bell, and while we waited for the drink to come the strange contrast of it all struck me. The ring of men in evening clothes, each of them absolutely fit according to our standards, and yet what chance would any of us have had against Bully Benton? But there, quietly lowering his pint of beer, was the man who, when it came to stark reality, had beaten him in the final test—a man who, but for Ronald, would now be sitting in a third-class carriage to all outward appearances a common sailor.

"I shan't be much longer now, gentlemen," he continued, putting down his tankard, "and then you must do with me as you sees fit. You belong to one class, I belong to another, but there's one thing where all of us meet on the same level—when we come to love a honest girl. Perhaps you won't believe it, that there was a time when Tom Dixon was a bit of a favourite with the women, but from the moment I first set eyes on little Alice Preston there was never room for another girl in my life. And now I knows it was the same with her, though for a time I didn't. God! I thank you for that!"

His great fists were clenched: the sweat glistened on his forehead: for the moment we were nonexistent.

"No," he repeated, "for a time I didn't. We were pledged, Alice and me, though her parents were not too pleased about it. They wanted something better for their sweet girl than a rough sailor man. I didn't blame them: she was worthy of the highest in the land. But she was true to me, and we were going to be wedded when I got back from my next cruise."

And once again did he forget we were there.

"I got back to Sydney," he went on a while, "and went round to her house at once. And there her father met me.

"'Tom, lad,' he said, 'I've got some terrible bad news for you.'

"My heart almost stopped beating.

"'Not Alice!' I cried. 'Don't say anything's happened to her!'

"'She's run away,' he said in a rasping voice. 'Run away with Bully Benton.'

"Gentlemen, I reckons I went crazy. I shook him like a dog shakes a rat; told him he was a liar and it was a trick to fool me But at last I understood that it was the truth: my Alice had run away to sea with Bully Benton. We didn't even know if they was married, but what did that matter? I'd lost her: Bully Benton had got her. She'd gone down to his boat happy and carefree—I found that out from one of the watchmen: gone willingly.

"It broke me up, mister; broke me up utterly. And I went to the devil in my own way. I'm not excusing myself; I was young and head-strong. But the finish of it was that I got three years. I didn't care; I came out more black-hearted than I went in. And the first thing I did was to look round for Bully, only to find that he'd quit the game and left Australia.

"'And the girl,' I said to the man I was talking to. 'Has she gone with him?'

"'Alice Preston?' he cried, looking at me strangely. 'Of course, you wouldn't have heard, Tom. The poor child fell overboard and was drowned?

"So she was dead, and serve her right, was my thoughts. She de-served it for playing me false, and I felt no pity for her. Until one day a week later when I happened to meet the cook who had been with Bully that trip. I was drinking hard, and feeling that I feared neither for God nor man, when he altered my life for me.

"'If only you'd been here, Tom,' he said, 'it would never have hap-pened.'

"'What d'you mean?' I cried. 'I couldn't have stopped her going: wouldn't have if she'd wanted to.'

"'Wanted to, you damned fool!' he shouted. 'Wanted to! You must be mad to think such a thing.'

"And then, gentlemen, I heard the truth. Heard how Bully had lured her on board his boat with a cock-and-bull story about me having put back because I was ill, and that he would take her to me. How or why she believed it, God Almighty only knows. Maybe it was that, with her mind, she was incapable of suspecting the devilry of that foul blackguard. Just a few hours' sail, he told her; she'd be back before nightfall. So she went with him—all blind trust and confidence."

He was speaking slowly now, was Tom Dixon, and you could have heard a pin drop in the crowded hall. For every one of us there realised that he was hearing the simply told story of one of life's stark dramas.

"Can you realise her feelings, gentlemen, when it first dawned on her that she'd been deceived? Can you realise her feelings when she went on her knees to that man and he just laughed in her face? Can you realise her feelings when he first flung his foul arms round her and soiled her with his lecherous kisses? One friend she had—the cook—and Bully split his head open with a belaying-pin; he showed me the scar.

"'So it was better that she fell overboard,' I said when he'd finished.

"And then, gentlemen, he looked at me queerly.

"'She didn't fall, Tom,' he said. 'She jumped.'"

For a while Tom Dixon was silent, staring in front of him, and seeing the ghosts of that tragedy of long ago. Then with a little shake he pulled himself together.

"I guess that's about all, gentlemen. There and then I vowed that some day, at the same hour that my girl went to her death, Bully Benton and I would settle accounts. For years I have been seeking him, and quite by chance a fortnight ago in Marseille I picked up an English newspaper of several months ago. And in it I saw a little paragraph saying that a Daniel Benton had been given three months for assault. I had found him at last: there could not be two of them.

"The rest this gentleman knows, though how he found it out can't understand, seeing that he wasn't there. I don't know how I stand with the law of England; I don't know what they can do to me: I don't care. I killed Bully Benton and I guess if they want to hang me for it they can."

"You take it from me, Dixon," said Ronald quietly, "that the law won't hang you for it. You'll have to go with the inspector and stand your trial, of course, but in view of the fact that you went to him un-armed and he flung the harpoon at you first, it will only be a formality. And may I say one thing more? I don't think there is a single man here who would not be proud to have acted as you did."

★★★★★★

"It makes one feel a bit small, doesn't it?" he said ten minutes later.

Dixon had gone with the inspector; Bill Maybury, Ronald and I were sitting down to a belated dinner.

"Little games of cricket and golf; nice food on nice plates; all the even tenor of our lives—and what we've just listened to."

"Agreed," grunted Maybury. "But we're still infernally curious, Ronald."

"Little fiddling clues," Ronald laughed shortly. "It was easy, Bill. From the word 'go' I was certain it wasn't young Drury. To throw a harpoon requires not only enormous strength, but very great skill—skill it was well-nigh impossible that a country lad could possess. Only a man trained to the sea could have done it.

"Then the rum; essentially a sailor's drink, and already I was fairly certain in my mind that a sea man was at the bottom of it, a conviction which was strengthened by what Betsy told us with regard to Benton's fear of strangers. Surely that must date back to his old life. But when we came to the remark she overheard I had proof positive.

"'Three bells in the second dog, you swine!'

"And there you see the danger of a preconceived idea. The inspec-tor, his mind full of the story of young Drury's dog, seized on the word dog—in a way, a very natural mistake. I, on the other hand, had already arrived in a nautical atmosphere and to me the remark had a totally different significance. The dog watch on board ship is from four to eight in the evening; the first dog from four to six; the second dog is seven-thirty—the time when Dixon entered the room; the time we now know when Alice Preston jumped to her death.

"By now I knew that the man who had killed Benton was a sailor: no landsman would have used such a phrase. Moreover, he'd killed him with one of Benton's own weapons. How had he got it down from the wall, with its owner sitting in the way? Obviously he couldn't have, so it must have been flung at him first. The rest was easy. I found the mark on the wall, and realising that Benton would have aimed at his chest, deduced that he was about the same height as myself. Inci-dentally, the fact that plaster was still on the floor was strong evidence

337

that the mark had been made recently. And finally, deep-sea sailors are invariably weather-beaten, walk with a slight roll, and frequently have beards. And when the landlord at the 'Greyhound' told me that just such a man had left a few minutes earlier walking to Tetterbury I knew we had him."

He lit a cigarette thoughtfully.

"But this night a man has talked with us."

The Man in Yellow

I had known little Marjorie Beaumont since she was a child of six, but of late years since both her parents had died in one of the epidemics I had rather lost sight of her. She was living, I knew, somewhere down in Kent with an elderly uncle. Where, exactly, I was not sure till I received the letter I now held in my hand, it ran:

> Groomley Park, Nr. Ashford.
>
> Dear Bob,
> Come and feed with me at the Six Hundred tomorrow (that's today when you get this) and meet Bungo. Also there is something I want to ask you about. Expect you one o'clock.
> Yours,
>
> Marjorie.
> P.S.—You have got a pal who does things, haven't you? You know, arrests people, and all that."

I smiled slightly. As a description of Ronald Standish, the postscript was not without humour. But what on earth could she be wanting to see him about? And who was Bungo? Points which doubtless would be settled at the Six Hundred, where I duly arrived at a little after one.

I saw her at once in a far corner sitting with a good-looking youngster. They were deep in conversation—so deep, in fact, that I had reached the table before she saw me.

"Bob, you old dear," she cried, jumping up, "it's great of you to come. This is Bungo."

I shook hands.

"His real name," she continued, "is Jack Ayrton, but it's used so little that he's almost forgotten it himself. And he and I are engaged."

"Splendid," I said. "All the usual and that sort of rot. But where," I remarked, glancing at her left hand, "is the outward and visible sign of this happy state of affairs?"

"That," remarked Bungo gloomily, "is where you butt your head into the snag. We are engaged, but Uncle Henry thinks otherwise."

"I don't think you know him, Bob," put in the girl. "But I've lived with him at Groomley Park ever since the poor old parents died. He's been my guardian now for ten years."

"And he doesn't approve of the nuptials?" I said. "Why not?"

"The Lord knows," answered Bungo. "I knew Marjorie has a spot of cash belonging to her, but so have I."

"Ayrton's Fabrics for All," explained the girl. "That's his father."

"I see where the cash comes," I remarked. "Thanks: I can do another of those. Does Uncle Henry give no reason?"

"Uncle Henry says I'm too young," said the girl, lighting a cigarette. "Of course, I know that it will be lonely for the poor old fish when I join up with Bungo, and I don't want to hurt his feelings, Bob. He's been awfully good to me all these years. At the same time, he's got to get used to the idea; and he no understands that when I come of age next November, Bungo and I are going to pull it off. But until then I've promised him I won't."

"But what has this got to do with my pal who arrests people, and all that?"

The girl laughed and then grew serious again.

"Seems a bit obscure, I must admit," she answered. "What we've been telling you up to date has nothing to do with him, but Uncle has—over something completely different. Shall I tell him, Bungo, or will you?"

"You're in the chair, old soul," he remarked. "Cough it up."

"It started about three weeks ago," she began. "We were having breakfast, just he and I, when the post arrived. Bungo wasn't down, and so he didn't see the beginning of it. But I suddenly heard a noise like a pig grunting, and there was Uncle Henry, half out of his chair, staring at one of his letters as if it was a bomb. He was plucking at his collar with one hand, and clawing at the air with the other."

"That's when I came tottering in," said Bungo, "and I thought the old chap was having a fit. At any rate, Marjorie and I clustered round, and when the commotion had died down a bit we asked him what had stung him.

"'They've found me,' he muttered. 'After all these years they've found me.'

"Which didn't convey much to us." The girl took up the story again. "So we laid him out to cool, and after a while tried to find out what the trouble was. But he wouldn't say anything more, and a few minutes later he left the room and went to his study, where he locked himself in, a thing I've never known him do before."

"Did you see the letter that had caused the trouble?" I asked.

"We got the envelope," said Bungo. "Here it is. But we didn't see the contents until much later."

I glanced at the envelope, but it did not seem to point to much. It was addressed to Mr. Henry Beaumont, Groomley Park, Nr. Ashford, in what was a childish rather than an illiterate hand. The postmark was Folkestone.

"Not much there," I said, handing it back. "What happened next?"

"Nothing till dinner that night," answered the girl. "He remained in his study all day, and had his lunch there."

"Which must have been considerably more liquid than solid," jut in Bungo. "When Uncle arrived for dinner he was quite-nicely-thank-you."

"So would you have been, my lad," she cried, "under the circumstances. Anyway, Bob, we tackled him about it again, as this is what we gathered. All his early life was spent in the East and it seems that when he was a youngster he was pretty hot stuff. At any rate, one night in the dim, dark ages—Swettypore in ninety-four sort of business—he and some pals were making whoopee."

"And they got gloriously sprung," said Bungo.

"And having got gloriously sprung," continued Marjorie, "they proceeded to raise Cain round some especially sacred Buddhist temple. In fact, according to him, they laid out some priests, and concluded the entertainment by dancing the Lancers with some of the girls attached to the place."

"Who were a particularly sacred brand of virgin," explain Bungo.

"What a dam' fool thing to do," I remarked.

"So they all realised the next morning," he said. "And so Uncle Henry admitted when he told us. The fact remained, however, that it had been done, and there was no undoing it. But they were only passing through the place on their way home on leave, so at crack of dawn next morning they beat it while the going was good. But not before one thing had happened. Pinned to the table in the rest house they found a note: 'Vengeance will overtake you sooner or later.'"

"It seems to have been some time on the road," I murmured

"Just what I said to Uncle," cried Marjorie. "But he didn't agree. He said that Time was a totally different thing in the East from what we Westerners understood, especially where the religious orders were concerned. Thirty or forty years mean nothing to them with their conception of life after death."

"And this was three weeks ago," I said. "Has anything happened since?"

"For ten days nothing happened at all," she answered. "Bungo had to leave, so that Uncle and I were alone except for the servants, who are all women. He locked up with the utmost care every night, and always slept with a loaded revolver under his pillow, but when I suggested going to the police about it he refused point-blank. He seemed to be afraid that if he did he would have to tell them about this episode of the temple, which is not a thing he wants made public.

"Ten days ago, Bob, a second letter arrived, this time from Ashford. It came at breakfast, like the first, and again Uncle Henry shut himself up in his study the whole day. I begged him show me the two notes, but he wouldn't. He seemed apathetic, almost resigned, and grew quite irritable when I once more suggested the police.

"'What good would the police be in a case like this?' he snorted. What use would they be when pitted against the mysteries of the East? If these men mean to get me they will get me even if the whole of Scotland Yard is round the house.'

"So I had to let the matter drop. Uncle is as obstinate as a mule when he wants to be; and to make matters worse a few days later he got a bad attack of gout which, by the way, he is still suffering from. And then the day before yesterday occurred an incident which threw him into a veritable panic.

"I had been sitting with him for about ten minutes in his room before dinner, when my maid came in to ask me some question. And when she saw me she looked very surprised.

"'I thought you'd already changed, miss,' she said.' 'I saw you in your yellow dress half an hour ago, and going into the master's bedroom."

"The effect on my uncle was electric.

"'Yellow dress!' he shouted. 'My God! Search the house, Marjorie Search the house! Take my revolver with you?

"He tried to get up, but his gout was very bad that night. And so, amazed beyond measure at this extraordinary outburst, Janet—that's my maid—and I went into his room. It was empty. There wasn't a sign of anyone, or of anything having been moved. And then I sent for the chauffeur, who lives in a cottage close by, and with him we went over the house. We looked into cupboards; we looked under beds—not a sign of a soul. And having told Uncle Henry I asked him what on earth it was all about, and why such a harmless remark as Janet's should have caused such a commotion.

"'Naturally you wouldn't understand, Marjorie,' he answered heavily. 'You've never been out East. But that yellow dress of yours is exactly the same colour as the robe which the Buddhist priests all wear.'

"I stared at him incredulously.

"'You don't mean to say,' I cried, 'that you think that Janet saw a Buddhist priest going into your bedroom?'

"'Then what did she see?' he said. 'It wasn't you. It couldn't have been one of the servants.'

"'But there's no one there,' I assured him.

"He smiled pityingly."

"'And you can't expect me to believe,' I cried, 'that they can vanish into thin air.'

"'I don't expect you to believe anything,' he answered quietly. 'Let us assume that Janet made a mistake.'

"But I could see that he did not think so, and that night after dinner I stuck in my toes. I took up the line that it wasn't fair to me; and that if he wouldn't tell the police the least he could do was to allow me to ask someone else for help. And at last he consented, though he obviously considered it useless.

"'Open the top drawer of my desk,' he said, 'and you'll find there the two notes that came by post.'

"I did so, and here they are, Bob."

She passed them over the table to me, and I examined them curiously. The writing was the same as that on the envelope, but the paper was different. It was a sort of parchment, about the size of a small luggage label, and it looked as if some sort of scratchy pencil had been used by the writer.

Do you remember Ranapore

So ran the first one, which had been posted in Folkestone.

The punishment will fit the crime

That was the second; which had come from Ashford. I handed them back to Marjorie, and shrugged my shoulders.

"It's beyond me, old thing," I said. "They look as if a child had written them when under the influence of drink. Did you uncle explain anything?"

"Only that that was the paper always used by the Buddhist priests, and that it was the leaf of some palm tree.

"'They're genuine, Marjorie, my dear,' he said. 'Only too well do I know it. No one but a priest would possess that paper; no one but a priest would understand how to do that writing, which is a special art. Go if you like and get anyone you wish to help but it is useless. They've found me, and there's no more to be said.'

"And so, Bob, I thought of you and that friend of yours."

"Whom I will get on the 'phone," I said. "And if he isn't playing golf or cricket we'll go along and see him at once."

Ronald was in, and ten minutes later we were all sitting in his room. He was dealing with a rusty niblick when we arrived, but Marjorie Beaumont retold her story he ceased operations on the club and listened intently.

"What's the verdict, Mr. Standish?" said Bungo, when she had finished.

Ronald was studying the two messages through a magnifying glass. "These are undoubtedly genuine," he remarked. "By that I mean that your uncle is perfectly right when he says that they are written by someone who has learned an art which is generally regarded as the exclusive property of the Buddhist priests. They scratch the words with a very fine pointed stylo, and then shake a dark powder over the leaf, which fills up the grooves of the letters. Then they wipe the rest of it off, leaving the writing showing up clearly."

"But do you really think the old dear is in any danger?" asked Marjorie anxiously.

"Frankly, Miss Beaumont, I am inclined to take the whole thing very seriously," he answered, "especially now that I have examined these messages. If it was just some silly joke they would have been written on paper. You see, except in a museum this palm leaf is unprocurable in England; also the implement with which the writing was done."

"What ought we to do about it?" she cried.

"Well, if you like, and you don't think your uncle would object, I'll come down and look into things on the spot," he said.

"Mind! I should think he'd kiss you on both cheeks," said Bungo. "When can you go?"

"This afternoon," answered Ronald. "There are one or two things

I must do first, and then I'll motor down with Bob."

"It's awfully good of you, Mr. Standish," said the girl. "And I know my uncle will think so too. Especially as even Bungo won't be there."

"Less of your 'even'," said Bungo, with a grin.

"I'll keep the two messages for the time being, if I may," said Ronald. "There are a few points I would like to verify. And we'll be with you in time for dinner."

Marjorie smiled at him gratefully and departed with Bungo.

"Nice children," remarked Ronald, watching them from the window. "What do you make of it, Bob?"

"There's only one thing that has struck me," I said. "If the writing was done by a genuine Buddhist priest there oughtn't to be much difficulty in putting one's hand on him."

"A very sapient remark, old boy," he agreed. "The only snag being that though the secret of this writing originated with the priests, there are other people who know it."

"You mean it may not be a priest at all, but someone else knows of this episode in the old man's past."

"Exactly," he said.

"But, then, how do you account for what the maid Janet saw?"

"I don't," he answered quietly. "For that, my dear Bob, is the most curious feature of a very curious case. A very curious case." he repeated, and seemed on the point of saying something Then he altered his mind and, crossing to a cupboard in corner, he took out a small bottle of dusting powder. He shook some carefully on to the second of the messages, and examined it through his magnifying glass.

I stared over his shoulder, and even with the naked eye I could see a confused medley of finger-prints, which was just what would have expected. Several people, including myself, had handled it, and I failed to see what he hoped to discover from such a blurred trail. But after a while a rather surprising thing occurred. Out of the jumble of marks, two prints began to stand out more clearly than the rest; one came directly under the centre of the word "punishment", the other midway between the words "fit the".

"We progress," he said tersely, "though I hardly expected such a clear result. Do you see those two prints, Bob? What do you make of them?"

"That two people have held the leaf more firmly than others," I answered promptly.

"Very nearly right," he remarked. "But it's one person, not two.

Those fingerprints are identical. Let's try the other."

Again, only less clearly, two stood out from the others—one under "you", the other under the last syllable of "remember".

"Once more the same gentleman," he said. "And so, old lad, we have in our possession four perfectly good finger-prints of the left thumb of the writer of these messages."

"How on earth do you know that?" I cried.

"I know it because I've seen this writing being done," he said. "The trouble is that I'm afraid it isn't going to help us much. It is most improbable that the writer is an old criminal, so we can't trace him at Scotland Yard. And, since we can't trot round the population of Folkestone and Ashford asking 'em for prints of their left thumbs, we're not much forrader."

"But if we can find a Buddhist priest," I cried, "that print gives the proof."

"If," he answered cryptically. "At any rate, let's go and look for him. You get the bus, Bob, while I go round to the Yard to make absolutely certain he's not an old lag."

I picked him up an hour later at the club, and as soon as he saw me he shook his head.

"As I thought," he said. "They can't help us. So we'll have to see what we can do on our own."

We arrived at Groomley Park at half-past six, and it was evident at once that there had been further developments. Marjorie was standing on the doorstep with News written large on her face.

"Uncle Henry has found out where they are," she cried.

"You mean the message writer?" said Ronald, staring at her.

"Yes," she answered. "But come on up and see him and he'll tell you himself."

We followed her up the stairs, and I could see that Ronald was surprised, though he said no more.

"This is Mr. Standish, Uncle Henry," she said, opening the door into a room that was obviously his study. "And Bob Miller, whom you've heard me talk about."

I studied Mr. Beaumont covertly. He was sitting in an easy chair with one foot well wrapped up, stretched out in front of him.

"Sit down, gentlemen," he said. "Sorry—but my damned foot prevents me getting up to greet you. Well—I gather Marjorie has told you the story."

"That is so, Mr. Beaumont," said Ronald. "But I now hear that you've solved the mystery."

"Solved it," he cried. "Of course I have. And if the police weren't such infernal fools, and this wasn't such a regulation-infested country, I'd have the whole lot arrested tonight. Snake charmers—pah! they're no more snake-charmers than I am."

"At the moment," said Ronald mildly, "it seems a little hard to follow."

"The circus, sir," barked the old man. "One of those cursed things with brass bands and merry-go-rounds and things. My fool of a parlourmaid told me about it after lunch, and happened to mention there were Indian jugglers there. So I sent her out to make inquiries—they've pitched their show in the village a mile way—and what do you think I've discovered? The circus was in Folkestone when the first note was sent, and in Ashford at the time of the second. Isn't that proof, sir?"

He thumped the table at his side and glared at Ronald.

"A good piece of presumptive evidence, Mr. Beaumont," said quietly, "but, I fear, hardly proof."

"Bosh!" snorted the other. "Do you know anything about Buddhist writing?"

"A little," said Ronald mildly.

"Well—you've seen those two messages, haven't you, so what more do you want?"

"Quite so," answered Ronald soothingly. "They were most certainly written by someone who is conversant with the art and has used the proper implements. But that is not to say that one of this snake-charming troupe is of necessity the culprit. It certainly a coincidence, and one that is well worth following up, but that is as far as we can go at present."

The old gentleman snorted again. Then he turned to his niece.

"Go down and see about some drinks, my dear," he cried, "I would like a word with Mr. Standish alone."

"You see," he went on as the girl left the room, "it's the second message that worries me, about the punishment fitting the crime. Marjorie has already told you what we young fools did, and I am so desperately afraid that these devils may try and do something to her by way of revenge. For myself, I'm an old man and it doesn't matter, but if they hurt a hair of her head I'd never forgive myself."

"Naturally, Mr. Beaumont," said Ronald gravely. "Some such idea had also occurred to me."

"She's a high-spirited child, and until she comes of age I feel she is my charge. Then, of course, she will have her own money and, I gather, proposes to desert me for young Ayrton. But until then I feel myself entirely responsible. And, if you will forgive my saying so, what I fear is that you are up against something you don't understand. Janet is an unimaginative girl. What was it then, that she saw? They have powers of which we Europeans have no conception. And against those powers ordinary methods are of no avail."

"Then we must try extraordinary methods," said Ronald. "By the way, Mr. Beaumont, does that door lead to your bedroom?"

"It does," said the old man in some surprise. "Why?"

"That, then, is the room into which Janet saw or thought she saw the individual in the yellow dress disappearing."

"Yes. There is another door to it leading into the passage, and it was through that one the man vanished."

"You were in here at the time?"

"I was."

"And you heard nothing?"

"Not a sound. One doesn't hear these people when they walk, my young friend."

Ronald rose.

"Perhaps not, sir. Well, I think I'll just have a look round, and later on, Bob, you and I might go to the circus and have a shot at the co-conuts. We'll report in due course, Mr. Beaumont."

We left the old gentleman muttering sarcastically to himself, and going along the passage encountered a quiet-looking woman of about forty dressed in black. Ronald stopped.

"Are you Janet—Miss Beaumont's maid?" he asked.

"I am, sir," she said.

"Would you please tell me exactly what happened that evening when you saw someone in yellow going into Mr. Beaumont's bedroom."

"There's nothing much to tell, sir," she said. "I was coming up the stairs, and I saw someone wearing a yellow dress standing just outside the bedroom door. It was exactly the colour of one of Miss Marjorie's evening frocks, and when whoever it was opened the door and went in I assumed it was her."

"Naturally," said Ronald. "And what did you do then?"

I did some sewing for half an hour, and then as I was returning to Miss Marjorie's room I heard her voice in Mr. Beaumont's study. So I went in to find out if there was anything she wanted, and I found that she hadn't dressed for dinner, so that it couldn't have been her I saw."

"So during that half-hour the passage, so far as you know, was empty."

"So far as I know, sir, it was."

"Thank you, Janet," he said. "That's all at the moment."

"A puzzling point, Bob," he continued as we went downstairs. "She doesn't strike me as the sort of woman who would imagine things. And if someone in a yellow robe was really there, why did nothing happen? What was the object in getting thus far and then going no further?"

We found Marjorie in the hall, and she waved her hand at the drink tray.

"Help yourselves," she said. "Well, Mr. Standish, what do you I think?"

"I don't know what to think, Miss Beaumont," he answered frankly. "In fact, I'm completely nonplussed. I shall go to the circus and see these Indian jugglers, and perhaps we may find something. In any event I would not, if I were you, go far from the house alone, at any rate while they are in the neighbourhood."

He reverted again to Janet's story on the way there.

"It baffles me," he said. "It seems so absolutely pointless. Clearly there was no difficulty over the fellow getting away, but what earthly use was there in going there and then doing nothing? If he'd introduced a snake into the bedroom, or something of that sort, we should have had a motive. But as it is I'm defeated."

★★★★★★

The circus turned out to be a small one, and we had no difficulty in finding the jugglers. There were four of them, and when we had paid our shillings and entered their booth we found them in a group of staring yokels watching a cobra swaying slowly and fro to the sound of a pipe whilst the player squatted on the ground in front of it.

"They're Tamils," whispered Ronald to me. "Fortunately I can talk a bit of their lingo. But we'll have to wait till their show is over. And then by means of a little ruse we may get some information. You didn't know I was something of a conjurer, did you Bob?"

We watched the mango tree grow, and all the other tricks familiar to those who go East, until at last the show ended and the audience departed. Whereupon Ronald, stepped forward and said something in a dialect which brought the four natives excitedly to their feet with broad grins on their faces. Next he produced from his pocket a pack of cards and I wondered what on earth was coming. Evidently he was going to show them some trick, but what good he hoped to obtain by that was obscure. And then suddenly the man's amazing ingenuity dawned on me, though I could not understand a word he was saying. For each of the natives had grasped one of the four corners of the pack with their left forefinger and thumb, so that four thumb-prints would be obtained on the top card.

I forgot even to look at the trick, so lost was I in admiration of his cleverness. And when a quarter of an hour later we were sitting in the neighbouring pub with the vital card in front of us he admitted that the trick had been a complete frost.

"However," he remarked as he sprinkled the dusting powder on the card's surface, "I dare say my reputation for sleight of hand survive the failure." The four thumb-prints came out perfectly, and from his pocket he produced the second message. And a few moments' comparison established the complete innocence of the jugglers. None of the four thumb-prints on the card bore the smallest resemblance to those on the palm leaf.

"That settles that once and for all," he said, draining his tankard of beer. "So we've got to start all over again, Bob."

"I feel I'm being a fool," he said at length. "I feel I ought to be able to get something out of Janet's evidence. And I can't. Why should this man, having got into Beaumont's bedroom, having done all the difficult part safely, leave without profiting by it? Making all allowances for times not being accurate, the old man was alone after our unknown entered the bedroom. Why, Bob, why? Did he hear or see something that scared him? Or did he do something in that room which hasn't acted yet, and which sometime will function and kill Beaumont? Or."

He fell into a deep reverie which lasted for ten minutes; then he beckoned to the landlord.

"How much longer is that circus remaining here?" he asked.

"It be going tomorrow morning, sir. Up to Tenterden."

"Thank you. Come on, Bob. Let's be getting back. And since I have a feeling that the very walls have ears, say nothing of our little effort in conjuring tonight."

A warning which proved unnecessary, for we found the whole house in a turmoil on our return. Another message had arrived. It seemed that Mr. Beaumont's gout being a little better, he had gone down to dinner. And on his return to his study he had found it lying on the table.

"There it is, sir," he roared, holding it out to Ronald. "The damned swine put there while I was downstairs. Take it, man, take it," he went on testily, "I can't hold my arm out the whole night."

I glanced at Ronald in some surprise, for he was staring at the little leaf of paper like a man bereft of his senses. Then in an instant his face was as expressionless as usual, and taking the note he read out the contents:

Be at Handel Corner at one tonight

"Where is Handel Corner?" he asked.

"About three miles from here," said Marjorie.

"And what do you propose to do about it?" asked Ronald.

"Do?" shouted the old man. "What the hell can I do with a foot like this? But you and your friend can do something. Go to Handel Corner and catch this devil. Find out who it is, and haul him here for the police to deal with."

"A very good idea, Mr. Beaumont," said Ronald thoughtfully "That should settle things once and for all."

"Take one of my revolvers and shoot the dog on sight." The old gentleman's wrath was rising.

"You had the house searched after you found this, I suppose?'

"Of course! Of course!" said Mr. Beaumont testily. "No trace of anyone. He vanished the same as he did last time. Don't take your car right up to the corner, Standish. Leave it some way off and walk. Then you'll trap the blackguard. Damn it!" he exploded, "what are you hesitating about? Surely two young men like you aren't frightened, are you?"

But Ronald did not even smile; I have never seen him look graver.

"No, Mr. Beaumont," he said at length, "not frightened, I assure you. Come along, Bob," he turned to me abruptly. "We shall have to be leaving shortly."

"And bring him back dead or alive," grunted the old man as we left the room.

"You're darned pensive, Ronald," I said as we went downstairs "What's the great idea?"

"Only that I've just solved the mystery of what Janet saw," he answered. "Where is Miss Beaumont?"

"Here she is," said Marjorie, appearing from the drawing—room.

"Do you want to speak to me?"

"Yes, Miss Beaumont, I do," he said. "I want you please to obey my instructions implicitly, and I think we shall catch the gentleman who has been causing the trouble. Now, I have the best reasons for believing that the note your uncle received tonight is a trap with the sole purpose of getting us out of this house. I didn't tell Mr. Beaumont so, as his condition at the moment; owing to his gout, he is so excitable that it could do no good. It is far better that he should believe that Bob and I have gone to Handel Corner or he might spoil the whole thing. Now I come to what I want you to do, and I don't want you even to tell Janet. Go upstairs in a few minutes and undress in your own room, as usual. When you've dismissed your maid, turn out your light and then, without making a sound, go to some other room and stay there. Turn out the light there, too, and lock the door. Have you got me?"

"Perfectly," she said quietly. "I will do just what you say. But what are you and Bob going to do?"

"Just for the moment we'll leave that," he said gravely. "How long will it take you before you're ready?"

"Twenty minutes," she answered, and he glanced at the clock. "That will do nicely," he said, and we watched her going up the stairs.

"The most damnable quandary I've ever been in, Bob," he remarked as she disappeared. "However, it's got to be gone through. Let's get to it."

First he walked, into the billiard-room, where he opened a window noiselessly; then he rejoined me in the hall.

"Time we started," he said. "Let's get the car."

"But," I began, "I thought you said—"

"You drive," he went on, opening the front door, "and I'll take the map."

Completely bewildered, I followed him to the garage, and we started off down the drive. But hardly had we turned into the main road, when he told me to stop.

"Now back to the house on foot," he said, "and keep on the grass."

Skirting the drive, we reached the open window in the billiard-room, and he put his lips to my ear.

"Take off your shoes," he whispered, "and don't make a sound." On tiptoe I followed him up the stairs, where the passage was in darkness, and he led the way to Marjorie's room. No light was shining through the keyhole, and very cautiously he opened the door. The room was empty. She had carried out her instructions.

"And now," he breathed, "we wait."

Screening his torch he flashed it round until he found a switch by the dressing-table.

"Sit by that, Bob," he whispered, "and for God's sake turn it on when I tell you."

Then he took off his coat and waistcoat, lay down on the bed and put out his torch.

Half-past twelve chimed faintly from the clock below in the hail. The house, save for the occasional crack of a floor board, was silent. A quarter to one; one, and I could hear the beating of my own heart. What were we waiting for? What was going to happen? And then quite suddenly came a much louder crack from just outside the door.

I heard Ronald move slightly on the bed, and with my pulse hammering and one hand on the switch I waited. Whatever it was, it was coming now. Old Beaumont had been right. It was Marjorie who was in danger.

The door was opening slowly, and I could see the faint outline of a cloaked figure standing there. Then, in a flash, it had disappeared and the springs of the bed shook. Came a sudden grunt and a snarl; then Ronald's quiet voice.—"Light, Bob."

I switched on, and stared in amazement at the scene. Standing by the bed was a man in a yellow robe. He was struggling furiously in Ronald's iron grasp, but after a time he grew quiet. His features were squat and almost Mongolian, but as I got up and went nearer there seemed to be something very odd about the face. Until Ronald put up a hand and pulled off—a mask.

"Well, Mr. Beaumont," said Ronald in a terrible voice, "Have you anything to say to excuse yourself for attempting such inconceivable crime as the murder of your niece?"

I stood rooted to the ground. Beaumont—her uncle. He stood there mouthing, helplessly. Then with a sort of strangled cry he bolted from the room. I turned to follow him, but Ronald stopped me.

"There is only one expiation," he said gravely. "Pray Heaven he takes it!"

He did a moment or two later, and the sound of the shot brought Marjorie rushing out of her room.

"What is it?" she cried wildly.

"I will explain things shortly, Miss Beaumont," said Ronald, laying his hand on her arm. "Please go downstairs now. Come with me, Bob."

We went to the study. There was nothing to be done. Ronald bent down and picked up a small bottle that was lying on the floor. And having pulled out the cork he sniffed it.

"The vile old devil," he said softly, slipping it into his pocket. "Prussic acid."

And so we went downstairs to the weeping girl through a crowd of frightened servants.

"Get the police and a doctor," said Ronald to the parlourmaid. "And no one is to go into the study till they come."

"It's very bad news I'm afraid, Miss Beaumont."

He drew her into the drawing-room.

"There is no doubt at all that this business has so preyed on your uncle's mind," he went on gravely, "that it sent him off his head. And tonight it came to a climax and he shot himself."

Which was the verdict ultimately returned at the coroner's inquest.

"Far better so, Bob," said Ronald to me after it was all over. "To tell the truth would only damage the girl and not hurt him."

"What made you get it first?" I asked.

"When he gave me that third note," he answered.

"I saw you staring at it," I said. "But you couldn't have spotted the thumb-print."

"No; but I spotted the thumb. In doing that writing the leaf is held firmly between the thumb and the first finger, and in the thumb-nail a nick is cut. Into that nick is put the implement the writer scratches with to keep it steady. And when I saw that he had just such a nick in his thumb I was completely dumbfounded. Up to that moment the truth had not even remotely dawned on me. And then I saw that it all fitted together, and that, at last, what Janet had seen became comprehensible. Naturally, nothing had been done by the man in yellow if he was Beaumont himself."

"But what was his idea in being seen?"

"To establish an atmosphere," he said promptly, "the atmosphere of the mysterious East. He started it with the notes and the story of his youth, and added to it as he went along. The circus was a golden opportunity to throw suspicion on the wrong person, but he overlooked the little matter of finger-prints. And since the circus was moving early the next day it was clear he would have to act that night. His gout, of course, was a fiction, though a very plausible one. In fact, Henry Beaumont was as pretty a damned villain as I've ever come across."

"But the main question is still unanswered," I reminded him. "Why did he want to murder Marjorie?"

"We shall have that proved for certain shortly," he said. "But in the meantime I'll hazard a guess. In a few months Beaumont would have been called on to give an account of his stewardship of his niece's money. The ultimatum had gone forth; she was going to marry Bungo. Doubtless she still will. But I'm open to a bet with you, Bob, that a hundred *per cent* of their combined income will come from Ayrton's Fabrics for All."

"You mean he embezzled Marjorie's money?"

"Exactly," he remarked:

And once again he proved to be right: every penny had gone.

The Man with Samples

"Can you spare a few minutes, Bob? Two heads are better than one, and, maybe, you'll be able to see a way out."

I had not seen Ronald Standish for some weeks, and as I put down the morning paper I saw he was looking worried.

"As many as you like," I said. "But if you can't solve the problem I'm not likely to be much good."

"It's nothing to do with solving a problem this time, old boy," he answered. "At least, not in the way you mean. By Jove!" he burst out savagely, "there ought to be a law passed allowing one to shoot a blackmailer on sight."

"So that's it, is it?" I cried. "Nobody getting at you, is there?"

"Not guilty, Bob," he said with a grin.

He grew serious again.

"Do you know Archie Maitland?"

"Sir Archibald Maitland, Bart? Yes, I know him slightly. Just got engaged to one of the Sussex girls."

"That's the bird," said Ronald. "And have you ever heard me speak of a man who calls himself Richard Mordon?"

"Can't say I have. Who is he?"

"Richard Mordon, amongst other things, is one of those kind hearted philanthropists who will lend you any sum from five pounds to ten thousand on note of hand alone. He trades under the name of John Grant & Co. His real name I have forgotten but his parents were foreigners who settled in England, where their precious offspring was born. He, therefore, speaks the language like a native. He has an office in the City, and lives in a house not far from Sevenoaks. I'll tell you more about that house later.

"To return to Mordon. I said, if you remember, 'amongst other things'. The gentleman, besides being the most rapacious blood sucker in London so far as his rates of interest are concerned, has a very paying side-line. It is one that he handles with great discretion, since a mistake would involve his being kept at His Majesty's expense for several years. He conducts it entirely from his private house, with the money-lending business quite separate And the side-line is this. He is prepared to buy any incriminating document which he considers worth his while.

"Setting to work with, I am bound to say, considerable skill, he let it be known amongst valets and ladies' maids that any compromising letters they chose to bring to him would be well paid for. And not being a damned fool he does pay well; he gets it back a hundred times over. And the result is that many a damning letter has found its way into Mordon's safe.

"Then comes the next step—blackmail the writers. And here Mordon again shows his devilish cunning. He seems to possess an almost uncanny flair for squeezing the maximum out of his victims, without overstepping the mark and asking the impossible. Knowing human nature, he realises that by so doing he is far more likely to get the money. Of course, there have been cases when Mordon has suggested the advantages of borrowing money from John Grant & Co., and has thereby got it both ways, but as a general rule he touches them for just what they can pay and no more."

"You seem to know a good deal about the swine," I said.

"I do," answered Ronald. "Four or five times he and I have crossed swords, and I regret to state he has won on every occasion. You see, the devil of it is, Bob, that with a blackmailer one is helpless. The police are helpless. Unless the victim will move, nothing can be done. And that's where this blackguard is so astute. He never touches a case which concerns one individual only; there is always someone else implicated. Since ninety *per cent.* of his cases concern love affairs the man has to think of the woman's reputation. What he specialises in is the case where a real scandal would ensue if the facts came out. And that is the state of Denmark so far as Archie Maitland is concerned. My hat! Bob," he added despairingly, "why are people such drivelling half-wits as to write compromising letters, and then to qualify still further for a lunatic asylum by leaving them lying about? However—to continue.

"Two years ago, Archie had a love affair with a girl who must be nameless, even to you. He was quite frank about it, and while it lasted it was evidently pretty hectic. Then, as has been known to happen before, the thing fizzled out, and a year ago the girl got married to a man some fifteen years older than herself. They are ideally happy, and a child is expected shortly.

"Now we come to the point. A week ago Mordon rang up Archie as he was dressing for dinner. Archie, of course, didn't know from Adam who he was, and when Mordon suggested that he should come down and visit him at Sevenoaks Archie told him to go to the devil. Then Mordon mentioned the girl's name, which gave Archie such a jolt that he could only stutter foolishly. He had almost forgotten the affair himself, so how on earth could complete stranger know anything about it? However, he evidently did, and so Archie made an appointment to go down and see the following evening.

"He found Mordon in the room in which he always transact his business, and at first he thought he'd come to a madhouse. Immediately on his entering, a large man of the professional pug type ran his hands over his pockets. But it wasn't that which surprised him; in fact, he hardly noticed it in his amazement the rest of the preparations. Seated against the farther wall the man he had come to see. In front of him was a desk, and set into the wall itself was a big safe, the door of which stood open. But the astounding thing was that a high open-work grille fenced him in completely, on the same principle that one sometimes in banks.

"'Pardon these small precautions, Sir Archibald,' said the blackguard affably, 'but I have a rooted objection to revolver bullets or physical force in any form. So I prefer to conduct negotiations from this side of the grille. Our business will not take long. Do you recognise this letter?'

"He held up a sheet of paper and Archie stared at it stupefied. It was in the girl's handwriting, and he could see that the address was that of her parents' house.

"'How the devil did you get hold of that?' he shouted.

"Mordon held up his hand.

"'I must really beg of you to moderate your voice, Sir Archibald,' he said. 'Such lack of control is shockingly bad for digestion.'

"The genuine Mordon touch, Bob: the swine always talks like that. "'I see that you do remember,' he continued. 'I don't wonder, either; it is not the sort of letter a man would forget. A little indiscreet, per-haps—but very affectionate. Have you had another week-end in Paris with the lady?'

"I gather that at that point Archie went mad. He cursed and swore at the sneering moneylender behind his desk; he seized the steel bars of the grille and shook them, and as he said to me, if he had had a gun he'd have shot Mordon dead on the spot. It was perfectly true that he and the girl had spent a week-end in Paris, but it had been quite innocent. It had been on the occasion of the Davis Cup, and they had decided to go over and see it. She had made a fictitious date with a girl friend for the benefit of her parents, and had then gone over by the midday boat. He had flown. And they had stayed at the same hotel, though on different floors. Which was where the devil of it all came in. Whatever it was in reality, it looked, on the face of it, just about as certain a cinch as could well be thought of.

"Archie pulled himself together, and explained the facts to Mordon, who began to laugh.

"'Really, Sir Archibald, you pain me,' he said. 'Perhaps I had better refresh your memory as to some of the choicer phrases in the letter. Passing lightly over the opening gambit of "My own darling boy," we arrive in a slowly increasing *crescendo* to the illuminating statement that "the memory of those two nights will be with me for the rest of my life."'

"Mordon put down the letter.

"'Now, Sir Archibald, as a man of the world, what would you understand by that sentence? I, of course, am only too relieved to hear that my unworthy suspicions are unfounded, but it is just possible that there are other people—to wit, the charming lady's husband—who will not be so trusting.'

"I gather Archie then went mad again, but Mordon must be used to scenes like that.

"'You can't, man,' Archie yelled, 'you can't! Don't you know she's going to have a baby very soon?'"

"'Yes, I was aware of that fact,' said Mordon placidly. 'And it was in anticipation of such an occurrence taking place that I have held up this letter until now. It has, I think you will admit, a somewhat higher market value at the present time than it would have had a few months ago. Any severe shock might be very prejudicial to her health. And,' continued this super-swine, 'there is one other little point that I would like you to bear in mind, Sir Archibald. I realise that matters being as they are at the moment it is more than likely that her husband would keep things to himself—at any rate, until it is all over. So that in the regrettable necessity of my having to send this letter to him, a copy will go by the same post to the lady with a covering note informing her who has the original.'

"To cut a long story short," went on, Ronald, "Archie had by this time realised what he was up against and demanded Mordon's price. It was forty thousand pounds."

"Great Scott!" I cried. "Forty thousand. It's iniquitous."

"Mordon is iniquitous."

"Can Maitland pay it?"

"He can and will, unless we can think of a way out. It's a sum even for him, but he's a wealthy man, and sooner than run the slightest risk of upsetting the woman in any way he is going to ante up. He regards the whole thing as being his fault for not tearing up the letter."

"How did this man Mordon get hold of it?"

"On that point Archie is not sure, though he thinks it must been through a valet that he sacked on the spot about a year ago. Anyway, Bob, how he got it doesn't really matter: he has got it. And for the life of me I can't think of any way out."

"When has the money to be paid by?"

"This day week," said Ronald savagely. "God! Bob, I'd give five thousand pounds to outwit that devil."

"Is there any use in going to the police?"

"Not an earthly. What can they do? In a blackmail case the only way of employing the police is for the victim to inveigle by some means the blackmailer into a room where the police are hidden. Archie has no chance of inveigling Mordon anywhere: all that side of his business is done in his own house. There's another thing that makes it impossible, too. Even supposing we could get the police to take action, we should be precipitating the very catastrophe which Archie wants at all costs to avoid. It might be kept as Mr. X. and Mr. Y. in the papers, but the husband bound to find out."

"Well, my definite advice, old boy, is that Maitland should g at once to the husband and make a clean breast of it. You say he's a decent fellow."

Ronald nodded.

"Quite. Though I don't know how he'd take it. He has—how shall I put it?—distinctly old-fashioned ideas. Anyway, there's no good thinking about it, Bob. Archie has absolutely made up his mind on the subject and nothing will move him. Sooner than do that he will stump up the forty thousand."

Ronald began pacing up and down the room.

"I'd do anything," he said, "anything criminal, even, to beat that devil. But he's so cursedly clever. I swear that it is easier to get into

Buckingham Palace than into his house. Every downstairs window is covered with steel bars, and at the slightest suspicious sound they let loose a mastiff that is the size of a donkey."

"You have been down there, then?"

"For the last three nights, trying to see if there's a possible chance of breaking in. Though what good one would do if one did I don't know. Even if I got into the holy of holies, what then?" said Ronald. "There's this grille to get through before you even begin to come to the safe."

"Pretty risky, old boy. It would be pure and simple burglary."

He looked me quietly in the face.

"I'd risk it, Bob: risk it every time, if I thought it had the smallest chance of being successful. I'd stick at nothing to do him down.

"If only there was some way of getting into the house, legitimately, so to speak. Through the front door, I mean. Then perhaps one might do something. But it's like entering a Masonic Lodge. I was hiding close by last night when a visitor arrived—evidently a manservant with something to sell. He rang the bell, and after a time the door, still on the chain, was cautiously opened a few inches, and the visitor was inspected. I heard him say: 'I've got some samples I want to show your master,' and after another prolonged inspection the man was admitted. That is clearly the Open Sesame, but it doesn't seem to help much unless you have got some samples. This fellow evidently had. I saw him counting notes the lamp-post by the gate after he'd come out ten minutes later."

"Just an idea, Ronald," I said. "Probably perfectly useless. Would it be impossible to get a search warrant?"

He shook his head.

"Quite," he answered. "No magistrate would sign one. And even if the police did manage to get one, what chance would they have of finding anything? Letters are very easily hidden, and they are his stock-in-trade. During the delay that would inevitably occur before they reached his room anything incriminating would have completely disappeared. No, bluff is the only thing. But how can we bluff?"

"Couldn't run him for being in possession of stolen property? After all, that letter was stolen from Maitland."

Ronald stood still and stared at me.

"It's an amazing thing, Bob," he said at length, "but do you know that that aspect of the case had not occurred to me? You're perfectly right. That letter is just as much stolen property as diamonds received by a fence. But—does it help us? Even to search a well-known fence's house the stolen goods have got to be traced to him. And it would be impossible in the case of that letter. Quite impossible. But—but—"

He paused, and suddenly the most extraordinary change came over his face.

"Bob," he yelled, "you blinking genius! And to think that all these long years I have misjudged you!"

He snatched up his hat, and dashed out, hurling a Parthian shaft from the door.

"Make no engagements. Stand by till I ring you up."

Mr. Richard Mordon was feeling at peace with the world. A sense of well-being pervaded his entire system. With one hand he was warming a glass of old brandy, in the other he held a Corona Corona. He had dined to his complete satisfaction. In honour of the occasion he had allowed himself a pint of Perrier Jouet. The shaded lights gleamed on the polished table; the flames from a log fire—it was distinctly chilly for so early in September—flickered in the grate.

Trade that day had been good: John Grant & Co., the old-established Scotch house, had excelled itself. A well-known sporting peer; two ladies of title with wealthy but mean husbands; and the heir to a big margarine business formed the main catch.

Not a bad bag, taking it all the way round, especially the margarine entrant. It would be many years before that young man got off the hook. But if these young idiots would go getting heavily into debt over some wretched chorus girl, then they deserved to be taught the error of their ways. In fact, as Mr. Mordon sipped his brandy a glow of self-righteousness spread over him. He was a public benefactor in teaching this youth and his like a well-deserved moral lesson. Only by sound business methods could the welfare and prosperity of the Old Country be built up.

The door opened softly, and Mr. Mordon glanced up. A pimply youth was standing in the entrance with an ingratiating smirk on his face.

"Well?" said Mr. Mordon.

"Following up your instructions, sir," began the youth.

"Shut the door," said Mr. Mordon curtly, "and come in. And be brief."

The youth obeyed.

"I again took the housemaid out to tea," he continued. "The nurse has already arrived, and the doctor is visiting her ladyship twice a day."

"You reported that before," said Mr. Mordon irritably. "Anything fresh?"

"Yes, sir." The youth took a few steps forward and became confidential. "Complications, sir: they're afraid of complications. His lordship is terribly worried."

"You're sure of that?"

"It's the talk of the servants' hall."

"When is it expected?"

"In a week or ten days, sir, but now they don't seem so sure. May be earlier."

Mr. Mordon examined the ash on his cigar.

"All right. That will do. Tell Mr. Benjamin to give you five pounds."

He waved the youth out of the room, and once again contemplated his cigar. Complications! excellent. That made his position even stronger, in case Sir Archibald attempted to haggle.

He glanced at his watch: nine o'clock. In another hour his man would be arriving. And then forty thousand pounds to cap the labours of the day.

He refilled his glass with brandy. Assuredly life was good. Mr. Mordon knew it was good. He felt it in every fibre of his being. And why was it good? Simply because he possessed the gift of making it so. Other people who specialised in his—er—line were stupid. They spoiled the ship for a ha'porth of tar. They didn't pay their informants well. At least, informants was the wrong word: those people who had useful information to sell in the interest of public morality—that was a better way of putting it. That man, for instance—Sir Archibald's valet—what was his name? The man who had brought him the letter. James Fulton: that was it. Fifty pounds had been the price he had paid the fellow. A big sum. Some men he knew would have tried to foist him off with a flyer. Richard Mordon did not do business on those lines. Hence the goods—the real goods. And it paid—paid every time. None of your messy little suburban scandals for him, but the big stuff.

Again the door opened this time it was Mr. Benjamin.

"It's O.K. about that flyer, Benjamin," said Mr. Mordon.

But Mr. Benjamin closed the door and advanced into the room.

"A man with samples, sir," he said quietly. "He asked me to give you this envelope as a proof of his *bona fides*. He said also that he heard about you from Fulton—Sir Archibald Maitland's late valet."

Mr. Mordon took the envelope and glanced at it. It had been

opened and was empty.

"The Earl of Bletcheley, Upper Bruton Street, W.," he read out thoughtfully. "And a coronet on the back. Where are the contents?"

"Those, sir, are the samples. Belman—that is the name of the earl's valet—thinks they may interest you. They are in his pocket at present."

The eyes of the two men met, and Mr. Benjamin nodded. "Very good, Benjamin. I will see this man. I will ring when I am ready, as usual, and should, by any chance, Sir Archibald Maitland arrive before I have finished, ask him to be good enough to wait a few moments."

Mr. Mordon made his way in leisurely fashion up the stairs to his office, feeling a glow of pleasurable anticipation. He did not know the writing on the envelope, but it was clearly feminine. Moreover, since it was in an educated hand, the writer, in view of the coronet, presumably belonged to the peerage. It was not a question of a servant borrowing notepaper. Which was all very, very good. The day was closing in a positive blaze of glory.

He took his keys from his pocket and opened the door of the grille surrounding his desk. Then picking up a copy of Debrett sat down.

Bletcheley, Earl of. Arthur George, 10th Earl. b. April 4th, 1900.

His eye skimmed down the page.

m. 1931 Lady Jane Mayhew, dau. of 5th Duke of Wessex.

So he was thirty-three years old and recently married. "Seat Grantchester Towers, Yorkshire. Clubs Marlborough, Turf."

Mr. Mordon closed the book. All very satisfactory so far, but there was one vital thing to find out—a thing not mentioned in that august tome. How stood Lord Bletcheley's finances?

From a drawer in his desk he extracted a small black book, which he opened at a section marked B. Methodical in all his ways, Mr. Mordon always made a note of the real financial condition of any celebrity or well-known man, if such information should happen to come his way. (Bitter experience had that him that the real condition was frequently very different from the apparent.) But in this case all was well. He could not remember when he had entered it up, but there it was. "Bletchley quite sound." He replaced the little book, and picking up the speaking tube, told Benjamin to bring the man up.

A few minutes later there entered a man who, to the expert eye of Mr. Mordon, was a typical gentleman's gentleman. The newcomer paused at seeing the somewhat alarming grille, but Benjamin having closed the door pushed him gently forward into a chair.

"Now, Belman," said Mr. Mordon, in his most affable voice. "That is the name, isn't it?"

"That's right, sir," said the man.

"Well, Belman, I gather that you think that the contents of this envelope addressed to Lord Bletcheley may interest me."

"You can bet your sweet life they will," answered Belman, with a coarse laugh.

"You are Lord Bletcheley's valet?"

"Was. Got the sack without notice this morning. Me, that's been with him five years. For doing a thing, too, that half the valets in London do."

"What was that?" Mr. Mordon always believed in adding to his store of knowledge.

"Wearing his evening clothes to go to a dance. Thought he was stayed put for the night, and walked straight into him as I came in."

"And he gave you the sack?"

"Without notice, and with a character that would keep me out of a Salvation Army band. But he didn't know what I'd found in the dress clothes."

He gave a cunning leer, and pointed at the envelope.

"Was it in the pocket?"

"No, sir. It was not. It was an old suit of his—one he hadn't worn for some time; and it had a hole in the inside breast pocket. I found that out as soon as I put my cigarette-case in, because it fell straight through into the bottom of the coat. And when I started to push it up again I realised that something else had fallen through before. So I got that out too. It was that letter."

"I see," said Mr. Mordon. "May I look at it?"

But now Belman began to get a little restive.

"Look here, sir," he said. "Fair's fair. You're sitting behind a great iron fence. How do I know if I pass this letter through to you that you won't keep it and tell me to go to blazes?"

"Because, my man, I don't do business that way. I gather it was from Sir Archibald Maitland's valet that you heard about me?"

"That's right."

"And didn't he tell you I treated him fairly?"

"Yes," said Belman reluctantly. "He did."

"Then why should I do otherwise with you? This grille is merely a measure of precaution for such occasions when I have other types of client to interview. However, if you prefer it, I will come to you."

He rose and came through into the room.

"That's all right, sir," said Belman sheepishly. "No offence meant. Here's the letter."

14, Delchester Square, W.1 Tuesday

Bimbo, my pet,—John has got to go to Berlin for three nights. From what Jane told me, she's going to stop with the male parent. What about it? The Five Feathers again. Not a chance of meeting anyone there.—Talie."

Mr Mordon studied it in silence for a while; then he glanced at Belman.

"Bimbo, I presume, refers to the Earl of Bletcheley?"

"That's right, sir. That's his nickname amongst all his friend Jane is, of course, her ladyship—his wife."

"And who is the writer of this? Who lives at 14, Delchester Square?"

The faintly contemptuous expression which gentlemen's gentlemen assume when dealing with lesser breeds without the law showed for a moment on Belman's face. What. social ignorance!

"14, Delchester Square," he said, "is the London residence of his Grace the Duke of Chiltington. He is the John referred to."

"And who is Talie?"

Belman permitted himself a smile of triumph.

"The duchess. Her real name is Natalie, but her friends call her Talie."

"Then this letter"—Mr. Mordon's voice was shaking with excitement—"this letter is a suggestion for a clandestine love affair?"

Belman stared at him.

"What else could it be? An invitation to go bird's-nesting?"

But Mr. Mordon ignored the impertinence. The stupendous nature of his haul had almost stunned him. A duchess and earl! It was incredible. Sir Archibald's mere baronet seemed very small beer. A duchess and an earl! What a day! What an amazing day!

"Where is the 'Five Feathers'?" he asked.

Belman took a packet of cigarettes from his pocket and lit one. "Somewhere in the Malvern district," he answered. "Look here, Mr Mordon, it's like this. I can put two and two together as well as anybody. If you look at the envelope you'll see that half the stamp and the postmark are missing. But it doesn't require that to date the letter. I know when her ladyship went to stop with her father, and the duke went to Berlin. It was the middle of July last. And it was then that the earl went away for two nights without me. Now I'd had my suspicions for some time—you see that word 'again' in the letter..."

"What had caused your suspicions?" asked Mr. Mordon.

Belman smiled—a faintly contemptuous smile. "You may take it from me, Mr. Mordon, that there's precious little goes on amongst that lot that we don't know. And though I had no proof like that letter, I'd been wondering for quite a while. So when we were staying down in Sussex for Goodwood I put a few questions to the duchess's maid, and found that her Grace had been away at the same time, by herself. She'd been staying with a friend near Malvern."

"How did the maid know that?"

"The duchess told her so. And there was a Malvern label on her trunk."

Mr. Mordon rubbed his hands together. Better and better. This man Belman was one after his own heart.

"So there won't be much difficulty in locating the inn," continued Belman. "And then you've got your case complete. Now then, sir, how much?"

Mr. Mordon hesitated. Even with this crowning gem added to his collection he ran true to type. "How much do you want?"

"A hundred pounds," said Belman promptly. "Not a penny less. And it's worth ten times that to you."

Which was certainly true, though it was five minutes before Mr. Mordon finally agreed to the figure.

"You needn't bother to count them," he said, handing over a wad of notes. "They're new, as you can see. All that you've got to do is to look at the first and last numbers."

But Belman was leaving nothing to chance. Slowly and laboriously he turned them over while Mr. Mordon watched him with growing irritation. He was in a fever of impatience to gloat in secret over his latest purchase.

At last Belman was satisfied, and pocketing the notes he rose to say "Good evening, Mr. Mordon," he said. "And I don't know which of us is the bigger scoundrel."

The door closed behind him, leaving the owner of the house frowning at such a piece of monstrous insolence. But the frown soon disappeared as he once again read the letter in his hand. A duchess and an earl! It staggered him. Properly handled, this ought to be worth eighty thousand at least—perhaps more. And he was just passing through the door of the grille to go to his safe when the sounds of a commotion below made him pause in surprise and annoyance. A man of orderly habits, he disliked anything in the nature of a scene. Was it Belman making trouble? He thought he recognised his voice. He hastily unlocked the safe and deposited the letter inside.

The noise grew louder. He could hear footsteps on the stairs. And the next moment, to his intense indignation, the door was flung open and a positive army of people poured into the room. There were a police-sergeant and three constables, two of whom were holding Belman by the arms. There was a good-looking young man in plain clothes whose face seemed vaguely familiar to him, whilst in the rear of the cavalcade Benjamin hopped about like an agitated hen.

"What on earth is the meaning of this?" spluttered Mr. Mordon.

"Caught him on your very doorstep, sir," said the sergeant cheerfully.

"Caught who?" said Mr. Mordon.

"Belman. His lordship's valet."

He nodded towards the young man in plain clothes, and a peculiar empty feeling began to assail Mr. Mordon in the pit of his stomach. It was one thing to deal with duchesses and earls on paper: it was somewhat different to have the actual earl in question in the room with a posse of police.

"What has he done?" He forced himself to speak casually.

"Stolen a lot of things from his lordship's house," cried the sergeant. "And quite by chance he was seen by his lordship getting into the train at Charing Cross. What's the matter, Smith?"

"Just found these in his pocket, Sergeant," said one of the constables, coming forward with the bundle of notes.

"You precious scoundrel," cried the sergeant. "Something more of yours, my lord."

The young man shook his head.

"Give the devil his due," he said, "for he's not guilty on that score. I don't know where he got 'em from, but they're not mine."

"How did you get these notes, Belman?" asked the sergeant sternly. "Come on, my lad. It will be better for you in the long run to make a clean breast of it."

And now Mr. Mordon's stomach was positively heaving.

"If you want to know, Sergeant," he said in a shaking voice, "I gave them to him. I wanted the poor fellow to have a fresh start in life."

He threw an agonised look at Belman. Surely the fool would take his cue. But Belman was staring at his late master, and suddenly, to Mr. Mordon's speechless horror, he took a step forward.

"Fresh start be blowed," he said. "I'm sorry, my lord, more sorry than I can say that I've done what I have. But I was fed up with being sacked. I got this hundred pounds for one of your lordship's letters that I've just sold him."

"You fool," screamed Mr. Mordon. "You blasted fool!"

But no one paid any attention to him.

"One of my letters?" said the Earl in a bewildered voice. "What the deuce are you talking about?"

"A letter from the Duchess of Chiltington to you, my lord," said Belman in a low voice. "I found it in the lining of your coat."

And at last the earl seemed to understand.

"You damned swine!" he roared. "You infernal blackguard! By God! I'll murder you for that."

"Hold hard, my lord," said the sergeant quietly. "This wants looking into." He turned to Mr. Mordon. "Has this man sold you a letter of his lordship's?"

Mr. Mordon moistened his dry lips, but seemed unable to speak.

"Come, sir, come," went on the sergeant sternly. "Yes or no?"

"Yes," muttered the other at length.

"And you bought it, knowing it to be stolen property?" He motioned to two of the constables. "You'll come along to the station, if you plea and explain to the inspector. I shall want you as well as Belman."

"But, Sergeant," stammered Mr. Mordon, "I assure you I can make the matter clear."

"Then you can do it to the inspector," said the sergeant curtly

"But I have an important engagement tonight."

"It must wait. Take him away; I'll be along shortly with Belman. One minute, though. He might destroy the letter on the way. Give it to me. I'll take charge of it."

"It's in my safe, Sergeant."

"Then open your safe. Come, sir, or do you wish me to take your keys from you by force?"

Stumbling like an old man, Mr. Mordon went to the safe and opened it. His mind was seething chaos. Stolen property! Police stations! And what was the sergeant saying now? Leave it open. Preposterous! Impossible!

"I will be responsible for all the contents."

The man's odious voice seemed to come from a great distance Was it all some hideous nightmare? He, Richard Mordon, take to the police station. And, most dreadful thought of all—he could not explain. There was no explanation; it was stolen property.

The sergeant watched him as he left the room pinioned between the two constables. Then he turned to Benjamin.

"Clear out," he snapped. "If I want you, I'll send for you."

The door closed. Mr. Benjamin's footsteps died away. And silence fell on the house a strange scene was enacted in Mr. Mordon's private study—a performance which would have caused that gentleman, had he seen it, such a rush of blood to the head that death would have been instantaneous. For a well-known member of the peerage, a sergeant, a constable, and a recently-sacked valet were sobbing gently with laughter in one another's arms.

"Bob," said the Duke of Chiltington, removing his constable's helmet, "you were magnificent."

"Nothing," I remarked, with pride, "to what I was during the private interview."

"Well, chaps, we must get on with it," said Ronald, unbuttoning his sergeant's tunic, and removing a false moustache.

"What is the first of the doings?" asked the Earl of Bletcheley.

"Find Archie's letter. And then burn every other damned blackmailing document in that safe."

"Give me Talie's letter to Bimbo," said the duke with a grin. "I want to have it framed."

And for those who require the epilogue, I cannot do better than to quote *verbatim* a paragraph from the *Daily Observer*.

Outrage on City Man Well-Known Financier

Tarred and Feathered

A dastardly outrage was perpetrated the night before last on Mr. Richard Mordon, the well-known financier. Mr. Mordon, who is a much-respected citizen of Sevenoaks, was discovered early yesterday morning wandering through some hop fields not far from Tonbridge completely covered from head to foot with tar and feathers. He is still somewhat dazed and incoherent, and from inquiries made at his house it was found that he was far too indisposed to see anyone. It is understood that the difficulty of finding out what happened has been greatly increased by the fact that the miscreants removed his false teeth.

.

The Empty House

Ronald Standish glanced at the card he held in his hand, and then at our visitor.

"Sit down, Mr. Sinclair," he said, "and let's hear the trouble. But first let me introduce my friend, Mr. Miller."

I looked at the old gentleman with some curiosity as he carefully deposited one of those antiquated hard felt hats, so beloved of our forefathers, on a chair. Pink-faced, with a small white beard, he was almost bald. He wore an old-fashioned frock-coat, and pepper-and-salt trousers. A massive chain adorned his waistcoat, whilst the large gold watch attached to it, which he consulted as he sat down, showed that he was certainly no pauper, whatever his clothes might be. He looked a typical example of a well-to-do retired tradesman who had high tea instead of dinner, called his wife "Mother" and handed round the plate in church on Sunday. In short, one of the last persons I should have expected to see in the room, and the faintest perceptible rise of his eyebrows showed that Ronald was thinking the same.

"I have been told about you, Mr. Standish," Mr. Sinclair began in a precise, rather mincing voice, "by a gentleman for whom you acted with some success a few months ago—Mr. Harper. And though I do not approve of private detectives—I consider the police, for whose upkeep I pay, should be perfectly adequate to protect me—I have decided on this occasion to consult you. To start with, what is your fee?"

It was not an auspicious beginning, and I stole a look at Ronald, whose face, however, was expressionless.

"I think that before we trouble you to continue, Mr. Sinclair," he said, "we had better understand one another. In the first place, I am not a private detective in the accepted sense of the word. If a case amuses me I may look into it; if it doesn't, I don't. In the second place,

I have no fee. If I decide to take up your case, I may, if they are heavy, charge you out-of-pocket expenses. But you must get quite clearly into your mind that, as you do not contribute towards my upkeep in the same way that you do for the police, it is I who am conferring the favour on you, should I act for you, and not you on me."

I suppressed a smile. Rarely have I seen such a rapid change in anyone's demeanour as took place in our visitor's. All the pomposity vanished as if by magic, and what was left was a little old man, rather pathetically frightened.

"I'm sure, Mr. Standish," he stammered, "I didn't mean to offend you. I had no idea...I...I..."

Standish smiled genially.

"That's all, right, Mr. Sinclair," he said. "Don't think about it any more. Now let's hear what has sent you to me."

"I do hope you will be able to assist me, Mr. Standish," he said earnestly. "I have been to the police and they don't seem to take it seriously."

Ronald pushed a box of cigarettes towards him.

"Thank you, no. I don't smoke. I suppose I'd better tell you all the facts that led up to the present situation."

"If you please," said Ronald briefly.

"I am a retired provision merchant, Mr. Standish," he began. "Many years ago I started in a small way, and by hard work I succeeded in building up what I may fairly claim to be one of the best-known chains of stores in the Midlands. I have a branch in almost every decent-sized town within a radius of thirty miles from Leamington, and up to a few weeks ago I retained full control in my own hands. But we none of us get younger, Mr. Standish, and some time ago my doctor warned me that I must take things easier. And so, to cut a long story short, I decided to give up active participation in the business, and enjoy a little well-earned leisure in the time that is left to me."

His self-assurance was returning to him, and I wondered what on earth this distinctly boring preamble could be leading up to.

"Now, while I was still in harness," he went on, "I had continued to live in the same house where I had first started. I had added a bit to it here and there, but I had never bothered to move, though my sister, with whom I live, had often suggested the advisability of doing so It had become, I admitted, hardly suitable in size or position, but you know what it is, Mr. Standish, to undertake all the discomfort and upheaval of a move. At any rate, I'd kept on putting her off on the plea that it was very convenient for my work, and that I hadn't got the time to bother with moving.

"Well, of course, when I finally retired that excuse no longer held water, and one day about two months ago she came to me with the announcement that she'd found the very thing for us—a big semi-detached house about two miles out of Leamington. The other half was let to an old lady called Miss Burton—who was almost an invalid.

"So I went and had a look at it, and I must say I quite endorsed my sister's opinion. The rooms were large and comfortable, and the house stood well back from the main road so that passing traffic would not disturb us. At the same time buses passed frequently, which is a very important matter where servants are concerned in the country."

I glanced at Ronald, but his face only expressed polite attention, and I remembered his invariable rule of letting people tell their story in their own way, however verbose.

"And so, Mr. Standish, I decided to take it. A lot of work was necessary as the house had been empty for some time. It had to be completely repapered, and I wanted another bathroom put in. However, I went into the whole question with a good architect and plans were prepared.

"Now, my first intention had been to rent it, and the house agents with whom I was doing the business—Messrs. Manfield and Pretty— were quite agreeable. Miss Burton, I understood, rented her half, and I proposed to do the same. And so we agreed provisionally at the figure of two hundred and fifty a year. Mark you, Mr. Standish, nothing was signed yet, and not deeming it necessary I hadn't even taken the trouble to get the first refusal.

"Judge of my surprise then when one morning Manfield rang me up to say that someone else was after the house and would I go round and see him at once. I did.

"'A very strange thing, Mr. Sinclair,' he said as I entered his office. 'There, has been no one after that house for years, and now, it has suddenly become popular. And the trouble is that, as far as you are concerned, it is more popular with my other client than with you.'

"'You mean he's prepared to pay a higher rent?' I cried.

"'Exactly, Mr. Sinclair.'

"'What have you done about it?' I asked him.

"'I haven't closed with him, of course. That wouldn't have been fair without first letting you know. But business is business, isn't it?'

"'Who is this newcomer?' I demanded.

"Naturally he refused to tell me, but I gathered it was no one I knew. And though I was annoyed, I saw that Manfield was, perfectly right. He was acting on behalf of his own client, the landlord, and it was up to him to get the best terms he could. And then I suddenly had an idea. What about buying outright? It was almost certain that the owner would prefer it, and it was more than likely it would put my rival out of the running. And so I suggested it to Manfield, who jumped at the notion.

"'I must, of course, inform the other gentleman who is after it,' he said, 'and I will let you know the result.'

"The price I had offered was four thousand five hundred pounds, and two days later Manfield rang me up to say that it, was mine at that sum. The other man wouldn't contemplate buying at all. And so work started right away.

"All this," proceeded our visitor, "must seem very irrelevant, I fear, but I thought it best to tell you everything that could have any possible bearing on the extraordinary events of the last few weeks. All my life I have endeavoured to do my duty as a law-abiding citizen. So far as I know, I have not an enemy in the world. And now, just as I am preparing to settle down and enjoy a few years of peace, I am subjected to what I can only describe as a series of dastardly attacks."

Ronald leaned forward attentively.

"Do you mean physical attacks, Mr. Sinclair?"

"I do, sir," said the other individual, "though really those were the least annoying. But when it came to my poor sister being subjected to insult and rudeness then I decided it was time to consult you, since the police seem unable to do anything. This persecution—for I can call it nothing else, Mr. Standish—started before the workmen even commenced the alterations."

He produced a bulky pocket-book and extracted a slip of paper. "This," he remarked, handing it to Ronald, "arrived by the first post one morning."

I got up and looked over Ronald's shoulder. On the paper, which looked as if it was a leaf torn out of a cheap notebook, were scrawled the words:

As you value your life do not go to Holmlea.

The writing was illiterate, there was no signature, and for a few moments Ronald studied it carefully through a magnifying glass. Then he put it on the desk in front of him.

"Holmlea," he said, "is presumably the name of your new house?"

"It is, Mr. Standish. I thought I'd mentioned that."

"And what did you do on receipt of this?" asked Ronald.

"Well, Mr. Standish, to be perfectly frank, I did nothing. I didn't wish to alarm my sister unnecessarily, and at first I thought it was some stupid hoax, or that someone was trying to get his own back on me. I said a little while ago that I had, so far as I know, no enemies, but I ought perhaps to qualify that statement a little. You see, I am a magistrate, and in the ordinary course I of events it may he that I have incurred the enmity of someone who has come before the Bench."

"Quite, Mr. Sinclair," said Ronald. "One more question before you proceed. Did you notice what the postmark was on the envelope?"

"I did. It was Warwick, which, as you know, is close to Leamington."

Ronald nodded and made a note.

"Go on, Mr. Sinclair."

"As I say, I took no notice. I very nearly tore it up, but I finally decided to keep it, though I mentioned it to no one. The workmen started next day, and the matter had almost slipped from my mind when, happening to go to Holmlea to see how they were progressing, I saw an envelope addressed to me on the drawing-room mantelpiece. And the writing was the same as before. There was no stamp. It had evidently been left by hand. I opened it and found this."

Once again he extracted a piece of paper from his pocket-book and passed it across to us. It was the same sort of paper as before, and this time the following words were written:

You will have one more warning. If you don't take that, God help you.

"I called the foreman," proceeded Mr. Sinclair, "and asked him if he knew anything about the note. He was an honest, conscientious man who had done work for me in the past, and I am convinced he would have told me if he had known anything. But he was just as much in the dark as I was. He said that he had seen the note on the mantelpiece when he started work that morning, and as it was addressed to me he had thought no more about it. And he was positive it had not been there overnight. At my request he got all his men together and asked them if they could throw any light on the matter, but they one and all professed complete ignorance of it."

"This grows interesting, Mr. Sinclair," said Ronald thoughtfully. "I suppose you didn't think of asking the foreman if he was certain that the front and back doors were locked and all the windows bolted when he left the night before?"

"But I did, Mr. Standish," cried the old gentleman triumphantly "You don't want to be a celebrated detective to see the importance of that."

"True," murmured Ronald gravely. "And what did he say?"

"Unfortunately, nothing helpful. He could swear to both doors being locked, but he was not prepared to swear to all the window being bolted."

"Did you show him the contents of the letter?"

"No. I thought it better not to. But this time I took it, with the first one, and showed them both to the police. I went to Inspector Crawley, whom I knew personally from my position on the Bench, and asked him what he thought. And he was quite positive that the whole thing was a stupid hoax perpetrated by someone who had a grudge against me.

"'What possible reason can anyone have, Mr. Sinclair,' he said, 'for trying to keep you out of the house? It's absurd on the face of it. Depend upon it, it's some man of low mentality who hast hit on this way of trying to frighten you. It's like the old stories one used to hear of threatening letters sent to people, signed with a skull and crossbones.'

"So at that I left it, until a week later the third thing happened. And this time it was not confined to a letter. I was reading my paper after breakfast, when the architect was shown in, and I saw at once that something had happened.

"'Will you come at once with me to Holmlea?' he said. 'I've got my car outside. I should like you to see the state of affairs for yourself.'

"He said no more during the drive there, but when we arrived it was obvious that things were not going well. The men were all standing about doing no work, whilst the foreman, looking very worried, was at the gate.

"'I've left everything, sir,' he said to my companion, 'for Mr. Sinclair to see—same as you told me.'

"Well, Mr. Standish," continued the old gentleman, "to say that I was dumbfounded is no more than the literal truth. The place was like a bear garden. Pails of distemper had been thrown down the stairs; the new papers that they had put up in one or two rooms had been pulled off and hung in festoons; rubbish that had been collected into neat little heaps now littered the entire house. It looked as if a party of children had been let loose indoors with orders to do the maximum amount of wilful damage they could.

"'It's incredible, Mr. Sinclair,' said the architect. 'In the whole course of my career I have never seen anything like it before.'

"'Nor me,' said the foreman. 'And while I think of it, sir,' he continued, 'there's another letter for you on the drawing-room mantelpiece.'"

He passed the third over to us, and this time it was more brief.

The third warning and the last.

"Once again it had been left by hand," continued Mr. Sinclair, "and once again no one could throw any light on how it had got there."

"Excellent," cried Ronald. "This is really one of the most intriguing stories I have heard for a long while. What did you do?"

"I asked the architect to send his car back to Leamington and get hold of Inspector Crawley. This had gone beyond a question of a stupid hoax, and something drastic would have to be done about it. He came at once and looked at the damage, and though he didn't admit it I could see he was completely nonplussed.

"'I'll have a man on duty here every night,' he said, 'and then we'll see if these goings-on continue. And, seeing that it's come to this, sir,' he continued, 'it's just on the cards that I've solved it. This house has been empty for years, and it may be that tramps have been in the habit of dossing down in it at night. And now they're angry at losing their shelter.'

"So at that it was left. The damage was repaired and work started once more. But though I had said nothing to the inspector, an idea had struck me and I went off to see Manfield. Was possible that my unsuccessful rival was adopting this childish method of getting his own back? But Manfield would have none of it.

"'Out of the question, Mr. Sinclair,' he said emphatically. 'Almost as much out of the question as a bishop robbing the poor-box in church. He was a perfectly respectable individual who saw Holmlea and happened to like it. But beyond a little natural disappointment when I told him you'd bought it, he showed no feeling on the matter. I mean there was no sign of any resentment.'"

"I hope I am making everything clear, Mr. Standish?"

"I wish everyone who sat in that chair was equally lucid," said Ronald.

"From that day a policeman was on duty every night," continued Mr. Sinclair, "and nothing happened. The work proceeded apace and I began to think that the inspector's theory was right. An then one morning about three weeks later came the next thing. The new bathroom had been finished except that some of the plumbing had still to be done, and unfortunately connecting up the waste pipe was one of the uncompleted jobs. Well, Mr. Standish, I don't know if you have any idea as to the damage that can be done in a night when a tap is left running full on after the bath has overflowed? I certainly hadn't until I saw Holmlea. The hall was inches deep in water; the plaster had come off the ceilings of most of the rooms, and several of the new wallpapers had peeled off.

"Now, of course, this may have been a genuine accident. The constable on duty heard nothing and saw nothing the whole night. And yet I can hardly believe that even the most careless plumber would be such a fool as to leave the water running into a bath when he finished work. The man naturally swore that he hadn't, but I quite realise he would have sworn that in any event. And so it is possible that it was an accident."

"If so, it was a very instructive accident," said Ronald quietly.

"It was a very costly one," said the old gentleman ruefully.. "It threw back the work at least a fortnight. And what was worse, Mr. Standish, the workmen began to get jumpy. Thought there was something queer about the house, and really, I didn't blame them. In fact, had it not been that I had already paid the money, I think I should have backed out of it myself.

"And now we come to a week ago. This time it was nothing to do with the house, and perhaps it had nothing to do with the affair at all. We have at one crossroads an automatic traffic control of the usual red and green light variety, and I pass the spot every evening going to the club. Last Tuesday I got there as usual, and seeing the green light showing I proceeded to cross the road. I was half-way across when a small van drove straight at me, though the red light was showing as far as he was concerned.. I give you my word, Mr. Standish, he missed me by inches as I jumped for my life. Then, absolutely disregarding the traffic signal which still showed STOP, he shot over the crossroads and disappeared, narrowly escaping a collision with another car. Unfortunately there was no policeman there—he has been dispensed with since the automatic device was installed—so there was nothing to be done. And I was so upset I could not even get the number of the van. But I am convinced, sir, in my own mind," he went on emphatically, "that it was a deliberate attempt to murder me."

"I shouldn't be at all surprised if you are right," said Standish gravely. "Your story grows increasingly interesting, Mr. Sinclair."

"I reported the matter to the inspector, but he was powerless. Moreover, he ridiculed the idea that it was anything more than an ordinary case of dangerous driving. And so I had to leave it, since there was no chance of catching the blackguard. Might I have a drink of water, Mr. Standish? All this talking makes my throat dry."

I got him a glass from the sideboard, and he took a sip. "Thank you," he said. "Because now we are coming to the incident which decided me to come and see you. It occurred yesterday morning. I had been for a stroll in town, and when I returned for lunch I found my sister in a state of terrible agitation—in fact, she was almost in hysterics, so much so that for some time she was unable to tell me what had happened. But at last I got it out of her. It appeared that she, too, had been for a walk, and had come back by a road which is very little used. Half-way along it she became aware that two rough men were following her. Considerably alarmed, she quickened her steps, but it was useless. They overtook her—one on each side, and one of them seized her arm.

"'Listen here, old woman,' he said to her, 'you tell that brother of yours to quit the idea of going to Holmlea, or it will be the worse for both of you.'

"Then they disappeared, leaving her half fainting with fright. And nothing that I could say pacified her. It had, of course, been impossible to prevent her knowing about the damage that had been done to the house, though I had told her nothing about the three notes. But when this happened to her she at once put two and two together, and refused to accept any more my explanation that it had been the work of some irresponsible tramp. In short, Mr. Standish, she is thoroughly alarmed and flatly refuses to go to Holmlea at all, which means that I lose my money, and, what annoys me more even, these scoundrels, whoever they are, have succeeded in doing what they set out to do."

The little man's jaw stuck out, and for a moment one could se the underlying character that had built up that chain of stores.

"Can you help me, Mr. Standish?"

"I will most certainly try to," said Ronald warmly. "But there are one or two questions I would like to ask you. Is that policeman still on duty at night?"

"So far as I know—yes."

"Are you a person of fairly fixed habits? For instance, do you usually go to the club at the same time every day?"

He nodded.

"Generally about half-past four. You mean, that the driver of that van might have known that fact?"

"Not might—but did know that fact," said Ronald dryly. "Now Mr. Sinclair, I want you to obey my instructions implicitly. Tell your architect to stop work; say that you've changed your mind about going to live at Holmlea; have a For Sale board put up in the garden; and, lastly—and this is important—tell the inspector you no longer want a policeman there at night."

The old gentleman looked at him with growing indignation. "But that will be giving in all along the line," he cried. "I intend to live in Holmlea."

"Possibly," said Ronald. "But unless you do what I tell you the betting is all against your ever doing so. The next time that van won't miss you."

"Oh! I see, just pretence."

"Yes." answered Ronald curtly; "but it's got to be pretence that will carry conviction that those are your genuine intentions."

"But what do you make of it, Mr. Standish?" he asked pathetically. "Why on earth should I of all people be signalled out for this persecution? Who are the scoundrels?"

"Well, you may take one thing from me, my dear sir," said Ronald gravely, "they are not tramps. You have been moving in deep waters, Mr. Sinclair; how deep, at the moment, I am not prepared to say. Do not tell anyone that you've come to me. Do just what I've said, and we'll see if we can solve your little problem. And one other word—should we by chance meet in Leamington, you don't know me. Good day to you."

The door closed behind him, and Ronald rubbed his hands together.

"We're going to have some fun, Bob," he said. "Put some rubber shoes in your bag and a gun. We'll motor down to Leamington this afternoon for a preliminary survey of the land."

"Got any ideas?" I asked.

"Only one," he answered. "And that is that the episode of the bath water is singularly instructive."

And not another word could I get out of him.

Holmlea proved to be much as I had pictured it, as we drove past that afternoon. It stood some forty yards back from the road, and a hedge separated its garden from that of Burnlea, which was the other half of the house. As yet Mr. Sinclair had not had time to carry out all his instructions, and work was still proceeding. But a board had been erected facing the road announcing that it was to be Let or Sold, and Ronald returned to Leamington in high spirits.

"I'll just ring up the old boy," he said, "and find out about the policeman."

He returned in a few moments even more pleased than before.

"Excellent," he cried. "The men are going to be discharged this evening, and the policeman removed. So it's just possible, Bob, that our vigil tonight may produce some result. If it doesn't, we shall have to try again."

"In Holmlea, presumably." I remarked.

He nodded, and summoning a waiter ordered two pints.

"Just so," he said. "And so I fear you will have to entertain yourself until it's dark enough to go there."

"Where are you going?" I asked.

"For a stroll," he answered. "There are one or two little things I wish to clear up, and you can't help me."

He finished his beer, and left the hotel whilst I sat on, puzzling over the problem. The whole thing seemed so strange and pointless. What could there be about Holmlea, which, so far as I had been able to see, was like scores of other houses, that so interested these mysterious individuals? Could it be that there was booty hidden somewhere in the house; the proceeds perhaps of some old burglary? That the burglars had just completed their sentence and now wanted leisure to recover their loot? Or was the inspector's theory of tramps correct in spite of Ronald's statement to the contrary?

Time dragged by slowly, and at last I went in to dinner. I knew there was no use waiting for Ronald: past experience had taught me what "one or two little things to clear up" meant in his case. And, sure enough, it was not until nearly ten that he appeared again, but a glance at his face showed that the clearing up had been successful. He was in a state of barely-suppressed excitement, and that for him was pretty remarkable. He was not a man who often allowed his feelings to show.

"A most interesting evening, Bob," he remarked. "And I trust there will be no falling off during the rest of the night. Has my good friend McIver arrived?"

"The Scotland Yard fellow?" I cried. "I haven't seen him. So you've found out something?"

"Even more than I anticipated, old boy," he grinned. "Assuredly it was lucky in more senses than one that our worthy Mr. Sinclair came to us this morning. Hallo! here is McIver at last."

"Evening, Mr. Standish," said a burly-looking man who had come up to the table. "I came as soon as I could. Are you sure you're right?"

"Absolutely certain, Mac. I went and called this evening, and there was no mistaking that deformed hand."

"Well, it's going to be a damned good night's work if we catch 'em," said McIver. "What about the local police?"

"I've seen Inspector Crawley myself," said Ronald, "and I told him we don't want an army of men. The small fry don't count when all is said and done, and if we have posses of policemen marching up the road we'll be stung. So he's sending half a dozen of his best men by a roundabout route and he's coming with himself. In fact—here he is."

The two inspectors shook hands, and then Ronald glanced at his watch.

"Time we went," he said. "Put on your rubbers, Bob, and bring your gun, in case it's wanted."

I rejoined them a few minutes later, and we all got into a waiting taxi.

"Stop half a mile short of Holmlea," Ronald told the driver as we started off.

And now I was beginning to feel excited. That something big was afoot was obvious, though what it was I had no idea. But a man in McIver's position would not have come post-haste from London for some trifling larceny.

"'Ere you are, gents," said the driver, pulling up. "'Olmlea's just round the bend there in front of you."

We paid him off, and then Ronald took charge.

"Got to do a bit of trespassing," he said, "for we can't possibly go along the road. Follow me. I explored the route this evening."

He turned into some undergrowth, and silently led the way. A slight wind was stirring the branches of the trees, and twice during our walk a motor-bus rumbled past on the road a few yards away. The night was dark, and there was no moon, which made the going difficult, but at length he stopped and we closed up on him.

"There's the house," he whispered, "just in front of us. I've got the key of the front door, but the difficulty is going to be in getting over this bit of open. They may have scouts round the place."

"You get the door open, Mr. Standish," muttered McIver "then we'll dodge across singly."

Like a shadow Ronald vanished, and a minute later a faint click told us he had been successful. Then one by one we flitted across the lawn and joined him in the hall.

The house was deathly silent. Not even the ticking of a clock could be heard.

"Be careful how you walk," whispered Ronald. "There may still be buckets and things about."

On tiptoe we followed him, until we found ourselves in a small vestibule leading off the hall. In front of us were steps going down to the kitchen premises, which we could dimly see by the light of a street lamp outside.

And then commenced an eerie vigil. No one spoke. No one even whispered. We merely stood and waited—I, at any rate, with no idea what for. And it was just as very faintly in the distance we heard a church clock chime midnight that a sudden sharp click came from below. I felt Ronald stiffen. The moment had come.

Scarcely breathing, we stood there. Stealthy footsteps were coming up the stairs. They passed our door, and continued up the next flight. And it was then that I became aware for the first time of a peculiar rhythmical noise that seemed to shake the whole house. *Thump: thump: thump*—it went on without cessation, just as if some big engine was working.

But another sound distracted my attention. The bath tap had been turned on above. The splash of water was clearly audible, though it did not prevent us hearing a creak on the stairs as the mysterious visitor descended again.

"Catch him as he passes us," breathed Ronald. "Silently, if possible."

But that was not to be. In the dim light we impeded one another, and the man as we sprang on him let out one wild shout before a heavy blow on the back of his head stunned him.

"Move!" shouted Ronald. "Before they get the opening closed." We fell down the kitchen stairs, and into the scullery. Through a hole in one wall light was streaming, and we dashed through to find ourselves in a long passage. And the thumping noise had ceased.

We raced along and burst open a door at the end. And then things happened. I had a fleeting vision of a hall with an oil lamp, swinging from the ceiling, of two furious-looking men and a wizened-up old woman standing underneath it. Then something red-hot seared through my chest, and I felt myself falling into blackness, punctuated by the crack of revolver shots.

★★★★★★

"My dear old Bob—thank God he didn't kill you. The bullet missed everything vital."

Ronald was leaning over the foot of the bed, in a strange room when I opened my eyes, and a hospital nurse was hovering around. I was bandaged up tightly, but otherwise I felt all right.

"Do you mind explaining what happened?" I said.

"You got plugged through the chest by one of the most notorious criminals in Europe, who is now safely under lock and key with several of his associates."

"But how did you spot it in the first place?" I demanded.

"You are not to tire yourself," said the nurse, coming forward.

"I promise I won't," I cried. "But I shall start biting the bedclothes unless this old scoundrel satisfies my curiosity."

Ronald grinned.

"Don't worry, nurse. I can do it very quickly. Well, Bob, from the word 'go' I dismissed the idea of tramps being at the bottom of it. One thing alone ruled them out absolutely. Tramps are not in the financial position to hire motor cars to kill people with. And so we were confronted with the plains bald fact that some person or persons were prepared to go to almost any lengths to prevent Holmlea being occupied. Obviously it had nothing to do with Sinclair himself. He only came into the matter because he was the prospective householder.

"Now, why do you want to keep a house unoccupied? For one of two reasons: either that you wish to use it yourself surreptitiously, or because you're afraid the occupier will inconvenience you in some way. And of the two the second is the more likely.

"To carry on again, who were the people most likely to be inconvenienced by the tenant of Holmlea? Quite obviously the tenants of Burnlea, and at an early stage in the proceedings I determined to have a close look at the invalid lady, Miss Burton. Because it seemed well-nigh impossible that a genuine old lady, however passionately she desired privacy, would hire a gang of hooligans to wreck someone else's property.

"Then came the episode of the bath, which, as I said, was very instructive, because it clinched almost for certain that in Burnlea lay the seat of the trouble, and that there was some communication between the two houses. While there was no constable on watch it didn't matter what damage they did, since it could be attributed to a man entering the house from outside. But once the policeman was there that was impossible. He would know that no one had got in from outside. And so the only damage they could do was what would appear accidental. They couldn't again upset the whitewash, for then it would be known that someone had been in the house, and if he hadn't come from outside he must have come from inside: that is, from Burnlea. But with the bath no one need have been in the house at all. It could be attributed to a workman's carelessness.

"Well, that's about all. When I left you that evening at Leamington I made a few changes in my personal appearance, and called at Burnlea. I did not see Miss Burton, but I did see the butler, and one glance was enough. He had a curiously distorted right hand, the result of a knife brawl some years ago, and I recognised him at once. It was a gentleman called Galliday whose speciality was coining, and the whole thing became clear. Coining is by no manner of me a silent job, as you heard yourself last night."

"You mean that thumping noise," I cried.

"Exactly. And they couldn't see old Sinclair and his sister standing for that either by day or night. So I got on to McIver, and the rest you know. The old invalid lady was one of the most dangerous anarchists alive—a Frenchman called Pierre Martin. In fact, the whole gang was just about as pestilential a sore as you'd find anywhere. That they would again try the bath trick never occurred to me; I wanted to hear that engine going so as to be absolutely certain."

He paused suddenly, a horrified expression on his face.

"What is it, old boy?" I cried.

"My dear Bob," he said, "something has just dawned on me. In the excitement of the moment nobody has turned the bath water off!"

The Tidal River

"The very person I've been wanting to see. I rang up your rooms, and your man told me you'd probably be dining in your club."

I glanced up from my coffee. A man by the name of Mervyn Davidson was standing by our chairs. I only knew him slightly, but Ronald Standish had shot with him once or twice.

"Could you possibly come down to my place tomorrow," continued Davidson, "or are you too busy?"

"Do you mean professionally?" asked Ronald.

"Yes," said the other, pulling up a chair. "Do you mind, at any rate, if I tell you the story?"

"Fire right ahead," said Ronald, lighting a cigar.

"The thing happened yesterday," began Davidson, "and at first everybody thought it was an accident. However, as you don't know any of the people concerned I'd better start by putting you wise to them and to the locality. You've been down my way, I think?"

"Only once," said Ronald. "So take it that I'm quite ignorant."

"I will," said Davidson. "My house is just five miles from the sea, and as you may perhaps remember, the River Ling forms one boundary to the property."

Ronald nodded.

"Yes, I recollect that. Tidal, isn't it, as far as you?"

"For three or four miles farther upstream. A muddy bit of water, but unfortunately it plays a big part in the tragedy which concerns my next-door neighbour, a retired business man named Yarrow. Do you want my estimate of the gentleman, or would you prefer to keep an open mind?"

"I want everything that bears on the case," said Ronald.

"His character certainly does that," said Davidson, "but I didn't want to bias you in any way. In short, then, he was a most unpleasant individual."

"Was?" Ronald raised his eyebrows.

The other nodded.

"I'm coming to that. Yes, he was a most unpleasant man, and one of the incomprehensible things of life is how his perfectly charming wife came to marry him. She is years younger than him, and an extremely pretty woman. He must have been well over fifty, whereas she is on the right side of thirty. Exactly what his business was I can't tell you: he was one of the most morose and uncommunicative men I've ever met. But it must have been lucrative, as there was no shortage of money about the *ménage*. I've dined with them off and on, and I know the style they lived in.

"It was not, however, an entertainment I indulged in more than I could help, because the atmosphere of the household was so damnable. He was frequently rude to her in front of the servants, and even if he wasn't that he had that cold, sarcastic manner that made one long to hit him.

"He had one hobby, and one hobby only, so far as I know—fishing in the Ling. Everyone to his own taste, and if it appeals to a man to sit on the bank of a muddy river fishing for uneatable fish with a worm and a float, by all manner of means let him do so. He certainly did, for hours on end. The river flowed past his place, but between it and his boundary was a right of way. And it was at one particular spot on this path that he always took up his position.

"Now, though the path is a right of way, it is very little used. Probably not more than two people go along it a day, though sometimes on Sundays the customary loving couples walk there. But on weekdays it is practically deserted. Well, it so happened that the day before yesterday I was down near the river giving instructions to my gardener about one or two things, when I saw a man called Stapleton coming along the path. His trousers were dripping with water, and the instant he saw me he gave a shout.

"'For God's sake come, Davidson. Yarrow has been drowned.'

"The gardener and I went at once, and sure enough it was so, Wedged against a sunken tree by the pressure of the water was his body, and a glance was sufficient to show that it was too late to do anything. His hat was on the bank, and a campstool and creel.

"'I tried to get him out,' said Stapleton, 'but he was too heavy for me.'

"'When did you find him?' I asked.

"'Five minutes ago,' he said. 'I was walking from Briggs's farm and as I passed I saw that hat, which I recognised as his. So I looked over the edge and there he was.'

"Between us we hoisted the body out and laid it on the bank. I sent my gardener back for a hurdle, and while he was away we made an attempt at doing some artificial respiration. But it was utterly hopeless, and we both knew it.

"'How on earth did it happen, I wonder?' I said after we had desisted.

"'The only thing I can think of,' said Stapleton, 'is that he fainted, or had a fit, and fell in. The water is comparatively shallow; if he'd been conscious he'd have had no difficulty in getting out.'

"Which was perfectly true, as the bank though steep was not high. No one would have had the smallest trouble in scrambling out, and it seemed to me that his solution must be the correct one.

"At last the hurdle arrived, and we put him on it. And then it struck me that somebody had better go on in advance to prepare Mrs. Yarrow for the news. Stapleton evidently did not want to, so I said I would. I didn't relish the job: with a woman, one never knows. He had treated her like a dog during his life, but for all that you can't tell how they'll take things. To my intense relief she kept perfectly calm. She turned white and swayed a bit; then she asked me quite quietly what to do.

"'I think the best thing would be to put the body in the billiard-room,' I said. 'You realise, Mrs. Yarrow, that he'll have to be seen by a doctor, and possibly the police may come into it. But, of course, it will be entirely a formality. It's obvious what happened.'

"'I repeated Stapleton's theory, and she listened in silence. And then, in view of subsequent developments, she made a rather strange remark: 'My husband has never fainted in his life.'

"At the time I thought nothing of it; they were just carrying in the body, and I went to see if I could be of any assistance. We laid it on the floor, and Stapleton put the hat and the creel on the table. And then we waited a bit awkwardly, nobody quite knowing what to do next. I dismissed the gardener and the man who had helped him, and Stapleton and I talked in the hushed tones one uses in the presence of death. Little pools of water were forming on the floor under him, but it seemed indecent to move him again.

"'I liked him, you know,' said Stapleton, 'though I know he was not popular. But it's a pretty mouldy end! And to think that I took a photograph of him on my way out to Briggs this morning. I never thought that the next time I saw the poor devil he'd be like this.'

"Half an hour later Dr. Granger arrived, and Stapleton and I left him to do what was necessary. Mrs. Yarrow had gone to her room, and I gave a message for her to the butler, to say that if there was anything I could do to help she must have no hesitation in ringing me up. Then, since there was nothing more to be done, I suggested to Stapleton that he should come over to my house and have a drink. I felt I badly needed one.

"An hour passed when suddenly the telephone rang. I went to it, and heard the voice of Sergeant Grayson at the other end. Being on the Bench, I knew him very well; a good man, distinctly above the average local policeman in intelligence. Would I go up to the Yarrows' house, and take Stapleton with me: some startling developments had taken place.

"We went immediately, wondering what on earth they could be, and the butler showed us into the billiard-room. The doctor was still there, with the sergeant and a constable, and all their faces were very grave.

"'Sorry to trouble you, sir,' said Grayson to me, 'but it was unavoidable. May I ask both you gentlemen to tell me all you know.'

"We did so, and when we'd finished he looked significantly at the doctor, who nodded.

"'The fact is, Davidson,' said Granger, 'that this is not a simple case of drowning. Yarrow was drowned all right, but it was the result of foul play. He didn't faint or have a fit, which was what I, too, first thought: he was stunned by being hit a heavy blow with some weapon on the base of his skull. He then pitched forward into the water, and probably was drowned almost instantaneously.'

"'Good God!' I cried, aghast. 'Are you sure, doctor?'

"'Quite sure, I'm sorry to say. The bruise is there plain for all to see, and by the feel of it I think something is chipped or broken inside. So you can guess how fierce the blow was.'

"'But who did it?' I said, staring at him.

"'That, sir,' said the sergeant, 'is what we've got to try and find out. And we have one very valuable piece of evidence. Mr. Yarrow's watch stopped at half-past two. Which proves conclusively that the poor gentleman met his end before that hour. Now, sir'—he turned to Stapleton—'as you seem to have been one of the last people to see him alive, can you add anything to what you have already told us?'

"'I can't, Sergeant,' answered Stapleton. 'I passed Mr. Yarrow just as he was packing up for lunch. It must have been about one o'clock, as I reached Briggs's house at ten minutes past. I had one film left in my camera, and as I wanted to get the roll finished I asked him to pose in the most characteristic attitude I could think of—sitting on his camp-stool fishing. I then had lunch, and the rest you know. I left Briggs's farm between five-and-twenty and twenty to three, and found the body in the river. I went in and tried to get him out, but I couldn't. And then Mr. Davidson came on the scene.'

"'Don't you think, Sergeant,' I put in, 'that it would be a good thing to get hold of the butler and find out about times from him?'

"So the butler was sent for, and it's his evidence that has brought me to you, Standish. I can't believe the boy did it, but I'm bound to say things look just about as black as they can be—Sorry: I'm jumping ahead too fast.

"It appears that Yarrow came in to lunch shortly after one to find a youngster called Christopher Stern having a cocktail with Mrs. Yarrow. And now comes the part that has got to be told, though naturally the butler said nothing about it. He knew, of course—we all did: you can't keep things like that dark in the country. Young Stern is in love with Mrs. Yarrow and has been for years, though what her feelings are on the matter I don't know.

"At any rate, it was quite clear from what the butler implied that his master was not at all pleased to find Stern there, and when he discovered that his wife had asked the boy to lunch he was even less pleased. Looking back now I remember having heard from other sources that Yarrow was very jealous of his wife, and it was obvious from what the butler said that the lunch was not a great success. We pressed him to be more explicit, but he is a good servant. And the most we could get out of him was that Yarrow was in a bad temper.

"Now comes the damning part. At a quarter past two Yarrow gathered his fishing tackle together, and the butler saw him standing in the hall talking to Stern. He was speaking angrily, though the butler did not hear what he said. But it ended in the two men leaving the house together and taking the direction of the river."

Davidson paused, and beckoning a waiter, ordered drinks. "More than that," he continued, "the butler could not say, but it was enough to make things begin to look ugly for Stern. And the boy's own statement of what happened didn't help much. We telephoned for him and he came round at once. And I think we all watched him as he came into the room. He saw the body, turned as white as a sheet and clutched the table as if he was about to fall.

"'What's happened?' he muttered.

"'I want you to tell me, sir' said the sergeant, 'exactly what took place this afternoon after you left this house with Mr. Yarrow!'

"'But I don't understand,' stammered the youngster. 'I know nothing about it.'

"After a while he pulled himself together and his story tallied exactly with the butler's. Yarrow and he had had words after lunch—he refused to say what about, but we all of us knew—and it had finished up with Yarrow forbidding him the house. They had gone out together and he had walked with Yarrow as far as the river. And there he had left him to his fishing.

"'Where did you go?' asked the sergeant.

"'Along a path somewhere: I really forget,' said Stern.

"'And what time did you leave Mr. Yarrow?'

"This again Stern couldn't remember: he supposed he'd stayed two or three minutes.

"'So, Mr. Stern,' said Grayson gravely, 'you know nothing about Mr. Yarrow's death?'

"'Absolutely nothing.'

"'You didn't have a struggle with him or strike him with anything?'

"'Good God! no. Why do you ask?'

"'Was anyone else there while you were with him?'

"'I saw no one.'

"'And you didn't pass anybody as you went along the path?'

"Again he shook his head.

"'Not that I'm aware of,' he said. And then, after a moment, he added: 'But I was all worked up and I might not have noticed. Anyway,' he cried wildly, 'what is it all about? Why are you asking me all these questions?'

"'I am asking you these questions, Mr. Stern,' said Grayson, 'because so far as we know at present you are the last person who saw Mr. Yarrow alive. And Mr. Yarrow was murdered.'

"'Murdered!'

"The word was just breathed—barely audible, and once again Stern clutched the table.

"'Who by? But—but, it looks as if he'd been drowned.' And then, wildly: 'Great Heavens! you don't suspect me?'

"Grayson stared at him.

"'I didn't say I did, Mr. Stern. But you left the house at a quarter past two with Mr. Yarrow; you must, therefore, have arrived at the river at about twenty past. You tell me you remained talking for two or three minutes.' He paused impressively. 'And Mr. Yarrow was murdered before half-past.'

"'You keep on saying he was murdered,' said Stern. 'How do you know that?'

"'He was hit on the back of the head and stunned,' answered Grayson. 'Then he fell into the water and was drowned.'

"And at that it was left for the time. Whether or not they have actually arrested young Stern yet, I don't know, but it's only a question of hours before they do so. And I wondered, Standish, if you would come down and run your eye over the country, so to speak. I'd like to do everything I can for Stern—he's an extra ordinarily nice boy. But I must confess it looks pretty hopeless to me.

"You think, then, that he did it?" said Ronald.

"What else can one think? We know that he was with Yarrow just before it happened; we know that they were having a quarrel over Mrs. Yarrow. We know also that the place where they were is usually entirely deserted, so that the chances of someone else being there are remote."

Davidson shrugged his shoulders.

"I am quite prepared to believe," he continued, "that Stern didn't even know he'd killed him. That in a moment of ungovernable rage he hit Yarrow and knocked him out, and that then, after he had gone, Yarrow rolled over and fell in the water and was drowned. In which case it might be possible to make it a case of manslaughter only."

"What does Mrs. Yarrow say?" asked Ronald.

"Nothing at all, so far as I know. I gather that she has admitted that her husband did not like Stern, but we knew that already. In fact, with regard to yesterday, the butler knows far more than she does."

"Well, there are certainly one or two very significant points," said Ronald, lighting a cigarette. "So, if you like, Davidson, Bob and I will come down tomorrow. I suppose there's a pub some where handy."

"My dear fellow, I wouldn't dream of letting you do that. I can put both of you up with the greatest of pleasure in the world. But I'm afraid it's pretty hopeless for young Stern. There's a good train from Liverpool Street at ten. I'll meet you at the other end."

"What do you make of it, Bob?" said Ronald, as Davidson went off to write a letter.

"Told as he's told it, I must say I agree with him. It looks black for Stern. Motive, opportunity, time—everything seems to fit."

"Almost too well," said Ronald. "However, we'll see?"

★★★★★★

True to his promise, Davidson met us at the station. "They've arrested him," were his first words. "I'm afraid it's a waste of time for you, Standish."

"When did they do it?" asked Ronald.

"Immediately after the inquest this morning. Hallo! there's Stapleton—the man who found Yarrow's body."

He waved his hand, and a good-looking, slightly-built man of about forty, who had just come out of a photographer's shop, came over to the car.

"Bad affair this," he said, "about young Stern. Still, I suppose it was only to be expected."

Davidson introduced us, and Stapleton looked at Ronald with interest.

"I've heard of you, Mr. Standish," he said. "Tom Ponsonby, who is a distant cousin of mine, is never tired of singing your praises."

"That's very nice of him," said Ronald.

"Have you come down here over this business, or merely to stay with Davidson?"

"A little of both," said Ronald, with a smile. "I hear they've arrested Stern."

The other nodded.

"I don't see how they could avoid it," he replied. "If ever there was an obvious case this is it."

He fumbled in his pocket.

"By the way, Davidson, I've just had that roll of films developed. Here is the last photograph of the poor chap taken an hour and a half before his death. Good, isn't it?"

"Very," said Davidson, passing it to us.

It showed Yarrow seated on his campstool watching his float. His face was in profile; his hat and creel were on the bank beside him.

"I'm glad I got it," said Stapleton simply. "It's just the pose I'd like to remember him by."

"I wonder if you would allow me to keep this," said Ronald "Or perhaps you would let me have another print made. My reason is that it helps one to visualise the scene in a way that mere imagination can't

394

do."

"By all manner of means keep it," cried Stapleton. "I can easily have another done."

"I suppose, Mr. Stapleton, that you saw no sign of any weapon on the bank when you found the body?"

"It never dawned on me to look for one. I assumed it was a common or garden case of drowning. The possibility of foul play never entered my head."

"Naturally not," said Ronald. "It wouldn't."

We stayed there talking for a few moments; then Stapleton got into his car and went off.

"Have you formed any plan of campaign, Standish?" asked Davidson. "Or do you think the thing is too hopeless to worry about?"

"Far from it," said Ronald.

Davidson glanced at him in surprise.

"You mean that you think young Stern has a chance?"

"I most certainly do," answered Ronald. "But until I've seen one thing I can't say more than that."

"And what is this thing you want to see?" asked Davidson curiously.

"The dead man's watch," said Ronald. "I take it you can manage that for me."

"I suppose Grayson has it," said Davidson. "It's a vital piece of evidence for the prosecution."

"Or for the defence," remarked Ronald with a faint smile. "However, we'd better wait and see."

"For the defence!" spluttered Davidson. "What on earth are you driving at, my dear man?"

But Ronald refused to elucidate further, or even to discuss the matter while we had lunch. But after the meal was over he suggested an immediate move.

"Let's go first to the place where it happened," he said. "And then if you'd ring through to him, Davidson, we'll go along and interview Sergeant Grayson."

"Certainly," answered our host. "I'll take you there at once. And I'll have the car waiting in the drive so that we'll waste no time."

He left us to go and telephone, and I tackled Ronald about the watch. But he was in one of his uncommunicative moods, and I could get nothing more out of him than the illuminating statement that it was damned rum. Then Davidson returned and we started for the river.

"That is where I was when I first saw Stapleton," said our host, pointing to a clump of trees in his park. "We've got about another quarter of a mile to go."

We turned into the path that ran along the bank. On our right through the bushes which fringed the river we could see the muddy waters of the Ling; on our left ran more bushes and a fence.

"Yarrow's property," remarked Davidson. "You'll be able to see the house soon through the trees."

At length he paused. We had come to a small clearing.

"Here's the spot," he said. "You can actually see the marks of the legs of his campstool in the ground."

Ronald nodded, and stood motionless studying the surroundings. The gap in the bushes on the bank measured about ten yards, and the river was some thirty yards wide. Behind us the undergrowth was dense. Up and down stream the path twisted, so that the place was completely secluded. On the right-hand side of the clearing a tree, half waterlogged, stuck out into the water, and Davidson pointed to it.

"It was against that the body had drifted." he said. "The tide was ebbing at the time and carried it there."

Ronald nodded again.

"I see it's just high tide now," he remarked. "Let's get the depth of the water."

He picked up a long stick and took some soundings.

"Three or four feet close inshore and a muddy bottom."

He straightened up and then for nearly half an hour he crept round on his hands and knees examining the ground at the bottom of the bushes. He went each way along the path, exploring it minutely, while Davidson watched him with curiosity tinged with slight impatience. At length he gave it up and rejoined us.

"I can find nothing," he said. "But, of course, the ground is very hard."

"What did you expect to find?" asked Davidson.

"'Expect' is too strong a word," answered Ronald. "All that can be said is that I thought it possible I might."

He lit a cigarette, and we waited.

"Let us try and size tip the situation," he said. "To start with an obvious platitude, either young Stern did it or someone else did. If it was young Stern we are wasting our time, because frankly, Davidson, your suggestion of manslaughter won't wash. A man who is stunned by a dunt on the head sufficient to break a bone lies where he falls. He doesn't wriggle about afterwards. Therefore, whoever hit Yarrow saw him fall into the river.

"So we'll consider the other alternative—that it was someone else who murdered him. Now, from what you have told us Yarrow was an unpopular man, so he probably had plenty of enemies. You further stated that fishing from this spot was his invariable hobby, a fact which other people must have been quite as well aware of as you were. Suppose, then, that this hypothetical some one else, desirous of seeing Yarrow, came here knowing that he'd find him. Suddenly he hears Yarrow approaching and quarrelling with Stern. He hides in the bushes, waits till Stern goes; then seizing his opportunity bashes Yarrow on the head and watches him drown."

I glanced at Davidson. His face expressed polite interest. And I must confess that I was a bit disappointed myself. Perhaps I had expected too much after such a prolonged examination, but the bald fact remained that an intelligent child of ten could have reached the same conclusion.

"And since," continued Ronald imperturbably, "the betting is four to one that that or something like it is what did take place, I thought I might find traces of his footprints."

And now we stared at him: this was a more positive assertion. "How on earth can you have arrived at that?" demanded Davidson.

Ronald smiled.

"Let's go and see Sergeant Grayson," he said. "And there is only one thing more I've got to say at the moment. If my theory is correct we are dealing with a very clever man, but one who is not quite clever enough."

"You'll be telling us you know who it is next," said Davidson, with mild sarcasm.

"I haven't a notion," said Ronald frankly. "Not the ghost of an idea. But it will be something if we can prove it wasn't young Stern."

Sergeant Grayson was expecting us, and with a genial and tolerant smile he produced the watch.

"I hear you want to see it, sir," he said. "Though what you think you'll get from it bar the obvious fact that it stopped at half-past two is beyond me."

"We'll see, Sergeant," said Ronald cheerfully, as he examined it. "By the way, it was in his waistcoat pocket, I suppose?"

"That's right, sir: attached to a button-hole by this leather guard."

The watch was a thin gold one, and the back fitted so tightly that it was only with the help of a penknife that Ronald prised it open. And when he had done so he sat staring at the works with a puzzled frown.

"Have you had this open, Sergeant Grayson?" he said at length.

"Can't say I have, sir. Why?"

"What do you think made the watch stop?"

"Water getting in, sir, of course."

"Then why is the whole inside bone dry?"

The sergeant scratched his head. "It's two days ago, sir, you know."

"Rot, man," cried Ronald. "If enough water had got into that watch to stop it, it would still be there after two weeks. It couldn't evaporate."

He was idly turning the swivel as he spoke, and suddenly a look of keen concentration came on his face.

"Great Scott!" he almost shouted, "the main spring is broken."

"Must have happened as Mr. Yarrow fell in," said the sergeant. "So that fixes the time exactly."

"My dear sergeant," remarked Ronald quietly, "I will, if you like, have a small bet with you. I will obtain for you a hundred different watches. You will go to the bank of the river or any similar spot and fall in a hundred times, with a different watch in your waistcoat pocket on each occasion. And if one mainspring breaks, I will present you with a bag of nuts."

"Well, it did this time," said the sergeant stubbornly.

"Look here, Grayson," said Ronald, "what makes a mainspring snap? Over-winding—ninety-nine times out of a hundred. Are you going to tell me that Mr. Yarrow during a heated interview with young Stern pulled out his watch and started to wind it up? It's ridiculous."

"Not more ridiculous than that someone else did," remarked Davidson.

"That's just where you're wrong," cried Ronald. "Last night I carried out a small experiment. I got into a warm bath wearing a waistcoat—and deuced absurd I looked, too," he added, with a grin. "In my waistcoat pocket was a watch. I stopped in the water for twenty minutes, and the watch was still going when I got out. It's the point that struck me the instant I heard your story, Davidson. This watch stopped too soon. If young Stern had done it, a watch that fits as tight as this one would have been still going at three."

No one said a word: we were all too keenly interested. "When I opened the back," he continued, "I expected to find it full of water. I was then going to suggest that we should have it thoroughly dried and carry out my experiment of last night with it. The murderer, however, was evidently unable to open it—you saw the difficulty I had—and he was in a hurry. So instead of filling it with water, he deliberately over-wound it, thereby breaking the mainspring, and hoped it would not be noticed. Then he set the hands at half-past two, and replaced it in Yarrow's pocket."

"But why should he put them at that hour?" said Grayson.

"Expressly to incriminate Stern," cried Ronald a little irritably. "That surely is obvious."

But the sergeant had become mulish.

"Theory—all theory," he snorted. "You go your way, Mr. Standish, and I'll go mine. And when you lay your hands on the man who, having just committed a cold-blooded murder, had the nerve to do what you have suggested, Mr. Stern will be free within five minutes."

"It's your funeral, Sergeant," said Ronald quietly. "But I tell you in all seriousness that you are barking up the wrong tree. The bit of evidence that you think most damning is, in reality, what completely exonerates young Stern. Who did it, I don't know; but it wasn't him."

The trouble of it was that it remained at that. Exhaustive inquiries in the neighbourhood failed to reveal the presence of any stranger, and so far as the local residents were concerned, it was impossible to single out anyone in particular. Moreover, since public opinion was unanimous that Stern was the murderer, interest in the case had flagged with his arrest.

Ronald grew more and more irritable. He spent hours on the river bank searching for possible clues without the smallest result. And, at length, even he began to give up hope.

"There absolutely nothing to give one a pointer, Bob," he cried to me in despair before lunch one day. "I am as convinced as ever that Stern didn't do it, but who the devil did? I feel it's leaving the youngster in the lurch, but there doesn't seem much use in our stopping on here. We're doing no good."

And Davidson agreed. Though he pressed us to stay as long as we liked, I think, at the bottom of his mind, he had come round to Grayson's opinion, that it was just theory. And so we took our departure, though it was like getting a dog away from a bone, so far as Ronald was concerned. He had told Stern's solicitor to subpoena him as an expert witness, but I knew he felt uneasy about the result.

"Even if he gets off, and I don't think they'll hang him, it's going to be a damnable thing for the youngster. If the trial was in Scotland, the utmost I should expect would be a verdict of Non Proven. They can't bring that in here, but it's what it will practically amount to. Not one person in a hundred will believe he is innocent, and he'll be under the stigma for the rest of his life."

★★★★★★

It was the evening before the trial, and I was round with him in his rooms. Never have I known him so depressed, and it was not difficult to understand. He felt he had failed, and though it was through no fault of his, the result was the same. And then, quite suddenly, the most amazing change came over his expression.

"My sainted aunt!" he shouted. "Let me think a moment." I glanced over his shoulder: he was studying the snapshot of Yarrow taken by Stapleton.

"What time was it when you and I and Davidson reached the river that first day we were down there?"

"We left the house at a quarter past three," I said. "So it must I have been half-past, as near as makes no odds!'

"Get Vickers on the 'phone," he cried. "Proof, Bob—proof under my nose all these weeks and I never saw it!"

Vickers was the K.C. defending Stern, and I got through at once.

"Tell him I'm coming round to see him immediately," said Ronald, and before I had time to speak he had dashed out, and I heard him shouting for a taxi. And that night it was touch and go that I did not find myself arrested on a similar charge to young Stern. For the irritating devil would say nothing. He kept grinning all over his face and rubbing his hands together.

"Wait till tomorrow, Bob," was all I could get out of him. "And then I can promise you the kick of your young life."

The court was crowded, but through Ronald's influence I got a good seat. And a glance at young Stern's face showed that the news, whatever it was, had been passed on to him. The atmosphere was tense, as it always is during a murder trial, but the prisoner seemed the least concerned person in the place. I saw Davidson and Stapleton not far away in the body of the court, but Ronald had been given a seat just behind Vickers. And then the trial began. Counsel for the Crown outlined the case for the prosecution, and though he spoke with studied moderation it was a pretty damning indictment. He admitted freely that the case rested on circumstantial evidence, but pointed out that ninety *per cent.* of murder cases did. Then he called his first witness—John Stapleton—who went into the box and took the oath.

He looked, I thought, strained and pale, but that was not to be wondered at. Yarrow had been a friend of his, but apart from that, to be one of the principal witnesses when a man's life is at stake is a nerve ordeal. However, he gave his evidence in a calm and steady voice, and when Vickers rose to cross-examine him, Stapleton gave him a courteous bow.

"Now, Mr. Stapleton, we have heard that you lunched with Mr. Briggs on the day of the murder. What time did you arrive at the house?"

"Between ten and a quarter-past one."

"And it is about ten minutes' walk, is it not, from where Mr. Yarrow was fishing?"

"That is so."

"You therefore left Mr. Yarrow at about one o'clock?"

"Yes."

"Before leaving him, did you take a photograph of him fishing?" Stapleton looked surprised, as did everyone else, including the judge; so far the fact had not been mentioned.

"Now you speak of it, I did," said Stapleton. "I'd really forgotten about it."

"But you remember now?"

"Perfectly. I had one exposure to complete the roll and I took one of him fishing."

"At about one o'clock?"

"Yes. It was just before I left him to go to lunch."

"Is this the photograph you took?"

Vickers held up the snapshot and Stapleton studied it.

"Yes. That is it."

"And is that tree that one sees half submerged in the water the one against which you found the body?"

"Yes. It is."

Vickers passed the photograph up to the judge.

"I would ask you to examine it carefully, m'lud. Now, Mr. Stapleton, is that tree downstream or upstream from the place where Mr. Yarrow was fishing?"

"Down-stream."

Vickers produced a book and opened it. And suddenly I glanced at

Stapleton. Ceaselessly he was wetting his lips with his tongue.

"I have here," continued counsel quietly, "a book which gives the times of high and low water for every day of the year in every part of the country. Would it surprise you to know, Mr. Stapleton, that on the day Mr. Yarrow was murdered, high tide in the River Ling was at one-fifty p.m.?"

"I will take your word for it," said Stapleton in a low voice.

"Therefore, when you took this photograph at one o'clock it was not yet high water; the tide was still coming in?"

"If high water was at one-fifty it must have been."

"Then why, John Stapleton," cried Vickers in a terrible voice, "is it going out in that photograph? You can see the swirl of the water against the tree."

For what seemed an eternity did the man in the box stand there mouthing, and one could have heard a pin drop in the court. Then came a sudden shout of "Stop him," but it was too late. Stapleton had cheated the hangman. And maybe as a point in his favour he confessed before he died.

"The motive—who can tell?" said Ronald, as we waited for lunch at Davidson's house. "But it was a devilish clever crime, though not quite clever enough. Somehow or other Stapleton must have known that Stern and Yarrow had had a row. Somehow or other he must have known that Stern left Yarrow a little before half-past two. The photograph which sealed his fate was probably taken to foster the idea that he and Yarrow were friends. And he forgot about high tide. If you remember, Davidson, it was just on the turn two days later at three-thirty. Now it gets about fifty minutes later every day, so that on the day of the murder high tide was an hour and forty minutes earlier—at one. His one slip. But as to motive. . ."

He shrugged his shoulders, and at that moment the butler announced Mr. Briggs.

"Won't keep you a moment, gentlemen," he said, "but there's just one point you might like to know. I thought no more about it till the trial today. At twenty-past two on the day Mr. Yarrow was murdered, someone rang Stapleton up at my house."

"Who?" said Ronald.

"Mrs. Yarrow."

Partial Salvage

My Dear Standish,

I don't know if you ever ran across Miles Parker. He died about two years ago, and, to everybody's surprise, left practically nothing, for we had all thought he was pretty comfortably off. He was a widower, so the only person affected by it was his son Terence, who was up at Cambridge: a darned good lad, as I think you'll agree when you meet him.

It was, of course, impossible for him to stop on at the 'Varsity, and since he has no uncles or near relatives, I suggested he should come and make his headquarters with us, at any rate until he found something to do. But, as you know yourself, jobs are not too easy to come by these days, especially for fellows who have no technical training. And it fridged the lad as month after month went by and nothing turned up: he felt he was sponging on me. At last, however, he answered an advertisement in the paper, and from this point Terence can tell you his own story. I may be several sorts of ass to take up your valuable time, but I'd like your candid opinion. I'm not quite easy in my mind.

Yours sincerely,

Graham Meredith.

P.S.—Probably wild horses won't make him admit it, but I don't think Terence is quite easy himself.

Ronald Standish passed the letter over to me and turned to the third occupant of the room—a cheery-faced youngster of about twenty-three.

"Well, what's it all about, young feller?" he said with a smile.

"I feel quite ashamed to worry you, Mr. Standish," said Terence Parker. "But Uncle Graham seemed set on it, so I've come along. He's not really my uncle, of course," he added.

"Courtesy title," cried Ronald. "I see. Let's hear about this mysterious job of yours."

"He's told you about my father, I suppose?"

"Yes: I'm wise up to the time when you answered an advertisement."

"Good: I'll start from there," said our visitor. "It was about three months ago, and I was getting desperate. Uncle Graham has been goodness itself to me, but I felt I couldn't go on living with him for ever. And suddenly, one morning, I saw this advertisement in the paper."

He took a cutting out of his pocket and handed it over to Ronald.

Secretary wanted. Must be unmarried man about five feet ten in height: average build. Shorthand unnecessary. Good salary to suitable applicant. Box 231.

Without comment Ronald put the cutting on the table, and waited for Parker to continue.

"As you can imagine, I had an answer in the post within ten minutes, and two days later I received instructions to go to a place called Fordham House, near Woking, where I was to interview a Mr. Charles Follitt. I'm afraid I haven't got the letter with me, as I tore it up when I got the job.

"I went down at once, and found the house without difficulty. And before I'd had time even to ring the bell the door was flung open and a fellow of about my own age was shown out by an elderly female. He looked a bit glum, so I concluded that he was an unsuccessful competitor, and that the place wasn't filled yet.

"'This way,' mumbled the old dame. 'And what's your name? '

"I told her, and she announced me. Standing on the hearthrug was a man of about fifty. He was swinging a pair of *pince-nez* to and fro, and as I came in he put them on and gave me the once over. I did the same to him. He was about my own height, clean shaven, and in his way not bad looking. But there was a shifty sort of look in his eyes that I didn't very much like.

"'Well, Mr. Parker,' he said, ' you are the thirtieth applicant I have seen. It is incredible how foolish some people are: no less than ten of them were married, whilst three of them were at least six feet. You are not married, I take it?'

"'I am not,' I assured him.

"'And your height, I can see, is satisfactory. So we will proceed to the other points. Do you live with your father? '

"'My father is dead,' I told him, ' and so is my mother.'

"'Indeed,' he said. 'You have my sympathy. An uncle perhaps? '

"By this time I was beginning to get a bit stuffy: I couldn't see what the devil it had to do with him who I lived with. However, I told him quite civilly that my nearest relative was a second cousin whom I'd never seen, and that the man whose house I was in was no relation at all.

"'Excellent!' he cried, rubbing his hands together. 'I, too, am almost alone in the world, and my only relative is a cousin. I feel we shall get on capitally together, Mr. Parker.'"

"I stared at him.

"'Do you mean you've engaged me? ' I cried.

"'I think I may say that you will suit me,' he answered. 'Subject, of course, to one small condition. There may come an occasion, Parker—I don't say it will, but it may—when I shall have to leave the house, and at the same time let it appear that I am still here. Nothing criminal, I assure you,' he added with a laugh when he saw me look at him pretty hard; ' it's merely a family matter into which I prefer not to go. What I am getting at is this, however. Should such an occasion arise I should want you to wear some suit of mine and appear just once or twice in the window of one of the rooms facing the road, so that only your back is seen.'

"Well, I must say, Mr. Standish, I thought that was a bit odd, but the money side came in and I agreed.

"'Splendid,' he remarked. ' Now as to salary. Shall we say five pounds a week?'

"'That suits me,' I said promptly. 'And what are my duties? '

"'To start with, I want my library catalogued,' he said. 'And there will be a few letters and things of that sort.'

"At that it was left, and I started work the next day."

"One moment, Parker," said Ronald. "What does the staff consist of?"

' The old woman who let me in, and she goes home every night.'

"So you and Mr. Follitt slept there alone. I see: go on."

"As I say, I started in next day, and having provided myself with pens, ink, and paper, I proceeded to tackle the library. And ten minutes' inspection was sufficient to show that the thing was simply farcical. I don't profess to know anything about books, but I can recognise absolute junk when I see it. There were piles of books all over the floor, and shelves full of them, but you've never thought of such a collection. To give you an example, there were four copies of that revolting tome, *Eric, or Little by Little*. There were old books of hymns mixed up with a treatise on spherical trigonometry: there was Mrs. Beeton's cookery tome next door to a table of logarithms. And this is what I was supposed to classify!

"So I interviewed Mr. Follitt and asked him how he wanted me to set about it. And then he told me how he had acquired his collection. Apparently one of his hobbies was to buy up the whole of the contents of a second-hand bookshop in the hopes of finding something good. And what he wanted me to do was to arrange and make a list of anything I thought possible and discard the rest. So I started off on those lines, and have been carrying on ever since. As he was doing the paying, he could presumably dictate the job.

"So much for that side of it: now for the other. After I'd been in the house about four days I was sitting in the smoking-room one night after dinner. Mr. Follitt had gone into the place he called his laboratory, a room which was separated from the rest of the house by a green baize door, and I was alone, when suddenly a most queer-looking customer came in. He still had his hat on, and for a time he stood there looking at me with his hands in his pockets. He was wearing dark glasses and had a ragged-looking black moustache.

"'Is Charles in his laboratory' he asked in a peculiar hissing voice.

"'He is,' I said. 'May I ask who you are?'

"'His cousin. I suppose you're the secretary?'

"And it was then I discovered what caused the hiss: his two central front teeth were missing."

"'Damned foolishness,' he grunted. 'What's he want a secretary for?'"

"With which he turned on his heel and left the room. I heard the baize door swing, and picked up my book again with some relief. Mr. Follitt's cousin was not my idea of a pleasant evening. After a while, however, it occurred to me that they might like a drink, so I walked along the passage and knocked at the laboratory. They were talking inside, but when I tried the handle it was locked.

"'What is it?' called out my employer.

"'I wondered if you'd like a drink, Mr. Follitt.'

"'No, no,' he said testily. 'Go away, Parker.'

"Which I thought a bit harsh: I didn't care a damn if he had a drink or not. However, to do him justice he apologised handsomely later on.

"'*I* fear I seemed a little irritable,' he said, 'when you came to the laboratory. But my cousin, James Palliser, and I were having a business discussion, and we could not see eye to eye.'

"'Has he gone?' I asked, for I hadn't heard him leave.

"'Yes: I let him out by the side door. And, by the way, Parker, whenever he comes, as he did tonight he always goes straight to the laboratory. And then we never wish to be disturbed.'

"I refrained from saying that so far as I was concerned nothing would induce me to disturb Mr. James Palliser, who had struck me as a positively leprous piece of work; and any time in the future when he came—and it's been pretty often—I've kept religiously out of his way."

Young Parker paused and lit a cigarette.

"I hope I'm not boring you, Mr. Standish," he continued, "but your sufferings are nearly over. About a week ago my bird came to me and said that the occasion he had alluded to when he engaged me had arisen, and that he wanted me to impersonate him that afternoon. He produced a suit he often wore, and in which I, personally, would not have been seen dead drunk in a ditch. But I'd agreed to do it, and so I put it on.

"'Show yourself four or five times,' were his instructions, 'but don't be recognised. Also—and this is very important—try and see if anybody appears to be watching the house.'

"Well, I carried out my orders, and after he'd been gone about an hour I found that somebody *was* watching the house. No less a person that Mr. James Palliser. I showed him my back view two or three times, and in between kept an eye on him through the curtains. He was passing and repassing the house, and kept lingering by the gate and peering in. And finally I'll be damned if he didn't stop a passing policeman and have a talk with him, evidently about the house, for the copper peered in too. Which struck me as pretty rum: what on earth could a policeman tell him with regard to the place or its occupant that he didn't know already? In fact, the more I thought of it the more extraordinary the whole thing grew. He'd seen what he thought was his cousin inside, and therefore he must have assumed that his cousin had seen him. So what sense was there in popping about outside the gate like an agitated hen ?

"I told Mr. Follitt, of course, as soon as he got back, and, to my amazement, he appeared to have expected it.

""I'm not surprised, Parker,' he said. 'You think you bluffed him into thinking it was me?'

"'I think so,' I answered. 'But the whole thing seems so pointless.'

"'Not if you knew the facts of the case,' he told me. ' A matter of business, my boy, and one thing I can assure you. It was imperative that James Palliser should believe I was here the whole afternoon.'

"And with that he went off to his laboratory, leaving me to wonder what was at the bottom of it all. It's all so queer, Mr. Standish. This so-called work I'm on is complete bunkum. I gave him two long lists and he never even glanced at them. I'm convinced he bought all those books merely as a pretext for giving me something to do."

"That," agreed Ronald, "is fairly obvious. Has he paid you regularly?"

"Every week," said Parker. "And that's another point. He's a mean man—very mean: at times one literally doesn't get enough to eat. So why pay a ludicrous salary for absolutely useless work?"

"He isn't," answered Ronald. "He's paying a ludicrous salary in order to keep you in the house. And the point is, why is he doing so? Has anything happened since you impersonated him?"

"Nothing, except that another avalanche of 'Erics' has descended on me," said the youngster with a grin.

"Does he know you've passed all this on to Meredith?"

"No: but he's never told me to keep it dark. What do you make of it, Mr. Standish?"

"Frankly, my dear fellow, I don't make anything at all of it at present. It's an odd story, but odd things happen in this world. Clearly his sole object is to have a man in the house who is of right build to impersonate him at a distance. Equally clearly Mr. James Palliser would appear to be the audience for the impersonation. But why? What the relations are . . . By the way, what are their relations? How do they get on together?"

For a moment or two Parker stared at him.

"Do you know, Mr. Standish," he said slowly, "it's a most extraordinary thing, and it's never struck me until this moment. I've never seen 'em together. I've heard 'em talking, but I've never actually seen 'em together."

"Hasn't Palliser ever stopped for a meal?"

"Not on your life. Old Follitt is far too stingy. It takes one back to one's old schooldays when one went and gorged at the tuck-shop. Hashes and muck of that sort every day. Says his teeth hurt him."

"Well, Parker," said Ronald after a pause, "the situation as I see it is this. You're getting a fiver a week and the run of your hash. I don't like this impersonation business at all, but it may be only a family matter, in which there's no harm in it. You are old enough and ugly enough to take care of yourself, and my advice to you is to hang on drawing your fiver and to keep your eyes skinned. And the instant anything occurs which you don't like—hop it. You know my address, and a line here will always get me."

It was a fortnight before the next development took place, and this time it was Mr. Graham Meredith who came to see us.

"Look here, Standish," he burst out even before the door was shut, "I wish you'd give me your advice. You remember young Terence, don't you? Now would you put that boy down as being a thief?"

"A thief!" echoed Ronald. "Most certainly not. Who says he is?"

"His employer—Mr. Charles Follitt," cried Meredith indignantly. "I was in my garden this morning when a man I'd never seen before drove up to the house. He turned out to be Mr. Follitt, and the first thing he said to me when he found out who I was left me gaping. 'Naturally I can't employ him any more,' he said, 'but if he lets me have the money back I'll say no more about it. Perhaps I was to blame in leaving it lying about.'

"'What the deuce are you talking about?' I cried.

"'Hasn't Terence Parker come back here?'

"'He has not,' I said. 'Why should he? Isn't he still with you?'

"'He went to bed as usual last night: he did not appear this morning. And his bed had not been slept in. In fact, he's gone. And I'm very grieved to have to tell you, Mr. Meredith, that a hundred pounds of my money has gone also.'

"'You mean to say,' I cried, 'that you're accusing young Terence of stealing a hundred pounds of yours. Because I don't believe it.'

"He shrugged his shoulders.

"'I can hardly believe it myself,' he said. 'Nevertheless, the fact remains that the notes have gone, and so has he.'

"'What about the servants?' I cried.

"'I have only one woman who comes by the day, and she wasn't there yesterday or today. It's a shock, I know,' he went on. 'It was a terrible one to me, because I liked him. But I really can't afford to lose a hundred pounds.'

"'The instant I am satisfied that Terence took your money,' I assured him, 'I will send you a cheque for that amount.'

"And with that he departed. What do you make of it, Standish? I'd stake my whole reputation that that boy is no thief."

"I agree," said Ronald. "And yet this man Follitt would hardly dare to make such an accusation unless he had good grounds for believing it. Have you heard nothing from Terence?"

"Not a word. I got quite a cheerful letter from him about three days ago, and that's the last I've heard of him. But nothing," he reiterated, "will make me believe that boy is a thief."

"Well, Meredith," said Ronald, "I'm extremely sorry for you. But it seems to me that there's nothing to be done except to wait and hear his side of the story. From what Mr. Follitt told you he's not going to call in the police, and that is something, at any rate. Because, however innocent he is, police inquiries are always unpleasant."

"An unexpected development, Bob," he remarked when Mr. Meredith, still vehemently protesting that the thing was outrageous, had gone. "He struck me as being a remarkably nice youngster."

"You think he took the money?" I said.

"If he didn't, the whole of Mr. Charles Follitt's story is a lie. And why should he lie? What is his object? The fact that young Parker has disappeared can easily be verified. And if for some reason or other they've had a row and Follitt wants to get his own back, he'd make his accusation of theft as public as possible. He wouldn't go to Meredith, as he did do, and announce his intention of keeping the whole thing quiet."

"And yet I don't believe that youngster would steal," I said.

"Sudden temptation. A hundred quid is a lot of money. May have been betting, or something of that sort. And yet I agree with you. Let us put on our considering caps, Bob. Let us try and evolve a solution, which would cover the facts as we know them, based on the assumption that young Parker is not a thief, and that therefore Follitt is lying."

"Thank you kindly," I said, "for the little word 'us.' I, personally, am going round to the club to have a drink."

He joined me there at lunch, and I asked him what luck he had had.

"None," he answered. "I've tried three possibles, but each of 'em fails on one point or another. You remember our assumption—that Follitt is lying. That being so one fundamental fact emerges. If young

Parker did not take that money, but just quit the job after a row, Follitt would never have dared to go to Meredith with a cock-and-bull yarn about stealing. He would naturally have assumed that Parker would have got there before him. Am I right so far?"

"Yes," I said. "You are."

"Let's go a step farther. Follitt did go to Meredith, therefore he *knew* Parker could not get there before him. How could he know that *unless young Parker has not disappeared?*"

"You mean . ." I began."

"I mean this. If Follitt is lying, that youngster is a prisoner somewhere. And I can think of no more likely place than the house itself."

"But what's the great idea?" I cried.

"I can think of two or three, Bob," he said gravely. "Are you on for a visit on the quiet to Fordham House?"

"Of course," I answered.

"Because I think we'll go after lunch. Mr. Follitt does not know either of us."

We found the house without difficulty, and strolled casually past it. It was a smallish place, standing back from the road, and there was no sign of life in any of the rooms.

"I'm going to take the bull by the horns, Bob," said Ronald. "It's acted before: I'm travelling in linoleum. You keep out of sight."

He produced a bundle of samples from the car, and walking up to the front door, he rang the bell. But a few minutes later he had joined me again.

"No answer," he remarked. "Which may or may not mean the house is empty."

"What are you going to do now?" I asked. "Because it rather points to Follitt's story being true."

"I know it does. And yet . . . Look here, Bob," he said suddenly, "it's not fair on you . . . You go back to Town."

"What the devil are you driving at?" I cried. "What are you going to do?"

"I'm going to wait till it's dark, and then have a closer look."

"I'm with you," I said resignedly. "We'll ask if we can share the same cell."

We put through the afternoon somehow, and then had dinner. But it was nearly eleven before Ronald deemed it safe to start. We left the car some way from the gate, and then stood in the shadow reconnoitring. The house was in darkness, and in the faint light of the moon that came filtering through the fir trees it seemed that all the windows were shut.

"Come on," whispered Ronald. "It's now or never."

He climbed the gate and I followed him, creeping along the grass verge that bordered the drive. The trees were creaking slightly in the breeze, and our footsteps made no sound, as we skirted round to the back of the house. This, too, was in darkness, and with infinite care we approached one of the windows. The curtains were drawn, but when one got close to, a faint glow came from inside. It was the dying embers in the kitchen grate.

And then I began to sniff, and Ronald put his lips to my ear.

"Smell it, Bob?" he breathed. "It's paraffin. I'm breaking in."

Came a sharp crack as he used a peculiar implement of his own on the catch, and cautiously lifted the bottom window. And the next moment we both recoiled involuntarily: the place literally reeked of paraffin.

"Something wrong here," he muttered, and switched on his torch. "My God! Bob," he cried, "look there!"

I could scarcely believe my eyes. Sprawling in a chair, his mouth and chin covered with blood, was young Parker. Stacked up around him was a mass of shavings and paper, whilst at his feet was an over-turned lamp. And the floor was swimming in paraffin.

"The devil!" snarled Ronald. "The foul devil! Come on, Bob, though I'm afraid we're too late."

And then he gave a cry of triumph as he reached the youngster.

"Not dead, Bob; not dead. Only insensible."

And as we carted him to the window something fell with a tinkle on the floor. I picked it up: it was a plate of six false teeth.

We laid Parker down on the grass and turned the torch on him. He was breathing deeply and regularly, but his mouth was a shocking sight. And Ronald examined it more closely.

"What's happened to him?" I said.

"Six teeth hauled out," remarked Ronald softly. "May heaven have mercy on Mr. Charles Follitt when I get hold of him. Let's get Parker to the car, Bob: then we will come back and await the gentleman."

But that was not to be. Hardly had we got the youngster in the car when a sudden blaze of light shone through the trees from behind us. We could hear the roar of the flames and see the smoke pouring out of the house.

"Just in time, Bob," said Ronald, even more softly. "Mr. Charles

Follitt will not return tonight. It did not occur to me that he was so well versed in scientific arson. We will now go to the police station, and doubtless in time we shall be able to return his *bona-fide* false teeth."

"To Mr. Charles Follitt," I remarked.

And Ronald's reply was enigmatic.

"A rose by any other name," was all he said.

I suppose I was dense, but even then the truth did not dawn on me. That Mr. Charles Follitt had deliberately set fire to Fordham House by means of some incendiary device timed for a certain hour was obvious. Further, that he had intended the wretched Parker's charred body to be mistaken for his own was also clear. He had been thorough, too. Realising that he himself had false teeth, he saw the impossibility of leaving a corpse that had not: he had therefore extracted six of the youngster's and left the plate of false ones to be found. The fact that it did not fit could never be discovered after the fire. Also he had spun the only story to Graham Meredith which would account for Terence Parker disappearing: the disgrace of having taken the money would prevent the boy going back to the man who had treated him so well. His insistence on his secretary not having any near relatives who might make awkward inquiries: all the details of the plot were clear, save the one crucial one. What was his motive? Why did he want the world to think he had been burned to death ?

It could not be a question of insurance, either fire or life. If he was supposed to be dead, claiming the money became a little difficult. And then Mr. James Palliser began to loom up in my mind. He might help there. As the only relation he would inherit anything his cousin might leave, and he would be in a position to claim the insurance money. Then, after a decent interval, he could join Follitt abroad and split the cash. A risk on Follitt's part, undoubtedly: he was putting himself completely at Palliser's mercy. And since, from what Parker had told us, there was friction between the two men, the risk seemed a large one. However, that appeared the only possible solution, and I said as much to Ronald, who smiled.

"The swine will lie doggo for a bit," I remarked, "and then get out of the country."

"Think so, Bob? Well, we'll see. Anyway, to make him easy in his mind I have persuaded the inspector to put up a little mild deception. Here it is."

He tossed over a sheet of paper, and I read the contents.

"Fordham House, near Woking, the residence of Mr. Charles Follitt, was completely gutted by fire in the early hours this morning. It is feared the unfortunate owner perished in the blaze."

"A nice little paragraph for the newspapers," he remarked, "which may help matters. And now all we can do is to get Parker back to Meredith's house and make him as comfortable as possible."

The youngster recovered consciousness the next day, and for a time, as was only natural, he seemed completely dazed. His mouth was hurting abominably; the teeth had been wrenched out in the crudest way. And even when he could speak coherently all we got out of him was that he had felt queer at lunch and after that remembered no more.

"That's when Follitt drugged him," said Ronald. "He was in the house when Bob and I called, and probably Follitt was, too."

"I'm very anxious to meet Mr. Follitt again," remarked Meredith quietly.

"And so you shall," said Ronald. "In the very near future."

"But, damn it," I cried, "the man is pretending to be dead. He's not going to show his nose anywhere."

"An even fiver, Bob," he grinned, "that with the help of Mr. James Palliser we lay our hands on him within the next few days."

"You mean Palliser will split," I cried. "What a precious pair of blackguards they are."

To be exact, it was three days later that Ronald rang me up.

"If you want to be in at the death, old boy," he said, "come round to the office of the South British Insurance Company in Pall Mall at midday."

I went there, to find the inspector I had seen at Woking, with Ronald and a stranger who proved to be one of the directors of the company.

"You were quite right about the insurance, Bob," said Ronald. "Follitt had insured his life for thirty thousand, and his house for five against fire. And Mr. James Palliser is coming shortly to claim his cheque. Will you and the sergeant wait in the next room, Inspector? We don't want to alarm our bird. And we may have to use unpolice-like methods."

He arrived almost immediately, and I must say I have seldom seen a more peculiar-looking man. He was dressed in black, and as he greeted us the two missing teeth were most noticeable.

"Mr. James Palliser, I believe?" said Ronald. "Please sit down."

He took a chair, and one could see his eyes blinking behind the dark glasses.

"A terrible affair," he remarked. "Terrible."

"I see from the policy in which you are mentioned a next-of-kin to Mr. Follitt," said Ronald, "that you live near Birmingham."

"That is so," said Palliser. "I have had a house there now for two years."

"But you frequently visited your cousin at Woking?"

"Frequently. And he came to see me. Not during these past few weeks, but before that he was often a visitor."

"You have been to his house quite a lot recently, I believe?"

"Four or five times, I suppose. To be frank, we have not been on quite such friendly terms of late. A private matter, connected with a lady on which we did not see eye to eye."

"You know he had engaged a secretary, don't you?"

"I do. I met the young fellow on two or three occasions. But my cousin telephoned me—let me see, it was actually the day of the fire—that he'd decamped with some money."

"Most fortunate for him he wasn't involved in the fire too," remarked Ronald. "Did you know, Mr. Palliser, that when your cousin engaged him he made the peculiar condition that his secretary must be prepared at times to impersonate him?" Mr. Palliser sat forward. "I did not," he said. "Impersonate him! Then that accounts . . ." He leaned back and sighed. "However, my cousin is dead. Let us not speak ill of him. It is the private matter I mentioned. One day when I thought he was at Fordham House, it must have been his secretary I saw. Poor Charles!"

He sighed again, and put his finger tips together.

"I suppose you couldn't tell us the name of the lady," said Ronald.

"Really, sir! What possible bearing can it have on the case?"

"I thought that perhaps she might like a little memento of your cousin," answered Ronald blandly.

"But I understand that the house was completely gutted."

"There is always partial salvage, Mr. Palliser," said Ronald, still more blandly.

And to my utter amazement he produced from his pocket the set of false teeth and put it on the table in front of him. But if I was surprised the effect on Mr. Palliser was electrical. A hoarse sort of gurgling noise came from his throat and he plucked at his collar with both hands.

"You seem upset, Mr. Palliser," continued Ronald, and his voice was no longer bland. "Strange, isn't it, that these teeth show no signs of the fire."

"I don't understand," stammered the other. "What have my cousin's false teeth to do with me?"

"That remains to be seen," remarked Ronald. "I was going to suggest that if the lady would not like them they might come in handy for you. Your own seem sadly wanting."

Mr. Palliser rose from his seat as Ronald approached him.

"Don't touch me," he shouted. "Don't dare to touch me."

And what happened then was, as Ronald had said, not strictly police-like.

"Hold his head, Bob," snapped Ronald, and in a second the transformation had occurred. Off came the moustache and glasses: out came a set of false teeth with the centre ones missing.

"Now, Mr. Charles Follit, you ineffable blackguard, you can put in the complete set or not, as you like."

"Mercy!" screamed the wretch. "I . . . I . . ."

"Did you show mercy to your secretary?" cried Ronald. "Luckily we got him out in time, which unfortunately saves you from the gallows. Take him away, Inspector. Attempted murder and arson should keep him happy for some years to come."

★★★★★

"You were very nearly right, Bob," he said to me later. "At first that was my solution, and then the incredible risk of Follitt putting himself completely in the hands of a distant cousin, with whom he was not even on the best of terms, ruled it out. Inquiries were made, of course, and, sure enough, a Mr. James Palliser was found to have a house near Birmingham, where he'd been for two years. He, too, had one old woman who looked after him, and from her we found out that he was frequently away for a month at a time. Then we went to Mr. Charles Follitt's servant and discovered that he, up to the time young Parker went to him, also indulged in these long absences. And it was then that I saw the immense significance of the fact that Parker had never *seen* 'em together. Heard 'em, yes—but not seen 'em.

"The whole thing was an elaborate and carefully planned plot to make Palliser a reality. When Follitt was not in Woking, Palliser was in Birmingham. And *vice versa*. Follitt, realising that there is nothing so noticeable about anyone as missing teeth, had two plates made, from one of which he removed two conspicuous ones. That also had the

416

effect of making him speak with that peculiar hissing intonation. And when Parker heard them, as he thought, talking to one another, it was Follitt talking to himself and changing the plate each time. As I say, just a carefully thought-out scheme to allow Mr. Follitt to be burned beyond recognition, and then draw the insurance money as Mr. Palliser. For the fact remains, Bob, that if we hadn't been in time and young Parker had been burned to death, the evidence of Follitt's dentist as to the false teeth would have been conclusive.

"You shall now stand me lunch and I'll let you off the fiver."

The Silent Victim

Petersdown Towers was a large, rambling, old-fashioned house lying in the heart of West Sussex. Elizabethan, it was one of the few places where the Virgin Queen was not reputed to have stayed the night, though Sir James Ardingley, the fourth baronet—if rumour was to be believed—had not been unpleasing in that august lady's eyes. The grounds were extensive: the shooting good without being first class. And, like most houses of similar size today, its capacity for absorbing money was incredible.

The existing baronet, Sir Hubert, had long discovered that annoying fact. As a captain in the Guards he found it increasingly difficult to combine his expenses with his income; the property seemed to be an inexhaustible sink for cash.

And yet nothing would have induced him to part with it, even if he could have found a purchaser. Sooner or later, it being bred in the bone, he would go back to the home of his forefathers, till in the fullness of time he was buried alongside them in the family vault. And until that day arrived who could look after the old place better than his uncle, William Ardingley? A blood relation, reared in the house himself, he loved it as if it was his own. And if sometimes his demands seemed extravagant, they were in a good cause.

William Ardingley was a man of fifty-five, and owing to a rather strange chain of circumstances he had spent fifty of them in Petersdown Towers. His elder brother John, Hubert's father, had come into the title when he was twenty, and the two of them had lived together till John married ten years later. Of that marriage two children were born—Hubert and, a year later, his brother Philip, who was now a lieutenant in the navy. And in giving birth to Philip, Lady Ardingley had died, leaving her husband with the two infants.

For three years he carried on alone, though her death had very nearly broken him up. He had idolized his wife, and small wonder; a more lovely girl it would have been difficult to find. And the mere thought of replacing her never even entered his head. But after a while the loneliness began to tell, and he suggested to William that he should come back again.

William had been agreeable, and for another three years the two brothers joined forces. Then came the next tragedy: Sir John was killed in a motor accident and his son, aged four, became the baronet. Very naturally William, after consultation with the family lawyers, stayed on in *loco parentis*, until Hubert came of age, when the two of them discussed the matter at length, though the upshot of the matter was a foregone conclusion.

Hubert, though he adored the place, did not want to bury himself in the heart of the country for many years to come. Philip was in the navy: Hubert was an Ensign, and though money was getting tighter there was still sufficient and more than sufficient for Hubert in his regiment, and a good allowance for Philip. So William remained on, ostensibly as agent, though practically as owner, and the two boys came down when they wanted to and leave permitted.

Such then, in brief, was the state of affairs in the Ardingley family during the years that followed the war. And such might have been the state of affairs today but for the terrible tragedy of last July. It is only after careful consideration, and fully discussing the matter with Ronald Standish, that I have decided to put on record the real facts. And though these words may never see the light of print, it will at any rate be something to have the truth available, in view of the mass of malicious rumour that still surrounds the whole affair.

It was on Eclipse day at Sandown—I remember that Ronald and I had argued as to whether we should go or not—that the story starts. We had decided not to and were just going in to lunch at the club when we ran straight into Hubert, who joined us at our table.

"Heard the latest?" he asked us as we sat down. "Uncle William has gone batty."

"What's the matter with him?" said Ronald studying the menu. "He was quite normal the last time I saw him."

Hubert laughed.

"So he seemed to me until he told me the news. My revered uncle is going to be married. Can you beat it?"

"Really!" said Ronald. "I must say that is a bit of a shatterer. I'd have put him down as one of the most bullet-proof bachelors I've ever known. Who's the lady?"

Hubert's grin faded, and I regret to state that his answer might have led one to suppose that our discussion concerned a kennel.

"She's the daughter of a retired doctor who has settled down in the neighbourhood," he continued. "By name of Plessey—Violet Plessey. She's a good looker for them who likes her type, but she's just about as hard as they make 'em. However, that's old William's funeral. As things stand he's running round in small circles eating out of her hand."

"How's this going to affect you, Hubert?" I asked.

"That's just the point, Bill," he answered. "Quite a lot, I'm afraid. One thing is certain: it will mean a complete change of our present *regime*. And that is always annoying."

"You mean you don't want the lady at Petersdown Towers."

"Just so. Even if she was one of the brightest and best it wouldn't be satisfactory. I shall probably do likewise myself some day, and by that time they'd be thoroughly settled in. Besides, there may be some little Williams. No—anyway it wouldn't do, but in this case it is out of the question. Nothing would induce me to have Miss Violet Plessey in the house, though I'm not exactly relishing the idea of letting her know same."

"Does she expect to stop on?" asked Ronald.

"I really don't know, old boy. So far I have held no converse with the lady on the subject. Nor do I propose to. It will have to go through Uncle William, and I'm afraid it is going to be a bit of a pill for him to have to uproot after all these years. Still, if he will go plunging into matrimony he can't hold me responsible."

"He'll probably suggest remaining on till you plunge yourself," I said.

"Well, he ain't going to, Bill. As a matter of fact, though this is between ourselves, apart altogether from this marriage I'm afraid there would have had to be a change. Things are so tight these days that I don't see how I can stop on in the regiment. It means I've got to keep a show going here in London, and my tastes have never been exactly of the ginger beer type."

"Still, if he wasn't getting married, he could have stayed on with you," remarked Ronald.

"Sure thing. We get on damned well together. Look here," he said, struck with a sudden idea, "are you two blokes doing anything this week-end? If not, why don't you come down with me and give me your moral support. You know the links, and there are always some bunnies."

"I'd like to, Hubert," said Ronald. "What about you, Bill?"

"So would I," I answered, and Hubert got up.

"Good," he said. "Come round to my place at four. I shall be interested to get your reaction to the fair Violet."

And so it transpired that at half-past five we rolled up to the massive doors of Petersdown Towers to find Walters, the old butler, waiting to receive us.

"This is a bit of a surprise, Walters," said Hubert as we got out.

"You mean about Mr. William, Sir Hubert. It is indeed, sir."

He turned away, and Hubert gave us a wink. Quite obviously Walters shared his master's opinion of the lady. And yet, when we met her shortly afterwards with William Ardingley, my first impression was favourable. She was of medium height, and her figure was superb. Good-looking too in a rather flashing style, and evidently determined to make a good impression on Hubert, who was going through the usual formalities of congratulation.

Then a third person appeared on the scene, and a glance at his face showed where he fitted in. The girl's likeness to him was obvious, but I found myself wondering whether he had given up doctoring or doctoring had given him up. The water shortage, so far as his diet was concerned, could not have affected him greatly.

Father and daughter went off shortly after to change, as they were returning to dinner, and we four men went into the billiard-room for a drink. Through the windows one could see the great stretch of rolling park, leading up to an avenue of magnificent copper beeches. In the foreground lay the lake, and on its surface floated two graceful swans with cygnets in attendance.

The home of the Ardingleys for centuries: assuredly Hubert was right. To leave it all after fifty years was not going to be an easy matter. And even as the thought crossed my mind I heard William speaking about it.

"I think I've found the very house that will suit us, Hubert," he was saying, and I glanced at the baronet. His face was expressionless, but one could sense his profound relief. To have the thing settled voluntarily by his uncle was more than he could have hoped for.

"Of course you will stop on here as long as you like, Uncle William," he said.

' Thanks, my dear boy. If I may I will stop till it is ready. It will be a bit of a wrench leaving here after all these years, but one can't have everything. Well—I must write a couple of letters before dinner."

He paused as he reached the door and looked at Ronald.

"You fellows know, don't you, about the dog? He lives near the stables and he's on a chain. Don't go near him, whatever you do."

"Rollo," explained Hubert as the door closed behind his uncle. "A mastiff the size of a donkey, and the most savage brute you can imagine. Uncle William and one of the grooms are the only people who can touch him. Like a game of anything?"

We played slosh till it was time to dress, and at eight o'clock we sat down to dinner. Two other people had come in, and I found myself sitting next to Violet Plessey.

There was no doubt about it: she was an extraordinarily good-looking girl. I admit that it did strike me—though I am a child over women's clothes—that she was a little overdressed for such a small party, but the fault was excusable. She was on Hubert's left, and once again she went out of her way to be charming to him. Sensing, as any woman would do, that he did not like her, she seemed determined to break down his prejudice, and towards the end of the meal she had succeeded, at any rate so far as appearances went. Once I saw William looking at them, and wondered if he was wise to his nephew's feelings; then an interminable story by the doctor on my other side necessitated some semblance of attention.

"I hear Mr. Ardingley has a house in view," I said to the girl when Hubert turned to the woman on his right.

"Yes," she answered. "A sweet little place. We shall be terribly poor, you know."

I murmured some conventional reply: actually that aspect of the case had not struck me. In my thoughts I had got no farther than the fact that William would have to leave Petersdown Towers, but now that she mentioned it I realised the financial side as well. Though the revenue from the estate had been entirely Hubert's since he came of age, his uncle had to a great extent enjoyed the benefits of it, as much as if it had been his own. He had lived rent free and food free; he had had no servants' wages to pay. And now all that was going to stop.

"It is about ten miles from here," she continued. "I do hope William won't miss this too much."

"He's been here a long time," I said.

"He adores the place," she answered in a low voice. "Positively adores it. Sometimes I think . . ."

But what she thought I was not to know, for at that moment Hubert stood up, glass in hand, and in a few words proposed the health of the happy couple. The doctor emitted a porty heart throb anent his little girl, and we all drank to their future prosperity. After which she again monopolised Hubert, and the doctor continued the history of his life.

Strange as one looks back now on that evening, how difficult it is to remember anything of interest. I suppose that it is because it was such a perfectly ordinary evening that there are no pegs which stick out. I remember that Philip was mentioned: I remember Hubert saying that there would be no difficulty about his coming to the wedding as he was only stationed at Invergordon.

I remember, too, that of all strange subjects the conversation came round to walking in one's sleep, and William asking Hubert if he ever did it now.

"You and Philip," he said, "were very bad at one time."

Which naturally the doctor, being that manner of man, found irresistible, and bet that Hubert had not given it up by a long chalk, it being a most convenient malady at times. It was then that I began to dislike the doctor actively, and to realise that if there was anything in heredity Hubert might be right about the girl.

But apart from those two things I remember nothing, because as I said before there was nothing to remember. The guests departed about eleven; half an hour later we all went to bed, Hubert in particular stating that he was most infernally sleepy.

I was not, and for quite a while I sat beside my open window, smoking. It was a pitch dark night, overcast and warm. Ronald and I had adjacent rooms in the west wing, and I could hear him moving about as he went to bed. At last he drew back his curtains and I saw his shadow outlined in the square of light on the ground below.

"Night, night, Bill," he called out, and at that moment we both heard it. Rising and falling in a hideous cadence there came from the other side of the house the deep-throated baying of a hound. Twice, three times; then we heard it no more.

"The Pekingese seems excited," he said. "I think there's going to be a storm."

His bed creaked: his light went out, but still I sat on feeling strangely awake. An owl was hooting mournfully and occasionally a little eddy of breeze made the leaves rustle in the trees near by. Save for that—silence: a brooding, oppressive silence.

Suddenly lightning began to flicker in the distance followed by the muttering of thunder. It was a long way off, and I was just wishing that it would come over us to cool the air when a very vivid flash lit up the grounds. And there, standing under a tree on the other side of the drive, was a man. I could not see his features, or anything else about him; all I knew in that instantaneous exposure was that someone was there.

For a while I debated whether I should wake up Ronald; a man in the garden at that hour of the night was probably up to no good. And then there came another flash; there was no one there. The nocturnal visitor had gone, and I began to wonder whether my eyes had deceived me in the first instance. At any rate it settled the question of arousing anybody; to look for someone outside on such a night would be like searching for the proverbial needle in the hay. And so, after one final cigarette, I switched off the light and turned in.

A hand on my shoulder awakened me, and I sat up blinking. Daylight was streaming in at the window, and Ronald, his usually ruddy face chalk white, was standing by the bed. Outside people were moving about, and instinctively I glanced at my wrist-watch. It was half-past five.

"What's the matter?" I asked.

"Hubert is dead," he answered in a shaking voice. "He's had his throat torn out by the mastiff."

Too stunned to reply I could only stare at him foolishly, and wonder whether I was dreaming. Then I got out of bed and pulled on some clothes.

The servants were standing about in little huddled groups as we went downstairs to the hall where William Ardingley was speaking to a groom. He turned round as we came up and in the early morning light his face looked ghastly.

"My God! Standish," he said. "I can't believe it. I simply can't believe it. It was Rogers here who found the poor boy."

And so we heard the story. Rogers, looking out of his window, had been appalled to see a sprawling figure in pyjamas lying on the ground near the mastiff's kennel. Blood was all over the place, and he could tell at a glance that the man was dead. He had rushed down and pulled the body out of the hound's reach, and then to his horror he had realised it was Sir Hubert.

"Let's go and have a look," said Standish quietly, and I followed him outside to the stables. In one corner stood the kennel, and on the ground covered with some sacks lay the dead man. And he was a terrible sight. His throat was torn and gashed in the most dreadful fashion, and the jacket of his pyjamas was saturated with blood. It had, of course, ceased to flow by that time, but an ominous pool near the kennel showed where the unfortunate baronet had met his end. His feet were bare, and I thought of the conversation at dinner. Obviously he must have been walking in his sleep.

"Do you mean to say, Rogers," said Ronald as the groom and William Ardingley joined us, "that you heard nothing at all?"

"Not a thing, sir. But a mastiff kills mute."

"It doesn't follow that the victim is mute too," answered Ronald.

"Well, sir, I heard nothing," said the groom stubbornly.

"Where is the dog now?"

"I've shut him up in his other kennel."

Ronald gently replaced the sacks over the dead man.

"What a ghastly tragedy, Mr. Ardingley. As you say, one can hardly believe it."

"To think that I should actually have alluded to sleepwalking last night. And then for this to happen. Get a hurdle, Rogers, and carry Sir Hubert into the house. I must go and telephone for a doctor: the death certificate will have to be signed."

He went indoors, and Ronald and I, with a last look at the motionless figure, turned away.

"It's amazing, Bill," said Ronald after a while. "And the more I think of it the more amazing does it seem. That Hubert came here in his sleep is easy to understand: there have been cases of people walking miles in that condition. But being killed by an animal is not an instantaneous death. So why on earth didn't he wake up while it was happening and yell the place down?"

And it was at that moment I remembered the man I had seen standing under the tree. I told Ronald about it and he stopped and stared at me.

"You're sure of that?" he said.

"Positive," I answered. "Though I don't see that it can have any bearing on the matter. It might even have been Hubert himself."

He walked on slowly with a deep frown on his forehead.

"Why didn't he wake, Bill? Why didn't he wake?"

Again and again he harped back to the point, and when I suggested that possibly he had, and that Rogers had slept through his calls for help, he shook his head irritably.

"It's unthinkable," he cried. "A man who is being mauled to death

425

by a hound would wake the dead."

We had come to a corner of the stable yard, where some rabbits blissfully unconscious of the tragedy were having their morning meal.

"Wake the dead," he repeated, as he stood watching them absent-mindedly.

"He evidently didn't wake Rogers," I retorted, feeling a little irritable myself. It certainly was strange, but the bald fact remained that that was what had happened. And that being so there was no more to be said about it.

"Terrible thing about the poor young master, sir."

Another groom had joined us, and Ronald nodded.

"Ghastly," he said. "Where do you sleep?"

"That's my room up there, sir."

He pointed to a corner of the building.

"And you heard nothing in the night?"

"The only thing I heard, sir, was a rabbit squealing. I reckons a stoat had got 'un."

And then a puzzled look came over his face; he was staring at the hutch.

"Well, that be main queer. Where be Susan, the old doe? She were here last night. Couldn't have been her I heard, for the stoat couldn't have got her out through the wire, and she'd have been dead inside there."

He scratched his head and recounted the rabbits.

"Five," he said. "And Susan not there."

He looked at us rather as if he thought we had abducted the lady. And somewhat to my surprise I noticed that Ronald seemed interested in this triviality.

"Do you look after them?" he asked.

"I feeds them, sir—yes."

"And there were six there last night and only five this morning?"

"That's right, sir. Susan's gone. Knows her name, she does. Follows me like a dog across the yard. Susan! Susan!"

But no Susan appeared, and the groom departed still calling for her.

"The somnambulist who didn't wake; the unknown man who watched the house; the rabbit that vanished." Ronald lit a cigarette thoughtfully. "Are they three disconnected facts, Bill, or . . .?"

He fell into a brown study, and after a time I left him and went indoors. I knew the futility of speaking to him when he was in one of those moods. In the hall William Ardingley was talking to a stranger, whom I placed correctly as the doctor, and leaving them together I went upstairs to complete my toilet.

Ronald I could see walking down by the lake evidently sunk in thought. And much as I liked him I could not help a certain feeling of annoyance over his attitude. The whole thing was tragic enough as it stood without making a mystery where no mystery could exist. What was more likely than that the mastiff, with the first snap of his jaws, had severed Hubert's jugular vein, and that to all intents and purposes death had been instantaneous? That would account for no sound having been heard.

It was the view that was taken by the doctor, who had completed his examination by the time I came down again. He was on the point of leaving and William Ardingley was standing by his car.

"There will be a few formalities, Mr. Ardingley," he was saying. "In view of the circumstances the police will have to come into the affair, and they will doubtless order the dog to be destroyed. But beyond that the whole thing is obvious. Sir Hubert was walking in his sleep, and unfortunately got within reach of the mastiff which killed him. The oppressive weather last night may have made it more savage. Once again—my deepest sympathy."

He drove off just as Ronald came up, and a glance at my friend's face told me that he was still not satisfied. But when he spoke to our host there were no signs of it in his voice.

"You will naturally want us to clear out, Mr. Ardingley," he said. "As we came down in Hubert's car perhaps we could have one a little later to take us to the station?"

"Of course, Standish. Whenever you like. But from what the doctor says there may be some police formalities. Had you not better wait for them ?"

"I hardly think it is necessary," said Standish. "Should they require to see us, or ask us anything, we can easily come down again. By the way, where have you put the body?"

"In the gun-room," said Ardingley. "It is still on the hurdle."

We walked indoors and our host went into the study leaving us in the hall.

"What about that man I saw," I remarked. "Oughtn't I to mention him?"

"Everything in due season, Bill," he said gravely. "And this is the wrong one. I am either talking through my hat, or this is one of the most amazing crimes of modern times. Come into the gun-room."

I followed him unwillingly: I had seen enough of that poor mangled body.

"Have you a large clean pocket handkerchief?" he asked, as he pulled back the sheet with which the dead man was now covered.

Completely mystified I produced one. And then, to my amazement, he carefully removed the blood-stained handkerchief from Hubert's pyjama pocket and wrapped it up in mine. Then he replaced the sheet.

"No one is likely to notice that it has gone," he said quietly, and without another word he led the way from the room and went upstairs.

The house, of course, was completely disorganised. Not that it mattered much, for no one could eat any breakfast when it did arrive. And at ten o'clock the car came for us and we started for the station. It was about four miles away and halfway there we met Violet Plessey driving a small two-seater. She stopped at once and we got out to speak to her.

"William has just telephoned through to me, Mr. Standish," she cried. "I simply can't believe it."

"It is only too true, I fear, Miss Plessey," said Ronald.

"Walking in his sleep. How ghastly. Do you think he suffered much?"

"As he didn't call out I should think not at all," said Ronald, and a look of relief spread over her face.

"That would have been too dreadful," she cried, and with that we left her.

"An enigmatic young woman," said Ronald as we resumed our drive. "She and William should get on well."

"What are you driving at?" I demanded.

"Even without the suffering it strikes me as being too dreadful," he answered.

We arrived in London just before one, and Ronald at once dashed for a taxi, leaving me to take our kit in another.

"Wait for me at the club, Bill," he said. ' I may be a couple of hours."

It was nearly three to be exact before I saw him again, and I knew at once that further developments had taken place. Never have I seen him look so stern as he did when he sat down beside me.

"So I was not talking through my hat, Bill," he said.

"Where have you been?" I asked.

"To the laboratory of the Middlesex Hospital," he answered.

"And what have you found out there?"

"That the most coldblooded murder I have ever come across in the whole of my career was committed at Petersdown Towers last night."

"Good God!" I cried. "What are you going to do about it?"

"I have done already, as I came in. I've put through a long-distance call to Philip at Invergordon. I couldn't get him, but I left an urgent message with one of his brother officers that Philip is to get in touch with me the instant he comes back to the ship."

"But can't you arrest the murderer now?"

"As I've often told you, Bill, there's a lot of difference between knowing and proving. I propose to let the murderer arrest himself."

"Who is he?"

"Need you ask? Mr. William Ardingley. He was the man you saw standing under the tree last night. He was waiting for your light to go out. And all I'm wondering is to what extent Miss Violet Plessey is concerned with the matter."

I felt a thrill of horror run through me: the thing seemed too monstrous to be possible. And yet I knew that Ronald was the last man on earth to make a statement of that sort unless he knew it was true. But when I asked him for further details he shook his head.

"All in good time, Bill," he remarked. "You'll know by tomorrow night at latest."

The hours passed and he grew more and more fidgety.

"Why hasn't Philip telephoned?" he said. "The officer I talked to said he'd gone ashore early this morning and was expected back at any moment."

And then at last a page appeared to say that the call had come through and Ronald went to the box.

"It's all right," he said when he returned. "It's the same bloke I talked to before. Philip has had a wire from his uncle telling him of Hubert's death, and he's left in a car to catch the night mail farther south. He's given him my message, and so he'll be round to see me tomorrow morning before he goes to Peters-down Towers. And that being so there's nothing more we can do at present."

The evening passed with maddening slowness, and though I tried to play bridge I was quite unable to keep my mind on the cards. Hubert murdered—and by his uncle! I simply could not get it out of my head. It seemed like an incredible nightmare. And so it was to the intense relief of my partner that I refused to play another rubber and rose from the table just before eleven to see Ronald come rushing into the room like a man distraught.

"Come, Bill. Hurry, for God's sake. Never mind your hat."

He hurled himself into his car which was outside the door, and I fell in beside him. And that run will linger in my memory while I live. He drove like a madman, and how we were not killed a dozen times I do not know.

"Had another call from Invergordon," he shouted above the roar of the car. "Man who motored Philip just returned. . . . He missed train and chartered aeroplane. . . . And he's flown direct to Petersdown Towers. . . . Tried to get him on the 'phone. . . . Line out of order. . . . Pray Heaven we're not too late . . ." The sentences came in jerks as with screeching brakes we skidded round corners.

"Never forgive myself. . . . Last thing I anticipated. . . . Have you got a gun? . . . Of course you haven't . . . I have. . . . There's the house."

The lodge gate was open, and we roared up the drive. The place was in darkness, but suddenly in the light of our headlamps there came a sight which froze the blood in my veins. Fifty yards in front of us by the corner of the stable a huge dog the size of a donkey was standing over something that lay on the ground. And even as we watched it shook something savagely. Then, alarmed by the lights, it lifted its great head and stared at us. We could see the huge slavering jaws, the heavy jowl; could see all its hackles come up as we ran towards it shouting. And then shot after shot into its skull from point blank range, till it sank down dead on top of Philip.

Men were appearing from everywhere as we pulled him out. His throat was torn, but he was still breathing though unconscious. And at that moment William Ardingley came on the scene.

"What has happened?" he cried in a shaking voice.

"Another case of sleepwalking," said Ronald quietly. "And this time a rabbit would not have been necessary, you . . . murderer."

The last two words seemed to pierce the night. A deathly silence settled on the group of servants, and for a space in which a man may count ten William Ardingley faced his accuser. Then with a quick movement he lifted his hand to his mouth, and a few seconds later his dark soul had passed before another tribunal.

★★★★★★

It was many days later before Philip was fit enough to sit up and talk. His throat was still bound up, and he looked weak and ill, but all danger of blood-poisoning was past.

"Explain things, Ronald," he said. "What made you suspect my uncle?"

"What I couldn't understand, Philip, as I said all along, was the absence of noise. A man can do the most amazing things when he walks in his sleep, but it's not difficult to wake him, though it may be dangerous. Therefore it seemed impossible to me that poor old Hubert had been sleepwalking. What, then, had he been doing? That he had walked there in pyjamas when awake was equally out of the question. So it boiled down to the fact that he must have been taken there. Now he couldn't have been taken there while conscious; therefore he must have been drugged, and drugged so heavily that he would not wake even though he was being mauled by the mastiff.

"Then came the extremely interesting point about the rabbit. How had it escaped? The groom was positive it was there over-night; it was not there in the morning. Now a bizarre fact of that sort may be intensely important. He had heard a rabbit squealing, and had put it down to a wild one caught by a stoat. But to me it started another line of thought, which, though it seemed preposterous at first, was no more preposterous than the sleepwalking theory. And so I took Hubert's handkerchief to a laboratory to have a test made.

"You know, of course, that there is a radical difference between human blood and the blood of animals or birds when viewed under the microscope. And I found, not altogether to my surprise, that the blood on the handkerchief was *not* human blood but might easily have come from a rabbit. And that one point established, it became clear that your brother's death was no accident, but plain murder."

Philip stared at him.

"It may have been clear to you," he said, "but it certainly isn't to me. Why on earth should there have been rabbit's blood on the poor old chap?"

"Because your uncle had made one big mistake. When he drugged Hubert he gave him too much and actually killed him. And then, having dragged his body within reach of the mastiff, he found the dog wouldn't touch it. No hound will touch a dead man. Which must have been a pretty nasty moment for Mr. William Ardingley. The whole of his carefully thought out scheme had gone west. There was Hubert dead on the ground, and the mastiff refusing to do his bit. So your uncle had to do it instead. He gashed up Hubert's throat with a knife—I didn't mention it at the time, Bill, but the marks didn't look to me as if the dog had made them—and once again found himself in a quandary. Your brother being dead the blood would hardly flow at all. So he got a rabbit and, having wounded it, let the blood run over Hubert. It was then the groom heard it squealing."

"The infamous old swine!" cried Philip.

"Not a nice piece of work," agreed Ronald. "However, it was obvious you would be the next victim. He would then become the baronet, and remain at Petersdown Towers. So I got through to you. I meant to put you wise over anything you might eat or drink—by the way, how did he drug you?"

"It must have been in a whisky and soda I had just before going to bed," said Philip.

"Probably. However, I was going to get you to pretend to be doped, and to allow him to drag you towards the kennel, when the police would have appeared on the scene and the case was complete. And then to my horror you came here before seeing me. By Jove, Philip, I've never had such a nerve-racking drive in my life! And I give you my word I could have shouted for joy when I saw that brute worrying your throat: it proved you were alive. But whether your uncle had purposely given you less, or whether you stood the same dose better than Hubert we shall never know."

"Supposing Hubert hadn't been dead when the hound smelt him," I said. "What then? The blood would have been human."

"True, Bill. But you can take it from me that even had that been the case Philip would not have spent his first night here alone. I just couldn't swallow that sleepwalking explanation, though it would have been infernally difficult to *prove* it was wrong."

"Amazing he should have the nerve to try it twice on successive nights," said Philip.

Ronald shrugged his shoulders.

"The murderer's mentality is a curious one," he said. "Mark well— it had to be done quickly; he couldn't in ordinary decency have kept that mastiff on here for long after it had apparently killed Hubert. And he probably thought he had a foolproof scheme. No one suspected him over Hubert; why should they over you? The tragedy had preyed on your nerves; what more natural for anyone at all addicted to walking in his sleep than to visit the scene of it? Touch and go, Philip, old lad; another two minutes and the title would have passed again. Though if it is any comfort for you to know, I can assure you the next holder would have been hanged as high as Haman."

"By the way," said Philip, "the Plesseys, *père et fille,* have departed suddenly."

"It isn't too easy to get dope," remarked Ronald quietly. "And old Plessey was a doctor. One wonders."

The Missing Valve

"One of the most extraordinary cases I have ever encountered, Bill," said Ronald Standish to me. "And since a lady, who has, as yet, not appeared in it officially, is coming to consult me on the matter shortly I'd like to run over the facts, so far as they are known, before she arrives."

We were seated in his rooms in Clarges Street early one morning in June. I had been out of London for some weeks, and was therefore out of touch with things. So I had no idea of the case he was referring to, and told him so.

"I am alluding," he continued, "to the death of Charles Sinley outside the lift on the top floor of a block of flats in Carimer Terrace. Now it will be of great assistance to me to give you the story up to date: not only in order to get your reaction but also to get things in sequence in my own head.

"Carimer Terrace, as you know, lies north of the Park. It consists of a row of those large houses in which, during the Victorian era, wealthy lawyers and stockbrokers used to live. Not fashionable, but the houses were big and comfortable, requiring a large staff to run them. Of late years they have fallen quite out of favour, and several of them have been converted into service flats. And it was in number nineteen that the tragedy happened three days ago.

"The top floor flat, which is the only one we are concerned with, is rented by a man called Raymond Tranton. He is thirty-seven years of age, a bachelor, and of independent means. Apparently he does nothing for a livelihood, and is very fond of the ladies. He dabbles mildly in art, and outside of that his only hobby appears to be things electrical.

"On the night in question he was throwing a small party, which on this occasion was eminently respectable. There were present Lady

Graddon and her daughter; a Mrs. Vrowson and her husband, and a friend of Miss Graddon's called Mary Baxford.

"It was a warm night, and the windows were wide open. The time was half-past ten, and the wireless was relaying an opera from Cologne. Suddenly there came a sound of an explosion, and they all looked up. It seemed close to, and was the sort of noise a backfire in an exhaust makes. Or it might have been a gun. . . .

"Tranton, who was standing by the door, opened it and peered out.

"'What the devil was that?' he said, and walked along the passage, leaving the others still in the drawing-room.

"He went to the front door, and a few moments later was back with an ashen face.

"'Vrowson,' he cried, 'for God's sake come. Will you ladies please stop here.'

"Major Vrowson—he's a retired soldier—at once and accompanied his host outside the flat. And there close by the front door, and opposite the entry to the lift was the sprawling body of a man. He lay face downwards, and a pool of blood had formed on the floor round his head. Beside him was a doublebarrelled twelve-bore.

"Very gently they turned him over and then Tranton gave another exclamation of horror.

"'Good heavens!' he muttered. 'It's Charlie Sinley. What on earth can have happened?'

"The poor devil was a horrible sight. Half his face was shot away, and it was obvious at a glance that he was dead.

"'You know him?' said Vrowson stupidly.

"'Of course I know him. He must have stumbled over something coming out of the lift and shot himself.'

"'Where is the lift?' said the major.

"'It goes down automatically when the door is shut,' said Tranton. 'My God! this is awful. We must get the police at once, and not touch anything till they come. Go to the women, there's a good fellow, and don't let 'em come out here. I'll get on to the police station.'

"So Vrowson returned to the drawing-room, and Tranton did the necessary telephoning. And ten minutes later the police arrived, during which time Tranton had been busy getting a room ready for the body.

"(As you will note, Bill, I am piecing the evidence at the inquest together in narrative form to make it clearer for you.)

435

"Inspector Mac Andrew, an extremely shrewd man, was in charge, and he at once began his investigations. The double-barrelled gun was found to contain one used and one unused cartridge, so the cause of death was obvious. One barrel was dirty, the other was clean, and that settled that. And then the inspector noticed a lot of fragments of coloured china lying about on the floor, which he picked up and carefully stowed away. After which he ordered his men to move the body into the flat, and having rung up the doctor, he proceeded to question the members of the party.

"It was a mere formality, since obviously none of them could tell him anything save that they all heard the shot, and after taking their names and addresses they were permitted to go.

"MacAndrew then interrogated Tranton, but he could throw no light on the matter either. He said that he knew Sinley very well, and that Sinley frequently came to his flat. They both belonged to the same club, and that very evening he had had a cocktail with him there. He had told Sinley he had a few people coming in, and had suggested that he should drop in too if he cared to. And that was positively all he could say. The thing was a complete mystery.

"It seemed evident that death had been caused by a barrel going off accidentally as he got out of the lift. But why Sinley should have been wandering round London with a loaded twelve bore in his possession was absolutely beyond him. He was a keen shot, and a good shot, which made it all the more mysterious. It was possible he had been bringing round the gun to show Tranton, but why he hadn't brought it in a gun case was simply inexplicable. Am I since the poor devil was dead the reason had died with him.

"Then came the inquest at which all that I have told you came out, with one more fact that made the whole thing even more bizarre. With infinite care MacAndrew had pieced together the fragments of coloured china. And though there were several missing, what remained formed part of a grotesque-looking mask.

"'What do you make of that?' asked the coroner.

"'I can only conclude, sir,' answered MacAndrew, 'that Mr. Sinley was wearing this mask as a joke. Had he been merely holding it in his hand, it would have fallen on the floor and we should have found all the pieces close together. As it is many of them were not I there, and the others were widely scattered about.'

"'So that the shot went through the mask?' continued the coroner.

"'Exactly, sir,' said the inspector, and on that a verdict of accidental death was brought in."

Ronald lit a cigarette. "So there you are, Bill; and I think you will agree that it is the most extraordinary case. Why should a presumably sane man, and one who is a good shot, carry a loaded sporting gun in London? Why—another small thing which I forgot to mention before—was he not in evening clothes?"

"What had the porter below got to say?" I asked.

"He goes off duty at ten, so he doesn't come into it. The entrance is deserted from then on."

"Has any taxi-driver come forward?"

"No. But there is nothing strange in that. Sinley lived in Merridew Terrace, which is the next street. He would therefore almost certainly have walked."

"Carrying a twelve-bore?" I cried incredulously.

"Just so," said Ronald. "It is amazing. But so far as I can see there is no other explanation that fits the facts. Suicide is out of the question: why should a man who wanted to commit suicide put on a china mask and do it outside a friend's flat?"

"Murder?" I suggested. "Isn't it possible there was somebody outside the door of Tranton's flat who shot him as he got out of the lift: left the gun beside him and then calmly went down in the lift himself?"

"I'd thought of that, Bill," said Ronald. "Anything is possible in this impossible case. But think of the difficulties. In the first place it wasn't certain that Sinley was coming at all, though it is conceivable he might have said he was to somebody who wanted to kill him. And then that somebody proceeds to run the appalling risk taking up his position, with a loaded gun, outside the door of Tranton's flat through which at any moment the party might emerge. Its possible, but it's darned unlikely. No; on the data in *our* possession at the moment accident seems the only possible solution. It may be that when"—he consulted a letter on his desk—"Miss Sheila Darby has said her piece we shall think otherwise."

"And who is Miss Sheila Darby?"

"I don't know. Her letter merely states that she is coming round to see me in connection with this affair. And, if I mistake not, here she is."

The front door bell rang, and a moment or two later Bates ushered in a girl of about twenty-five. We both rose.

"Miss Darby, I assume," said Ronald with a bow. "May I introduce Mr. Leyton?"

He rushed forward a chair and I studied our visitor. She was distinctly pretty, with fair, auburn hair and blue eyes which showed traces of tears. She was dressed in black, and there was a ring on her engagement finger. So it was not difficult to see where she fitted into the picture. Obviously the dead man's *fiancée*, and I waited with interest to hear what she had to say.

"Cigarette?" said Ronald, offering her his case.

'No, thank you," she answered. And then she burst out suddenly: "Mr. Standish, you *must* do something. That verdict is all wrong."

"Take your time, Miss Darby," said Ronald quietly, "and tell me all about it. Why do you think the verdict is wrong?"

"Because Charlie and that brute Mr. Tranton hated one another like poison," she cried.

Ronald leaned forward in his chair.

"The devil they did," he said softly. "But Tranton in his evidence said that Sinley was a friend of his. Called him Charlie."

"Lies: all lies. Raymond Tranton may have called him Charlie, but that was the extent of their friendship."

"How do you know that?"

"Because I was engaged to Charlie, and . . ."

She hesitated a moment and Ronald smiled faintly.

"And Tranton was not pleased. I see."

"He's worried my life out for years," she continued, "and I loathe the man. Mr. Standish, I know that verdict is wrong."

"What do you suggest it should have been?" asked Ronald.

"Mr. Tranton murdered Charlie," she said fiercely. "I know it."

"Come, come, Miss Darby," said Ronald gravely, "that's a very serious accusation to make in view of the proven facts. When the shot that killed your *fiancé* was heard, Tranton and five other people were in the drawing-room. You mustn't make wild statements of that sort, you know: it won't do any good."

"I don't care," she answered stubbornly. "I know I'm right. How he did it, I don't know. And that," she added fiercely, "is in have to find out. Mr. Standish," she continued earnestly, "I know you must think I'm letting my feelings run away with me, but I beseech you to listen to me. Knowing Charlie as I do"—she gave a little dry sob—"did I tell you the thing is impossible. Going about with a loaded gun is amazing enough; but that Charlie, being on the terms he was with Mr.

Tranton, should have proposed to go into his flat with an idiotic mask on his face, I cannot and will not believe."

"It certainly seems very strange, Miss Darby," agreed Ronald. "Even stranger now that you tell me what the relations were between the two men."

She clenched her hands together fiercely.

"It isn't strange, Mr. Standish: it is impossible, Charlie would *never* have done such a thing."

Still, Miss Darby, one must go on facts, mustn't one? I admit that the only ones I know are those that came out at the inquest. But it is absolutely certain that at the moment the shot was fired Tranton was in the drawing-room with the door shut."

"I know: I know. But still . . ."

"I suppose you didn't see your *fiancé* earlier that night? I was only trying to see," he continued when she shook her head, "if by any chance we could verify Tranton's statement that he asked him to look in that evening. Find out exactly what he said . . ."

"That's another point, Mr. Standish," said the girl. "I can't swear that Charlie *never* used to go to his flat, but to imply, as Mr. Tranton did, that Charlie was frequently there was false. He wasn't: that I know."

"So we arrive at one new and significant point, Bill," remarked Ronald thoughtfully. "Tranton, for some reason or other, wished the world to think they were friends, when they weren't. Why, unless . . ."

He fell silent, drumming with his fingers on the desk, while we both stared at him.

"What do you want me to do, Miss Darby?" he said abruptly.

"Go and find out the truth," cried the girl with her eyes blazing. "*I know Charlie didn't kill himself accidentally.*"

'Bless her darling heart," said Ronald a few moments later, when the door had closed behind her. "It doesn't seem hard enough, does it, Bill?"

He was pacing up and down the room, his hands thrust deep in his pockets.

"It does throw a new light on the thing—that they were enemies not friends. But how does it help? How does that alter the main incontrovertible fact that Tranton was in the drawing-room with the door shut when the shot that killed Sinley was fired? It is impossible that that is not true. If it were a lie five perfectly respectable people have committed perjury, and connived at murder. No: no: that *must* be true. I wonder if there would be a chance of getting hold of MacAndrew. He's a good fellow, and through him it might be possible to have a look at the scene. Though what . . . Good Lord! talk of the devil . . ."

In the doorway stood the bulky form of Inspector MacAndrew, holding a small suitcase in his hand.

"My dear Mac," he cried, "what fortunate chance brings you here? I was just talking about you."

"And I'll lay a shade of odds you were also talking about what has brought me here—the Sinley case," answered the inspector.

"You win," said Ronald. "There's whisky in the sideboard, and tell me why I am thus honoured."

"Entirely because of your last visitor—Miss Darby."

The inspector splashed some soda into his glass and sat down.

"I want to know, Mr. Standish, if you'll be good enough to tell me what she has said to you."

Ronald raised his eyebrows.

"It's rather an unusual request," he said. "At the same time I don't think anything she said can be regarded as confidential. But fair play is a jewel. If I tell you, will you let me in on the whole thing?"

"I will," answered MacAndrew.

"I score on it," laughed Ronald. "Because what she told me is merely feminine intuition. In short, she was engaged to Sinley."

"I knew that," said the inspector. "That is why she has been shadowed. She was marked down here, and I came along at once."

"She was engaged to Sinley," repeated Ronald, "and the fact did not please Mr. Tranton. He has apparently been badgering her for years to marry him. So—and this is the only piece of news I can give you—Tranton's pose of friendship with Sinley is a lie. So much for hard tack. As for intuition, she is certain that the verdict at the inquest was wrong, and that it should have been one of murder against Tranton."

The inspector puffed thoughtfully at his cigarette.

"This is one of the most baffling cases, Mr. Standish," he said at length, "that I have ever handled. You may have guessed that everything did not come out at the inquest?"

"I thought it possible," grinned Ronald.

MacAndrew picked up his suitcase, and put it on the desk.

"I have here," he said, "the china mask which the papers have been so intrigued about."

We bent over him eagerly as he gently undid the wrappings, and placed it on the blotter. It was a strange looking object with a big jagged hole in the centre. Coloured fantastically, it represented the face of a gargoyle from which the nose and part of the mouth were missing. At the top a small triangular piece of metal enabled it to be hung on a nail. The bits had been seccotined together, and the whole effect was grotesque.

"Examine it, Mr. Standish," said the inspector, "but for heaven's sake handle it gently."

Ronald picked it up and studied it through a magnifying glass; then with a shrug of his shoulders he put it down again.

"I confess I see nothing here which controverts the evidence we've heard. And yet there must be something. I can see you chuckling, you old devil. Wait a moment . . ."

He turned the mask over so that the inside white surface was uppermost. And the next instance he gave an exclamation.

"Great Scott!" he cried. "So that's what you mean. D'you see, Bill?"

He was pointing to a faint black smear which stretched all round the jagged hole.

"Sorry to be so dense," I said.

"The scorching of the powder, boy," he cried. "So the gun was let off from *inside* the mask, and not from the outside."

"Good man," said MacAndrew. "I thought for once I'd caught you, Mr. Standish. As you say, the gun was discharged from the inside, and therefore Sinley cannot have been wearing the mask."

"Even so, Mac, I don't see that that helps much. In fact if anything it makes it easier. He was taking it round to show Tranton. He wasn't wearing it, which was the one thing Miss Darby by refused to believe. By some extraordinary accident the gun went off; the shot passed through the mask and hit him in the head. As I see it, it strengthens the case for the verdict."

Without a word the inspector replaced the mask in his suitcase; then with twinkling eyes he picked up his drink.

"Possibly," he said. "Possibly. So now I will come to my second little surprise: the extraordinary phenomenon of the finger-prints on the gun."

"What was extraordinary about 'em?" asked Ronald.

"There were none."

We stared at him blankly.

"None!" said Ronald.

"None. And, Mr. Standish, the dead man had no gloves on."

"Good Lord! Mac—this beats cock-fighting," cried Ronald.

"I'm going to beat it still further," cried the inspector triumphantly. "On the mask you've just been examining there were finger-prints. On the big bit up by the hook."

"Whose were they?"

"That I don't know. But they were *not* Charles Sinley's. And"—he paused impressively—"they were made after it was broken. They point towards the hook and not away from it."

"Well, I'm damned," said Ronald, getting up and going to the sideboard. "This requires alcohol. What do you make of it, Mac?"

"That the verdict was wrong. That someone murdered Sinley. That, in view of what Miss Darby has told you, that someone was Tranton. But how he did it I have absolutely no idea."

"Then, my dear Mac, the sooner we have an idea the better. If between us we can't solve the matter we'll go into the country and grow tomatoes. Can we get into Carimer Terrace?"

"We can. Very fortunately Mr. Tranton is staying with friends in the country."

"Then," said Ronald, "we might avail ourselves of his absence." He rang the bell. "Bates—a taxi."

★★★★★★

A small crowd of morbid sightseers was standing round the door as we drew up, though it was now three days since the tragedy.

"Can't get rid of 'em, sir," grumbled the irate hall porter, touching his cap to MacAndrew. "Though wot the 'ell they think they're going to see, I dunno."

"I'm going up to Mr. Tranton's flat, Johnson," said the inspector. "We think something may have been lost out of Mr. Sinley's pocket when he was carried in," he continued, winking at Ronald. "Can you lend me the master key?"

"Certainly, sir," and thus armed we proceeded up in the lift.

"Grossly irregular," said the inspector with a chuckle. "But there are times when one must take the law into one's own hands."

The lift stopped and we stepped out on to a narrow landing about four feet wide. On our right was a big window overlooking Carimer Terrace, whilst immediately in front of us a small pane of glass which could not be opened was let into the wall.

"That," said the inspector, pointing to it, "is the window of the cloak-room in Tranton's flat."

Close beside it, and about a foot to the left was an open ventilator covered with the usual metal grille; and two yards more to the left was the door of the flat facing the top of the stairs.

"The body," said the inspector, "was lying with the head towards the lift and diagonally across the landing. The gun was by the right side; the bits of china were scattered all over the place, but no fragment was more than a yard from the body. Now, if you'll come inside, Mr. Standish, you can get the lay-out of the flat: then you can put on your thinking cap."

He opened the door and we entered a small hall. In front of us ran a passage, and the inspector led the way along it.

"This," he said, pointing to a door on the right, "is the room in which the body was put. And this," as we came to the next one, "is the drawing-room, in which the whole party was sitting when the shot was fired. With the door shut," he added.

"Draw a rough sketch. Bill." said Ronald, as he studied the room. "Get your measurements approximately right. Now look here, Mac," he continued, "let us sum up so far as we have gone at the moment. The absence of any finger-prints on the gun is conclusive proof that Sinley didn't bring it with him."

"Practically conclusive," agreed Mac Andrew. "Then someone must have placed it beside him after the shot was fired, and that some-one was wearing gloves, or using a pocket handkerchief, to prevent his own finger-marks appearing."

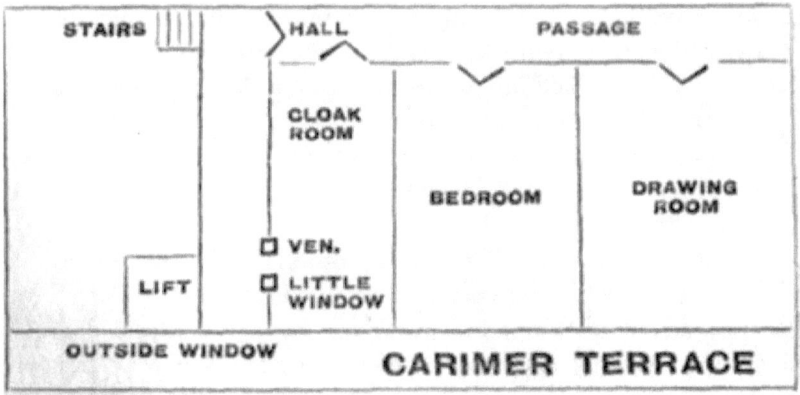

443

"Agreed," said the inspector. "Since the finger-prints on the china are not Sinley's it is clear that he didn't bring the mask either. And as the prints on the china were made *after* it was smashed, it seems a fair assumption that whoever put the gun there touched the china. The fact that there are prints on one and not on the other could be accounted for in many ways. He was flustered and replaced his hand-kerchief in his pocket after arranging the gun; then for some reason he picked up this one broken bit of the mask with his bare hand."

"Quite feasible, but far from proven, said MacAndrew. "Still we can take it as a working hypothesis. But who fired the gun, because he must be the man who did the rest? Unless we assume a confederate. And if I'm not going dippy that lets out Tranton. You can't fire a gun through a door and round four corners. Apart altogether from the audience."

"Come, come, Mac. Many a gun has been fired when the stock has not been against a man's shoulder. No one is suggesting that the shot was fired from this room."

"Well, where was it fired from?"

"Obviously somewhere near the lift. That's our hunting ground. Come on."

I followed them to the landing outside, where for a quarter of an hour Ronald prowled about muttering to himself.

"Must have been a place to which Sinley would certainly go . . . About his own height. . . . He wouldn't be stooping . . . Not cloak room window or glass would have been broken . . . Not . . . Hullo! Hullo!"

He whipped out a magnifying glass and focused it on the plaster above the ventilator. Then with a match he began probing gently.

"Mac," he cried, "come here. There's been a nail in this plaster. And the hole has been filled in recently. It's still soft. And, ye Gods, man—look at this." His voice was vibrating with excitement. "The top of this ventilator is scorched. The shot was fired through there."

MacAndrew was equally excited.

"But—how, man—how?"

"Steady," said Ronald. "Don't let's go too fast. The nail. Supposing the mask had been hung over that ventilator? Supposing Sinley, his attention caught by such a bizarre object on the wall, stopped a mo-ment to examine it, and at that moment the gun was fired? Does that meet it?"

"Yes—but . . ."

"Wait a moment. Just supposing—does that meet it? The mask was hit from the inside and shattered. Sinley was killed. The big bit of china attached to the nail did not come off the wall. The man who placed the gun beside the body saw it and took it off himself. What about it, Mac?"

"But who fired the gun?" persisted the inspector stubbornly.

"The murderer," grinned Ronald. "Let's consider that later. Does that meet it, so far as it goes?"

"So far as it goes, I suppose it does," admitted MacAndrew cautiously. "In fact I believe you're on the right track. There's no doubt the top of the ventilator is scorched; and there's no doubt a nail has recently been removed from the plaster. But we're still a long way from home, Mr. Standish. Are you suggesting the murderer was in the cloak room the whole time? For that again lets out Tranton, at any rate, as the actual murderer."

"Supposing the gun had been previously fixed in position and was fired electrically?"

"How would he know when to fire it?" demanded MacAndrew. "He was in the drawing-room."

"Arrangement of mirrors," said Ronald tentatively.

"But the door was shut, man. The drawing-room door was shut. You can't see through walls."

"Supposing he'd fixed up some system of wires," persisted Ronald, "by which he could know in the drawing-room when the lift reached the top?"

"You mean ring a bell, or show a light? Think of the risk. All his guests would have heard it or seen it, and then immediately after there's a shot, and a man is killed. Besides think of the practical difficulties. I'll give you that he can play about with his electrical gadgets as much as you like inside his flat, even to the extent of firing the gun electrically, and no one will be any the wiser. But not outside in a public passage. A thing like that can't be fixed up in a minute. . . . What are you grinning at?"

"Mac—we're being too clever. I've got it, Bill—go downstairs, and come up in the lift. Mac—come back to the drawing-room with me." They went into the flat, closing the door behind them, and I descended the stairs. Then I went up in the lift, and sent it down again.

"Hoyo!" I called out. "Let me in."

The door opened slowly, and I saw Ronald looking distinctly crestfallen.

445

"Not a sound," he said glumly. "I expected to hear the damn thing, or at any rate the gate shutting. But not a sound."

"And we weren't talking," remarked MacAndrew. "He had a party, and the wireless going into the bargain."

"Couldn't you hear anything at all?" I asked.

"Not the hint of a whisper," answered Ronald. "It's absolutely silent. And yet, Mac, we *must* be on the right tack: we *must*."

Once again he studied the ventilator and the nail mark above it.

"It all fits," he went on. "Look, you can even see that that metal grille has been recently moved. There's a fresh scratch on the plaster. We're hot, Mac; we're hot. Don't you think so yourself?"

"I do. But how did he know when to fire?"

' You'll admit, won't you, that *if* he knew when to fire he could have done it from the drawing-room?"

"Ye-es. I'll admit that."

"Therefore that is what the problem narrows down to. Assuming for the moment it was Tranton, how did he knew when to fire? Mirrors—out of the question: a system of wires on the lift giving some signal inside the flat—possible, but I admit very dangerous; the noise of the lift—nothing doing. What is left? Damn it, you fellows—surely three sane men can hit on the solution between 'em?"

He was walking restlessly up and down the room as he spoke. Tastefully furnished, it left no doubt in one's mind that Tranton was a man of means. Even the wireless was of the super type that combines itself with an electric gramophone capable of playing a dozen records on end, and mechanically I switched it on. Somewhat to my surprise nothing happened, and looking inside I saw that one of the valves was missing. And I had just mentioned the fact when there came the sound of a key in the front door; Raymond Tranton had unexpectedly returned. Undeniably the situation was awkward, as he stood in the passage staring at the three of us.

"May I ask to what I owe the pleasure of this visit?" he remarked coldly. "Johnson told me you were here. I was always under the impression that a warrant was necessary before you entered a man's house. I presume you have one, Inspector?"

"I have not," said MacAndrew calmly. "But we had reason to believe, Mr. Tranton, that a very vital paper had been dropped from Mr. Sinley's pocket when he was carried in here, and we assumed you would have no objection to our looking for it."

"Indeed! And who are these two gentlemen?"

"Friends of Sinley's," said Ronald promptly. "What a sad affair."

Tranton's eyes narrowed momentarily.

"We were talking to him the very evening it happened," lied Ronald cheerfully, and I could have laughed at the effect of the bluff. Tranton was obviously rattled; and why should he be if everything had been as he said?

"Of course, any friend of poor old Charlie's is welcome here," he said after a pause. "Did he tell you he was coming to see me?"

"He said he had an engagement at ten-thirty," answered Ronald. "And he mentioned something about that strange china mask."

"Really! What did he say?"

I glanced at MacAndrew; the situation was intriguing. Tranton was fencing blind; could Ronald get through his guard ?

"I suppose I must have misunderstood him," said Ronald. "I gathered he was going to have a look at one belonging to his host. Have you got one yourself?"

We had drifted back into the drawing-room.

"I?" cried Tranton. "No."

"Strange. I certainly got that impression."

"As you say, you must have misunderstood him," said Tranton. "Well, gentlemen, if you have seen all you want to . . ."

He paused, his hand on the door knob.

"Just a minute, Mr. Tranton," said the inspector quietly. "You were a great friend, I believe, of Mr. Sinley's."

"I was."

"Well, it may interest you to know that we have come to the conclusion that the verdict at the inquest was quite wrong."

"Indeed!"

"Mr. Sinley was murdered."

"Murdered! Good God! Who by?"

"That is what we are trying to find out. You know of no one, I suppose, who had a grudge against him?"

"Good heavens, no. Charlie was a very popular man."

"I ask you particularly," continued the inspector, "because, amazing though it may seem, we think the murderer must have been in your flat."

"Impossible," cried Tranton. "The flat was empty save for the party in here. But in any case, what on earth makes you think that he was here?"

I was watching him narrowly, and I gave him full marks for his manner. If our suspicions were right, and he was implicated in the matter, no trace of guilt showed in his face.

"Certain indications," said MacAndrew. "But before I go into them there is one rather important little point that might help us. When you found all that broken china lying near the body, did you pick up any of the pieces?"

"Quite positively—no. I touched nothing."

"And Major Vrowson touched nothing either?"

"I can't actually swear to that, but I am convinced he didn't. But surely that is a detail. What I want to know is how Charlie could have been shot by someone who was in this flat, seeing that he met his death on the landing outside."

"Through the ventilator in your cloak room," said MacAndrew quietly.

Tranton laughed.

"Really, Inspector, this sounds like detective fiction gone mad. Are you seriously suggesting that a man was concealed in the cloak room with a twelve bore? Why, I should have seen him leaving the flat."

"You went straight outside, Mr. Tranton. He might have remained there unnoticed and escaped later when you went back to the drawing-room."

"What about the gun?" cried Tranton. "It was beside the body when I got there."

"He might have passed that through the ventilator," answered the inspector.

"That is true," agreed Tranton. "But if I may say so, it all seems most unlikely."

"When you think of it, no more unlikely than Mr. Sinley coming to see you with a loaded double-barrelled gun."

Tranton shrugged his shoulders.

"I agree; that was inexplicable. Well, gentlemen, if you are right I trust you discover this man. I can't help thinking myself that the verdict was correct, and that it was just one of those amazing accidents that can never be accounted for. May I offer you a drink? '

"Thank you," said MacAndrew. "I should like one. Whisky, please."

"Say when," remarked Tranton, going to the sideboard and holding up a glass.

"Just right," said the inspector, as he took it. "Sorry to have intruded in this way, but we thought perhaps we might find some litter or paper which would throw light on this man."

"My flat is at your disposal any time you wish," said Tranton politely. "Nothing would give me greater pleasure than to see poor Charlie's murderer caught, if indeed he was murdered."

And a few minutes later we were in the street.

"A cool customer, Mr. Standish, if he's guilty," remarked MacAndrew. "I'll let you know the result of the finger-prints shortly."

"What's that, Mac?" said Ronald, staring at him.

"I've got the glass in my pocket," said MacAndrew with a wink. "What do you suppose I had a drink for?"

But it was not until six o'clock that we saw him again.

"You're right, Mr. Standish," he greeted us gravely. "The marks on the glass and the china are identical. Further, I took advantage of his absence this afternoon to pay the flat another visit. The metal grille of the ventilator is loose, and there are the same finger-prints on that. Tranton did it: but how? How? How did he know when to fire the gun? Until we can find that out he's got us euchred. A clever counsel would tear our case to shreds. And I confess I'm beat. Can't you think of anything, Mr. Standish?"

Ronald stretched out his legs.

"A possibility has occurred to me, Mac," he said. "A bare possibility. When can we get into his flat again?"

"He's away this weekend," said MacAndrew. "But what's your idea?"

"So vague that I'll say nothing about it at the moment," answered Ronald. "There's just one thing we haven't tried. I propose to do so."

And not another word would he say.

★★★★★

I did not see him again till the following Monday.

"Like to be in at the death, Bill?" he said. "We've got him. My bare possibility was a bull's-eye."

"How did he do it ?" I cried eagerly.

"You wait and see, old boy," he grinned. "Come to my rooms at nine."

I found MacAndrew there, who was as much befogged as I was.

"I've got a warrant," he said. "But I'm still completely in the dark."

And at that moment Ronald entered carrying a small parcel.

"Leave him to me, Mac," he said. "The fish is hooked, but the tackle is light. He'll require careful playing."

449

He was surprised to see us, was Tranton, and not too pleased.

"Surely," he cried irritably, "you don't want to search the flat again. I have an engagement."

"We shan't keep you long, Mr. Tranton," said Ronald quietly. "But some further facts have come to light. Now," he continued, when we were in the drawing-room, "I want to reconstruct the whole thing. You were in the drawing-room with the door shut talking to your friends when the shot was fired. You dashed out, and along the passage; you went to the front door and there you found Sinley lying dead. Do you mind if we do that? A substitute is taking the part of Sinley."

"This is absurd," said Tranton. "However, if it affords you any satisfaction, I will."

We followed him to the landing outside, where a constable lay sprawling on the floor with the gun beside him, and broken china lying about near him.

"That's right," said Tranton, and suddenly gave a little gasp. I glanced at him; his face was dead white. He was staring like a man bereft at the ventilator, where the top bit of the broken mask hung on a nail.

"Quite right, isn't it?" agreed Ronald.

"But you seem surprised. Wasn't that piece on the nail when you came out the other night?"

Of course not," he stammered. "How could it have been?"

"How indeed," said Ronald pleasantly. "You at once took it down."

"A lie," shouted Tranton.

"Then how come your finger marks on it?" asked Ronald quietly.

"I may have touched it as it lay on the floor," said Tranton sullenly.

"'Quite positively—no,' was your answer to the inspector's question," remarked Ronald.

"Good God! man, with a tragedy like that one may forget a trifle." Tranton with a great effort had recovered his self-control. "In any event, what has it to do with me? I was in the drawing-room when it happened."

"Let us return there," said Ronald. "As you say you were in the drawing-room talking to your friends."

"And if you'll tell me how anyone in the drawing-room could know when a man arrives on the landing outside I shall be obliged," he sneered.

"Just what I am going to tell you," answered Ronald, unwrapping his parcel. "For that is the very point that has been worrying us. You see, Tranton, you murdered Sinley by firing a fixed gun electrically through the ventilator. You had asked him to examine that strange mask you had suspended on a nail . . ."

"Are you mad?" spluttered Tranton.

"But our difficulty, in view of the fact that the lift is absolutely silent, was to find out how you knew when he was in position so to speak. And then it suddenly dawned on me that not only were you talking, but you were playing the wireless. Shall we turn it on now, Tranton?"

The colour of chalk, Tranton plucked at his collar ceaselessly.

"When trying it before we found a valve had been removed," continued Ronald. "Which struck me as strange, since it was playing all right on the night of the party. So I obtained another. Here it is. Hold him, Mac."

Struggling like a madman in the grip of the inspector and the constable who had joined us, Raymond Tranton strove to get at Ronald, who was imperturbably adjusting the valve.

"Now," he said, "let's hear the news."

He switched on; then, going to the window, he waved his hand.

"Another constable representing Sinley is about to come up in the lift," he said. "Listen."

It started suddenly; a clear piercing note from the wireless. Then it stopped.

"The lift is up," said Ronald quietly.

Came a pause; then the noise started again.

"Now it's going down. And now Sinley is looking at the mask. And now you killed him, Tranton. That is how you knew when he'd arrived on the landing."

The shrill note stopped, and in the room there was dead silence.

"The lift was inaudible, save when the wireless was playing. Then, the lift being electric, *that* noise took place. Ingenious, Tranton, very ingenious."

"You can't prove it," snarled the other.

"At any rate," said Ronald affably, "we can have a damned good attempt."

The Paper Stamp

"Show the gentleman in, Sayers," said Ronald Standish, tossing the card his man had just given him over to me. I glanced at it and saw that our visitor was a Mr. Alfred Humber of Humber, Jones and Humber, Gray's Inn; and a moment or two later a typical family solicitor entered, who looked from one to the other of us in doubt.

"Take a chair, Mr. Humber," said Ronald, rising and pulling one forward. "This is Mr. Miller."

Mr. Humber sat down and mopped his forehead with a handkerchief.

"Cooler in here than it is outside, Mr. Standish," he remarked in a deep, rather pleasant voice. "But as I expect you are a busy man, I'll get down to the reason of my visit right away. It was Mr. James Marrowby from whom I heard about you some two years ago, and I docketed your name for future reference should the occasion ever arise."

Ronald bowed. "I remember Mr. Marrowby's case well," he remarked. "How can I be of service to you?"

Mr. Humber drew some papers from his pocket and adjusted a pair of spectacles.

"I should like to make it quite clear at the beginning, Mr. Standish," he said, "that I can only give you a bare outline of what has happened. The details I do not know myself, but I am hoping that if you are sufficiently interested you will come forthwith to Ashington Manor and go into the matter more fully. Have you by any chance read the morning papers closely? You haven't. Then you will not have seen the small paragraph that contains the news.

"Ashington Manor lies not far from Tenterden, and it belongs—or rather belonged—to a Mr. George Sinclair who has been a client of my firm for years. And it is in connection with his sudden and very unexpected death yesterday that I have come to see you.

"But before I come to that part of it, which I have only heard in brief over the telephone, it will be necessary for me to give you some details as to his circumstances generally. He was a man just rising sixty-five, in excellent health save that recently he has been having some little digestive trouble for which a doctor has been treating him. He was unmarried, and for the past four or five years his nephew John Sinclair has been living with him. His hobbies were a strange mixture, gardening and toxicology, and for the purposes of the latter he had built a room at the end of the garden which he used as a laboratory and study. It was in this room that he was found dead by his nephew at four o'clock yesterday afternoon.

"I must now deal with another aspect of his affairs, which, as things have panned out, is a very important one. I allude to finance. Mr. Sinclair some years ago was a quite wealthy man, but he was one of those dear fellows who was under the fond delusion that he was a financial genius. And it soon became apparent to us that unless he was watched carefully he wouldn't remain wealthy for long. So we persuaded him to put his investments in our hands, where they have remained ever since. We also advised him to take out an insurance policy on his life, which he did. And it is over this policy that the trouble, if any, is going to arise. I have it here with me and I will give you the details.

"The business was effected with the Southern British, and the policy was for a certain number of years or earlier death. You are doubtless familiar with similar schemes."

"I am," said Ronald. "How many years was it?"

"Twenty-five; of which twenty-four and nine months have already elapsed."

"And for what was he insured?"

"The sum which would have fallen due, had he lived, in three months from now is just under twenty-five thousand pounds."

"Which now that he is dead falls due at once," remarked Ronald.

"Now we are coming to the point, Mr. Standish." The lawyer leaned forward impressively. "Again I must remind you that my information is of the scantiest, and that what I am about to tell you is what I heard in an agitated conversation over the 'phone with his nephew. John told me, that amazing though it might seem, the circumstances pointed to suicide."

"In which case the company won't pay up," said Ronald.

"Exactly. But as John said to me, the thing is incredible. What possible reason could there be for him to take his own life? His finances were sound, though like all of us he had felt the draught during these past few years. And in three months from now he would have received twenty-five thousand pounds."

"Come, come, Mr. Humber," remarked Ronald, "there are other reasons for suicide beside financial ones."

"I would be the last to deny it," said the lawyer. "But in his case I can think of none. He thoroughly enjoyed life; he was healthy; there was no question of the loss, say, of a devoted wife. There is nothing, Mr. Standish, that I can think of which could have caused my old friend to take his life."

"How did he do it?" asked Ronald.

"I understand from John that he drank poison," answered Mr. Humber, and Ronald raised his eyebrows.

"That looks a pretty deliberate action," he remarked. "I mean, I take it, that since there is no question of foul play . . ."

"Good heavens! no," cried the lawyer.

"Then the only alternative to suicide is that it was an accident."

"Precisely. Precisely, Mr. Standish. And it is in order to try and establish the fact that it was an accident that I have come to you. Your trained eye will notice things that ours will miss. It is not only a question of the company paying up, believe me; though naturally one doesn't want to lose the money. But it is the stigma of the thing that I want removed. And so I am venturing to ask you if you will be good enough to accompany me down to Ashington Manor, and go into things first hand on the spot."

Ronald rose.

"All right, Mr. Humber; we'll come. Though I must frankly confess that from what you have told me up to date things don't look too bright. One would hardly expect a man whose hobby is toxicology to drink poison by accident."

★★★★★★

Ashington Manor was a medium-sized house lying some distance back from the road, down to which the property stretched. Some fine old trees fringed the lawn, and partially hidden amongst them was a low building which was obviously the laboratory to which Mr. Humber had alluded.

Standing by the front door as we drove up was a young man of about thirty, and with him was a short thick-set companion who I instinctively put down as belonging to the police.

"My dear John," said Mr. Humber as the car drove up, "my very

454

deepest sympathy. I can hardly believe it even now."

"I can hardly believe it myself, Mr. Humber," said the young man. "The whole thing was so tragically, so unbelievably sudden. By the way, this is Inspector Durrant."

"And this is Mr. Standish," said the lawyer, "who has kindly come down to help us if he can."

John Sinclair bowed.

'Very good of you," he remarked. "We want all the assistance we can get, don't we, Inspector?"

Inspector Durrant gave a non-committal grunt.

"Assistance won't alter facts, Mr. Sinclair, I'm afraid," he said. "And it's facts that we have to put before the coroner."

"At any rate," put in the lawyer, "it will do no harm to hear the facts. Shall we go inside?"

We followed John Sinclair into the house.

"They can be told very shortly," he said, when we were settled in his study. "My uncle, as perhaps you have heard, Mr. Standish, was a very ardent toxicologist. And yesterday afternoon he announced his intention of continuing some experiments he was engaged upon down in his laboratory, which is the building you see across the lawn. He was working, so he told me at lunch, on a little known African poison belonging to the group with which the points of darts and spears are sometimes impregnated by the natives—I believe *curare* is one of the family—a group of probably the most deadly poisons in the world.

"The old man had seemed a bit moody and irritable during the morning, so as I had to go into Tenterden myself I was glad he had something to take his mind off."

"Have you any idea why he was moody and irritable?" asked Ronald.

"I don't think he was feeling very fit; that's what he told Ames the butler. He's been having trouble with his digestion, and as I told you, Inspector, I'm convinced my theory is right."

"Take it in order, sir," said the inspector. "That comes later."

"I returned from Tenterden about four," continued Sinclair, "and as I was passing the laboratory I put my head inside to see how he getting on. To my horror I saw the dear old chap lying contorted on the floor in a corner of the room, and quite dead. For a moment I was completely stunned; I could hardly believe my eyes. Then I rushed to the house and telephoned for the doctor, though it was obvious that my uncle was beyond human aid.

"Doctor Streatham came immediately, and together we returned to the laboratory. Everything, just as it is now, was as I had found it, and while the doctor made his examination I took stock of things. The desk was in its usual state of untidiness, but there was one most unusual feature about it. My uncle was the most abstemious man, and he rarely touched spirits. But standing on the desk with the stopper out was a decanter of whisky and a siphon, and a half-filled glass of what appeared to be whisky and soda was on the blotting-pad in front of his chair. In addition to that a tiny bottle, also with the stopper out and marked 'Poison,' was beside the glass.

"I had just finished investigations to that point when the doctor called me.

"'Bend down and smell your uncle's lips,' he said gravely, and somewhat unwillingly I did so. And at once I perceived what the doctor was driving at. A faint but very pungent odour hung round them, and I was not surprised when the doctor beckoned me over to the table again, and pointed to the bottle of poison. I sniffed it; the smell was the same, though infinitely stronger. So with the whisky and soda, this time faint but still unmistakable.

"'*I* am afraid there can be no doubt as to what has happened,' said Streatham after a while. 'For some inexplicable reason your uncle has put this poison, whatever it may be, into a whisky and soda and has drunk it.'

"And then the full implication of his words struck me.

"'Good Lord! man,' I cried, 'you aren't suggesting that he did it on purpose. That he committed suicide?'

"He stared at me in silence; then he shrugged his shoulders.

"'I'm devilish sorry to have to say so, my dear fellow,' he said at length, 'but it's difficult to see any other solution that fits the facts. We must send for the police.'"

Sinclair thumped his fist into the palm of his hand.

"Gentlemen," he cried violently, "I don't care what anybody says: I don't care how black it looks, I am convinced that my uncle did not commit suicide."

"What then is your theory?" asked Ronald quietly.

"He may have been experimenting," answered Sinclair. "The man who discovered chloroform experimented on himself."

"As an expert!" said Ronald. "With a poison he knew was deadly?"

"Then I have another solution," cried Sinclair. "One I have already mentioned to the inspector. My uncle, as I have told you, has been having digestive trouble for some months past, and the doctor prescribed some drops which he had to take if he got an attack. Now he was not at his best at lunch yesterday, and it may be that he got worse in the afternoon. The bottle with the drops is standing on his desk, as you will see, and I believe he absentmindedly muddled up the two. They are not unlike—the two bottles."

"Except," put in the inspector dryly, "for a staring red label of 'POISON' on one of them."

"You don't know how absentminded my uncle could be," said Sinclair. "And it is clear he was so yesterday afternoon."

"How do you know that?" cried Ronald.

"Very simple, Mr. Standish. My uncle had a peculiar trick, one which I think Mr. Humber will remember. You know how some people when they are thinking deeply will draw little pictures on blotting paper. He had another mannerism—you recall it, Mr. Humber?"

"I do: perfectly," said the lawyer, turning to Ronald. "He had on his desk one of those implements for stamping an address on note-paper, and if he was engrossed in something or talking he would go on using it ceaselessly. Is that what you mean, John?"

"It is," was the answer. "It was a piece of foolscap yesterday that he was stamping; it is still there on the desk. Gentlemen," he continued, "I firmly believe that that is what really happened. My uncle was the last man in the world to take his own life. Mr. Humber knows, and I dare say he's told you, Mr. Standish, that he had a considerable sum falling due to him from an insurance company in the near future. And only last week he was telling me the result of inquiries he'd made with regard to purchasing an annuity with the money. Does that look like the action of a man who is proposing to commit suicide?"

"The impulse to do so sometimes comes very suddenly," said the inspector.

"Damn it, Inspector," cried Sinclair half angrily, "I believe you want that verdict brought in."

"Not at all, Mr. Sinclair," said the inspector quietly. "I knew your uncle and respected him far too much for that. But there's no good blinding one's eyes to the fact that it isn't what you think or I think, but what the coroner and his jury will think. In addition to that, the insurance company will most certainly be represented. And on the face of it, putting aside for the moment all personal bias, I am bound to say that the evidence as it stands points to suicide, and not accident. I'm afraid it will be very hard to make the coroner believe that your uncle could have made a mistake in those two bottles, however absentminded or engrossed he was at the time. What do you think, Mr. Standish?"

"That I would like to go to the laboratory," said Ronald. "Where, by the way, is the body?"

"Upstairs," answered Sinclair. "The post-mortem is to be held this afternoon."

We trooped into the hall, and while crossing the lawn Ronald fell behind with me.

' I don't see that we're going to do much good, Bob," he said. "As the inspector says, everything depends on the coroner's interpretation of certain facts. But if I was young Sinclair, I should be optimistic about the result. His uncle was well known and liked in the district, and a local coroner will bring it in as an accident if he possibly can in spite of anything the insurance may say."

The laboratory was a large airy room. A big sink with running water, and a bench covered with the usual paraphernalia of the chemist occupied one wall. Shelves with rows of bottles were above it, but it was to the desk that our instinctively turned.

It was in a state of orderly disorder. A whisky decanter and siphon stood at the back; on the blotting-pad was the half-filled glass just as Sinclair had described. Also the phial of poison. In one corner was another little bottle marked "The Prescription. To be taken as ordered," and Sinclair pointed to it.

"You see what I mean," he cried. "Those bottles are very similar except for the labels."

To the left of the chair was the paper stamp, with a sheet of foolscap close to it. And there on the side of the paper—not even on the top, which showed it was a subconscious trick of the dead man—the address was stamped.

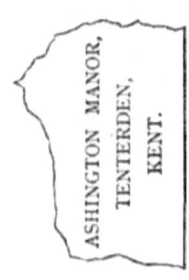

ASHINGTON MANOR,
TENTERDEN,
KENT.

The paper had slipped away from the machine and was lying near the blotter; and again Sinclair spoke :

"I've seen the dear old chap use sheet after sheet stamping all the way round the margin."

"But," said Ronald slowly, and then he paused. "By the way," he continued casually, where did you find the body?"

And only I, accustomed to his ways as I was, knew that that was *not* what he had originally intended to say.

"Over by the door," said Sinclair. "He had evidently attempted to go for help, and had collapsed."

"I see," answered Ronald. And then he shrugged his shoulders. "Well, Mr. Sinclair, I fear all I can do is to tell you to hope for the best. I would stress, if I was you, his cheery outlook recently, and the fact that so far as you know there was no conceivable reason why be should have taken his life."

He was moving towards the door, and Sinclair and the lawyer took no pains to conceal their disappointment.

"But is that all you can say?" cried the young man.

"Honestly, I fear it is," said Ronald; and at that moment I realised he was going without his stick. I was just picking it up when he flashed me a look from the door which said, "Put it down, you damned fool" as clearly as if he'd shouted it. Wondering greatly, I did so; he had spotted something quite obviously. But if he had, why not say? What could be the need for secrecy?

He discovered his loss halfway across the lawn, and with a muttered exclamation of annoyance went back for the stick while we strolled on.

"I confess I'm a little disappointed, Mr. Miller," said the lawyer. "He hasn't wasted much time, has he?"

I murmured some conventional reply just as Ronald rejoined us.

"I wonder," he remarked, "if I might see your uncle's body, Mr. Sinclair?"

Sinclair raised his eyebrows.

"Certainly—if you wish to," he said. "I don't suppose there would be any objection, Inspector, would there?"

"None at all," said the officer. "Though I don't think you'll learn much, Mr. Standish. I will show you the way."

Mr. Humber declined to come with us, and we followed the inspector up the broad flight of stairs to a big bedroom overlooking the lawn. The blinds were drawn, and on the bed, covered with a sheet,

459

lay the body of the dead man. Reverently John Sinclair drew back the covering, revealing his uncle's face quiet and peaceful in his last sleep. Ronald bent over it, and then straightened up.

"I wonder, Mr. Sinclair," he said, "if I might trouble you to ask your butler to go to my car and get the small bag off the back seat."

"Certainly," said Sinclair, going to the door. "I'll tell him."

He left us, and the instant he had gone to our complete amazement Ronald whipped back the sheet and very gently raised the old man's right hand.

"Light," he said urgently. "Switch on the light."

I did so, and from the bedside came an exclamation.

"Do you see, Inspector?" he cried. "That deep prick in the palm?"

"What of it?" answered the officer. "It looks as if he'd cut a thorn out."

"Yes," said Ronald slowly. "Perhaps that would account for it. By the way, have you examined the glass with the whisky and soda in it for finger-prints?"

"I can't say that I have. It didn't seem necessary."

"I wish you would. And if you could stretch a point and give me a little poison out of that phial on the desk I would be very much obliged. I would like to add it to my museum."

He strolled to the door as Sinclair returned. "There doesn't seem to be a bag in your car, Mr. Standish," he said.

"You don't mean to say that fool of a man of mine forgot it? It doesn't matter; I'm sorry to have troubled you. "Well," he continued, as he reached the top of the stairs, 'I fear I can only say what I said before. Stress his cheerfulness at the inquest; bring Out strongly his remarks about the annuity and I firmly believe they'll dismiss the idea of suicide. Goodbye, Mr. Sinclair; my deepest sympathies are with you."

' Won't you both stay to lunch? I have to go to London immediately afterwards, but I Shall be delighted if you'll stop for some food."

"Impossible, I fear," said Ronald. "I have a very important case which I can't leave. Can I give you a lift as far as Tenterden, Inspector?"

He accepted, so we bade goodbye to Mr. Humber and entered the car.

"I think after all I shall stay here to lunch," said Ronald, as we swung out of the drive. "What's the best hotel in the place, Inspector?"

"The Swan," was the answer. "And if you like I'll bring you the poison there."

"Thank you. And the finger-print result. Don't say anything about it; my request might seem callous."

We dropped him at the police station and turned into the yard at the Swan."

"What did you go back to the laboratory for?" I demanded curiously as we entered the bar.

He pulled an old bill out of his pocket and handed it to me. On the top it was stamped :

ASHINGTON MANOR,
TENTERDEN,
KENT.

"To see how nicely the paper stamp stamped paper," he remarked. "A very curious fact, Bob, and one that I've often noticed, is how hard it is to spot an obvious thing when it is presented to you in an unusual setting."

"Well, it's clear you've spotted something," I said, "but what you've seen is beyond me."

His reply consisted of asking the lady behind the bar if it would be possible to obtain a live guinea-pig. She opined that it would; that, in fact, there were some next door. And I, completely dazed, had another gin and French. Then we went in and had lunch, during which meal Ronald refused to talk about anything except cricket.

At three o'clock Inspector Durrant arrived and it was clear from the expression on his face that he was puzzled.

"I would very much like to know, Mr. Standish, why you raised that point about finger-prints."

"What have you found out?" asked Ronald.

"A very amazing thing. There are none at all."

Ronald rubbed his hands together.

"Excellent," he cried. "I verily believe, Inspector, that we're going to prove quite conclusively that Mr. Sinclair did not commit suicide. Have you brought any of that poison with you?"

The inspector laid a tiny test tube on the table.

"Splendid," said Ronald. "Bob, go and ask Amaryllis for the guinea-pig. Don't harrow her feelings, but I fear there is going to be a casualty in the guinea-pig world."

I got the little animal, and when I returned with it I found Ronald had taken out his hypodermic syringe.

"I'll inject a mere drop," he said, "and we'll see the result."

It was the nearest thing to being absolutely instantaneous I have ever witnessed. One convulsive jerk and it was stone dead. And the inspector, who had watched in silence, gave a sudden exclamation.

"By Jove! Mr. Standish, I believe I see daylight. That mark on the old man's hand! You think he may have pricked himself accidentally with something impregnated with the poison."

"That's more or less the idea." said Ronald gravely.

"But how about the smell that lingered round his lips?"

"How about the absence of finger-marks on the glass?" was Ronald's reply. "Has young Sinclair gone to London yet?"

"Yes. He went while I was in the laboratory with Mr. Humber."

"Did he see you there?"

The inspector shook his head, and Ronald again rubbed his hands as if he was pleased.

"Well, Inspector, only one thing now remains to be done, though that, I fear, may prove the hardest. And as I think it will be easier if I do it alone, I will now go up to Ashington Manor. And then later on when Mr. Sinclair returns from London I think I shall be able to show to nearly everybody's satisfaction that it was not suicide."

"Why nearly?" I queried.

"The Insurance Company, of course," said Ronald with a faint smile. "They'll have to pay up. Stand by, both of you, and when the time comes we will reconstruct the whole affair."

And with that he left us scratching our heads.

★★★★★★

It was not till seven o'clock that a message came through telling us to go to the Manor. The inspector had his own car outside, and when we arrived Ronald was talking to John Sinclair in the drive.

"I think I can show beyond doubt, Mr. Sinclair," he was saying, "that your uncle did not commit suicide. And my suggestion is that we adjourn to the laboratory for my demonstration. Inspector Durrant must see it because he will be occupying an official position at the inquest, whereas I am merely an outsider. Now I want," he continued, as we entered the room, "to try and visualise everything as it was. Your uncle was experimenting with the poison, and then I think we can assume that in an absent-minded way he sat down at his desk. Inspector, you stand by the door; Bob, you over there against the wall, and you, Mr. Sinclair, will you just play the part of your uncle."

"Sit at the desk, you mean?"

"That's right," said Ronald, as Sinclair sat down. "Now, let's get this right." He cocked his head on one side as he studied the effect, and we all watched him breathlessly. "The glass was there; the poison there: siphon and decanter. Good. Let's continue. Feeling *distrait* he picked up a bit of foolscap and put it in the stamping machine. Just do that, will you, Mr. Sinclair. Then he banged down the handle of the stamp."

John Sinclair did so; then with a shout of terror he sprang to his feet. His face was chalk-white, and he was staring hypnotised at a mark in his hand from which blood was already beginning to drip.

"Am I right, John Sinclair?" said Ronald in a terrible voice. "Then staggering in his dying gasp your uncle went to the door and collapsed. Just as you will collapse . . ."

"The antidote," screamed Sinclair, and Ronald laughed.

"It's only plain water this time," he said, "and a gramophone needle. But I think we have proved it was not suicide. Murder, Inspector— and there is the murderer."

Almost dazedly the inspector laid his hand on John Sinclair's shoulder.

"Warn you anything you say used evidence against you," he mumbled.

But I doubt if Sinclair heard; he was glaring vindictively at Ronald.

"You devil," he muttered. "You clever devil!"

★★★★★★

"What utterly beats me, Mr. Standish," said the inspector, "is what put you on the track in the first instance."

He had dined with us at the "Swan"; John Sinclair, realising he had given himself away hopelessly, had confessed and was lodged in a cell.

"An obvious thing in an unusual setting, Inspector," said Ronald. "It was very easy to miss, and you'd all missed it. So had John Sinclair. Otherwise he'd have pulled off a perfect crime. Will you cast your mind back to what will be one of the principal exhibits in the case— the piece of foolscap with the address stamped on the side. There is the unusual setting—an address on the side of a piece of paper. And so the obvious thing escaped attention; *the address was upside down.* The word "Kent" was nearest the edge instead of being farthest from it."

"Well, I'm damned," muttered the inspector. "Go on, sir."

"I happened to spot it, and it at once struck me that it must be a very peculiar paper stamp. So I left my stick behind and went back and tried it. And I found the thing worked perfectly when I stamped a letter of my own. The address was the right way up. Thus at the very outset of the case one was confronted with a fact so bizarre and extraordinary that I felt there must be something vital in it.

"Now those paper stamps have two detachable blocks, one with the address embossed, the other with it countersunk. And they are fastened to the machine by two screws. Either therefore old Mr. Sinclair had unscrewed the blocks, turned 'em round, stamped the paper, and then again altered the blocks—an extremely improbable contention—or *there was a second stamp.* So at once the paper stamp, instead of being an ordinary article of desk furniture, became a very sinister feature of the case. And the mark on his hand confirmed my opinion. There was still however a long way to go. If I was right and the poison had been injected through the hand the glass of whisky was a blind. So also was the smell round his lips. That is why I asked you about finger-prints. There were none, because the man who planted the blind used gloves. That glass was placed on the desk after the old man was dead. It was then, too, that the drop of poison was put between his lips. And when the guinea-pig showed that injecting was instantly fatal, I knew I was on the right track.

"There still remained however the second stamp, and it was that that I went up to find. It wasn't difficult; it was in the study. An identical machine with rubber round the handle; just like the one in the laboratory. And with my magnifying glass I could see the tiny hole in the rubber through which the needle had come. Then very carefully I tried it and found that it stamped upside down.

"Here was proof; the stamps had been changed. But an inconvenient fact obtruded itself; what firm in the world would send out a stamp in such a condition? And in any event why had this idiosyncrasy not been discovered before? Still pondering, I stripped off the rubber handle—and then I understood. The metal part of the handle had been hollowed out, obviously to allow of the introduction of a little bag of poison. And since Mr. John Sinclair could not do that himself, he'd got someone else to do it for him. What excuse he'd made for such an unusual request, I can't tell you— you may be sure it was not done locally. But, realising it was *very* unusual, he had taken the precaution of removing the address blocks to avoid being traced. And when he replaced them he made his one incredible mistake; he replaced them so that they stamped upside down.

"That, I think, is all; the rest is clear. He saw the possibility of a suicide verdict; therefore he left the paper as proof that his uncle was in one of his absent-minded moods. And the only thing he did after he found the old man dead, except to stage the whisky red herring, was to change the two stamps back again."

"I congratulate you, Mr. Standish," said the inspector. "The only remaining point seems to be motive."

"My dear Inspector," cried Ronald, "that surely is obvious. Mr. John Sinclair saw twenty-five thousand of the best vanishing into an annuity which would die with his uncle. And that, from his point of view, was not so funny. No: the whole thing is only one more proof of what astoundingly foolish mistakes a clever man can make."

The Mystery at Styles Court

Of all the cases in which I have had the privilege of working with Ronald Standish, I think the most amazing was the one which had for its setting the historic old house of Styles Court. Much water has flowed under the bridge since the events I am about to relate took place: it is, in fact, only for that reason that it is permissible for me to commit them to paper. And even today some of the actors in the drama must be veiled under fictitious names, though to many the task of identifying them will not prove difficult.

Styles Court is a charming Elizabethan manor situated in the gently undulating country which lies north of the South Downs between Pulborough and Petworth. Originally the home of an old Sussex yeoman family it had continued in their possession from father to son for over two centuries, until increasing taxation and decreasing revenue had enforced its sale. It had passed into the hands of a wealthy stockbroker named Cresswell who, fortunately, had excellent taste as well as a considerable bank balance. This gentleman, in addition to installing running water and other necessities of modern life, also added a large room which started life with the intention of being used for billiards and finished its career as a sitting cum dance cum general utility room. He spared no expense over it.

On the outside it conformed exactly to the rest of the house in a way which did credit to the architect; inside it provided all that the most comfort-loving individual could demand. It was completely separate from the rest of the house, being connected with it by a short passage, and so possessed four outside walls. But an excellent system of central heating and a huge log fire made it perfectly habitable on even the coldest winter's day. And if I seem to have devoted over much space to the details of a mere room, the time has not been wasted, since it was to prove the scene of the whole tragedy.

It was on a morning in early September, 192—, that the telephone rang in Ronald's flat. I was with him at the time and we were debating on the rival merits of our respective links for a day's golf, when the interruption occurred. It was Cresswell himself who was on the line—we both knew him fairly well—and he wanted to know if he could come round immediately.

"Moreover," said Ronald as he put down the receiver, "I am inclined to think, Bob, that our golf is not likely to materialise. There was a note of urgency in Tom Cresswell's voice that I fear means business."

He arrived in a quarter of an hour, and with him was another man whose face seemed vaguely familiar to me. Cresswell introduced him as Sir James Lillybrook, and then I remembered that I had seen him at a City dinner some months previously. He was the guest of honour: one of those Powers behind the throne in the Treasury of whom the public rarely hears. And it was easy to see at a glance that, on this occasion, the usual unemotional expression of the highly placed permanent official was only maintained with difficulty.

"Can you chuck everything, Ronald," said Cresswell, "and put yourself at the disposal of Sir James?"

"Everything, at the moment," said Ronald with a smile, "consists of where Bob and I were going to play golf today. So fire ahead, Sir James. I hope no miscreant has been tampering with the Income Tax."

"I see, Mr. Standish," answered the other gravely, "that you know who I am. So I will not waste my breath by pointing out that at such a time as this, only the gravest emergency would have brought me to consult you."

Ronald held up his hand.

"One moment, if you please, Sir James. Bob and I are only humble readers of the newspapers, and are not behind the scenes. Is anything of special import brewing? From your words, I gather it is. And"—as he noticed a certain reticence on the other's face—"I need hardly point out to you, that if you desire my assistance, it is essential that I should be in full possession of all the facts. All," he repeated quietly.

"I quite appreciate your point, Mr. Standish," said Sir James. "And I will put all the relevant facts in front of you."

He paused for a moment or two as if marshalling his thoughts: then speaking in the concise, almost legal manner of a senior Civil servant, he began.

"Two months ago, my chief, the Chancellor of the Exchequer, rented Styles Court from Mr. Cress ell."

"I saw that Mr. Bignor had done so," said Ronald. "He is there at present, I understand—and not in the best of health."

"Precisely: he is not in the best of health. Now, even from a superficial study of the newspapers, you are probably aware that the condition of affairs in Europe today, is very unsettled. And it is no exaggeration to say that the Press, with their usual loyalty, have not divulged one half of what they know. In a nutshell, conditions have seldom been graver, and, as usual, finance is at the root of half the trouble. Problems of security and boundaries play their part, but, *au fond* everything comes back to money.

"Realising this fundamental fact, Mr. Bignor some months ago started tentative negotiations with the representatives of certain foreign powers for a joint discussion on the position. And the essence of his idea was secrecy. No Press, however devoted, could be expected to refrain from comment on a conference such as we have become accustomed to since the war. And so, through channels into which I need not go at the moment, except to say they were not the usual diplomatic ones, his plans gradually took shape and the thing was arranged. No whisper of the thing escaped: the papers are still in complete ignorance of it.

"Under normal circumstances the meetings would have taken place in London, but the unexpected indisposition of the Chancellor rendered that impossible. And so it was decided to hold them at Styles Court. Do you by any chance know the house?"

"I do," said Ronald.

'Then you know the annexe Mr. Cresswell has built on and I need not bother to describe it to you. The first of the meetings was held a fortnight ago in that room. The delegates had come separately, and by devious routes, and I am certain—or I was then—that no inkling of what was taking place leaked out."

"One point I would like cleared up," interrupted Ronald. "What are the countries concerned?"

Sir James hesitated: then drawing a piece of paper towards him he wrote some words on it.

'I see," said Ronald, concealing a smile at such an excess of caution. "So there were just the three delegates, Mr. Bignor and yourself at the meeting?"

"Each delegate was accompanied by one adviser, who filled the same position as I did."

"Therefore there were eight of you in all?"

"That is correct. The meeting commenced after lunch, and lasted till dinner, when the delegates motored back to London, having arranged the date for the next meeting. And though this first discussion had only been on general lines, even at that one many things had been said which it was essential should not be divulged. For I need hardly point out to you, Mr. Standish, how invaluable inside information would be on matters of that sort to international financiers. You may judge then of our amazement and dismay, when it became obvious to us the next day, that that was just what had happened. Either a certain group on the Continent had pulled off an almost incredible fluke, or—"

"Someone had blown the gaff," put in Ronald quietly.

"So it seemed at the time. Which put everyone, as you can well imagine, in a very awkward position. The three principals were as much above suspicion as Mr. Bignor: their three advisers were occupying positions as responsible as I was myself. In short, the only solutions that occurred to us were that someone had, quite unintentionally, been indiscreet, or that, during the afternoon some of our conversation had been overheard by a listener outside. And so at our next meeting we decided—I should say Mr. Bignor and I decided—to eliminate, at any rate, the second alternative. As you know, the room has four outside walls, and two Scotland Yard men were posted so that no one could approach the annexe unseen.

"With regard to the other solution the matter had, of course, to be alluded to. and the ground was delicate. But with that characteristic directness which marks one of the nations represented, we got over the awkwardness more easily than I anticipated. Without any preliminary beating about the bush, and with a smile which robbed the remark of any offence he said—'Wal, gentlemen, I guess that someone, without intending to, has spilt the beans. We'll have to watch it this time.'"

Sir James shrugged his shoulders.

"I'm sorry to say that his words had no effect on the culprit. To use his own phrase, the beans were spilt again. The Scotland Yard men were satisfied that no one had been near the annexe; the possibility of it having been a fluke on the first occasion was eliminated, and we were left with the unpleasant impression that one of us was a traitor."

"One might almost say certainly," said Ronald.

"At the time I would have agreed with you: I did agree with you.

Now—and this is my reason for coming here—I don't know. I have heard of your great reputation, Mr. Standish," he continued courteously, "but even you would have been powerless, I venture to think, to have kept such track of several people in London that you could have spotted the culprit. A word over the telephone, spoken in code from a bedroom was all that was necessary to convey the information. But at the time, as I say, I thought it was a certainty: we all did. Which rendered the atmosphere almost intolerable.

"It was again the American who saved the situation with his usual blunt candour. I will not attempt to repeat his actual words, but shorn of trappings his remarks boiled down to this. One of us eight was giving the show away—he could not even exempt Mr. Bignor, who, though he was confined to the house had easy access to the telephone. And if that was so it was useless to continue the discussions. But in order to make absolutely certain, before taking such a drastic step as calling the conference off he suggested the following plan, if Mr. Bignor approved. We should all make Styles Court our headquarters, and remain there for the night and day following our next meeting. And if no information leaked out the case would be proved and there would be nothing for it but for everyone to return home. He pointed out that as we were all under equal suspicion, no one need feel any offence should that suspicion prove wrong.

"Mr. Bignor agreed, and suggested the further precaution that the telephone should be disconnected."

Sir James lit a cigarette.

"I suppose I should say the scheme was a success. Certainly it seems to have cleared all of us, even if it has deepened the mystery. As you can imagine, everyone was ostentatiously careful of what they did. The telephone was out of action: no letter was sent: no one left the house save for a stroll in the garden and then he took care not to go alone. Additional men were drafted in from Scotland Yard, and it is certain that no stranger approached the house. And yet, next day it was obvious that all our precautions were in vain: the information had been passed on. How? Where is this leakage?"

"The servants," said Ronald thoughtfully.

"A C.I.D. man was seated during the whole meeting at the entrance to the passage leading to the annexe."

"Tell me, Sir James," said Ronald after a while, "the nature of the information. What I am trying to get at is this. For it to be of value to the people at the other end would it have to be a long and complicated message? Or would some simple order such as Sell so-and-so short: Buy such-and-such a stock, be sufficient?"

"Undoubtedly, that would be enough."

"Under those circumstances an easy code with an electric torch from a bedroom window would do the trick."

"Would anyone risk it knowing the house was watched?"

"True," agreed Ronald. "And yet it has got through somehow."

"I am asking you to find out how that somehow is. If, Mr. Standish, it was only a group of financiers pulling off a scoop it wouldn't matter so much, though it would be very annoying. But bigger things are involved: international problems of far-reaching importance."

"You are proposing to hold more meetings?"

"More or less continuously over next weekend," said Sir James. "And since they will be the last, decisions may be taken then which must *not* be divulged."

"I see," said Ronald. "Well, Sir James, if I come down I take it you will be able to give me every facility for making enquiries."

"Short of being actually present at the meeting, Mr. Standish, you can do what you like and go where you please. All we ask is that you should solve the mystery."

He rose, and shortly afterwards left with Tom Cresswell.

"A bit of a teaser, Bob," remarked Ronald, as he stuffed his pipe. "What do you make of it?"

"That you hit the nail on the head when you suggested signalling from a window."

"Almost too obvious to be correct. Sir James was right there. Would the guilty man have dared risk it knowing the house was being watched by a cordon of the keenest eyed men in the world? Still, it remains a possibility, and about the only one I see so far. So let's get down there at once, Bob; we've got a couple of days to spy out the land."

★★★★★★

Mr. Bignor having evidently been put wise to our arrival, received us with the greatest courtesy.

"I sincerely hope," he said as he shook hands, "that you will be able to solve it, though I confess that I see no ray of light myself."

He apologised for not being able to put us up, but Ronald assured him that we were quite comfortable at the local inn. And with that we left to start investigations. And the first man we ran into was Inspector McIver, an old friend of ours. He grinned when he saw us.

"Horse, foot and artillery all mobilised," he remarked. "But honestly, Mr. Standish." he grew serious again, "it is a bit of a poser."

"So it seems," said Ronald, leading the way towards the annexe, where a man was seated in an armchair quietly smoking. He sprang to his feet as the inspector entered.

"All correct, sir," he reported.

"This room has had a man in it day and night, Mr. Standish, ever since the last meeting," said McIver. "And during the coming conference someone will be here up to the moment the gentlemen arrive, and will take over again the instant things are finished for the day."

"You examined the room, of course?"

"Almost to the extent of ripping up the wainscotting," grunted McIver.

"Naturally, I need hardly have asked. How many men did you have round the house that night?"

"Enough to keep every room under observation," said the inspector. "If you are thinking of the possibility of someone signalling, rule it out."

Ronald nodded.

"And how many inside?"

"A man at the foot of the staircase; a man at the foot of the servants' staircase, and two men doing a general patrol all night. Though really the gentlemen themselves were their own best detectives; each of them is watching his next door neighbour as if he was a convicted murderer."

"I gathered that from Sir James," said Ronald with a smile.

"Now, of course, it is better. They feel they have been given a clean bill of health, and are certain that the information has been obtained from an outside source."

"And what do you think yourself, McIver?"

"Just this," said the inspector grimly. "Whatever may have happened last time, there is going to be no outside source this next one. Excuse me, Mr. Standish, I'm wanted."

He bustled away, and we strolled out into the garden. The afternoon was hot, and throwing myself on a shady bank I took off my hat and let the faint breeze play round my forehead. In the distance a small river wound its way through the fields, whilst just below me the owner of a neighbouring farm was cutting his corn. He worked by hand in the old-fashioned way, and the field—for the job was nearly finished—was covered with neatly arranged stooks. And as I watched him the contrast struck home forcibly. Behind me, the might of a great police force mobilised to prevent international complications; in front, not a hundred yards away, one of the real fundamentals of life—unchanged for thousands of years. And in all probability the diplomats would have felt scandalised had it been suggested to them that they and all they stood for were the less important of the two.

A tall man came striding across the field, and pausing for a moment to speak to the farmer, came on up the slight rise towards us. It was Sir James, and he stopped as he reached us.

"I am glad you have been able to come so promptly," he said. "It is too early, I suppose, to ask if you've come to any conclusion?"

"None, I fear, Sir James," answered Ronald. "And I see no chance of doing so until the next conference begins. I have talked to McIver, but the scent is altogether too cold to arrive at any conclusions at present."

"He's the Scotland Yard man in charge?"

"Yes. And a very able officer. I have worked with him often. By the way, when was Mr. Bignor taken ill?"

Sir James thought for a moment.

"Two days before the first meeting."

"So that it was only just before that meeting that it was decided to hold the conference here and not in London?"

"It was decided on the actual morning," said Sir James.

"And how was the decision communicated to the delegates?"

"By my secretary personally."

"No possibility of any leakage there, I suppose?"

"Absolutely none," cried Sir James emphatically. "Merriman is beyond suspicion."

He strode away towards the house, and Ronald knocked out his pipe and got up.

"Let's go back to the pub, Bob," he said.

"A pint of ale is indicated. We might walk over the fields."

Our direction lay via the cornfield. And as we came abreast of the farmer he greeted us cheerily.

"Nearly finished, I see," remarked Ronald. "You've got good weather for it."

The old man nodded.

"Might be worse," he conceded. "Be you gennelmen staying up at the Court?"

"No, we're at the Angel. I suppose," he went on casually, "a good

473

many tourists and strangers come down to these parts?"

"A tidy few; mostly earlier in the year though. And we had some of them dratted hikers a few days ago."

"But they don't do any damage, do they?"

The farmer snorted.

"Not 'xactly damage; but silly nosensical mischief. But what do they want to upset the stooks for? That's what I want to know."

"Why don't you tell them to put ''em up again?"

"They were gone before I got here in the morning," said the old man.

"Well, we all have our worries," said Ronald with a smile. "Good day to you."

We strolled on, Ronald deep in thought.

"A definite snorter this, Bob," he said at length. "Since it was only decided on the actual morning of the first meeting to hold it here, how could any outside agency get the news in time to alter their plans, unless there is a traitor in the camp?"

"One of the servants at Styles Court would have been in a position to pass that on."

"Granted. But in view of the fact that, but for the Chancellor's indisposition, the conference was to have been held in London, what would have been the object of an outside agency squaring a servant here? If the original plan had been adhered to, none of the servants here would have been any use."

"That's so," I agreed. "Well—I give it up. Thank heavens, here's the pub! I can do with that pint."

I hardly saw him at all during the next two days. He disappeared after breakfast and only returned in time for dinner each night. Moreover he was not communicative, and I could tell by various little signs that things were not going well. He would discuss anything except the point at issue, and even then periodically he would fall into a brown study, staring out of the window, and drumming on the table with his finger nails.

I knew of old the futility of questioning him, so I possessed my soul in patience till he should choose to be more talkative. Twice McIver came to the inn and they had long consultations, but it was not until Friday that Ronald alluded to the matter again with me.

"Now we start the doings, Bob," he said. "And it is a lucky thing that the weather is set fine. For the next few days we join McIver's merry lads."

"Delighted to hear it," I cried. "The last two days have not been a scream of gaiety."

"Sorry, old boy," he said. "Afraid it's been damned dull for you. And the trouble of it is that I may be on the wrong line now."

"You've got an idea anyway?"

"The vaguest," he said briefly. "Bring your little camera with you."

I slipped it in my pocket and we started off.

"Are we going to take pictures of the delegates?" I asked.

"No, my dear Bob, we are not. We are, if luck is with us, going to take pictures of the sleepy English countryside."

We reached Styles Court and McIver joined us.

"They've all arrived, Mr. Standish, and the conference begins after lunch."

"You examined the room again thoroughly this morning?"

"Every nook and cranny of it. There's nothing there. Would you like to walk round the defences?" he asked jocularly.

"Hardly necessary," laughed Ronald. "I can see 'em bristling. No— I'll just take a photograph. Come along, Bob."

We went to the bank where we had rested three days before.

"A charming view," said Ronald. "I see that the farmer, who re-joices in the delicious name of Buzzle, has finished his labours, and the golden corn, if not actually waving, looks delightful in the foreground. Take a picture, Bob."

"I don't see anything particularly charming about it," I remarked.

"That's because you lack the artistic sense," he grinned. "And now we can go back to the pub."

"But I thought we were joining the party here."

"Only at stated intervals, old boy," he answered. "McIver is quite capable of holding the fort in our absence. Provided we are back here before dawn tomorrow all will be well."

And not another word would the aggravating blighter say, save a few vague generalities which only increased my curiosity.

"It can't be coincidence, Bob, and yet . . . Anyway, we'll know for certain tomorrow."

"What?" I demanded.

"If it's coincidence," he grunted.

He woke me at four o'clock next morning, and waited with barely concealed impatience whilst I put on some clothes.

"Don't forget your camera," he cried, as I bolted a cup of tea.

And then he led me, almost at a run, back to our vantage point in the grounds of Styles Court. We passed two of the C.I.D. men, yawning and stiff from their night's vigil, and after a while McIver joined us. The first faint streaks of dawn were showing over the downs: a low lying mist covered the country in front of us like a carpet. And then the sun itself showed over the ridge of hills. The mist eddied in thin wisps and began to lift, and glancing at Ronald I saw his eyes were gleaming with excitement. Slowly the sun crept up above the horizon: the white blanket rolled sluggishly back from the little hill on which we stood. And suddenly Ronald gave a cry of triumph.

"So it wasn't coincidence! We've solved the first part of the problem. Take a photo, Bob."

"But I'll only get the cornfield," I protested.

"That's all I want," he answered.

I focused the camera, and as I did so there came the drone of an aeroplane in the distance. The noise came nearer and nearer and glancing up I saw the machine. It was a Puss Moth flying low, and with a roar it passed over the house and disappeared.

"Now then, McIver," cried Ronald, "it's up to you. There's not a moment to be lost. Get to the village and fuse the bally telephone wires if necessary."

"I hope to Heaven you're right, Mr. Standish," said the inspector.

"Of course I'm right, man. For God's sake get a move on."

McIver hurried away and Ronald turned to me.

"Take another photo, Bob, now that the light is better, to make sure. And then we'll rout the local chemist out of his bed and force him to develop them."

I made a second exposure, and still feeling completely bewildered followed him back to the inn.

"Perhaps you will now condescend to enlighten me," I remarked peevishly.

"All in good time, old boy," he answered. "The method we know: the culprit we don't—as yet."

★★★★★★

The snapshots were ready by ten o'clock, and slipping them into an envelope I stepped out into the street just as McIver passed in a car. A youngish man was with him, and when I got back to the hotel, the car was standing empty outside the door. Of Ronald there was no sign, and I sat down in the lounge to wait for him. Ten minutes passed—a quarter of an hour, and then I saw him coming down the stairs. And a casual remark died on my lips: never had I seen him so grave and so stern. Behind him was McIver with the other occupant of the car, who was now looking thoroughly frightened.

"You have the prints, Bob?" said Ronald, coming across to me.

I handed him the envelope.

"Good. Then come in here with me. I am expecting a visitor shortly. McIver—will you wait in the bar."

He led the way into a small parlour and I followed. Then, having examined the snapshots, he flung himself into a chair.

"My God! Bob," he said heavily, "the end of this hunt is a bit of a nerve shatterer."

He sat smoking moodily till the landlord opened the door and ushered in Sir James Lillybrook.

"I got your message, Mr. Standish, and since it was so urgent I came at once. Have you discovered anything?"

"I have," said Ronald.

"Well, please be as quick as possible," remarked Sir James. "We are meeting at eleven today."

"Will you look at those two snapshots, Sir James," said Ronald quietly.

The other glanced at them, and for an instant his eyes dilated.

"With special reference to the cornfield," continued Ronald.

"Well," said Sir James. "I am looking."

"Do you notice any difference beyond the obvious one of the mist?"

"I can't say that I do."

"One of them, Sir James, was taken last night, and all the stooks of corn are standing upright. The other was taken this morning and three of the stooks are lying flat."

"Now you mention it, so they are. But what is the significance of that?"

Ronald went to the door.

"McIver," he called, "will you both come here."

And as Sir James's eyes fell on the young man he gave a strangled gasp and swayed as if he was going to fall. Ronald closed the door again, and with his back to it stood watching the other who was struggling to regain his self control.

"I see you recognise the pilot of the aeroplane," said Ronald gravely. "Well, Sir James, it is not for me to ask what induced a man in your position to act as a traitor to his country: presumably it was money. All

I am concerned with is my own course of action. When you all dispersed after the earlier meetings and went back to London, the thing was easy. Then, when you remained here, you had to think of another plan. So by knocking over different numbers of stooks of corn you arranged to send different messages to the men who are in league with you, through the pilot outside—who I am glad to say had no idea what he was really doing. And my plain duty is to report what I have discovered at once to Mr. Bignor."

"For God's sake don't, Mr. Standish," cried Sir James in a shaking voice. "Think of the disgrace. I could never stand it, I had been speculating: I was desperate. My son: he's just left Sandhurst. My wife. . . . ."

But Ronald's expression showed no sign of relenting: in his particular code some things were beyond the pale.

"Because of your wife, and because of your son, and even more because of the hideous public scandal which would be involved, I am going to make a suggestion to you. There is good rough shooting round Styles Court. . . ."

While a man may count ten they stared at one another: then Sir James Lillybrook rose, and without a word walked through the hall to his waiting car.

★★★★★★

I got things out of Ronald that afternoon. He spoke in jerky, clipped sentences—sentences punctuated by long pauses when he stared with sombre eyes over the fields at Styles Court.

"Buzzle, the farmer, and the hikers. Hikers wouldn't knock down stooks. . . . Besides, the mist. . . . They wouldn't sleep out in the open at this time of year if they could avoid it. . . . Then the aeroplane. . . . Buzzle remembered it flying so low over his farm that he looked out, and it was then he saw that some stooks had been knocked down. . . . And that morning was the only morning they were knocked down. . . . And that morning was the morning of the conference when special precautions were taken. Coincidence perhaps: but it used to be done in the war if you remember, signalling to aeroplanes by signs on the ground. . . .

"I was sure it was somebody engaged in the conference: no outside agency could have got on to things so promptly without inside information. . . . But I never dreamed it was Sir James. . . . Once the delegates had given up returning to London after the meetings he had to act quickly. . . . Told young Ramsden, the pilot, that the number represented a code message to a bookmaker. . . . Gave him a telegraph-

478

ic address to send it to, and pitched a yarn about liking his flutter but not daring to send betting wires from Styles Court. . . . Appealed to the boy's sense of sport. . . . And, of course, he has no idea even now of the real meaning of the messages. . . ."

"How did you get Ramsden?" I put in.

"McIver had a man at every aerodrome within a radius of ten counties. . . . Picked up the right one on the telephone this morning."

He rose and walked up and down with his hands in his pockets.

"Just luck. If Buzzle hadn't mentioned hikers that first day we saw him the plan would have succeeded. No outsider would notice a few stooks lying flat, or attach any importance to it. And it only took half a minute after dark for Sir James to stroll into the field and upset 'em. The poor devil was so sure he could not be found out that he actually came to me when Bignor proposed outside help. God! Bob—was I right in what I suggested to him? Hallo! landlord, what's the matter?"

"Accident up at the Court, sir. One of the gents staying there— Lillybrook the name is, I think—was out shooting. And the gun went off when he was getting over a fence. Killed him on the spot. Shockingly careless some gentlemen are with guns. Some beer, sir?"

But Ronald Standish did not seem to hear the question. And after a while he turned on his heel and swung away down the village street. For there are times when it is well that a man should be alone.

The Man in the Saloon Car

"Come in, Bob, and take a pew. Philip has just returned from a rest cure in Paris, and he's feeling a bit hot and bothered. Tell us the tale again, Philip."

Ronald Standish waved his hand towards the sideboard, and Philip Hardy, his long legs stretched out in front of him, lit a cigarette.

"How are you, Bob?" he said. "You look your usual repulsive self."

"When did you cross, Philip?" I asked.

"Boat train this morning, old boy. Why, Heaven knows: I usually fly. And if I had this time, I shouldn't be here now boring Ronald."

"You aren't, Philip," said Ronald. "Not a bit. He's been having adventures, Bob, and I want you to hear 'em."

"Who is she this time?" I asked resignedly, knowing Philip's habits.

"It isn't a she; it's a he—or rather a bunch of them. I can't tell it all over again, Ronald; probably the whole thing is imagination on my part."

Ronald strolled to the window and glanced out.

"It's not imagination, Philip, that you've been followed here," he said quietly. "Sit down. I'll do any observation that is necessary. There's a good-looking gentleman on the other side of the road who arrived just after you did. He's still there. I must admit that he's not very good at his job. In fact we might send him out a camp stool. But that doesn't alter the main situation; somebody is very solicitous about your movements."

I confess I was surprised. Philip Hardy was a well-to-do young gentleman, with a pretty taste in horses and girls, and possessing the most extensive wardrobe I have ever seen. But since his brain was completely negligible, and he had never done, and never intended doing, a day's work in his life, what possible source of interest he could be to anyone else was beyond me.

"All right, old lad," he remarked wearily. "I will tell him the whole ghastly story. You see, Bob, I wasn't at all well this morning—not at all. I'd lowered some perishing hell-brew last night, and when I got to the Gare du Nord, I thought I might die at any moment. So I had a great idea; I would die lying down. Apart from the fact that you can't in decency die in a Pullman, I felt that the strain of contemplating a face from close range all the way to Calais would be more than I could bear. So I staggered up and down the platform looking for an empty compartment.

"Luckily the train was not full, and I managed to get one. I told the *conducteur* that I was a suspected case of bubonic plague; bribed him with inordinate quantities of silver, and by the time we left Paris I had sunk into an uneasy doze which lasted as far as Amiens. There I awoke feeling, if possible, more unutterably ghastly than before.

There is a short little tunnel just this side of Amiens station, and it was in that that I woke up. And as I opened my eyes I knew that something had caused the awakening—something had brushed my face. What, I didn't know. It wasn't there when my eyes were open. I could see nothing when we got into the light. But that something had touched me I was certain.

"The door into the corridor was open, and I was lying on the seat facing the engine with my head nearest the door. And suddenly there came into my range of vision a spectacle so repellent that I sat up with a jerk. It was a man with hair sprouting all over his face apparently searching for something in the corridor. He came nearer so that I saw him more distinctly, and he was far, far worse close to. He was an outrage: definitely for adults only; a child would have yelled with fright.

"He paused by my door, and a series of explosive noises issued from the face fungus. It appeared that he had lost a piece of paper. It had fluttered out of his compartment, and blown along the corridor. Had I seen it?"

"One moment, Philip," said Ronald. "This man was a foreigner?"

"He was, though he spoke English."

"All right. Go on."

"You must remember, Bob, that I was still partially unconscious," continued Philip. "Further, what little sanity had come back to me was numbed by the sight of this human gargoyle. At any rate I completely forgot about the thing that had brushed my face in the tunnel. So, with the best will in the world, I assured him I knew nothing about any piece of paper, that I had been asleep, and that at any moment I might be violently sick. On which, mercifully, he vanished from my gaze, and I slowly recovered. In fact, by the time the restaurant bloke came along ringing his bell I was just capable of movement, and picking up my newspaper I followed him to the luncheon car, passing on the way the compartment containing blackbeard.

"There were three other men in it, and as I got opposite the door I glanced in casually. Which was the moment selected by the train for a rather worse lurch than usual that threw me almost into the carriage, so that I blundered against one of these blokes' legs. I apologised, and having resumed a perpendicular position was about to move on when I noticed that the fellow I had barged into was making a clumsy sort of attempt to conceal something in his hands. If you get me, it was only noticeable because it was so clumsy. And out of the corner of my eye, as I got into the corridor, I saw it was a sheet of an ordnance survey map of England."

Philip Hardy lit another cigarette.

"The whole thing, you understand, Bob," he continued, "was over in a second, though I have taken longer to describe it. And by the time I'd reached the restaurant car it had passed from my mind. I did wonder vaguely why a man should want to cover up the fact that he was studying a map; it seems a comparatively harmless pastime. But the whole thing was so trivial that I forgot all about it until I opened my newspaper. For as I did so there fluttered out a single sheet of paper which fell on the floor. I bent down and picked it up. On it were written four meaningless words.

"Now the old grey matter was still partially seized, but as I toyed with a more than usually revolting omelette, it began to creak a little. There could be no doubt at all that the slip of paper was the one the gargoyle had been looking for. And then I remembered my feeling when I woke that something had brushed my face. Obviously it was this very piece of paper that had blown along the corridor while the train was in the tunnel, and by some chance had drifted *via* my face into the newspaper beside me on the seat.

"I again studied the words, and came to the conclusion that they were some sort of code. Anyway, they meant nothing in my young life, and I had just made up my mind that I would return the paper on the way back to my carriage when I happened to look up. Sitting two tables away on the other side of the gangway and facing me was the map-studier. And he was glaring at me like a wild beast; or rather he was glaring at this blasted piece of paper which I, of course, had made no effort to conceal. I was examining it, quite openly, above the table.

"For an instant he caught my eye; then he immediately looked away. But it was too late; my curiosity was thoroughly aroused. The expression on his face had been so ferocious that I felt it couldn't be some harmless business message. And so I slipped the menu on my knee, and whilst pretending to read the newspaper I copied out the message. Just in time as it turned out. Hardly had I done it, and got the menu in my pocket, when map-reader rose from his seat and came over to my table.

"'Excuse me,' he said, 'did my eyes deceive me, or were you studying a piece of paper a few moments ago that seemed to cause you a certain amount of perplexity? Pardon my impertinence, but I think you are the gentleman whose seat is in our carriage, and since we have lost a very valuable—valuable to us, I mean—message, I was wondering if by any extraordinary possibility it could have blown into your clothing, and that you have only just discovered it.'

"His tone was suave and perfectly courteous, and it seemed to me that since he had actually seen the damned thing in my hand, it would be" fatuous to deny it. There was always the likelihood now of my suspicions being wrong, and its being a genuine business message in code. In any event I had a copy. So I said the exact truth; told him that unknown to me it had lodged in my newspaper; that I had only that moment found it. With which I handed it back to him, and we resumed our respective meals.

"Bob, I was intrigued. You know how incredibly boring that journey is from Paris, and as the temperature in my head slowly decreased, I began to weave fantastic yarns in my imagination to pass the time. Map-reader had not waited for the end of lunch. He had disappeared shortly after our interview, but I sat in the restaurant car until we were running down the long hill into Calais. Then I went back to my own compartment, which I found exactly as I had left it save for one thing. I had shut the door on going to feed, and the window was shut too. But the instant I opened that door I spotted a faint smell of cheap hair grease—the sort of muck a third-rate hairdresser stuffs on Bert's quiff for Sunday best. Well, whatever my sins are I don't put stuff like that on my hair, so I thought I'd investigate. I went straight along to black-beard's compartment, where I apologised to him for having unintentionally deceived him at Amiens. And no further investigation was necessary. They'd got everything hermetically sealed, and the place reeked of the same filth. One of them, therefore, had given my stuff the once over, which would have put them wise to my name and address. Nothing was missing, nothing apparently had been touched. But attached to one of my bags is a card in a leather case, so they knew who I was.

"And so far as I was concerned they were quite welcome to the information. At the same time, seeing that I'd given 'em back their rotten bit of paper, their interest in me seemed a little strange. However, in the bear garden at Calais I forgot all about the blighters, and as soon as I got on board I tottered down below to have a quick one when I butted into Jimmy Prendergast and proceeded to do a bit of bar-propping.

"After a bit Jimmy says to me, 'Who are your boy friends, Philip?'

"Sure enough there they all were in the dining-saloon which you could see into through the opening at the back of the bar.

" 'I've been watching 'em,' he went on, 'and they're talking about either you or me. I don't know 'em, thank God, so you must be the lucky one.'

"At which I told him what had happened, keeping the old optic skinned on the beauty chorus while I did so. And Jimmy was right: their loving interest in me had not waned. They were having the hell of an argument about something, and from the way any one of them who caught my eye immediately looked away, I knew I came into it.

"'You mind your step, Philip,' said Jimmy. 'That man with fur on his face would eat his mother.'

"By Jove! Bob, Jimmy was right. And it's because of what happened next that I came round to see Ronald. When we got to Dover I waited as I always do for the mob to get off. I'd lost Jimmy, and I was standing near the top of the disembarking gangway and to one side of it. Suddenly I became aware of a very seductive scent beside me, and perceived a dame, pleasant to the eye, who was fumbling in her bag. And the next instant her landing ticket dropped on to the deck just inside the guarding rope. I naturally got underneath to pick it up, and as I was bending down I got the deuce of a blow in my back which shot me forward into the gap between the gangway and the ship's rail. In fact, as near as a toucher, I went overboard between the dock and the side of the ship.

"To put it mildly I was not amused, but when I'd recovered my balance and was on the point of giving tongue, I saw what had happened. Lying prone on the deck was one of the four men, with the other three bending solicitously over him.

"'You're not hurt, I trust, sir?' said map-reader to me. 'My poor friend here is subject to sudden fits of vertigo.'

"Bob, I stared at him for about five seconds, and then I made the only possible answer—'Oh! yeah.'

"Fit of vertigo! I couldn't prove anything, of course, with the blighter lying there on the deck giving a spirited imitation of a half-dead codfish. But I knew, and he knew that I knew, he was lying. The whole thing was a deliberate attempt to kill me. If I'd gone overboard there was every chance of my being crushed to death between the ship and the wharf.

"However, there was nothing to be done about it, so I returned the ticket to the lady who it was obvious must be in with them. Then I expressed my deep regret at the gentleman's lack of equilibrium, and departed to my seat in the Pullman. Give me a drink, Ronald: my throat's like a lime kiln after all that talking."

"Did anything happen coming up in the train?" I asked.

"Not a thing. Didn't see any of 'em again. The car met me at Victoria, and having dumped my kit I came round here. What do you make of it, chaps?"

"That you've acted pretty wisely, Philip," said Ronald. "If you are right—and I'm inclined to think you must be—and the episode on board was an attempt to murder you, you've butted into something considerably bigger than a mere business deal. The presence of the watcher outside confirms it."

"How the devil did he get there?" asked Philip. "No one knew I was coming to see you."

Ronald gave a short laugh.

"On your own showing, they knew your name and address before you reached Calais. A wireless from the boat, or even a telegram handed in at Dover, would give ample time for their friends in London to have your flat watched before you got there. After that it was merely a question of following you here."

"Where is this mysterious communication?" I asked. "Have you got it here, Philip?"

"There you are," said Ronald, throwing it on the table. "See what you can make of it."

Scrawled on the menu card was the following cryptic message :

485

"Ask me another," I remarked. "Anything like that gives me a pain in the neck. Have you got it, Ronald?"

"I haven't tried yet," he answered. "Been too busy listening to Philip's spot of bother."

Our visitor looked at him anxiously.

"Do you really think that it's serious?" he asked. "Even granted they had a dip at me on board the boat, they can't do anything in London."

"My poor idiot boy," said Ronald kindly, "your remark only shows how very little you know of what can go on in London. I don't say they will have another go at you, but they may. The fact that you came here at once has prevented them doing so already, but unless I'm much mistaken you had better watch your step. They are obviously a bunch of desperate and unscrupulous men, and they know that you have had the original of this message in your hand. That you can't make head or tail of it is beside the point; they can't be sure that you haven't deciphered it."

"What do you suggest that I should do?" asked Philip.

"Leave this card with me, and go to your club. Dine at your club, sleep at your club, and don't leave your club till you get permission from me."

"But, damn it, old boy," spluttered Philip, "you don't know what our smoking room is like after dinner. The only members who aren't snoring are the ones who have died during the day."

"Sorry, Philip, but it's got to be done," said Ronald gravely. "If it wasn't for that man outside there, I wouldn't feel uneasy. But the mere fact that he is there proves that they don't propose to let the matter drop. I believe you are in considerable danger, and therefore I want you to go somewhere where, humanly speaking, you are safe. No one can get at you in a London club. But if anybody calls to see you whom you don't know personally, you're not in."

"But what about you, Ronald?" said Philip, impressed in spite of himself. "My coming here has put you in the danger zone."

"Don't worry about me, Philip," laughed Ronald. "I have ways of my own of chasing people who think they're chasing me. But until I've solved this message—if I do solve it— I shall remain here. Then I'll telephone you. You push off now; you're safe in daylight. Get straight into a taxi"—he paused for a moment—"any taxi except the one waiting on the other side of the road."

He was peering cautiously out of the window. "The plot thickens, my hearties. Our opponents lose no time. But the watcher has blotted his copy-book; he should not have spoken to the taxi-driver. I will ring up the rank. And remember, Philip, *you are not to leave your club.*"

He put through a call, and having done so again repeated the order.

"Under no circumstances whatever, until I say you may. 'Phone me when you get there to say that you've arrived; then sit tight. Here's the car. I'll come down with you. Give the driver the address of your flat, and re-direct him when you get into Piccadilly. Bob, you hold the fort for a moment."

He returned almost immediately.

"So far, so good. The watcher heard the address all right, but the dud driver is following Philip. So, unless some lucky intervention of red and green lights occurs to separate them, they will trace him to his club."

"You really think it is as serious as you say?"

"I do. This *can't* be a mere business communication."

He picked up the menu card and studied it.

"RARPA...Turn it round...APRAR...That's no good," He was talking half to himself. "No good at all ...And the others look worse ...Unless ...Bob!"

He gave a sudden exclamation and seized a pencil.

"It is, by Jove! Bob: the second word is Berengaria spelt backwards. That's sense at any rate. NODYA is the third. No *bon*. And the fourth—well, it's a word anyway. CORNSHEAF. But what about one and three? Berengaria and Cornsheaf. It's a bit hard to follow, but we must be on the right track."

"Hold hard a moment," I said. "I've heard the word Cornsheaf quite recently. It's a pub somewhere or other; quite a well-known one. I passed it the other day coming up from Bournemouth."

"The devil you did," he cried, getting out an ordnance survey map. "By Jove! Bob, you're right. It's between Basingstoke and Winchester. Which accounts for Philip's map-reading friend. On the way up from Southampton to London, you note. *Berengaria.* . . . Look up in the paper and see where she is at the moment."

I opened a copy of *The Times*. The *Berengaria* was due in Southampton that night.

"So that if we are going to find the connexion between her and the Cornsheaf we haven't too long to do it in," he said quietly. "There must be a connexion, Bob: it's quite impossible that there shouldn't be. Is it a harmless one? If so, why their agitation over Philip? And if it isn't harmless . . ."

He broke off and sat drumming with his fingers on the desk.

"If one and three are in cipher, why aren't two and four? Perhaps they are not in cipher. They may be code words—insoluble unless you know the code. A five-letter code. Let us start with the best known of them all—our Mr. Bentley. Get him off the shelf, old boy, and see if they have an APRAR."

I turned the pages eagerly.

"They have," I almost shouted in my excitement. "APRAR . . . Arriving on.

"Arriving on *Berengaria*," he wrote. "Go on, Bob. What is NO-DYA?"

I looked it up.

"NODYA . . . Await orders."

"So there's our message," he said quietly. "'Arriving on *Berengaria*. Await orders Cornsheaf.' Interesting, Bob; very interesting. Who is arriving in the *Berengaria* tonight? Who awaits orders? And why at the Cornsheaf Inn, which appears to be a matter of some twenty-five miles from Southampton?"

The telephone shrilled suddenly, and he stretched out his hand for the receiver.

"Hullo . . . Speaking . . . What's that? My God! Is he badly hurt? . . . Oh, . . . No report heard? . . '. Listen. . . . Tell him from me that we've solved the message, and on my personal guarantee we will repay in full. No, I won't come round now."

He replaced the receiver and stood up, his face grimmer than I had seen it for a long while.

"This, Bob, has definitely ceased to be funny. Philip was shot through the upper part of the arm as he crossed the pavement to go into his club. No report was heard so it must have been some form of air gun, fired presumably from that following taxi."

For a few moments he stood deep in thought.

"If they'd killed him, I'd never have forgiven myself. But it proves one thing, Bob, if further proof was necessary. This matter is desperately serious. Ring up the Yard, will you, and ask for McIver."

I did so, and as I waited for the number Ronald crept cautiously to the window and peered out.

"Still there," he remarked, coming back into the room. "We're going to have some fun tonight, Bob."

"Here's McIver," I said, and he took the receiver out of my hand.

"That you, Mac?" he asked. "Standish speaking. Is anybody of extra importance arriving by the *Berengaria* tonight? Anybody who would cause the police a bit of alarm and despondency in case they might get hurt? . . . No? . . . I can't say. . . . I don't know whether it's male or female, or whether he's come from New York or Cherbourg. . . . No, Mac, I'm not fooling. There's something damned funny going on. So funny that a pal of mine who stumbled into it first and came and told me about it has just been plugged through the arm in broad daylight going into his club. . . . I knew you'd have heard of it, but it's the same show. . . ."

At that moment I happened to glance at the door; inch by inch it was opening. Glanced at Ronald; saw that he had noticed it too, and that his right hand was feeling in a drawer for his revolver . . . Saw him make an imperative sign to me to get out of the line of fire: then watched him crouch behind the desk, while his level voice continued the whole time, though his eyes were bright and watchful.

"And it's a funny show, Inspector, as you'll hear for yourself in a moment. . . . I've solved the cipher, and this is how it reads . . ."

It brought the thing to a head as he intended it should. The door was flung open, and for the split fraction of a second the man who dashed in stood bewildered, his gun in his hand, looking for Ronald. And in that split fraction Ronald fired and stood up, while the man, cursing venomously, dropped his revolver from a hand already dripping blood.

"Leave that gun where it is," snapped Ronald, "or I'll plug you through your other arm. Get behind him, Bob, and belt him over the head with a poker if he tries any monkey tricks."

Then he began to grin; a noise like a gramophone record was coming from the receiver.

"All right, Mac," he said, "I wasn't talking to you. We've got a visitor. Like to come round and see him? Yes, it was my shooting party, not his. Thanks very much all the same. I'll keep him here till you arrive. All part and parcel of the same affair."

He replaced the receiver, and came slowly round the desk.

"Get the handcuffs, Bob," he said. "I'm getting tired of carrying the howitzer about the room. Put one round his left wrist. . . . Thanks."

489

With a quick heave he jerked the man into a corner, and the next moment the other handcuff snapped round the leg of a vast arm-chair.

"I don't think you'll get far attached to that little bit of furniture," he remarked quietly. "And now—who the devil are you?"

Crouching on the floor, his teeth bared in a snarl, our prisoner looked like an animal. He was young, in the early thirties. His face was sallow; his chin needed the attentions of a barber. But his eyes arrested one. They burned like coals of fire; the eyes of a madman or a fanatic.

"Well, who are you?" repeated Ronald. "Do you usually go round trying to shoot complete strangers?"

But the only answer was a snap of his jaws.

"Nice little thing to have about the house, isn't he, Bob," continued Ronald, and at that moment there came a frantic peal at the bell.

"Sounds like old Mac's fairy finger," he grinned, and even as he spoke the inspector came charging into the room.

"Great Scott! Mr. Standish," he cried, "what's all this about?"

He paused, staring at our captive.

"So that was your caller, was it? What's your game, my man?"

"Do you know who he is, Mac?" asked Ronald.

"I don't. But it won't be difficult to find out." He bent down, and the next instant drew his hand back sharply, as the man's teeth missed it by a quarter of an inch.

"So that's the line, is it?" he said grimly. "I don't want hydrophobia yet, my lad."

Which gave me the privilege of seeing what an extraordinarily effective gag a handkerchief can be when placed inside the mouth like a bit, and knotted behind the head. It is, of course, at the discretion of the gagger how tight the knot is drawn, and McIver was merciful. He only put one knee in our prisoner's back when pulling. . . .

"Bite me, would you," he muttered. "Now let's see what we can find."

He ran an expert hand over him, and the first thing he produced was an ugly-looking stiletto.

"Quite fitted to run a babies' *crèche*, isn't he?" he remarked. "What's this? Looks like the badge of some society. . . . And here's a letter addressed to P. Thompson. French stamp. Postmark, Paris. Address—ah! yes, I know it. Accommodation address. That damned little tobacconist makes quite a steady income out of that game. . . . But Thompson . . . Accommodation name, too, no doubt, Mr. Standish. What's inside?

Single sheet of paper. *Il est arrivé*. Which, unless my French has deserted me, means 'He has arrived.' Who?"

He stared thoughtfully at the man on the floor.

"If I take that handkerchief off, will you speak?"

The other shook his head and his eyes gleamed venomously.

"If I'm any judge of human nature," said Ronald quietly, "you'll never get that man to speak. If you try to you'll only be wasting time, and I don't think we've got any to waste."

"But what on earth does he want to shoot you for?" cried McIver, scratching his head.

"Because as I was telling you over the telephone I have, quite by chance, butted into something pretty big. That's why I was asking you about the *Berengaria*. . . . Ah! did you get our friend's reaction to that, Mac? I was watching him purposely. . . . A code message was mislaid in the boat train from Paris this morning, by some friends of this specimen. I have decoded it. Arriving *Berengaria*. Await orders Cornsheaf. Which is an inn on the Southampton-London road. *Il est arrivé*. It is pretty obvious that the man who arrived in France is the same man who is arriving in the *Berengaria*, and whom our friend here and his pals seem anxious to meet—and to meet privately. And from what I've seen of this ornament's proclivities I shouldn't think the meeting is for the purpose of presenting the mysterious arrival with a birthday present."

"What do you suggest we do?" asked McIver.

"Do you see that good-looking man on the other side of the road? The one gazing everywhere except at this room. Get him arrested at once as a loiterer."

McIver, who knew Ronald of old, went straight to the telephone.

"Get a couple of men round here to remove this little bunch of joy to somewhere safe," advised Standish. "And then, McIver, two car loads of trusty warriors in plain clothes, armed and ready for the road. We don't know how many there are at the other end, which as you already know is the Cornsheaf."

McIver was giving clear and rapid orders over the line, whilst our prisoner, writhing impotently, struggled to free himself. If looks could have killed us we would all have died painfully, and I found myself feeling almost sorry for the poor devil. His position was so incredibly ignominious.

"All fixed, Mr. Standish." McIver replaced the receiver. "What are you and Mr. Leyton going to do?"

491

"See the fun, Mac," grinned Ronald. "As soon as our visitor here has been removed, Bob and I will hit the road for the Cornsheaf too."

"Is it political, do you think?"

"More than likely, I should say. This badge is a new one on me, but judging by its owner I should hardly imagine it betokens the International Society of Dart Throwers. You say you know of no one in the *Berengaria* who would be likely to attract attention?"

"Not from New York. But if you're right our man got on at Cherbourg."

He smiled suddenly as he glanced out of the window.

"You must admit we don't lose much time, Mr. Standish."

I looked out. Protesting furiously, the watcher was being hustled into a car that had drawn up beside the pavement, and even as he departed a ring at the bell announced the arrival of our own reinforcements.

"Here's your man, Sergeant Latimer," said the inspector. "Feloniously entering a house, and unlawful possession of firearms. And watch him: he bites."

"You bet he does, sir. I know the customer."

"You do, do you? Who is he?"

"I wouldn't care to swear to his mother's name—or to his father's. But he passes as Georgio Pozzi. Half-bred Italian anarchist. Was in my district. And"—he caught sight of the card—"that's the badge of his damned society. A branch of the Mafia. I put in a report about 'em, sir, but of course, it's not your department. A bad gang, the whole lot of them—but so far the lodge over here have kept within the law."

"Well, they haven't this time," said McIver grimly. "Lock him up, and we'll get a move on. I'll come with you, Mr. Standish, if I may."

"What orders have you given the police cars?"

"To wait for us in Basingstoke."

Ronald roared with laughter.

"I was under the impression you asked me what I was going to do."

A smile twitched round McIver's lips.

"A matter of form, Mr. Standish. Just a matter of form."

Of all the strange adventures I have ever had with Ronald, I think this one was the queerest. True, it called for none of that detective ability on his part which in other chronicles I have tried to portray. The solution of the so-called cipher was so simple that it can hardly be said to count. In fact, as Ronald himself has frequently remarked, the cardinal error of the opponents was their attempt to murder Philip on board the cross-channel boat; had they not done that no one would have bothered about the thing at all. And another throne in Europe would have changed its occupant.

It was growing dusk as we reached Basingstoke. Drawn up in the square were two cars, whose passengers were strolling about, looking at the shops, and who, the moment we stopped, came up and grouped themselves round the car.

McIver issued his orders, which, by the very nature of things could only be provisional.

"We don't know what to expect," he said. "But something is brewing at the Cornsheaf Inn. Number One car will take up its station beyond the inn, but in sight of it. Number Two will remain this side, and in sight of it also. Park your cars so that you can go in either direction immediately. After that you must act on your own initiative. I am going to the inn itself."

It was Ronald's suggestion that only he and I should actually enter the pub. At first McIver refused flatly; he felt it was contrary to his professional dignity. But at last he was compelled to admit that there was every possibility of his being recognised, and he agreed to remain in the car outside the door.

And so, twenty minutes later, Ronald and I entered the bar of the Cornsheaf Inn, to find an atmosphere which would have been comical but for the fact that every suspicion was confirmed. The British yokel does not take kindly to strangers, and when those strangers consist of five of the most obvious foreigners one could hope to meet, the kindliness is even less in evidence.

"Two pints, please," cried Ronald cheerfully, and it sounded like a man laughing at a funeral. Elderly men raised rheumy eyes from tankards of ale, and having gazed at us pessimistically returned to the contemplation of the group in the corner. No dart was thrown; no halfpenny was pushed. Intense suspicion hung like a pall over the assembled company.

The foreigners were aware of it. One of them was evidently Philip's black-bearded friend, and he kept glancing uneasily round the room. But always his eyes came back to the door, and he continually looked at his watch.

"Fine day it's been," said Ronald affably.

"Might 'a been worse," conceded the barman.

"Ay," acknowledged the oldest inhabitant. "That's right, Joe."

After which conversational high spot, silence again settled on the bar.

Suddenly, from afar off in the distance, there came three short blasts on a motor horn, and the foreigners grew tense. Blackbeard half rose then sat down again. And, gradually growing louder, came the roar of a powerful car. It stopped outside the inn, and a moment later the door was flung open, and a man looked in.

Instantly the five of them rose and left the room.

"Come on, Bob," said Ronald. "This is our cue."

They were already in the car by the time we got outside, and as we joined McIver they started off at speed towards London. "That our bunch?" asked McIver.

"You've said it, Mac," said Ronald. "Hallo! Here's another car."

Travelling fast, also towards London, came a big saloon. The inside light was on, and in the back a man was sitting reading. The red tail-lamp of the first car had already disappeared, and we followed the saloon.

"Not too close, Mr. Standish," cried McIver, flashing his torch as a signal to the police cars to follow. "What the devil is it all about?"

"Search me," said Ronald. "But the crowd in the first car are pretty tough."

The saloon in front swung over a hill, and dipped out of sight. Behind us were the two police cars, and as we breasted the rise we saw at the bottom of the hill the saloon car stationary. Two red lights gleamed in the road: a STOP sign barred the way.

"Easy," repeated McIver. "Not too close."

And even as he spoke the saloon, disregarding the traffic signal, ran through the control and proceeded on its way.

"Rum," said McIver, as we slowed down. The STOP signal still showed; the red lights still gleamed. And it was Ronald who let out a sudden shout.

"That control is new. It wasn't here when we came down."

We drew up beside it; there was no watchman. Only a board in the middle of the road, and a pair of legs sticking out of the ditch—legs encased in black gaiters. We pulled him out, that poor devil in a chauffeur's livery, and there was a lump on his forehead the size of a hen's egg. But he was breathing, and leaving one of the men with him McIver got back into the car.

"Stamp on it," he said curtly. "Someone is going to get hell for this."

Up the next hill, and then in front of us a long stretch of road. But of the saloon car, no trace.

"There she goes," I cried, pointing away to the right, where we could see lights moving.

"Good for you, Bob," said Ronald. "Taken a by-road."

We came to it in about a quarter of a mile— a narrow twisting road between high hedges. And with the two police cars sitting on our tail Ronald drove all out. So much so that he had to ditch us to save ramming the back of the saloon car, which we came on suddenly round a corner.

"Put out all lights," cried McIver, and as we tumbled out of the cars there rang out from close by a scream for help. It came from a barn which one could see through a gap in the hedge, a barn from which a dim light filtered through the door.

We burst in. Dangling from a beam was the man in the saloon car; round him on the floor were; our friends of the Cornsheaf. Even though taken completely by surprise they fought savagely, but it was hopeless. In half a minute they were handcuffed in a circle, and the show was over.

"Well, sir," said McIver to the man they were just hanging, and who had been instantly cut down on our entry, "we were just in time it seems. They don't appear to like you. What's it all about?"

"Are you the police?" he gasped.

"We are," said McIver.

"Thank God!" he muttered and pitched forward unconscious.

It was a strange story that he subsequently told us. A member himself of this secret society, which he had joined in ignorance of its true character, he had learned the full details of a plot to assassinate a certain foreign prince on the occasion of his state visit to England the following month. And it was to give away the whole thing that he had come over. But somehow or other he had incurred the suspicions of the other members, and they had decided to kill him.

Believing himself to be safe owing to the precautions he had taken, he had not bothered to inform the police of his intentions, and the first moment he had realised his folly was when the car stopped, the chauffeur was knocked out in front of his eyes, and the two men he dreaded most got into the car with him.

His name is immaterial, and as all the world knows the Royal visit passed off without a hitch. But though the particular gang we caught are never likely to trouble him again, there are others. And I do not think I would care to be in the shoes of the man in the saloon car.

The Fourth Bottle

Admittance to the Pointed Shoe presents but few difficulties to those who wish to enter. On a payment of five shillings you become for the evening a guest of the proprietors, and a partaker—at a price—in the festivities, which last as a general rule till about five in the morning.

And here let me state at once that the Pointed Shoe is not one of those reprehensible establishments which sell forbidden liquor out of hours, and are invariably raided, sooner or later, by hordes of detectives in regulation boots.

The Pointed Shoe is run on absolutely legal lines, and furnishes yet another example of the futility of trying to enforce unwanted legislation. Attached to it, though ostensibly quite a separate undertaking, is a wine merchant whose hours for opening are midnight to five a.m. From this gentleman then, on the production of much money, may be obtained a bottle of whatever drink the guest may desire.

To buy an ordinary whisky-and-soda is impossible; it would render the proprietors, the staff and the consumer liable to execution in the Tower. To buy a bottle of whisky, however, and have twelve whiskies-and-sodas is a great and meritorious deed. Which is a remarkable state of affairs, but I feel sure it has made somebody happy.

Now, if I have written at some length on this peculiar anomaly of the licensing laws, it is because there may be people who know not the Pointed Shoes of London, and who would rightly regard such an artificial absurdity as an invention on my part. And it is essential that they should realise the conditions that existed at the Pointed Shoe if they are to appreciate one of the cleverest murders ever planned, and still more the brilliant manner in which it was detected.

On the night in question the place was almost full up at two o'clock. The room is long and narrow, and is especially adapted to allow the minimum of people to dance with the maximum of discomfort. Which, as all the world knows, is the goal aimed at every nightclub. At the end opposite the entrance door a gaily-uniformed band was playing really well. From table to table moved Captain Coombe—late of His Majesty's Royal Lancashires—chatting with his guests, most of whom were regular *habitués* of the place. A haze of tobacco smoke hung like a pall. At times the conversation drowned the music.

Taken as a whole, the crowd was a smart one. Quite a number of the sweet girlish faces that are repeated week by week in the society papers could be seen; a couple of earls, two well-known actors, and a sprinkling of guardsmen supplied the male attendants. And it was during one of those sudden lulls that sometimes occur that the door was flung open and a large, rather red-faced man came in with a woman. Coombe was at my table at the time, and I heard his muttered "Damn!" And the reason was not far to seek.

The red-faced man was John Forfar, and it was clear at a glance that he had not confined himself to water during the evening. His blustering "Hi! you to a waiter came distinctly across the room; then the babel of conversation broke out again.

But the cause of Captain Coombe's annoyance was not the fact that John Forfar was a little in liquor. Such a condition was not unknown in the Pointed Shoe. Nor was it due to the fact that the lady with him was one of those that the Greeks had a word for. Again, such ladies were not unknown in the Pointed Shoe. The reason of his expletive lay in the composition of the party seated at the next table but one to ours. For amongst that party was Tony Elgin.

And now I must once again digress for the benefit of those whose paths lie far from London.

Everybody knew that Tony Elgin was in love with John Forfar's wife. Including John Forfar. Of the lady's feelings on the matter no one was quite so sure. Being a woman, she was naturally aware of the fact; but whether she reciprocated the sentiment I, for one, am unable to say.

Certainly, she gave no hint of it in public, whereas Tony's every movement proclaimed his state of mind from the housetops. His eyes followed her from the time she entered a room till the time she left it. Never a bright conversationalist, his mind became a complete blank on such occasions, so that he mumbled incoherently, and men fled from his presence.

Admittedly, Sheila Forfar was an adorable creature, and why she had married her husband John was one of those insoluble mysteries that everyone had given up trying to solve years ago. He was flagrantly unfaithful to her, and took not the slightest pains to conceal his infidelities. But for some strange reason she would not divorce him.

It was no question of money—she had plenty of her own. I do not think it was religion—she certainly was not a Catholic. But she was not a woman who gave her confidence easily, and so to the mystery of why she married him in the first place was added the even greater one of why she did not get rid of him now.

Fortunately, she herself was not in Tony Elgin's party, and he had his back to the table which John Forfar had taken. But it could only be a question of time before the two men saw one another, and one had an uncomfortable feeling that then there might be trouble, in spite of the publicity of the place. Everybody knew Tony Elgin's opinion of John Forfar. Including John Forfar. And though Tony was one of the most delightful men you could meet, he had the devil of a temper when it was roused.

A bottle of whisky and one of champagne for the lady had appeared on Forfar's table, and it soon became evident that he was proposing to make a night of it. In rapid succession he lowered three of the very strongest, so that even his fair companion began to shake her head at him. And still Tony was oblivious of his presence.

Then Forfar got up to dance, and almost simultaneously Tony rose too.

"The fat," said little Anne Dornoch, "is shortly going to be in the gas-stove, my pet. Only the Crystal Palace would be big enough for those two tonight."

And she was right. At no time a brilliant performer, when in wine Forfar was positively a menace. He seemed to regard the floor as a space on which he could move at speed in a straight line. If anybody got in his light, so much the worse for the other. And fate decreed that just as Tony was passing our table Forfar, backing across the room like a bull, took him and his partner fairly amidships, and literally almost knocked them down.

Now, let it be clearly understood, in justice to everyone, I am quite convinced that Forfar did not purposely run into Tony. He did not purposely run into anybody. But as an exhibition of execrable dancing it would have been hard to beat, especially on that tiny floor. And Tony, quite naturally, was not amused, even before he realised who it was who had done it. But when he did he lost his temper. He thought, as he told me afterwards, that Forfar had meant to do it.

"Confound you, Forfar," he said angrily, "if you do that again I'll smash your face in."

Forfar dropped his partner, and his face grew mottled with fury.

"Will you really, Mr. Elgin?" he answered thickly. "Give my love to my wife when you see her again tonight."

It was an unspeakable thing to say, and it was said in an unspeakable way. And once again, in justice to everyone, I do not think even Forfar would have said it had he not been slightly drunk. But no one could blame Tony for standing not on the order of his answer.

"You ineffable swine," he said in a very clear voice. "Some day some lucky man is going to kill you."

And then Captain Coombe came hurrying up. Though not many people heard the actual words used, all heads were craning in our direction, and conversation had practically ceased. Tony's partner had hurriedly sat down; the lady friend had gone back to Forfar's table. And Coombe, who was a little man, performed a deed of great valour. He got between the two men who were glaring at one another over his head.

"Gentlemen," he said quietly, "I must really ask you to control yourselves. It makes it so unpleasant for all my other guests."

He half led, half pushed Tony to his seat, and after a moment's indecision Forfar resumed his. The band played a new tune; the tension relaxed. And in a few moments the Pointed Shoe had resumed the even tenor of its way.

"It's a funny thing," remarked Ronald Standish thoughtfully, "how near the primitive we all are. Had Tony had a gun then, he might easily have shot that swine dead. For from such a situation does murder so often arise."

"But they'd never have hanged him," cried Anne.

"No, Anne, they wouldn't have hanged him. At least probably not. But they'd have given him a nice long spell at His Majesty's expense. And you must always remember that in the eyes of the great British public, Tony is the villain of the piece. Sheila is Forfar's wife. Do you feel like shaking a leg?"

They rose to dance, and I sat on, watching covertly. Tony was being petted and cajoled into a better temper, but he was obviously still in a towering rage. And suddenly he saw me and came over.

"Did you hear what that——" said, Bob?"

"I did, old boy," I said. "I couldn't help it. But don't forget he's half tight."

"I don't give a damn whether he is or not," he answered. "But he and I are going to have things out before the night is through."

He returned to his seat, and I glanced at Forfar's table. He was still punishing the whisky, and it seemed to me that the woman was trying to get him to leave.

"Very awkward," said a voice in my ear. "What was it about?"

Coombe was standing beside me.

"Forfar barged into Elgin at a rate of knots," I said, "and darned near knocked him down. But I think it was accidental. Do they often come here?"

"Elgin very rarely. But that man Forfar is in here two or three times a week, and I wish to Heaven he'd stay away. He's never actually given any trouble before, but the staff detest him."

"Who is the woman with him?" I asked perfunctorily.

He shrugged his shoulders.

"A new one on me," he said. "What is it?"

A waiter had come up, and for a moment or two I stared at him. Seldom have I seen a man who looked so desperately ill. His face was dead white, save for an angry spot of colour in each cheek, and his eyes glowed with an unnatural brightness.

"Mr. Forfar wants to speak to me?" Coombe was saying. "All right; I'll come."

"That waiter looks pretty sick," I remarked as the man left.

"I didn't notice," said Coombe. "They come and go, these fellows. I wonder what the deuce Forfar wants to see me about. Hallo! the lady is going."

I looked across the room. Coombe was right. She was standing up, putting on her wrap, and was obviously giving Forfar a bit of her mind. I grinned happily. Most assuredly was she of the type who would call a spade a spade. Also most assuredly was she doing so now.

She paused, and evidently seemed to be giving him one last chance of going with her. But he shook his head sullenly and sat on. And with a snap of her fingers in his face, she swept out of the room just as Coombe approached the table. Then Anne and Ronald returned, and my attention wandered. Periodically during the next half-hour I saw him drinking morosely, with his heavy features set in a permanent scowl, but I was no longer interested.

And then it happened. The whole thing was so sudden that it almost stunned one. No one was dancing; two entertainers were singing

501

an extremely *risqué* song. The waiters were standing motionless at one end of the room; everyone was seated at their tables. Came the most dreadful bellow of pain, and John Forfar lurched on to the floor. His face was distorted with agony; animal-like noises were coming from his lips. Tottering, staggering, he got halfway across the floor towards Tony Elgin's table. Then with a final croak of "You . . . murderer!" he pitched forward on his face and lay still.

For a space there was silence, utter silence. The whole room sat petrified, as if turned to stone. Then came a woman's piercing scream, instantly stifled, as Coombe walked slowly up to the body and turned it over. Then abruptly he knelt down, and I saw him take a deep sniff.

"Standish," he said curtly. "Come here, will you?"

Ronald crossed the floor, and Coombe whispered something in his ear.

"Not a doubt about it," answered Ronald gravely. "Will you tell them, or shall I? No one must leave the room."

"Ladies and gentlemen," said Coombe quietly. "I'm afraid you will all have to remain here until the police come. I realised at once, and Mr. Standish confirms it, that this is not a case of natural death. Mr. Forfar has been poisoned with prussic acid, which means it is a question of suicide or—murder."

And as Ronald covered the dead man's face with a pocket handkerchief, I noticed a piece of paper clutched in Forfar's right hand.

I have spent many unpleasant quarters of an hour in my life, but I think the one that elapsed before the arrival of the police was the worst. People talked in whispers, trying not to look at the thing that lay sprawling on the floor. And then some fool woman had hysterics, which might have started the whole lot off had not the man with her thrown a glass of water in her face and told her to shut up.

"How did he do it?" asked Anne as Ronald came back to the table. She was sitting holding my hand very tight, and her eyes seemed enormous in her little face.

"It's in the whisky, Anne. The bottle reeks of it."

"But—but was it murder?"

"I can't tell you, dear. I don't know. But it points that way."

"Why?" she whispered.

"Because if Forfar had wished to commit suicide he'd have put the poison in the glass and not in the bottle."

"Who could have done it?" I barely heard the half-breathed question.

"'That," said Ronald gravely, "is what the police will have to try to find out."

"Could it have been that woman who was with him?"

"No," I remarked. "It could not. I personally saw him drink at least three times from that bottle after she left him."

"You're certain of that, Bob?" asked Ronald quickly.

"Positive," I said.

"Because that is a very important piece of evidence. It conclusively lets her out. And I'm thinking this may be a question of elimination."

'You've dismissed the idea of suicide entirely?"

"Not entirely. But as I said to Anne, why put the stuff in the bottle?"

And at that moment Tony Elgin came over to our table.

"May I interrupt?" he remarked gravely. "It's rather important."

"Sit down, Tony," said Ronald.

' That note in Forfar's hand. Is it necessary that the police should see it?"

"Essential," said Ronald. "It may have a very important bearing on the case."

"It hasn't."

"How do you know?"

"Because I wrote it."

Anne's grip tightened on my hand.

"Sorry, Tony," said Ronald after a pause.

"But it would be quite out of the question to remove it now. Apart from any other reason, the whole room would see it being done, and someone would most certainly tell the police. Is there anything very private in it?"

"Yes. A woman's name."

And once again there was a pause. We all knew who the woman was.

"I'm afraid it can't be helped, old man," said Ronald. "The police will have to see it. Incidentally, here they are now, with McIver in charge."

Inspector McIver, followed by two plain clothes men and a uniformed constable, had entered the room and was talking to Coombe. Then with a curt nod he crossed the floor and bent over the body, while a breathless silence settled on the room. It was as if the curtain were going up on the first act of a play.

His examination was brief but thorough. Then, prising open the dead man's fingers, he extracted the note. He read it, and glanced round the room.

"Ladies and gentlemen," he said quietly. "I gather that you realise what has happened. Mr. Forfar has died as the result of swallowing prussic acid. It may have been self-administered; it may not. May I ask, to start with, who is the writer of this note?"

"I am," said Tony, and McIver came over to our table.

"Good evening, Mr. Standish," he remarked on seeing Ronald. "I take it you saw the whole thing?"

"I did," said Ronald. "It was I who told Captain Coombe that no one must leave till you came."

"Thank you. You did perfectly right. Now, sir," he continued, turning to Tony, "you say you wrote this note. What is your name?"

"Anthony Elgin."

'Who is the Sheila you refer to?"

"Mrs. Forfar."

"The dead man's wife?"

Tony nodded, and McIver gave him a penetrating glance from under his shaggy eyebrows.

"You say in this note, Mr. Elgin: 'You foul blackguard, how dare you bandy Sheila's name about in public?' I gather you know the lady well?"

"I do," said Tony.

"Am I to understand that it was tonight Mr. Forfar was bandying his wife's name about?"

"That is so," answered Tony.

"What exactly took place?"

"He barged into me while I was dancing, and then made the most offensive reference to Mrs. Forfar."

"Yes. And what did he say?"

"He asked me," said Tony after a momentary pause, "to give her his love when I saw her again tonight."

Once again came that penetrating look from McIver.

"Indeed. But that hardly seems to me to be very offensive, Mr. Elgin."

Tony hesitated and Ronald cut in quietly:

"Don't try to hide things, Tony. It will do no good."

'Very well. It was peculiarly offensive, inspector, because Forfar knew that I had taken his wife home from a theatre, and that she had retired for the night."

"I see. May I ask if there is any reason why that remark should be peculiarly offensive to you personally?"

"I am a very great friend of the lady," said Tony curtly.

McIver glanced at the note again.

"You go on to say: 'If you have the guts of a louse, come outside and take the thrashing you so richly deserve.' Did you have any reply?"

"No. I saw him come back into the room and read it. Then he picked up the bottle of whisky and took a drink neat. And the next moment he was dead."

"So that when you sent the note over to his table he was not in the room?"

"I didn't send it over. I took it myself."

"You took it yourself?"

"I did. I wasn't sure if he had gone for good, but when I saw his cigarette-case on the table I knew he hadn't."

"So there was no one at the table?"

"No one. The woman who was with him earlier in the evening had gone."

"There had been a woman with him, had there? Do you know who she was?"

"Not an idea."

"She's no help, McIver," put in Ronald.

"She left about half an hour before it happened, and Mr. Leyton saw Forfar drink on two or three occasions out of the bottle after she had gone."

"That is so," I corroborated.

"Have you any idea," McIver asked me, "how long it was before he died that he took his last drink in safety?"

"I can't say if it was his last," I said, "but he certainly drank from that bottle a quarter of an hour before the end."

"One more question, Mr. Elgin." He turned back to Tony. "Do you remember if the cork was in or out of the bottle when you took the note over?"

"I am almost sure it was out, but I would not swear to it."

"Thank you." McIver closed his notebook, and Tony, getting up, went back to his own table.

"I gather," continued the inspector to Ronald, "that the dead man's last words were 'You . . . . murderer' Have you any idea to whom he was speaking?"

"To be perfectly frank, McIver, I think he was speaking to Mr. Elgin," said Ronald promptly. "I think he believed Elgin had poisoned him. Which, on the face of it, is absurd."

"Why, Mr. Standish?"

"My dear fellow, does one come to a place of this sort with a bottle of prussic acid in one's pocket?"

"Not a very good argument, Mr. Standish, for someone evidently *has* done so. The prussic acid was not in the bottle a quarter of an hour before he died; it was there when he died. It can't have got there by itself."

"I say, Inspector," said Coombe, coming over to us, "can you let some of these people go now? They're getting very restless."

"In a few moments, Captain Coombe. Just now I would like to speak to the waiter who was looking after Mr. Forfar."

Coombe made a sign, and the same waiter whose appearance I had noticed before came up.

"You were waiting at Mr. Forfar's table?" said McIver.

"I was, sir."

"What is your name?"

"George Parsons."

"Now, Parsons, I want you to answer a few questions. After the lady who was with Mr. Forfar left, who, if anyone, went to his table?"

"I saw Captain Coombe, sir, talking to him."

"That is so," interrupted Coombe. "He wanted to know when the singing was going to begin."

"And except for him," continued the waiter, "I saw no one come to the table except that gentleman over there."

He indicated Tony.

"Was Mr. Forfar at the table then?"

"No, sir."

"Did you see what that gentleman did?"

"He put a note under Mr. Forfar's cigarette-case."

"Anything else?"

"He took his handkerchief out of his pocket, sir."

"What do you mean? To blow his nose or what?"

"No, sir. He did not blow his nose. I don't know what he did with it, because he half turned his back to me."

"And how long did he remain with his handkerchief out of his pocket while his back was turned to you?"

"A few seconds, sir."

"Have you no idea what he was doing?"

"None, sir."

"Could he have picked up the bottle of whisky?"

"He might have, but I can't say that he did."

"When was the last occasion on which you saw Mr. Forfar take a drink from the bottle in safety?"

"Just before he left the room, sir. I brought him another siphon."

"Did anyone except Mr. Elgin go to the table while Mr. Forfar was absent?"

"No, sir. Of that I am positive."

"All right, Parsons, thank you. That will do. You can tell your guests, Captain Coombe, that they may go now. Keep all the staff, and if you would care to stop, Mr. Standish, I shall welcome your assistance."

He walked over to Tony's table and said a few words to him. It was not difficult to guess their purport, for Tony turned as white as a sheet.

"Surely he can't think that Tony did it," cried Anne indignantly.

I said something reassuring, but I noticed that Ronald looked a little worried.

"I wish he hadn't gone over to the table when Forfar was out," he said. "No one in their senses could believe he'd do such a thing, but the bald fact remains that somebody put the stuff in the bottle while Forfar was absent."

The room had emptied, and suddenly Tony got up and came to our table.

"That police merchant suspects me," he said quietly. "He hasn't told me that he does in so many words, but it's sticking out a yard. It's farcical, Ronald," he continued angrily. "A bloke doesn't go to a night club with bottles of poison all over him. What the devil are they looking for now?"

McIver and his satellites were making a thorough search of the seats and chairs, and I noticed that McIver himself was concentrating particularly on those at which Tony's party had sat. And suddenly, to my unmitigated horror, he plunged his hand into the space between the seat and the back and withdrew a small bottle. He took one sniff at it and then came over to us.

"How do you account for this, Mr. Elgin?" he asked gravely. "It is obvious from the smell that it contained prussic acid, and I found it just where you were sitting."

"I can't account for it," said Tony steadily. "I certainly did not put it there. And I can only say that whoever did is merely trying to throw suspicion on me. He knows I quarrelled with Forfar, and that's why he has singled me out. Confound it all, Inspector, I didn't even know Forfar was coming here tonight. So how could I have brought prussic acid to kill him? And I suppose you're not going to suggest that I brought it to kill anyone else. The whole thing is a plant; it's obvious."

"Of course it is, Tony," cried Anne.

"Look here, McIver," said Ronald. "I've got an idea which may help us. Test the bottle of whisky, and that empty bottle in your hand for fingerprints. Not that you'll get much, I'm afraid, but it can do no harm."

"I was naturally going to do that in any event, Mr. Standish," remarked McIver a little stiffly, and beckoning to the sergeant he crossed the room to Forfar's table.

"It's a positive nightmare, Ronald," said Tony. "God knows I had no cause to love the man, but to be accused of poisoning him seems like a fantastic dream. I keep pinching myself to make sure I'm awake."

"My dear Tony," said Ronald, "don't you get hit up about it. It is obvious, of course, that someone has taken advantage of an unusual set of circumstances to try to make you the scapegoat. We'll euchre him somehow. Well, McIver, what luck?"

"None, Mr. Standish. I hardly expected it. On the empty poison bottle the only finger-prints are my own. On the whisky bottle, the only prints are Mr. Forfar's. Five perfect ones as clear as you could want. But naturally a glove or a handkerchief was used. What on earth is the matter?"

For Ronald was standing up, literally shaking with excitement.

"Five," he shouted. "*Only* five."

"What more do you want? Four fingers and a thumb."

"And no others?"

"No. Why should there be?"

"McIver, you're mad. Coombe—come here. You keep a record, I take it, of all the drinks bought each night?"

"Yes. And it can be checked next door at the wine merchant's."

"How many bottles of Haig whisky have been ordered tonight?"

"Louis can tell us."

He summoned the head waiter.

"How many bottles of Haig have you ordered tonight, Louis?"

"Three, sir. One for Lord Glasstown; it is there on his table. One for Mr. Jacobstein; there it is on his table. And one for Mr. Forfar, which the inspector has in his possession."

Ronald looked nonplussed, and we all stared at him in bewilderment.

"What's the great idea, Mr. Standish?" said McIver with faint derision.

"I can't be wrong," cried Ronald, "I can't be. Coombe—can you get hold of the wine merchant's place?"

"Easily. Louis, ask Mr. Tracy to come down here, will you? And to bring his record of sales."

"What's stung him, Bob?" said Tony eagerly. "Is he on to something?"

"Looks like it," I answered. "Though what it is is beyond me."

"This is Tracy," said Coombe as a clean-shaven young man came in with a book in his hand.

"Good evening, Mr. Tracy," said Ronald. "Can you tell us how many bottles of Haig whisky you've sold tonight?"

"Four," answered the other promptly. "Three to Louis, according to the ordinary routine, and one to a waiter."

"So," said Ronald quietly. "Can you identify the waiter?"

"Easily, if he's here. He said he was feeling ill, and he looked it. There he is." He pointed to George Parsons.

"Well, Parsons," said Ronald, "what have you got to say? Where is that bottle of whisky?"

"Come forward," ordered McIver curtly, as the man hung back. "Where is that bottle of whisky?"

"I've drunk it," muttered Parsons sullenly.

"Send the sergeant, McIver," said Ronald, "to search for an empty bottle of Haig in the back premises. Or there may be a little left in it. Tell him to use a glove, for it will be covered with Mr. Forfar's fingerprints. In other words, he will find the bottle out of which Mr. Forfar has drunk the whole evening, until Parsons substituted the one that was found on his table after his death, and in which he had previously inserted the prussic acid."

And suddenly the waiter drew himself up defiantly.

"You've got me all right," he said, "though I don't know how. Yes, I murdered him, as I always said I would. And I don't regret it. The only thing I regret is trying to saddle the blame on Mr. Elgin. I only did that because they had that quarrel. I'm sorry. I've no excuse for that."

"I warn you," said the inspector, "that anything you say may be used as evidence."

Parsons laughed.

"Let it be," he said. "You'll have to try me mighty quick, inspector, if you want to try me at all." He pointed to his chest. "One of them has gone, and the other is as full of holes as a colander. I knew Forfar came here a lot, so I got a job as a waiter. And I've been lying up for him for weeks. At first I meant to tip the poison into his own bottle, but I found it was too risky. Someone would be bound to see me do it. Then I got the idea of substituting a bottle of the same brand, just as that gentleman has said—though how he found out is beyond me.

"But what you want to know, I suppose, is why I killed him. It's an old story now, but some stories remain new—with the principal actors. It had all the ingredients of full-blooded melodrama. A girl: the man she was engaged to as the youthful hero—you wouldn't think I was under forty, would you? And the villain, top hat and all. But it didn't end as stage melodramas end. No happily ever after business this time. It ended in a poor, bedraggled thing being pulled out of the slime of the Thames. I heard he was ostracised at his club for a bit over the matter. Then it was forgotten, except by me."

He laughed again.

Sorry I can't be more original. Sorry I can't even make a good story out of it. You see—I'm tired; terribly tired; tired, thank God— unto death. And now that I've put 'Paid' to the account, nothing else matters."

And with one last look at the motionless thing on the floor, Parsons, with the inspector's hand on his shoulder, passed through the silent staff and was gone.

"Poor devil," said Tony gravely. "I'm sorry for him. But how did you spot it, Ronald?"

"Five fingerprints, Tony; and *only* five. On a bottle from which Forfar had been drinking the whole evening! It was impossible. The bottle on his table could only have been drunk out of once. Therefore it was *not* the bottle from which he had been drinking; it was one that had been substituted. And the problem, instead of being the very difficult one of who added the poison, became the extremely simple one of who did the substitution. Simple, because it was almost a certainty that the stuff would be bought from Mr. Tracy, since it couldn't be obtained until Forfar himself had decided what he was going to drink. Still, I agree with you: I'm sorry for the poor devil."

The Music Room

"I'm afraid I must be terribly materialistic and dull, my dear Anne. I quite agree with you that the house ought to have a ghost, and if I could I'd order one from Harridges. But the prosaic fact remains that so far as I know we just aren't honoured."

Sir John Crawsham smiled at the girl on his right and helped himself to a second glass of port.

"We've got, I believe, a secret passage of sorts," he continued. "I've never bothered to look for it myself, but the legend goes that Charles the First lay hidden in it for two or three days. The only trouble about that is, that if His Majesty had hidden in all the secret rooms he is reputed to have stayed in he'd never have had time to do anything else."

"We must have a hunt for it one day, Uncle John," sang out his nephew David from the other end of the table.

"With all the pleasure in the world, my dear boy. I've got a bit of doggerel about it somewhere, which I'll look up after dinner."

"How long have you had the house, Sir John?" asked Ronald Standish.

"Two months. Incidentally. Standish, though I can't supply a ghost, I can put up a very strange story which is more or less in your line of country."

"Really," said Ronald. "What is it?"

Sir John pushed the decanter to his left.

"It happened about forty years ago," he began. "At the time the house was empty; the tenants were abroad, the servants had either been dismissed or put on board wages. The keys were with the lodge-keeper, and two or three times a week he used to come up to open the windows and generally see that everything was all right. Well, one morning he arrived as usual and proceeded to unlock the doors of all the rooms, according to his ordinary routine. Until, to his great surprise, he came to the music-room and found that the key was missing. The door was locked but there was no key.

"He searched on the floor, thinking it might have fallen out of the keyhole; no sign of it. And so after a while he went outside, got a ladder, and climbed up to look through the mullioned windows. And there, lying in the middle of the floor, he saw the body of a man.

"The windows in that room are of the small diamond-paned type and are not easy to see through. But Jobson—that was the lodge-keeper's name—realised at once that something was badly amiss and got hold of the police, who proceeded to break open the door. And there an appalling sight confronted them.

"Stretched on his back in the middle of the room was a dead man. But it was the manner of his death that made the sight so terrible. The lower part of his face had literally been battered into a pulp; the assault must have been one of unbelievable ferocity. I say assault advisedly, since it was obvious at once that there could be no question of suicide or accident. It was murder, and a particularly brutal one at that. But when they'd got that far, they found things weren't so easy.

"From the doctor's examination it appeared that the man had been dead for about thirty-six hours. Jobson had not been to the house the preceding day, and so it was clear that the crime had been committed two nights before the body was found. But how had the murderer escaped? The door, as I've told you, was locked on the inside, which showed that the key had been deliberately taken from the outside and placed on the in. The windows were all bolted, and a very short examination proved that it was impossible to fasten them from outside the house. Therefore the murderer could not have escaped through a window and shut it after him. How, then, had he escaped ?

"Wait a moment!" Sir John laughed. "I know what you're all going to say. Through the secret passage, of course. All I can tell you is that the most exhaustive search failed to reveal one. Short of actually pulling down the walls, they did everything they possibly could, so I gathered from the man who told me the yarn."

"And no trace of any weapon was found?" remarked Ronald.

"Not a sign. But apparently, from the injuries sustained, it must have been something like a crowbar."

"Was the dead man identified?" I asked.

"No. That was another strange feature of the case. He had no letters or papers on him, and his clothes proved to have been bought in a big ready-made shop in Birmingham. They found the assistant who had served him some weeks previously, but he was of no help. The man had paid on the spot and taken the clothes away with him. And that, I'm afraid, is all that I can do for you in the ghost line," he finished with a smile.

"Did the police have no theory at all?" asked Ronald.

"They had a theory right enough," said Sir John. "Burglary was at the bottom of it; there is some vague rumour that a lot of old gold plate is hidden somewhere in the house. At any rate, the police believed that two men broke in to look for it, bringing with them a crowbar in case it should be necessary to smash down the walls. They then quarrelled, and one of them bashed the other in the face with it, killing him on the spot. And then somehow or other the murderer got away."

Sir John pushed back his chair.

"After which gruesome contribution to the evening's hilarity," he remarked, "who is for a game of slosh?"

There were a dozen of us altogether in the house-party, and everyone knew everyone else fairly intimately. Our host, a good-looking man in the early fifties, was a bachelor, and his sister Mary Crawsham kept house for him. He was a man of considerable wealth, being one of the partners in Crawsham's Cable Works. The other two were his nephews, David and Michael, sons of the late Sir Wilfred Crawsham, John's elder brother. He had died of pneumonia five years previously, and when his will was read it was found that he had left his share of the business equally to his two sons, who were to be automatically taken into partnership with their uncle.

As a result, the two young men found themselves at a comparatively early age in the pleasant possession of a very large income. Wilfred's share had been considerably larger than his brother's, and so, even when it was split into two, each half was but little less than Sir John's portion. Fortunately, neither of them was of the type that is spoiled by wealth, and two nicer fellows it would have been hard to meet. David was the elder and quieter of the two: Michael—a harum-scarum youth, though quite shrewd when it came to business—spent most of his spare time proposing to Anne Horley, who had started the ghost conversation at dinner.

The party was by way of being a house warming. Though Sir John had actually had the house for two months, the decorators had only just moved out finally. Extra bathrooms had been installed and the

513

whole place had been modernised. But the work had been done well and the atmosphere of the place had been kept—particularly on the ground floor, where, so far as was possible, everything was as it had been when the house was built.

And especially was this true of the room of the mysterious murder—the music-room, into which everyone had automatically trooped after dinner. It possessed a lofty ceiling from which there hung in the centre a large and immensely heavy chandelier. Personally, I thought it hideous, but I gathered it was genuine and valuable. It had been wired for electricity, but the main lighting effect came from lamps dotted about the room. A grand piano—Mary Crawsham was no mean performer—stood not far from the huge fire-place, on each side of which were inglenooks with their original panelling. The chairs, though in keeping, could be sat on without getting cramp; there was no carpet on the floor, but several valuable Persian rugs. Opposite the fireplace was the musicians' gallery, reached by an old oak staircase. Facing the door were the high windows, through which Jobson had peered nearly half a century ago and seen what lay in the room.

"The bloodstain is renewed every week, my dear," said Sir John jocularly to one of the girls.

"But where exactly was the body, Uncle John?" cried Michael.

"From what I gather, right in the centre of the room. Of course, it was furnished very differently then, but there was a clear space in the middle and that was where he was lying."

"What do you make of it, Ronald?" said David.

"Good Heavens! My dear fellow, don't ask me to solve the mystery," laughed Standish. "Things of that sort are hard enough, even when you've got all the clues red hot. But when they're forty years old—"

"Still, you must have some idea," persisted Anne Horley.

"You flatter me, Anne. And I'm afraid that the only solution I can see might spoil it as well as solve it. Providing everything was exactly as Sir John told us—and you must remember it took place a long time ago—I think that the police theory is almost certainly correct as far as it goes."

"But how could the man get away?"

"I am quite sure they knew how he got away, but that part has been allowed to drop so as to increase the mystery. Through the door."

"But it was locked on the inside."

Ronald smiled.

"I should say it would take a skilled man with the right implement five minutes at the very most to lock that door from the outside, the key being on the inside. Which brings us to an interesting point. Why should he have troubled to do so? He had just killed his pal; so his first instinct would be to get away as fast as he could. Why, therefore, did he delay even five minutes? Why not lock the door from the outside and put the key in his pocket? He can't have been concerned with staging a nice mystery for future owners of the house; his sole worry at the moment must have been to hop it as rapidly as possible."

He lit a cigarette.

"You know, little things of that sort always annoy me until I can get, at any rate, a possible solution. Why do laundries invariably send back double-cuffed shirts with the holes for the links at least an inch apart? Why do otherwise sane people persist in believing that placing a poker upright in front of a fire causes it to draw up?"

"But of course it does," cried Anne indignantly.

"Only, my angel, because at long last you leave the fire alone and cease to poke it." He dodged a book thrown at his head, and continued. "Why did that man take the trouble to do what he did? What was in his mind? What possible purpose did he think he was serving? That, to my mind, Sir John, is the really interesting part of your problem. But then I'm afraid I'm a base materialist."

"Then you don't think there is a secret passage at all?" said Michael.

"I won't say that. But I think if there had been one leading out of this room, the police would have found it."

"Well, I think you're quite wrong," remarked Anne scornfully. "In fact, you almost deserve to be addressed as my dear Watson. What happened is pathetically obvious to anyone except a half-wit. These two men came for the gold plate. They locked the door to ensure they should not be disturbed. Then they searched for the secret passage and found it. There it was, yawning in front of them. At the other end— wealth. On which bright thought Eustace—he's the murderer—sloshes Clarence in the meat trap, so as to get a double share, and legs it along the passage. He finds the gold, and suddenly gets all hit up with an idea. He will leave the house by the other end of the passage. So he goes back; shuts the secret door into this room, and hops it the other way. What about that, my children?"

"Bravo!" cried Ronald, amidst a general chorus of applause. "It's an uncommonly good solution, Anne. It gets rid of my difficulty, and

515

if there is a secret passage I wouldn't be at all surprised if you aren't right."

"If! My poor child, what you lack is feminine intuition. Had women been in charge of this case it would have been solved thirty-nine years and eleven months ago. I despair of your sex. Come on, children: let's go and dance. I'm tired of ancient corpses."

The party trooped out into the hall, and Ronald strolled along the wall under the musicians' gallery, tapping the panelling.

"All sounds solid enough, doesn't it?" he remarked. "They certainly didn't go in for jerry-building in those days, Sir John."

'You're right," answered our host. "Each one of these walls is about three feet thick. I was amazed when I saw the workmen doing some plumbing upstairs before we moved in."

He switched out the lights and we joined the others in the hall, where dancing to the wireless had already started. And as I stood idly watching by the fireplace, and sensing the comfortable wealth of it all, I found myself wishing that I was a partner in Crawsham's Cable Works. I said as much to David, who looked at me, so I thought, a little queerly.

"I wouldn't say it to everybody, Bob," he remarked, "but I confess I'm a trifle surprised at things. I'd heard all about the new house, but I did not expect anything quite like this. Crawsham's Cable Works, old boy, have not been entirely immune from the general slump, though we haven't been hit so hard as most people. But that is for your ears only."

"He's probably landed a packet in gold mines," I said.

"Probably," he agreed with a laugh. "Don't think I'm accusing my reverend uncle of robbing the till. But this ain't a house: it's a ruddy mansion. However, I gather the shooting is excellent, so more power to his elbow. Which reminds me that it's an early start tomorrow, and I've got to see him on a spot of business. Night, night, Bob. That cup stuff is Aunt Mary's own hell-brew. I think she puts ink in it. As the road signs say—you have been warned."

Which was the last time I saw David Crawsham alive.

Even now, after a considerable lapse of time, I can still feel the stunning shock of the tragedy that took place that night. Big Ben had sounded: National had closed down, and a general drift bedwards took place. Personally, I was asleep almost as soon as my head touched the pillow, only to awake a few seconds later, so it seemed to me, with the sound of a heavy crash reverberating in my ears. For a while I lay listening. Had I dreamed it? Then a door opened and footsteps went past my room. I switched on the light and looked at my watch; it was half-past two.

Another door opened and I heard voices. Then a shout in Sir John's voice. I got up and, slipping on a dressing-gown, went out. Below I could hear Sir John talking agitatedly to someone, and as Ronald came out of his room, one sentence came up distinctly.

"For God's sake keep the women away!"

I followed Ronald down the stairs: Sir John was standing outside the music-room in his dressing-gown, talking to the white-faced butler.

"Ring up the doctor at once, and the police," he was saying, and then he saw us.

"What on earth has happened?" asked Ronald.

"David," cried his uncle. "The chandelier has fallen on him."

"What?" shouted Ronald, and darted into the music-room.

In a welter of gold arms and shattered glass the chandelier lay in the centre of the floor, and underneath it sprawled a motionless figure in evening clothes.

"Lift it off him," said Ronald quietly, and between us we heaved the thing clear. And a glance was sufficient to show that nothing could be done: David was dead. His shirt-front and collar were saturated with blood; his face was crushed almost beyond recognition. And one hand was nearly severed at the wrist, so deep was the cut in it.

"Poor devil," muttered Ronald, covering up his face. "Somebody had better break it gently to Michael. Keep everybody out, Bob. Ah! here is Michael."

"What is it?" cried the younger brother. "What's happened?"

"Steady, old man," said Ronald. "There's been a bad accident. The chandelier fell on David and crushed him."

"He's dead?"

"Yes, Michael, I'm afraid he is. I wouldn't look if I were you; it'll do no good."

"But in God's name how did it happen?" he cried wildly. "What on earth was the old chap doing here at this time of night? He was with you when I went to bed, Uncle John."

"I know he was," said Sir John. "We sat on talking over that tender for about half an hour, and then I went to bed, leaving him in my study. He said he would turn out the lights, and I can tell you no more. I fell asleep, until the frightful crash woke me up. I came down and

517

found this. For some reason or other he must have been in here: he said something jokingly about the secret passage. And then this happened. Of all the incredible pieces of bad luck—"

Sir John was nearly distraught.

"I'll have that damned contractor ruined for this," he went on. "He should be sent to prison. Don't you agree, Standish?"

There was no answer and, glancing at Ronald, I saw that he was staring at the body with a look of perplexed amazement on his face.

"What's that?" he said, coming out of his reverie. "The contractor. I agree; quite scandalous."

He walked round and examined the top of the chandelier.

"Funny a chain wasn't used to hold it," he remarked. "Though this rope is obviously new, and should have been strong enough. What room is immediately above here, Sir John?"

"It's going to be my bedroom, but the fools put down the wrong flooring. I wanted parquet, so I made 'em take it up again. They're coming to do it next week."

"I see," said Ronald, and once again his eyes came back to the body with a look of absorbed interest in them. Then abruptly he left the room, and when I went into the hall, where the whole party were talking in hushed whispers, he was nowhere to be seen.

"It's that room, Mr. Leyton," said Miss Crawsham to me between her sobs. "There's tragedy in it; something devilish. I know it. Poor Michael! He's gone all to pieces. He adored his brother."

And certainly the pall of tragedy brooded over the house. It was the suddenness of it; the stupid waste of a brilliant young life from such a miserable cause.

The doctor came, though we all knew it was merely a matter of form. I heard his report to Sir John.

"A terrible affair," he said gravely. "I must offer you my deepest sympathy. It is, of course, clear what happened: so clear that it is hardly necessary for me to say it. Your nephew was standing under the chandelier when the rope broke. He must have heard something and looked up. And the base of the chandelier struck him in the face. I am sure it will be a comfort to you to know, Sir John, that death must have been instantaneous. Of that I am certain. I shall, of course, wait for the police."

And at that moment I felt a hand on my arm. Ronald was standing beside me.

"Come into the billiard-room, Bob," he said in a low voice.

I followed him and threw a log on the dying fire. Then in some surprise I looked at him. Rarely had I seen him more serious.

"That doctor is a fool," he said abruptly.

"Why? What makes you say so?" I asked, amazed. "Don't you agree with him?"

For a space he walked up and down the room, his hands in the pockets of his dressing-gown. Then he halted in front of me.

"David's death was instantaneous all right; I agree there. But he wasn't standing underneath the chandelier when it fell."

"What was he doing then?"

"He was lying on the floor."

"Lying! What under the sun do you mean? Why was he lying on the floor?"

"Because," he said quietly, "he was dead already."

I stared at him in complete bewilderment.

"How do you make that out?" I said at length.

"That very deep cut in his hand," he answered. "Had he received that at the same time as he received the blow in the face it would have bled profusely, just as his face did. Whereas, in actual fact, it hardly bled at all. There are some other scratches, too, obviously caused by breaking glass which show no signs of blood. And so I say, Bob, that without a shadow of doubt, David Crawsham was already dead when the chandelier fell on him."

"Then what killed him?"

"I don't know," said Ronald gravely. "But it is a significant point that if you eliminate the chandelier, David's death is identical with that of the man forty years ago. Both found lying in the centre of the room with their faces bashed in."

"Do you mean that you think there's something in the room?"

"I don't know what to think, Bob. If by something you mean some supernatural agency, I emphatically do *not* think. That wound was caused by a very material weapon, wielded by very material power."

"You think it quite impossible that for some strange reason the wound in his wrist did not bleed? That all the blood that flowed came from his face?"

"I think it quite impossible, Bob, that those two wounds were administered simultaneously."

"His face would have been hit first," I pointed out.

"By the split fraction of a second. Damn it, man, his hand was almost severed from his arm. He ought to have bled there like a pig—"

"In that case what are you going to do about it?"

He again began to pace up and down the room.

"Look here, Bob," he said at length, "as I see it, there are two possible alternatives. The first is that somebody murdered David by hitting him in the face with some heavy weapon. He then placed the body on the floor under the chandelier and, going up above to the room without floor boards, deliberately cut the rope."

"But the rope wasn't cut," I cried. "It was all frayed."

"My dear man," he answered irritably, "use your common sense. Would any man be such a congenital fool as not to fray out the two ends after he'd cut the rope? The whole thing must appear to be an accident. The top end which I went and had a look at is frayed just like the bit on the chandelier. But *that* proved nothing. It's what you would expect to find if it was an accident or if it wasn't. That's the first alternative. The second is, I confess, a tough 'un to swallow. It is that something—don't ask me what—struck David in the face with sufficient force to kill him. He fell where we found him, and later the rope supporting the chandelier broke, and the thing crashed down on him."

"But if something hit him, not wielded by a human agency, that something must still be in the room," I cried.

"I told you it was a tough 'un," he said. "And the first isn't too easy either. The blow wasn't on the back of the head. He must have seen it coming; he must have seen the murderer winding himself up to deliver it. Can we seriously believe that he stood stock still waiting to be hit? It's a teaser, Bob, a regular teaser."

"Well, old man," I remarked. "I have the greatest respect for your judgment, but I can't help thinking that in this case you're wrong. Who could possibly want to murder David? And though I realise the force of your argument about the wound in his wrist, it's surely easier to accept the doctor's solution than either of yours."

"Very much easier," he agreed shortly, and led the way back into the hall. The police had arrived and were taking notes in readiness for the inquest; the doctor had already left The women had all gone back to their rooms. Only the men, with the exception of Michael, still stood about aimlessly.

I wondered if Ronald was going to say to the police what he had said to me, but he did not mention it. He gave his name, as I did mine—but as they obviously agreed with the doctor that the whole thing was an accident, the proceedings were merely a matter of routine.

At length they departed, having carried David's body to his room. And after a while we drifted away. The first streaks of dawn were beginning to show, and for a time I stood by the window smoking. And when at last I lay down it was not with any thought of sleeping. But finally I did doze off, to awake in a muck sweat from a nightmare in which some huge black object had come rushing at me out of space in the music-room.

The result of the inquest was a foregone conclusion. The building contractor produced figures to prove that the rope which had been used was strong enough to carry a weight twice as great as that of the chandelier, and that therefore he could not be held to blame for what must evidently have been a hidden flaw.

And so a verdict of accidental death was brought in, and in due course David Crawsham was buried. Only his aunt remained unconvinced, maintaining that there was a malevolent spirit in the room who had cut the rope deliberately. And Ronald. He did not say anything; on the face of it he acquiesced with the coroner's finding. But I knew he was convinced in his own mind that the verdict was wrong. And often during the months that followed I would find him with knitted brows staring into vacancy as he puffed at his pipe. But at last in the stress of other work he forgot it, until one day Michael caught Anne at the right moment and they became engaged. Which was the cause of our being again invited by Sir John to a party to celebrate the event.

The guests, save for ourselves and Anne, were all different from those who had been there when the tragedy occurred, and somewhat naturally no mention was made of it. The music-room was in general use, but there was one alteration. The chandelier had been removed.

"My sister insisted on it," said Sir John to me. "And I think she was right. A pity though in some ways; of its type it was very fine."

"Have you got any farther with finding the secret passage?" I asked.

He shook his head.

"No. Since the poor boy's death I haven't given the matter a second thought. What a ghastly night that was. I believe I've still got the paper somewhere," he said vaguely.

But one thing was clear; whatever Sir John had done, Ronald was giving it several second thoughts. Returning to the scene of the accident had brought the whole matter back to his mind, and I could see he was still as dissatisfied as ever.

"Not that it cuts any ice practically," as he said. "For good or ill, David was killed by the chandelier falling on him, and by no possible means could that verdict be shaken. Moreover, it would be a grave mistake to try and shake it now; the only result would be to upset Sir John and his sister, and lay oneself open to a severe rap on the knuckles for not having spoken at the time. But I'd give a lot, Bob, to know the truth about that night."

"Well, you're never likely to, old man," I answered, "so I'd give up worrying."

Which was where I went down to the bottom of the class; though even now the thing seems impossible. And yet it happened—happened the very evening I left. Ronald, who had stayed on, told me about it when he got back to London. Told me in short, clipped sentences with many pauses in between. Rarely have I seen him more savagely angry.

"I'm not a rich man, Bob, but I'd give ten thousand pounds to bring that swine to the gallows. . . . Who? . . . Sir John Crawsham. . . . He murdered David and, but for the grace of God, he'd have got Michael. . . . There's only one thing to be said in his favour, if it can be regarded in that light; it was, I think, the cleverest scheme I have ever come across.

"We were all sitting in the hall after dinner last night, and the conversation turned on the secret passage. After a while, Sir John was prevailed on by Michael to go and get the paper on which the clues were supposed to be written, and Anne and Michael went into the music-room and started to try to solve it. I was playing bridge and could not go with them, and I'd have liked to.

"Suddenly, I heard Michael give a shout of triumph, and by the mercy of *Allah* I was dummy. Otherwise—'"

He bit at his pipe angrily.

"I got up and went to the door of the music-room; Michael was standing in the right-hand inglenook, his hands on the panelling above his head, with Sir John beside him.

"'He's got it,' cried Anne triumphantly, and there came a loud click. And then, Bob, number two solution flashed into my brain and I acted mechanically. I think some outside power made me move; I don't profess to say. I got to Michael, collared him round the knees and hurled him sideways, just as the panel slid open and out ' something ' whizzed over our heads.

"Good God!" I muttered. "What was it?"

"The most wickedly efficient death-trap I have ever seen. As the door opened, it operated a catch in the roof of the passage behind it. As soon as the catch was withdrawn, a jagged mass of iron weighing over sixty pounds was released, and, swinging like a pendulum on the end of a chain, hurtled through the opening at a height of about five feet from the ground. Anyone standing in the opening would have taken it in the lower part of the face, and literally been hit for six.

"We stood there white and shaking, watching the thing swing backwards and forwards. As it grew slower we were able to check it, and as it finally came to rest, the door shut. The room was normal again. . . .

"I won't bore you, Bob, with a description of the mechanism. That it was of great age was clear; it had been installed when the house was built. Anyway, that's not the interesting point; *that* began to come in on me gradually. I suppose I was a fool; one is at times. But for a while the blinding significance of the thing didn't strike me. Then suddenly I knew. . . . Involuntarily, I looked at Sir John; and he was staring at me. . . . For a second our eyes held; then he looked away. . . . But in that second he knew that I knew. . . ."

Ronald rose and helped himself to a drink.

"I may be dense," I remarked, "but I still don't quite see. It is clear that that is the thing that killed David, but even then there's no proof that Sir John was aware of it. From what you tell me, the door shut of its own accord."

"As you say, that is the thing that killed David. As it killed that man forty years ago. And it lifted the body through the air with the force of the blow, and deposited it in the centre of the room. So much is obvious; the rest is surmise.

"Let us go back a little, Bob, and put a hypothetical case. And let us see how it fits in. A certain man—we will call him Robinson—was senior partner in a business. But though the senior, he drew but little more money from it than his two nephews. Which galled him.

"One day, Robinson happened to hear of a certain house—it is more than likely he got hold of some old document—which contained a very peculiar feature. It was for sale, and little by little a singularly devilish scheme began to mature in his mind. He studied it from every angle; he tested it link by link; and he found it perfect.

"He gave a house-warming party, where he enlarged upon an unsolved murder that had taken place years before. And late that night, after everyone else had gone to bed, he sat up with his elder nephew.

After a while he turned the conversation to the secret passage, and they both went into the music-room to look for it. Robinson, in spite of his statements to the contrary, knew, of course, where it was. And very skilfully, by a hint here and a hint there, he let his nephew discover it, as he thought, for himself. With the result we know.

"Had it failed, Robinson's whole plan would have failed. But no suspicion would have attached to him. He knew nothing about this infernal device. It did not fail; there in the centre of the floor was one of his partners dead. Robinson's third had become a half.

"Quietly he goes upstairs and gets into pyjamas. Then he cuts the rope of the chandelier. You see, the essence of his scheme was that the death trap should not be discovered; he wanted to use it just once more. For the whole is much better than a half. I've told you how he did it; fortunately without success."

"But can't you go to the police, man?" I cried.

"What am I to say to 'em? What proof can I give them *now* that David was dead before the chandelier fell on him? Exhumation won't supply it; this isn't a poison case. I merely lay myself open to thundering damages for libel. Why, if I knew it, didn't I speak at the time?"

"How I wish you had!"

"Robinson would still have got off. Even if the chandelier hadn't killed David, it had fallen accidentally, and he knew nothing about the other thing."

"I suppose it isn't possible that it *did* fall accidentally, and that Sir John *did* know nothing about the other thing?"

Ronald gave a short laugh.

"Perfectly possible, if you will answer me one question. Who replaced the weight in position?"

The End Justifies. . .

Ronald Standish threw the paper across the table at me.

"You'd better get the outline into your head, Bob," he remarked. "We'll be hearing the details shortly."

I glanced at the open page: there was no doubt as to what he referred :

TERRIBLE TRAGEDY IN MIDLANDS.
WELL-KNOWN HUNTING BARONET
MURDERED.

A shocking outrage occurred last night at Horsham Grange, near Melton Mowbray. Sir Peter Denne, a well-known figure in the hunting field, was brutally murdered in his study after dinner.

It appears that the baronet, who was sixty-five years of age, retired to his study, according to his invariable custom, at nine o'clock, leaving his niece, Miss Muriel Padston, in the drawing-room at the other end of the house. At ten o'clock the butler, William Sinton, took the whisky tantalus and a siphon to his master as usual. On opening the door of the study he at first thought Sir Peter had gone out, as the French windows were wide open, and there was no sign of him in the room. But on going to the desk he was horrified to see the body of the unfortunate baronet lying on the carpet. A glance was sufficient to show that he was dead, and that the cause of death was a terrible wound in the head, which lay in a welter of blood.

He rang up the police, and within a short time Inspector Drury and Dr. Deacon were on the scene. And it was at once apparent that a brutal crime had been committed. No trace of any weapon could be found, and it was therefore obvious that it was a case of murder and not suicide or accident. Sir Peter had been shot in the head at close range, by some form of sporting gun, probably, according to the doctor, a twelve-bore. The pellets had scattered very little, but there were no traces of scorching on the face. It is therefore estimated that the shot was fired at a range of some five or six feet. "Inquiries amongst the staff, and of Miss Padston, elicited the fact that no shot had been heard by anyone. But since the study is at the far end of the house, and a considerable wind was blowing at the time, this is not surprising. The matter is a complete mystery, since Sir Peter was one of the most popular men in the district; but further developments may be expected shortly.

I put down the paper.

"Seems clear enough so far as it goes," I remarked, "but it doesn't go very far. Who are you going to hear the details from?"

"Miss Muriel Padston herself," he answered. "She telephoned me this morning. I met her two or three years ago at a shooting party."

"Good looker?"

"Quite, so far as I remember. And a very good sort. I wonder what she can want with me."

"Presumably to consult you over this affair."

"My dear Bob," he grinned. "I didn't imagine she was coming up to London to ask me to choose her a hat. But as you so succinctly observed, the case does not seem a very difficult one, and it rather surprises me that she should come so post-haste. Anyway—*nous venom.*"

"Have you ever heard of Sir Peter before?"

"Never. But I've looked him up in *Who's Who.* Thirteenth baronet, J.P., and all the usual dope. His son—the only child—was killed in the war. His wife died seven years ago."

"Who is the heir?"

"A nephew, Charles Denne."

"And the Padston girl is presumably his wife's niece."

Ronald nodded.

"Yes. Sir Peter married a Miss Mary Padston in 1895. So now you know as much of the family history as I do myself."

The bell rang as he spoke, and a moment or two later Parker announced Miss Padston. She was a tall, pretty girl of about twenty-five, though her eyes looked a bit swollen from weeping. But her voice was quite normal when Ronald introduced me.

"A shocking tragedy, Miss Padston," he said. "You have my deepest sympathy."

"A worse one may take place, Mr. Standish," was her somewhat surprising answer. "That's why I rushed up by car to see you."

"Take your time," said Ronald quietly. "And please begin right at the beginning."

He pushed over a box of cigarettes, but she shook her head.

"You've seen the account of it in the papers, of course?" she asked.

"I have seen that your uncle, Sir Peter Denne, was killed by being shot through the head. I have seen that the police consider it was murder, and that the weapon reputed to have been used was a twelve-bore. I have seen that the crime took place between nine and ten last night, and that nobody heard a shot. Now let's hear the rest, and as I said, take your time."

"Five years ago," she began, "I went to live at Horsham Grange with my uncle. It suited me down to the ground as I'm mad on hunting, and it suited him to have someone to run the house. Besides, we've always got on most awfully well together. He was such a dear—"

She paused for a moment and her lips quivered.

"Last night," she continued steadily, "we had dinner together as usual. But it was obvious that something had upset him. There is no good disguising the fact because I am sure Sinton, the butler, noticed it too."

"But why should you disguise the fact, Miss Padston?" asked Ronald. "It may have an extremely important bearing on the whole case."

"That's what the police think; but I know they're wrong," she cried. "You see, Mr. Standish, there has been one big bone of contention between my uncle and me for the past few months—my cousin, Charles Denne. In reality he isn't a cousin at all; at least, there is no blood relationship. At any rate, last December he came home from abroad, and being just as keen on hunting as the rest of the family, he took a small house about a mile from Horsham Grange.

"Unfortunately from the first Uncle Peter took a dislike to him. Why, I don't know; the whole thing was too unreasonable for words. Charles goes magnificently; he's very good looking, and he's the best of company. It's true he threw one or two parties where they played pretty high, but that would never have affected Uncle Peter in normal circumstances. Moreover, Charles went out of his way to break down this curious dislike, but without any success. It just was there—inexplicable, unreasoning.

"Sometimes I've thought it was because Charles was his heir. His son was killed on the Somme, and he may have subconsciously resented Charles as an interloper. He idolised his boy Harry, and he saw Charles coming into all that was rightfully his son's. But as Charles said to me, it wasn't his fault. It was nothing to do with him that he'd been born Sir Peter's nephew: it was nothing to do with him that Harry had been killed. And after a while Charles began to get fed up himself. And since the two men were continually meeting on the hunting field the situation grew more and more awkward.

"Then came the culminating blow." She gave a sudden very delightful smile. "I fear I don't quite know how to cast down my eyes modestly."

"But you and Charles fixed matters up," laughed Ronald.

' Exactly. And Uncle Peter was not amused. In fact, there was the most unholy row. Both men lost their tempers and abused one another like bargees, until I walked into the room and sent Charles home. Then I had a talk with Uncle Peter.

"Mr. Standish, one might as well have argued with a mule. He was adamant. He pulled out all the old stuff about being my guardian: said that Charles was a damned fortune-hunter—that, mark you, about his own heir—"

"One moment, Miss Padston," interrupted Ronald. "Is your money your own, or was it controlled by your uncle?"

"My own."

"Thank you. Go on."

"And finally wound up by informing me that never under any circumstances would he give his consent. Well, that was a bit too much, and I told him so. I pointed out that as I was over age he had no means of stopping me marrying whoever I liked, and that I proposed to do so. And with that the party broke up."

"How long ago was this?" asked Ronald.

"About two months. Now, as you will understand, Mr. Standish, I was awfully upset over the whole thing. Save for this one amazing bee in his bonnet over Charles, Uncle Peter was just the same old dear as ever. And I hated the thought of hurting his feelings. Charles was all for telling him to go to blazes, and getting married with or without his consent. But I talked it over with him and, after a while he agreed, rather reluctantly, to let me try and get round him."

She shrugged her shoulders.

"It's been quite useless. Honestly I believe the poor darling was literally insane on that one point. The mere mention of Charles's name was enough to send him into a fit of ungovernable fury. And he would give no reason; that was the infuriating part of it all. If only he had mentioned some specific cause for his dislike I might have been able to cope with it, but he wouldn't. And so at last I realised it was useless going on, besides being unfair to Charles. So we decided we'd get married a month from now.

"I wanted to tell Uncle Peter myself, but Charles preferred to do it so that there should be no question of his appearing to funk it. And two days ago he did so. Apparently it was an accidental meeting in the village, and George told me about it."

"George? Who is George?" asked Ronald.

"Charles's cousin. He lives in London, and had stayed the previous night with Charles. And on his way back to Town he called in and saw me. Evidently there had been a hideous scene which ended in Uncle Peter actually going for Charles with his walking-stick. And the trouble is that it was witnessed by several people."

"Let's get these dates clear," said Ronald. 'Today is Thursday, so that it was on Tuesday that that happened."

"'That's right."

"Did Charles come and see you that day?"

"No. I rang him up when George had gone, but he was out."

"When did you next see Charles?"

"Last night—after the tragedy. I was out myself all yesterday till dinner-time."

"But I think you said, Miss Padston, that it was yesterday evening that your uncle seemed upset at dinner. What had caused that?"

"Apparently they'd had another row yesterday afternoon."

"They certainly do not seem to have liked one another," remarked Ronald. "Where did this one take place?"

"In the park."

"And did anyone witness it?"

"Charles doesn't know. You see, when Sinton told me that Uncle Peter was dead I rang up Charles at once."

"That would be just after ten o'clock last night. Was he in?"

She hesitated for a second.

"No. There was no answer at all."

"What about the servants?"

"A man and his wife look after him. And they go out every Wednesday."

"So you rang him up again later?"

"Yes. About twenty past ten. He answered, and I told him what had happened. He came over at once. And it was then he told me about the row yesterday afternoon. Oh! Mr. Standish, I *know* he didn't do it."

"My dear Miss Padston," said Ronald reassuringly, "I think you're alarming yourself most unnecessarily. On what you've told me there is no earthly reason to suppose that he did. Because two men have a quarrel—even a very bad quarrel—there is no reason for thinking that one of them is going to shoot the other hours afterwards in cold blood. Had he killed him in the heat of the moment the thing is understandable. But to walk a mile, as I say hours after, is a different matter. What object had he in killing your uncle? You and he were going to get married anyway."

The girl bit her lip.

"I haven't told you everything yet," she said. "While I was talking to Charles, Inspector Drury came into the room.

"'Have you been here long, Mr. Denne?' he said.

"Charles told him he'd only just arrived.

"'Have you been round to the study?'

"'No,' said Charles.

"'Nor outside the window?'

"'I came straight in here to Miss Padston,' Charles said a little irritably. "What are you driving at, Inspector?'

"'Mr. Denne, are your initials C. T. D.?'

"'They are,' answered Charles.

"'Then how comes a handkerchief bearing those initials to be in a rhododendron bush just by the study window?'

"He held it out, and Charles took it.

"'It's my handkerchief right enough, Inspector," he said. ' But how it came there I know no more than you.'

"And then it suddenly dawned on him what the inspector was driving at.

"'Good God! man,' he cried, 'you don't suppose I murdered my uncle, do you?'

"'I suppose nothing, Mr. Denne,' said the inspector. 'But a terrible crime has been committed, and it is my duty to investigate it. Can you tell me your movements since eight o'clock?'

"'Most certainly,' answered Charles. ' I fed at home at eight o'clock, and at about half-past nine I went for a walk, returning to my house at a quarter past ten. For that you will have to take my word since my servants always go out on Wednesday nights. Miss Padston rang me up five minutes later, telling me what had happened, and I came up here post-haste in my car.'

"'Merely as a formality, Mr. Denne,' said the inspector, 'may I ask if you met anyone during your walk?'

"'Several people,' said Charles quietly. 'But since the implication in your question is obvious, I may as well say at once that I spoke to no one who can confirm my story. And since it was dark there is nobody who could have recognised me.'

"With that the inspector left us, and Charles turned to me. Naturally he was most frightfully upset; it was evident that Drury suspected him. And that's why I've come straight to you, Mr. Standish."

"Did anything more happen last night?" asked Ronald.

"Nothing of any importance. We rang up George in London, but found that he had caught the eight o'clock train from King's Cross to York. His man didn't know where he was staying there, but he'd gone up on business."

"And nothing more this morning?"

"Not before I left. You will help Charles, won't you, Mr. Standish? You see, it's not enough, as he said to me, for them not to be able to prove that he did it. He's got to be able to prove that he didn't."

"That is so," agreed Ronald gravely. "Otherwise on the facts as you've told them to me suspicion will stick to him for the rest of his life."

"But you don't think—you *can't* think—he did it," she cried indignantly.

"Does it very much matter what I think, or don't think?" said Ronald. "Though if it's any comfort to you, I don't think he did it. But what we've got to do—if we can—is to prove that to the satisfaction of other people. And that may not be very easy. Have you any ideas yourself?"

"I believe it was a poacher," she said. "Or someone Uncle Peter had had before him on the Bench, and sentenced. But probably a poacher, because he'd be more likely to have a sporting gun. But you'll come down, Mr. Standish, won't you? You will help him?"

"I will. I'll come down this afternoon. And then we'll see what we can do."

"Well, Bob," he said after he had shown our visitor out, "what do you make of it?"

"Much the same as you," I answered. "I can hardly believe that any sane man would have done such an insane action just after two violent quarrels."

"He gets the title. He gets Horsham Grange and a lot more money. It is arguable both ways, you know. Supposing Charles Denne said to himself exactly what you've just said. Supposing he reasoned it out that the thing would appear so insensate, so obvious, that that in itself would be a proof that he couldn't have done it."

"Yes," I said doubtfully. "I suppose it is possible."

"It's certainly possible. Whether it's likely is a different matter. And in that case the episode of the handkerchief loses any significance. He dropped it accidentally and it blew away. But if it isn't the case then the matter of the handkerchief becomes of supreme importance."

"In what way?"

"Because it narrows our field down to someone who wished not only to murder the old man, but also to foist the crime on to Charles Denne. And that rather precludes a stray poacher, who is not as a rule a man of high mentality. Would the average vagrant go to the length of planting a handkerchief? How would he get the handkerchief in the first place? Still, there may be some further developments when we get down there."

His prophecy was destined to be fulfilled: further developments there were indeed. Charles Denne had already been arrested and charged with the murder of his uncle. And I must confess that the new fact that had come to light and had caused the issue of the warrant seemed pretty damning to me. For it proved conclusively, if it was true, that Charles Denne had lied over at least one point.

The evidence had been volunteered by a man called John Dillon, a very respectable farmer in a small way, who was a pillar of the local church and a man whose integrity was above suspicion. He stated that at about nine-forty the previous evening Charles Denne had passed him in the road carrying a gun under his arm, and had spoken to him. He had been standing just outside his own gate at the time, and the remark which Denne had made to him was, "Good evening, Dillon. Mr. George and I will be having another whack at your rabbits soon."

Pressed as to how he knew it was a gun, he stated that he had seen the faint glint of the barrel. Moreover, it was being carried as a man carries a gun, and not a walking-stick. What type of gun it was he could not say, but nothing would make him budge from his statement that it was some form of weapon.

Now the most superficial glance at the topography of the place revealed that if Sir Peter had been killed round about nine-thirty, the murderer, should he have been walking towards Charles Denne's house, would pass Dillon's door ten minutes later. And this, coupled with the fact that Charles and his cousin *had* shot rabbits over Dillon's ground a few weeks previously, seemed to clinch things conclusively. It was true that Dillon had not actually recognised Charles in the darkness, but if it was not he who else could it have been? Who but he would have alluded to George Denne as Mr. George? And if it was not George Denne who had been alluded to, who was it? He was the only George who had shot over Dillon's ground.

Strangely enough Ronald did not seem as worried as I expected.

"Proceeding on the assumption, Bob, as we are, that Charles Denne is innocent, this is merely another attempt to foist the crime on to him. It has of course been obvious to you all along that the murderer must be conversant with Denne's habits. The significance of Wednesday night being selected cannot be overlooked: the one night when the servants are out and their master can't rely on them for an alibi. So is it surprising that he should also have known that Charles Denne and his cousin George shot over Dillon's land? And made use of the knowledge?"

Which was perfectly sound, but it left the solution of the main problem as far off as ever. Who was the man who had impersonated Charles Denne? The inspector, conscious that his case was by no means foolproof, had not stopped his investigations. But nothing further came to light. The staff at Horsham Grange could, one and all, account satisfactorily for their movements between nine and ten on the fatal night. Two men who lived in the neighbourhood and who had recently been released from prison after serving a sentence for poaching, were equally convincing. And there seemed to be no one else who could possibly desire Sir Peter's death.

He even went so far as to check up George Denne's movements, once again to come up against a brick wall. The evidence was absolutely conclusive that at 11.45 p.m. on Wednesday he had arrived in York on the eight o'clock express from King's Cross. The ticket collector who knew him, since he often did the journey, was positive of the day because of a remark he had made when handing up his ticket. It had concerned a horse which had won that afternoon, and so had impressed itself on his memory. Further, there was the evidence of the hotel where he had stayed, and of the business deal he had put through on the Thursday morning.

In fact, every single being that Drury knew of who could possibly be interested in Sir Peter's death had a perfect alibi. And so the only logical conclusion was that it was someone he did not know of or that it was Charles Denne. The mere thought of Muriel Padston being the culprit—though it was undeniably true that there was no one who could vouch for her movements—he dismissed as too horrible to contemplate.

After the first stiffness had worn off Drury had got along well with Ronald. He realised they were both working in a common cause— the finding of the criminal. And no one would have been better pleased than he were Ronald able to prove it was not Charles Denne.

"A more open-handed gentleman, sir," he remarked on the day after our arrival, "I've never met. Everybody knows that he and his uncle didn't get on, but that he should have been guilty of such a dastardly crime is beyond me. And yet, if it wasn't him, who the devil was it? If it was someone from Sir Peter's past life—someone we haven't even heard of—how comes it that he was so glib with his local knowledge? If he'd been knocking around the place here he'd have been noticed; a stranger in a village like this is everybody's business in ten minutes."

But there had been no one. Muriel Padston could throw no light on it, nor could Charles Denne. And nor could George, living as he did in London. He had arrived in time for dinner on the Thursday, having motored post-haste from Town.

"I was busy this morning in York," he said, "and never read the paper. Actually, the first thing I heard of it was when I reached London and a man sympathised with me in the club. What a ghastly thing! Uncle Peter of all men."

The funeral was attended by the whole county, a striking tribute to the dead baronet's popularity. And a few days later Charles Denne was formally committed for trial on the charge of murdering his uncle. No further evidence had come to hand, and opinion as to his guilt was divided. A few loyal friends never wavered in their belief in his innocence. But the majority were floored by the same difficulty that had defeated Inspector Drury. If it was not Charles Denne, who was it ?

The date of the trial approached, and Ronald's irritability increased. We had long left Horsham Grange, as there was nothing further to be done there. But as the days passed his conviction of Charles Denne's innocence strengthened, till it became almost unreasoning. And he felt it was his fault that the truth had not been arrived at.

"A verdict of what is tantamount to Non Proven is no good, Bob,"
he said again and again. "We've got to *prove* him innocent, otherwise
he's finished for the rest of his life. And every instinct I possess rebels
against the idea that he did it."

And then one evening, about ten days before the trial was due to
commence, he walked into my sitting-room and solemnly bent over
a chair.

"Do you mind giving me a dozen of the best,

Bob, as hard as you can lay in, and then sending for a mental specialist."

A sudden wave of excitement came over me.

"You don't mean to say you've solved it?" I cried.

He lit a cigarette.

"The Lord has created fools, damned fools, and me," he remarked.
"Though, 'pon my sam, you're all in the same boat. I believe I once
said to you, Bob, that it is the obvious thing one is so liable to overlook. I even gave you the homely illustration of the two women, one
of whom entered a room with a baby in her arms, and the other with
a sucking pig. I asked you which you would be most likely to remember, and with unerring accuracy you got the answer right. It's been
the same in this case: we've all been concentrating on the lady with
the sucking pig."

"For Heaven's sake stop drivelling," I cried in exasperation. "Who
did kill Sir Peter?"

"All in good time," he said. "But I promise you shall know very
shortly. And since I have been driven into outer darkness by plumbers
and people, I have taken the liberty of asking a few people round here.
I trust they will keep to their time-table as it is rather important."

The bell rang and Inspector Drury came in.

"Good evening, Inspector," said Ronald. "I have asked you round
so that you can hear a very important development in the case."

"So I gathered," answered the mystified officer. "What is it?"

"And here," continued Ronald, "is Mr. Jacobson, the proprietor of
the Bull garage in Grantham."

A respectably dressed middle-aged man had entered, and stood
looking about in some surprise.

"Have you brought the book, Mr. Jacobson? And the other
thing?"

"Here it is, sir," he said, handing a ragged and rather dirty small
book over to Ronald. "I've got the other here, too."

"The most valuable witness in the case, Drury," remarked Ronald, holding it up. "And now, if you don't mind, would you both retire into Mr. Leyton's bedroom, where you can hear without being seen."

The bell rang again, and as the two men disappeared, Sir Kenneth Paine, K.C., the brilliant counsel briefed for the defence, came in.

"Evening, Standish," he said. "I got your message at the club. What's it all about?"

"Some fresh facts have come to light, Sir Kenneth," answered Ronald, "which I think are going to make your task a very easy one. But before I give them to you, we'll wait for Mr. George Denne, who will naturally be interested in them, too. And here he is."

"Good evening, Standish," cried Denne, entering. "Evening, Sir Kenneth. What's this I hear: you've found out something that will help poor old Charles? Excellent."

"I'm sure this information is going to be of the very greatest assistance," said Ronald. "So I thought we'd better have a conference at once with Sir Kenneth."

"Quite right; quite right," remarked the K.C., lighting a cigar. "For I'm bound to say, gentlemen, that though I don't think they'll hang him it's going to be a near thing on facts as they stand at present. That particular defence that no man could be such a crass idiot as to commit such a crime in such a way is weak. And if I rely on the line that someone was deliberately impersonating him, I'd prefer if I could," he concluded with a short laugh, "to produce the someone."

"Precisely, Sir Kenneth," agreed Ronald. "And since I felt that way myself, I decided to produce that someone for you. There he is."

His outstretched finger pointed at George Denne, who with an ashen face was swallowing repeatedly.

"You're mad," he stuttered at length. "Mad. I was in the train going to York. Is this some damn fool trick?"

His self-control was coming back, and he rose to his feet.

"I don't know much about the law, Mr. Standish, but I believe there's one on libel. How dare you make such an accusation against me?"

Ronald Standish was balancing the little book in his hand.

"Do you know what this is, Denne?"

"I don't; and I don't care."

"This is the book in which Mr. Jacobson, who owns the Bull garage at Grantham . . ."

With an oath, George Denne hurled himself on Ronald, only to be met with a straight left on the jaw, that knocked him half senseless to the floor.

"Here's your man, Inspector," called out Ronald. "He murdered Sir Peter on the night of Wednesday the twenty-first of last month by shooting him through the head from close range with a sporting gun."

With venomous eyes, Denne glared at Ronald from the carpet.

"It's a lie," he said thickly.

"It looks it," remarked Sir Kenneth dryly. "Your face at the moment is enough to send you to the gallows, without further evidence. But having made the accusation, Standish, it's up to you to substantiate it. I understood, I must confess, that he was in the eight o'clock express from King's Cross to York."

"That's what we all understood, Sir Kenneth," said Ronald quietly. "And beyond any question of doubt he arrived in that train at York where he handed up the first half of a return ticket from London to York. Naturally, under such circumstances, the assumption would be that the passenger boarded the train in London, thereby giving a cast-iron alibi for a murder committed between nine and ten. And what we all overlooked, every man jack of us, was the fact that the train stopped at Grantham."

The inspector gave a whistle of disgust.

"It seems incredible, I know," continued Ronald, "that such a blatant and obvious point should have been missed. I suppose it was because it *was* so obvious. But the instant it penetrated my fat skull the whole case changed.

What was a cast-iron alibi became no alibi at all. The train arrived at Grantham at ten, which left ample time for you, Denne, to murder your uncle and catch it there."

"Have I no redress against these monstrous allegations, Sir Kenneth?" snarled Denne.

"I take it you can prove this, Standish?" said Sir Kenneth gravely. "What you are saying is pretty serious."

' Is the number of your car VCT480, Denne?"

"It is."

"Where was your car on the night of Wednesday the twenty-first?"

"In London to the best of my belief."

Ronald turned over the pages of the little book.

"Would it interest you to know that VCT480 was taken in by the

Bull garage at Grantham at nine-forty-three that night?"

A muscle in Denne's neck was twitching.

"Very much," he said. "If what you say is the case somebody must have been joy-riding, I suppose."

"Really," remarked Ronald. "By what train did you leave York on Thursday, the twenty-second?"

"Go to hell," shouted Denne. "What the devil has that got to do with you?"

"If I were you, Mr. Denne," said Sir Kenneth quietly, "I would answer the question. If you don't it is apt to give a false impression."

"By the noon train," said Denne sullenly.

"Which arrives at Grantham at one-forty," continued Ronald, again consulting his book. "Would it interest you to know that VCT480 was removed from the Bull garage at one-forty-seven that day, by the same man who had put the car in the preceding night and who stated he had just come from York?"

Denne scowled but said nothing.

"The reason I can say that with confidence," went on Ronald, "is that the man rather impressed Mr. Jacobson by his almost morbid interest in Sir Peter Denne's death which he had read about coming down in the train. And so he remembered the whole conversation and the man."

"Well, it couldn't have been me," snarled Denne. "I knew nothing about my uncle's death till I reached London."

"I am quite aware that that is what you have always maintained," said Ronald gravely. "Which is not quite the same thing, is it? Because, Mr. Denne, a most unfortunate thing took place. As VCT480 drove out of the garage Mr. Jacobson saw, lying on the ground, an international driving licence, which had obviously fallen out of one of the pockets. He ran after the car but he couldn't stop it, and so he kept the licence expecting the owner would write for it."

Denne's face was ghastly to look at; his forehead was covered with sweat.

"That doesn't prove that I was driving the car," he muttered.

"Mr. Jacobson," called out Ronald. "Come in, will you? Is that the man?" he asked, as the garage proprietor came in with the blue licence book in his hand.

"It is, sir," he answered without a moment's hesitation.

"It's a lie," screamed Denne. "He's making a mistake. How could he remember a man after all this time?"

538

"Surely you forget, Mr. Denne," said Ronald, "one essential feature of an international licence. Your photograph is pasted in it."

For a tense five seconds there was dead silence; then George Denne crumpled up and collapsed.

"I did it, God damn you," he croaked. "I did it."

★★★★★★

"Smart of you, Standish," said Sir Kenneth a few moments later when Denne had been removed by the inspector. "I still don't quite see the whole thing."

"From the word 'go,' Sir Kenneth, it was obvious that Mr. George Denne was what might be described as an interested party. Of all the people we *knew* about he stood to benefit most. With Sir Peter dead and Charles hanged, he became the baronet. But since, in my fatuous stupidity, I thought he *couldn't* have done it owing to his being in the train, I dismissed him from my mind. When I realised that he *could* I set to work to review the whole thing from that angle. And at once everything began to fit in.

"He knew of the bad feeling between his cousin and uncle. He could easily have obtained one of Charles's handkerchiefs when staying with him. He knew that Charles's servants were always out on Wednesday night. He, more than anyone else, would have been likely to make that remark to Dillon; and his voice is not unlike his cousin's.

"So far so good, but we weren't over even the first hurdle, yet. If he'd done it, how had he done it? There were two methods: by train entirely, or by train and car. He buys a first return to York some time on Wednesday; at another pigeon-hole he gets a third to Grantham. Then he goes to Grantham by an earlier train; murders Sir Peter, and joins up on the eight o'clock express for York. Now I said by train entirely; I must amend that a little. Horsham Grange is ten miles from Grantham; therefore, he would have had to hire a car. Would he have dared risk it? In addition to that he would have been carrying a gun. Further, he would have had to tell the driver to stop somewhere while he killed the old man. No; that method was impossible.

"So I come to number two: train and car. He still buys his first return from London to York; then he motors up to Horsham Grange, and leaves his car hidden in some safe spot. Don't forget he knows the country. Then having shot Sir Peter, he goes on to Grantham and buys a return ticket to York. Then he catches the express; arrives in York, and goes out of his way to draw attention to himself with the ticket collector, whilst handing him the London ticket. Next day, having concluded his business, he catches the noon express and, utilising the return half of the ticket he bought at Grantham, he gets off there and picks up his car. Then he disappears into the blue until it is time for him to appear at Horsham Grange, having ostensibly motored up from London. That method was possible, but—and it was the hell of a but—could it be proved ?

"It was obvious he would have to drive his own car up; no one else must know anything about it. Equally it was obvious he must garage it somewhere in Grantham. Could I find the garage, and if I did would there be any record? For if I couldn't check in on that point we were no better off. My theory was purely academic, and would be torn to shreds by a clever lawyer.

"As luck would have it, Mr. George Denne had garaged at Jacobson's, near the station. And they keep counterfoil tallies of every car that comes in. There was the entry as large as life; my theory had ceased to be academic."

"For all that," said Sir Kenneth, rising, "it's fortunate for us he dropped that international driving pass. Otherwise identification after such a long gap of time would have been a ticklish affair. Admittedly, if it hadn't been Denne driving the coincidence would have been remarkable; but once again it would have been the old question of the difference between knowing and proving."

"Or confessing," remarked Ronald thoughtfully, after Sir Kenneth had gone and we were alone. "I must say Jacobson played up splendidly."

"What on earth do you mean?" I cried.

"Knowing and proving; Sir Kenneth was right. When I saw those entries in the book I knew. The coincidence of a joyrider taking Denne's car to Grantham on that particular night was simply too fantastic to contemplate. George Denne was the murderer."

"But what do you mean about Jacobson playing up?"

"How often do you look in the pockets of the doors of your car, Bob?" he asked.

"Very rarely. Why?"

"Nor does anyone, and that's why I chanced it. You see, that international driving licence never fell out in the garage at all. I stole it from Denne's car three days ago."

The Tenth Earl

Lady Ranelagh was an extremely lovely woman. Almost one might say girl, for she was only twenty-five. And as it so happened that I had seen a good deal of Kitty Barberton, as she then was, before her marriage to the earl, it was with real pleasure that I ran into her at the Savoy one morning just before lunch.

"How goes it?" I cried. "It must be a year at least since we last met. And now that I look at you, Kitty, you seem a bit fine drawn. Anything the matter?"

"Order a cocktail, Bob," she said. "My party won't be here for ten minutes yet."

We sat down and I beckoned to a waiter.

"I believe it's Providence that I butted into you," she went on. "Is that nice friend of yours, Ronald Standish, still in London?"

"He was last night," I said. "Why?"

She hesitated for a moment, and I noticed her hand was trembling a little.

"Does he still go in for detective work?"

"If a case interests him, and he's asked to take it up, he does," I told her.

She waited while the man put the drinks on the table: then she leant forward.

"Bob," she said in a low voice, "I'm terribly uneasy. Things are going on down at the Towers that I don't understand."

"What sort of things?" I asked.

"There's no time to tell you now," she answered. "I see that awful cow of a Melshot woman arriving already. Are you lunching here?"

"In the grill-room," I said.

"Do you think it would be possible for us to go round and see Mr. Standish this afternoon?"

"Perfectly. He's lunching at his club, I know. I'll get through to him on the telephone."

"Send a note in to me by a waiter to say if it's all right," she said. "Any time after three will do me. And it's rather urgent, Bob."

"I'm sure I can fix it, my dear," I told her. "I'll ring him up now."

I got on to Ronald at once and fixed three-thirty: then having sent her a message to that effect I ordered another cocktail and sat down to wait for the man I was lunching with. What, I wondered, could be the trouble at the Towers ?

Henry, tenth Earl of Ranelagh, had been married to Kitty Barberton for eighteen months. About twelve years older than her it had seemed and, so far as I know, had proved an ideal marriage in every way. He was a charming man, good looking, cultivated and a fine sportsman. In addition to all that, unlike many less fortunate members of the aristocracy, he had no worries over finance and was able to keep up the Towers in the semi-regal magnificence of his ancestors. It was a huge house, and only an extremely wealthy man could possibly have maintained it. The gardens were famed all over England: the avenue of copper beeches was historic. In fact the house was historic. Charles the First had made it his headquarters tor a considerable time during the Civil War: all down the centuries royalty had honoured it with periodical visits. In short it was one of England's show places, and the last spot where one would anticipate trouble of any sort.

The present earl had succeeded to the title three years before he married Kitty. He had two younger brothers one of whom was in the navy, the other out in Canada. His sister Muriel, who was older than him, was strangely enough unmarried. She had all the family good looks, and the reason, one gathered, of her still being single was a war-time tragedy. Before his marriage she had lived with the earl: now she occupied the dower house some two miles away.

Such, then, was the *ménage* into which Kitty Barberton had married, and all the way through lunch my mind kept reverting to what she had said. What could it be that was making her uneasy? What could be going on that she did not understand? But since every possibility that occurred to me was more absurd than the one before, I gave it up and possessed my soul in patience till we arrived at Ronald's rooms at half past three.

"Would you like me to leave you two alone?" I said when they had shaken hands.

"Not a bit, Bob," she cried. "I don't in the least mind you knowing all about it. Not that there's really very much to know, and I think that because of that, because it is so indeterminate that it's got on my nerves. You've met my husband, Mr. Standish, haven't you?"

"I have," said Ronald. "I can't say that I know him at all well: Bob knows him much better than I do. But we've shot together once or twice."

"It's about him that I'm worried," she began. "However, I'd better go right away back to when the thing first started. And it's only comparatively recently that little episodes which occurred at the beginning have fitted into their proper place: at the time I thought nothing of them.

"About a fortnight after we came back from our honeymoon I was in the library one morning looking for a book. And it so happened that I was standing in an alcove out of sight of the door, which suddenly opened and Henry came in with someone else.

"'Come in here, Doctor,' I heard him say, and then the door shut.

"'It's out of the question, Henry,' said the other man, and I recognised the voice of Doctor Frobisher. He is the local doctor, who has attended the family for years and who is regarded as an old friend rather than as a doctor.

"'But, my God! how much longer is it going on?' cried my husband, and then I stepped out into the room.

"They both swung round, and for a moment or two Henry looked annoyed.

"'Hallo! dear,' he said, ' where have you sprung from? '

"'I was looking for a book,' I answered, wondering whether I should say anything about the remark I had just heard.

"'I hope you had a pleasant time in France, Lady Ranelagh,' said Doctor Frobisher, at the same time opening the door for me.

"I made some perfunctory reply, and left them. And since it so happened that Henry had to go up to London that afternoon for a few days, I had no opportunity of asking him about it at once. Then when he came back I put it off, until finally it was too late, and the whole episode faded from my memory."

"That would be about fifteen months ago, Lady Ranelagh," said Ronald.

"That's right," she answered. "Well, as time passed by, it began to strike me that Doctor Frobisher came to the house rather more frequently than one would expect. He was continually coming either to dinner or lunch, and on two or three occasions I saw his car in the drive in the middle of the morning. So one day I mentioned it casually to Henry, who turned it off with a laugh.

"'My dear girl,' he said, 'the old chap loves my port. And seeing that he brought the whole lot of us into the world he can have as much of it as he wants, bless his heart.'

"But it seemed to me, Mr. Standish, that he looked at me a little queerly, and I wondered if his answer was quite the truth. Certainly there was no one ill in the house, and so there was no reason for a professional visit: at the same time I had an intuitive feeling that there was something that was being kept back from me. And though I can truthfully say that I'm not a particularly curious person, it piqued me a little. With the result that I kept my eyes open more than I should have done normally. But I found out nothing until one day about a fortnight ago.

"Happening to look through the window I saw the doctor's car outside. Now it was eleven o'clock in the morning, and the old man had dined with us the night before. And it struck me that, port or no port, this was a little excessive. So I went out into the hall just in time to see Henry and him disappearing into the library. And as they closed the door I heard my sister-in-law's voice.

"'Well, Doctor Frobisher, what do you think?'

"For a moment or two I hesitated: then I'm ashamed to say that I deliberately tiptoed across the hall and listened outside the door. But they were talking in low voices, and I could hear nothing until I suddenly caught one sentence of my husband's.

"'She must know nothing; under no circumstances must she ever find out.'

"And at that moment I looked round to find Weston, the butler, watching me from the door that leads to the servant's quarters. There was nothing to be done about it, and I don't think I've ever felt more embarrassed. To be caught red-handed eavesdropping by a servant is not funny, especially when that servant was Weston who has been with the family since the dawn of history. So I did the only possible thing: I opened the door and went in.

"The conversation ceased abruptly.

"'Hallo! Kitty dear,' said Muriel. 'I was just coming to see you. I'm stopping to lunch if I may.'

"'Delighted,' I replied. 'Am I interrupting a family powwow?'

"'Of course not, darling,' cried Henry. 'This old rascal has come for a hair of the dog that bit him last night.'

"'Playing the deuce with my gout, too,' laughed Doctor Frobisher. 'But if your husband insists on keeping such an infernally good cellar,

544

Lady Ranelagh, what on earth is a poor country practitioner to do? '

"I laughed too, and left them. But now, of course, all my suspicions were confirmed. Who could the 'she' be who must never find out except myself? Something *was* being kept back from me, and I determined to tackle Henry direct. The opportunity came that very night.

"'Just before I came into the library this morning, Henry,' I said, 'I overheard a remark you made. You said, "She must know nothing: under no circumstances must she ever find out." You were alluding to me?'

· "'My dear Kitty,' he answered, ' that shows how dangerous it is to listen to a conversation and only hear one remark.'

"'I wasn't listening,' I said, putting down the indignation pedal.

"'Weren't you?' he answered quietly, and in a flash I knew that Weston had told him. 'Anyway the "she" I referred to was not you. but somebody quite different. If you must know, Charles'—that's his youngest brother—'has been making a fool of himself over a woman, and we're trying to get him out of it.'"

She paused and lit a cigarette thoughtfully.

"Mr. Standish, that was a lie. I knew it, and Henry knew that I knew it. I didn't say anything, of course, but it hurt—hurt considerably. As his wife surely I had as much right to be taken into his confidence as Muriel or Doctor Frobisher. And Weston, too. How dared he go to Henry and tell him he'd seen me listening outside the door unless he was in it, too. It would be as much as any butler's place is worth to say such a thing under normal circumstances.

"As I said, that was about a fortnight ago, and since then Henry has been most odd. I can tell he's worried to death about something, and he seems to get worse and worse every day. And then two mornings ago it came to a head. I don't think you know the house, Mr. Standish, but Bob does. It is an enormous barrack of a place: there are old box-rooms and lumber-rooms that even I haven't been in to. And it so happened that on the day in question I was walking along a passage in the east wing which I'd never been along before. As a matter of fact parts of that wing are never used; they are supposed to be damp or something.

"Suddenly walking towards me I saw Henry, and as he came up I made some commonplace remark about the passage wanting dusting. Then I looked at his face and gasped. It was quite white, and his voice when he spoke was shaking—shaking with rage.

"'What are you doing here?' he said.

"'I really don't know,' I answered. 'Is there any reason why I shouldn't be here?'

"As you can imagine, I was a bit fed up: there didn't seem to me to be anything peculiar in the mistress of a house going round it. And I suppose the same idea occurred to Henry, for he pulled himself together and gave a sort of sickly smile.

"'Sorry, darling,' he said. 'No reason at all, of course. I'm a bit nervy today; didn't sleep very well last night.'

"'What is this mystery, Henry?' I burst out. 'There's no good pretending there isn't one, because it sticks out a yard. Muriel knows about it, and Doctor Frobisher and Weston. Why can't I be told?'

"He took me by the arm, and led me back to the main part of the house.

"'You're imagining things, my dear,' he said. ' There's no mystery at all. I was a little surprised at finding you in this unused part of the house—that's all.'

"'Then what were you doing there?' I demanded.

"'Just having a look round,' he answered. 'There's a bit of dry rot starting, and I don't want it to go too far.'

"'The dry rot is what you're talking,' I said angrily. 'Do you imagine I'm a fool, Henry, or a baby? Once and for all, will you tell me what this mystery is?'

"'Once and for all I tell you there is no mystery,' was his reply. 'You're imagining the whole thing.'

"And that's how it stands at the moment, Mr. Standish, and it is upsetting me terribly. I'm frightfully fond of him, but this beastly barrier between us is ruining everything. And I wondered if you could help me."

Ronald raised his eyebrows.

"It's rather a tough proposition, Lady Ranelagh," he said. "To help you I should have to come to the Towers, and if I did so it would be the most unwarrantable impertinence on my part if I started prying into your husband's private affairs. Besides, what possible excuse have I got for going there at all? To be quite frank I haven't the pleasure of knowing either of you at all well. . . ."

"I've thought of that, Mr. Standish," she interrupted. "And that's where Bob comes in, for he knows Henry very well and me too. This morning two guns failed us. What about you and Bob coming in their place?"

"I can assure you," said Ronald with a smile, "that an invitation to shoot your coverts would *not* be thrown in the paper basket. But what will your husband say? He's almost certain to have already invited two other guns to fill the vacancies."

"He hasn't. He asked me to get hold of Tony Ditchling at lunch today, but I didn't. Anyway he's a foul shot. I'm going to tell him that I asked Bob, and that he suggested you."

She rose.

"So that's settled. I'll write you a line confirming the invitation tonight. And it is sweet of you to have listened so patiently."

"A remarkable woman, Bob," said Ronald, as he came back from seeing her off, "and three days' shooting is not to be sneezed at. But if the dear thing expects me to go nosing round the house I fear she's going to be disappointed. It would be an unpardonable thing to do."

"I wonder what the deuce it can be," I remarked.

"He's always been a healthy bloke, hasn't he?" said Ronald.

"So far as I know, perfectly."

"Because it did occur to me to start with that he might have some illness which had to be kept from her. That would account for the doctor's consumption of port, and the old family butler being in it."

"But hardly for the agitation in the passage," I remarked.

"No; not for that. Well, let's hope at any rate that we hit 'em in the beak."

★★★★★★

I had not seen Henry Ranelagh since his marriage, and I confess that I was shocked at his appearance. He looked a sick man, so much so that I began to wonder whether Ronald's idea had not been right, and that he was suffering from some disease himself. At times he was his old self, but it always seemed to me that it was forced.

As usual the shooting was wonderful, but only on one day did our host come out with us, which was a most significant thing in itself for he was a magnificent shot. And somewhat naturally his mood communicated itself to the party, so that it was with a feeling of relief that one realised it was drawing to a close.

It was on the last night but one of our visit that Ronald came into my room for a final cigarette. There was thunder about; the atmosphere was sultry and oppressive. Heavy clouds drifted sluggishly across the sky, and through them the moon made a fitful appearance. He was in his dressing-gown, and drawing up two chairs we sat down by the open window.

"I had a long talk with Lady Ranelagh after dinner," he said. "She's worried to death, poor soul, and I'm only sorry I can't help her. I had to tell her that I was afraid I'd earned a shoot under false pretences."

"His nerves are certainly all to hell," I remarked. "I've been wondering if you weren't right and that he's ill."

He shook his head, and looked at me curiously.

"Did you hear anything last night, Bob? Round about three o'clock."

"No; I didn't. I was tired, and never batted an eyelid till I was called. What was it?"

"I can't say. But I had one of those nights when one can't get to sleep. The house was deathly still; nothing was stirring outside, when suddenly from a long way off there came a harsh call—rather like the call of a bittern. But there are no bitterns in this neighbourhood. It was not repeated, and I was just beginning to doze off when I heard a strange sort of slithering noise going past my door. It was so peculiar that I got up and looked out. And in the faint light—the moon was just setting—I saw what looked like a shadow move. It was there one moment and gone the next. And in the distance a board creaked. For a moment or two I hesitated: should I follow? And then I heard steps—ordinary human footsteps. So I closed my door, save for a tiny crack, and waited. Two men came past, walking along the passage, and going in the direction in which the shadow had vanished. One was Ranelagh; the other was the butler Weston."

"Good Lord!" I cried. "Did you say anything to Kitty about it?"

"No; I thought it better not. There's no good frightening her with vague stories."

"What do you make of it, Ronald?"

"Just this. That were it possible in my position as a guest to do such an outrageous thing, I would very much like to have an hour alone in the wing where Lady Ranelagh unexpectedly met her husband that day."

He pitched his cigarette out of the window and got up.

"But since it isn't possible . . . My God! Listen. The same noise."

From outside there came an eerie, wailing cry, harsh and discordant. It rose and fell, then ceased abruptly.

"Switch out your light, Bob," said Ronald quietly.

I did so, and side by side we stood at the window peering out into the darkness. And at that moment a vivid flash of lightning split the sky. It was like the instantaneous exposure of a camera. For in that fraction of a second the picture was printed on our brains. In the middle of the garden two men were bending over something dark that lay on the ground between them; one was Henry Ranelagh, the other was Weston the butler.

Came the crash of thunder, and we waited tensely for the next flash. At last we got it, more vivid even than the one before. The garden was empty; of Henry and his butler and the thing that had lain between them there was no sign.

"What was it?" I muttered.

"I don't know, Bob," said Ronald gravely. "But whatever it was it's none of our business. I'm going to bed."

And so did I—but not to sleep. Try as I would it eluded me. I could not keep my mind off what we had seen. Was it imagination? Had there been something out there, or was it a trick of the light? But if that was the case what had taken Henry and his butler to the garden at that time of night? And still puzzling, at last I dropped off.

It was broad daylight when I woke, to find Ronald fully dressed standing by my bed.

"I've been taking a spot of exercise, Bob," he said. "And where do you think my footsteps led me?"

To the garden?" I hazarded.

"You've said it. I wanted to see if the ground would tell us anything."

"Has it?"

"Yes. There were three distinct sets of footprints on one bed. One was the earl's; one was Weston's."

"And the third?"

"Were the footprints of a child," he answered.

"A child!" I echoed. "Is that then the mystery?"

"You know as much as I do, Bob. There is certainly no question of there being any child in the party."

"But that awful noise?" I said, staring at him.

"Just so. That noise." He shook his head gravely. "I'm afraid we're treading on rather dangerous ground, old boy."

"So you think that somewhere concealed in this house there is a child, and that that is the secret which is being kept from Kitty?"

"I can't see what else there is to make of it."

"But why on earth hasn't it been seen before? It is obviously free to walk about."

"Ask me another," he said.

"Can it have only just arrived?"

"Possibly. It may be that the conversation Lady Ranelagh interrupted a fortnight ago was when they were making the original plans to bring it here. Be that as it may, I can't help thinking that it is most unfair on her to keep her in ignorance. If she does run into it the shock will be infinitely greater."

"Where can they have hidden it, I wonder?"

"My dear Bob, in an old house of this vast size there is almost certain to be a secret room. That's why I said I'd like an hour in that wing alone."

"What are you going to do about it?" I said.

"Nothing," he answered promptly. "As I said to you last night, Bob, it is no business of ours. To interfere in such a matter would be unpardonable."

"I suppose it would. And yet I wish we could put Kitty wise. She's worried to death."

"If you get a chance find out from her if she heard that noise last night," said Ronald as he left the room.

As it happened I did get a chance, just before we were starting out.

"Of course I heard it, Bob," she said. "And I tell you I can't go on like this. Henry was out of his room practically the whole of last night. It's getting on my nerves. Doesn't Mr. Standish see that something is wrong?"

"Naturally he sees it," I said guardedly. "But he's in a very difficult position, Kitty."

"But has he said nothing to you?"

"He's a very uncommunicative bloke," I temporised, but she shook her head.

"I'm sure he knows something," she said. "Or at any rate suspects."

"Isn't Henry coming out today?" I asked.

"No; he isn't. And don't try and change the conversation, Bob. Listen to me. If Henry is out of his room again tonight I'm going to follow him. Will you and Mr. Standish come with me?"

"My dear," I said, "it's really devilish awkward, you know. Henry is our host, and to spy on him is a gross abuse of his hospitality."

"And I'm your hostess," she answered. "Bob, this can't go on. I must know the truth. If you won't come with me I shall go alone."

"I'll talk to Ronald about it, Kitty," I promised. "But you do see, don't you, what a very embarrassing position we are in?"

Strangely enough, when I mentioned it to him during the course of the morning he viewed it rather differently.

"I think that if we go with her, Bob—at her request, so to speak—it puts the matter on another footing. It's totally different to our prying round on our own."

"Then I'll tell her that we'll both be in my room," I said.

And so for the second time did we settle down to a vigil by the open window. We sat in the darkness, and gradually the house grew silent. And then just as my head was beginning to nod there came a gentle knock on the door. Kitty was standing outside.

"Henry's dressed," she whispered. "He's gone out into the park."

"Come along," said Ronald briefly. "Though we may have a job to follow him."

We crept down the stairs, and through a side-door.

"Have you the slightest idea where he's gone?" asked Ronald, and even as he spoke a light shone out suddenly through the trees. It was two or three hundred yards away, and Kitty gave a little gasp.

"It's the mausoleum," she said. "They're all buried there—the Ranelaghs."

"Is that so." Ronald's voice was grave. "Let's go there, but don't make a noise."

Our feet made no sound on the springy turf, but for the last thirty yards we had to cross a gravelled drive that led to the door. And it was when we were half-way across it that Kitty stumbled, and only just saved herself from falling. But the noise was plainly audible in the still night, and the light inside the mausoleum was instantly extinguished. A few seconds later the door opened and Henry Ranelagh's voice came out of the darkness.

"Who's there?" he said.

"It's me, Henry," answered his wife quietly.

"What are you doing here at this time of night?" he cried. "Go back to bed at once."

He flashed on his torch, and discovered the three of us.

"So, gentlemen," and his voice was icy, "this is the way you behave when you are guests in a house."

"They came with me at my express wish, Henry," said his wife. "They didn't want to—either of them."

"I don't think you quite realise, Lord Ranelagh," said Ronald gravely, "how worried your wife has been. And now that things have come to this pass, if you take my earnest advice you'll cease making a mystery of things and take her into your confidence. Neither Bob nor I wish to hear; at the same time . . ."

He stepped forward and whispered something to the earl, who gave a violent start.

"How do you know that?" he cried.

"Am I right?" said Ronald.

"Up to a point. But you don't know all."

"Wouldn't it be better if we did? Or at any rate tell Lady Ranelagh. There will be permanent mistrust between you till you do."

For a long minute he stood motionless; then abruptly he turned round and entered the mausoleum.

"Come inside," he said curtly. "Shut the door, please; I'll turn on the light."

He did so, and a strange sight met our eyes. On a raised dais in the centre of the room was a small coffin; beside it stood Doctor Frobisher and the butler Weston. And inside it lay the body of a boy.

"Perhaps it is better so, Henry," said the doctor gravely. "I am sure we can trust these two gentlemen not to speak."

"Most certainly," answered Ronald equally gravely. "At the same time it is obvious, I think, that some explanation is necessary. Who is this boy?"

"My brother," said the earl, and his wife gave a little gasp.

"But, Henry," she cried, holding out her hands to him, "why couldn't I have been told that? Poor little chap!"

"Listen, my dear, and you'll understand. John was one of the most lovely children it would be possible to imagine. He was the apple of my father's eye; my mother worshipped the ground he walked on. One day, when birds'-nesting in a tree, a branch broke, and he fell to the ground. As diabolical luck would have it, he fell in such a way that he became paralysed. Not only that, but he lost the power of speech.

"My parents were heartbroken. Specialist after specialist was brought in, but none of them could do any good. And at last it was left to my old friend here"—he laid his hand on the doctor's shoulder—"to break it to my father that the case was hopeless. There was nothing that could be done. He might partially recover the use of his limbs, but he would be a terrible cripple for life.

"And so my father took a decision, a decision only rendered possible by the help of this other old friend Weston. John died, and was buried in the tomb of his forefathers. That was what the world thought. That was what I thought till I came of age. In reality he was smuggled away into a secret suite of rooms in the wing where I met you that day, Kitty. There, tended by Weston, he has remained ever since, and only we three and my sister knew that the story told to the world was a lie. He has never grown since his fall; you see him now as he was then.

"And then, one day shortly after we came back from our honeymoon, Weston came to me with the most disquieting news. So long as he was completely paralysed it was easy to keep the secret. But Weston told me he had seen signs of returning animation. We watched and we waited; the weeks passed by, and the months. And at last we knew the worst: I use that word advisedly. The incredible was happening; John was partially recovering the use not only of his limbs, but also of his vocal cords. You must have heard that terrible noise two or three times lately. And from that moment our vigil has been ceaseless. But not always successful. The night before last he escaped; last night, too, in that thunderstorm he managed in some amazing way to get into the garden. And that, I suppose, proved too much for him, for this morning he died."

For a long space there was silence, and then Kitty went to him.

"But, Henry dear," she said, and there were tears in her voice, "I still can't see the reason for it all. Why couldn't the poor little chap have been put into a nursing home?"

His answer was a strange one: he flashed the torch on to the end of the coffin—

John, Viscount Laverton
1895—1905

"You see," he said quietly, "he was my father's eldest son."

The Footsteps on the Stairs

Ronald Standish glanced at the card which his man had just brought in, and raised his eyebrows slightly.

"M. Ivolsky. Agent," he read out. "What on earth can he want with me? However, show him in, Bates."

The newcomer proved to be a dapper little man of about five-and-forty. He was on the plump side, and as he entered he looked from one to the other of us with quick, bird-like glances.

"Sit down, Mr. Ivolsky," said Ronald. "What can I do for you?"

The little man seated himself, and carefully deposited his hat on an adjacent chair. Then, in a voice so curiously high that I smiled involuntarily, he began his story.

"I have come to you, Mr. Standish, on the advice of a friend of mine who I think you know—Mr. Laver, the stockbroker."

"Yes; I know Mr. Laver," said Ronald.

"I was having dinner with him last night," continued our visitor, "and when I told him of the curious—I may say very curious—incident, which occurred to me yesterday he suggested that I should consult you about it."

His English was perfect, though he spoke with a faint accent which proclaimed him a foreigner.

"I shall be pleased to hear about it, Mr. Ivolsky," said Ronald, pushing over a box of cigarettes.

"As you can see from my card," he went on as he helped himself, "I am an agent, though perhaps a more accurate description would be to say that I am the London representative of several large Hungarian firms. They work their commissions through me, and that constitutes the bulk of my work. But in addition to that I do a certain amount of buying and selling on my own account in the antique line. I have a small shop not far from Mr. Laver's office, and it was over one or two business dealings that I first made his acquaintance. The shop is run by a manager, and I only come in from my office in the event of some very important deal.

"Yesterday morning, at about eleven o'clock, I was engaged in decoding some cables from Budapest when I heard the sound of voices below in the shop. I thought nothing of it, when somewhat to my surprise, since he knew I did not want to be disturbed, Mr. Hudson, my manager, entered my office with a card in his hand, which he placed on my desk. The name on the card was Mr. Alfred Smithson.

"'He is downstairs, sir,' said Hudson, 'and he is very anxious to see you. In fact he refuses to leave the office until he has.'

"'What does he want?' I asked irritably.

"'He won't say anything,' answered Hudson, 'except that it is very important. But ...'

"He paused with a peculiar look on his face.

"'What is it?' I cried.

"'Just this,' said Hudson. 'I'll stake my bottom dollar that he was never christened Smithson. He speaks English perfectly, but he's not an Englishman.'

"'Tell him I'm engaged,' I said, 'and that I can't see him. He must tell you first what his business is.'

"And at that moment Mr. Smithson walked into the room.

"'Mr. Ivolsky,' he remarked, 'I am quite aware that this is an impertinence on my part. Nevertheless since it is essential that I should see you, my action is unavoidable.'

"I at once noticed what Hudson meant: the man was not English. But before I could speak he continued:

"'I shall not detain you for more than ten minutes, and I think I can promise you a fee so substantial that you will find that ten minutes well spent.'

"Well, Mr. Standish, there was nothing for it but to listen. Short of throwing him out— which incidentally would have been quite beyond Hudson's and my power, for he was a great big man—there was no way of getting rid of him. And a substantial fee is a substantial fee wherever it comes from. So I told him to sit down, and tell me what he had to say.

"'Alone, please,' he said, and I signed to Hudson to go back to the shop.

"'You are a Hungarian, Mr. Ivolsky, are you not?' he began.

"'I am,' I assured him.

"'It is a language of which I fear I only know a smattering,' he said. 'And that is the reason of my call here this morning.'

"'Good Heavens!' I cried, 'you aren't proposing that I should give you lessons in it, are you?'

"'Hardly that,' he said with a smile. 'Something very much simpler, and which will only take you this afternoon. I trust you are free?'

"'Before we discuss that,' I answered, 'it would be as well if you told me the object of your visit.'

"'That is only fair,' he agreed. 'And I will explain the situation in a few words. I am in the middle of a certain business deal with one of your fellow-countrymen. As I have told you, I only speak your language very indifferently, and the negotiations have been conducted up to date by a friend of mine who speaks it well. This has been essential since the Hungarian with whom we are dealing knows no language but his own. Now, at the eleventh hour, when the matter is almost settled, my friend gets involved in a motor accident and is lying in hospital dangerously ill. You see the situation, Mr. Ivolsky. Thus am I unable to continue owing to the fact that neither of us can talk to one another. Or, rather, shall I say that I am unable to talk to him: he, poor fellow, is dumb. Would you therefore be prepared to take my friend's place for this afternoon and act as interpreter? Naturally I would not dream of asking you to give up your valuable time without a substantial honorarium. And I suggest that a fee of fifty pounds might prove adequate.'

"Well, Mr. Standish," continued our visitor, "I stared at him. He had spoken plausibly enough, but the whole thing seemed a bit queer.

"'Why didn't you bring the Hungarian here to my office with you?' I asked.

"'He is not in the best of health,' he explained. 'At the moment he is recuperating at my house in the country.'

"'And where may that be?' said I.

"'In Hampshire, not far from Alton. And my idea was that we should motor down together after lunch. The actual business will only take a few minutes, and I can then send you back in the car.'

"'Why did you come to me particularly?' I asked.

"'I happened to see your name in the directory,' he said. ' Come, come, Mr. Ivolsky, it is surely a fairly simple matter to decide. I am offering you a fee of fifty pounds for a few minutes' work and a pleasant drive into the country. If you are unable to accept the commission I must find someone else who will.'

"And put that way it certainly sounded madness to refuse. I had nothing particular to do yesterday afternoon, and fifty pounds are not to be sneezed at these hard days. So I accepted, and agreed to meet him at Hyde Park Corner at two o'clock."

"Before you continue, Mr. Ivolsky," said Ronald, "had you formed any opinion as to what nationality this so-called Smithson was?"

"German, perhaps, or Dutch. Possibly Swedish."

"I see. Please go on."

"The drive down was quite uneventful. The car was a big limousine with a liveried chauffeur, and we made very good time. Smithson was not talkative, but once or twice I had the impression that he was watching me covertly out of the corner of his eye. He made no further allusion to the business in hand, and when I tentatively remarked about it he turned it aside with a smile.

"'All in good time, Mr. Ivolsky,' he said. ' I can assure you that you won't find it at all complicated.'

"At about half-past three we arrived. The house was a big one with lodge gates and a long drive, and the first thing that struck me was the shocking condition the whole place was in. The drive was overgrown with weeds; the bushes and trees on each side were nothing but a tangled mass of undergrowth. I suppose he saw me looking, because he made a remark about it.

"'Terrible thing these days having a place of this size to keep up,' he said. 'But gardeners' wages are quite prohibitive.'

"The house itself was in keeping with the approach. One could see at a glance that there had been no work done on it for years, and I confess, Mr. Standish, that I began to regret having come. But it was too late to draw back then, and so with considerable misgivings I followed my host into the hall.

"'You won't forget, will you, Mr. Ivolsky,' he said with his hand on a door, ' that the poor fellow is dumb. And he's very sensitive about it. He will just nod or shake his head, as the case may be, in answer to your questions.'

"On that we entered the room, and I took a quick look round. It was most inadequately furnished, with a round table and a few chairs. But there was one unusual feature. Stretched right across it from side to side, and cutting it in half, were heavy black curtains reaching to the ceiling.

"The occupant of the room rose as we came in. He was a middle-aged man with grey hair, and Smithson introduced me to him. His name was Pilaudi, and I greeted him in Hungarian.

"'Shall we begin?' said Smithson. 'Will you sit here, Mr. Ivolsky?'

"He indicated a chair at the table with its back to the curtains. I sat down and Pilaudi took one opposite me. Then Smithson came and stood beside me.

"'I think the simplest way,' he said, 'is for me to give you the questions written in English, and for you to translate them. Here is the first.'

"He laid a piece of paper on the table in front of me; on it was the following sentence:

"'Do you realise that what I have is useless without the other?'

"I translated it into Hungarian and watched Pilaudi. For a while he appeared to take no notice, and merely stared vacantly over my head. Then suddenly he nodded, and Smithson put down a second slip :

"'Will you produce the other?'

"Once again I watched Pilaudi; once again for an appreciable time he seemed not to have heard what I said. Then he shook his head.

"Came the third slip, this one not a question!

"'I will pay you the same amount that you can get elsewhere.'

"There was no delay this time; Pilaudi at once shrugged his shoulders, and I looked at the fourth sentence:

"'I will give you twenty-four hours to think things over. If at the end of that time the other is not forthcoming the result will be fatal.'

"'I glanced at Smithson.

"'Fatal,' I said.

"'Only to our negotiations,' he remarked.

"So I translated the last sentence, and Pilaudi again shrugged his shoulders immediately.

"'That is all. thank you, Mr. Ivolsky,' said Smithson. 'And I'm very much obliged to you for your assistance. Here is an envelope containing the sum we agreed on, and the car can take you back to London at once.'

"I rose, and so did Pilaudi. Smithson was already at the door, and since there seemed nothing more for me to do, I shook hands with both of them and got into the waiting car. The whole affair had barely taken five minutes, and it all seemed so bizarre and fanciful that I felt I had been dreaming. I had expected a long and possibly complicated business interview; instead of that, four simple remarks of a most general nature. But the envelope contained ten five-pound notes, and I can safely say I have never earned money more easily."

The little man paused and looked at Ronald and me almost apologetically.

"I really feel quite ashamed to have taken up your time," he said. "All the same, the whole thing was so strange that I couldn't help telling Mr. Laver about it. And when he suggested my coming to you I felt I'd risk it. What do you think, Mr. Standish?"

"In the first place," said Ronald, "I think that a man who can afford to pay fifty pounds for such a trifling service, and cannot afford to keep a gardener, is a peculiar customer. Tell me, Mr. Ivolsky, about this man Pilaudi. Did he strike you as being a Hungarian?"

"I really didn't think much about it at the time. I assumed he was, and there was nothing in his appearance to make one think he wasn't. But what do you mean, Mr. Standish? If he wasn't what was the object of my going down there at all?"

Ronald lit a cigarette thoughtfully and answered the question with another.

"Did you see anybody else except Smithson and the dumb man?"

"Nobody. Except of course the chauffeur."

"And what impression did the interior of the house give you?"

"Well, I only saw the hall and that one room. But they gave me the impression of extreme discomfort."

"You did not, of course, see what was behind the curtain?"

"No. I did not."

"You realise the significance, Bob, don't you?" he said, turning to me, "of the delay in answering after the two questions, and the prompt reply after the two statements?"

"I can't say that I do," I answered. "He had to think over the questions, whereas the other two remarks were, as you say, statements."

"Possibly. I wonder. You said he was staring over your head, Mr. Ivolsky, when you spoke to him."

"That is so. But what has that to do with it?"

Ronald got up and began to pace up and down the room.

"Let us briefly recapitulate the whole thing at its face value," he said. "A man, posing as an Englishman, comes to Mr. Ivolsky and offers him a big fee to go down to his house in the country. He has a large limousine; a liveried chauffeur, and yet the condition of the house and grounds is one that indicates great poverty. Arrived at the house Mr. Ivolsky meets a dumb Hungarian, who is in the throes of an important business deal with the owner of the house. He makes four remarks to him: he sees no servant: he is offered no refreshment. He then returns to London the richer by fifty pounds."

He paused and stared at us.

"It doesn't sound sense to me, you know. Dumb men who are in a position to make big business deals don't travel in foreign countries unattended."

"Well, he was certainly dumb," cried Ivolsky.

"Was he?" said Ronald calmly.

"But if he wasn't, why didn't he answer when I spoke to him?"

"Were you speaking to *him?* That's the point."

He resumed his restless pacing. "Yes: that's the point. You thought you were: in reality I believe you were speaking to someone you couldn't see, and who was a genuine Hungarian. And I'd lay a small wager that Pilaudi was neither a Hungarian nor dumb. The delay in answering your two questions, of which he, of course, knew the English equivalent, was due to waiting for the reply from the other side of the curtain. And that reply he had to pass on to Smithson."

"But why the mystery?" expostulated our visitor. "Why not take me behind the curtain and let me speak direct?"

"It's when we try to answer that 'why,' Mr. Ivolsky, that the matter becomes more sinister. If I am right: if this so-called Pilaudi was merely pretending to be dumb because he realised he'd immediately give himself away if he spoke, then the whole affair assumes a very different complexion."

"I am completely bewildered," said the little man. "Even now I do not quite see what you are driving at, Mr. Standish."

"There are too many glaring inconsistencies in the story you have told us, my dear sir, for it to be the truth. Please don't misunderstand me: I am not suggesting that you have said anything but what actually happened. Why should you? You have no object in wasting my time as well as your own. What I am suggesting is that the whole story of this business deal was a lie from start to finish. That the four remarks you made consisted of two questions, an offer, and a threat. That they were addressed to someone who was behind the curtain out of your sight. And if that is so there arises at once a very unpleasant question. Why did this someone make no sound, and say no word? Why, indeed, was it necessary for him to be hidden at all? And there can be only one answer. He is being held as a prisoner. There may have been half a dozen men behind the curtain with him. Somebody certainly was—the man who passed the answer to the so-called Pilaudi. Yes, Mr. Ivolsky, I'm inclined to think that you have been moving in far deeper waters than you imagined. Could you find this house again?"

"I think I could. In fact, given time, I'm sure I could."

"That's one up to us anyway. But the point is what we are going to do."

"Would it not be as well to go to Scotland Yard?" said the Hungarian.

"What are we going to say to them? I've told you what I *think*, but I haven't a vestige of proof. Supposing I'm all wrong: supposing Pilaudi really is a dumb Hungarian, and that, incredible though it sounds, the whole story is correct, we should look pretty average fools. We haven't got a single peg to hang our hat on, except that this man Smithson is not an Englishman though he pretends to be one. But having a bogus visiting card printed is not illegal, unless it is used for perpetrating a swindle or obtaining money. And all he has done is to present you with fifty of the best. No one would grant a search warrant on the story we've got to tell. And so if we're going to do anything in the matter we've got to do it ourselves. In other words take the law into our own hands."

Our visitor paled visibly. "Will not that be very dangerous?" he muttered uneasily.

"Cheer up, Mr. Ivolsky," laughed Ronald. "Your share of the performance will end when you've shown us the house. But twenty-four hours was the time mentioned, and that expires at four o'clock this afternoon. So we haven't got long."

He glanced at his watch.

"'Phone round for the car, Bob, will you? And I expect after all that talking, Mr. Ivolsky, you'd like a drink. There's whisky or beer."

"Thank you, I think a small whisky and soda. Tell me, Mr. Standish, what do you propose to do?"

"Have a closer look at the house," said Ronald. "From what you tell me of the condition of the grounds it shouldn't be difficult. And when we have reconnoitred we'll see what we can do next."

"There's going to be an outsize in blots on the copy book," I remarked, "if by any chance the whole thing is genuine."

"Sufficient unto the hour, old boy," said Ronald cheerfully. "You didn't by any chance notice if the house had a name on the gate, Mr. Ivolsky?"

"I specially noticed that it had not," answered the Hungarian. "I looked as we went in, and again when I left."

"A pity. We might have made inquiries locally."

561

"Here is Seymour with the car," I said. "Are you going to take him?"

Ronald nodded.

"He's quite a good man in a scrap if by chance it comes to it. Take this, Bob: it's better than a gun."

He handed me a loaded stick, and took another himself, whilst our visitor watched the proceedings apprehensively.

"I am beginning to wish, gentlemen," he remarked, "that I had not followed the advice of the excellent Mr. Laver. I trust you will not expect me to become involved in—what do you call it—a scrap?"

"You'll probably lead the vanguard," said Ronald, smacking him on the back. "Come along, *mes enfants: en voiture.* You come in front with me, Mr. Ivolsky, and tell me the way."

Which unfortunately was what the little man proved unable to do. Arrived at Alton the direction had to be left to him, and it soon became obvious that he was completely at fault.

"And I could have sworn," he cried almost tearfully, "that I could have led you straight to the house. But your roads to me they all look the same."

"Take it easy, Mr. Ivolsky," said Ronald soothingly. "You're sure at any rate that you came through Alton? Good. And that the house was two or three miles beyond? Right. Then all we can do is to try them one by one."

He spoke quite quietly but I could tell he was seething with impatience. Time was valuable, and to waste it motoring up and down country lanes was infuriating. For it was not till the third attempt that the Hungarian gave a sudden shout of triumph.

"That cottage! I recognise it. We are right this time, Mr. Standish. The house is about a mile farther on."

And the time was a quarter to four. "What are you going to do with the car, Ronald?" I asked.

"Drive past the gates, and leave it in the road. Then you and I, Bob, will walk in. The lodge is still presumably empty, but we can see that as we go past."

"There it is," cried Ivolsky, pointing ahead, and Ronald slowed down.

"Shutters up," he remarked as we drove by. "No danger to be anticipated there. Now, Mr. Ivolsky, I want you to stay here with my chauffeur. You can do no good with us, and if we want you we'll know where to find you. Come along, Bob: there's no time to lose."

The drive had a bend in it, so that for the first two hundred yards the house could not be seen, and we were able to get along without taking to the undergrowth. And assuredly the little Hungarian had not exaggerated in his description of the condition of the place. It did not look as if a hand's turn of work had been done on it for years, and when, before reaching the bend, we had to take cover it was almost a question of hacking one's way through.

"Let's hope they're occupied indoors," said Ronald. "We're making enough noise to waken the dead."

And then suddenly he stopped abruptly, his hand raised in warning. We had arrived at the edge: in front of us stood the house. I wormed my way cautiously forward: then side by side we crouched down staring at it. To all appearances the place was deserted. The windows were shut, and so was the front door. Dusty ivy trailed drunkenly down the walls: the whole place was dilapidated to a degree.

"That settles it, Bob," said Ronald. "Smithson was certainly lying when he said this was his country house, and so the whole story he told Ivolsky was a plant. But it looks remarkably as if the birds had flown, and that we're too late."

"Shall we have a closer look now that we are here?" I remarked.

"I was just going to suggest it," he said. "And if by chance there is anybody at home we've come to look over the property."

He stepped out on to the grass verge bordering the drive, and walked boldly up to the front door. The question of concealment no longer came into it: we were two *bona fide* prospective tenants. The iron bell pull was old and rusty, and stuck when he tried to use it. Then it went with a jerk, and the reverberation of the bell could have been heard in Alton.

Gradually it died away, and we listened intently. No sound came from the house: the place might have been a tomb.

"They've gone, Bob," said Ronald. "We're wasting our time. Hallo! the door is not locked. That's strange."

He pushed it open, and we stepped into the hall. The unpleasant musty odour of a long disused house at once assailed our nostrils: dust lay thick everywhere and Ronald's keen eye searched it for footprints.

"Five people at least," he remarked, "have been here recently. And that room on our right is obviously where our little friend did his interpreter stuff. There are the curtains now pulled back: there's the table. Let's see if we can find anything in the part of the room that was shut off."

We walked through and suddenly Ronald halted staring at the floor.

"Bad, Bob: very bad," he muttered. "Blood, and recent blood. It's not even dry. And look at that coil of rope in the corner. There's been devilry here. Good God! What's this?"

He bent down and picked up a strange looking metal implement, which was stained a bright crimson.

"I am beginning to feel a strong desire to meet Mr. Alfred Smithson," he said quietly. "This, unless I am much mistaken, is a form of thumb screw. They've been torturing the wretched fellow. Come on, Bob: this is very definitely a police job."

He was standing by the door taking a final look round the hall. And suddenly he gripped my arm.

"Look at the stairs, Bob: look at the stairs," he muttered. "One set of footprints, only."

"What of it?" I said.

"They go up, man: and they don't come down. Get hold of that coil of rope: the police will have to wait. There is someone upstairs."

On tiptoe we crept up, and as we reached the top we heard it. Rising and falling there came from a room in front of us an ever swelling cadence of snores. The door was open, and we peered in. And a strange sight met our eyes. In one corner lay the motionless body of a man: in another, sprawling on a pile of old sacks was one of the drunkest individuals I have ever seen in my life. The room reeked of whisky, and an empty bottle was on the floor beside him. So drunk was he that he never stirred when we lashed his arms and legs: then we turned our attention to his companion.

"The swine," muttered Ronald savagely. "Look at his thumb. However, he's alive, though they've doped him. See if you can find a bucket of water, Bob, and we'll see what we can get out of this drunken sot."

I found one in the back premises, but it was not until the third application that his eyes opened and he stared at us.

"Wot the 'ell," he began thickly; then he realised he was bound. And with the realisation the drink died out of him and fear came.

"Strike me pink, guv'nor," he quavered, "'oo are yer? Wot 'ave yer got me trussed up like this for? I ain't done no 'arm."

"That's what we want to find out," snapped Ronald. "Where are the other men who have been in this house?"

"Gone aht, guv'nor: gone aht two hours ago."

"Where have they gone to?"

"I dunno, guv'nor: strife I don't. But they're coming back."

"They are, are they? You're sure of that?"

"Sure as I'm a'lying 'ere."

"Who are these men?"

"I dunno, guv'nor. They're furriners though they speaks English: that's all I can tell yer abaht them."

"Is one of them dumb?"

"Dumb. Gaw lumme—no."

"What about this poor devil here? How did that happen to his thumb?"

"It wasn't me, guv'nor: I swears it. It was them other two wot did it."

"While you looked on and cheered. Why did they do it?"

"They was trying to make 'im give them something. You see, guv'nor, they couldn't speak 'is langwidge. That's why a bloke came dahn from London yesterday."

"I know all about that. So having tortured him, they then doped him, and you carried him upstairs."

The man's odious little eyes shifted uneasily. "That's right, guv'nor, though I dunno 'ow you knows."

"What orders did they *give* you when they left?"

"To wait 'ere with 'im, guv'nor, till they comes back."

"Did they say what time they'd be back?"

"Didn't give no time, guv'nor. Just said wait 'ere. Can't yer let me aht now?" he whined. "I've got the cramp, I 'ave."

"Delighted to hear it," said Ronald. "Long may it continue. So we were right, Bob," he continued. "I'm inclined to think that this beauty is speaking the truth, and that he is merely in on this as a guard. The people we want are the other two. Is there a cellar or some place downstairs where we can put him?"

"There are some outhouses," I answered.

"That'll do."

He unlashed the man's legs.

"Get up, you swine. And don't try any funny stuff, or you'll have a taste of that thumb screw yourself. Bob, you lead the way."

It was beginning to get dark as we took him across to the stables. And there having re-lashed his legs, and dumped him in a loose box we locked him in.

"Now for that other poor bloke," said Ronald, and even as he spoke there came the sound of wheels on the drive.

"By jove! Bob," he muttered, "they're back already. Keep out of sight while I reconnoitre."

He faded into the gathering dusk, and I crept after him keeping in the shadow of the house. By the front door an empty car was standing, and suddenly I saw Ronald approaching it on hands and knees. Came the hiss of escaping air repeated twice, and then after an interval twice again.

"I've punctured all four of their tyres," he chuckled as he rejoined me. "Which will make 'em cough a bit. I wonder how many there are of them."

From inside the house a man's voice could be heard shouting "Carter" furiously: evidently our drunken acquaintance was wanted. And then a lamp was lit in the room with the curtains.

"By God! Bob," muttered Ronald as a man came to the window and looked out, "this is big stuff. That's Baron von Huyter—the most unscrupulous of all the European agents. And he's a gentleman who doesn't hesitate to shoot."

Another man joined him, elderly and grey-haired—obviously the dumb Pilaudi. And a moment later two men, one of whom was the chauffeur, appeared carrying the unconscious Hungarian.

"Dump him there," snarled von Huyter. "Now then, you." He turned on Pilaudi. "How long will it take to bring him round?"

"Five minutes," answered the other, and Ronald gripped my arm.

"Sprint like hell, Bob, and tell Seymour to go for the police. Then come back here."

When I returned Pilaudi was bending over the Hungarian doing something with a hypodermic syringe.

"He's not recovered yet," whispered Ronald, "but they'll torture him again when he does. We've got to stop 'em somehow, Bob. And quickly," he added, "he's conscious."

The wretched man was sitting up staring round the room dazedly. And then he saw von Huyter and shrank back in terror.

"Don't you want the interpreter again, Mr. Smithson?" sang out Ronald, and the German swung round as if he had been shot. "He'll be here soon with the police."

Like a flash von Huyter blew out the lamp, and we heard his muttered orders.

"Into the car—all of you. Lift him in."

And Ronald laughed softly. Came the whirr of the self-starter as the chauffeur leapt into the driving seat. And then came the other three half carrying, half pushing their prisoner.

"Police," roared Ronald.

"Here we are," I shouted back.

Bump—bump—bump: the car had started. Often has one heard it with one punctured tyre: rarely, I imagine, with four. And to the accompaniment of hideous blasphemy from von Huyter the car stopped.

"Police," yelled Ronald again, and this time it worked the oracle. Doors were flung open: the occupants of the car dashed out and bolted, leaving their prisoner behind. And when the last footsteps had died away down the drive Ronald laughed again.

"Which settles Baron von Huyter's hash," he remarked. "A word to Scotland Yard will not be wasted. Let's go and see if we can do anything for that poor devil."

★★★★★★

But it was not to be, and the true story will never be known. For the Hungarian relapsed into unconsciousness again, and remained in that condition till he died two days later. They had overdosed him, and his secret died with him. Months after it transpired that he was an inventor who had specialised in aeronautics, and that he claimed to have discovered something which would revolutionise flying and which he wished to sell to the British Government.

But how von Huyter got him in his clutches: how, unknown to the agents, he had obtained possession of an empty house will for ever be a mystery. Only von Huyter could have explained it, and his body was washed up on the Belgian coast a week later with fragments of wreckage of an aeroplane. Or the "dumb" Pilaudi. But his body was never found, though a grey-haired elderly man left Weston aerodrome with the baron.

Mr. Marbury's Hands

"Good afternoon, Colonel. Been shooting anybody lately?"

A choleric-looking little red-faced man swung round and grinned cheerfully when he saw Ronald Standish.

"Hallo! my boy," he said. "Glad to see you again. How's the golf?"

"Not too bad," answered Ronald, which in view of the fact that he had just been round in seventy-one hardly seemed an overstatement. "The course is in grand condition. By the way, you don't know Bob Leyton, do you? Colonel Fortescue."

We shook hands, and having had one for the road, we all left the club house together.

"Are you staying at the dormy house?" inquired the colonel. "If so, there's no good my offering you a lift."

"None, thanks," said Ronald. "We must have a game some day soon."

"Not on your life, my dear boy," chuckled the old man. "I've got to the age now when I like my opponents to have double-figure handicaps. But I insist on your both coming to have a bit of dinner with me. I've still got a few bottles of the old Cockburn left."

He paused suddenly, one foot on the running-board.

"Good Lord! I hadn't thought of that." He was frowning to himself. "I don't think he would object to your knowing. Look here, Standish, there's something which might be in your line going on down here. It concerns a neighbour of mine, and naturally, I can't tell you about it without his consent."

"Sounds mysterious," said Ronald lightly.

"It is. Deuced mysterious. It's the sort of thing one reads about in books. Now can you both dine tomorrow night? If so, I'll get hold of Marbury—he's the man concerned— and I'll persuade him to tell you."

"Seems good to me, Colonel. And I'm sure Bob is on."

"Excellent. Eight o'clock. Short coat, of course. Just the four of us."

"One of the characters of Slindon-on-Sea, Bob," said Ronald, as the little man drove off. "But I've never heard of Marbury. He must be a newcomer."

"What lay behind your remark to the old boy about shooting people?" I asked.

"It's a fact," said Ronald, lighting a cigarette. "And since we're dining there I'll tell you about it. As you see, he's a man of about seventy, and he's lived here ever since he retired from the army. He's unmarried, and provided you can keep him off the Swetty-pore in 'ninety-four tack, he's extremely good company. He's got a lot of money, and a charming house about half a mile from the links.

"To come, however, to the gun-work. The family have always been soldiers, and old Fortescue's grandfather held some high command in India, in the year dot. And though it is advisable not to go too closely into the matter, the bald fact remains that when he returned to England he brought with him a collection of precious stones of immense value. That collection was passed on intact, and is now in this old chap's possession."

"Have you seen it?" I asked.

"I have. He showed it to me the last time I was down here."

"Does he keep it in his house?"

"You're getting warm, Bob. He does. He's been told a score of times that he's a damned fool for doing so, but he's as pig-headed as a mule on that one point. He keeps it in his smoking-room, but no one knows where. He's got some secret hiding-place installed in that room, which nobody has ever been allowed to find. If he wants to get his collection he'll go and shut himself in there, and then bring it to another room. Even his confidential servant, who has been with him since his service days, has no idea where it is. But you could hardly expect a trifle of that sort to put off a burglar. And it was over that that the shooting took place.

"A man broke in, and the colonel heard him. He came rushing down the stairs with a twelve-bore, and he peppered this fellow in the seat of his pants so badly that the man was in hospital for weeks. In fact, it was touch and go whether he would pull through or not. And burglar or no burglar, it would have been awkward for Fortescue if he'd killed him. The general feeling at the time was that it's not fair to have things of such value in an ordinary house which a child could break into. Like leaving your money about; it's just putting temptation in people's way. However, even that didn't budge him; the stones are still there, and if you want to see 'em, he'll be only too delighted to show them to you tomorrow night."

"Presumably we shall be occupied in listening to Mr. Marbury's troubles."

"I'd forgotten about him. John."

He beckoned to the dormy-house steward.

"Do you know anything of a Mr. Marbury who has come here to live?"

"Very little, sir. He plays a good deal of golf with Colonel Fortescue, and he came to Slindon about six months ago. Their houses are next to one another. A pleasant spoken gentleman, sir, of fifty or so."

Which proved to be a very just description of the man. He was there when we arrived, genial, stoutish, grey-haired, and while we sipped our sherry I found myself wondering what mystery it could be that had come within his orbit. But no allusion was made to it until Dyer, the taciturn manservant, had placed the port before the colonel and withdrawn. Then our host brought the subject up.

"I've been telling Marbury about you, Standish," he said, "and I've persuaded him to put the whole story in front of you. My own candid opinion is that he's a fool not to go to the police about it, but that's his affair."

"Told in cold blood, Mr. Standish," began Marbury, "the thing seems so fantastic as to be ludicrous, I'm afraid. But I can assure you it's beginning to get on my nerves. To begin at the beginning, then, I came to live here just five months ago. I'm a retired business man, and my idea was to enjoy what years are left to me pottering in my garden and playing a little mild golf. Most fortunately, the house next door here was vacant, and when I found that my neighbour the colonel was also keen on those pursuits I considered myself very lucky. I like the locality, and when I managed to get hold of a very respectable man and his wife to look after me I felt that Fate had treated me kindly. And then out of the blue, about a month ago, there fell the thunderbolt.

"Glancing through my letters on the breakfast table I saw one with a typewritten envelope. It was addressed to Henry Marbury, without the customary Esquire, and assuming it was a bill I left it till last to open. A bill!" He gave a short laugh. "Would to heaven it had been. A

570

demand for ten thousand pounds would have been preferable."

He leaned forward in his chair, and I noticed his hand was shaking.

"Inside that envelope, Mr. Standish," he continued, "was a sheet of single paper. On that paper was written a single sentence. And that sentence was as follows: 'You have thirty days to live.'"

Ronald sat up with a jerk.

"Good God!" he said. "What an amazing thing. Have you the letter on you?"

Marbury laughed mirthlessly.

"I have twenty-seven letters on me. The following morning, Mr. Standish, an identical envelope arrived. This time the message inside was more laconic. Just one number—'29.' The next day it was '28.' This morning it was '4'."

Ronald, his cigar still unlighted, stared at him.

"You have had a letter every day?" he asked.

"Except Sundays, when there is no delivery. Two have arrived together on the Monday."

"And the postmarks on the envelope?"

"Always London."

"Have you these letters with you?"

Henry Marbury extracted a bundle from his pocket and handed it over the table. Then we waited in silence while Ronald examined the contents.

"This is the most extraordinary affair, Mr. Marbury," he said at length. "May I ask if you have the faintest idea as to who could be the sender? Have you any enemy who would be likely to do such a thing?"

"Few men who have reached my time of life, and been, if I may say so, successful financially, can say they have no enemies. But there is no man living, to my knowledge, who dislikes me enough to murder me."

"That's the whole point," cut in our host. "Is this a serious threat, Standish, or is it a damned silly hoax?"

"Precisely," said Ronald. "As you say, that is the whole point. And if it is a hoax the perpetrator of it should be flogged, for a more wicked one could scarcely be conceived. I understand, Mr. Marbury, that you have said nothing to the police about it?"

"I have not. The only man that I've mentioned it to until this moment is the colonel. The way I look at it, Mr. Standish, is this. What good can the police do? To trace the sender of a typewritten letter posted somewhere in London is beyond anyone's power. The paper is quite ordinary, and I can give them no hint or assistance of any kind as to a possible writer. Whichever it is, a serious threat or a hoax, the police are equally powerless, and in the event of it being the latter I shall be made to look a perfect laughing stock."

"There is a lot in what you say," agreed Ronald. "What are you proposing to do?"

"Today, Mr. Standish, is Friday. So next Tuesday is the fatal day. Once that is over the question as to whether it is a hoax or not will have been answered. And on Tuesday the colonel has promised to stand by me the whole day."

"Trust me, Marbury," barked our host. "We'll play golf morning and afternoon. Damn, I'll break my invariable rule and lunch at the club. And if the port kills you, my boy, I'll die by your side. Probably that's at the bottom of it all. Have you ever drunk the club port, Standish?"

Ronald smiled politely, but I could see he hardly had heard the old man's well-meant badinage.

"I think that's a very good idea, Mr. Marbury," he said. "And with your permission we'll make it a foursome. And then we'll come back here, or else to your house and see midnight over together."

"Have to be yours, Marbury," said the colonel. "Tuesday is Dyer's annual bean-feast. It was fixed six weeks ago. He says it is a reunion dinner in London: my own belief is that the dirty dog is lying through his back teeth."

"I cannot say how grateful I am to you, Mr. Standish," said Marbury quietly. "I try to persuade myself that it is some stupid hoax, but those inexorable letters turning up every day tend to shake one's nerve."

"I can well believe it," answered Ronald "They would shake anybody's. By the way, Mr. Marbury, might I ask what your business was before you retired?"

The other raised his eyebrows as if a little surprised at the question.

"I was in the hardware line up in the North country," he answered. "But I can assure you," he added with a smile, "that my goods were not sufficiently bad to account for this business."

We all laughed, and the colonel pushed back his chair.

"Let's forget it," he said. "How about a rubber of bridge?"

It was after midnight when we left and we dropped Marbury at his front gate.

"It's only three now," he said. "Tell me the truth, Mr. Standish," he went on, with a note of desperation in his voice, "I'd sooner know it. What *do* you think? Is this a hoax or is it not?"

"Whichever it is," answered Ronald reassuringly, "I'm sure of one thing. You need not worry about it until Tuesday. And then you'll have three vigilant guards with you. Goodnight, Mr. Marbury. I advise you to do what the colonel said. Try and forget it till then."

"Easier said than done," I remarked, as we drove away. "It really is the most extraordinary thing I've ever heard of."

"Most," agreed Ronald absently. "You'll have to get someone to take my place in that four-ball tomorrow, Bob. I'm going up to London."

"To London," I cried. "On a Saturday! What on earth for?"

"To see if I can find the sender of those letters," he answered.

"A pretty tall job," I remarked. "Are you serious?"

"Perfectly," he said. "Did anything strike you particularly about Marbury?"

He ran the car into the garage and switched off the lights.

"I can't say that it did," I answered, as we strolled back to the dormy house. "I was so interested in his story that I didn't pay much attention to the man himself. What are you alluding to?"

"His hands," said Ronald. "Always look at a man's hands, Bob: they're a much more reliable guide than his face."

"What did you learn from them?" I asked curiously.

"That he hasn't spent the whole of his life sitting at a desk in a hardware store. Mr. Marbury has done more than his fair share of manual labour during his time."

"What of it?" I said.

"Perhaps nothing; perhaps a lot." I had followed him into his room. "I have a notion, Bob, that Tuesday is going to be an entertaining day."

"You are an irritating devil," I cried. "Why can't you be more explicit?"

"Because I don't know myself," he answered gravely, as he emptied his pockets and took off his coat. "But if my vague guess is correct I think our friend may require all the assistance he can get."

"You definitely think it is not a hoax?"

"Definitely. Further, I think that in spite of what he said, Marbury knows it isn't, too."

"Then why hasn't he gone to the police?"

"Precisely. Why? You puzzle it out for yourself. Don't touch that card, I beg of you."

I was staring in amazement at one of the playing cards we had used that night, which was lying on his dressing-table.

"What on earth have you pinched that for?" I cried.

"Bob, old boy," he said kindly, "the hour grows late. That keen and scintillating brain of yours is not at its best. Goodnight; and may angels watch round your little bed."

Ronald caught an early train and I had lunch at the club-house. Try as I would I could not get the strange story we had heard overnight out of my head. Neither the colonel or Marbury was there, and I sat with the secretary, a retired naval officer called Gamage. It was impossible, of course, to mention the story—to do so would have been a breach of confidence—but I brought the conversation round to the teller.

"Dined with old Fortescue last night," I said. "A man named Marbury was there. Newcomer, isn't he?"

"Yes," answered Gamage. "Only been here a few months. Quite a nice fellow: he and the colonel have become great friends."

"Standish was telling me some yarn about the old man nearly killing a burglar," I said.

Gamage laughed and lit a cigarette.

"It's a fact. He did. And though I laughed when you mentioned it, it was no laughing matter at the time. He's a very rum-tempered old blighter, you know; he's apt to go off at half-cock at any moment. And it's mighty lucky for him that that man of his, Dyer, puts up with him. He's never been able to keep another servant for more than a few weeks."

"Does Dyer do the whole work of the house, then?"

"Practically. A woman comes in in the morning, I believe. The old colonel hates the sight of the whole sex. At least, he always swears he does. He was badly let down in his young days, I gather."

"I shouldn't think he's everybody's cup of tea," I said idly.

"My dear fellow," chuckled Gamage, "at one time or another he has insulted every member of this club either singly, in pairs, or in droves. And if there's no one else I am the invariable standby. He resigns regularly once a month, and one of these days he'll get the shock of his life. The committee will take him at his word. Did you think that was a bad lunch ?"

"Very good. Why?"

"If old Fortescue had eaten it he'd have described the mutton as shoe leather, the vegetables as garbage, the beer as undrinkable, and the port as poison. But everyone likes the old boy really, though he swindles in the most barefaced manner at golf. It's a standing jest. He'll tee up his ball in a bunker without a blush. And he becomes apoplectic if anyone says anything about it. In fact, it really was getting beyond a joke. Everybody was refusing to play with him, and if he got hold of an unwary stranger it gave the club such a damned bad name. So it was very fortunate when Marbury came along, for he doesn't seem to mind. Incidentally, here they both are. Afternoon, Colonel. Afternoon, Mr. Marbury."

"You've got to sack the caddie master, Gamage," cried the colonel. "Will you believe it, I've just been round to get two. The place is crawling with the little brutes, and the blithering idiot tells me they're all engaged. Preposterous."

"Saturday afternoon, Colonel," said Gamage mildly. "And there's a match on into the bargain."

The irate old gentleman stumped away, breathing fire and blood, and Marbury gave me the faintest signal to follow him into a corner.

"I thought you might like to see it," he said wearily, showing me a piece of paper with a "3" on it. "Heavens, Mr. Leyton, I'll be glad when Tuesday is over one way or—the other. Where is Mr. Standish?"

"He had to go up to London most unexpectedly," I said, following Ronald's instructions. "He'll be back again tonight."

"He won't let me down, will he?" he cried anxiously. "He'll be here on Tuesday?"

"I can promise you he will," I assured him. "He was most annoyed at having to go at all."

Marbury was lighting a small cigar, and with Ronald's words in mind I studied his hands covertly. Now that my attention had been drawn to it I at once saw what Ronald meant. In one respect they were well shaped. But the skin was rough and calloused; the nails were short and had evidently been uncared-for in the past. And suddenly I became aware that their owner had his eyes fixed on me.

"Relics of my early days in Australia, Mr. Leyton," he said quietly, and I almost blushed. To have been caught so blatantly was most embarrassing.

"A country I have always wanted to go to," I murmured fatuously.

"Are you playing this afternoon?"

"Only if Colonel Fortescue can get a caddie," he answered. "He won't play without one, though I have no objections to doing so."

He spoke casually enough, and yet I know he was studying me; knew, too, that he was annoyed. Clearly a matter he was touchy about: it was stupid of me to have been found out. I was glad when my opponent appeared and we started out.

I did not see either the colonel nor Marbury on my return, but Ronald was propping up the bar.

"You're back earlier than I expected," I cried. "What luck?"

"Excellent," he answered. "Though quite different from what I anticipated."

"You mean you've found the writer of the letters?"

"I have."

"And have you told Marbury?"

"No. I think it is very much better to let events take their normal course. Marbury will be amply protected; no harm will come to him. And we shall catch the other sportsman in the act. Whereas if Marbury knew, he wouldn't be able to go through his part. He'd be sure to give the show away, and the attempt would not be made."

"I see," I remarked. And then I asked him how on earth he had found the man. "It's amazing," I said. "I don't see what you had to go on. Is he an Australian?"

"An Australian!" Ronald stared at me in astonishment. "Why under the sun should he be an Australian?"

"At any rate, it was something to do with Marbury's hands," I said.

"It is possible, Bob, that you know what you're talking about, but I don't."

"Only one thing. Marbury's hands, so he told me, are the result of his early days in Australia."

"Indeed! Did he volunteer the information ?"

"More or less."

"What do you mean by more or less? Did he catch you staring at his hands?"

"Er—well," I said a little guiltily, "I suppose he did."

"Really, Bob," he said at length, "there are times when you ought to be attended by a nursemaid. This, believe me, is one of them. I go out of my way last night to explain to you that Marbury's hands are the crux of the situation. Your next act is to study them through a magnifying glass! I am not partial to strong language, Bob; but I here and now inform you that you're a damn fool."

"Confound it all, man," I cried. "I'm sorry. I didn't know. But it's very largely your own fault. You're so cursedly secretive."

He laughed suddenly.

"Sorry, Bob; I apologise. Let's hope there's no harm done. How went the game this afternoon?"

But I was not to be so easily mollified, and I regret to say that my only answer was to tell him to go to hell. After all, how *could* I be expected to know that sort of thing if Ronald did not tell me? He always seemed to think that because he had certain information in his possession, other people must have it too. But after a while I could no longer stifle the uneasy conviction that he had been justified in what he had said. My own feeling of embarrassment at the time when Marbury caught me in the act, so to speak, was in itself a proof that I had done a very foolish thing. But it could not be undone, and so the only thing to do was to hope for the best.

On Sunday nothing happened of note; on Monday Marbury showed us at the club-house the two letters that had arrived that morning— "2" and "1."

"And tomorrow '0'." he said grimly. "I'm staying at the dormy house tonight; I daren't face my own house. Cowardly, I suppose; but my nerve has gone."

"As a matter of fact I was going to suggest that you should," said Ronald. "I think it very much wiser from every point of view. There's not much sense in forming a bodyguard for you from nine in the morning till midnight and neglecting the rest of the twenty-four hours. Further, I'd bolt your window and lock your door."

And so the dreaded morning dawned. I was awake early, conscious of a tingling sense of excitement. All my attempts overnight to pump Ronald had proved futile; the utmost he would say was that he had taken every possible precaution and that I should know in good time.

I got down soon after eight to find that Marbury was there before me. He was going through the pretence of eating some breakfast, but his hand was shaking so badly that he could hardly lift his cup to his mouth. And I could not blame the poor devil.

"I didn't sleep a wink," he said, and I nodded sympathetically.

"If you take my advice, Mr. Marbury," I said, "you'll have a large whisky and soda. I know it's a bit early, but I think it is excusable to-

577

day."

"Hear, hear," remarked Ronald, who had come in and overheard. "It won't do you any harm at all. Any letter this morning?"

"It's probably at my house," said Marbury. "That's to say, if he's thought it necessary to send one at all today."

At nine-thirty we walked to the clubhouse, with Marbury peering fearfully over his shoulder at every step he took. At nine-forty-five the colonel arrived, and I noticed a suspicious bulge in his hip pocket.

"Pray heaven," muttered Ronald anxiously to me, "that the old gentleman doesn't discharge his lethal weapon at some completely harmless stranger. There is always the possibility that he might hit him."

At ten we started out, and that round will live in my memory for all time. Marbury played a shocking game, but it was the colonel who was the most trying. He was just like a child playing Red Indians. Every bunker held a possible murderer; every bush concealed an assassin. In fact, I could hardly help laughing in spite of the gravity of the situation. Only Ronald seemed quite unperturbed, and played his normal game.

At length that nightmare round was over, and we returned to the clubhouse.

"Now then," said Ronald cheerfully, "sherry? Gin and French? What's the matter, Mr. Marbury?"

"The steward has just given me this," he answered. "It has come, you see. Delivered by hand."

It was the usual letter, marked with the fatal "0."

"Who delivered this, steward?" said Ronald.

"A small boy gave it to one of the waitresses, sir. About half an hour ago."

"So it means he's in the neighbourhood," muttered Marbury. "And it means it isn't a hoax. Oh God, what shall I do?"

"Have a drink," said Ronald prosaically. "Cheer up, Mr. Marbury; we're not going to desert you."

. But the poor devil was beside himself with fear; every time the door opened he started like a nervous cat. And it soon became obvious that golf that afternoon would be out of the question. He could hardly hold his glass, much less a club. So, to my great relief, the idea of it was abandoned; anything would be better than a repetition of the morning.

We dawdled through a miserable meal, at which only the greatest tact on Ronald's part prevented the colonel putting his revolver on the table. Mercifully there were very few members lunching, because Marbury's condition of nerves was obvious. And then for an interminable hour we sat outside pretending to read the papers. At a quarter past three Ronald was called to the telephone; at half-past he suggested we should go back to Marbury's house.

"We can't go on sitting here the whole afternoon," he pointed out. "And if anything, you'll be safer there, Mr. Marbury."

So to his house we went. And the first thing we saw as we entered was a man's hat and stick lying on a chair.

"Whose hat is that?" yelled Marbury, and as if in answer there appeared, to my surprise, the well-known figure of Inspector McIver.

"Good afternoon, Dick," he said genially. "I'll bet you didn't expect to find me here. At Mr. Standish's request I've come specially to guard you."

"Dick!" spluttered the colonel. "His name is not Dick. And who are you, anyway?"

"Inspector McIver of Scotland Yard, sir. A rose by any other name, you know. And to me he is always Dick."

I glanced at Marbury: his mouth was opening and shutting like that of a codfish. And then the inspector continued :

"A very pretty scheme, Dick. Honestly, I congratulate you on it most heartily. It's sheer bad luck that you should have told the story to Mr. Standish of all people."

"What the devil is the fool talking about?" howled the colonel.

"Are you Colonel Fortescue, sir?" asked McIver politely.

"I am."

"You have, I believe, a very valuable collection of jewels."

And from Marbury's lips there floated one crisp "Damn."

"What of it?" barked the colonel.

"Only that I have it here."

McIver was holding a chamois leather bag in his hand, and for a moment I feared the old soldier was going to have an apoplectic fit.

"You scoundrel," he shouted. "How did you get hold of that?"

"Come, come, Colonel," said Ronald with a smile, "that is hardly the way to speak to a distinguished officer from Scotland Yard, who is returning your stolen property to you."

And once again from Marbury's very soul there came a weary "Damn."

"Well, Dick," said McIver, "we might as well be getting along. Pete is waiting for you at the station, and I want to be getting back to London."

★★★★★★

"I'm defeated, Standish: absolutely defeated. How on earth did you spot the scoundrel?"

We had adjourned to the colonel's house, after having broken the sad news to Marbury's servants that their wages were a very problematical asset.

"It's my job to notice small things, Colonel," said Ronald, "and in this case, as I told Bob, it was his hands. I noticed them that night when he dined here, and though, of course, I couldn't be sure, they struck me as not being what I would expect in a retired business man. And that, coupled with the fact that he had not informed the police of these threatening letters, as ninety-nine men in a hundred would do if their consciences were clear, made me wonder if Mr. Marbury was telling us all he knew. A hardware business in the Midlands! Very vague, you know, and impossible to verify.

"So before leaving I obtained his fingerprints on one of your playing cards—you'll find the ace of spades is deficient from one of your packs—and on Saturday I went to Scotland Yard. What I believed was this. I thought that Marbury had spent a considerable portion of his time, not as he told Bob in Australia, but at His Majesty's expense in England."

"That he was an ex-convict," cried the colonel.

"Exactly. And I thought the writer of the letters was some other old lag he had fallen foul of. In short, when I went to London all that I was accusing Marbury of in my own mind was that he had been in prison and that he was not telling us all he knew about the letters.

"The real truth had not dawned on me. It did not until we identified the gentleman, which was not difficult. He was none other than Dick Turner, a burglar right at the top of his profession. He generally worked with a man called Pete Simpson, and they had come out of Dartmoor a year ago. So far as the police knew, the two men had not quarrelled, and were running straight. Which put a different complexion on matters. What was Dick Turner doing down here posing as Henry Marbury? The answer stuck out a mile—your jewels. And the whole plot was clear. Moreover, as McIver said, it was a very pretty scheme—the prettiest I honestly believe I've ever come across.

"Turner came here to spy out the land. He was a public school man and went down with the locals all right. You yourself asked him

580

to dinner frequently. But he soon discovered one or two uncomfortable snags about the business. The first was your penchant, if I may so, Colonel, for letting drive at intruders with a shotgun. The second was Dyer, a large and powerful man who rarely left the house. It was an impasse, but they could afford to wait. And at last came their chance—Dyer's reunion dinner, the date for which was fixed six weeks ago. They knew that unless something unforeseen occurred Dyer would be in London today and tonight. So that only you remained, and their problem was how to get you out of the house for at least four or five hours to enable Pete Simpson to have undisturbed possession of your smoking-room for that time.

"The scheme they evolved we know. And but for my long shot it would have succeeded beyond their wildest dreams. Pete Simpson would by this time have been well on his way to London with your collection of precious stones. You would still be sitting in Marbury's house with a revolver in each hand and the light of battle in your eye. And tomorrow I venture to guess that Marbury would have received another note concluding the series, and couched something as follows

I swore I'd pay you out, and I have. We'll cry quits.

"And in a few weeks' time, I venture further to guess, Marbury would have found some good excuse for folding up his tent and fading gently away from the neighbourhood."

"And I might not have discovered the theft for a month," cried the colonel.

"Precisely. By which time the jewels would have long been out of the country. As it is they're back in your hiding-place. But you'll have to find another one, Colonel. McIver, who watched the whole show from his hiding-place in the garden, told me when he telephoned through to the club that it took Pete one minute to find it and half a minute to get it open."

www.ingramcontent.com/pod-product-compliance
Lightning Source LLC
Chambersburg PA
CBHW030741030726
47497CB00001B/80